FLAPPER
AND THE
CAPTAIN

and Other Flights of Fancy

DAVID LANGE

Contents

Part One
Anthology Submissions

Part Two
Mixed Bag & Random Thoughts

Thematic Index

ADVENTURE/FANTASY

AUTOBIOGRAPHICAL

CHILDREN'S FICTION

COMEDY

DYSTOPIAN FICTION

HORROR

MYSTERIES

OTHER/MISCELLANEOUS

POETRY

ROMANCE

SCIENCE FICTION

THEMED ESSAYS

Stephanie Larkin, Founder & President, Red Penguin Books

When the world stopped in 2020, so did many of the things we'd come to rely on for comfort, connection, and purpose. But for some, the stillness sparked something unexpected—creativity. David Lange was one of those rare individuals who not only found his voice during the global pandemic, but used it to bring light to others during one of the darkest chapters in modern history.

At Red Penguin Books, we launched The Red Penguin Collection to give writers—new and seasoned—a platform to express, to connect, and to create in community. Little did we know that one author would go on to contribute to nearly every anthology in the series. David Lange's work has been a steady, inspiring presence across our publications, bringing insight, humor, and heart to topics ranging from travel and childhood memories to science fiction, heartbreak, and hope.

In *Flapper and the Captain and Other Flights of Fancy*, David curates a powerful collection of the work he created throughout the COVID-19 era—a time of global uncertainty, personal reflection, and unexpected reinvention. These stories, essays, and thought pieces do more than entertain—they chronicle resilience. They are a window into a mind that refused to sit idle, a heart that sought connection, and a spirit determined to create.

As a publisher, it's rare to witness such dedication and range from a single author. David approached each anthology prompt not as a challenge to be met, but as an opportunity to stretch, to surprise himself, and to grow as a writer. His versatility is matched only by his authenticity. Each piece carries his signature warmth, wisdom, and a sincere desire to make sense of the world through story.

It is my absolute pleasure to introduce this anthology to you, dear reader. Whether you've followed David's journey through the pages of our anthologies or are meeting him for the first time, you're in for something special. These are stories born not just from imagination, but from lived experience, deep introspection, and a profound love of storytelling.

Settle in. You're about to embark upon an exciting trip—with one of the most thoughtful, engaging, and heartfelt narrators you could ask for.

Enjoy the journey.

Stephanie Larkin
  Founder & President
  Red Penguin Books

Introduction

In late September 2019, I parted ways with my employer. Technically, it was a layoff—but truthfully, we both sensed it was time to move on, and we did so amicably. Having previously navigated job transitions with relative ease, I wasn't overly concerned. I was ready for a break after years on the road and looked forward to unwinding through the holidays before beginning my job search in the new year.

What I didn't anticipate was the arrival of a highly contagious and deadly virus—COVID-19—that would soon engulf the world in a global pandemic. First identified in December 2019, COVID-19 reshaped every aspect of daily life. Businesses shuttered, workers were sent home, and the economy spiraled. As a military retiree with little civilian corporate experience and a limited network in New York after decades of global travel, I quickly realized that the job market I had planned to enter no longer existed.

Confined to my apartment, I watched days blur together, marked only by meals and television. Even casual walks felt risky amid the fear and uncertainty. In that bleak and isolating time, one bright light emerged: writing.

In August 2020, I published my memoir with Red Penguin Books. Shortly after its release, I was excited to learn about their newest venture: The Red Penguin Collection—a fast-paced series of anthologies featuring new and emerging authors across genres. When editor J.K. Larkin and founder Stephanie Larkin encouraged me to contribute to the first volume, I decided to write an original piece. I submitted two—and both were accepted. I was hooked.

Over the next few years, I contributed regularly to the collection, submitting work for every anthology, even as competition grew. Not every piece was selected, but the process of writing to each prompt became a welcome creative challenge. In total, my work was published in over 30 Red Penguin anthologies, including their travel series and two Best Of compilations.

Each new anthology inspired me to stretch creatively, explore unfamiliar genres, and craft stories that might offer a moment of joy in otherwise difficult times. I wrote not for recognition but for the joy of storytelling—and the hope that my words might resonate with someone, somewhere. The feedback I received from friends and strangers alike was a wonderful reminder that this time behind the keyboard was indeed well spent.

Now, with the pandemic behind us and retirement offering a new kind of freedom, I've gathered many of those pieces—both published and unpublished—into this collection. I've also included several shorter works written for social media during the pandemic, along with a few earlier pieces. Where appropriate, I've added notes after each entry to share the backstory: how the topic inspired me, what influenced the characters or setting, and how the work came together.

These stories, essays, and poems were written between December 2019 and December 2023—during a time of upheaval, uncertainty, and unexpected creativity. Given the tight timelines (Red Penguin released anthologies every two weeks during the first year and a half) and the specific submission guidelines, I'm proud of what I created.

The entries are presented chronologically to offer a sense of how my writing may have evolved throughout the journey. From my earliest childhood stories (not included herein) to this latest anthology, one thing remains unchanged: my love for storytelling and my hope that my words bring a smile to your face.

So, settle in and enjoy the ride. Welcome to my world of imagination.

Part One

Anthology Submissions

Quid Pro Quo – A Cruel Betrayal

(Written August 27, 2020)
Published by Red Penguin Books in *"Realiteen: Reflections on Growing Up"*
(September, 2020)

Middle School heartbreak and resulting disillusionment—early lessons on the importance of kindness.

I look back with incredibly fond memories upon my elementary school experience. In fact, my views are so one-sided that I cannot help but believe that the clouds of time must have obscured the majority of the unpleasant happenings that inevitably creep into all of our lives. One thing I remember with crystal clarity is that I was dreading—and I mean ABSO-FREAKIN-LUTELY DREADING—the move to Junior High. In Sixth Grade (my last year of elementary school), we read an article in class about bullying and I was convinced that I was about to deploy into a veritable war zone with my upcoming move across town to the Junior High School. It didn't help when my father related his own dramatic stories about challenges at that age. His advice to me—"keep a low profile." Literally, that's what he said. At a time in life when I should have, perhaps, been putting myself out there and trying to establish myself within a new environment, I became convinced that the key to survival was digging a deep foxhole and taking cover. Friends from elementary school remember me as a nice kid; a fun-loving class clown who loved to write silly stories and make people laugh. I had a personality. All this was about to change. My new motto (borrowing a term from submarine warfare) was "Run Silent, Run Deep." In short, shut down the engines and hide silently well below the surface until the enemy passes. And that's exactly what I did. I grew increasingly quiet and non-interactive.

I remember showing up on the first day of school—my heart was racing. Kids from a half dozen different schools were poured through the funnel and deposited in a completely random fashion within the turbulent waters of our new ecosystem. Beyond this, those 9th graders were big—and a bit scary. It was not unusual to have one of them randomly punch you in the gut as they walked by or otherwise try to intimidate you just for the thrill of the power play. Even within my own 7th grade class, there was no shortage of bullying. Like lions on the African plains, predators were constantly watching for any signs of weakness amidst the herds of zebras, antelope, and wildebeests who struggled to survive from day to day. It was brutal and it was unfair. As a quiet kid, I sometimes invited probing engagements. It didn't help that my allergies left me prone to random sniffing as I attempted to clear my airways so that I could breathe. Who would have thought that a classmate struggling for air was somehow funny? Apparently, it was disturbing to a few individuals with fine sensibilities. I sluffed off the verbal teasing, to a point. The bullies quickly found out that I was not afraid to fight back. I knew too many people who couldn't or wouldn't defend themselves. Where I could, I tried to defend others against bullying attacks. I knew how to handle myself with the guys. I had absolutely no idea how to deal with "mean girls." We had some of those.

I remember my biology class where a few nasty girls were sitting behind me and they constantly made fun of my sniffing. I was not appreciative. When I blew my nose, it was, of course, incredibly disgusting to them . . . and they'd be sure to let me know. The "nice approach" and attempts to explain my medical condition resulted in no remedy whatsoever. I just took the harassment, begrudgingly. I was miserable and hated coming to class. Had I known at the time that I was only seeing the tip of the cruelty iceberg that Seventh Grade had to offer, I might have skipped school altogether.

The early teen years can be especially challenging as new relationships are forged, old relationships are lost, and puberty and hormonal craziness abound, unabated. In a strange ritual that was unfamiliar to the typical denizens of the elementary school world, I began to notice boys linking up with girls and girls linking up with boys. This was a brave new world! At this point in my life, I was negative on the scale of self-confidence when it came to amorous engagements with the opposite sex. And by "amorous," I'm talking date night at the ice cream parlor. Anything beyond that was best left to those magazines I wasn't supposed to be looking at. With that said, I was starting to feel a certain longing to connect. Wouldn't it be nice to have a girlfriend of my own?

I didn't have a car, or a driver's license, and my allowance was about a buck and a half a week but those were merely trivial matters. Love conquers all, right? And then there were my father's words—"keep a low profile." I was a little confused. We all were. If any girl was even remotely nice to me, I was thrilled. I wouldn't have known a pickup line if one had hit me in the face—until one did.

Reva came out of nowhere. Shoulder-length auburn hair, nice eyes, and a pretty smile--Reva was pretty and I did kind of like her but, otherwise, I hadn't given her much thought. She wasted no time cozying up to me and I was stunned by the sudden show of affection. Was this really happening? Is this how romances begin? The closest I had ever come to a romance was when, in 5th grade, I retrieved a stolen playground ball and returned it to the French girl who then gave me a lovely kiss on the cheek. Those French girls! Wow! She was a couple years younger and in my sister's class. A May-December romance! I knew it was never going to work (wink). I had to let her go. So, yes, I knew nothing of the ways of love. But Reva was lovin' on me something fierce and . . . I liked it. Maybe I wasn't a social zero, after all? The flirting continued. I fought through countless blushes over the coming days as Reva continued to express her affection while classmates looked on with interest. What was it that she liked about me? Was it my smile? The flash in my eyes as I laughed? Perhaps my engaging personality? I was about to learn yet one more lesson in my biology classroom.

It was time for the big science test. I was glad not to be sitting near the mean girls anymore. With a plethora of assorted biology facts racing through my head, and tests being handed out within the classroom, I'm pretty sure mixed-gender bullying was the last thing on my mind. Today was my lucky day—Reva was sitting at a desk right next to mine! O, my Muse of Academic Exceptionalism, fail me not at this hour of my greatest need! I look to you for the inspiration I need to conquer this, my latest trial. And Reva was looking at me, too! And then she slowly slid her desk closer to mine. And then closer, still. She leaned in and whispered to me. Ah, how gentle was her voice as she lovingly asked me to turn my test booklet a bit so that she could see it better. What?! What was happening?! I didn't respond. She looked directly at me and whispered a little bit louder, perhaps thinking that I hadn't heard her well enough the first time. Where my nose and sinuses left something to be desired, my ears were high performance instruments and I heard Reva's plea the first time . . . like a clash of thunder. My stunned silence had nothing to do with auditory comprehension. I sat there in disbelief. The clock was ticking. This was no longer just a test about biology. This had become a test on life. My grade hung in the balance. Love hung in the balance. Most importantly, for me, my integrity hung in the balance. I had never cheated on any test. I had never assisted others in cheating. Tick-tock, tick-tock, tick-tock. My heart was breaking. I took one more glance over towards Reva. It had to be quick—I didn't want my Science teacher to come rolling in on this mess. I just shook my head no and pulled my test in closer, guarding my work. I don't recall what my grade was on that test. It didn't really matter. I will never forget the crashing end of my first "romance." It was never about me, after all. This whole "relationship" which, thank heavens, couldn't have lasted more than a couple weeks, had all been an elaborate setup to steal test answers from a "smart kid." After the test, Reva wanted absolutely nothing to do with me. My last memory of our interaction was at a Bar Mitzvah reception where a number of my classmates were dancing and a few girls suggested that Reva should dance with me. She just looked over and said she had no desire to dance with me. At that point, I had no desire to dance with her, either. I wasn't angry at Reva. I was just sad. Sad and disappointed.

Decades later, I have never forgotten Reva. No, not like that. She wasn't the love of my life and she definitely was not my "dream girl." I was a young man, a kid really, struggling with self-confidence and unsure of myself, especially in matters regarding love and relationships. She offered me something I wanted so very much . . . and then she took it away. Her affection was conditional—it had a price; an exchange of goods; a quid pro quo. Were I less kind, I might equate Reva with the working girls on the street corner. But, then again, even they are sacrificing something of themselves to make a living. Reva was sacrificing her integrity to survive a test. No, I couldn't hate Reva—certainly not for that. Even though my heart suffered grievously, I walked away with my integrity intact . . . and I have never regretted my decision. I felt sorry for Reva. She moved on and I haven't seen her since Junior High. I often wonder about her. However, when I share this story, it's not with affection. Reva's trickery left a deep scar that never fully healed. I became very suspicious of the opposite sex. To be honest, I became very suspicious of peoples' motives, in general. My natural shyness often kept me from making advances towards girls that I liked and my memories of the Reva incident made me all but blind towards any and all signals of interest. I felt completely invisible to the opposite sex. Whether or not I was, I could not say. I lost all confidence with women and retreated even further into my shell. While I can hardly blame Reva for the growing unhappiness that characterized the following years, I'm certainly not appreciative of the shove she gave me at the top of the stairwell. Issues at school, issues at home, loneliness and self-doubt—I continued to fall deeper into the abyss. It was not until three years later that a beautiful princess would rescue me from myself and restore my faith in humanity and in the goodness within this world. And she did it within the span of a couple weeks, simply by showing kindness and compassion.

I have seen the hurt that we can inflict upon each other. I have also seen the beauty of the human spirit as we care for those in need, helping to uplift the fallen. I tell this story in the hope that all who read it will choose to offer warmth and compassion to others without the expectation of reciprocation. Helping others simply for the sake of goodness—that's the mark of a true hero. We all have it within us to be a hero and it's a true privilege to have that ability to make a positive change in the life of another human being. Please consider your inter-actions—what you give, and what you take . . . it makes a difference. You can change a life. Change lives for the better.

The Story Behind the Story

"Realiteen: Reflections on Growing Up" was the first book of the Red Penguin Collection. As the title suggests, this anthology includes an array of short stories, essays, and poems where authors reflect upon experiences from their teenage years— the challenges and anxieties as well as the liberating feeling of evolving into an independent adult. Submissions were limited to 5,000 words. It was initially suggested that I might offer up an excerpt from my recently published memoir and, certainly, that would have been a viable option. Rather than cutting and pasting part of my memoir, I thought I'd work up an original piece based on a story from my life that I seldom shared but one that had a definite impact on my psyche and view on relation-ships for many years to come. Names were changed to protect the innocent (and

guilty), but the rest was a factual recounting of a near-traumatic social debacle from my teen years. Like with most things I write, I tried to leave with a positive message about the importance of kindness. Although some 40 years in the past, I could still feel the emotions resurface as I visited this unpleasant experience from my Junior High School days.

What I Learned About Myself While Doing Underwater Push-ups

(Written August 28, 2020)
Published by Red Penguin Books in *"Realiteen: Reflections on Growing Up"*
(September, 2020)

*Life lessons I learned during a challenging
experience in Basic Training.*

When, in the fall of 1983, I went to interview for a senatorial nomination to the Air Force Academy, the interview panel asked me a fair but challenging question. Simply stated, the question was "What makes you think you can take it? Have you ever done anything like this before?" I hadn't. I'm not sure how many 17-year-olds had. I tossed out a few lame anecdotes about some Boy Scout adventures but, in truth, I hadn't really been tested...at least not in the way I was anticipating being tested during Basic Training. I had worked through some emotional challenges and I had worked through some physical chal-lenges. But getting yelled at while low crawling under barbed wire in the mud was not something I could relate to. Jumping off a 10-meter tower, then swimming underwater, under a bulkhead, coming up and treading water for several minutes and then swimming to the other end of the pool, all while being timed, wasn't part of my life resume. So many of the things I knew I would face had absolutely no equivalent in my life experience. I thought I was a pretty tough kid. I didn't know.

My initial days as an Air Force Academy Basic Cadet were not pleasant. In fact, my first year at the Academy was pretty much a continuous haze. But that's another story. I wish to confine this tale to a single, memorable, incident.

During the second half of Basic Training, the Cadet Wing traveled out to Jacks Valley. No, not "Jack's" but "Jacks," named after the Jacks family. Jacks Valley was home for all sorts of obstacle courses and phys-ical challenges. During our time in Jacks, Basic Cadets lived in tents and received all manner of field training. In truth, for many of us, these challenges were more enjoyable than our Basic Training experi-ences back in the Cadet Area. I got yelled at in both places and I kind of preferred getting yelled at while scaling walls, swinging on ropes, and jumping over logs. You could "fight back" by tackling the obstacles with an increased level of passion and aggressiveness. For all that, the lack of sleep, stress, limited food intake (which actually improved in Jacks Valley), and everything else contributed to the spread of sickness. I came down with Bronchitis and I was hurting. And this forms the context for my story.

On this particular day, we were to participate in "Recondo" training. That's short for "RECONnaissance and commanDO." It was a pretty cool day making our way through the woods and engaging with enemy parties. Though feeling quite ill, I did a good job keeping up and enjoyed the training. As the day wore on, the sky got darker and darker. A storm was on the way. In the late afternoon, feeling quite exhausted, we came upon a really nasty, swampy looking, lake. At that point, our trainer informed us that it was time for some "underwater push-ups." WHAT?!! Underwater push-ups?!! I could barely breath as it was. There was not a one among us who was excited about the prospect of wading into the swampy lake to do push-ups while completely submerged. Did they even know what brain-eating amoebas were in those days??? Besides struggling with my bronchitis, I had always had a bit of a phobia about being submerged underwater. Growing up with allergies, the ability to breath was not something I took for granted. The notion of not having oxygen available was somewhat terrifying for me. I did swim (in fact, I swam in high school), but I still did not like the idea of being submerged beneath the surface. The Recondo cadre member in charge of our group, Cadet Gonzales, knew I was pretty messed up and told me that I did not have to do it if I didn't want to. I didn't want to. I stepped back. But I didn't feel very good about the decision. In fact, I felt pretty awful about it. I had a dozen reasons not to participate. As I saw my classmates start to head towards the edge of the lake, I knew I couldn't just stand there and watch. I had to take part. I think I muttered a few curse words under my breath and I approached Cadet Gonzales. I told him that I had to do this. He looked at me, as if to say "are you sure?" and then approved. I joined our small group in that lake. We waded out until the water was at our waistline and then we assumed the push-up position, under water. There was absolutely nothing fun about the experience. I don't know if there was any real training value or not. But for me, there was value. I had been at the end of my line. I was sick and exhausted and facing a personal phobia...but I was not going to quit. Part of it was about keeping team integrity but, I believe, an even larger part of it related to a personal struggle. For better or worse, I have never been good at giving up...on anything. This is not always a virtue. It's just part of who I am. I felt a certain crazed pride as I did those push-ups in the lake. I think I would have beat myself up for a long time afterwards, had I not participated in that experience. As we waded back to shore, I could hear my Senator's Nomination Panel interviewer question reverberating through my head--"What makes you think you can take it?" My answer? "I can take it."

We formed up and began our march back to the tent city. The storm I referred to earlier? That's when it hit. We were getting dumped on! At least the rain may have helped to wash away some of the swampy smell from the lake push-ups. We were still quite muddy by the time we arrived back at our tents. I was coughing up a lung and really looking forward to a nice warm shower that night. Then a voice came over the Public Address System in the tent city. Due to the lightning hazard, we were not permitted to transit to the shower building. No shower that night. I toweled myself off, as best I could, and laid down in my cot, still damp, and went to bed.

Many months later, Cadet Gonzales, who remembered the day, asked me if my health improved any after my Recondo experience. I was glad he remembered. In truth, my health deteriorated even more-- but I kept on going. I completed Basic Training and all associated activities. I finally did get better, after Basic Training was over. From a medical standpoint, my decision was not a very smart one. My medical professional friends would probably tell me I was stupid. I probably was. Like I said, I don't always make smart decisions but I try to follow my heart and make decisions that I will not regret.

I don't share this story to try to prove some point about what's inside of my heart. I have some incredible friends who are battling major health issues and they are as brave or braver than I ever was or had to be. We really don't know how strong we are until we face adversity. Talk is cheap. Speculation is meaningless. We don't know until we face "that moment." For some of us, the "moment" lasts a very long time. I gave up...briefly. A minute or two of doubt at the side of a stupid little lake in Colorado Springs. But then something kicked in. I reflected on who David Lange really was and what he was about. Each of us needs to make very personal decisions in life--when is enough really enough? Are we at that point where we really can't go on? There's really only one judge--the person you must share your story with when you look in the mirror. I wish all of you strength as you fight your own personal battles. Sometimes, circumstances are beyond our control. There is, however, something truly beautiful and inspiring about the human spirit--that unquantifiable magic that helps us to carry on when it seems like we've been beaten. I wish you strength and the courage to persevere over adversity.

The Story Behind the Story

As the Red Penguin Collection was just getting started, and seeing as how I had been solicited for a contribution, I wasn't sure how many pieces would be submitted from interested authors, and I thought that I might help with the launch if I offered an additional story for consideration. With time, Red Penguin Books would receive many more submissions than they had the ability to incorporate—works that would come from authors across the globe. The selection process would grow increasingly competitive which, of course, yielded anthologies of great quality. "What I Learned About Myself While Doing Underwater Push-ups" was the only piece I submitted to Red Penguin that was not specifically created for the anthology. This essay was based off of a Facebook post from a year or so before. I felt my experience in over-coming fear and pushing my limits as a 17-year-old going through Basic Training was a tale that might help others facing challenges in their lives, and the corre-sponding doubt we all have as to whether or not we really have what it takes to make it through.

OVER AND OUT – THE LAST JOURNAL ENTRY OF THE MARS CLIPPER

(Written September 10, 2020)
Published by Red Penguin Books in "*What Lies Beyond: Sci-Fi Stories of the Future*" (September, 2020)

A routine interplanetary mission proves that there's never anything routine about space travel. Protagonist reflects upon life priorities.

SEPTEMBER 15ᵀᴴ. So, I guess this is it. Phoebe (Commander Carter) told me the news this morning—our journey to Mars has become a one-way trip. Apparently, that unpleasant warbling tone coming from the master warning panel last week and the impressive display of flashing red and amber lights was not, in fact, a friendly reminder to balance out the fuel quantities between our various tanks to normalize the center of gravity. How would I know? I'm not "crew;" I'm a passenger—the lucky "lottery winner"—the second artist to be welcomed aboard a Martian Clipper space ship headed for the Red Planet. The first was a songwriter and she's on her way back home after spending a month at the Martian Exploration Center on the planet's surface. I hope she sells some albums or maybe wins an MTV Video Music Award. Space flight has become so routine that everyone seems to take it for granted. It was decades ago that we first stepped foot on the Martian surface. Next came a small outpost and refueling station. The footprint just grew from there and, before you knew it, we had a full-blown Exploration Center established on Mars, much like the national research outposts in Antarctica that have been collecting data since the middle of the 20ᵗʰ Century. Most of Earth's citizenry fully expect there to be shopping malls on Mars before the end of this century. But they all forget a critical point--space is not easy! It never was and it never will be. Space is a forbidding medium and we were never meant to master it. If anything, we were meant to place offerings at the altar and pray to our Gods to grant us mercy so that we might then offend the laws of nature with impunity as we rocket through our atmosphere and into the darkness of the endless void. If I've learned one thing, it's that space travel is one-part science and three-parts prayer. I didn't know that when I tossed my name into the hat. Somebody in the upper echelon of the space travel bureaucracy decided that Mars missions were so reliable that it was time to prove the point by putting a select group of common folks on the roster. We were chosen for our excellence in various arts so that we might effectively spread the message—whatever message the marketing folks and politicians felt was important to be spread. Mostly, "give us more money and we will ensure a better future for all denizens of planet Earth." Me? I was the author—the honored guest who was going to write brilliantly about my experience as I traveled through the solar system. My words would serve to inspire generations of future adventurers and hopeless romantics. Well, I hope they like folk songs back home because that's what Norway's Anja is going to give them after she and her crew land back on Earth. Figures they'd pick the pretty blonde for the first ride out of town. Maybe she'll write a poignant song in remembrance of me and the crew? I hope she gets my name right.

What happened? It's simple math, really. Space was "trending." It was going "viral." It's what everybody wanted to talk about. Create a space motif on a t-shirt, handbag, or cell phone case and name your price. People loved our space missions. For a while, at least. With time, the thrill fizzled and enthusiasm slowly morphed into a thinly veiled disinterest. That's right about the time that federal taxes increased to help subsidize the private sector space companies with the government funding required to keep them viable. Here on planet Earth, there were a million and a half problems that needed to be remedied and, no matter how spectacularly the sales pitches were embellished with virtual reality videos and glossy brochures, there was no hiding the fact that Mars missions did not seem to be improving the everyday life for any kid growing up hungry or any parent fretting over where the next paycheck was going to be coming from after getting laid off from the factory, or the school, or the hotel staff, or a million other positions that found themselves suddenly vulnerable after the economic downturn. Space seemed like the rich man's playground. I can't say that I fault their logic. It's hard to be inspired by the thought of saving mankind a few thousand years from now when you're struggling to keep your family viable through next Tuesday. So, this is where the math comes in. More missions. Less Cost. Tighter time lines. Something had to give and program managers and engineers worked their darndest to find ways to shave time and expense off the projects laid before them. They succeeded—mostly. Redundancies were eliminated and processes and materials were adjusted to eliminate any excess. It was all business. If I learned one thing from my grandfather, a military aviator from a bygone era, it's that an over-engineered aircraft is your best friend. In his mind, there was simply no such thing as having too much thrust or too much redundancy. Several of the major aircraft manufacturers must have looked on in horror as their jets approached the century mark. They wanted Uncle Sam to buy a new jet every 10 years—you know, because everyone loves that new car smell. I guess they took the lesson to heart and began to use advanced computer engineering programs to precisely construct their craft so that they met the basic thresholds of performance, and not an iota more. Shame on them. Shame on all of us. We did it to ourselves. And here we are—a computer glitch and a faulty nozzle have sent us off course— irreparably off course. When the lights started flashing, we really needed Buck Rogers to leap into the seat and save the day. We had no pilot—none—only a wonderful array of academically brilliant "mission specialists." Pilots were deemed unnecessary—testing at the labs proved it time and time again. No one bothered to mention that the computer algorithms at the testing lab were inherently stacked against our pilots and the occasional computer autopilot anomalies were conveniently left out of the reports that went up to key decision makers. It's an old story. Too old. Chuck Yeager is gone—now we're all about "Siri, take me to Mars."

Hope springs eternal in the human breast and I have to admit that I was incredibly impressed by the professionalism of the entire crew as they rallied to discuss options. I almost fell for it when Phoebe confidently proclaimed that she was going to get us all home. Sure, she would—that's her job. Thereafter, followed a dazzling array of scientifically irrefutable discussions regarding orbital mechanics, thrust and vectoring analysis, distance versus time calculations, and all manner of lofty topics for which the attending PhDs were well-equipped to engage on. It was like watching a flickering candle on a windy night. Just as the flame seemed all but extinguished, it would bravely leap forth again, defying the forces of nature seeking to snuff out the light. Again, and again, the cycle of hope and despair played out upon the dimly lit stage . . . but without the theatrics, without the pathos. Until the oxygen report, that is. Defeat was signaled not by a trumpet upon the hill but by silence; a deafening and terrifying silence. After the science and math jars were emptied, I was again included in the conversation. We now had to decide how we wanted to die. In this matter, my vote counted.

So, the good news was that within about 34 years we would become the first manned spaceship to ever depart the solar system. Voyager 1 held the honor of being the first unmanned vessel to depart our home solar system, back in 2012. The bad news was that we would run out of oxygen, oh, about 33 years before then. While the Mars Clipper was equipped with the wonderful OGS, or Oxygen Generation System, it still was unable to generate more than about a year's worth of breathable oxygen before imminent system failure. It was primarily designed to make the relatively short 250-day trip to Mars before being serviced for the return flight. Once the scientific debates had concluded, I began to see something I had been waiting for over three months to witness—humanity.

Throughout months of training, I have grown very close to my four astronaut partners. I'd like to say they had all become close friends but, alas, I would be lying. They had all the qualities I could hope for in a friend—integrity, intellect, bravery, and a slew of other wonderful traits that stemmed from the remarkable lives they all had lived. But there was always something missing. They executed their duties with robotic efficiency as they called off checklist items and pushed a sundry of multi-colored buttons upon impressive arrays of touch screens. Everything was efficient and timed to the second. I don't hang out with people like that. My friends were a scurvy crew of miscreants and deviants, scratching and clawing their way through life with a beer in one hand and a book of poetry in the other. They laughed and they cried and they shouted in anger against any and every manner of infraction that threatened their freedom to be the uniquely eccentric people they were convinced that they were. I loved them all. Onboard the Mars Clipper, not a laugh, or a tear, a clenched fist, or an angry stare. I worked on them, as if I was working on a guard outside of Buckingham Palace. My results were nearly the same. Sure, I'd get the occasional chuckle and smile but these seemed to come after a few internal checklists had been run inside their brain to clear them to execute the smile release protocol. It was unnatural. Then things changed, maybe an hour ago. The electronic checklists got returned to their holsters as did the handheld remote calculating devices. To call them calculators would subject one to charges of heresy. These beauties could get you to Mars and back. Well, on a good day they could. This was not a good day. Ennio was crying. Barry was praying. Anika was fidgeting with some sort of worry beads that emerged from one of the dozens of pockets on her flight suit. Phoebe just sat in her chair with a thousand-mile stare. There wasn't anything to see within a thousand miles. Not even within ten-thousand miles . . . or a hundred thousand. Nothing.

Passages from old sailing stories began to creep into my thoughts as I admired the blossoming humanity around me. Maybe we could be friends! But back to the "lost at sea" stories. I've read of sailors drawing straws to see who the crew would eat so that others might live. Was that applicable here? Maybe we would cook our shoes and eat them, too? I seem to remember reading about such things—or was that from Charlie Chaplin's "Gold Rush" film? My memories are clouded. Our high-tech space boots probably aren't even edible. I'll bet they taste better than "space toast." Would we sacrifice members to gain the oxygen for another month of flight? Two months? My mind raced through countless ridiculous scenarios. I was no longer thinking rationally and, for the first time in their lives, I suspect my new-found friends may not have been, either. One suggested we just shut down the OGS immediately rather than spend months dwelling upon our certain doom. Another suggested that we create an electrical spark to ignite a fatally explosive fire within the system itself. One simply suggested that we pray for divine deliverance until it came. Phoebe listened to all of this with an open mind and, apparently, free of judgment. Ultimately, she would have to be the judge for that is a commander's burden. More so than ever before, I saw the people behind the patches . . . and they were beautiful, each in his or her own way. I saw bits and pieces of myself in all of them and, for the first time, I think they began to see parts of me within their own psyche. We were becoming one. It's at this point that a unique revelation struck me. This is what life on Earth is supposed to be about in the first place. It should never have been about competition and judgment. It was supposed to be about harmony—different people from different backgrounds coming together for a greater good and possessing a common understanding of our shared experience. Anika. She was born in India and got to where she is today by being the hardest working person in every school and within every program and on every job she ever held. And she never stepped on anyone to get the job done. She freely gave of her talents to help others rise to their potential. There's a statue of her in the square of her little hometown. Ennio was from Italy. He is a deeply religious man and his faith inspired him to be more than his parents ever thought he could become. It was difficult for him to tell his father that he was not going to take over the family business. That honor would have to go to his younger brother. Much like with Anika, Ennio's natural brilliance propelled him to great heights and he never looked back. Barry was an American, like myself. Unlike me, he was born in a pretty rough neighborhood in Philadelphia but he defied the odds. A consecutive series of miracles enabled Barry to attend a private school where he was challenged in a way he was unlikely to have experienced at the school around the corner from his home. He resented being used as the poster child for the "ghetto kid done good, first college graduate in his family" marketing campaign but he tried not to let it show. Forever proud of where he had come from, Barry always made sure to return to his roots to help inspire the next generation of leaders. Perhaps it was because we both grew up in eastern cities, albeit under different life circumstances, but I certainly felt closest to Barry during training. We seemed to understand each other on a somewhat deeper level. Finally, our fearless commander, Phoebe. I liked her and I certainly respected her but she always seemed a little bit aloof. She'd occasionally talk about the positive impact her grandparents had on her life but she never mentioned her parents. I'm a writer, my mind wanders and creates stories to fill the void when questions linger, unanswered. I was writing Phoebe's life story in my mind though I really knew next to nothing about her. I think she was a military brat, that is to say the daughter of a military father . . . or mother . . . or both. She was born in Texas but it's unclear whether or not she actually considered the Lone Star State as home, or not. Phoebe expertly avoided personal questions, preferring always to engage in conversation within the confines of professional air and space discussions. Her leadership qualities were phenomenal. She was incredibly insightful and sharp as a tack. I knew about her educational degrees and a little bit about her time in the military. I knew about her published articles and books. I knew about her thoughts on the future of our space program. I knew a lot about Phoebe "the professional" and yet I really knew nothing about Phoebe "the person." I wanted to know. She was commanding this one-way trip to our doom so I figured it was the least she could do to fill me in on some of the missing pieces of her life story which was, pretty much,

her entire life story. I looked out the small windows into the vast emptiness of space. A hand touched me on my shoulder and gave it a
squeeze followed by a gentle shake. I looked backed and saw Phoebe
standing behind me. She looked deeply into my eyes, penetrating in a
way she had never entered before. I felt a stirring in my heart. I felt a
connection. "So," she said, "you're probably wondering what brings a
girl like me to a dingy joint like this?" I was wondering, and I absolutely
wanted to know—everything. I have to know. Before I die, I want to
know absolutely everything there is to know about Phoebe Carter and I
want her to know absolutely everything about me. I want our first date,
our first dance, our first kiss, and our wedding vows all to happen in the
short span of time we have remaining together. These are the only
remaining items on my mission checklist. I've spent too many years
observing and recording life when, perhaps, I should have spent more
time living it. Is there still time to make amends? It's time to close out
this journal. I will make the most of my remaining time. Over and out.

SEPTEMBER 10TH. I can't even remember what I was doing when
I fell asleep last night. I think I was writing. Commander Carter had to
shake me to get me up this morning. I awoke feeling rather drained,
like one woken prematurely from a dream that hadn't yet run its
course. This morning began much as the mornings before—powdered
eggs, toast that more closely resembled stale crackers, and something
remotely reminiscent of coffee in my cup. My heart nearly jumped out
of my chest shortly after 0830 hours when these crazy sounds began to
emanate from one of the panels up front and some lights started
flashing on the screens. Ennio says it's just the ship's friendly way of
reminding them that a fuel transfer was required to adjust the center of
gravity of our ship. It's all good. I'm looking forward to some smooth
sailing out to the Red Planet and then, hopefully, getting home in time
to see the World Series next season. More later on the finer points of
constructing the perfect piece of "space toast."

Flapper and the Captain

The Story Behind the Story

It had been a long, long time since I had written anything that even resembled science fiction. I wrote one fantasy piece in college that had elements of time travel, but nearly everything I'd ever written that could be considered Sci-Fi was created during my elementary school years and involved robots and monsters or very angry fruits and vegetables. As a long time Sci-Fi fan (regrettably, mostly a film viewer with only a few novels in the mix), I thought I'd try my hand at creating a story for the second anthology in the Red Penguin Collection which would be entirely populated by Science Fiction stories. While Science Fiction writing spans a wide range of environments, I considered sticking to a basic spaceflight story. I was very familiar with our space program and the challenges it experienced along the way. I also knew, only too well, how the exciting and death-defying soon became, in the public's eye, routine and mundane. There's always risk when we take impossibly complex machines into the air, or out of our atmosphere, and I wanted to tell a tale that spoke to these risks in a creative and interesting manner. As a long-time diary author, the previous anthology's essays about my life experiences were a relatively easy ask. I knew I'd have to put in some effort, and even do a little bit of research, to pull off a decent science fiction story. I was very happy when my efforts were rewarded and my short story was accepted into an anthology that included lots of great stories.

THREE SUMMERS: MEMORIES OF CHILDHOOD ROAD TRIPS

(Written September 30, 2020)
Published by Red Penguin Books in "*A Trip for the Books*" (October, 2020)

Personal reflections upon childhood cross-country trips with my family.

I recently read an article about all the ways the American road trip has changed over the years and how they're better now on all accounts. I'm not sure that I agree. Granted, my memories of several summer trips in the mid-70s are likely painted with the colorful brush strokes of an idealistic child through whose mind and body I experienced these adventures. It seemed like a simpler time; a period more connected with the 1950s and 60s than with any of the years that followed. Three trips merge into one, in my mind. My age? Somewhere between 7 and 9. My sister was a few years younger and my brother 10 years older. My Dad was older than I ever thought I'd be and considerably younger than I am now. My mother joined us on one of the three trips. I don't recall her being particularly enthusiastic about the journey. Maybe that's why my mind has largely written her out of the narrative—not because I didn't want Mom along but because my memories have written the script for four. We traveled west from New York to see my grandfather in Chicago, Illinois. Getting on in years, it was no longer prudent for him to travel east to visit us. The last time he did so is recorded in photographs but largely lost from the memories that I retain. On one of the trips, we traveled even farther west to visit my Great Uncle and Great Aunt in Edgemont, South Dakota. This was my first memory of seeing Uncle Gib. It was the last time I would ever see him. Our conveyance was the stalwart 1970 Chevrolet Impala. Oh, how I loved that car. It was a tank! A million tons of indestructible American steel painted blue with a black vinyl top. The interior seats were all black vinyl and would set your pants on fire if you settled on them too quickly on hot summer day. Its legendary status was cemented in my mind as an elementary school child when we got rear-ended at the bottom of a hill on the way to school. The road was slick

21

and the offending driver waited too long to get on his brakes as he zipped down the hill towards where we sat waiting on the traffic light. We all felt the jarring bump. The man driving the car quickly got out and came forward to apologize to my mother who was behind the wheel of our carpool ride full of school-age children. All passengers were fine. The car that struck us . . . not so much. The front had crumpled in and the hood popped open. Steam emanated from the wreck. When we pulled forward, the damage to our mighty Chevy was apparent—a tiny dent, about the size of a quarter, in our rear fender. We drove on to school—no insurance claim was filed. The Impala was all business. The car had a radio but I have no memory of it ever actually being turned on. There was no air conditioner. Cooling, if you can call it that, was achieved with vigorous turns on four cranks to lower each window. Besides having an automatic transmission, there was absolutely nothing automatic about the car. It was perfect—at least in the mind of an eight-year-old boy.

We'd set out from Long Island on a hot summer morning, my father driving and my brother helping out in the passenger seat. I sat behind the driver's seat and my sister sat on the right. Those were our proper places and were non-negotiable. The trips always began slowly. Getting off of Long Island and through the New York City traffic was always like a street brawl. There was nothing poetic about it. There was no point in breathing until we made the New Jersey Turnpike. It's at that point that things opened up a bit and my father got to settle back into his seat. The next main kid highlight was going to be lunch followed by the ultimate highlight, the impossibly long tunnels through the mountains along the Pennsylvania Turnpike. Back in the 1970s, there were no electronic devices to keep kids occupied. I'd pull out my little notebook and start searching for license plates. My goal was always to collect all 50 states. I think the best I ever did was 39 different plates. I kept my eyes peeled. Seeing a license plate from Guam was so impossibly miraculous that I still remember the thrill, nearly fifty years later. We didn't really bring much in the way of toys with us so my sister and I would readily engage in a variety of back-seat skits, playing the voices and personalities of a number of mischievous junior characters. The most notorious of the lot were Elbis Jackknifer and his sister, Elbis Deary. If somebody crossed Elbis, LOOKOUT! Yes, he owned a jackknife and was not afraid to use it. Ah, the innocence of childhood! My sister and I had all kinds of fun. I'm not sure the trips would have been bearable without my travel companion. Jen held up very well, especially considering she was two years younger than me. Occasionally, we'd stop for a rest break at one of the roadside rest areas. They weren't nearly as built up at they are now. There were no McDonalds or Burger Kings, no KFC or Arby's. There were some picnic tables and bathrooms. Without my mom along, my poor sister was subjected to the somewhat humiliating ritual of having to relieve herself in a plastic bucket that was brought along for the purpose. I don't believe my father felt safe sending his young daughter into a public restroom alone so he'd take Jenny out of view and allow her to do her business. He would then rinse out the bucket with some water from a thermos. Jen never complained but I still felt badly for her. I sure didn't want to use a bucket every time I needed to go to the bathroom. Occasionally, at rest stops, Dad would give us a quarter or two to get trinkets from one of the vending machines. I remember cherishing my Pez dispenser. It was a little plastic candy dispenser with a recognizable character head that you would tilt back to push forward a tablet of flavored sugar from the spring-loaded magazine. I had a Woody the Woodpecker dispenser. I also got a few plastic animals from the vending machines; each dispensed in an egg-shaped plastic container. These animals became travel toys.

Our first food stop was typically at a Howard Johnson restaurant. Before the McDonalds/Burger King Coup, Howard Johnsons were a regular site along the Turnpike and Interstate. I would almost always order a hot dog. I never used relish at home but their pickle relish was delicious and, following some mustard, would finish off the culinary masterpiece. The real highlight of the meal was, without fail, the absolutely magnificent chocolate milkshake. I loved HoJo's chocolate shakes —they were out of this world! Meals were a wonderful break from the monotony of the never-ending road. The endless green pastures and gently rolling hills of Pennsylvania were lovely but not exactly of great interest to an elementary school kid. The black and white dairy cows were the only thing that could hold our interest before the afternoon tunnel excursion.

We pressed on, the intent being to drive until it made sense to stop. Depending upon traffic and my father's level of alertness, we usually tried to get somewhere near Toledo, Ohio on the first day of driving. Having an awake driver was, of course, very critical. There weren't any car seats in those days and my sister and I liberally unbuckled to sit on the floor of the vehicle and use the seat as a play table. Fortunately, along the long stretches of open road, there weren't many threats to be concerned with, especially during summer daylight driving. Eventually, our vehicle would start to climb and the gradual change in elevation and changing scenery was like Thanksgiving to our Christmas—heralding the upcoming tunnels through the mountains. We had plenty of tunnels in New York but nothing like this. My heart was racing by the time I saw the large sign directing drivers to "Turn Headlights on Now." Cars emerging from the other direction still had their lights on. And then, like something out of a cool science fiction movie, we entered into the seemingly endless tunnel; the first of several. It was amazing! I made sure to soak in every minute of it because I knew this was as exciting as it was going to get until we reached Chicago. Ohio and Indiana still lay ahead but they didn't have anything to rival the super tunnels of Pennsylvania!

Late afternoon and another rest stop. Dad would usually make this a quick one. He might get a cup of coffee but the intent was always to gas up, use the restroom (or bucket!), and continue our forward progress. By the time we stopped for dinner, we were all feeling a little bit hot, tired, and stiff. I was stiff so I have to imagine my father desperately needed to stretch his legs. My brother, at six-foot-two, was probably really in need of a good stretch. We'd grab dinner along the way at some convenient exit and, again, try to minimize our delay. My Dad might buy a pack of peppermint Lifesavers to help get him through the after-dark driving hours. Using the refreshing candy to invigorate me during night drives is a technique I still use to this day and one I trace back to those early road trips with my dad. Another less desirable trick that I picked up from my father (don't tell Mom!) involves using the ice in my drink to give my hands a cleaning after a meal. If my hands were sticky or otherwise soiled following eating, I'd pick an ice cube out of my water glass and let it slowly melt in my hands as I rubbed my hands together. Finally, I'd dry my hands off with my napkin. Makes sense, right? Thanks, Dad. Now my boys do it, too. Their Grandmother would be so proud! Shhhh.

Back on the road, we enjoyed the setting sun. Well, I enjoyed it, as we drove west. For our chauffer, sunset was preceded by an agonizing hour of driving directly into the sun. My father never used sunglasses but I imagine he got pretty good at positioning the sun visor in the late afternoon.

By around 8pm to 9pm, everyone was getting pretty tired. I'm glad my brother was along to keep my dad company and to talk with him during the drive, especially during those late hours. Eventually, everyone knew it was time to seek lodging. We nearly always went the low budget route, looking for places under $20 a night. In the days before major hotel chains devoured the market, there was a wonderful array of privately owned motels spanning across the country. I can't remember any of the names other than they ended in Motel. Collectively, I've always referred to them as "The Color TV / Air Conditioning Motel." In those days, these were big selling points and these features were prominently highlighted on the bright neon signs that formed a beacon for weary travelers. Also, the signs would often note if there were vacancies. In one instance, we had an extremely difficult time finding any vacancies. There was a large auto show taking place in the Toledo area and, at each exit, the hotels and motels were booked solid. This was not good. I fell asleep in the car and, when I finally awoke, I was laying in a motel bed. Speaking of motel beds, we used to love the vibrator beds. Sometimes, to wake us up in the morning, my dad would insert a quarter into the slot under the bed to start it shaking. That was always so much fun. The whole purpose for those beds was to thrill small children, right? Of course, it was. They performed their task admirably.

After retrieving a change of clothing from my father's old brown leather suitcase, which I can only presume had followed him across all his adventures from the past forty years, it was time to get some breakfast. I'm typically not a breakfast eater but I could never turn down the diner faire that we'd get on the road. It seems they were all the same. We'd take a short walk from the motel to the nearby diner. We'd sit in a little booth with a mini-jukebox at the end of our table. We'd never play any music but it seems there was always some country song playing in the joint. And I'm talking old school country—Patsy Cline, Loretta Lynn, Johnny Cash, etc. As we listened and soaked in the ambiance, which usually involved a strong cigarette smoke smell, we perused the laminated single page menus and made our breakfast choices. Before long, a waitress, wearing a stereotypical waitress outfit, would make her way over to us with her little notepad. I almost always opted for the two egg (any style) breakfast which came with toast and two slices of bacon. I'd usually add on a glass of orange juice, or grape-fruit juice if I was feeling especially feisty. The two-egg combo was an easy choice and hard to mess up. Sometimes, it'd come with some hash brown potatoes. This is where I first grew to appreciate hash browns—especially when they're done right. The diners always got it right.

After breakfast, it was back to the room. We packed up and Dad took care of whatever, um, business Dads need to take care of in the morning. Jen and I would occasionally plead for another quarter in the vibrating bed. Sometimes Dad would humor us but, as a child of the Depression, sometimes he wouldn't. A quarter had value and was not to be squandered. Before long, we were on the road again. If we worked the timing right, we would be in Illinois by late afternoon.

The second day of driving was not much different from the first except for the fact that Ohio and Indiana seemed to transition more quickly into the rearview mirror than did Pennsylvania which seemed to go on, and on, and on. Gas was pretty cheap in those days but I do remember a time when we stopped to refuel and, for the first time ever, my father saw the cost of regular gas exceeding 50 cents a gallon. He was furious! This was highway robbery, literally. We didn't fill up but pushed on until we came to the next station where, happily, the cost was just slightly below the 50-cent mark. It was reminiscent of the first time I went to a barber shop with my father where the cost per cut exceeded $5. He was not happy. The world was changing and prices were climbing. Good thing he didn't burn that quarter on a bonus ride for the kids at the Color TV / Air Conditioning Motel! My sister and I just shrugged and continued our games. Jen would help keep a lookout for license plates, too. It helped to have two sets of eyes searching. Eventually, the unmistakable skyline of Chicago would come into view in the distance and we'd work our way to our hotel. When possible, we'd stay in the old hotel where Grampy (our name for our grandfather) lived. It was a classic place, a hotel that belonged in an old movie. It was dark inside and I recall a beautiful dark mahogany staircase that descended into the imposing lobby. It was a cool place but it definitely felt, and smelled, ancient.

After several days with Grampy, we'd hit the road again. Twice we returned directly to New York. Once we pushed on, through Iowa, to western South Dakota. The road trip was similar but, instead of Howard Johnsons, we might stop at a Stuckey's. I liked Stuckey's. They had great hamburgers and, of even greater interest, a little store with trinkets for purchase. I still own a little Iowa flip calendar that I purchased at Stuckey's which is, perhaps, my only real connection with the state of Iowa (well, besides the best man at my wedding). The only remarkable driving tale from South Dakota was my father nearly running out of gas in the Black Hills. Did he bypass that gas station with the 51-cent gas??? We were so low, riding on "E", that my dad literally put the car in neutral and shut off the engine as we reached the top of the large hills so that we might coast down without burning any fuel. It would not have been good to be stranded out in the middle of nowhere. I'm happy to report that we finally did find a gas station before we ran dry. I wasn't too worried. I wouldn't have been the one who had to explain that little misadventure to Mom. While in South Dakota, we visited with family and saw a few tourist sites, much as we had in Illinois. It was a great visit. Wonderful as it may have been, we were all anxious to make our way back home. The return trip went much as the trip out. Again, the tunnels were the main thrill of the journey. A final highlight, however, were the rest stops in New Jersey. There were several, and the structures spanned across the Turnpike like a welcome home banner. We all knew this was the last stop before reaching our house. From there, it was just a matter of hours. The return route was familiar so the fold out road maps could be safely stowed. The final welcome home was the Fiddlestix Toy Store. While not precisely co-located with the border, it was always my kid reference signaling we were back in my hometown. Our house was just over a mile away. My sister and I would begin singing: "We're almost home but we're not home yet!" That was the only line to the song. And we'd keeping singing it until we reached our driveway.

I miss those trips. Driving across country is a different experience these days. Cars have all the bells and whistles and GPS units are squawking directions as satellite radio stations play select playlists of targeted music. Drivers leap frog from McDonalds to McDonalds, all part of giant road-side complexes. The Color TV / Air Conditioning Motels are disappearing as the major hotel chains litter the roadsides with fancier lodging options that, ultimately, all belong to one or two major companies. Likewise, the little privately owned diners are vanishing from the landscape as large trucks deliver pre-fabricated foods to all their franchisees. I'm not saying it's all bad. In many ways, things have become safer and the needs of the traveler are better catered to. But it is different. I'm sure, a few hundred years ago, a cowboy looked on sadly as a railroad car filled with cattle raced along the tracks, disturbing the quiet of a summer sunset on the plains.

Flapper and the Captain

Times change. I tip my hat to that cowboy and to the remarkable road trips of yesteryear.

The Story Behind the Story

Once more, an anthology's theme took me right back to my wheelhouse—writing stories about my life experiences. "A Trip for the Books" called upon authors to submit stories relating to travel adventures. As an Air Force veteran, having traveled the United States and the world, I had a nearly infinite quiver of arrows to launch against this project. The trick was going to be selecting a story that would be unique and interesting to the audience. I had a couple ideas in mind—stories that didn't read like the standard "road trip." I elected not to use my military-specific travel experiences, instead opting for "something else." The first of my two submissions, "Three Summers," took me back to a special time in my life and happy memories of childhood trips out west to see my grandfather. As I did not start my diary until 1982, I had to rely upon my childhood memories—many of which remain surprisingly vivid in my mind. At some point in the future, I realize I may lose some of these mental pictures so this piece was somewhat of a labor of love—a preservation of images. I thoroughly enjoyed writing this story of a simpler time when families traveled together across the country enjoying a uniquely American experience before the days when chain restaurants and hotels swallowed up the competition and each town started to look much like the one before.

THE HALLOWEEN BLIZZARD: TWO HILLS AND THE ICY PLAINS OF DOOM

(Written September 30, 2020)
Published by Red Penguin Books in "*A Trip for the Books*" (October, 2020)

Recounting of the most harrowing drive of my life.

Diary entry, October 28, 1991: "The mountain conditions are very questionable but I'm going to try to get across anyway—it's the prettiest route and by far my preferred routing. It'll be a tough drive."

My Instructor Upgrade Training Program was over. The Air Force gave me five days to get from Atwater, California back to my home base in Wichita, Kansas. I was going to try to make it home in three with a slight detour to visit my old college in Colorado Springs, Colorado. I knew friends who made the drive in two days. I'd heard of idiots who made it in one. My only company on this journey was my Chevy S-10 Blazer 4x4. Through three perilous days, a blizzard tracked eastward with me. I nearly died a half dozen times and I vowed, upon my return, that I would never own a vehicle without four-wheel drive—it saved my life, again and again.

I set out early on the morning of October 29th—my goal for day one was to conquer the Sierra Nevada Mountains and recover for the night into Salt Lake City, Utah. An older and wiser me would have elected to take the southern route home. At 25, I was more interested in reliving the breathtaking vistas that were etched in my brain following several spectacular trips across the mountains, especially a beautiful stretch of I-70 that wound its way through the Rocky Mountains. It was still fall and I gravely underestimated the brutality of the storm that was fast on my heels. In 1991, I had no cell phone to call for help or to check weather or road conditions up ahead. I navigated using my road atlas and, as necessary, my pocket compass. GPS units for automobiles were still years away.

A series of backroads took me north. The early morning drive was uneventful. As if fleeing before the tempest, the sun had long since disappeared from the daytime sky and an ominous darkness accompanied me as I made progress along some eerily desolate stretches of road. Where was everybody? Did they know something I did not? I intercepted I-80 somewhere north of Sacramento and felt a little more comfortable before detours took me, once again, across barren landscapes. Eventually, I reached the familiar foothills and began my ascent. The gentle snowflakes were hardly a portent of things to come. It wasn't long before the snows came in earnest. Between the fog and the blowing snow, visibility went down dramatically. I strained to see out ahead of me. Lane markings disappeared from view. My inclination was to reduce my speed significantly but I also knew that many trucks traveled these roads and I had no desire for an 18-wheeler to come barreling into me on a downhill stretch of interstate. If I couldn't see ahead, then neither could they. I was more confident in my ability to decelerate my small SUV than in a truck's ability to brake for me. So, I kept on at a moderate pace, just below the speed limit. While visibility was my primary concern, on this first leg of the trip, I did encounter a number of slick spots on those mountain roads which definitely got my attention. My entire body was tense as I wound my way through the mountains, four-wheel drive engaged. By the time darkness fell, I was exhausted. I popped some peppermint Lifesavers into my mouth to help revive me and they seemed to do the trick. Through the darkness and the mist, I was finally able to make out the distant lights of Salt Lake City. I made my way into town, my eyes stinging, and I hoped that there would be vacancies at the first hotel I found. Happily, there was. Little did I know that my winter driving experience had barely just begun.

Not wasting time for breakfast, I checked out of my hotel early in the morning and made a quick stop at a gas station to fill my tank. The degrading weather conditions filled me with a sense of urgency and I began to believe that every minute saved would help to keep me just ahead of the severe weather. My plan seemed to be working throughout the early hours of the morning. I tracked south along I-15 in order to reach I-70 where I would pick up my eastbound heading. Despite my concerns about the weather, I was still anxious to enjoy some mountain views along a familiar stretch of road. By the time I reached the Rockies, there was nothing to see. Again, the snows came and the lanes disappeared. My car fish-tailed, fighting for traction again and again, as I perilously passed a number of trucks, all creeping at a horse and buggy pace around the winding mountain roads. This was no longer a sightseeing pleasure drive; it had become a battle for survival. Ice was accumulating on my windshield wipers and the spray reservoir outlet nozzle quickly froze over. My wipers were doing the best they could to provide at least a limited amount of forward visibility; as much as was possible considering the blowing snow. I felt very uncomfortable but I continued my progress towards Denver. I can't overstate the sense of relief I felt as I began to slowly work my way back down the mountainous roads taking me into Denver. Denver, Colorado was reporting a record low temperature at five degrees Fahrenheit and, with the winds, the effective temperature was well into the negative range. Refueling my vehicle was pure misery. I was not equipped with a cold winter coat as I was not anticipating an October drive to turn into an Arctic expedition. As I held the icy-cold metal trigger on the gas pump, my hand nearly froze. The wind and blowing snow were tearing at my face. Could my eyeballs freeze? I wasn't sure. I squinted hard and tried to turn away from the direction of the wind. I considered my detour to Colorado Springs and quickly concluded that I had assumed enough risk for the day and could do without an icy rush hour detour two hours south of my primary route. The light was fading and, fortunately, I had enough sense not to let the temptation of a sentimental excursion cloud my judgment.

Retiring for the night in Denver, I went to bed with a false sense of security, having conquered two mountain ranges in less-than-ideal road conditions. I wasn't too worried about the long, straight, shot along I-70 into Kansas. That was plains country and there was little risk of sliding off a cliff. I'd sleep in a little bit longer just to give the plows a chance to clear the roads of the night's snow. I was sure my final day of driving would be the easiest and I was anticipating an afternoon recovery back at my apartment in Wichita.

I made no diary entry on October 31, 1991, Halloween. When I type the date into my computer's search engine, the first thing that pops up is "The Halloween Blizzard." A day later, my diary begins "We all can point to a day and say 'those were the worst driving conditions I ever saw' – October 31st, Halloween, was that day for me. I'm glad I lived through it and, if I thought roads might improve in the next few days, I might have called it quits—but I figured things would only get worse."

It was an incredibly frigid morning and the snow continued to fall heavily. Denver's temperature was the lowest recorded temperature ever for Halloween—a record only broken 28 years later, in 2019. This would be my third day of driving with no visible lane markers beneath the accumulated snow and ice. Visibility was awful and I kept telling myself that I'd break out into the clear sooner or later. I never did. I had no way of knowing that one of the most powerful "winter" storm systems in this nation's history was tracking right along with me and would be my traveling companion for the remainder of my journey. My car stayed in four-wheel drive mode the entire day as snow gradually transitioned into an even more dangerous freezing rain and sleet. The icy precipitation, layered upon the accumulated snow and slush, turned the entire interstate into a giant ice rink. My wiper blades worked furiously to maintain an aperture of sight but even their heroic efforts could not fend off the impressive ice building up upon my windshield and upon the wipers themselves. My eyes desperately strained to see the road ahead. I noted in my diary that if there had been any significant curves along the highway between Denver and Salina, Kansas, no one would have been able to keep to the road. As it was, an ever-increasing volume of vehicles lay motionless off to the sides of the interstate where they had slid into ditches, guard rails, or simply off into the shoulder. Smoke emanated from their tailpipes indicating that the hapless travelers were burning their fuel to keep warm rather than to attempt any more forward progress on their journeys. The highway patrol was their last hope and the increasing number of flashing lights were proof that the first responders were out in force and attending as many stranded drivers as they could while others waited and hoped for rescue before their life-sustaining fuel ran out. Those who were able to maintain enough traction to stay on the road plodded along cautiously knowing that their fate could just as easily be that of the unfortunate host of adventurers who succumbed to the brutal hand of Mother Nature.

As if things weren't bad enough, I encountered nearly unbearable road conditions between Hays and Salina, Kansas. It was the most dangerous stretch of road yet—something seemingly impossible to fathom considering the long, straight, stretch of flat earth separating the two cities. There were no places to stop and the freezing rain continued to pour down. Through some strange combination of snow, plowing, slush, more plowing, and then topped by freezing rain, the road had turned into a rutted and uneven surface that I can only equate to moguls on a ski slope. For 100 miles, and over four hours, my

car bounced and jumped as if I were driving over a series of continuous ice-covered speed bumps, one after the other. I had never experienced anything like that in my life. Even at 20 to 30 miles per hour, my
car was bouncing and vibrating wildly and I had to fight to keep my
vehicle on the road. The miles to Salina seemed infinite. My hands
tightly gripped the steering wheel, my teeth were clenched, and my
entire body was tense—it was absolutely exhausting. The darkness of
the night only added to the dread. My hopes of a late afternoon return
to Wichita had long-since faded. My new focus was on trying to keep
myself alive, and sane, until Salina where I hoped I might find lodging
for the night. My concern was that everyone else on the road was going
to have the same idea. There aren't a lot of towns with hotels in that
neck of the woods and I knew travelers would be scrambling for what
rooms were available.

As I approached Salina, feeling like I had reached the limit of my
endurance, I began to pick up my favorite Wichita radio station on my
car radio. Less than 100 miles to go—maybe I can make it? The
internal debate began. While I thought calling it quits right then and
there was the safer option, I had serious doubts about finding lodging
in Salina and it also seemed a shame to charge Uncle Sam for another
night of hotel lodging when my own bed was a stone's throw away. As
it turns out, it was going to be a really, really, really long stone's throw
—I pushed on.

I was not on I-135 South for very long before I picked up on some
burning flares in the road up ahead. With my windshield still heavily
iced, I was struggling to assess the situation. I slowly followed the car
ahead of me, not seeing any signs to indicate what I should be doing.
The flares seemed randomly placed and absolutely confused me.
Moments later, I saw the flashing lights of a police vehicle behind me. I
pulled over. Expecting some helpful safety tips from the police officer
who got out, I was instead rebuked for not turning off at the exit near
the flares. "Yes, Sir; no, Sir; no excuse, Sir." I ran through all my basic
military responses. I wanted to complain that the flares did nothing to
advise drivers and that I had merely followed the path of the vehicle in
front of me. Ultimately, I knew it was better just to take the heat and
get on my way than to argue with a jerk who was probably having a
pretty awful day, too. I didn't need any more stress in my day although
spending the night in a warm jail cell was seeming like a fairly decent
option at that point. Apparently, I-135 was now closed. They should

have closed I-70. I think they eventually did. Rather than turn me around, the highway patrol officer directed me to depart the interstate at the next available exit and I did just that. The detour only complicated my night's journey. As the entire interstate was shut down, I was going to have to somehow figure out how to get down to Wichita, Kansas using a series of backroads that were unfamiliar to me. Zigging this way, zagging that way, I worked my cardinal directions south and east until I saw the appropriate signage to get me back to Wichita. I breathed a huge sigh of relief as I finally entered the familiar city and, from there, memory took over and I cautiously made my way the remaining few miles towards my apartment. I was totally wiped out and the only thing I could think about was getting into my warm bed. And I was just about to do so when the phone rang. I must re-emphasize that I was not even supposed to be back home until Sunday night, November 3rd. I picked up the phone—it was my aircraft commander with one final Halloween night surprise for me. I was informed that I needed to come in the next morning (Friday) to mission plan for a flight out to California on Monday and a week-long TDY (Temporary Duty) in California. The irony was not lost on me. I did my best to hold back the anger. I had just spent three days driving from California, in blizzard conditions, ne'er a lane marker to be seen, and having nearly lost my life on several occasions . . . and now the Air Force wanted me to head right back?! Worse still, several other navigators were going to be on the flight so I could have easily just met up with them in California as my services were not required to get the jet out to the West Coast. After a deep sigh, I told my aircraft commander that I'd be there. Phone receiver down, blankets pulled back, I was sound asleep within minutes.

I've been on countless road trips across the years. I've seen majestic mountains and beautiful stretches of southwestern dessert; I've experienced lovely views of the ocean and passed through many historic towns, occasionally stopping to visit sites of interest. But if there's one journey that really stands out in my mind, it's the great Halloween nightmare drive in 1991. An older me looks back and questions my judgment—I certainly didn't choose the safest options and, in some ways, my decisions might make for some powerful talking points in a "what not to do" case study on winter driving safety. That aside, it was truly a memorable saga. That which does not kill us . . . often makes for a pretty decent story. Buckle up and drive safely!

The Halloween Blizzard: Two Hills and the Icy Plains of Doom

The Story Behind the Story

"The Halloween Blizzard," my second submission for "A Trip for the Books" was an equally enjoyable piece to write. Unlike with my first story, I had the benefit of my detailed diary account to bolster the authenticity and accuracy of the narrative. Outside of my experiences during combat and flying through severe weather systems, the story I recounted in this piece recalled one of the most harrowing experiences of my life. Beyond the building drama, I thought this story might also give pause to younger audiences, many of whom never experienced the solitude of truly being "alone and unafraid" on isolated stretches of road with only a map to guide you and without the benefit of a cell phone to call for help or a GPS unit to help you navigate across unfamiliar winding mountainous roads and the various detours directed following Interstate highway closures. What should have been a routine drive home turned into something much more—a modern day saga, of sorts. That which does not kill us . . . makes for a pretty good story.

DAPPER MAN

(Written October 10, 2020)
Published by Red Penguin Books in *"I Can't Find My Flashlight"*
(November, 2020)

*Young adults stumble into a nightmare when they fail
to accord proper respect to a New York City street
performer.*

It was a beautiful October day and I couldn't have asked for a better stage to show off my beloved Manhattan to a couple friends whose lives were sadly unfulfilled, never having experienced the splendor of a Big Apple autumn. Cynthia and "Don't Call Me Chuck" Charles were classmates from USC and stayed local, both finding jobs in the Los Angeles area, following graduation. I had actually dated Cynthia during my first year in college and I was convinced we had something going. Then I moved on. Actually, "Cynth" moved on . . . and I waited a year or two before I decided I would, too. We stayed friends, neither of us wanting to part with the good vibes or wonderful conversations that made our platonic bond so uniquely special. Charles transferred in during our junior year and his larger-than-life personality immediately attracted Cynthia. I convinced myself that I was happy for the two of them and supportive of their growing intimacy. A real friendship blossomed between the three of us and I willingly joined in on outings and touring excursions. Cynthia and Charles always did their best to make me not feel like a third wheel. If I had only let go sooner, I might have found my peace. Instead, I will forever be haunted by the day I met the stranger . . . the day we all met The Dapper Man.

With only the three-day Columbus Day weekend to work with, I developed a rather aggressive touring schedule for my friends and they were game for all of it. Empire State Building, Statue of Liberty, Times Square, China Town, a few museums, and, of course, the beauty of Central Park; the leaves were bursting out in brilliant hues of autumnal glory--oranges, reds, yellows; even purple. A smattering of fallen leaves made a lovely crunching sound beneath our feet as we walked the paths throughout the park. Up ahead, in a clearing, several performers took advantage of the favorable climate to earn a few more tips before the cold winds of November drove them from the park. We sat on a park bench and listened to a guitarist who did some very nice renditions of several Beatles songs. When he started to repeat his four-song set, I knew it was time to move on. I walked over and dropped a five into his guitar case. Charles joked that it was worth only a buck-fifty, at best. It was really worth $10, or better, but I didn't have that kind of money as a junior associate with my company; a guy trying to scrape by in one of the most expensive cities on the planet. $5 would have to do.

A street mime approached Cynthia and re-enacted a strike to the heart from Cupid's arrow followed by the gracious gifting of an invisible rose to our lovely friend. We all got a kick out of that and Charles insisted we get our photo taken with the mime. He was good about it. I would have preferred we just got on our way. The mime acted out the motions of wiping a tear from his eye as we left. Photo and all, we really should have given him some money. I was running low but it was clear that my travel companions weren't about to cough up any dough. I turned around and ran back to give the mime a five-dollar bill. I had nothing left now but a couple twenties. We continued to walk the path on the outskirts of an open field. The sky was a magnificent sapphire blue and several picture-perfect fluffy clouds slowly drifted across the scene, in no hurry to reach their final destination. Artists only dream of recreating this kind of splendor upon the canvas.

Out ahead, just before our path re-entered a wooded section of the park, there appeared a finely dressed man who, upon closer inspection, seemed like something out of a 1930s musical. As we drew nearer, we heard the distinct tapping of his tap shoes upon the pavement. He was an older gentleman but cut an elegant figure in his black full-dress tailcoat tuxedo, white gloves, top hat, and dancing cane. Occasionally, he would stumble a bit as his knee seemed to give way attempting to land a twirling jump or recover from a dramatic leap off the nearby park bench which he expertly incorporated into his routine. Several older women and one couple, who I imagined to be newlyweds on their honeymoon, applauded the dancer as he performed for them. Cynthia was very interested so we decided to stop for a bit to watch. The dancer tipped his hat, acknowledging us. Invigorated by the growing audience, he seemed to step up his game—throwing in even more daring dance moves. The theatrical makeup which was now clearly visible upon his face did little to conceal the wrinkles that betrayed his true age. Cynthia was spellbound but Charles was growing increasingly impatient. He'd clearly had enough of street corner musicians, mimes, and dancers and was eager to find a place where he could grab a couple beers. "Hey Cynthia, let's snap a couple pics and get going, I'm getting thirsty and Pat promised he'd buy the first round." I had made no such promise.

"Come on, Charles, let's just watch for a bit. This guy is really good." Cynthia tried the nice approach first. She always does.

"Um, hello, Earth to Cynthia. We came here to feel the vibe of the City not to watch a washed-up Broadway bit player stumble over himself." Charles spoke a little too loudly and the old ladies gave him an angry glare. We were rapidly becoming unwelcome interlopers on their excursion down memory lane. Worse yet, I think the dancing gentleman may have heard, too. He looked over briefly, following Charles' rude comment, but, rather than taking offense, he re-doubled his efforts to put on a good show. Unfortunately, his knee buckled as he leaped up onto the park bench and he flipped over the backrest and crashed spectacularly on the grass behind. The poor old ladies gasped and the bride softly uttered a concerned "Oh no!" Charles was less sympathetic.

"Dude, you should not be dancing at your age. Does your insurance even cover death by dance?" Cynthia and I walked over to see if we could help the man up but Charles just pulled out his phone and filmed the poor fellow as he tried to pull himself up using the bench as an aid. Charles couldn't stop laughing as he embarked upon the creation of a video clip he hoped would go viral on YouTube before the night was over. Worse yet, he added in his own condescending narrative. "We're here in New York City's Central Park where the Ghost of Fred Astaire has just completed the spectacular debut of his new production aptly entitled 'Fall in New York.' The question on everyone's mind is whether or not all the king's horses and all the king's men can ever put Humpty Dancer together again?"

"Stop it, Charles. That's not cool. I think he's hurt." Cynthia always was the compassionate one. I think the dancer was hurt, but he refused to take my outstretched hand. Instead, he eventually returned to his feet under his own power. There were distinct mud stains upon his lapel and on both of his trouser legs. The man was visibly shaken. His hand trembled as he pulled out his handkerchief and began to address the mud. Charles came closer, still filming until Cynthia literally yelled at him "turn that damn thing off, already! Let the poor guy have his dignity."

Almost imperceptibly, at first, the clouds seemed to cease their peaceful ambling and, instead, conspired most purposefully to blot out the sun. An eerie overcast subsumed the park. Charles certainly picked up on the emotion in Cynthia's voice but completely missed the disgusted looks of the attending audience. "Okay. Sorry. Let's snap a couple pics and then let the assisted living facility take care of Uncle Charlie here." Charles grabbed the dancer and pulled him in close to take a few "selfies" with the old man. "Say Cheez—y dance routine." Cynthia just shook her head, fighting back a few tears. I urged Charles to stop and come with us.

"Come on, Charles; first round's on me, remember?"

"Okay, okay, I'm coming. This dude ain't gonna smile no matter how hard I try. Hey, Fred, what's your real name? I want to make sure you get credit when this video wins an award." The man said nothing. He did his best to ignore Charles but our friend kept taunting. "Can you even talk or are you like from the silent movie era? You should get together with the mime on the other side of the park—you guys would have some rockin' conversations."

The dancer turned back towards his audience and started to dance again but he barely got a few steps in before his leg completely folded under him and he fell on the pavement, scraping his chin and nose upon impact. He stumbled to his feet only to fall again. Charles was filming it all on his phone. "Ladies and gentleman, turn off the stage lights, this show is over."

Tears were rolling down the cheeks of the two older women. They both walked over and left some money in his top hat, laying on the ground beside him. They waited to make sure he was able to return to his feet. Well, Charles was right, the dancing was done for the day. The young couple also placed a generous tip in the old man's hat before they turned to walk away. The skies seemed to be darkening ominously and a strong wind created an unpleasant chill in the air. I could see the bride covering herself with a sweater as the groom ushered her away from the scene. With his audience departed, the old dancer stood there, trembling, and looking very unsteady. Were it not for his cane, now operating as a functional third leg, I'm not sure he would have kept his balance. Charles seemed unmoved and motioned for us to be on our way. "Let's get going, there's nothing more to see here and I think the old fella's going to be just fine." Charles turned away and began walking. Cynthia was clearly troubled but was struggling to find a remedy beyond a nearly inaudible inquiry as to the man's health. The inquiry, if heard, was never answered. I reached back for my wallet and slowly approached the dancer. When I opened my wallet, I remembered that I had given away my smaller bills earlier in the day. I felt very badly but I wasn't about to drop a twenty-dollar tip for a few minutes dancing.

"I'm sorry. I'm out of cash. We really enjoyed the show. Thanks. Um . . . bye." I ran to catch up with Charles and Cynthia. "Hey, Cynth, do you happen to have a fiver on you? I think we really ought to tip that guy. Cynthia shrugged.

"Sorry, Pat, all I've got is plastic today." Charles made a silly face and shook his head.

"Maybe he's got a card reader in his pocket? I'm guessing grandpa isn't going to fare well with a PayPal transfer." Cynthia shot an angry look over at Charles.

"Seriously, dude, you need to chill. I hope that poor guy has a nice home somewhere near and a family to go home to. I feel really badly for him." Charles was unmoved.

"He's probably like some Wall Street mogul who just does this for kicks on the weekend. He does remind me a bit of Mr. Monopoly—well, without the mustache that is. Okay, Pat, set us on a course for the nearest watering hole." As we walked, the old man's eyes never left us.

Even though it was only late afternoon, the lights were already coming on in the park and the winds were howling. This change in weather is not something the forecast had warned of. Before making a direct line for a park exit, I led my companions through a colorful forested pathway so that they could further appreciate the glory of the fall leaves which, unfortunately, were losing some of their vibrancy in the dimming light. With no other park goers in sight, I began to feel a bit uneasy. My anxiety was clearly not shared by my companions who had no memories of perilous nighttime crossings through Central Park in the darkness. I had a few unpleasant experiences during my younger days that stayed with me through the years. My senses were now on high alert. Up ahead, I saw a shadowy figure leaning against a lamp post. Cynthia and Charles kept gabbing away like unwitting tourists but I slowly placed my hands in my pockets and quietly assessed the situation as we approached. My heart all but stopped when I realized it was him . . . the dancing man. How did he even get here? A second or so later, Charles and Cynthia identified the man and they, too, got quiet. Charles just laughed. "Yeah! Encore." He jogged down the pathway to where the gentleman stood. Cynthia began to mutter the words "Please stop," but never got past a mumbled first syllable. Then, much to our horror, Charles took the man's hat and placed it on his head. He also grabbed his dancing cane and started to perform an outrageously silly routine.

"Charles, what the Hell are you doing? Cut that shit out!" He wasn't listening. Charles was lost in his own self-centered world and having the time of his life. Cynth and I walked at an increasingly rapid pace towards where the scene was playing out. The wind was really blowing now and it blew the cap off of Charles' head and carried it down the pathway where it rested at the feet of old man. His eyes were burning with rage. The violence of the wind, now whipping the tree limbs to and fro, seemed to reflect the intensity of the anger of this once gentle man.

When Charles walked over and offered the cane back, Cynthia and I breathed a deep sigh of relief. And then our jerky friend quickly pulled the cane back and taunted "You didn't say please." The old dancer carefully replaced his top hat which somehow withstood the tremendous winds that should have carried it all the way to 5th Avenue or, more likely, the East River. He was trembling with rage as he outstretched his hand to reach for his cane. Once more, Charles pretended to offer it up, only to pull it back. The old dancer's body shuttered frighteningly, as if some demon had possessed his spirit, and he let loose the most horrifically blood-curdling shriek imaginable. This ungodly utterance was unlike anything I had ever heard . . . not even within my worst nightmares. So thunderous was this cry that hundreds of jet-black crows, frightened from their resting perches in the branches above, took to the air with an equally disconcerting chorus of frantic cawing. Charles' face went pale and he dropped the cane where he stood. He stepped back a few paces, still visibly in shock. The old man lithely bent over to retrieve his cane; his face now expressionless. Charles quickly returned to us. No longer the class clown, he seemed dead serious about quickly finding an exit to the park. Our once pleasant stroll along the wooded paths of Central Park had become a frightening excursion into darkness. We reversed our course and back-tracked along the route we had taken until I got my bearings. I have to admit, I was panicking a bit and decided to head off the path and make a direct line east towards the edge of the park. No words were spoken as we negotiated the hills, rocks, and trees that stood between us and the safety of 5th Avenue. The familiar sounds of traffic could not have been more welcome. We all took a deep breath when buildings and cars appeared through the trees. Charles and I helped Cynthia up over the stone wall that was our only remaining barrier. Once over the wall, we all looked at each other and laughed, albeit nervously. Catching her breath, Cynthia asked "What the Hell happened in there?" I just shook my head.

"No freakin' idea. Are you guys still up for some drinks?" Charles still wasn't talking but he nodded his head and gave me a thumbs up. We had hardly walked ten paces down the sidewalk when a rather disheveled homeless man approached us. He was wearing a torn Army field jacket and some baggy pants that must have been three sizes too big for him. His hair was completely white as was his unkempt beard. Charles and Cynthia weren't as used to seeing homeless people so they withdrew back a few steps leaving me to do the talking. "Sorry man. Got nothing for you today." The man looked at me with an expression of annoyance upon his wrinkled face.

"I didn't ask for no money, young man." I immediately felt guilty.

"I'm really sorry. I didn't mean to . . ." Before I could complete my sentence, the man lost interest and walked right past me until he stood directly in front of Charles. Charles took another step back, repulsed by the appearance and odor of the unfortunate drifter standing before him. The retreat offered him no reprieve—the old fellow just closed the gap once more. He stared into Charles' eyes with a disturbing intensity.

"What are you looking at?!" asked Charles. He was now posturing in an attempt to intimidate the aging vagrant. The homeless man was not intimidated. He just shook his head and laughed.

"Mmmm mmmm, you shouldna fucked with Dapper Man." All the color left Charles' face.

"What?" asked Charles, confusion and fear robbing him of his confidence.

"Dapper Man. You . . . should . . . not have . . . fucked . . . with . . . Dapper Man. Nothin' good ever comes from fuckin' with Dapper Man. You're gonna regret it, son. I don't need your money. I'm just thanking the good Lord that I ain't in your shoes." He laughed again and gave a half-hearted salute as he turned to walk away, mumbling as he went. "You all have a good evening now. Enjoy the Big Apple." We could faintly hear him humming the New York, New York song as he slowly trudged away. We stood there quietly, for a while. Cynthia nervously tried to reassure us all.

"He must have seen us with that dancing guy. He was kind of dapper. Well, at first. That crazy primal scream thing kind of freaked me out but, hey, he was a little upset so . . ."

"Have you ever heard anyone scream like that, Cynth," I asked. "I mean, ever?"

"Okay. Well, let's put that in the past. We could have been nicer to the old guy but it's not like we committed any heinous act of inhumanity." Charles agreed with Cynthia.

"Right, I was just having some fun with the old guy. The mime didn't seem to have an issue with a little bit of fun so why should this Dapper Guy?" I feigned my best serious look, just to mess with Charles."

"Dapper Man, Charles. His name is The Dapper Man." Charles seemed somewhat taken aback. Mission accomplished! I finally cracked a smile and the game was up. We all started laughing as we turned back up the street, on our way to Tabby's Bistro for some drinks. The place had a good atmosphere and I knew it was just what the doctor ordered to set the stage for some more fun in the City.

With drinks in hand and a platter of Tabby's Deluxe Nachos to share, the mirth and frivolity was rekindled. Memories of many happy outings in California came flooding back. My head was in a good place. In the spirit of the conversation, I fired off a great zinger at Charles, waiting for some approving laughter and more than ready to respond to his counter attack. I was met by silence. I repeated my joke. Had it somehow offended my friends? My mind was reevaluating the last twenty seconds when I noticed that both Charles and Cynthia were no longer looking at me but had their gazes fixed directly towards a street light across the road. My distance vision wasn't quite what it was a few years ago so I squinted to try to make out the details of the scene. I joined my comrades in stunned silence when the unmistakable figure of Dapper Man materialized at the very outskirts of the soft glow of the street lamp. Inside the well-lit bistro, we must have shone like a beacon to all passersby. And, just like that, my appetite was gone. We were all feeling very uneasy but Cynthia was the first to express our shared concern.

"Okay, now this is getting a little creepy. Let's say we just get the check and head on down to Times Square, as you recommended. Pat, are you listening?" I was listening, but it took me a few seconds to process Cynthia's words as my mind was elsewhere.

"Yah, right. Great idea. I doubt he's following us but I'm all for putting more space between us and that Dapper Guy."

"Dapper Man!" Charles replied, winking.

"Right. Dapper Man." I raised my arm and gave a quick wave to our waitress to signal her that we were ready for our check." A few minutes later, the waitress arrived and handed us the check. Cynthia quickly snatched it.

"This one's on me." She smiled and turned the check over to assess the damage. Her smile disappeared completely and her eyes widened.

"That much?" I joked. Cynthia held the check so that we might all see it clearly. Written in bold red letters across the paper were the unmistakable words "Dapper Man does not suffer fools gladly." Charles' reaction was immediate. He yelled across the bistro for the waitress and she signaled that she'd be over momentarily. Once she had finished with the table she was attending, the waitress came over to see what we needed.

"Anything wrong with the bill, Sir?"

"Not with the bill," responded Charles, angrily, "but I'd like an explanation about this!" Charles menacingly outstretched his arm until our check was only six inches from the waitress' eyes. She backed away, a concerned look upon her face.

"Oh, that," she responded calmly, trying to defuse the situation. "It's simple really." She paused as she considered her words. It means you shouldn't screw with Dapper Man. Ever." A voice from across the establishment called out for more coffee and our waitress politely excused herself. Charles was clearly not satisfied. He yelled out across the restaurant.

"This is a bunch of BS!" Charles was about to head after the waitress but Cynthia grabbed his arm, motioning with her head that we should just head out. "Okay. Let's go. But no tip. Nothing."

We hastily departed Tabby's and stopped briefly to look across the street. Dapper Man was gone. With my friends in tow, I headed for the 96th Street station to catch a downtown train. The crowded street provided me with a reassuring sense of comfort and safety that I'm not sure my friends shared. Using my MetroCard, I swiped Charles and Cynthia through the turnstile and continued leading them towards the downtown platform. Even though I was used to waiting on subways, on this night, every minute seemed excruciating. I kept looking at the stairs, half expecting Dapper Man to make an appearance. Charles and Cynthia didn't say a word but I know my friends were uneasy, as well. Once on the train, I took a deep breath and slowly exhaled. I hardly noticed the stench of urine and vomit that permeated the car. 86th Street. 77th Street. 68th Street, Hunter College. I mentally checked off the stops as we made our way south on the island. At 68th Street, our car emptied. This early in the evening, on a holiday weekend, the sudden departure of our fellow riders seemed unusual—the emptiness seized my attention. I didn't want to alarm Charles or Cynthia so I didn't say a thing. Charles looked at me and smiled, joking that it was about time we got some room to stretch out. Cynthia asked if we might move down a bit, away from the horrible smell. I nodded but I was fairly certain that the entire car wreaked of human excretions. The subway doors closed and we slowly pulled away from the station. When our train arrived at the 59th Street station, my heart rate went up exponentially—the station appeared to be completely abandoned. Despite this, the train remained stationary, its car doors open. Cynthia let out a terrified shriek and pointed towards one of the support pillars. Standing beside the steel support beam, as straight and erect as the pillar itself, was the Dapper Man. His lifeless eyes and expressionless face added to his terrifying visage. Slowly, he began to walk towards us. Cynthia was completely freaking out at this point, screaming that we needed to get out of the train and leave the station. Despite our combined prayers, the doors remained open and the train motionless. I choked on my words as I bid my friends to follow me. We raced to one end of the car and through the doors into the next car. I peeked out the window and Dapper Man was still approaching the train. We hurried through two more cars, all abandoned. There was something terribly unnatural about the scene but the only thing on my mind was putting some distance between us and the Dapper Man. I poked my head out of one of the doors just in time to see the Dapper Man entering the car we had previously been riding in.

"Quick, let's get out!" I shouted. Before I could even take a step towards the car's exit, the doors whooshed shut with incredible speed. "Shit!" I was rapidly assessing the situation. Looking through the scratched little window at the end of the car, I was fairly certain I saw some motion from a few cars down. Was Dapper Man coming towards us? My fears were realized when I saw the door open between the car behind us and its predecessor. Dapper Man was slowly ambling our way, still somewhat unsteady on his feet. "Let's go!" We quickly moved forward through the cars. I was fairly confident that we would reach the next stop, at 51st Street, before Dapper Man could reach us. We did. The train slowly rolled into the station and stopped at the platform. And we waited. The doors did not open. I yelled as loud as I could, hoping the train operator might hear me, "Please open the doors, we want to get off at 51st Street!" Nothing happened. I didn't have to look to know that Dapper Man was continuing his slow but steady progress between subway cars. "Keep moving." We rapidly transited cars until we reached the front of the train. Lights flickering inside the car, our train continued its southbound journey all the while a light show of sparks, born of wheel on track contact, danced upon the darkened walls of Manhattan's underground labyrinth. By this time, tears were streaking down Cynthia's cheeks and she was clutching onto Charles' arm. Charles tried to comfort her but empathy was never his strong suit. My eyes rapidly transitioned between the inter-car door and the darkness of the tunnel. My prayers were answered when the bright lighting of the 42nd Street station came into view. A large crowd awaited the coming train. Seeing all the familiar visual cues one might expect on a crowded holiday weekend in the heart of New York had an immediate calming effect. Exiting, we worked our way through the gathered crowd waiting to board the downtown train. Once clear of the mass of humanity, we all looked towards the train to see if Dapper Man would follow us. He was nowhere to be seen. "Well, I was going to suggest we catch 'the 7' over to Times Square but, if you don't mind a little walk, I'm thinking we could all use a little fresh air." There was no disagreement there. On our way, we got to talking about Dapper Man. Although my initial inclination was to avoid the topic, it was pretty clear that we wouldn't be able to consider anything else until we had worked through the bizarre circumstances of our multiple encounters. As bewildered as my friends, I had no great insights to offer. Finally, my "rational mind" checked back in from its coffee break. "I think there's probably a really easy explanation for all of this. There are tons of character players in New York and you're likely to find half a dozen Mickey Mouses or Spider Men on any given day in the City. I'm not really familiar with this Dapper Guy character . . ."

"DAPPER MAN!" my friends simultaneously interjected. I was glad they still found some humor in the situation.

"Yes, I mean Dapper Man character. But if he's some new social media icon then it makes perfect sense that actors might be playing that role from South Ferry all the way up through Harlem. With that theatrical makeup on, it'd be really hard to tell the actors apart. Right?" I looked at both of my friends and was pleased to see a more relaxed expression come over their faces. I had convinced them. I almost convinced myself. "That guy in the Park was clearly a nut case but the rest of these Dapper Men are probably just out of work actors trying to earn a few bucks from some sponsor." As we were walking down 42nd Street, the famous New York City Public Library came into view.

"Is that the library?" asked Cynthia.

"Let's see now. Ginormous white marble edifice. Imposing lions guarding the stairs. A grand entrance way, bracketed by pillars and the words 'The New York Public Library' etched in stone above the entry. Yes, by George, I think it just may be!" Cynthia punched me on the shoulder.

"Jerk," she said playfully as she smiled. "Let's go look up Dapper Man."

"Are you nuts?"

"No. Now you've got me interested. Let's go see if we can find out what this whole Dapper Man craze is all about."

"Cynth, I'm pretty sure the library closed a couple hours ago." She looked disappointed. I was nearly 100% sure but, to humor Cynthia, I was willing to take a closer look. As we approached, it became very clear that no one was coming or going. For some reason, I felt the need to state the obvious. "And . . . it's closed."

An old woman, sitting on the library steps, called over to us. She looked somewhat disheveled but I couldn't discern whether she was a homeless woman or merely one of the many eccentrics that gave New York its rare flavor. Her sweet "little old lady voice" was very comforting. We all desperately needed a couple of grandma's homemade cookies and a glass of warm milk.

"I'm so pleased to see young people interested in a library. It seems everyone just wants to walk around looking at their little screens these days."

Cynthia immediately warmed to the old woman. "I love libraries!" There's nothing like the feel of an old book in your hands."

"Now you're talking," said the old woman, with a big grin. That's what I've always said. I used to work as a reference librarian in this very library. The look, the feel, the smell—there's something magical about old books. It looks like you were planning to visit. I'm so sorry. The library closed a couple hours ago."

"Sorry we missed it," said Cynthia. I've never been to this library but I've heard it's spectacular. You must have all kinds of great stories from your time working in the library. I'm Cynthia, by the way. These are my friends Charles and Patrick. Pat's our local guide here, today. Charles and I are in from California for the long weekend." Charles and I both added in our hellos.

"Charles, eh? That's terrific. I like the old names. It seems like these days everyone wants to jazz up their names or use nicknames. Chaz. Chuckie. C-Rod." The old lady chuckled, sweetly, reflecting upon 'C-Rod'. "I'm Doris. Doris Wiggins. Very pleased to meet you. So, were you here just to look around or were you on a special mission?"

"A special mission," replied Charles. We met this strange guy in the park and then he showed up a couple more times through the night. A couple folks mentioned that he might be called the Dapper Man so we thought we'd research to see if he was, maybe, advertising some upcoming film or some new product. We were just kind of interested."

The old woman sat quietly for a moment, reflecting. "Ah, S.C. Montague. A darling of a man."

"So, you're familiar with him?" I asked, my interest peaking. "We'd love to hear more if you've got the time."

"Oh, I don't know. There's a lot to tell and I imagine you kids have a hundred places you'd like to visit during your night in the city."

"Oh please," injected Cynthia. "We'd love to hear more. The Big Apple is about stories, after all, not about neon signs and skyscrapers." Her words seemed to inspire the woman.

"Well then, have a seat and buckle up." We all sat on the stone stairs near the woman. She pulled her shawl in closer to keep out the night air as the temperature was quickly dropping.

"S.C. Montague was a well-known performer in his day, right here in New York City. He was quite successful and was adored by theater-goers. But, like many in his day, he watched jealously as the motion picture industry grew and began to get all the attention. Being a star of the stage no longer held the same allure when compared to being a big movie star. They were making silent pictures in those days. He went through a very dark time. He took to the bottle and it only made matters worse. Soon, he found trouble getting work here in New York. He lost his love of life. He lost his fear of God. There are many rumors about what happened next but, cutting out all the ridiculous speculation, I'll just say that fortune took a turn for the better. Much better. He came into a great sum of money. He then received an unsolicited invitation to sign a major motion picture deal for several films with one of Hollywood's largest motion picture studios. Out there, in California, Mr. Montague met and married a beautiful actress, Agnetha Anne Lockborn. She was so stunning that all the Los Angeles papers called her 'The Belle of the West'. This was a very happy time in his life. S.C. Montague rose to national prominence; his clever dance routines held movie goers spellbound from coast to coast and then in Europe and Asia. His career was at its peak. At some point, in the early 1920s, he developed a nagging cough. He visited all the best doctors but none could pinpoint the cause of the affliction nor find a cure. All we know is that his voice became increasingly raspy until, finally, he couldn't speak at all. The only vocalization he was capable of making was a very disturbing screeching noise. The papers said of his voice that it was so hideous it would make babies cry and dogs howl. You should know, the press was never really fair to Mr. Montague."

"Why, what did they have against him?" asked Cynthia.

"Oh, it's hard to know exactly where the falling out occurred. I suspect there was some jealousy of this handsome and talented newcomer from the East Coast who seemed to suddenly rise to fame and glory. Maybe they felt he should have paid his dues for a while and worked his way up the ladder? But, you know, with all his time on stage in New York, he wasn't exactly a rookie. The horrible stories they told. Heartbreaking. Total garbage."

"Like what?" replied Cynthia, completely immersed in the tale.

"Well, there was this one crazy paper that wrote that he had cut a deal with the Devil who offered him the success he dreamed of, on a golden platter, and asked only his soul in exchange. They say the Devil never cuts a fair deal and that it was the Dark One, himself, who reclaimed the voice of S.C. Montague and cursed the poor man with the voice of a demon. Absolute rubbish!" Doris was clearly getting a little upset now. Cynthia, the most empathetic of us, put her hand upon the woman's shoulder and agreed with her that the attacks were ridiculous. Doris took a deep breath and continued.

"In October of 1927, "The Jazz Singer" was released. It was the first major motion picture with synchronized sound and it ushered in a new era in Hollywood. It was no longer good enough to have an expressive face and graceful movements. If you wanted to be a star, you had to have a voice built to steal hearts. I suppose I don't need to tell you what happened next. S.C. Montague's star came plummeting back to earth and his life completely fell apart. Thanks to the bad press, what you kids would probably call "fake news" now, he wasn't even able to find work as a backup dancer in the musicals of the day. His wife left him for one of the up-and-coming Hollywood glamour guys and S.C., broken of heart and spirit, used his remaining funds to buy a train ticket back to the East Coast. He lived for a while at the Algonquin Hotel, on 44th Street until . . ."

"Where?" said Charles, choking on his words. We all recognized the Algonquin as the place Charles and Cynthia were staying during their visit. Doris didn't seem to hear the question. She was lost in her thoughts and trying to fight back the tears.

"Until 1937. He hung himself in his room. A terrible, terrible tragedy. He was only 37 at the time." What followed was an uncomfortable silence. We all wanted to ask Doris about whether or not she was familiar with any kind of revival or show that might be honoring the legend of S.C. Montague but, given her emotional state, we thought it better just to let it go. About that time, an unusual yellow taxi pulled up. I had only seen cabs like that in old copies of Life Magazine. It was definitely a vintage model . . . maybe late 40s or early 50s. Doris apologized for having to leave but she expressed gratitude for keeping her company while she waited for her ride. The driver came around and opened the door for her and she gave a farewell wave, her white cotton glove highlighted against the night sky, before she slid into the back seat. Nice lady. The cab slipped away into the darkness. Hidden from view, behind the taxi, we now saw the figure of the Dapper Man, standing silent and still across the street.

"Hey, do you want to go talk to that guy?" asked Cynthia? If anyone can tell us about these mysterious Dapper Men sightings, it's a Dapper Man."

"Fuck, no!" Charles had no desire to learn any more. He was still freaking out about the Algonquin Hotel. "Let's go."

"Times Square?"

"No, Pat. I want to go back to the hotel and I want to catch the first flight back to L.A."

"What?!" said Cynthia, shocked by the sudden change of plans. "We still have another couple days to hang out with Pat. There's a ton of things I want to see."

"We're done, Cynthia. We're going home. If you want to stay, you can hang out with Pat; but I'm outta here."

"You wouldn't mind if I stay?" asked Cynthia.

"Whatever. Knock yourself out." Charles' voice was trembling with fear.

"Okay, follow me." I knew the hotel was within easy walking distance and I also knew that no amount of coaxing was about the change Charles' mind."

We arrived at the hotel and Charles made a direct line to the front desk where he told them he was planning on checking out that evening. The desk attendant explained that the holiday lodging fee was not refundable but the warning had absolutely no impact on my friend. He was a driven man. Cynthia and Charles headed off for the elevator; I decided just to wait in the lobby. I looked around a bit but then curiosity got the better of me. I slowly walked up to the front desk.

"Excuse me. I know this is a strange question but did anyone ever hang themselves in this hotel?" The attendant gave me a strange look.

"You sure know how to start a conversation. Well, it's an old hotel. I couldn't say whether or not anything like that ever happened here."

"If it did, would you tell me?" The attendant considered my question.

"Sir, it's hotel policy not to discuss incidents involving our guests."

"Sooooo . . . no?"

"No. Probably not."

"Probably? Ever hear of a guy called S.C. Montague?" The woman shouted back to the room behind the counter.

"Hank, have you ever heard of a guy called S.C. Montague?" An older gentleman, quite well dressed, slowly emerged from the door.

"You don't have to yell, Charise. I may be old but I can hear just fine. S.C. Montague? The Dapper Man? Yes, I've heard of him."

"Did he hang himself in this hotel?"

"I'm sorry, but it's company policy not to discuss . . ."

I cut the man off before he could finish and completed his words for him "'incidents involving our guests.' I know. Look, this is pretty important and, if I were to maybe donate a substantial tip towards the hotel staff maybe . . ."

This time, it was I who was cut off in mid-sentence. "That would be bribery, wouldn't it? No, I'm sorry, but I can't."

"Look, I'm sorry. This is just really important right now and I can't explain why. I won't tell anyone a thing and, to be honest, I doubt we'll ever see each other again after tonight so," I paused, "what do you say?"

"That was many years ago. All I know is that my predecessor lost two weeks of pay for joking that he only assigned "The Montague Suite" to people he didn't like. The owners didn't take kindly to the remark. First off, it's not a suite. Second, Mr. S.C. Montague was a long-time resident and, although he was rarely seen, he always paid his bills and he always tipped the hotel staff well. Finally, the owners were very disturbed about the whole incident. They were pretty superstitious and felt that Mr. Montague traveled with a dark cloud surrounding him. Frankly, he spooked them and they preferred his name not be mentioned at all. You know how some people are."

"Two weeks of pay? That's a lot. Did they eventually fire him? Is that how you got the job?"

"He was hit by a cab while crossing the street, just a couple blocks down from the hotel. He died in the hospital the next day. That's how I got the job." I swallowed deeply.

"That's awful. I'm sorry to hear that." I held back my follow-up questions long enough to pass for a respectful silence. "The Montague Suite? And which room might that be, Mr.," I squinted as I read his nametag, "Simpson."

Mr. Simpson shook his head in exasperation. "Room 313. But don't you tell anyone I told you." He looked over at the young attendant, "And that goes for you, too."

"Yes, Sir, Mr. Simpson. Silence is silver."

"Golden. Silence is golden." Mr. Simpson retired to the safety of his cave. I returned to the cushy easy chair in the lobby.

Before long, Charles and Cynthia returned. Charles left the bags beside my chair as he and Cynthia went to the desk to check out. In the quiet hotel lobby, I couldn't help but overhear the conversation at the desk."

"Checking out of 313 and, if you wouldn't mind, could you please call me a cab for the airport."

"Absolutely, Sir." The attendant tried to maintain composure but she seemed a bit shaken. She took a quick glance over at me and, no doubt, observed the stunned look upon my face, as well. I debated whether I should say anything about the Montague Suite. I finally concluded that it wouldn't serve any of us to travel down that road. It was best to leave well enough alone.

As a final cherry upon this Twilight Zone evening, it was another strange vintage taxi cab that showed up to take Charles to LaGuardia Airport. I suggested that he request another cab but I had no desire to explain why I was letting my superstition get the best of me . . . so I quickly conceded upon Charles' protest. We said our farewells and then Cynthia and I headed off towards my apartment. I had a little futon in my place that I knew would meet my friend's needs. I was concerned about Charles but looking forward to a little one-on-one time with Cynth, over the next few days.

Cynthia and I did have a wonderful time exploring the city. The weather was pleasantly cool and we got around to see many of the tourist attractions that had been on Cynthia's bucket list. We each sent text messages to Charles and, between stops, tried to call. His failure to respond was a little concerning but we both knew that Charles had a way of "checking off the grid" when he didn't want to be disturbed. I was just hoping that he wasn't upset about Cynthia and me hanging out together for the weekend.

Mid-day, on Monday, I escorted Cynthia back to the airport and saw her off. I missed both my friends. I'd be lying if I said I missed them equally.

Wednesday night, I received what I can only describe as the worst phone call of my life. It was Cynthia and she was in tears. She described how she had visited Charles' apartment on numerous occasions but that he wasn't there. None of their mutual friends had seen him. After a heroic battle with the airline bureaucracy, she finally ascertained that he never actually boarded his flight back to Los Angeles that Saturday night when we parted ways. In short, he had simply disappeared. I tried to comfort Cynthia but I was as much in need of succor as my friend.

Weeks of police investigations followed. The last time anyone had seen Charles was when he got into his taxi at the Algonquin. Cynthia thought that maybe the Dapper Man might have some connection to the disappearance but none of us had any idea how to even bring that up with the authorities. Beyond this, Cynthia was becoming more and more obsessed. She was pouring through any old newspapers archived online to try to find out more about the life of S.C. Montague. As Doris had warned us, many of the papers were not kind. One trashy rag even called him Satan's Child Montague. Beyond the litany of terrible accusations, Cynthia desperately tried to sort out fact from fiction. Occasionally, she'd call me to report her latest findings. In truth, I had heard about all I wanted to hear on the topic. She did gain my full attention when she ran through Mr. Montague's family tree.

"Pat, you remember the woman we met at the library?"

"Right. I don't recall her name but she sure seemed like an expert on the Dapper Man."

"So, when S.C. Montague married Agnetha Anne Lockborn, you know, the Belle of the West, they had two daughters—Gladys and Patience. Gladys and Patience remained with Agnetha in California. Eventually, Patience came east, to New York. Her father had already passed away by that time but she attempted, briefly, to establish a career on Broadway. Unfortunately, she wasn't finding enough work to pay the bills. So . . ."

"Where is this going, Cynth?"

"Just hear me out. So, she marries this cello player with the New York Philharmonic and they have a couple kids—a boy and a girl. The girl gets married to Charles Wiggins, a banker. The oldest daughter from that wedding is named Doris. Doris Wiggins!"

"Doris Wiggins?"

"Yes, Doris Wiggins! That was the name of the old lady we met on the stairs at the library."

"So, Cynth, you think we were talking to the granddaughter of S.C. Montague?" The line was silent for a bit.

"Okay. So, I did. But then I did some more research. Doris Wiggins was, in fact, a librarian with the New York Public Library. She tried to restore her grandfather's reputation as best she could but the public had moved on and nobody gave the matter much mind."

"My turn," I said, impatient to get to the point. "So, let me guess, she decided to create a Broadway play called 'Three Cheers for S.C.' to honor her grandfather and it's due to open next week and a dozen

Dapper Men are running around the City to advertise the upcoming shows?" The line was silent.

"Pat, Doris Wiggins died in 1987."

"Okay. Look, Cynth, I want you to let this thing go. It isn't doing you any good to obsess about this. I miss Charles, too. I know how close you were and I can only imagine the pain you're going through but this is not helpful. There are no ghosts sitting on the steps of the New York Public Library and no tap-dancing demons entertaining visitors in Central Park. We saw some weird stuff during your visit but that's all it was—weird stuff. The world is full of weird things and weird people and yet we continue on our journeys and make the best of it." I went on and on and on. Sometimes, I felt like I was working as hard to convince myself as I was to convince Cynthia. Finally, she conceded, and made a kissing sound through the phone to show her affection.

"Love ya, Pat."

"Love ya, back, Cynth."

I waited for Cynthia to hang up first. I didn't want to risk cutting her off if she had anything more to say. After a lengthy pause, she ended the call.

At this point, I just really needed to clear my head. Although I had given a wide berth to Central Park since the Dapper Man incident, I thought it might be beneficial to confront my silly fears and take a little stroll through the park before all the holiday crowds arrived for the Thanksgiving experience in New York City. I was just praying to God that they didn't fly a Dapper Man balloon in the Macy's Thanksgiving Day Parade this year.

Although it was quite cool, the park was very inviting and I derived a strange pleasure from kicking at the small piles of dead leaves I encountered as I wandered the grounds. I emerged from the woods near where we first saw the Dapper Man. I stopped dead in my tracks. There he was! Dancing with renewed vigor and entertaining the small pre-holiday crowd that had gathered to admire his footwork. Just turn and go. Just turn and go. I swayed back and forth as my fear drove me one way and my curiosity beckoned me towards the familiar stage. I squinted, trying to make out the features of the Dapper Man's face. My heart was gripped with pure terror as the features came into focus. It was Charles! I began to run towards him but my legs locked up and I fell. I quickly returned to my feet and continued running as I yelled "Charles! Charles! It's me, Pat!" The dancer continued. I ran up to him and grabbed him by both shoulders. "Charles! What the Hell! What in God's name are you doing here?! Everyone thinks you're dead!" The dancer just looked at me with hollow, expressionless, eyes. I know I was not mistaken. There was no doubt that this was Charles. I spoke again, my voice frantic, "Charles, what's happened to you, man?" The crowd grew very unsettled and I started to gain their ire.

"Hey, Dude, leave the Dapper Man alone. Let him do his dance," shouted a rather burly looking fellow who appeared to be a construction worker on break. The sentiment was echoed by a chorus of assorted pleas to get out of the way and stop ruining the performance.

I took one last, long, look into the familiar face. And then I realized . . . this was no longer Charles. Any part of the friend I once knew was long gone from the shell of humanity that danced before the gleeful crowd of spectators. The Dapper Man looked right through me, his face void of any expression. I slowly backed away. I just stood there and watched the dance. He was quite good. Very good, to be precise. I looked into my wallet to see if I had any money to offer as a tip. All I had was two twenty-dollar bills. I pulled them both out and left them in a little tin box next to the performer. Dapper Man tipped his hat, ever so slightly, acknowledging the donation. I turned and walked away. A couple beer guzzling ruffians passed by me, as I walked. They were singing a mocking version of Elton John's "Tiny Dancer" and joking about beating the heck out of the dancing performer.

I stopped and turned around. "Hey! Assholes!" That got their attention. They stopped abruptly and looked at me, assessing whether I was someone they wanted to mess with or not. I stood silently for a bit. I hadn't really thought through my plan. Finally, I said the only thing that came to mind, the only piece of advice I wish Charles, Cynthia, and I had received sooner than we did. In my loudest voice I shouted "DON'T FUCK WITH DAPPER MAN!" And then I walked away.

Dapper Man

The Story Behind the Story

Where did this one come from? I'm not exactly sure. I really hadn't written a true horror story before. Generally speaking, I steered away from truly spooky or disturbing topics in my writing. My elementary school "horror stories" were more laughably funny than they were frightening. I knew it would be a challenge to create a story that had a true element of dread but I was eager to give the task a try.

With most of my short stories, I first envision an environment and then try to place interesting characters within that world allowing for a free flow of interactions that is rarely pre-scripted. I then allow the story to meander toward some notional endpoint, the likes of which is often not clearly defined and only attains focus as I near the terminus. In some instances, the story's ending is a complete surprise to me. Writing against the clock to meet the deadline, I knew I'd have only limited time for research, so I opted to set the story in a familiar location—New York City. I did have to do some research regarding the hotel while also refreshing my memories about the transition from silent films to "talkies."

New York City seemed like a great backdrop for my horror story for multiple reasons. Having grown up in a suburb of the City and traveled within Manhattan on countless occasions across the years, I harbored several countervailing impressions. In most instances, it was an exciting place filled with interesting museums, buildings, cuisine, shows, and so forth. On the flip side, especially during some of my trips in during the 70s and early 80s, it could take on a darker aspect. The City was, at times, dark and dirty and filled with homeless people and a range of strange characters who set the wary traveler on their guard. Likewise, Central Park could be a bright and cheery place, filled with picnicking friends and families, joggers and bikers, artists and wonderful street performers, and happy tourists during the sunny days of spring and summer. Yet, after sunset, especially during the cold and dark days of late autumn and winter, the park could become a somewhat foreboding place, filled with interesting (and occasionally frightening) characters. Walking through the park, on such days, my heart rate was usually elevated and I was keenly aware of any movement within my peripheral vision that might indicate the approach of some potential threat. I was never mugged. I knew people who were. Finally, the transit system, likewise, seemed to have two poles. Most of the time, the subway was my magic carpet ride to adventure—an incredible feat of human ingenuity racing me toward some fantastic destination. However, there were times when the subway ride could turn into a bit of a terrifying experience. I've seen some scary characters stumbling through the cars. I've seen swindlers and conmen, drug addicts and angry patrons who wanted to share their rage with all their fellow passengers. In the late hours of the night, when the crowds disappeared, one could not help but dread being trapped in a speeding subway car with someone who felt they had nothing more to lose and decided to target whoever was luckless enough to find themselves in their destructive path. All of these thoughts bounced around in my head as I began to write.

Finally, regardless of the genre, where possible, I like to add some element of morality. I suppose it's not unusual in popular horror for the "victims" to be snotty kids, lecherous old men, or corrupt business moguls—you know, people who we won't feel too sorry for if they meet an untimely demise. In "Dapper Man," the character of Charles most closely approximated my own notion of someone just itching to find himself on the receiving end of some unpleasant karma consequences. I recalled many times, in many countries, traveling with a group of people who, frankly, seemed disrespectful of local customs and tended to stick out like sore thumbs, further solidifying the unfortunate reputation of "the ugly American." I wanted to include an element of that frustration that I've felt into this story, and so I selected Charles to embody the cliché. He wasn't bad, per se, or evil, but he was a bit of a bull in a china shop and his insensitivity would put him in the crosshairs of the late S.C. Montague who, likewise, was not necessarily evil. As it turns out, the "Dapper Man," suffering from his past wrongs, takes on the role of judge—less the vindictive villain, randomly targeting victims, than a soul looking to hold others accountable and, perhaps, finally break a curse that has held him bound to his hellish existence for the better part of a century.

I had a great deal of fun writing "Dapper Man," in some cases writing through the night, because I felt so compelled to continue the story and find out where it was going. I was thrilled when "Dapper Man" was not only selected for publication in the horror anthology but was also selected for inclusion in "Stand Out: The Best of the Red Penguin Collection." I was very pleased with the positive reception for this, my first contribution to the world of horror fiction short stories.

WELCOMING LIFE

(Written October 19, 2020)
Published by Red Penguin Books in "*The Moments*" (December, 2020)

*Reflection upon the uniquely beautiful births of my
children and the joy those memories still bring.*

My life is full of special moments. There are four that rise above all others. The four moments each have a name and they share that name with each of my four children. There is nothing more beautiful, or more perfect, than the blessing of welcoming a child into the world. Where there is life, there is hope. Hope for a better tomorrow.

Altus, Oklahoma. Lakenheath, England. Omaha, Nebraska. These were places we lived but I don't cherish them for this. These were places of birth . . . and they will live forever in my memories.

Our first child was two weeks overdue and the doctor elected to induce the delivery on a specific day. We arrived early in the morning and spent the entire day in the hospital with a Pitocin drip feeding into my wife's arm. A medical professional herself, my wife timidly advised the attending nurse that the IV was incorrectly positioned and the fluids were not going into her veins but into the soft tissue of her arm, which was starting to swell. With little fanfare and hardly an apology, the situation was remedied. At the end of the day, there was still no labor. The doctor was working up the paperwork to release my wife back to home when our first-born decided it was time to make his entrance into the world. Things got busy and I stepped back to get out of the way. And then he arrived! The doctor beckoned me over and I was handed some medical scissors. Cutting the umbilical cord was exciting and also a bit nerve-racking. The cord was stiffer than I had imagined—it felt like cutting through a rubber hose. Our baby was free —he was now an individual. It was the first step of many along the road towards independence. Sight. Rolling. Crawling. Walking. Car seats and strollers to reading and studying to college and employment. With care and with blessings from above, the seeds we water grow into beautiful trees, steady against the winds and raising their arms toward the sky with hope and aspirations.

England. Number two elected to visit us on foreign soil. My parents made the trip "across the pond" to assist, where possible. I told my father that, in a pinch, he might have to drive my wife to the hospital . . . driving on the left side of the road. I took Dad out for a practice drive —he had a tendency to ride up on the curb as many American drivers do when they first try to drive in Great Britain. My father was dreading the thought of having to convey a pregnant woman via English back roads and through complex "roundabouts" towards a military hospital, a good twenty minutes away. I was summoned to the phone at work on that cold and dark January day—the race was on. I made my rounds to explain my absence and, rather than having to detail how I had delegated the day's tasks, my leadership simply said "Get going. Now." So, I did. I made it back to our cottage and collected my wife. With steely-eyed focus, I expertly negotiated the country roads and roundabouts and gate checks on the way to the hospital. This baby was coming and coming fast. The doctor, with a false sense of calm, casually set about some preliminary set-up. This child was her second and my wife knew the time was now. The doctor and nurses seemed unimpressed . . . until a head broke through—then the chaos ensued. People pushing this way and that, the doctor rushed over—he hadn't even the time to put his latex gloves on. I held my wife's hand—as she vomited on me—and looked on in amazement as our beautiful girl, our British Princess, completed her journey from the womb into her new kingdom. It happened in the blink of an eye; no stopwatch required to time that delivery.

A year and nine months later, a spooky Halloween night. I was wandering the neighborhood with my children, Trick-or-Treating within Base Housing at Offutt Air Force Base. I had agreed to periodically check back home where my mother was attending to my pregnant wife. I did not have a cell phone in those days. So, dutifully, me and the costumed cuties accompanying me returned for a mid-tour wellness check at our house. My wife looked at me with a dead serious gaze and told me it was time. "What? You're kidding, right? Halloween?" What kind of "trick" was this? I wasn't really sure I wanted a baby born on Halloween and I convinced myself that these were just some mild tremors—not the big quake. All the same, I wasn't about to take chances. I left the kids with their grandmother and I drove my wife to the base hospital, still skeptical that this was the real deal. The nurses and doctor were skeptical, too. They gave us this long speech about how many moms think they're going to deliver on holidays just because it's kind of a special event. Halloween? Really? So, the doctor vanished and the nurses went about some routine business and started to get my wife's vitals when BAM! Go time! Once again, the hospital room became a scene of frenzied action. It happened so fast that no doctor ever made it in for the delivery. Our third child, the greatest Halloween treat ever, was delivered by the attending nurse. My wife had tried to warn them that she was a pro at quick deliveries (we all learned our lesson in England) but the good hospital folks weren't buying it. We proved them wrong. But none of this mattered with our sweet little pumpkin-girl in our arms. Years later, I always worried that my daughter would be bothered that she had to share a birthday with the Halloween spirits, conducting her party as doorbells rang, and then quickly costuming up to join the little pirates and superheroes raiding the neighborhood. My concerns were ill-founded. My daughter absolutely loved it! She thought it was the best way to spend a birthday—cake, presents, nighttime adventuring with her costumed siblings, and a bag full of candy before the night was done.

Several years later, we were blessed with one more surprise. After enduring two sisters, who he truly loves, my first-born burst forth in ecstatic joy when, while watching a video of an ultrasound my wife brought home, he saw letters appear on the screen that spelled out "It's a boy!" He would finally have a brother! This was the first time we knew the sex of our child before delivery. Previously, we wanted it to be a surprise. By the time #4 was "baking in the oven," we were more interested in actionable intelligence than in surprises. With three children to our name already, we were fully prepared for our fourth and final birthing experience and, for the most part, everything went as advertised. My wife was 38 at the time so she was in a higher risk category—the docs kept a close eye on her throughout the entire pregnancy and they did a wonderful job. They were calm. We were calm. The only one who had a tough time was me. My wife had previously elected not to use anesthesia but, this time, the pain was too much so she requested an "epidural." For some reason, the doctor thought it was a good idea to have me help with that process. Getting up close to assist as a needle was shoved into my wife's spine—sure; why would that bother me? It did. I started to get very light-headed and finally suggested that, perhaps, the medical professionals might want to take it from here. And then, finally, we all heard that sublime cry of a newborn, a freshly-minted human breathing his first breaths from our world, sharing our air. It was beautiful. They all were beautiful.

Life is filled with ups and downs. I am no longer married to the woman who will always be the mother of my children, but we will forever be bonded through the creation of four beautiful children. I was proud of my wife then and I have lost no respect over the years for the woman who carried four Lange children through three-trimesters, each, and who lay stoically, propped up in a delivery room bed, as I carefully handed the creation of her labors, and of our love, into her awaiting arms. These are the memories that bring me the most joy. That's love.

The Story Behind the Story

The assigned task for the upcoming "The Moments" anthology was to craft pieces that described moments or occasions from the authors' lives that were uplifting and worthy of celebration. The responses were as diverse as the authors. For me, this was an easy one...at least from a mechanical standpoint. The emotional aspect was somewhat more challenging. Immediately, I knew the moment, or moments, I celebrated most, and I was confident I could craft an essay without much effort and without having to do any research. The birth of my four children was an obvious choice for the topic, but it was challenging to write on an emotional level as I had to reconcile some of the most beautiful memories of my life with the fact that, following my divorce in 2016, I rarely get to see my kids anymore as they followed my ex-wife to her small hometown in South Dakota. We had been living in Seoul, South Korea, at the time of the divorce. While no longer a "whole family," we were still a family, and I regularly had to wrestle with the challenge of being a long-distance father. In writing this essay, I had to work through some of that pain and a feeling of loss as I focused on the great joys of fatherhood and acknowledged how proud I was of my ex-wife for carrying, delivering, and mothering our four wonderful children. None of that changed on account of the divorce. Sharing the moments of personal joy was an enjoyable experience and reconciling my own emotions through the process was a cathartic experience.

DIVINE WIND

(Written November 1, 2020)
Published by Red Penguin Books in *"The Beauty Within: Stories of Spirituality, Faith, and Love"* (November 2020)

Essay regarding the universality of faith and the power of divine inspiration.

A Divine Wind blows. It fills our souls. It gives us hope. I've felt it. You have, too. Do you remember where it first touched you? Do you remember when? Have you forgotten? Were you too busy to notice the way it caressed your face and soothed your heart? There were more important things going on at that time, weren't there? Was it money? Was it your reputation? Perhaps a relationship that needed tending to? There were a million distractions and there'll be a million more. Who am I to ask that you quiet the noise and open your mind? I am nobody. I have no degree in counseling nor am I an ordained minister. I might be completely wrong in everything I say and do. I admit it. I can only offer my truth. I won't ask that you believe me. You will believe what you choose to believe. That's okay. I won't think the less of you. Will you think less of me? You won't be the first. Nor the last. Will you chastise me? Will your words save me? Or is it important for you to ensure that I know that my path will lead me towards damnation. Will it? Am I without hope, then? Perhaps I will find your blessing if I sit next to you next Sunday at church, shake your hand, share your hymnal? Will I find God's blessing? Will you respect me more if I drop a hundred-dollar bill onto the collection plate? Will God respect me more? Maybe. But I'm not so sure. You who are so quick to judge, is that not the pride you were warned of? No matter. I have felt the Wind—the Wind that bursts through the chapel doors, howls in chorus with the singing voices in the grand cathedrals; the Wind that whispers tales of old in synagogues and calls Muslims to prayer; the Wind that embraces the standing stones of old; the same Wind that reaches the lonely upon snow-covered mountains and touches the sailor far out at sea. This is the Divine Wind that has inspired countless men, women, and children of every imaginable faith, known and long-forgotten, across the entire span of human existence. I have felt this Wind yet it touches me like it touches no other. It touches you in a unique way, too. From the East or from the West, racing up from the valleys or down from the mountains, it makes contact with each of us in a different and special way. I wish we would all understand this and learn to appreciate it. Faith is about hope. It is not about who is better than who or who is more worthy in the eyes of God. I'm pretty sure of this. None of us own the Divine Wind. It's a blessing shared equally with all. What we do with this blessing—well, it's up to each of us, I suppose. I don't mind sharing how I feel. I like to know how you feel. I won't tell you how you should feel. I would ask that you reciprocate. Live and let live. Believe and rejoice that we have all found strength in our faith. Let's hold hands and agree. Can we? I hope so. Much depends upon it.

I've seen too much hate. I've seen swastikas spray painted upon the beautiful columns of my school. I've heard people mock others for their beliefs. I've been told I was going to go to Hell because I did not go to church on Sunday. I've been told that I was a terrible leader for my family because I did not regularly accompany my family to church—it was not enough that I encouraged them to follow their hearts and open themselves spiritually for the Divine Wind, however it might touch them. The criticism hurt. I got over it. My critics might have been right. But, then again, they may have been terribly wrong. Sometimes, leadership is knowing when to let the ones you love travel their own roads. That's what I believe but I don't need to convince you because you know what is right. You do, don't you? I'm glad you do. I don't always know what's right but I know when I need to be still and quiet and look, listen, and feel. When I am, the Divine Wind finds me, even in my deepest, darkest, hiding spots. When I believe all those who wish to hurt me and I curse myself for being so much less than I am, the gentle Wind finds me and kisses me gently upon the cheek like a beautiful angel assuring me that I am worthy not only of life, but of love, as well. My heart fills and I am strong again. I don't pray much but, when I do, I pray that the Divine Wind will save others as it has saved me. We all see it differently; we all feel it differently; and we all are touched in a uniquely special fashion by its gentle caress. I think this is what makes the Divine Wind so very beautiful. I celebrate that which brings us together. I celebrate that which gives us hope. I celebrate a Divine Wind that makes us whole—it makes us human.

Divine Wind

The Story Behind the Story

Committed to trying to submit a piece for consideration in every anthology, I had to put some thought against this particular prompt. My thoughts regarding faith and spirituality are at once simple yet interestingly complicated. I was raised without any religion and, in truth, coached to be somewhat suspicious of organized religions. Certainly, there were enough examples throughout world history of the darker aspects of religious fervor. Yet, for all that, I have always been a spiritual person, and I did feel a connection with the "spiritual world" that developed naturally over time. This connection was uniquely simple as a young child—a notion that I was part of something much bigger—a small part of a greater universe ruled over by a benevolent "It" and watched over by my invisible friend, aptly named "Mr. Invisible." I knew exactly what he looked like, and I knew he was there with me. After reading countless books on the Age of Chivalry (Arthurian legends, Don Quixote, and so on), my terminology changed and my diary entries, eventually, refer to God and angels (or my "Friends"). My faith was developing yet the basics remained unchanged from my earliest days. It wasn't until I left home for college that I began to feel the uncomfortable tension that occasionally exists between people with different belief systems. I was told, for the first time in my life, that I was going to go to Hell because I didn't go to church or believe in a Christian God. I was frequently marginalized and led to believe that I could not possibly be a good and moral person without conforming to someone else's religious paradigm and these attacks hurt because I felt I was a good and moral person. As complicated as all this was, I firmly believed that God, in whatever form one believed in, universally accepted people of all faiths and reached out to them in the language they would most understand. I felt that faith shouldn't be a dividing line between the peoples of the world but that a common spirituality should unite us all. These tenets of faith and spirituality that I believe to be true helped inspire this essay. I envisioned this unifying power of faith as a "Divine Wind."

LAST WALK HOME FROM SCHOOL

(Written November 19, 2020)
Published by Red Penguin Books in *"Tis the Seasons"* (December, 2020)

*Recalls the exuberance of the final walk home and the
beginning of Christmas break.*

Anxiously fidgeting, furiously scribbling
Doodles upon the page
Barely listening, second hand ticking
The clock owns the key to our cage

School bell now ringing, the children all singing
Holiday songs as they dress
While boots are now buckling, the teachers are chuckling
Forgiving their young pupils' mess

Parting words said to Jeff, Jim, and Ed
I sprouted some wings and I flew
But once in the snow, I just had to throw
A holiday snowball or two

Ouch! One in the face, freezing the place
Where it struck me just over the eye
Principal alerted; the school yard deserted
We ran as we shouted goodbye

Glistening alabaster, the snow falling faster
I purposely slowed down my pace
Fulfilling my duty to admire nature's beauty
There was no need to make this a race

Soon walking alone, I started for home
Down a path framed by snow-covered pine
Reveling as I go, privileged to know
That the very first tracks would be mine

Last Walk Home From School

Enjoying the breeze, I throw snowballs at trees
Only stopping when I hit five or six
Then nearing the pond, that lay just beyond
I gather some stones and some sticks

Throwing rocks way up high in the pale winter sky
I eagerly await their return
I'll hear either a rock-on-ice smash or a watery splash
Upon re-entry, the verdict I'll learn

The water's frozen today so the sticks go away
I slide stones from near shore to far
I wander about when my ammunition runs out
I am happy with things as they are

With freezing numb feet, I return to the street
The cars splashing slush as they pass
I get a bit wet but never upset
No, not on the last day of class

Up over the ridge, I soon cross the bridge
The sign for my village ahead
I'm now moving fast, my patience won't last
I neglect to watch where I tread

I soon pay the price on a cruel patch of ice
I fall back and land on my rear
It seems I'm okay so I get on my way
Thank God my mother's not here

It's a sure bet she'd worry and fret
Had she seen me fall to the ground
But she's three blocks away and I'm thankful to say
She'll never know I was downed

Now feeling the chill, I ascend one final hill
Stepping aside for a plow
Taking greater care yet, since it's a fair bet
That my mother is watching me now

Flapper and the Captain

Up the driveway I go, through unshoveled snow
My mother's beautiful smile now in view
She races for the door, across our white tiled floor
And greets me just like mothers do

It's been a long walk, I'm not yet ready to talk
I just say the day went okay
But when I see our big tree, something comes over me
And I feel like dancing away

There'll be Christmas shows on TV and hearts filled with glee
My sister and I will make gifts
And if the snow is persisting, there'll be no resisting
Sledding down hills and snow drifts

We'll have small parties at night and Christmas tree lights
Joy and excitement on Christmas Eve
Santa will come, before it's all done
My sister and I we believe

This all lay ahead after some more nights in bed
Boots and coat must come off first, as a rule
Not a morsel of grief, I sigh with relief
I love that last walk home from school

The Story Behind the Story

Poetry! My arch nemesis! Okay, maybe it's not that bad but I had my doubts when Red Penguin Books announced their upcoming anthology which would be a collection of holiday-inspired poetry. This would be my first attempt at creating a poem for competitive selection. Over the years, I had written a few poems, but they were mostly simple affairs with rhyming verse—some were very private reflections of inner turbulence or disgust with certain aspects of society while others were humorous poems written to cheer up friends during difficult times. I'd never written a free-verse poem. In fact, until recently, I wouldn't have even considered these works as poetry as my unschooled mind thought that all poems had to adhere to some form of meter or rhyming scheme. I know better, now. I had a few ideas in mind, and so I decided to try my hand at both a standard rhyming poem and a free-verse poem. I actually completed both on the same day. While both poems met the requirement of tying into the winter holidays, they were very different in nature. The one you just read was a poetic translation of vivid memories from my childhood—the joy of completing the last day of school before Christmas break and the relaxed and carefree walk home, sometimes through a winter wonderland of snow and ice, to officially begin my Christmas vacation. The second poem is very different—a bittersweet reflection on what was and what will never be again.

NEEDLE IN THE CORNER

(Written November 19, 2020)
Published by Red Penguin Books in *'Tis the Seasons* (December, 2020)

Bittersweet reflection upon holidays past.

I close my eyes; my world comes alive.
Trumpets ushering in the holidays as angels sing.
Roasted turkey waftings, only recently turned memory, replaced by cookies and cakes yet made.
Cloaked and ambitious, I navigate the oceans of shoppers.
I hear the clang, clang, clang of Salvation Army Santas and the jingle of coins deposited.
Cabs honking, seasonal favorites played by street performers, the City all aglow in festive holiday colors.
Prizes claimed, I return in secret.
Scissors meeting little resistance, cut cleanly through rolls of festive paper.
Folding here and there, treasures concealed; tape dispensers and brown pasteboard rollers scattered like autumn's dying leaves.

Anticipation; excitement building, my children try to show restraint but their eyes betray them.
I remember that feeling of hope; the belief that somehow my dreams might be fulfilled on a day.
I knew better.
Good enough was always good enough.
I was happy with what was; never disappointed by what was not.
I wanted more for my children.
The displeased face of my wife spoke the words she could not—too much.
Who was I pleasing?
I'm not sure I knew.
I was trying to add magic in a world that denied it—for my children; for me.

Needle in the Corner

Late night shuffling; all rooms checked for signs of consciousness.
Green leaf bags emerging from hiding.
Silent and deliberate foot placement; hoping not a single floorboard
might creak beneath my weight.
Flashlights shielded; gifts slowly removed and placed around a beautiful
tree.
Lights of rainbow hue set afire, blazing with holiday cheer; the stage
is set.
Wait; what have I forgotten?
A cookie on a plate is attended to with crumbs carefully left for the
forensic investigators.
Flat ginger ale sipped and the job is done.
The silent Ninja returns, brushes his teeth, slides into bed with a shiver.

A few hours of sleep before the shuffling begins.
Muffled voices as child speaks to child; flashlight beams dance across
the scene.
Who gets the big box? I can almost remember when this mattered
to me.
We gather around the tree; the curtains are drawn open; the play
begins.
Children create their own traditions, uniquely theirs—I am glad.
Each collects their gifts, building a box fort about them—strange but
endearing; I admire the creativity.
Gift opening remains as I remember from my own childhood; a tradi-
tion passed on.
Youngest to oldest; Mom before Dad; each gift a gift for all.
Children look for approval to open the next; parents attempt to
manage the pace.
Christmas songs play quietly in the background.
Our dog's attention is focused on tasty bribes; it seems to work.
He'll soon have gifts of his own, chosen by the children.
We all give.
We all receive.
We share the beauty of the day.

Gifting complete, there's a sense of relief.
Eggs fry, bacon sizzles, biscuits rise.

Flapper and the Captain

Children investigate gifts meriting additional attention.
I ready tools; my work is not yet done.
Breakfast, alas, a formality and a distraction.
Soon the savory aroma of roasting turkey shall return to our home.
Connect part A to part B using screw Y and clip Z.
Doll houses take shape; robots spring to life.
There is peace amidst the chaos.
We are connected with generations long departed.

Snow falls, gently.
I feel loss and I don't know why.
Perhaps the crescendo was too grand? The fall back to reality too steep?
Yet I am satisfied; satisfied because my family seems satisfied.
But happy? I don't know.
I hope.

Christmas cheer extended; we try to make it so.
I look towards the new year; I'm the only one.
We have the party; it's preordained.
I look towards the new year; I'm the only one.
Children to bed; wife to bed.
I look towards the new year; I'm the only one.
California to Korea, England to Saudi Arabia, countless time zones—
my year always ends in New York.
I tolerate the festivities; music I don't care for; celebrities I do not celebrate.
My eyes are focused on the clock . . . and on the ball.

I see myself, a child.
My watch ready for its annual setting.
My heart rate picks up.
Where music and media personalities have failed, the movement of time has not.
I am . . . inspired.
I do care.
I mourn the passing of time yet I am filled with the hope that comes from new beginnings.
I am filled with hope.

I open my eyes; that world dies, washed away by a tear.
An empty home.
The tree stood here.
The children sat there.
A thousand memories; ten-thousand; a million!
The moving truck pulls away.
I am alone.

My children . . . a thousand miles away.
My wife is free.
I am free but I am dying.
I will not die; not yet.
Spotless floors, spotless windows, spotless spots—I have done well.
I turn to go but I cannot.
Kneeling; I've missed something.
A needle in the corner, a gift from a Christmas pine.
I wipe the tears from my eyes as I reach to cleanse the scene of its only debris.
I pull back and I stand.
The needle in the corner remains.
Not a gift to those who come next but my statement to the universe.
I was here; we were here.
We knew love, fresh and green.
Love faded, brown, dry and dead.
Like the needle in the corner, we had our time, we faded, we are resurrected in memory.
Summer heat burns as I open the door.
I need not look back.
The needle remains.

The Story Behind the Story

    As previously mentioned, "Needle in the Corner" is a very different poem than "Last Walk Home from School." Not only is this free-verse poem unconstrained by rhythm, it takes a slightly more melancholy look at the holidays. For many, the holidays are not a happy time. We become better friends when we understand this and seek to lend comfort, where possible, to those for whom the holidays only bring bad memories or elicit a sense of loneliness and despair. There is no question that the holidays are no longer the same for me as they once were. In many ways, this poem is very much biographical...right down to finding the dried-up pine needle in the corner. I loved Christmas as a kid—it was at its most magical in my elementary school years, but the magic seemed to fade as time went on. As a father, I occasionally went a bit overboard trying to recreate the magic for my own children, making Christmas an even larger and more elaborate extravaganza than anything I had experienced as a child. Like most parents, I wanted to take the best parts of my childhood, make them even better, and gift these to my own offspring. My wife and I did not always see eye to eye regarding the holiday experience. I was clearly the one driving the train through the holiday season and it did, occasionally, feel awkward not to have my wife by my side blowing the train whistle as we went. For all that, Christmas day with my children was always a beautiful and love-filled occasion. I felt satisfied that all the effort was worth it, and I never felt like I was spoiling our children even if my wife and I had different visions for the holiday. Our last Christmas together, in December of 2015, was a very hard one for me. We were living in South Korea at the time and had decided upon the divorce in early spring. My wife wanted to hop the next plane out with the kids but I told her that, as the father, I got a vote, too. I insisted that we stay together through New Years...and we did...just barely. We did the best we could to make a normal Christmas of it but this was easier said than done with all the children aware that they were heading back to the States on January 3rd and our family would never be the same. Even through the horrible pain, I did my best to make it a good Christmas, and I think it was. It was as normal as it could be, given the circumstances.

After the new year, my family left. Then the movers came and collected the many boxes of stuff that would be shipped out to South Dakota, including our Christmas tree and decorations. The holiday glee ended with a brutal finality. Shortly thereafter, I was informed that I would have to move out of the house as it was military FAMILY housing, and I no longer had a family. I was given only days to make this happen and I was required to clean the house to an impossibly immaculate level before turning it back over to the government. The reminders of our life together, across the many years and many assignments, kept hitting me like a sledgehammer. Things would never be the same. The dried-out Christmas tree needle incident was actually from our previous assignment where we had owned a real tree, and I discovered the needle while cleaning our government furnished home prior to our move. In each instance, I took a last walkthrough of our empty home—a home once filled with the laughter of my children—and emotions overcame me. Things would never be the same. *"Needle in the Corner" was my attempt to capture some of these emotions on paper.*

RECOVERY

(Written December 6, 2020)
Published by Red Penguin Books in "*It's the End of the World as We Know It*" (January, 2021)

*A fictional story about an Air Force tanker crew,
launched on a nuclear mission, attempting to make
their way home.*

"NAV, PILOT, give me a heading." Silence. "NAV, you up on headset?"

"NAV's up," I said.

"I need a heading, please." The frustration was, uncharacteristically, noticeable in Major Thompson's tone.

"We're about fifty K short on fuel so there's no way in Hell we're making it to our recovery base. Where would you like to go?" I immediately felt bad for letting my own frustration show through but, in the end, it was Major Thompson who thought it was a good idea to give away all our additional fuel to the B-1 bomber. In fairness, they had requested it. During our Strategic Air Command certification briefings to the Wing Commander, we always said we would transfer whatever fuel the bombers needed to hit their targets. The theory of Strategic Deterrence relied upon the credibility of a forceful response to any enemy aggression. To be credible, there had to be no doubt of our willingness to do whatever it took to get the mission done. Most of us wondered how we'd actually perform if "the balloon went up." And by balloon, I'm talking full scale global nuclear war. It's what we had trained for. It's what we had prayed would never happen. It was happening. There were a million things to consider but, right now, I was only considering a thousand plus miles of icy ocean that lay between our current position and a destination we were mathematically unable to reach.

Three years ago, I felt like I was on top of the world when I arrived at Castle Air Force Base in California. It was a beautiful spring day and I was incredibly excited to begin my training as a KC-135 Stratotanker navigator at the Combat Crew Training School. My training patches were off and I was now wearing the distinguishable iron gauntlet patch of the Strategic Air Command (or "SAC"). My friends were always amazed when I described my new job of passing jet fuel to receiver aircraft while traveling at speeds in excess of 400 knots (or nautical miles per hour). As the navigator, it was my job to get our aircraft together, effecting a rendezvous between our tanker and whatever receiver aircraft we were assigned to refuel. Once we were within visual range, the receiver aircraft would maneuver to a "pre-contact" position, just behind our tanker, and then our boom operator, the only enlisted crewmember on our aircraft, would expertly fly the boom until it was just above the receiver aircraft's fuel receptacle. The hose would then be extended until a contact was made and then jet fuel would be passed at 6,500 pounds per minute (somewhere around 1,000 gallons per minute). When the required fuel was offloaded to the receiver, the two aircraft would separate and both would continue along their assigned mission routing. I loved my job!

After three months of training, graduates of the Combat Crew Training School departed Castle Air Force Base for their assigned units; primarily SAC bases across the United States. Once arrived, new crew members were put through a rigorous "mission qualification" program to certify them to conduct the unit's Emergency War Order, or EWO, mission. The culmination of our training was an intense several-hour briefing and question and answer session before the wing's commanding officer. It was the Wing Commander who blessed you to join the long line of SAC warriors whose heritage dated back to 1946 and, ultimately, to the brave airmen of the World Wars before. Strategic Air Command was, without question, the most powerful and lethal force on the face of the planet. The SAC motto, "Peace is Our Profession," was sometimes mocked. I suppose it's understandable considering our "peaceful" objective was to drop thousands of the most devasting weapons known to mankind on the enemy; each weapon exponentially more powerful than the miniscule "Little Boy" bomb that was dropped on Hiroshima during World War II. To be honest, the mere thought of actually pulling the trigger on this kind of destructive power is a little bit terrifying. And that's the idea. The whole notion of Strategic Deterrence was that any government would have to be completely insane to invite this kind of destruction to their doorstep. With bombers upon bombers and Intercontinental Ballistic Missiles (ICBMs) and Submarine-Launched Ballistic Missiles (SLBMs), it would be impossible to defend against the vast redundancy of attacking systems; more so considering many targets were covered by multiple options. So, ideally, governments would avoid war all-together and the carnage and destruction unleashed during World War I and World War II would be a thing of the past. There's been no major world war since the end of the Second World War. Maybe Strategic Deterrence works? As "SAC Warriors," we each ran through the ethics and morality of our chosen profession, profiting from both the philosophical works of those long dead and the more current briefings and speeches of our commanders. In the end, we reconciled discrepancies as best we could and committed ourselves to the mission. Every third week, we sat SAC Alert. Huddled in Alert facilities near the Alert Ramp where our aircraft were parked, we awaited the blaring klaxon that summoned us to run to our jets and decode classified messages that would either confirm the training exercise or serve as a preamble to the end of the world as we knew it. Our every movement was evaluated to ensure maximum efficiency and the quickest launch possible—the idea being that nuclear warheads were minutes away from destroying our airfield. I was single. Those with family members living in the nearby base housing had an extra dimension of emotions to work through. This was our life. And it eventually became mundane. The excitement faded with the years. I still ran at a full sprint to my aircraft, whenever the klaxon blew, but the adrenaline rush wasn't quite what it used to be. Until yesterday. Then, everything changed.

It was just before midnight when the klaxon sounded in the Alert Facility. My eyes opened but my mind was not yet processing the signal. On my nightstand, a warbling tone came over my Tactical Aircrew Alerting Network (TAAN) radio. Now, I was awake. "FOR ALERT FORCE, FOR ALERT FORCE, KLAXON, KLAXON, KLAXON." Damn! I was not alone in my anger—I could hear curse words reverberating throughout the facility as I quickly slid into my flight suit and laced up the boots purposefully placed at the side of my bed. As I bolted out my door, winter flying jacket in hand, I nearly ran into my co-pilot who was, likewise, only half awake. We followed the rush of humanity towards the entrance of the Alert Facility and burst through the doors into the darkness of the night. The powerful Kansas wind nearly knocked me off my feet as I sprinted towards my aircraft, my lungs struggling to process the cold air. A light snow was falling and the Alert Pad lighting cast an unnatural glow over the scene. Latches popped, I pulled the crew entry door open and slid the ladder into place, locking it for entry into the aircraft. Message traffic was coming over my radio as I clamored up the ladder, hitting the switch to start up the auxiliary power unit as I went. I proceeded over to the CMF Container, a solid steel receptacle protecting all our classified documents; documents I had carefully inventoried and signed for at the start of our Alert tour, on Wednesday. Opening the box, I pulled out the decode documents I would need to translate the series of seemingly random characters coming across the radio. Sliding on my headset, I felt like I had just secured two blocks of ice to my ears. My breath was fogging the air. I was shivering. The aircraft commander (pilot), co-pilot, and boom operator ascended the ladder and quickly leapt into action at their respective stations. I jotted down the encoded message and translated the instructions as the pilots were starting the engines. I was expecting either a START ENGINES, DO NOT TAXI message or, if the exercise guys were feeling very feisty, maybe a START ENGINES, TAXI, AND SIMULATE TAKEOFF instruction. The "movers" always got our attention because no crew wanted to be the first to taxi out of parking; just in case there was an error in message translation. There's no "reverse" gear on the jet so a botched response movement would result in a lengthy and embarrassing trip around the alert pad to return to parking. Likewise, no one wanted to be the last jet out of parking, either. Response times were recorded and a quick response reflected the crew's proficiency. During peacetime, this proficiency was a source of pride. In a real-world scenario, a quick response might mean the difference between life and death. It had been several years since tankers supporting bomber Alert lines had actually taken off while on Alert. Someone probably figured out it wasn't a great idea to send half-asleep aircrews into the night sky just for training. I referred to the decode documents and began breaking out the message. I was hoping for a simple START ENGINES—this would get us back to bed that much sooner. I was quick but careful. I never knew a navigator who messed up a message decode and I sure didn't want to be the first. This couldn't be right. I re-checked my work. Then I called the Command Post to authenticate the message. "Command Post, Sortie One-Zero-Niner, authenticate BRAVO YANKEE." I waited. The controllers were now diving into their own authentication challenge-and-reply documents.

"Sortie   One-Zero-Niner,   Command   Post   authenticates

CHARLIE." That checked good. They weren't messing with us. This was real. This was no exercise! The pilots had run their initial checklist and were anxious to know what the plan was.

"NAV, whatcha got?"

"Positive Control Launch. This is real!"

"What?! Are you sure?"

"Yah, I'm sure. I checked it three times." The co-pilot asked me to hand him the decode documents and I did so. Co-pilots usually only decoded messages during our certification training but, given the growing gravity of the situation, I wasn't about to question the request. At this point, all eyes were focused on our co-pilot. The aircraft commander quickly looked outside to see if anyone else was moving. There was no motion.

"Nav's right," said our co-pilot, choking on his words. Our boom operator was now visibly upset. He started to mutter curse words under his breath. A dead-serious expression came across Major Thompson's usually pleasantly placid face.

"Pass me the books, CO." Again, there was silence as Major Thompson carefully broke out the code. One of the bombers was already rolling out of its parking spot. Major Thompson shook his head in disbelief and then spoke--"Okay. Let's get moving." I can't even begin to count the number of "F-bombs" dropped by our boom operator as we rolled out of parking. Several more tankers followed soon after. There was no time to align my Inertial Navigation System so I knew I'd have to attempt an airborne alignment once we were on a straight-and-level portion of our flight plan. While we were rolling, I unlocked the sturdy padlock that typically kept the main portion of the CMF Container locked. It was time to pull out flight plans and charts that I never thought I'd have to use for real.

Using Minimum Interval Takeoff (MITO) procedures, we took to the air just behind a departing bomber. Major Thompson steered to the right, on a fan heading, to avoid the wake turbulence of the jet just ahead of us.

We were passing through 15,000 feet when we experienced an intense buffeting that was unlike any turbulence I'd ever felt. The pilots struggled furiously to regain control of the aircraft. Had we just passed through the wake of another jet? It was unlikely at this point on the departure. Major Thompson yelled back at the boom operator, Staff

Sergeant Hurley, asking him to head aft to see if he could see anything through the boom sighting window.

"PILOT, BOOM, I'm up on headset in the boom pod."

"See anything?"

"It's glowing back there."

"What do you mean glowing?" asked Lieutenant Chenders, our co-pilot. His second wedding anniversary was just days away and his wife was expecting their first child in the spring.

"Glowing, Sir. It's really hard to see anything through the snow and clouds but there's a weird orange tint to the sky at our six."

"NAV, could you please get a comm check with Command Post?" Maj Thompson was already running through a multitude of scenarios in his head. We all trusted him and his judgement. He was an experienced Instructor Pilot with several thousand flight hours under his belt.

"Roger that, PILOT. SHOCKER CONTROL, SHOCKER CONTROL, Sortie One-Zero-Niner requesting comm check." We were still well within radio range and I was hoping the reply would be quick. It wasn't. "SHOCKER CONTROL, SHOCKER CONTROL, Sortie One-Zero-Niner requesting comm check on primary." Still nothing.

"NAV, PILOT, let's give 'em a try on the alternate freq."

"Roger that, PILOT." I repeated my radio call on Command Post's alternate frequency. There was still no reply.

"CO, why don't you see if you can get a hold of Kansas City Center. See if they have any reports to pass. Use our tactical callsign."

"Kansas City Center, this is TURBO One-Fife, climbing through flight level Two-Seven-Zero for flight level TREE-FIFE-ZERO, over." Similar to my recent attempts to call the Command Post, our co-pilot repeated the radio call several times. We heard no reply. And there we were, climbing higher and higher into the darkness of the night, leaving everything we knew and loved behind; on course and on speed towards an uncertain future. This is the point where training took over and Major Thompson made sure we had our heads in the game.

"Crew, listen up. I need you all to focus on the mission. I don't know what's happening back home right now but we can't afford to fixate on things beyond our control. So, stay sharp and keep your head in the game. Let's back each other up, get to the refueling track, pass some gas, and bring this jet home. Questions?" We all responded, in turn. This was the real deal and the only way back was to go forward.

I kept busy taking radar positions over the land and resolving celestial positions over the water; all along keeping up my dead reckoning position on the navigational charts provided with our mission package. All compass headings, airspeeds, and drift information were carefully entered onto my flight log. Conversations were kept to a minimum. No one was in the mood for chitchat and, although we couldn't block the thoughts from our mind, we knew it would not be helpful to discuss the fate of family members and friends back home. It was hard. Outwardly, we all displayed a cool, professional, demeanor but the reality was that each of us was struggling to keep our attention focused on our respective flying duties.

RZCT. Rendezvous Control Time. We arrived at our designated air refueling point but there was no bomber in sight nor any calls on the primary or backup air refueling frequencies. So, as directed in our mission folder, we established an orbit, flying an oval racetrack pattern in the sky, and we waited. Many thoughts were running through our heads. Was this all just a big mistake? Had the bombers been recalled? We used to joke about using the extra gas to fly down to the Bahamas to wait out the nuclear winter. We were running the response matrix when the HF radio crackled—it was our mated receiver. He was running late due to weather deviations and some threat-driven mission re-routing. Not good. This meant he was going to be thirsty. He was. When our receiver was within UHF radio range, BONE 70, our mated bomber, contacted us on the Air Refueling Primary frequency and made the request we all were dreading. Major Thompson, without hesitation, approved the request for additional fuel.

"PILOT, NAV?"

"Go ahead, NAV."

"Sir, the requested offload is going to put our recovery base out of range."

"Copy, NAV. Thanks." Major Thompson understood the ramifications of the increased offload even before I told him. A mental calculator inside his head was constantly running through aircraft performance data. Knowing full well that the bomber would not have asked for the fuel unless it was necessary to complete their mission, he still radioed back to verify the request. The call was made more the benefit of his own crew. "BONE Seven-Zero, confirm you require the addition Six-Zero-K give for your mission?"

"Standby, TURBO," replied the bomber pilot. I envisioned the bomber's co-pilot furiously checking over his numbers and re-confirming readings on the fuel panel. Our hearts were racing and each minute seemed like an eternity. All the while, our liquid lifeline was pouring into the B-1B Lancer bomber positioned just aft and below our aircraft. "TURBO One-Fife, affirm. We're going to need the gas. Sorry, fellas." Although I couldn't hear him in back, over the engine noise, I already knew Sergeant Hurley was yelling every obscenity he could conjure up. Still, he did his job and he did it flawlessly.

"Copy, BONE Seven-Zero. Plus Six-Zero-K on the offload." There was no emotion in Major Thompson's voice. We were still on our air refueling track as I pulled out a virgin Jet Navigation Chart and began my search for possible divert fields. The prospects were not looking good.

"Disconnect," advised our boom operator. The requested fuel offload had been transferred and we owed nothing more to national security. Now we were flying for ourselves.

"Offload Complete. Good luck, BONE."

"Copy. God speed, TURBO."

"NAV, PILOT, give me a heading." Silence. "NAV, you up on headset?"

"NAV's up," I said.

"I need a heading, please." The frustration was, uncharacteristically, noticeable in Major Thompson's tone.

"We're about fifty K short on fuel so there's no way in Hell we're making it to our recovery base. Where would you like to go?"

"NAV, PILOT, understood. Please give me a heading."

"Tree-Tree-Zero. I'll update."

"Copy, NAV. Right to Tree-Tree-Zero."

The heading would take us in the direction of our recovery field but, since we weren't even close on the gas we needed, I was really just buying some time to look for a better option.

I could hear the stream of expletives coming from the mouth of our boom operator as he made his way back up to the cockpit.

"Hey NAV, are we going to have to ditch?"

"Maybe, BOOM. I'm not seeing much out ahead but I'll keep checking."

"Crap! Okay, I'm checking off to get the poopy suits." "Poopy suit" is aircrew slang for the anti-exposure suits; protective outer garments that were designed to help insulate us from the chilling effect of cold water. We knew it would just delay the inevitable hypothermia we'd experience from prolonged exposure in the icy waters below. Several minutes later, Sergeant Hurley returned and handed each of us an anti-exposure suit. Thereafter, he wasted no time in donning his own suit. I knew we were still hours away from running out of fuel so I elected to wait. Then, looking at my chart, I noticed a small island with a runway. Would it be long enough? I pulled out the IFR Supplement book from my publications bag and read through the airfield description. Just barely! In any event, it was better than taking a bath in the Arctic Circle. I briefed the plan to the crew. This was not part of the playbook but it seemed to be our best option. Unfortunately, the winds aloft were heavier than forecast and our ability to make even this alternate airfield was questionable. The pilots set the throttles for our "Best Range Airspeed" and we prayed. When the island appeared as a blip at the outer edge of my radar scope, I knew we had a chance. Major Thompson pulled the throttles back to idle and we began our descent. We had been unable to contact any human since leaving our refueling track and there was no traffic coming across on the HF radio. We were flying blind into an unknown field. Fortunately, there was enough daylight remaining to make the landing at an uncontrolled, and likely unilluminated, airfield possible. Although we were flying on fumes, Major Thompson wanted to execute a low pass over the runway to inspect it for damage before circling for the full stop landing. As we passed overhead, the field looked like a ghost town. There was very little visible damage but there was also no trace of human life. With the runway much shorter and narrower than what we customarily landed on; Major Thompson had to fall back on several thousand hours of flight experience to safely land the jet. As we taxied to the empty parking area, our right outboard engine shut down due to fuel starvation. We were incredibly lucky to be alive.

Shutting down the jet, we walked back to the cargo bay, opened our mobility bags, and pulled out our cold weather gear. Donning our heavy parkas, we returned to the cockpit, installed the ladder, and departed the aircraft. The icy wind greeted us like a thousand needle pricks upon our exposed skin, as we hastily searched for an entrance to the nearby terminal building. The doors were locked but with all the windows shattered, entry was assured. After clearing away the remaining glass fragments, we climbed into the building. Inside, the room was dark. Lieutenant Chenders pulled out his pocket flashlight and scanned the walls for a light switch panel. We found the switches but the building lacked power. Papers were strewn about here and there and the building gave the appearance of a facility that had been hastily evacuated.

The sun was starting to set and the temperature was dropping outside. We were all very tired from the ordeal we had just gone through and Major Thompson knew it. He stopped using ranks and crew positions and addressed us now by our first names. "Dave, see if you can scrounge up some wood and any loose paper or cardboard that will burn."

"Yes, Sir. I'm on it." I was not about to call Major Thompson by his first name. Only his wife called him John.

"Paul, you still smoking these days?"

"I'm a boom operator, Sir. It's part of the job description."

"Okay. Good. I mean, not good that you smoke but we're going to need your lighter."

"It's yours, Sir."

"Rick, go scrounge around and see if you can't find any cushions that we could use for makeshift mattresses. I have no desire to sleep in the jet tonight and I think we should get some rest before we get too carried away and start making bad decisions. If any of you see any vending machines, crack 'em open and bring whatever food you can find back here."

We all set out on our missions. This was easy stuff compared to what we had just been through. I found several bookshelves and desks that I was able to break down. It took several trips to carry all the wood back to the terminal area. I considered bringing some of the books I found in one of the offices but, even on the brink of a nuclear Armageddon, I couldn't bear the thought of burning books. I carefully piled the books on the floor and then made quick work of the book-case. Fortunately, there were plenty of old newspapers and magazines lying around—more than enough tinder to get the fire going. When our crew got back together, Paul Hurley regaled us with his animated tale of smashing in the glass fronts of several vending machines to secure us a feast. He also acquired food from one of the airport conces-sions. I was glad. I wasn't overly excited about the prospect of surviving on candy bars and soda pop for the next few weeks. All things consid-ered, we had a pleasant meal together, sitting around a roaring fire we built in a less exposed corner of the terminal building. We talked about a lot of things. There were a million unanswered questions. When we settled in to sleep, on our makeshift beds, I was wondering how many weeks it might be before we were rescued from our dilemma. Rescue was not part of John Thompson's mental calculus. He drifted off to sleep with grander plans hatching in his mind.

We awoke on our own time, the next morning. As far north as we were, we weren't anticipating sunrise for another three or four hours. Worse yet, we'd only have a handful of daylight hours to work with before the Arctic night enshrouded us once more. Major Thompson wasn't going to waste a moment of light. Like a scene that might have unfolded a hundred thousand years ago, we circled the blazing fire in our modern cave and discussed our plan. Fuel and hydraulic fluid. It sounded simple enough. We had all completed our semi-annual "Aircraft Servicing" training class but, in truth, none of us felt particularly comfortable messing around with jet fuel and having to worry about static electricity causing a big explosion if we somehow neglected to follow the proper grounding procedures. No, we all preferred to leave that business to our highly proficient crew chiefs and the expert POL guys. Major Thompson didn't blink; we were going to turn our own aircraft and we were going to get off this desolate island. We returned to our jet, collected a few more flashlights and the aircraft servicing job guide, and set out in two groups of two on what seemed like a hopeless mission. Sergeant Hurley and I managed to break into a hangar and found a number of containers of hydraulic fluid. We were much more skeptical of our pilot team finding a means to refuel our jet. Major Thompson proved us wrong again. Why did I even doubt? Major T and Rick stumbled upon several fuel trucks which, miraculously, survived whatever tragedy had befallen this little airport in the middle of nowhere.

"Dave, I need you to work up a rough flight plan back to home station and another one to the nearest CONUS Air Force base; preferably a SAC base."

"WILCO, Sir." I ran through the darkness, back to our plane, and grabbed up my nav bag. All the mission planning materials I needed to plan our next mission were contained within this well-worn leather briefcase. When I returned, I spread my charts on the floor of the terminal building and started drawing lines and calculating headings and distances while shadows danced across the scene, choreographed by our life-sustaining bonfire. At the same time, Rick was calculating takeoff data and trying to determine how much fuel weight we could accommodate before we'd run out of runway during our takeoff roll. The runway length was already shorter than the minimum specified in our regulations but, since there was clearly no waiver authority to appeal to, Major Thompson accepted the risk and made the call. Too little fuel; we don't get home. Too much fuel; we become a smoking fireball at the end of the runway. The only thing working in our favor was the temperature. Like some great mythological creature, our beloved tanker roars furiously into the Heavens, climbing ever-higher through the chilled air of a winter's day. In short, the jet climbs better in the cold.

"65,000 pounds is the max we can take, Sir," said Lieutenant Chenders. "And that's without the engine failure safety factor." Typically, takeoff data was calculated based off of three-engine performance data, allowing a safety pad if one of the engines should fail during the takeoff.

"Thanks, Rick."

"Dave, how are those flight plans coming?"

"First one's done. Working on the second. If we fly a great circle route, we might just have enough gas to make it home. If you're looking for something up in Michigan, you might even be able to get in a few practice approaches." I was kidding about the approach work, of course, but Major Thompson seized on the opportunity to rib the co-pilot about his needing some work in the pattern to improve his proficiency.

"Okay, great. We'll bring the trucks around and get everything in place before the sun rises. We'll need to move very quickly if we want to get out of here today. Without airfield lighting, there's no way I'm attempting a short field takeoff on this narrow runway."

"Today?!" we replied in unison.

"Yes, today. We need to get this jet turned and back into the lineup for any follow-on missions." We could hardly believe what we were hearing. If General Curtis LeMay had been here, he would have pinned a medal on Major Thompson's chest right then and there. This was the fighting spirit SAC Warriors were supposed to be brimming with. Major T put us all to shame and, at least for that moment in time, had us buying into his vision that, somehow, everything was going to turn out okay. "We need to get this right so I want everyone back here in thirty minutes to "chair fly" this plan and knock out our mission brief." Even though it struck me as a little bit superfluous to conduct a formal mission briefing given the apocalyptic circumstances, I have to say that the return to routine set everyone a little more at ease—this was just another mission and we were going to treat it like the countless other sorties we had successfully completed.

As expected, we gathered just before 0930 Local Time. Major Thompson looked at me, "Time hack, NAV."

"Roger that, Sir. On my hack, the time will be Ten-Thirty Zulu." "Zulu" is the designation for Greenwich Mean Time and all flying activities use GMT as the standard reference time. My eyes closely followed the passing seconds on my watch. "Fife, Fower, Tree, Two, One, Hack. Ten-Thirty Zulu."

"Thanks, NAV," Major Thompson acknowledged with a nod as all crew members synchronized their watches. He then promptly began the formal mission briefing. Following the brief, all crew members briefing their respective parts, we launched into a detailed discussion of the aircraft servicing plan. Satisfied that everyone understood their roles, the crew was dismissed for any last-minute personal activities before the real "fun" began. I put all my mission planning materials back in my nav bag and went to visit the terminal restroom.

The sun had barely broken the horizon before we were racing about in the sub-zero temperatures, trying to prepare our bird for flight. Lieutenant Chenders was watching the fuel panel in the cockpit as Sergeant Hurley and Major Thompson maneuvered the fuel trucks, connected grounding wires, and ran the fuel hose from the truck to our aircraft's refueling point. Meanwhile, I was trying not to get blown off the wing of our aircraft as I opened the hydraulic fluid servicing panel and poured an errant stream of hydraulic fluid from multiple cans into the fill point trying, with only limited success, to keep to fluid from spilling on the wing or on my flight suit. Once I was done, I climbed back in the jet and secured the over-wing exit hatch. I was glad to be out of the wind. There really wasn't much I could do to help with the fueling process so I prepared all my mission materials for the upcoming flight and cross-checked all the data I had hastily calculated during our rushed mission planning. Perfect! The servicing process took us well over an hour—we weren't breaking any records.

Trucks cleared, cables and ground locks removed, it was "go time." Major Thompson called for each checklist, in-turn, and we completed the required items on our individual crew position checklists. The jet sprung to life as we started engines and prepared to taxi out to the runway. Major Thompson positioned our jet as close to the end of the runway as possible—we'd need every inch of available concrete. Throttles pushed all the way forward; he released the brakes and we were rolling.

"Four-thousand feet remaining. Three-thousand." Lieutenant Chenders called off the distances, clearly marked along the side of the runway. "Two-thousand. Shit! One-thousand." This was going to be close. I couldn't tell if Sergeant Hurley was praying or cursing behind me. An undiscernible stream of passionately mumbled words flowed freely from his lips. At this point, we were well past our "refusal speed" —a takeoff abort was no longer an option. I clenched the edge of my table. With only a dozen feet to spare, our beautiful jet took to the air and we barely cleared the fence line just beyond the outer edge of the overrun. Landing gear and flaps up, it was now my show.

"NAV, I'll take a heading now."

I drew a deep breath and released my death grip on the Nav Station table before replying. "PILOT, turn left, heading Two-Two-Zero." The familiarity of our office in the sky, and of a routine etched within our collective memory, was comforting. As we climbed up to 38,000 feet, I began the first of many attempts to reach any station on our HF radio. We heard no transmissions on any channel and I was unable to make contact with any other aircraft or ground station. Beyond the deafening silence on the radios, the flight went smoothly. Weather was good and an extra bit of tailwind was helping our fuel burn situation. We were all relieved when we re-entered the Air Defense Identification Zone into Canadian airspace. It would have been a great tragedy to be intercepted and shot down by friendly forces so close to home. Morale improved as we entered the airspace of the United States. There was a solid cloud deck below and we were unable to make out any features on the ground as we overflew Lake Superior into Wisconsin.

About an hour out from landing, I made several attempts to contact our command post on the radio. None were successful. Although none of us said a word about it, our minds were all racing to dark places; each of us imagining what horrors were awaiting. We had little spare gas to speak of and our divert options were going to be extremely limited. Major Thompson called for the Descent and Before Landing

Checklists. As there were no navaids operating in the area and the Instrument Landing System was almost certainly out of service, Major Thompson asked me to provide vectors to set him up for a visual straight-in approach to Runway 19R at our home base. I complied.

20,000 feet. Still in the clouds. 10,000 feet. Clouds. The closer we got to the ground, the denser and darker the clouds seemed to be. These weren't happy clouds, anymore. We were flying through the dark billowing smoke of a fire of unimaginable proportions. We could smell it. Major Thompson directed the crew to go on oxygen and we all donned our masks, flipping the regulator switches to "On, 100%". Finally, at just over 2,000 feet on the altimeter, we began to see the ground. Burning fires raged all the way out to the horizon. All eyes were fixed ahead, gazing through the windscreen, searching for anything that looked remotely familiar. It seemed as if time, itself, had slowed, as we gently banked left and right to survey the destruction below. "Two miles out," I called, over the intercom. I was waiting to hear the familiar "runway in sight. Continuing." It never came.

"Oh, dear God." The tone of absolute despair coming from our leader was enough to suck the air out of our lungs. I turned my head to look out front and Sergeant Hurley unstrapped and stood up to get a better look. What we saw might well have been an alien landscape. A giant crater, perhaps a mile wide and a thousand feet deep, was all that remained where our beautiful airbase once graced the Kansas plains. Within, we could see nothing to remind us that mankind had ever existed here. We thought about the friends and family members who probably never knew what hit them. We considered that a similar scene of death and destruction may well have played out in cities across the county. We wondered who, if anyone, was left to tell the tale. Perhaps that task would fall to us?

Major Thompson circled the area. Our fuel was running low.

"PILOT, NAV, do you see any fields out ahead that might be suitable for an emergency landing?" My question was followed by a minute of reflective silence.

"There's nothing out there, Dave. And even if we did find a place to put the jet down, we'd all be dead of radiation poisoning within a day or two. There's nothing to return to." Aside from the gravity of his words, I was somewhat taken aback by Major Thompson calling me by my first name in the aircraft. That was a first. I guess he was no longer Instructor Pilot Major John H. Thompson. He was John. We all shared

John's tears. "What have we done?! Dear God, what have we done? We've destroyed our home. We've washed away the beauty you bestowed upon us with rivers of blood. Gone. All gone."

"PILOT, NAV. Sir, have you got a plan? We're running low on fuel here." Major Thompson wiped away the tears. He sat up straight and keyed the microphone.

"Okay. Since they started this war, we're going to finish it. Here's the plan. We're going to build up as much speed as we can and then pull the nose up and head straight at the sun. If we time it right, we'll impact with enough fuel left to cause a massive chain-reaction explosion that will destroy that damn star. We're going to make sure nothing lives on this God forsaken planet. It's the only way to ensure we kill all our enemies. Questions?"

"Negative, CO."

"No questions, BOOM."

"What the Hell?! PILOT, NAV, what are you talking about? That's crazy!"

"You heard the plan, NAV. I need a heading towards the sun, ASAP."

"Sir, even if we had the gas for the climb, we'd top out around Flight Level Fife-Fife-Zero. This is ridiculous!"

"Never mind, NAV. I've got a visual on the sun. PILOT has navigation." I was beside myself. Was I the only one who had a problem with our aircraft commander losing his marbles? I unstrapped and started to get out of my seat but Sergeant Hurley put his hand on my shoulder.

"Hey, NAV, it's better this way. Besides, you don't want your last moments in the Air Force to be marred by an act of mutiny." The boom operator's words almost made sense. Now, I was the one who was cursing like a sailor and Sergeant Hurley was calmly assuring me that things were going to be okay. I sat back in my seat, buckled in, and tightened the straps on my harness. Major Thompson pushed the throttles all the way forward and our jet rapidly accelerated. Faster and faster and faster. Major T was pushing hard against the yoke to keep the nose down. And then, when our venerable Stratotanker refused to cooperate any longer, he released the pressure and, oh, how she climbed! Sixty, maybe seventy degrees nose high; she was gaining altitude like a moon-bound Apollo flight. 10,000, 20,000, 30,000. How much higher would we go before the jet stalled and fell back towards mother earth? With little fuel to weigh us down, it was as if our tanks were filled with helium. Even so, the nose began to fall as our jet resisted the thin air of the upper atmosphere. Major Thompson's folly was almost at an end. Did he plan to nose it over and dive towards the crater, taking all of us with him?

"Rick, passing Flight Level Fower-One-Zero, I want you to engage the warp drive. One quarter impulse power. Wait for my call."

"Roger, PILOT. CO-PILOT copies. One-quarter impulse on your mark." Lieutenant Chenders reached up and pulled back the red cover over a guarded switch I had never noticed before. I was confused. What was going on? I strained my eyes to read the lettering below the switch. I could swear it said "Warp Drive Engage." The first Stratotankers rolled off the line at Boeing in the mid-50s. A Warp Drive was not part of the engineering design. I was half expecting Scotty, from Star Trek, to appear out of the darkness of the cargo bay and warn us about the health of the dilithium crystals.

"Okay. Standby, CO." Lieutenant Chenders dutifully rested his finger upon the uncovered metal toggle switch.

"Standing by."

"Fife, Fower, Tree, Two, One, ENGAGE!"

"Warp Drive engaged, Sir." We accelerated rapidly. Sergeant Hurley tumbled backwards through the cabin door and into the cargo bay. I was saved only by my seat's harness system—the inertial reel locking nearly instantly after the Warp Drive was engaged. The needles on my altimeter were spinning so fast that they were impossible to read. Free from the clouds, the sky turned a deep sapphire blue. Stars began to appear as we left our atmosphere behind. Our tanker started shaking violently and I heard a loud banging sound. Our old jet was never designed to handle this much stress. I knew it was only a matter of seconds before she was ripped apart under the strain. Bang, bang, bang! Louder and louder. Bang, bang, bang! I began to scream.

"No! No! You're going to kill us! You crazy bastard, you're going to kill us all!" Bang, bang, bang!

"Dave, are you okay?" Bang, bang, bang. "Nav, are you okay?!" The shaking was getting worse. "Dave, wakeup!" Major Thompson was trying to shake me out of my deep sleep. My eyes slowly opened. I was still trembling as I tried to process my surroundings. I was laying in my bed in the alert facility.

"Holy cow! Dave, are you okay? What in the world were you dreaming about? I could hear you from across the hall. You weren't answering when I knocked on your door and you didn't even hear me yelling in your ear."

"I am so sorry, Sir. I usually don't have dreams this realistic. I really apologize."

"It was the T-Rex dream, wasn't it? Gets me every time." Major T chuckled.

"Um, yes, Sir . . . something like that."

"Okay. Well, you might want to get some sleep, I'm expecting an interesting morning briefing tomorrow in the auditorium." I started to get out of bed as I realized it probably wasn't appropriate to be talking to a major while I was lying down. Major Thompson motioned for me to remain as I was. "Relax, Dave." I considered Major Thompson's words about the upcoming briefing.

"Interesting how, Sir? Why will tomorrow be interesting?"

"Oh, you didn't see the President's news conference last night?"

"No, Sir. Sorry. I was studying my Emergency Procedures and then I read for a while before turning in for the night."

"Wow! You missed a doozy. President Bush said we're done—he directed that all United States strategic bombers immediately stand down from their alert posture and he directed a large portion of the ICBM forces to, similarly, come off alert."

"You're not serious?" I couldn't believe it. We'd been sitting nuclear alert since the mid-50s and we assumed our grandchildren's grandchildren would be carrying the torch well into the future.

"Dead serious. Peace is breaking out all over the world."

"So, we won? SAC won?" My question was a bit naïve but Major Thompson understood where I was coming from.

"We all won. Now get some rest. Tomorrow could be a big day." As he turned to leave, Major Thompson looked back at me with a smile. "Warp Drive? You're going to have to explain that one to me someday." He smiled, closing the door behind him.

The next day was, in fact, a historic one. The news was true. With the fall of the Berlin Wall in 1989, most of the Soviet Union's forces withdrawing from Eastern Europe, and with the dissolution of the Warsaw Pact in July of 1991, the United States saw an opportunity to work with Soviet President Mikhail Gorbachev to cooperate in backing the world off the edge of a nuclear precipice. On September 28, 1991, U.S. nuclear armed bombers downloaded their weapons, started their engines, and taxied out of the Alert parking areas on all SAC bases across the country, effectively ending over thirty years of continuous nuclear alert. Strategic Air Command was deactivated on June 1, 1992, the morning I pinned on my new captain's rank. Those who know what war is love peace more than most.

The Story Behind the Story

Write about what you know. I frequently heard this advice being given to authors. While it's fun to read and immerse ourselves in strange new worlds, it is no easy task to write convincingly about topics we know little about or environments we've never experienced. When the submission requirements came out for "It's the End of the World as We Know It," an anthology dedicated to catastrophic stories, devastating dystopian societies, and tales of survival in a post-apocalyptic world, I knew I had my work cut out for me. What did I know about the end of the world? And then it dawned on...for several years, I was to be an agent of global nuclear Armageddon. That's not what our mission statement said—officially, the Strategic Air Command (SAC) motto was "Peace is Our Profession." We used to joke that part two of that motto was "War is Just a Hobby." We joked a lot because this was serious busi-ness, and when we were "at work," we had to be deadly serious and 100% focused. As a tanker crew member in the Strategic Air Command, we regularly sat "SAC Alert," confined to an Alert Facility next to the alert aircraft parking area. We'd do daily pre-flight inspections on our aircraft to make sure they were free of maintenance issues and ready to go in the event of a klaxon horn which would either indicate the beginning of yet another readiness drill or the unthinkable...the beginning of the end of the world. Sitting just feet from us, their noses pointed toward our jets, were B-1B bombers loaded with nuclear weapons. The United States philosophy on establishing world peace had, for many years, revolved around the concept of Strategic Deterrence —the notion that no nation would be foolish enough to attack us knowing that we had the capability of responding with devasting effect using the three legs of our nuclear deterrent 'TRIAD"—Nuclear bombers, Intercontinental Ballistic Missiles (ICBMs), and Submarine Launched Ballistic Missiles (SLBMs). Together, they formed a survivable insurance plan against a third world war which, given the weapons of the day, few thought the world would survive. Apparently, it worked— hostilities shifted to clandestine operations seeking to undermine opposing governments through an array of activities falling well below the threshold of major nation-on-nation conflict. Conflicts remained conventional and were fought between proxy states or secretly carried out using covert operations, information warfare, or within new domains such as space and cyber. The evolution of national strategy in the nuclear age is a fascinating topic but well beyond the scope of this discussion. Clearly, there's been fervent proponents and opponents but most agree that it's difficult to "put the cat back in the bag" and just pretend that nuclear weapons don't exist or believe that any country possessing nuclear weapons would seek to totally disarm. Several infamous dictators who were convinced to abandon their weapons of mass destruction programs did not meet with encouraging ends…and the rest of the world took note. My story, "Recovery," takes us back to a simpler time, toward the end of the Cold War, when the world was still largely bi-polar—the Soviet Union vs. the United States, in the simplest of terms. Ultimately, the equation was infinitely more complex. Most of us were, by this time, fairly confident that we were no longer on the brink of a nuclear war (as had been feared during the Cuban Missile Crisis (1962). Still, it was our job to be prepared for nuclear war and we trained vigorously to be able to execute our mission. Our capabilities were frequently tested by both local leadership and the SAC Inspector General. This was a no fail mission. Our worst nightmare was that we would be called upon to execute our mission "for real." My short story travels this path. Due to classification issues, I kept this tale as generic as I could to avoid divulging any national secrets but to be safe, I still elected to send this story in for an official Department of Defense security review prior to submitting it for the upcoming anthology. The review was completed expeditiously, and my story was given the green light for publication. Happily, Red Penguin Books selected "Recovery" for one of the pieces to be included in "It's the End of the World."

Drawing to a Close

(Written December 11, 2020)
Published by Red Penguin Books in "*We Made It!: Essays Reflecting on the New Year*" (January, 2021)

Considers the significance of a passing year and the hope we carry into the new year.

What is life but for hope of better days ahead anchored by memories of roads we have traveled and touched by those who have played their roles, large parts and small, upon the stage that is our existence.

I frequently consider life but, even in my youngest days, my thoughts grew increasingly profound as the waning year drew to a close. I spent the final days of last year visiting my childhood home. I slept in my old bed; a single bed with three wooden slats supporting the mattress. By my junior year in high school, the bed was already several inches too short to accommodate my long legs. In my childhood sanctuary, I reflect upon days past. My room, a time capsule with four walls, is frozen in time dating back to 1984 when I left home to join the Air Force. Circus posters from the early 1970s still hang upon my door, just where I taped them after returning from a fun-filled outing with my mother to see the Ringling Brothers and Barnum & Bailey Circus at New York's Madison Square Garden. I was in Kindergarten. Several dusty latch hook rugs hang upon the wall—gifts from my younger sister, crafted when she was but a small child. Posters of cinema and sports heroes have replaced several wildlife posters from my earlier youth much as cities are built upon the ruins of their predecessors. Time marches on, relentlessly, leaving archaeologists to decipher countless riddles. Trophies upon my bookcase proudly stand above a collection of reading material ranging from *The Three Little Bears* (my very first book) to *The Hardy Boys* mysteries to books on airplanes and animals, my two passions at the time. I chose to follow the former, back in 1984 —I wanted to fly. It all makes sense to me—everything I see tells a story. I absorb it all, as the new year approaches. The knight statue upon my dresser! My prized possession; it hasn't moved from the spot where it was lovingly placed, back in 1982. It didn't seem right to relocate this reminder of my faith and my aspirations. His story is best told from where he has held vigil, these past thirty-eight years. I open my desk drawer and I carefully remove an old Timex watch. I got the watch as a Cub Scout. The Cub Scout logo on the dial reminds me of the pride I felt, as a young scout. I wore that old watch throughout my school years--it accompanied me on trips abroad and survived the abuse of countless sporting events. I used to set it once a year—when the ball dropped in Times Square. The countdown on television made it easy to synchronize the time on my watch. No matter where I lived in the world, the new year always began with the lowering of the lumi-nous ball in Times Square. The watch is idle now—lifeless. The motionless hands still tell a story—one only I would understand. The hour and minute hands, and date, are deliberately positioned atop the frozen internal gears as part of an encoded message to myself—a reminder of a special moment from my past. I do things like that.

Moving over to my night stand, and a drawer I rarely revisit these days, I remove a large folder that contains all my childhood artwork. On the eve of a new year, it seems appropriate to look through this lens upon my past. Within the folder, there are plenty of drawings of robots, airplanes, ships, animals, and such . . . but there are also some interest-ingly complex pieces betraying deep emotions and sentiments about my changing life and the world I perceived to be changing all around me. Some still evoke emotional responses when I view them, over four decades later. Long before I began a diary, the drawings expressed my feelings about environmentalism, wealth, the loss of childhood inno-cence, loneliness, betrayal, and a myriad of other topics that I regret were weighing heavily upon my mind at those tender ages. I guess I wasn't a simple kid, even back then. However, more relevant to the upcoming celebration, there is one simple stick-figure sketch that expressed my concern on New Year's Eve in 1979. In those days, a decade was forever. I was uneasy about the approaching 80s. All the happy memories of my childhood resided in the 1970s. The 70s seemed safe and protective although, in reality, I was not without burdens, even back then. The 80s were filled with frightening prospects —new schools, new relationships (or lack thereof), college, leaving my home and my childhood behind, etc. As I look upon the sketch, it's not the crude drawing that impresses me but the memories that come flooding back. I can literally see myself creating the drawing and my stomach tightens as I recall the gloom that filled my heart. It was not a happy time. In truth, the 80s were difficult . . . but they were also spectacular. From great despair, I found wings and soared above the clouds, gaining confidence and new perspectives on life even as I struggled through the inevitable challenges that life put before me.

And here we are, on the verge of turning yet another calendar page. Somewhere, some young boy or girl is struggling with this. Perhaps some young man or woman? Maybe an aging couple? I don't feel the gloom anymore. I know there will be good and bad, happiness and sadness, new beginnings and difficult losses, and the little bits and pieces of the entire human experience that become the stories of our lives. I look forward to it—I no longer fear it. While it's difficult to avoid the thousands of clichés regarding the passage of time and our journeys through life, I think it's worthwhile considering the road that lays ahead.

For my part, I view life as a journey. I see myself adrift upon a beautiful river that meanders its way through the forest of life. The trees and hills restrict my vision so that I'll never know what's at the journey's end nor am I likely to know what lurks around each bend in the waterway. As the river's flow varies, I may find I have less time to spend in the places I love and more time to appreciate scenery I'd rather forget. I may paddle furiously, attempting to alter path and pace but, ultimately, I'll be carried out to sea. I may look back, now and again, but I know that my destiny belongs to the future and not the past . . . and so I return my hopeful gaze to the waters ahead.

It's an adventure, really. Life's and adventure. Even before the sun rises on the new year, I know there will be times when I'll be cold and there'll be times when I'll be tired, and sick, and lonely, and sad. I am sure of it. Knowing, yet not fearing, gives me STRENGTH. I will survive. I also know there will be times when I'll feel happy and inspired and loved and courageous and noble. Knowing this gives me HOPE. Others can seek the crystal ball—I honestly don't want to know what's hidden from my view. I'll know when the time is right. What I do want is to enjoy the journey—to appreciate all of it—the peaks and the valleys. And, when the journey is done, I wish to take my rest with no regrets, knowing that I did my best to live my life on my terms; living with integrity and honor.

Paper browning at the edges and brittle, I carefully replace my drawing from December 31st, 1979 in my artwork folder. It's instructive to look back upon what we once dreaded and revel in the magnificence of our own resilience and upon the innumerable twists of fate that keep life interesting. I'm ready for another year. I wish you the best for the coming year, and in the years that follow. I hope you're not disappointed on your journey and I hope that our paths may cross as we travel. We all have stories worth sharing and it's life that provides the fertile ground for the greatest tales of all. Strike out with confidence into the unknown. Happy New Year!

The Story Behind the Story

In the wake of a difficult pandemic-defined year, Red Penguin Books elected to create an anthology filled with essays, poems, and prose aimed at celebrating the various ways authors found to cope with what was one of the hardest years in recent history. The anthology also sought out stories of hope related to facing a new year and new beginnings. There were a number of approaches I considered to creating a piece to submit for this anthology but, ultimately, I thought to tie it back to a childhood memory—a feeling of gloom I had on the eve of the 1980s that inspired me to draw a picture representing my trepidation. In the end, the 80s turned out to be one of the best decades of my life, but I could not have known it at the time. As such, my short essay sought to convey a sense of hope for the coming year(s) in the wake of one of the most awful years many of us had experienced. During the heart of the COVID-19 Pandemic, many were isolated from friends and family and fed a constant diet of fear through the general media which, while well-intentioned, only served to add to the growing hysteria that we might die a horrible death at any moment if exposed to the unchecked COVID-19 virus. Instructional news stories about scrubbing down all your groceries with soap and water and treating Amazon.com packages like discarded nuclear waste now seem ridiculous but, in the early days of the Pandemic, nobody knew what was real and what was media sensationalism. Though the losses were real and tragic, for most of us, the future turned out to be quite a bit brighter than our fears would allow us to believe it could be.

(Written December 26, 2020)
Published by Red Penguin Books in *"Feeding the Flock"* (February, 2021)

It's not rocket science; it's a recipe passed down from my Mom and my go-to dish for holiday meals. Brief story about the recipe's origin and associated family traditions is included.

Basic Stuffing Recipe
By David Lange

Prep Time:15 minutes
Cook Time:40 minutes
Servings:12 servings

Ingredients:

- 1½ loaves of bread
- 1 stick of butter
- 2 eggs
- 1 onion - diced

- 2 cups of turkey or chicken stock (may substitute water if cooking inside turkey)
- ½ cup of milk
- 2 tablespoons of poultry seasoning
- 1 teaspoon salt (or to taste)
- 1 teaspoon pepper (or to taste)

Instructions:

1. Preheat oven to 350°F
2. In a large bowl, hand shred bread into small pieces
3. Add in diced onions and toss with large spoon
4. Slowly melt 1 stick of butter in saucepan
5. Crack two eggs and whisk
6. Add ½ cup of milk to the bread and onions and mix with spoon
7. Add 2 cups of turkey stock to the bread bowl and continue to mix
8. Pour in melted butter and eggs and mix to ensure all bread crumbs are wet
9. Slowly add in poultry seasoning, salt and pepper, stirring the mixture to ensure distribution throughout the stuffing
10. Line either a cookie sheet or large cake pan with aluminum foil leaving extra foil at the ends to fold up over the stuffing
11. Spoon stuffing evenly across the aluminum foil covered pan and fold foil edges up over the center to cover the stuffing
12. Bake 40 minutes in the oven, checking occasionally to make sure top is browning but not getting too crusty.

The Story Behind the Dish:

I've always loved Thanksgiving and Christmas. Besides the family togetherness and beauty of the holidays, there was always the anticipation of a delicious meal. In my family, that meant Turkey with all the fixings. There was only one "fixing" I was truly interested in—my mom's stuffing. Mashed potatoes with gravy, green beans, rolls, cranberry sauce, and even the pumpkin pie with whipped cream could all go by the wayside so long as I had my stuffing. As a small child, I would envelop pieces of turkey in a veritable cocoon of stuffing before eating them. If I was going to get seconds, or thirds, of anything; it was always going to be stuffing. It's not surprising that when I left home, living on my own, I truly missed the delicious meals of my childhood. Store bought stuffing never lived up to expectations. I rarely cooked a big meal as a bachelor, but I was intent upon mastering the design of a homemade stuffing, it being a critical component for bachelor holiday cheer. When I asked my mother for her recipe, she had no written directions to offer. Instead, I hastily jotted down a list of ingredients with nearly all components being measured out "to taste." This was not the scientific formula I was hoping for but it gave me enough to begin the experimentation. All I knew for sure was the taste I was trying to recreate. It's a simple recipe, devoid of complex arrays of spices from the far east or the requirement to visit a farmers' market in New Delhi. It's simple but effective! Once I mastered the stuffing, my holidays came alive again. After I got married, I continued to be the stuffing chef of the family. Sometimes, my children might assist. One of my favorite photographs from my time living in England was of my young son "helping" me to make stuffing on Thanksgiving morning. As we tore up the slices of bread, together, he would occasionally pilfer a piece of bread and pop it in his mouth. The photo shows us sitting together next to a large bowl of shredded bread and, sure enough, my boy is chewing on a chunk of torn bread. Great memories! Where did my mother acquire her stuffing recipe? From her mother? From her grandmother? In truth, she has no recollection. So, the romantic in me will attribute the design to a prehistoric ancestor. Perhaps the proof is etched upon an undiscovered cave wall in western Europe? Regardless of its origin, I can only hope that my kids may, someday, pass the recipe down to their children, perhaps adding their own twist to the recipe to make it uniquely theirs.

The Story Behind the Story

I never thought I'd be submitting anything for publication in a cookbook. However, when Red Penguin Books announced that their next anthology was going to be a collection of recipes from authors along with a brief narrative describing the story behind the recipe, I knew there was only one option if I was going to try to keep my unbroken streak of anthology submissions going—it was time to tell the story of my favorite Thanksgiving side dish—my mother's bread stuffing. It wasn't a compli-cated recipe, but it was always my favorite across the years. I made a batch while I was home visiting my parents for the holidays and had my cell phone ready to take the photo, steam still rising from the bowl, so that I might include it with my recipe (requested as part of the submission requirement).

Twisted Sky

(Written December 26, 2020)
Previously Unpublished

*A free verse poem reminiscing about the power of
nature and the serious business of taking an aircraft
up into the chaos of a stormy summer night in the
Midwest.*

The sun rises to greet the day; springtime glory unfolds before my eyes
Nature is delicate; fragile; vulnerable to the whims of man
Flowers turn toward the morning light as dragonflies skip across tran-
quil ponds
Fragile; beautiful; our senses betrayed—a demon lurks; I have seen it
I know the cloak it wears; I've known the dread of this peace soon
broken
Tonight, I fly! I will test my skill against forces beyond your compre-
hension
Tonight, I shall sail the Twisted Sky

Children blow dandelion seeds; they waft along the breeze
Gardiners manicure flower beds with exquisite attention
Dogs playing, neighbors waving, pies baking, lives being lived
Am I the only one who feels the sinister thickness in the air?
Humid and warm; fuel for the fire
I take my rest
Tonight, I must sail the Twisted Sky

I have not slept—my mission, rehearsed in a thousand variations,
captures my thoughts
My sleeplessness shall avail me not—tonight's flight is beyond my ken
Weather reporting on the news blends into the background of my
consciousness
I needn't look to know I'll be slugging my way through bands of deep
red and orange
Flight suit zipped; boots laced; navigator's bag packed

Twisted Sky

Tonight, I must sail the Twisted Sky

I take a moment beside my vehicle
The air, thick with moisture; winds are picking up
Clouds form on the horizon; billowing ever-upward
It's coming; storms approach
There's no turning back
We shall lock arms before the day is done
Soon, I must sail the Twisted Sky

We sit; the four of us—my crew
I brief my plan—an air refueling; a navigation leg; approach work in the pattern
RNT; Refueling, Nav leg, Transition—simple
We'll be lucky to get out of this alive
The enemy awaits
She is beautiful and we shall sail the Twisted Sky

To the weather shop!
We're not surprised by what we hear
Visibility limited; crosswinds; windshear; microbursts; weather on the track
Neglected in the narrative—hail and tornados; they'll be there—I can feel it
We nod; our ambition sapped; each secretly hopes for a mission cancellation
Yet, tonight, we are tasked to sail the Twisted Sky

Standing outside, awaiting our bus
Cumulonimbus clouds are growing; racing upward with vengeful ferocity, anvils forming
Thunder is rumbling; the sky turns a dreadful green
The sergeant starts his stopwatch, timing flash to bang—storms are drawing nearer
We are amused—NEXRAD radar and satellites, yet a man with his watch tells the tale
They write a story I have already read—severe weather approaches
The blue bus arrives
Tonight, we shall sail the Twisted Sky

105

Flapper and the Captain

Checklists running; an aircraft coming to life
We find refuge in the routine
Track change—the planned air refueling track is laden with thunderstorms
I hastily replan the entire mission; connecting the dots
Track change—the alternate air refueling track is weathered out
I hastily replan the mission and advise our mated receiver
He's delayed!
Tonight; he'll join us upon the Twisted Sky

We nervously fidget
We converse
We look out the windows
The green sky is darker; the thunder louder; the flashes more dramatic
A wall cloud forms
We need to get out; the tempest feeds upon the lost time
Receiver calls and requests an hour delay; each passing second
increases the peril
The Twisted Sky awaits; ever-patient

Night falls
There is terror in the void
Flashes briefly illuminate the towering monsters hidden in the darkness
The pilots grow uneasy; their 20/20 vision will no longer avail them
All eyes turn to me; master of a forty-year-old radar system
She's a temperamental creature; a thin line between life and death
I place my faith in her; the crew places their faith in me
We'll all place our faith in God, as we tempt the Twisted Sky

Cancel, please cancel; we hope
Receiver is in the green; the tertiary track is no longer usable
I replan, I coordinate, we taxi
We takeoff
It's happening
We're going to challenge the Twisted Sky!

Lightning grows more intense--chasing us; daring us to dance
Altitude, airspeed, heading; my attention rapidly shifts between gages
and the radar

Twisted Sky

I adjust; I translate; green blobs become rain showers, thunderstorms, or worse
One eye on a watch, one eye on a scope, one eye on the instruments
Accelerating and climbing into the clouds; we lose all visual references
Buffeted about through an angry flashing maze of tempest-spewn clouds
We are not welcome in the Twisted Sky

Turbulence, cruel and unrelenting, punishes our daring
Weather deviations! I shout headings; co-pilot coordinates with Center
Banking left and right; we dodge death
Watch ticking; each deviation eating time
I amend the route; we push up the throttles; we regain precious seconds
The receiver calls in late; the Twisted Sky mocks us

Together at last! We lower the boom; fuel transfer commences
St. Elmo's fire dances across the windscreen—a blinding web of brilliant pink light
Feet apart; two aircraft attempting to Tango whilst the dance floor trembles
"Contact," "BREAKAWAY, BREAKAWAY, BREAKAWAY"
"Contact," "BREAKAWAY, BREAKAWAY, BREAKAWAY"
Fuel gradually transfers as we fight our way along the track
Electrical arcing between the aircraft; visibility reduced; we part ways
Our defiance angers the Twisted Sky

Climbing, we seek the stars
Celestial navigation demands a star, a planet, the moon—any light in the darkness
Higher and higher; the clouds are unkind
Our jet bucks uncomfortably like some spirited rodeo bronco
I fight the distraction as I work my computations
We all long to be home
The Twisted Sky offers no sanctuary

A break in the clouds; a miracle!
I leap to the sextant and steady the device
Peering through the eyepiece I see the moon
Bright and welcoming; shot started, timer running

Flapper and the Captain

Precariously balancing upon the stool through turbulent air
One hand on the sextant, the other grasping the strap above, as if
riding the subway
The moon dances a jig across the leveling bubble
Pilots look on in fear; the moon's rays spotlight towering anvils angrily
spitting fire
Behemoth mushrooms emerge like giants from the impenetrable cloud
deck below
The Twisted Sky offer's its final warning

The moon is gone; swallowed whole by the seething blankets of
moisture
My radar has no comfort to offer; massive glowing returns defy passage
We concede; no training is worth our lives
We turn for home; fighting for every inch of progress
The Twisted Sky pursues

Radios come alive with calls to Air Traffic Control and Command Post
This will be a close-run thing
Lightning reported in the area; cross-winds and wind shear; tornado
warnings
Rain streams across the windscreen
We descend, bouncing as if a child tumbling down the stairs
Every parameter approaches limits
The Twisted Sky refuses to release us

First approach; aborted for cross-winds
Second approach; aborted for visibility
Finally; "Field in sight; continuing"
We land; we breath, we taxi
No ground crew to meet us; lightning has cleared the area
The Twisted Sky has made us orphans

Returning to the squadron; we hastily complete paperwork
We shake hands; we complement; we offer thanks
We are done
So, we tell ourselves
The Twisted Sky is not

Twisted Sky

Thunder rumbles and shakes the earth
Lightning paints the sky with formidable brush strokes of electric
brilliance
The road all but disappears; torrents of horizontal rain sweep away all
references
Only a few miles to go
Home is all but assured
The Twisted Sky follows, spewing an icy vomit of hail

I slow as a hundred icy hammers beat my vehicle mercilessly
Finding parking, I steel myself for the sprint to my apartment
Marble sized pellets become golf balls
Golf balls transition to baseballs
I close my door behind me; turn on the lights
I have won
The Twisted Sky is not done

Tornado sirens wailing; power failing
Hail accumulating upon my porch;
No shelter here; my heart races as the roof is pounded by icy globes
Run the drill; just as you've rehearsed; run the drill
When the sky bellows like a freight train; say your prayers
The Twisted Sky seeks retribution for those that dared to defile her
sanctity

Climbing into the tub
Flashlight in hand; battery operated radio providing a play by play
Tornado spotted—it's heading down my street
Ripping and tearing; tossing and smashing; vengeful and merciless
Softballs replace the baseballs that replaced the golf balls that replaced
the marbles
Windshields give way and aluminum hoods surrender to the onslaught
The Twisted Sky wreaks a terrible toll

It's time; the symphony of destruction reaches its brutal crescendo
I pull the mattress over my head and pray as I lay helpless in the tub
Thundering; pounding; winds screaming with murderous rage
My radio as inaudible as my thoughts; I curl into a fetal position amidst
the tempest

Flapper and the Captain

The Twisted Sky has come to take me home

Silence
The still of the morning
Mattress tossed aside, I roll over the edge of the tub and stretch
Stepping out upon my deck, damaged but stable; I survey the
destruction
Cars bent, flipped; roofs gone; centurion trees uprooted and tossed to
next county
Shock and despair as lives are upended; fortunes changed in a night
I have survived; not through intellect or skill
The Twisted Sky has spared me

I walk outside
Birds are singing
Flower stems are petalless; spared trees stripped bare; but the sky is
blue . . . and clear
Forecast calls for severe weather on Thursday
Of course; I am to fly again that night
I breathe deeply; I exhale; I enjoy this day
Delicate beauty; unimaginable power—a photo and it's negative—
nature inspires awe
I accept one with the other
I admire a lone surviving flower; we share a common bond
On the morrow, I shall sail the Twisted Sky

The Story Behind the Story

"Twisted Sky" was written as my submission for an upcoming poetry anthology entitled "The Flower Shop Around the Corner." The assigned task was to submit "poems of all styles and lengths, centering around the theme of nature." It was further suggested that authors should "write about flowers, memories of walks in nature, the seasons changing, or whatever makes you look forward to the Spring..." I decided to go out on a limb. I knew they were probably looking for lovely poems about blooming flowers and chirping birds, but I decided to write on the darker side of springtime weather—something I was very familiar with after many years of living

in the Midwest. As if that wasn't a stretch already, I decided to use the poem to recount my heart-pounding experiences navigating a military aircraft around the severe weather of a stormy spring night. I was tasked to do this on numerous occasions, especially during my four years in Kansas (1990-1994) followed by three in Oklahoma (1994-1997). Especially in Kansas, I remember numerous evenings sheltering in my apartment and listening to the radio as tornado sirens sounded. My base in Kansas, McConnell Air Force Base, took a direct hit from an F5 Tornado in the spring of 1991 (April 26th) which devastated the base and destroyed many of the houses in military family housing. There were numerous injuries but, thankfully, no fatalities on base. Tragically, the nearby town of Andover, KS was not so fortunate. Seventeen people lost their lives as the same tornado swept across the little town.

I can't say I was surprised that "Twisted Sky" didn't make the cut for "The Flower Shop Around the Corner" anthology, but I still had fun creating this poem and I hope that you enjoyed reading it.

Unrequited in the Park: Aphrodite with a Salad

(Written January 15, 2021)
Published by Red Penguin Books in "*A Heart Full of Love*" (February, 2021)

Reflections on learning to love again.

Bryant Park, New York City. The year is irrelevant. I suppose it was probably a couple of years ago, now. I do recall that it was a lovely spring day. Do my eyes betray me? Perhaps I should start over. I know exactly when it was. It was just after 2pm, on June 25th, 2018. She was Aphrodite with a salad. She reminded me of many things I had forgotten about love. We never spoke.

In search of an apartment to position myself near a job that I would eventually be offered . . . and ultimately turn down, my brother and I had spent the better part of the morning and early afternoon wandering about Manhattan, looking at potential residences on my list. A former messenger in Manhattan, there was no one I trusted more to provide insights on neighborhoods, travel challenges, and places to rest. And it was definitely time to rest. With tired feet, we arrived at the beautiful Bryant Park. I'd been by there many times, primarily on trips to and from the New York Public Library, but had never found a reason to stop. Part of the park is built above the vast underground archives of the library. The lovely 9.6-acre patch of green, amidst of a sea of concrete and steel, featured a fair amount of outdoor seating, walkways, and beautiful gardens. It was the perfect place to catch our breath and continue our conversations about life.

My brother and I settled at a small table, benefitting from the shade provided by several trees. We sat; we talked; we watched people. That's when Aphrodite descended from the sapphire blue sky and took up her rightful position upon a glistening golden throne. The world about her, to my astonishment, seemed unaffected. People continued to walk by and the pigeons carried on with their scavenging efforts. Perhaps if she had arrived upon her jewel-encrusted chariot, borne forth by a team of ivory-white doves and heralded by the trumpet fanfare of a thousand angels, those around me might have been as wonderstruck as I. My brother might have noticed her, too. As it was, the goddess radiating with celestial glory a mere twenty feet behind him, my brother was woefully unaware of the divine presence nor the reason his brother's gaze drifted continuously over his left shoulder. My brother spoke and I tried to stay engaged . . . but I was drifting. No, not merely drifting—I was being swept away by flood waters carrying my helpless heart towards a sea of bliss; restoring a hope for love that I thought to be long dead within my breast.

Who was she? I wanted to know. She opened the lid to the vessel containing her sustenance and began to eat her salad. I tried, unsuccessfully, not to stare. There was something that drew me towards her like a brilliant sun pulling the orbiting planets ever closer. What was the attraction? It wasn't gravity? Could it be love?

Love or infatuation? I suppose it depends upon your perspective and which dictionary you rely upon to add structure to your thoughts and your descriptions of life's experiences. Sometimes, I prefer to leave words behind and peacefully coexist with my feelings. Maybe that's why I seldom discuss the topic of love. And yet, here I am. And there I was—gazing longingly upon a lovely urban professional on her lunch break. She was pretty but, more so, seemed to have an intelligence about her, and a worldliness. I think that's what grabbed me most. There are beautiful models traipsing all about Manhattan; exotic beauties being photographed in front of every monument and iconic New York backdrop. I acknowledge and appreciate their physical beauty but rarely do I feel inclined to introduce myself and never have I "made a pass" at any. Maybe I should have? I guess I never wanted to be one of the multitudes of male admirers who was constantly grab, grab, grabbing—that must get old very quickly. If I didn't think I would come across as just another guy hitting on them, I might have asked one of these models that very question: "Doesn't that bother you?" I digress. I think smart is sexy. I've always found intelligence to be a critical element of attraction. Kindness, integrity, and a good sense of humor are also major selling points. But these attributes often take time to ascertain. As I considered the stranger transfixing my gaze, my heart was checking boxes well before the interview and evaluation. She had it all. I just knew it. This fetching woman was probably ten years younger than me. Maybe fifteen? Would that be a problem? I didn't think so. Would she? What would she say, should I approach? I desperately scanned the park. I needed a flower vendor to be right over there. The scene played out in my head, again and again, until it was perfected. I would excuse myself from the table. My brother would understand. Brothers are good like that. I'd purchase a single rose—the best of the lot. I would walk over to where Aphrodite sat, consuming her salad, and I would bow as I carefully placed the rose upon her table. "For beauty." That's all I would say. I'd have to get it right. With only two words, this was all going to be about the delivery. But what next? That's the kicker, isn't it. The first date; the first kiss; making love at sunset; the laughs and tears as experiences are shared; the commitment; the legal bonds and rings exchanged; the growing together and evolution of love into something deeper and more meaningful than either partner had ever envisioned possible. That's what I hoped for. Allow me to replay this thought—that is what *"I"* hoped for. *"I, me, my, myself."* A relationship is not about my hopes and dreams. A relationship is about our hopes and dreams. A relationship is caring enough to compromise; and sometimes caring enough to concede. Was I capable of surrendering my dreams? Towards the end of my marriage, I found it increasingly difficult to concede and utterly impossible to communicate regarding such matters. Preserving hope for the future--wasn't that what my divorce was about? Letting go of the dying embers to keep hope alive so that, one day, a fire might burn brightly again? The pain of my divorce had not yet subsided and I was unsure whether I was ready to ignite what little fuel remained about the scarred tissue of my injured heart. Protected behind an imposing stone wall, I had all but thrown away the key to the formidable door that guarded my heart from the death blow that any further onslaught would surely inflict.

"For beauty." This must be about giving and not about receiving. Again, I looked all around, hoping to find a flower vendor; perhaps a florist shop on the perimeter of the park. There had to be something. I would leave the rose and I would turn to walk away. I wanted to acknowledge her presence and to say thank you—you have inspired me. What would she think? What would she say? I wondered. A smile and a thank you? Silence? A rebuke? Would she invite me to sit? If she did, how long should I wait before I asked if my brother might join the meeting? I should ask my brother, shouldn't I? I mean, if this was about giving and not receiving then why shouldn't I introduce Aphrodite to my amazing brother and best friend?

"For beauty." Would my words usher in the beginning of a relationship or expedite the abrupt end of a fumbled attempt to turn an infatuation into something more substantial and enduring. I was ready to buy the flower. My courage was building and I was ready to take that leap. I was ready.

Was this merely a crush? I've had crushes before. Crushes are brief yet intense cases of infatuation for a person who, more often than not, is unattainable. Here I was, dancing about with words off the pages of my dictionary—infatuation, crush, love—where were the boundaries? Was there a natural progression? I wish I knew. I'm sure I could have paid someone well to explain this all to me; and then another to refute what the first psychologist had posited. Where are the darn flowers! What's New York City's fine for picking flowers from a garden?

"For beauty." She was beautiful. She wasn't Aphrodite; she was better. She was of this earth (I think) and she might actually have been attainable, in so much as any person can be "attained." There was hope that a relationship might blossom. She looked smart and worldly and very lovely in the beautiful way that mortals do, far from the columned porticos of Mount Olympus.

I looked, once more, towards the gardens. And I considered the entirety of the scene as my brother and I pushed back our chairs and stood. City ordinance or not, what right had I to remove a flower from the gardens of Bryant Park? Not all flowers need be picked. Better that some might be left for all to enjoy. Those flowers did not belong to me and I had no right to claim ownership. I turned my eyes towards Aphrodite and I sighed deeply. Not all flowers need be picked.

Was I wrong for not addressing the woman who had captured my heart for the better part of a half hour? Perhaps I would have brightened her day? But then again, I might have caused her stress? Maybe it was never about right or wrong. On that 25th day of June, 2018, I chose to leave the garden exactly how I found it. Nothing moved; nothing changed. But something was moved. Lock undone, deadbolt slid to the side, the creaking of an impenetrable oak door within my breast bore witness to a change within my core psyche. It was Aphrodite that handed me the key to my heart, a key I had misplaced following my divorce and seldom considered seeking. I smiled. I looked to the sky and I smiled. Infatuation, crush, love? It didn't matter, not on this day. What was important was the feeling within my heart and the glowing embers of hope, brought to life once more as oxygen poured through the opening door to my heart. For the first time in years, I knew that I was capable of love and that I might, someday, learn to love again.

This was a joyous revelation. This was hope. Before returning my gaze back upon the earthly world below the vastness of the clear blue sky, I whispered under my breath: "for beauty." We left the park. I didn't find an apartment that day. I found something better. Love, or at least the hope of love. Either was a blessing worthy of all my gratitude.

The Story Behind the Story

With Valentine's Day approaching, Red Penguin Books put out the call for short stories exploring various facets of love and romance. This one was a bit tricky for me because I had never read any romance novels, and I was generally unfamiliar with the genre outside of several movies I had seen and my own limited experience. I had only had one partner in my life, my wife of 22 years. At the time the call went out to submit entries for this anthology, I was five-years divorced and had not dated since separating from my wife. In short, I felt completely unequipped and uninspired to write a love story. With that said, I wasn't quite willing to throw in the towel just yet. After much consideration, I decided to open up a bit and share the kind of tale that usually made it no farther than the pages of my Diary. This piece is a true recounting of a trip I took into New York City with my brother to look at apartments and a special respite stop at Bryant Park. The story tells the tale. It was a watershed moment for me because I realized that my heart was still open to the possibility of romance and an attractive and intelligent looking woman, eating her lunch alone in the park, could still capture my imagination.

FLAPPER AND THE CAPTAIN

(Written January 27, 2021)
Published by Red Penguin Books in *"The Roaring '20s: A Decade of Stories"* (March, 2021)

A physically and emotionally challenged former Army Air Service pilot encounters a mysterious woman in New York City and is swept up in a world of extravagance . . . and adventure.

I slowly made my way along 42nd street, heading toward Grand Central Station, intent on purchasing a one-way ticket back to a town I knew would not understand me. Staying in New York was a bad idea. In a city so large, I thought I might blend in; disappear. And I did, for brief moments here and there. Like thousands of other veterans returning from The Great War, I disembarked the ocean liner that carried us back from Europe, and I was hypnotized by the bright lights and excitement of New York City. The economy was booming and I knew I would eventually find my niche. With cane in hand, I hobbled the streets in search of a place where I belonged. Sure, I'd find a joint, here and there, that was willing to toss a few coins at me, but it was always barely enough dough to pay my rent. Just when I thought I had picked a winner; my horse would come up lame and I'd be out on the street again. I tried to sign on with the post office, delivering airmail. I had flown during the war and, even with my bum leg, I thought I could still fly. I got as far as an interview once, and then a door slammed in the next room and I fell to the floor, screaming, curled up in a fetal position. The docs called it "shell shock" and no employer wanted to have anything to do with me. My body was only partially broken—I'd been splinted back together after two serious crashes. They told me I was lucky to be alive. I wasn't so sure. The gunfire; the shelling; the explosions and the smoke; the smell of death in the air—it takes its toll, don't it? I had hocked nearly all of my possessions, hoping to reunite with them when my fortune took a turn for the better. I knew better days were just beyond the horizon. I've been telling myself that for five years now. I'd seen those sheiks driving Broadway in their ritzy automobiles and those gorgeous dames, bedecked in jewels and furs, and I wanted a taste of that life. I felt the world owed it to me. The world threw a wet blanket over that dream in a hurry. The only thing I had left was my Army Air Service flying jacket and, if the winter wind wasn't biting, I'd have probably hocked that, as well. 1923 had been an exciting year for many New Yorkers. The New York Yankees and the New York Giants played each other in the World Series and that fella Ruth really made a showing with a .368 batting average and three homeruns to his name. He helped lead the Bronx Bombers to their first World Series win. I shared in the excitement but the joy was only temporary and I knew it wasn't going to sustain me through a cold and rainy winter.

As if on cue, the rain started falling moments after I had checked out of the hotel. It was a dark and cold night. Rain began to soak through the canvas of my pack, threatening the only change of clothes I had available. I quickened my pace but my cane slipped as I stepped off the wet curb and I stumbled and fell into a puddle in the street. I felt utterly defeated as I lay there, curled up; honking horns and angry shouts roaring like thunder in my ears. I was frozen. My tears were diluted by the rainwater streaming down my face. And that's when I felt the warmth of her hand.

"Pool's closed, Fly Boy. Here, take my hand and climb on out." It was an angel's voice. Had I been hit by a car? Was I dead? The cold pavement and rain felt real enough. No dice . . . this flier was still grounded. I regained my feet, never letting go of the stranger's hand yet fearing to look her, or anyone, in the eyes. I was still trembling and I learned, years ago, to hide my darkness. With her free hand, my rescuer slowly turned my chin until my head was facing hers. I looked down, still reluctant to make eye contact. "Once you're done checking out the goods, how about you send those baby blues back up here?" I immediately felt embarrassed. I was blushing as I lifted my head to look her in the eyes. What a dish! She was stunning! Her short, black, bobbed hair formed a sharp contrast with her fair complexion and ruby red lips. And those eyes! So blue and filled with a mischievous excitement! I was transfixed. She gently squeezed my hand and led me, willingly, along the wet sidewalk toward a nearby hotel. "What do you say we move out of the rain?" I still wasn't speaking so I just nodded and accompanied her beneath the fringed canopy at the entrance of an extravagant hotel.

Collecting myself, I finally spoke. "Hey, I suppose I should thank you for rescuing me from drowning. I'm Jimmy, by the way. What's your name?" The woman briefly considered my question and then, with flirtatious eyes, responded.

"What would you like it to be?" I was taken aback.

"Well, you kind of look like a Trixie."

"Gosh, you're a regular Harry Houdini, aren't you! You guessed my name on the very first try." I was skeptical.

"Sure. That's what they all call me . . . Houdini."

"I like Jimmy better. Okay if I just go with that?" I took her hand and kissed it gently.

"Jimmy it is." Trixie seemed a little surprised by the kiss. She curtsied and smiled.

"Well now, 'Jimmy-it-is,' the night is young and I couldn't bear to face it alone. How about we get you into some dry clothes and you escort me through my evening of drunken debauchery."

"That's all well and fine but aren't you forgetting about one little thing?"

"What's that, dearest?"

"A little thing called the 18th Amendment . . . Prohibition." A devious grin slowly formed upon Trixie's lovely face.

"Let's get you dry."

"Where do you intend to do that?" I asked. Trixie's eyes drifted upward to the hotel towering above us.

"This is my hotel. We'll just get you a room for the night and I'll have the concierge dry out all your clothes and find you something suitable for the evening." I was surprised, and a little confused, but I wasn't about to turn down this charitable offer from one of the most beautiful creatures I've ever seen. I nodded my approval.

We walked into the hotel lobby and the staff immediately treated Trixie like royalty. Hardly a moment passed before we had a room and assurance that fresh clothes would be delivered within the next 30 minutes. We entered the elevator where the smartly dressed operator tipped his hat and greeted Trixie. "Good evening, Miss Beauchamp. Seventh floor?"

"Lucky seven, Reggie." Trixie winked at the operator who coyly looked away.

"You might want to be careful where you flash that smile, Miss; you're likely to be breaking hearts from here to Los Angeles."

"You're sweet, Reggie. Thank you, dear." Trixie pulled some money from her purse and stuffed a few bills in Reggie's vest pocket. "That's for the heart doctor. You can keep the change."

Trixie's room was just across the hall from mine. I asked if she wouldn't mind if I took a warm bath before our night out. I was still chilled to the bone from my aqueous winter mishap. Trixie told me that she'd expect no less. She instructed me to leave the wet clothes outside my door, to include any wet clothes in my bag. The hotel provided robes that would serve me while I awaited the turnaround. I must admit, it had been a very long time since I had such a wonderful bath; and never in such luxurious accommodations. The hotel was warm and welcoming and my room was spectacular. I was surveying the art upon the wall when a knock came at the door. It was Trixie, bearing a pressed tuxedo upon an oak hanger. I suggested she pass my garment through the partially opened door since I was only wearing a robe but she was undeterred. Trixie practically pushed her way in. I wasn't used to the brashness but I wasn't about to turn her out. Her long fur coat was unbuttoned, revealing a tightly fitting short black dress; the hemline just above the knees. Several strings of pearls adorned her neckline. A jewel-encrusted headband with a colorful feather protruding completed the look. My jaw dropped. Without me ever saying a word, Trixie smiled and told me she was flattered. My expression spoke the words I could not.

Retreating from view, I changed into the tuxedo. Trixie seemed amused by my modesty. I had to wonder what kind of fellas she usually associated with. I suppose it didn't matter.

"You look like a million dollars, Fly Boy. The fit's not bad. I had to guess at your sizes but, well . . . I'm pretty good at sizing up a man." Again, her expression was slightly suggestive. "The night isn't getting any younger; let's hit the town." And that's exactly what we did. The rain was subsiding as the hotel doorman hailed us a cab. I was a willing passenger on this voyage to the unknown—an excursion of growing peculiarity being led by a beautiful and mysterious stranger whom I had only just met. My curiosity was peaking as Trixie led me to a small barber shop in a less traveled corner of the city. She held my hand, giggling as she led me around the corner to a side door in the adjacent alley. I might have thought this to be some clever mugging scheme but I didn't believe that even Trixie was mad enough to dress me up in a Tuxedo so that she could make off with the twelve dollars in my tattered wallet. She had me step back and muttered a few words at the formidable iron door. The door slowly opened and Trixie motioned me to join her. We descended a dingy cement stairway, dimly lit by a single bulb. As we approached another sturdy door, at the bottom, I could faintly hear the unmistakable sounds of jazz music. Once through the final portal, I was awestruck by not only the size of the room but also the intensity of human energy within the large subterranean cavern. So, this was one of those "speakeasies" I had read about. I had never been to one. They were illegal. They were, as I understand, also very common. I have to believe the police turned a blind eye to most of the establishments; more so if the owner had the right connections in Tammany Hall or slipped a little dough to the underpaid cops walking the local beat. The atmosphere was vibrant and the booze ran freely. I offered to buy Trixie a drink, fearing that she'd be beating me to the punch if I didn't, but before either of us could drop any coin, the owner appeared and gave Trixie a big hug, yelling over to the bar tender that our drinks for the night were to be on the house. Who was this girl?!

We grabbed a corner table and sat down with our drinks. Trixie asked a lot about my flying experience and I dutifully answered, leaving out all of the darker memories that still haunted me from the war. Before I realized, I had nearly provided my complete biography and had yet to learn a single significant fact about the woman I was sharing the evening with. I was about to turn the tables when I noticed Trixie's feet tapping uncontrollably beneath the table.

"C'mon, Jimmy, let's dance," she beckoned, with a youthful excitement. Oh, how I wanted to. But, after having recently failed to negotiate a curb with my bum leg, I thought it best I turn down the offer. Trixie was disappointed and she let me know it with her best pouty face. "Oh, lover. Mind if I do? You may need to beat the wolves away with that cane of yours." I laughed and shooed her off to the dance floor just as a waiter was bringing us a second round of drinks. Boy, did that taste good. It'd been too long.

Trixie lit up the room. Fox Trot, Shimmy, the Charleston; she seamlessly transitioned between dances and all her admirers stepped back to watch the show. I watched, in awe. And then I slowly got to my feet. Trixie saw me and skipped over to the band leader, whispering something in his ear. She returned to the center of the room, reached her hand out across the emptiness toward where I was standing, and called my name. "Jimmy?" I stood there, contemplating. A slow, repeating chant grew in volume throughout the establishment.

"Jimmy, Jimmy, Jimmy . . ." Trixie just stood there; her arm outstretched; her eyes enticing me ever closer. With my cane steadying me, I walked toward the center of the floor where I joined Trixie. The speakeasy erupted in applause and cheers. Trixie carefully took my cane and gently set it on the floor as the band began to play a slow tune. Trixie held me tight and I retuned the affection, occasionally having to steady myself in hold. She didn't mind. As we slowly swayed across the floor, Trixie was more than happy to be my emotional and physical support. After the music ended, we just stood there, holding each other tightly, our eyes locked in meaningful union. Across the room, a table tipped over, shattering several glass bottles and the blissful serenity of the moment. I fell to the floor, my heart racing, sweat pouring down my face. The proprietor yelled over at the offenders and then ran over to attend me. Trixie waved him off.

"I've got it from here, Louie. Thank you, darling."

"Sure thing, Trixie. I'm really sorry about that."

"Don't be sorry. I had a lovely evening." Trixie knelt down beside me and grasped my hand. She looked back at Louie. "We had a lovely evening." The band resumed their vibrant jazz tunes as Trixie and I made our way up the stairs and back to the street.

"I'm so sorry, Trixie. I didn't mean to spoil your evening. If you want to go back without me, that's fine; I understand."

"You didn't spoil a thing. I loved the way you held me as we danced. Besides, I'm not done with you yet."

"You're not?"

"No. If you're willing to stick around another day, I think I can promise you an experience you'll never forget." Well, that sure sounded enticing. I wonder what Trixie saw in me? How did a glamorous dame like her get stuck with a broken man like me? She could have gone home with anyone in that club. New York was her oyster.

We hailed another cab and returned to the hotel. Trixie refused to release any more details of her master plan until we were alone together in the hotel. Up on the seventh floor, Trixie accompanied me to my room. Once there, she reached into her purse and pulled out two impressive monographed envelopes. Each was sealed with red wax; a heraldic figure embossed upon the seal.

"What in the world are those?" I asked.

"My ulterior motive. I hope you're not offended." I looked at Trixie, confused but definitely not offended. "You see, I have two invitations for a grand gala at the Meyer Mansion on Long Island and I am sorely in need of an escort."

"And you chose me?"

"I needed a dashing co-conspirator and, unfortunately, Rudolph Valentino was otherwise engaged this weekend. Besides, in your smashing new tuxedo, I'm not sure even Rudy could measure up. Please tell me you'll come." I paused, for dramatic effect, but my mind was made up even before Trixie's formal invitation was complete.

"Sure thing. It would be an honor. But no falling tables, okay?"

"I can't swear to the steadfastness of the furniture but I can promise you I'll be there to lend a hand."

"Deal." I smiled and extended my hand.

"Deal." Trixie ignored my hand and pulled me in for a long hug and a kiss on the cheek. We chatted for a while longer before Trixie kissed me goodnight. I watched as she danced across the hall to her room, stopping only briefly to wave and blow me a final kiss before exiting the scene. What a gal!

I did not sleep well. My nights were still haunted by the irrepressible images of my wartime experiences. All the same, I was awake and ready for the bugle sounding Reveille—a wakening call I'd not heard in a great many years. Old habits die hard. I was fairly confident that I wouldn't see Trixie until later in the day. We had prearranged to meet in the lobby at half past five. At six, I returned to the seventh floor and knocked on Trixie's door. An elderly man opened the door, awoken from his afternoon nap. I gracefully absorbed his retribution, apologized, and beat a hasty retreat toward the lobby. I pulled out my pocket watch and considered whether or not I had been stood up by the prettiest girl in New York City. I wouldn't have blamed her. Was it the alcohol speaking when she offered the invitation? I made up my mind to maintain my position until forcibly removed. Fortunately, it never came to that. At a quarter to seven, Trixie returned, looking absolutely ravishing in a shimmering white gown that hugged the curves of her body as it draped its way down toward her ankles. Lovely silver snowflakes were embroidered across the gown and I'm quite convinced that Venus, herself, might have been jealous were she to behold the vision before me. I half expected an apology for her late arrival but I should have known better. I had lived by the clock for too many years

—it drove my actions; the ticking gears pounding in my head and reminding me of time lost and dwindling possibilities for the future. Trixie was no slave to time. Time bent to her will and bowed before her as she confidently strode by.

"Be a dear and retrieve my coat, would you? And no flirting with the coat check girl." Trixie handed me a receipt and I forgot all about the time.

"But of course, good lady." I bowed, regally. Trixie got a kick out of that.

"See, I knew Valentino had nothing on you."

With coats in hand, we set off on our adventure. Trixie had arranged for a private car to take us across the Queensboro Bridge to the ritzy Gold Coast of Long Island. She wasn't about to show up, dressed to the nines, in a taxi cab. Trixie was all class.

The Meyer Mansion, presently ruled over by investment banker Franz Meyer, sat upon a sprawling 400-acre estate, bejeweled by fountains and gardens. Meyer was well known for his lavish parties and celebrated each season with an appropriately themed event. The silver snowflakes on Trixie's gown and the white feathers adorning her sparkling tiara now made sense—I was escorting the Snow Queen to the Winter Ball. Of course.

As we pulled into the large, circular driveway, an attendant leapt forth and opened the door on Trixie's side of the vehicle while another attended to my door. Out of the corner of my eye, I saw Trixie whisper something to our driver and slip him what looked to be a hundred dollar note—more dough than most honest working men earned in a week. I still wondered where Trixie came by her money. I thought it better not to ask.

Ascending the spectacular marble stairs leading to the grand entry, I could already see that the booze was flowing freely. I would not have been at all surprised if the spectacular fountains on the premises were spewing liquor. With that kind of dough, I'm sure all the police departments within a hundred-mile radius were incentivized to overlook indulgences on the Meyer Estate. Half undressed women were chased by amorous suitors as the band set the musical tone for frivolity. Ice sculptures adorned the interior of the home, watching over impossibly fantastic buffet tables set beneath luminous crystal chandeliers. Marble and gold; silk and fine lace. Every corner of the mansion screamed excess. I felt terribly uncomfortable. This was Trixie's world, not mine.

What was I thinking? I grew more taciturn while Trixie swept us through the corridors, winking and waving. The laughing and shouting; drums beating and trumpets blaring; a thousand unnamed faces shouting inaudible greetings—it was too much. I could feel the sweat soaking my shirt. My hands were starting to tremble. I wasn't sure I was going to be able to keep it together, yet I had to try—for Trixie.

"Trixie, I'm not sure I can do this." I felt awful but I didn't want to embarrass Miss Beauchamp in front of her social friends. For all I knew, they were the source of her inexhaustible financial reserves. With each passing moment, the crowd seemed to grow denser and the noise more intense. Trixie pulled me through a hallway that led to a fantastic balcony overlooking Long Island Sound. We stood there for a while, admiring the stars and ignoring the occasional gleeful screams coming from the nearby garden as frolickers set about destroying Eden. "Trixie, I . . ." I hadn't finished my apology before I felt the warmth of Trixie's hand tenderly squeezing mine.

"Shhh. I know." Her voice was gentle and soothing. "It's alright . . . truly." We stood together in silence. Eventually, she released my hand and we turned toward each other. "I need you to fight for me, just a little bit longer. Please fight." I was confused. What did she mean by "fight?" "Jimmy, do you think you can find your way through this rat maze and to the field beyond the statuary garden?"

"I suppose so." I would have found my way through the Minotaur's Labyrinth if Trixie had requested it.

"I need you to do this for me, Jimmy. Go to the field and find the car that we came in. It'll be parked near the statue of Icarus. The doors will be unlocked. In fifty minutes, I need you to start the engine and keep it running."

"Is that fifty minutes of Trixie time?" I quipped. Trixie gave me a friendly shove which, I'm embarrassed to say, nearly knocked me over.

"No, lover. That's fifty minutes of Captain Douglas time." It was the first time Trixie had actually used my former rank. Outside an off-hand remark I made the day before; it never came up in conversation. Trixie hadn't forgotten. I stood a little taller.

"Five zero minutes. You got it. Should I even bother inquiring?"

"No." Trixie paused for a moment to consider. "Cold night, and all —a little extra engine warming never hurts, right?"

"Sure. It'll be warm." I welcomed the assignment, even as my mind grappled for an explanation.

Flapper and the Captain

We parted and I fought my way upstream against the flood waters of humanity pouring toward the back end of the mansion. Trixie disappeared below the waves. I could feel my heart pounding and the symptoms of another attack coming on. I was suffocating within the unchecked sprawl of humanity. Like a Doughboy on the front lines, I was fighting for every inch of progress. I was fighting to keep my head together. I can't crack. I can't give up. I've got to pull through for Trixie. It was a close-run thing, but I finally made my way out of the Meyer Mansion and beyond the grasping arms of a half dozen fried flappers who seemed ready to engage in amorous escapades with any gentleman who would have them. Making whoopee was not on my agenda for the evening. Clear of humanity, I searched in the lamplit darkness of the night for Icarus. Icarus, the chump whose wings melted when he flew too close to the sun—he fell from the sky, drowning in the sea below. I could empathize.

I found our vehicle, a 1923 Maxwell Model 25. I was surprised it was still here. Trixie must have paid the driver to stick around. Perhaps he was one of the fellas chasing dames through the garden? Thirty minutes remaining. I searched the vehicle for keys. There'd be no warm up without the keys. On the passenger side, I was surprised to find my leather flying jacket. What was that doing here? Even more surprising, the keys to the Maxwell were in the pocket of my jacket. I strained in the dim light to read the hands of my pocket watch. With key in hand, I waited. I could see a stream of headlights flowing along the drive leading to the property. This party was far from over and was unlikely to reach its crescendo until the wee hours of the morning. I was honestly surprised that Trixie wasn't planning on dancing through to dawn. Ten minutes remaining. Five. Four. Three. I could swear I heard some gunshots coming from the mansion. That was probably fireworks. Two. One. With no one to evaluate my precision, I still took great pride in firing up the Maxwell at fifty minutes, to the second. The car shuddered back to life, like a lion shaking off the night's chill. I admired the night sky, my "challenging" assignment complete. More shots. Bells ringing. Indiscernible shouts emanating from here and there. I was losing it. I was fighting but I was losing it. My demons would not let go. My hands were trembling and tears were streaming down my cheeks when I saw a shadowy figure running rapidly toward the car. It was Trixie! Heels in her left hand and a leather satchel in her right, she was making

126

record time across the grassy field. She reached the car, gasping for air.

"Can you drive? Jimmy, can you drive?" I fumbled for words. More shots rang out through the night. Search lights were panning the grounds and I could hear the distant sound of police sirens. "Slide over, baby. I think I'd better take the wheel. You've had too much to drink." I hadn't touched a drop all night but I scooted over to the passenger side and let Trixie take the wheel. A spray of mud flew from the rear tires as Trixie put the car in gear and floored the accelerator. We were off the property in minutes and heading south on back roads. I was beside myself. I felt a terrible shame for failing. I was completely bewildered by Trixie's actions and the significance of the events of the past hour.

Up ahead, we saw the headlights of several vehicles approaching us at a high speed. With sirens wailing, there was no doubt these were responding coppers. Much to my dismay, Trixie pulled off the road, sliding in behind some trees, and turned off the headlights on our vehicle. The police cars had no sooner passed than Trixie was back on the road and doing some high-speed driving of her own. A fog was beginning to settle upon the island but Trixie raced onward, undeterred. I felt uneasy about the situation.

"Trixie, what have you gotten us into? What did you do?" Trixie was silent. I thought she may not have heard my question above the roar of the engine or perhaps because she was focused on negotiating every bend in the road without sacrificing speed. Despite my concerns, my anxiety seemed to be fading—the movement and the roar of the engine had a strange calming effect upon me. I looked out ahead. The stars had long-since disappeared; the fog was thickening. Several minutes later, Trixie finally responded.

"Do you trust me, Jimmy? Please tell me you trust me."

"Well, sure I trust you, Trixie." My response was more a reflex than a considered position. The truth was, I wasn't sure who to trust anymore and I had little reason to trust the mysterious beauty who appeared out of the dark just the night before; told me nearly nothing substantial about her own affairs; whisked me away upon a surreal journey into the lifestyle of the rich and powerful; and now appeared to be fleeing from the police.

"You do? You trust me, Jimmy? You really trust me?" I knew I wasn't going to pull the wool over this dame's eyes. She was too smart for that. Trixie could read me like a book.

"I don't have to trust you. I love you. I love you and I believe in you."

"You're a fool for falling in love me with, Jimmy." Trixie reached over with her right arm and gently squeezed my shoulder, never taking her eyes off the road.

"Then let me die a fool." The conversation stopped. I'd follow Trixie to the sun even though it meant my wings of wax would melt and I'd fall to my death. I would die for this woman, a thousand times over.

Roosevelt Field?! What were we doing at Roosevelt Field? Trixie slowed the vehicle and slowly drove over to one of the hangers on the quiet airfield. At this time of night, the airfield was nearly lifeless. She turned off the engine and sat there in silence.

"Well now, I guess this is the moment of truth." Trixie was searching for words; she seemed uncharacteristically ill-prepared for the moment. "I stole something, Jimmy; something that didn't belong to Franz Meyer and his crooked mob; something that my family swore to protect. I know you think we're running from the coppers but the cops are the least of our worries. By now, there's probably two dozen cars searching the Island for us . . . cars filled with men who don't ask questions; men who don't value life. If they find us, they'll bump us off; both of us. And they've got connections. They've got the police and the local government in their pocket. They're going to shut down the bridges and set up checkpoints along all the major roads. They'll be monitoring the ferries and tightening the noose around us until we've got nowhere to run. They'll trap us like rats in a barrel and then . . ." Trixie stopped to wipe a tear out of her eye.

"What's in the hanger, Trixie?"

"Come on, let me show you." We walked through a side door and I couldn't help but smile when I looked upon a beautifully maintained war surplus Curtiss JN-4 biplane; a "Jenny." I had flown Jennys during my training here in the States before I got shipped overseas to fly fighters with the Air Service in the war. I knew how to fly her; but that was years ago. I grew anxious as I understood my purpose. I was the missing puzzle piece. I was Trixie's ticket off this island prison; I was the guy supposed to carry her and her prize over the moat around the citadel. Maybe I should have felt used . . . or betrayed. But I didn't. Instead, I felt as if I had been given purpose. This was my last chance to be the knight in shining armor that I hoped I might be as a naïve second lieutenant heading off to war. Trixie looked over at me, assessing my condition, physically and mentally. "Can you fly her, Captain Douglas?" Captain Douglas. She called me Captain Douglas again.

"Get the door on that side of the hanger, Trixie; I'll get this side." We opened the hanger doors. I still had no idea what the plan was but the clock was ticking in my head and I knew every second mattered. "Where to, princess?" Trixie pulled out a folded chart with two spots marked. The destination appeared to be along the coast in southern Maine. That was a long haul.

"We're not going to make it there on a tank of gas, Trixie."

"No, we won't. This middle mark is a refueling stop. The landing zone will be marked by three bonfires. The destination field will also be marked by three bonfires." The chart had towns, roads, and rail tracks marked but, in the darkness and haze, I wasn't confident I would have the required visual references to safely navigate the route. I was going to ask if Trixie would consider waiting until morning but the distant sound of multiple car engines removed any doubt that we were in a "now or never" moment. My hand began trembling but I hid it behind my back.

"Trixie, I'm going to need your help to get this bird breathing."

"Wait, you're not ready yet." Trixie ran to the car and came running back with my leather flying jacket. She slid off my tuxedo jacket. My hand was still trembling and it was getting worse. Trixie didn't say a word as she helped me into my flight jacket. She held both my hands and leaned in to kiss me on the lips. "For Le Capitaine." Her French accent was nearly perfect. I was in seventh heaven. She spoke softly, "I trust you, too, Jimmy." I could have stared into those beautiful eyes all night long but I knew we had only minutes.

"Thank you." I paused. "Trixie, I'm going to need you to pull down quickly on that side of the propeller when I signal you. After you give it a good pull, I'm going to try to start the engine. Once I do, back away quickly and come around to this side and climb up the wing into the front seat." In the distance, we could see the headlights from at least three vehicles rapidly coming down the road. "On the seat, you'll find a leather cap and some goggles. I suggest you put those on to help keep any leaking oil off your face." I looked out the hanger door and then back toward Trixie. "Well, I suppose there's not much more to say and not near enough time to say it, so let's get to dancing." I hopped in the back seat and, when I was ready for the start, signaled down to Trixie. Like an old pro, she spun the wooden propeller blade counter clockwise and smoke spewed from the engine as it came to life. Trixie quickly made it into the front seat with her mysterious satchel and we were on the move. I expeditiously taxied the aircraft toward the runway. The ominous black cars were now heading directly toward us. I could faintly hear the rat-tat-tat of Tommy guns over the familiar music of the Jenny's engine. A bullet whizzed by my head; I could hear it. I remained focused. Reaching the runway, I pushed the throttle forward and accelerated, bullets still racing past. Finally, the wheels left the earth and we were flying. The gunfire faded as we disappeared into the fog and I gently banked right to pick up a northeasterly heading. I thought to calm myself only to realize that my mind was already at ease. I was caught up in the euphoria of the moment—the sheer joy of flying. I gently banked to the left and right; the engine purring beautifully up front; the controls responsive and obedient. Occasionally, Trixie would turn to look back at me—her excitement radiating through her glorious smile. I didn't need to ask—this was her first time.

I flew low, straining to pick up the lights of towns along the way or any vehicle headlights that might indicate a major road. A set of railroad tracks proved to be a godsend—I followed them along the coast of Connecticut and into Massachusetts. When no visual cues were available, I relied upon a compass heading and elapsed time to determine my approximate location. The cloud deck seemed to be thinning out, as I progressed along my route. Finally, as promised, I saw the glowing flames of three large bonfires in the distance. I breathed a sigh of relief as I began the gentle descent back to earth. I flew toward the flames until I saw a small airstrip in a clearing. I circled once to look for obstructions and then began my approach for landing. We bounced, ever so slightly, upon contact with the ground but I have to admit, I was pretty darn pleased with my first landing in half a decade. I stopped the aircraft at the end of the field, near a small shack. I had no sooner cut the engine than two burly looking brutes came running out of the shack, waving pistols and yelling for me to get out of the aircraft and keep my hands in the air. Trixie shouted back at them, in French, and the atmosphere quickly changed to a more congenial one. The two men, speaking in English but with French accents, both apologized and helped Trixie and I out of the aircraft and over toward a small campfire where we shared bread and Brie cheese along with a glass of wine.

One of the men set about refueling the Jenny. Our conversation remained cordial but nondescript. Who were they? What was going on here? Had I somehow involved myself in an international spy ring? Was I the good guy or the bad guy? Was I Trixie's fella or just some stooge, duped into being an accomplice in some fantastic heist?

As we sat by the fire, I was offered another glass of wine. The man thanked me for my help and told me that a car would be made available for me in the morning.

"What do you mean, a car will be made available for me?" I waved off the second glass of wine.

"Monsieur, you have done us a great service, tonight. Your job here is done and we all thank you. I'll be taking over from here." Over my dead body! I didn't actually say that. I quickly got up from my position by the fire and nearly fell over. My cane was still sitting in the corner of a hanger on Long Island. My feeble attempt to stand wasn't helping the cause.

"Now listen here," I objected; but Trixie cut me off, mid-sentence, and turned to the man, speaking forcefully in the silkiest French accent I had ever heard. I didn't understand a word. Clearly, Jacques did. He slowly stood, bowed, and apologized for the misunderstanding.

"Forgive me, please, mon capitaine, I was not aware that you would be continuing on from here. A thousand pardons." Jacques saluted me from where he stood.

Trixie looked at me and smiled. "I can only imagine you must be having a hard time with this. Would you mind if I drop the New York accent?"

"You're not from around here, are you? Who are you?"

"Later, my love." She spoke softly now with a beautiful French accent. "I've given you little reason to trust me but I beg of you, please, don't give up on me now." Trixie extended her hand and I accepted it. I wasn't going to let her down . . . not now. Her expression turned from serious to silly as she asked us not to look as she went behind the shed to relieve herself. We were gentlemen and we gave the woman her privacy. With the Jenny filled with gas and ready for the next leg of the journey, we climbed onboard and Jacques gave the propeller a good spin to help get the engine started. Having previously reviewed the navigational chart, I was confident I could use the brilliant light of the moon to follow the coastline to our final destination, provided the clouds cooperated. They did. Sunrise was still several hours away but a glorious moon lit our way, casting a million sparkling gems upon the surface of the waters below. The coastline was easily visible. I followed it north. At one point, I passed abeam a large flock of geese. Both Trixie and I admired the beauty of the scene. Just before dawn, I picked up the glow of fires out ahead. At first, they burned as one before eventually resolving themselves into the familiar pattern of the three marker beacons that would guide us home. Again, I descended and circled the area. There was no airstrip; only a large grassy field amidst a clearing in the trees. Trixie pointed downward; her voice inaudible over the engine. I responded with a thumbs up. The landing was a little bumpier than the last, as the field was not a prepared airstrip, but, as they say, any landing you can walk away from is a good one.

A sea fog was rolling in with the tide and I thanked my lucky stars that it was gracious enough to follow me through the door. Trixie lithely hopped out of the Jenny and ran off toward the wooded area just to the side of the field. I was tired and very stiff; I felt twice my age. Slowly, I climbed out of the cockpit and down off the wing. I had barely made it down before Trixie came running back with a large stick.

"You're cane, mon capitaine." Her smile was lovely and made me forget the pain. I thanked Trixie and steadied myself with the walking stick. I looked around the field. No shack; no Frenchmen sipping wine around a warm fire; just the still of the early morning. The visibility was rapidly degrading. There wasn't going to be a third flight. I shivered and looked over toward Trixie. I wasn't sure what to say.

"Looks like we made it." That was the best I could come up with. Trixie smiled and took my left hand.

"Walk with me." We walked to the edge of the wood and then followed a small dirt path that worked its way through the pines. We ascended a hill and then continued through the trees, descending into a thickening fog. I heard it first—the sea—the soothing music of waves kissing the shore. We were hardly free of the woods before the beautiful Atlantic came into view. Trixie led me, carefully, over to a large rock where we both sat to take our rest. I had a sinking feeling that our time together was nearing an end. I no longer desired to know the answers to the thousand questions racing through my brain; all I wanted was to keep the dream alive.

"This is it? Isn't it?"

"Not quite. I believe I owe you a story." I sat quietly, reveling in the presence of the lovely flapper who had won my heart. I wanted to memorize every feature of her face; the way she spoke; the way she made me feel. I dreaded losing a single detail to the onslaught of time. Trixie looked down and laughed. "You're never going to believe what I tell you. You don't have to."

"Then I'll believe in you." Trixie blushed at my words and held my hand as she spoke.

"Permit me, then, to take you back in time . . . a great many years ago. Two French pilgrims returning from the Holy Land took their rest in the ruins of a small abbey along the pilgrimage route. The night was cold and wet and what remained of the abbey afforded them protection from the elements. In the far corner of the abbey, they heard a man sobbing. The pilgrims went to investigate and found an inconsolable beggar, hunched over the lifeless body of a young girl. The beggar explained that the child was his granddaughter and that she had been foraging for food when she was set upon by a band of thieves who stole the fruits she had collected and beat her cruelly, leaving her for dead beside the nearby stream. The old man searched for days before finally coming upon his granddaughter's body. Death had stolen all but her last heartbeat. The man carried his beloved granddaughter, not quite fourteen years of age, back to the ruined abbey that they had made into a home. The child remained unconscious and withered slowly, her breath becoming ever-shallower. The pilgrims begged the old man to let them attend her. He was weak and had not eaten in days, himself. He refused to let the child leave his arms. The pilgrims prayed that night and each was visited by a fantastic dream whilst they slept. When the dawn came, the pilgrims thought to share the details of their dreams with one another. They were stunned to find the dreams were one and the same. Each dreamed of unearthing a beautiful chalice of gold, buried beneath a stone lily, and that the powers of that vessel might return life to the withering body of the beggar's grandchild. When they shared the details of their extraordinary dream with the beggar, he sobbed uncontrollably. But these were not the lamenting tears of a grieving guardian but the joyous tears of one touched by angels. With a quivering hand, he pointed a bony finger toward the northeast corner of the abbey and informed the pilgrims that there was, on that spot, a large stone with a carved lily upon it. The pilgrims fashioned makeshift digging tools from the remains of an iron gate and set about excavating around the lily. They dug for the better part of the day until they uncovered a lavishly decorated rosewood box. When they opened the box, they were astonished to see the beautiful golden chalice from their dreams. The cup glowed with an unearthly light. The old beggar pleaded for them to waste no time in filling the cup with water from the nearby stream. The men raced to the stream and complied with the beggar's wish. They returned with the chalice, filled with the cool, clear water, and handed it to the old man. He slowly poured the water across his granddaughter's parched lips and into her mouth. Dipping his finger into the water, he made the sign of a cross upon the young girl's forehead and then he kissed her, lovingly. The girl's eyes slowly opened and she gasped for air. Her body shuddered as Death fled to reap his harvest upon other fields. The pilgrims looked on, in disbelief. The old man cried and thanked the pilgrims for saving his granddaughter's life. In return, he offered the men the chalice. Grateful as they were, these pilgrims were not greedy men. They not only turned down the offer but they left nearly all their food supplies with the old man and his granddaughter. The next morning, they continued on their journey toward home. That night, as they camped just off the road, they were startled to see the beggar's granddaughter running toward them, tears in her eyes. Her clothes were tattered and she bore a leather satchel over her shoulder. She raced over to the pilgrims and embraced them both, telling an awful tale of how the bandits had returned and killed her grandfather. Hearing their approach, the old man placed the golden chalice in the leather satchel and bid her to run as fast as she could to find the pilgrims who had showed them kindness; for only in their care could he be sure the child would be protected. Together, they returned to France. The pilgrims not only held true to their oath to protect the young girl but they carefully hid the chalice in a small abbey not far from the city of Lille. And there it remained, protected through the centuries."

I was spellbound by Trixie's story; more so by the sparkle in her eye as she shared the tale. Her lovely French accent just added to the mystique. "What happened next, Trixie? Did anyone ever find the chalice? What happened to the girl?"

"Ah, so I haven't put you to sleep with my little bedtime story. I'm glad." Trixie continued. "The abbey prospered for years but, eventually, was abandoned when the order that cared for it disappeared. Some say they left when a plague devastated their order; others claim they were persecuted and forced to flee. There are no remaining records to tell us the true story but legend maintains that some members survive and that these few persist in protecting the secrets of the chalice. Lovely story, no? What we do know is that the German forces occupied that part of France during The Great War. Wherever they went, the Germans collected artwork and treasures from the lands they pillaged. The 'spoils of war.' The old abbey was turned into a fortification of sorts and it was severely damaged during an engagement with French forces. This holy ground is now littered with shell casings and unexploded ordnance—it's far too dangerous to visit. It's very sad. Very sad."

"So, do you think the chalice is still there, buried under all the rubble?"

"Oh no, it's not there. It's safe now."

"How do you know, Trixie?"

"Well, you see. After the war, the Germans sold off much of their captured booty to help pay for their war debts. Rich collectors, of questionable repute, were willing to pay top dollar for the masterpieces and treasures being sold on the black market. Our host last evening, Mr. Franz Meyer, was one of these collectors."

"So, Meyer has the chalice?"

"Meyer had a beautiful porcelain vase. He was quite fond of it. If he had realized its true value, he might have protected it better. As it was, he paid a substantial sum for the piece and he wasn't pleased when he spotted one of his guests climbing out a window with the vase secured under her arm."

"Was that you? Did you steal the vase? But I don't understand—what does the vase have to do with the chalice?"

"The vase was constructed about the chalice. In this way, the Order of the Chalice thought they might protect their treasure. I threw the vase out the window and shattered it. Mr. Meyer was not happy. The vase was worthless to me—I only wanted what was inside."

"The chalice?" Trixie's eyes brightened and she smiled slyly. She reached across to grab her satchel and stroked the bag as if it were a kitten.

"To some."

"What do you mean? Can I see it?" Trixie slowly unbuckled the straps of her leather satchel and reached inside. She pulled out what appeared to be a large rock and held it for me to admire.

"I don't know. Can you?" I closed my eyes and looked again. All I saw was a rock. In the distance, coming from the sea, I heard the unmistakable piping of a bosun's whistle. Trixie pulled a whistle from her pocket and responded to the call with a series of whistles. "I'm afraid our time is short, mon amour." Trixie replaced the rock in the satchel.

"Wait, that's it?" Trixie looked at me, her eyes watering up.

"No, my dearest; not quite. Permettez-moi le plaisir d'un baiser."

"What?"

"Allow me the pleasure of a kiss." Trixie slid off the rock and reached out both her hands, helping me to my feet. She pulled me in tightly and I wrapped my arms around her and we kissed. I'd never experienced anything like that in my life. We held our embrace, kissing passionately. At that moment, there were only two of us in the world. Gradually, we peeled ourselves apart, still looking into each other's eyes. I felt a tear roll down my cheek but Trixie caught it with her finger. She reached back into her satchel and pulled out a magnificent chalice of gold. I stared in disbelief. Trixie winked and put her finger to her lips to hush me, saving me the embarrassment of fumbling for words. None were necessary. She scampered across the rocky beach to where the sea met the land and lowered the cup into the sea, filling it with water. A voice cried out, in French, as a small rowboat appeared out of the fog, slowly making its way to the shoreline. Trixie responded, "Bienvenu!" as she was returning to me with the chalice. Clasped in both hands she offered the chalice to me, silently bidding me to take a sip. I prepared myself for the salty taste of the sea but, instead, my palate was blessed by a sweet and indescribably divine flavor unlike anything I had ever tasted before. Instinctively, I knew that one sip was all I should ingest. To sample any more would be folly. I handed the chalice back to Trixie. She dipped her slender finger into the water and then formed a cross upon my forehead with the wet finger. I stood there, motionless. Trixie returned to the water's edge and emptied the remaining contents of the chalice into the sea before replacing the vessel within the satchel. The rowboat reached the shore and the two oarsmen pulled the boat up onto the beach. Trixie approached the men and handed the satchel to the fella with a prodigious mustache. She then returned for what I knew would be our final goodbyes.

"You're leaving now, aren't you? I swear, I'd die a thousand times over for you, Trixie. You know that, right? If I thought it would help,

I'd beg you to stay. I've never met a gal as classy as you and if you get on that boat . . . if you get on that boat, my heart's just going to break and there's nothing that'll ever fix it." Trixie embraced me and we kissed again.

"I'm taking the chalice home, Jimmy. I can't take you with me. Know that I love you. I always will. You weren't an accomplice, a pilot for hire, or a means to an end. You are a soulmate." Trixie gently wiped a tear from my face. And I wiped one from hers. She slowly backed away, her eyes never leaving me as she moved toward the boat. Once she was seated, her comrades pushed the boat back into the surf and pulled themselves aboard. They lifted the oars and began to row against the tide. From the boat, Trixie shouted "Bravo pour le capitaine!" Her comrades responded with a rousing "Bravo pour le capitaine!" I watched in anguish, straining for every last moment of visual contact with Trixie Beauchamp. I yelled into the fog.

"Hey, Trixie, you never told me the name of the girl in your story —the girl who went with the pilgrims!" Trixie's reply found me through the fog.

"Beatrice. Her name was Beatrice."

"Will I ever see you again, Trixie?" There was silence; a painful silence.

"Oui, mon capitaine. Look for the white lily. Au revoir, for now, my love." Her voice was now barely audible. There was no point in shouting back. Au revoir, dearest friend.

Author's note:

I found this strange tale in an old cedar chest in my aunt's attic. After her passing, I was assigned the unenviable task of settling her estate. There was a little note attached claiming that the pages were torn from the diary of one James Douglas. Beneath the yellowing pages from the diary, I discovered a small notebook, apparently belonging to my aunt. Within the partially filled notebook were dozens of cryptic scribbled notes along with some additional details regarding the origin of the story in question.

After Mr. Douglas abandoned his Manhattan apartment, for reasons unknown, the landlord collected what little remained to either sell or discard. Assessing the two diary volumes he came upon as having no value, he tossed them in the trash bin. Fortunately, his wife, who was there assisting in the purge, appraised the books differently. She chastised her husband and moved quickly to recover them from the garbage. She was very curious about the stranger in the leather flying jacket who came and went but said very little. The diary merited further investigation. She retained them for several weeks but, being a superstitious man, her husband finally insisted that they be thrown away. He thought it was bad luck to keep the journals of a dead man. While there was absolutely no indication that their former tenant had met his demise, his wife consented . . . but not before carefully removing a number of pages describing the strange relationship between Mr. Douglas and a mysterious flapper girl who he met one winter's eve in the City. Those pages were carefully preserved over the years in my aunt's chest of special memories until they found their way into my hands. Aunt Sally always was a sucker for a good love story. I enjoyed the story but I was left unsatisfied by the abrupt ending and unanswered questions.

I carefully reviewed the notes my aunt had made in her notebook. Most had no meaning to me but my curiosity was piqued by references to several small towns in the northeast of France. The connection to the story was not clear. Like a slow burning candle, the story dimly lit a corner of my mind, all but forgotten but never extinguished. For me, the tale was interesting but not compelling. I had become so focused on developing my career that I had little room for flights of fancy or far-fetched tales of romance. I was content to walk the here and now and leave the day dreaming for those with less drive to succeed. I was a fool. I soon discovered that promotions and professional accolades brought me little joy. There was something missing. When an opportunity for a business venture in the north of France was briefed at the executive round-table, I felt strangely compelled to volunteer to lead the team. Business negotiations were successfully concluded, after a week of meetings, and I released my team to return to the U.S. while I remained. Officially, I was enjoying several days of vacation to cele-brate our successes in closing a multimillion-dollar deal with the French automotive company we'd been courting. My true purpose was so far out of character that I doubted my own intentions. With my aunt's well-worn notebook in hand, I would attempt to complete a senti-mental journey that she, sadly, never had the resources to embark upon. And thus, I found myself dreamily staring out the window of a passenger train in the north of France.

I was pleased to have the entire row of seats to myself. It's interesting now to recall the frustration I felt when, at the very next stop, I had to stand and step into the aisle so that an older gentleman could join me in what I inappropriately assumed was my row. It wasn't long before I humbly conceded that it was our row. No, that's not it either. I was a guest in his row.

The old man greeted me warmly. His English was fairly good. I nodded and responded, reflexively. I regretted not having a paper to read—burying my head in a copy of the Wall Street Journal was a time-honored tradition employed by those who had no desire to interact with the humanity surrounding them. Instead, I pulled my aunt's notebook from my overcoat pocket and studied the notes. The old man seemed fascinated by the little book and he was not going to give me an easy out. He introduced himself as François and inquired as to the contents of the notebook and the purpose of my travel. It's funny how you can talk to a stranger, someone you know you'll never see again, and share things that you might never share with those closer to you. As I told the tale of Captain Douglas and Miss Beauchamp, his eyes lit up. He seemed to be hanging on every word. François was a diminutive French gentleman with a heart so large I'm surprised his tiny frame could bear the load. I didn't realize it at the time but he was about to become part of my strange pilgrimage.

After a considerable period of silence, François looked upward and recited some form of prayer, in French. He then rested his hand upon my shoulder and told me that it was fate that brought us together. I was skeptical. My doubt soon faded as he shared that he was familiar with the story, albeit he'd heard it told from a different perspective. He explained how the tale was relayed to him by a monk he met at a hospital while being treated for a life-threatening illness, a number of years ago. The doctors called his recovery nothing short of miraculous. François insisted the story had given him the will to live. He became obsessed with the tale and had spent many years investigating the story. That I should meet a man on a train in northern France who shared my interest in an otherwise unknown love story was beyond fascinating. Perhaps we might assist one another on our quests? I began to pick the old man's brain for every scrap of information he had about the two protagonists—I had to know more. What became of Captain Jimmy Douglas? Did he ever see Trixie again? What became of the mysterious chalice? Was it the Holy Grail or, perhaps, another otherworldly vessel?

With no shortage of time on our journey, François went on to tell the remainder of story; so much as was told to him.

After Trixie disappeared into the fog, Jimmy remained at the beach and was greeted by a sunrise of incredible beauty. As he returned to the path between the trees, he found that he no longer had need for his walking stick. The pain in his legs was gone. He kept the stick, all the same, as it was a gift from his beloved Trixie. After a good thirty minutes of hiking, Jimmy found a road and eventually hitched a ride to the nearest bus station where he was able to work his return to New York. While sliding his bus ticket into the pocket of his flight jacket, he was shocked to discover a large stash of hundred-dollar bills—a secret gift from Trixie to help him get by. With renewed confidence and a sense of purpose, he landed a good job working at a children's hospital in New York City. There were lean times, especially during the Great Depression, but he managed to scrape by and did what he could to help others get through the many challenges in their lives. The years passed but Jimmy never stopped looking. Every time he saw a white lily, he stopped and thought of Trixie. He followed signs and portents; most leading nowhere—but it didn't seem to matter. So long as he was thinking of Trixie, he was happy. Ever so thrifty, Captain Douglas was saving every nickel so that he might, someday, take a trip to France. Though the years passed, he never lost hope that he might be reunited with Miss Beauchamp. He wondered if she thought of him. When the Second World War wreaked death and destruction across much of the globe, Jimmy prayed and prayed hard. He prayed for an end to war and he prayed that Trixie would come through it, unharmed. And all the money he'd been saving—he gave it all away to charities supporting the countless orphans of the war.

The details of Jimmy's post-war life were sketchier. François claims to have spoken to a woman who lived in his apartment and who frequently dropped off Jimmy's mail. She told of a perfumed letter that arrived one day—it came in a white linen envelope with a lily embossed upon the exterior. There was no return address on the letter. Since she'd never seen Jimmy bringing women to his apartment and never knew him to date, it got her attention. Within days, he was gone. He paid a month's rent in advance and simply walked out the door. After that point, according to François, the trail went cold. No one in New York ever heard from Jimmy Douglas again. Not only that, but no one he interviewed had ever seen Jimmy show any symptoms of Post-

Traumatic Stress Disorder, or "Shell Shock," as they called it back in the day. Perhaps the magic waters of the chalice had cured that, as well? It was a lovely thought.

I was fascinated by the story and, like my new friend, François, hoped that, somehow, things worked out for Trixie and Jimmy. I like happy endings. I was happy to leave it there. François drifted off to sleep and I occasionally readjusted his blanket so that it wouldn't fall to the floor. Sweet man. My mind drifted to wonderful places. The story of Trixie and Jimmy filled my thoughts. When our train stopped at a small town, just outside of Lille, I was startled to see a white lily upon the station sign. My heart raced. My rational brain told me to keep my seat; my destination was still over an hour away. My heart got the better of me. I stood and pulled my bag off the rack above the seats and made my way down the aisle. As I watched the train pull away, I began to wonder what I had gotten myself into. I didn't speak French and I knew absolutely nothing about the town. Eventually, I found lodging in a Bed and Breakfast and asked the proprietor if they were familiar with any ruined abbeys in the vicinity. Apparently, there were several. The next morning, I rented a bicycle and began my excursion. I must have biked nearly a hundred and fifty miles between the six sites I investigated before I saw the light. Bursting forth from a rift in the clouded sky, a ray of hope-inspiring sunlight seemed to be illuminating a wooded area in the distance. My legs were tired but I pedaled furiously toward the spot. Pulling my bicycle off the road and leaning it against a tree, I worked my way inward through the woods. It was there, in an overgrown clearing, that I saw the ruins of what appeared to be a very old abbey. I was investigating several graves marked with stone slabs when I nearly jumped out of my skin, startled by a voice coming from behind me. It was François, wrapped in the blanket that I had been readjusting while he slept. "I thought I might find you here," he said. "May I join you?" I thought to ask him any number of the hundred questions that were dancing around in my head but my heart won over my rational brain, yet again, and I merely thanked him for his companionship. He followed me as I walked, inspecting each marker. I was trying to make out the worn name on one stone when François gently placed his hand on my shoulder. "Perhaps you might try looking over there," he said. He pointed to an area away from the foundation of the abbey that appeared as a brilliant white patch amidst the lush green grass. I walked toward the spot and was astonished to see a garden of white lilies. A single stone slab, made of white marble, stood apart from any of the other markers at the site. "James M. Douglas and Beatrice B. Douglas." The remainder was in French. I looked to François for assistance with the translation. "Bound forever in love and free to fly upon wings of joy, uplifted by unbreakable faith." Beautiful. As I walked around the grave, I stumbled, nearly tripping over another stone hidden within the vegetation. I cleared the area to discover a marble block with a lily depicted, in relief, upon the top. I looked back at François. He said nothing but a slight smile made an appearance upon his aged face. I carefully replaced the concealing cover and stepped back. François nodded in approval. We both stood there for a while, absorbing what I can only describe as "the magic" of the moment. Eventually, we returned to the road. François flagged down a passing van and, after some negotiating in French, convinced the driver to take me and my bicycle back to town. François remained. We waved farewell as my van pulled away from the site.

I don't know how much of François' story is true. I'll never know if the events described in Captain Douglas' diary occurred as he described. The truth is often elusive. I do know that I'm prepared to take it all on faith. I will likely never see François again but I owe him a debt of gratitude just as I owe my aunt, and James and Trixie Douglas. I owe them all for opening my heart to a beautiful world I have never known; one I shall never part from. What of the abbey? you ask. I never went back. I don't plan to. I don't need to. It'll be there, just where it's meant to be. And, as for what secrets lay hidden beneath the Lily Stone—well, that's for you to decide.

The Story Behind the Story

"Flapper and the Captain" is one of my favorite short stories! The upcoming Red Penguin Books anthology, "The Roaring '20s: A Decade of Stories," set authors a task of creating short stories based in the 1920's but later, the aperture was widened to permit pieces based in other past decades. I imagine that given the rapidly approaching deadline, there just weren't that many authors with a 1920s themed work in hand or the desire to rapidly construct such a piece. Added to this, for most, some degree of research was probably required before a believable story could

even begin to take shape. I must admit, I had to do my share of research and note taking to make sure that not only were the facts historically accurate but that I was also able to accurately recreate the language of the period in my dialog. This became a labor of love, and I knew the preparation work would help to make the story something special.

In fiction writing, they sometimes describe authors as being either a "plotter" (someone who carefully maps out their story, start to finish) or a "pantser" (a "by the seat of your pants" author who just starts writing and lets the story take on a life of its own as the characters lead the author on an unexpected journey). People who know my professional background usually assess that I'd be a natural "plotter" when it comes to creative writing. Actually, I'm quite the opposite. "Flapper and the Captain," especially, illustrates this. When I began, I had only two characters in mind and a notion of the environment within which they would interact—i.e., 1920s New York City. I knew I wanted them to embark on some form of adventure, but I really had no idea what that adventure was or how it would end. I just started writing. And I wrote, and I wrote, and I wrote…into the early hours of the morning. I literally could not step away from my computer. Even halfway into the story, I didn't know how it was going to end. I fell in love with the characters, and I wanted them to fall in love with each other. I had always fantasized about meeting a beautiful, exciting, and mysterious stranger and being whisked away on some grand adventure, and that theme clearly comes across in the story. I love Trixie's confidence and moxie, and I absolutely identified with Captain Douglas, a former military aviator who is struggling to overcome his physical and emotional challenges, regain his self-confidence, and be the person he knows still lives inside his broken body. Thankfully, I've never had to deal with PTSD, as a number of my fellow veterans have, but I felt it was important to highlight the condition and tell a story of hope and perseverance.

It wasn't until I was well into the story that my mind began to wander and supernatural plot twists began to work their way into my mind and then onto the page. I've always loved the interesting twists found within shows like "The Twilight Zone" and I saw absolutely no reason to restrain my short story to a world of mundane normalcy. I was going to let it all fly and follow the storyline wherever it wanted to lead me. My love for Arthurian legends and medieval tales of romance and chivalry seized hold of the unsuspecting plot line and really shook things up. I began weaving together the threads of this 20th Century adventure story with an original Holy Grail inspired tale of faith and chivalry.

As the story was evolving, I became increasingly aware that I might well come up against the word count limit that had been established by Red Penguin Books for submissions to this anthology. The limit placed upon this anthology was 10,000 words (later anthologies dropped the word limit down to 7,500 or 5,000 words to enable inclusion of works by a larger number of authors). I was initially inside the 10,000-word limit but, as I finished my story, I had this feeling that the story really wasn't finished. I had grown so fond of the two protagonists that I could not simply leave them at a tearful yet love-filled parting on the shoreline. So, sometime in the early hours of the morning, I created what can best be described as Part II of the story. The second part, a modern-day investigation by a narrator who, himself, was in need of a life change, would pick up upon the grail lore teased during the final segments of the main storyline. Carefully, and with great love, I sought to bring closure to a beautiful love story, in my own unique fashion. The additional segment pushed me significantly beyond the 10,000-word limit set for the anthology but, after several reviews, I knew it had to stand as is, regardless of whether or not it was accepted for publication. Thankfully, Red Penguin Books graciously accepted the story. When my publisher was compiling a "Best of the Red Penguin Collection" anthology, some time later, "Flapper and the Captain" was nominated for inclusion, and I was asked if I would be willing to have it published without its Part II. I didn't have to think very long on that question. No. The two parts were meant to "travel" together much as Trixie and Captain Douglas were destined to journey through life, hand in hand. Happily, Red Penguin Books decided that they'd accept the entire story, and it was included in "The Best of…" anthology.

I hope that you enjoyed reading "Captain and the Flapper as much as I enjoyed writing it!"

I Believe in a World of Possibilities

(Written February 28, 2021)
Published by Red Penguin Books in *"An Empty Stage: A Collection of Monologues"* (March, 2021)

*Monologue relating a perspective on life and the
human experience that allows for the remarkable and
enables hope through an undying belief that the
impossible may just be possible.*

The Loch Ness Monster, space aliens, and everything in between. I believe. It's as simple as that. And because I do, you discount my position on every other topic under the sun. I have become irrelevant . . . in your eyes. More's the pity, for I might have opened your mind to a world of wonders and limitless possibilities.

As a child, I was an avid reader of any book or article concerning my favorite sea monster, Nessie, the famed monster of Loch Ness. In my youth, on vacation in the United Kingdom, our tour director found me out and began loaning me copies of booklets on the monster, in preparation for our visit to the Highlands of Scotland. I eagerly read each booklet and pamphlet, returning the material the following morning. Our planned Loch Ness "drive-by" transitioned into an unscheduled stop and I believe, to this day, the agenda modification was a gift from our kind guide to a young boy. I went to the lake's edge and placed my hand in the cold water. It was a magical moment. I scanned the surface of the lake for any ripple that might betray the presence of a fast-traveling sea serpent. The world was ripe with possibilities. There was hope that tomorrow might be more exciting than today as the unexpected and unknown progressed from fiction to fact. Mankind has made countless discoveries over the ages. Why do you doubt the presence of a prehistoric creature in Loch Ness? Why do you doubt that Sasquatch wanders the vast woodlands of the Pacific Northwest? And you doubt the existence of extraterrestrials yet you've failed to establish the borders of the universe. In this infinite expanse of space, I see infinite possibilities. Do you see a cold and lifeless vacuum?

I know. I was to outgrow these "childish" notions, casting them aside as fairy tales and myths, on that very day that I stopped believing in Santa Claus. Are you sure that I did? What if I didn't? Am I now a candidate for referral to a mental health clinic? I assure you, there are many in greater need than I; let them profit from these resources, I have other matters that need attending and those matters rely upon a youthful optimism and hope that the world might be more than we imagine and that, in life, we may do more than simply live and die.

Offer me proof? you say. Why? Why do I need to prove anything? Perhaps you should prove that I'm wrong. I've been down this road before. You point to studies, and formulas, and those pesky laws of physics. You tell me how they've scanned the entire volume of Loch Ness with sonar sweeps, sampled the waters for unrecognizable DNA traces, sent countless robotic submersibles equipped with advanced camera systems to scan the depths; they've exhausted all modern research methods . . . and yet nothing. No sign of a monster. I am fascinated by all of this. My mind remains unchanged. You see, I know something that you don't. Mankind's entire volume of knowledge is based upon observation and experimentation. We've sampled, and measured; quantified and documented. We've established thresholds for certainty and we have promoted theories to facts. I applaud all these efforts. I have a scientific mind. I also have a philosophical mind. And I know that our tomes of irreputable facts are born of our fanatical desire to control our surroundings and predict the future. We shut out the truths we simply don't wish to hear. I do not.

Who's to say that the laws of gravity might not flip head over heels every billion years? Newton's apple might one day accelerate upward into the sky. The sun might radiate a beautiful purple light and man might walk upon the surface of water as he now treads upon the firm pavement beneath his feet. Do you believe a man can walk on water? Do you believe a man once did? I hope I have not offended, but I ask you, please, to consider all that you believe and all that you do not. What is real? What is possible? I am quite content that you should shape the world in the manner you choose; I won't deny you this. I will, however, respectfully, request that you allow me to shape my world as I see fit—to apply my own brush strokes upon the empty canvas that I have been given.

I've met people who have seen Sasquatch. They've told me so. I have no reason to doubt them nor do I feel any compulsion to prove them wrong. I've read stories about "monster" sightings on Loch Ness, and upon a number of other bodies of water. I understand that if you look hard enough; if your search is that desperate; your senses might betray you. I get it. But why should I crush hope? Why should I doubt the fantastic when the fantastic makes this world that much more exhilarating? In the boundless reaches of space, I have no doubt there are beings of equal and, most certainly, greater intellect than our own exalted human race. They might, occasionally, desire to take a vacation to our planet, and dip their appendages into the cool waters of Loch Ness, much as I did. Why not? Perhaps they did lend a hand during the construction of Stone Henge, the great pyramids of Egypt, and who knows what else. My world view will never depend upon believing that these things are true. My world view absolutely depends upon my conceding that they might be.

In 1938, an expedition purposely sent to uncover the facts behind a wild rumor discovered a monster of a fish that was supposed to have gone extinct some 66 million years ago. Somehow, the coelacanth eluded our discovery through all recorded history. Similarly, the okapi, a mammal of great stature that looks like a strange cross between a zebra and giraffe, is now familiar to most naturalists. Yet this large creature remained hidden for centuries and was deemed a preposterous myth until its discovery by British explorer, Sir Harry Hamilton Johnston, in 1901. Fiction becomes fact. Legends inspire our imagination and those brave enough to step beyond the borders of our current understanding are often hailed as heroes . . . or fools. I applaud the heroes and the fools; I cheer for those who seek and those who believe. Perhaps, one day, someone will sing my praises? I'll not hold my breath. When I lay down for my final rest, I can assure you that I shall do so with hope and an unbroken faith that Shakespeare's Hamlet was not far off the mark when he advised Horatio that there are more things in Heaven and Earth than are dreamt of in your philosophy. I believe in a world of possibilities.

The Story Behind the Story

"I Believe in a World of Possibilities" was written for an anthology entitled "An Empty Stage: A Collection of Monologues." I wasn't quite sure how to

approach this piece, initially. I knew the editor wasn't looking for an actual play (a later anthology would solicit short plays) but the theme for the book was to celebrate solo performances that "cover a wide range of short works for the theater." In the end, I determined the aperture was wide open. With that said, my vision was to create something that a solo artist, standing in the spotlight upon an otherwise darkened stage, might boldly proclaim to the audience or, perhaps, to a silent pupil standing just outside the spotlight. I elected to toss out a little bit of Dave Lange's personal philosophy—a way of thinking that has formed an integral part of my understanding of the world since my childhood days. This way of looking at life has always made my world a more vibrantly colorful place—a world full of nearly infinite possibilities—and hope.

Katie Chen and the Twisted Blade

(Written February 28, 2021)
Published by Red Penguin Books in "*Behind Closed Doors*" (April, 2021)

*A spunky teenage figure skater races against time to
uncover the perpetrator of a heinous act during a
national figure skating competition.*

Long before graduating summa cum laude from Harvard and becoming a renowned sports medicine doctor and published author; long before her work as an Ambassador of Hope with the United Nations; and even before winning gold at the Olympics in Lake Placid, New York; Katie Chen was a girl with a dream and a pair of second-hand skates. Her rise to skating prominence is well documented but few people know about the time this effervescently cheerful ingénue cracked the second biggest case in figure skating history. It was twenty years ago, now. I remember it like it was yesterday.

Standing a slight four-foot-ten, and barely more substantial than a canary's feather, Katie stood behind the boards and watched the nation's best throw down an impressive array of skating brilliance. It was the U.S. Figure Skating Championship and, after winning the Junior Championship, this was Katie's first time competing with the Senior Ladies. Grinning from ear to ear, with her winning smile, Katie considered herself more of a fan and spectator at the event than a competitor. Medals were the last thing on her mind. Perhaps the second to last thing? Solving a mystery wasn't even on the radar.

Katie's heart raced when her hero, Agnetha Andersson, took the ice. Agnetha, Anna to her friends, was looking to win her third national title and a trip to the Olympics in Oslo, Norway. It would be a stretch to say Agnetha was a favorite for Olympic gold but everyone knew she was the only person on the ice that day who stood a chance to seize the prize from the reigning Russian figure skating champion, Nikita Leonova, much less beat Nikita's primary rival, Irina Dobrowskaya, the previous year's World Champion. Both had skated flawlessly at the recent Russian Figure Skating Championship and both racked up technical scores never before seen in the history of the sport. Competing against the younger "jumping beans" that were taking over the skating world by storm, it was a pretty sure bet this would be Agnetha's last opportunity to be competitive at the Olympics. A once every-four-year's event, few skaters were able to maintain the competitive edge into their mid-twenties and Agnetha knew it. She left nothing on the table this season and no one on the U.S. team could touch her consistently flawless performances. While not including quite as many quadruple jumps as some of the younger girls, Agnetha perfectly executed every triple jump and the two "quads" that were included in her program. Beyond the technical expertise which earned her an impressive Technical Element Score; her artistic mastery put her Program Component Score out of reach of even the greatest skaters in the world. Katie marveled at Agnetha's technical proficiency but she was most captivated by the eye-watering artistry of her idol's routines. Her performances were masterpieces the likes of which Michelangelo, Beethoven, and Shakespeare would have been envious of.

Katie was scheduled to skate with the fourth group on the ice during the Short Program, the first of the two events that were part of the overall competition. She looked over toward the gate where Agnetha was completing some limbering exercises while the third group of Ladies were waiting for the Zamboni to finish its rounds, smoothing out the ice following the last group's performances. Brittney Star, skating with the first group, nailed her routine, even without her conspicuously absent trademark sparkling gloves. Katie wasn't worried; she knew Agnetha was going to blow her out of the water. Mariah McPherson, due to skate with the fourth and final group, was going to be Agnetha's primary concern. If Agnetha skated cleanly, Mariah would not be a problem. Katie could barely contain her excitement, nervously fidgeting and bouncing about as the skaters took to the ice for their four-minute warm-up. Agnetha looked spectacular in her elegant chartreuse skating dress. The six skaters zipped about the rink, getting a feel for the ice and taking care not to collide with their fellow competitors. Agnetha built up speed to practice one of her triple jumps but something went awry; she stumbled on the landing and fell. Like a true champ, she picked herself up and continued her warm-up. A second attempt also resulted in a failed landing. Katie was somewhat alarmed—she knew all too well from her Junior competitions that a good warm-up was an essential confidence builder while a choppy practice could taint your thoughts with damaging doubt. Beyond the physical power, timing, and balance required; skating was simultaneously a huge mental game. Those who failed to manage their own psyche were destined for failure, no matter how capable their bodies were. Katie reassured herself that Agnetha had cleared off the rust and would be ready once her music started.

The warm-up over; the skaters cleared the ice. Riya Chandra skated to the center of the rink as her name was announced over the public address system. Riya was a second generation American and, dressed in her lovely Indian-themed skating outfit, would be skating to a medley of modern Indian music inspired by Bollywood films. Riya was only a year older than Katie and the two had bonded over the course of the year and become good friends. Riya stood at center-ice, waiting for her music to start. The solemnity of the moment was shattered as Katie, almost out of reflex, shouted a passionate "Go Riya!" There were a few chuckles from the audience and Katie immediately felt a little embarrassed. Riya looked over toward her, smiled, and winked, setting Katie's mind at ease. Once the music started, Riya leapt right into character and put on quite a show. While her technical skill wasn't going to earn her a spot on the podium, Riya was a fan favorite and received a rousing ovation after the end of her performance. Katie was very happy that her friend skated cleanly. She could tell by Riya's smile that she was bursting with joy. Her marks, the best scores she had ever earned for a Short Program performance, put a cherry on the cake.

Bonnie Gould was next up and she skated well. Katie didn't know Bonnie but she enthusiastically supported all her fellow competitors. Finally, Agnetha took the ice. If her confidence was shaken, it didn't show. She gracefully glided to the center of the rink and assumed her starting position, looking more like a Grecian statue than the fierce competitor who had been decimating her competition since the age of three. Although she normally left her cell phone with her coach, Katie decided to bring it with her, just this once, so that she could take some video of her idol skating at the Nationals. Katie pulled the phone from the pocket of her fleece jacket, pushed the red "record" button, and began recording Agnetha's routine; an upbeat program set to a medley of Gershwin tunes. Still concerned with the unsteady warm-up jumps, Agnetha decided to skip her planned Quad Toe Loop in favor of a triple-double combination. Her landing on the triple was so shaky that she had to abandon the second jump in the combo. Katie sighed,

Flapper and the Captain

"C'mon Agnetha. You've got this." The footwork sequence looked good but the following jump pass was a disaster. Agnetha lost her footing, attempting to land the difficult Triple Axel, and slid into the boards with an inglorious thud. Even Agnetha's typically spectacular Biellmann Spin looked off center and sloppy. Katie was nearly in tears, watching her idol falter so terribly during the two minute and forty second Short Program. Agnetha must have been bitterly disappointed but she gracefully ended the routine and took her bows before an audience who, for all their great encouragement, were unable to will Agnetha to success. It was all Agnetha could do not to break down in tears as she awaited her scores in the "Kiss and Cry" area. Only the top three U.S. skaters would earn a spot on the Olympic team and that dream now seemed like it was swirling down the toilet. Graceful, as always, Agnetha stood to wave at the many fans who had come to see her skate. Meanwhile, Brittney Starr looked on with interest. She could taste blood in the water. A fierce competitor herself, Brittney knew that Agnetha's lackluster performance had opened the door for her shot at the podium and a possible trip to Oslo. Agnetha would need to skate flawlessly in the Free Skate event to even stand a shot at recovering from the disastrous Short Program.

Katie was troubled by what she saw but knew she needed to stay focused. When the fourth group was called to the ice for their warm-up, she took a deep breath and cleared her mind of any thoughts that did not involve her music and movement across the ice. Skating to the center of the rink, Mariah McPherson was the first to skate in the group. Skating to music by famed Polish composer Frédéric Chopin, Mariah left the audience in awe; the hushed silence interrupted by a rousing applause at the end of her routine. Her only flaw was a slight under-rotation on a jump that only the judges and coaches noticed. In the Kiss and Cry area, Mariah's face lit up as her scores were posted—she easily moved into first place with a convincing margin, knocking Brittney down to second, but still within striking distance; the majority of points still hanging in the balance with the Free Skate the following day.

As her name was called, Katie skated out to the center of the rink and awaited her music. This was her big moment—the Nationals! With nothing to lose, Katie fearlessly launched into her routine set to several cheerful songs from *The Sound of Music*. If there were any butterflies at all, they swiftly flew away when Katie landed her first of two planned quadruple jumps. Each successfully completed element added to her growing confidence and joy. Her effervescent smile was reaching fans in the back of the mezzanine and the judges were noticing. A river of positive comments was flowing from the broadcast booth across the airwaves and helping to endear the young Asian-American skater to countless skating fans watching from home. Katie was oblivious to it all. "Silver-white winters that melt into springs, these are a few of my favorite things…" She was immersed in her music and in the moment. Ending with a final layback spin, Katie was absolutely dumbfounded when the arena erupted with a standing ovation. Her only thought: "That was fun." Several stuffed animals were tossed onto the ice by fans, at the end of her routine. A team of young girls in skating outfits leapt into action to gather the gifts but Katie glided over to retrieve one of the bears that landed in the corner of the rink. The network skating analysts in the media booth were commenting about little girls and their teddy bears while Katie was bending down to look at the scratches on the ice from where Agnetha had taken her bad spill. Something wasn't looking right. She made a mental note, and then lifted the bear in the air to thank the fans. In the Kiss and Cry area, Katie's coach, Jason Bryne, met her with a big congratulatory hug that virtually swallowed her up. Judges' calculations complete, Katie was speechless to see that she had moved into second place, just below Mariah. At the end of the Short Program, the top three competitors were Mariah, Katie, and Brittney. Agnetha had fallen to seventh place and a nearly insurmountable point deficit. After retrieving her cell phone from her coach, Katie made her way back to the locker room, watching several replays of Agnetha's performance on the device. Agnetha seemed to skid into the jumps which hurt the launch and rotation but, worse yet, something seemed terribly off in the landing—the blade was kicking up ice like a snow cone machine even though Agnetha's boot seemed aligned with her momentum as her foot returned to the ice. Katie shared the video with her West Coast friend and mentor, former Olympic gold medalist Kristi Yamaguchi, and asked for her opinion. In the locker room, Katie began unlacing her boots, glancing occasionally over at Agnetha who stoically braced herself for the dreaded post-performance interviews. This was not going to be enjoyable. Katie had just changed into her street clothes when her phone buzzed with a text message from Kristi. It said simply, "Check the boots." The second opinion from an

Olympic and World champion gave Katie the confidence she needed to approach her idol.

"Hi Agnetha! I've been a huge fan for a long time and I was wondering if you might, um, autograph my skate." Agnetha seemed to snap out of the fog she was lost in, her face lighting up with a lovely smile.

"You skated beautifully out there, Katie. I loved your routine. And, please, call me Anna. Do you have a marker on you?"

"You bet, I do," said Katie, smiling, as she passed a black Sharpie marker and her right skate boot to Agnetha."

"Jackson Premiere Fusion Boot. Jackson Ultima Apex Freestyle Blade. Nice choices, Katie. They're definitely working for you." Agnetha appreciated good equipment. Katie saw her opportunity.

"Hey, Anna, what are you skating on these days?" Katie knew exactly what skates Agnetha was using. She knew everything from what hairband Agnetha wore during practices down to the brand of boot-laces she preferred. After signing Katie's skate and returning it to her, Agnetha pulled her own skates out of her skate bag and passed them over to Katie.

"Maybe I should have you sign my skates? I may be looking at the next Olympic and World Champion and I'd love to tell the interviewers that I knew you 'back when.'"

Katie carefully took Agnetha's skates in her arms, hugging them like a puppy.

"They're awesome! And I absolutely love those fuzzy pink soak-ers! Would you mind if I..." Katie motioned to indicate she wanted to remove the soakers (cloth coverings for the skate blades designed to wick away the moisture and prevent rusting). Agnetha smiled and nodded her approval. Katie slid off the soakers on both skates, turned the boots upside down, and carefully inspected the blades. She then looked down the length of each blade, as if sighting-in a rifle.

"What in the world are you doing, Katie?" Agnetha laughed, barely able to contain her amusement.

"Anna, something's not right with your blades. Look here at the left skate; the blade is misaligned. Somehow, it's been twisted off at an angle."

"What?" responded a bewildered Agnetha, the smile fading from her face.

"Here, take a look at how the left blade looks compared to the right." Katie handed both skates back to Agnetha.

"Oh my God, you're right, Katie. How in the world could that happen? The last time I had my skates sharpened was two days ago, just before I left Connecticut. They were fine yesterday, during my practice session. At least I think they were fine. They sure felt good."

"Anna, may I take another look at that left skate?"

"Sure thing. Here you go." Katie carefully inspected the bottom of the skate boot, taking a few photos with her cell phone camera.

"It looks to me like the screws were removed, the blade rotated, and then re-secured to the boot. Have these skates recently been out of your sight?"

"No. I mean I keep my skates in my hotel room until the competition day and then I carry them to the arena and leave them in my locker until I'm ready to skate."

"Hmmm. Well, you might want to go with your backup skates tomorrow. It's probably better if we keep this quiet for a little bit. If someone is messing with you, they might try something even worse if they realize we've uncovered the twisted blade scheme."

Katie and Agnetha gave each other a hug before parting ways. Katie had a lot on her mind. Agnetha did, too. Both girls knew this wasn't going to help Agnetha's focus tomorrow—the damage had already been done. Katie was very surprised to hear that the NBC Skating Correspondent was interested in interviewing her after Agnetha. It would be her first televised interview. She passed by Brittney Starr on her way out of the locker area and Brittney made a snide comment about beginner's luck. The poke bounced right off Katie's youthful shoulders and drifted off into space. While it might be inappropriate to characterize Brittney Starr as being mean, she definitely waged an unrelenting psychological campaign against her rivals during competitions. She considered it part of the game. Katie poked right back, "Maybe you should skate more often without your sparkly gloves; that's definitely working for you."

"Rookie!" Brittney yelled back, as Katie continued on her way, a mischievous smile on her face.

During the interviews, Agnetha was a rock—poised; a class act, as always. Katie stumbled upon her words in an excited display of youthful exuberance which only endeared her more to the television audience. When she returned back to the locker area, to grab her remaining things; the room was already swarming with U.S. Figure Skating Association officials and a few security personnel. So much for "keeping it quiet." In truth, Agnetha had every intent of following Katie's advice but she thought it was important to let her coach know about the twisted blade. Her coach, Greta Baronclau, a former German national figure skating champion, was not about to let the incident sit. She insisted that an investigation be conducted immediately before the culprit had a chance to do further harm. There was pandemonium in the room as guards sifted through trash cans, opened lockers with a master key, and scoured every inch of the area. It was not long before one of the security officers shouted out "Hey, I think I've found something!" She asked for assistance from two guards who helped her pull a row of lockers away from the wall. Though ushered out of the room, several of the competitors, including Katie, peered through the open door, astonished at what they saw. Officer O'Grady slid between the wall and the relocated lockers and carefully removed two gloves and a screwdriver. The skaters gasped. The gloves had no significance to the security personnel but Katie and her peers instantly recognized them as Brittney's famous "sparkly gloves." Only Katie made the connection to the incident seeing as how the other girls were, as of yet, unaware of the skate blade tampering.

"Holy cow!" exclaimed Katie.

"What do you mean, Kat," asked Jolene Kennedy. "What's going on?"

"I'm not sure," responded Katie, working through a dozen permutations in her head.

It wasn't long before word got out. First, the coaches and officials were informed, and then the skaters. Before long, the story was leaked to the local news and the scandal took on a life of its own, coursing through media channels like an unabated wildfire during the dry season. Detractors reveled in the damage to a sport they thought unworthy and prissy while diehard fans felt like the air was knocked out of them. Was this going to be the next Tonya Harding/Nancy Kerrigan incident? Most of the skaters had little sympathy for Brittney; they'd seen her clever psychological games in action and they were convinced she would stoop to any level to gain an edge against her competitors. Katie was more than familiar with Brittney's antics and the lengths she might go to in order to secure a competitive advantage. She was clever, alright. And that's what bothered Katie. Why would someone as brilliantly diabolical as Brittney Starr use her own skating gloves to prevent leaving finger prints on a screw driver, locker door, or skate blades, much less carelessly toss the offending evidence behind some lockers at the scene of the crime? Something didn't smell right and it wasn't just the chili cooking at the concession stand down the hall.

The Figure Skating Association scheduled an emergency meeting for the following morning. They would convene to discuss the fate of Miss Starr. With the Free Skate scheduled for tomorrow night, the possibility of a disqualification before the competition loomed heavily on Brittney's mind. As bureaucracy is a slow-moving leviathan, a more realistic outcome would be a post-competition removal from the team or, worse yet, a life-long ban from competing in sanctioned events.

As the skaters awaited the DV shuttle buses that would take them back to their hotel, Katie saw Agnetha standing apart from the group with her coach. She ran over to say hello and was warmly received by Agnetha who formally introduced her to Greta.

"Ms. Baronclau, it's an honor to meet you, Ma'am," greeted Katie. Katie's bubbly enthusiasm stood in stark contrast to Greta Baronclau's Old World solemnity. Greta's greeting was flat but not unkind. As they stood there in the bright light of the foyer, Katie noticed several small particles of pink fuzz upon Greta's black slacks. "I hope I'm not putting you out but you would totally make my day if I could take a photo of you and Agnetha." Greta and Agnetha both agreed and Katie took a few shots on her cell phone.

"Hey, Katie, how about you and me pose for a photo?" Agnetha asked.

"Bless you, Anna! I'd love that," replied Katie. Katie handed her phone over to Greta who took several pictures, hoping that at least one of them might turn out well. She returned the phone when the job was done. "I can't thank you enough; these are great," said Katie, admiring the photos on her phone; only one of which was an awkward, eyes-closed throwaway. Through the large glass windows of the Arena, the girls saw the two DV buses pull in. Thinking quickly, Katie added, "Hey, how about I AirDrop this pic over to your phone so you can have a copy of it, too?" Agnetha sighed.

"Sorry, Kiddo, but I never bring my phone to the Arena. It's kind of a superstition of mine, you know."

"Oh really?" Katie had read all about Agnetha's routines and rituals in last October's *International Figure Skating* magazine and she was counting on her not having a phone. "Well, how about I push these to you, Ms. Baronclau?"

"Well, I don't know, Miss Chen. I don't even know what an AirDrop is. How about we just wait until…"

Katie broke in, "Oh, it's easy cheesy. I'll just zip them over and then show you how to pull them up." Before Greta could even finish her opening arguments, Katie had fast-fingered her photos across the air gap between the two devices and then instructed the confused former skating champion on how to accept the images and pull them up on her phone's photo gallery.

"My, oh my. You kids are something else."

"Well, you know, we live for this kind of stuff. Now you can email them over to Agnetha later." Greta's jaw dropped open and Agnetha had to quickly come to the rescue.

"I'll show you how to do that later, Coach."

The skaters all boarded the buses with their coaches, along with any family members who were accompanying them, and the buses made their way back to the hotel. The lobby of the hotel was all abuzz with speculation about the twisted blade incident. Sentences were being doled out by dozens of teenage judges before the case had even been to trial.

Back in her room, which she was sharing with her mother, Katie prepared to change for dinner. The two would join Katie's coach for dinner at a highly recommended restaurant. A few of the other girls were planning on heading there, too. Mrs. Chen was always nervous when her daughter skated and made it a point to stay in her room during competitions. Katie was disappointed that her mother wasn't there to see her amazing Short Program, but she knew only too well what an emotional wreck her mom could be at the rink. Mrs. Chen was always supportive of Katie's skating and certainly played a large part in her meteoric rise from Snow Plow Sam basic skills classes to regional competitions and, eventually, Junior National champion. To have her little sweetheart competing at the Senior level was a source of tremendous pride. As Katie peeled off her skating tights, she noticed several pieces of pink fuzz stuck to the snow-white legwear. Her Mom asked her what she was up to when she saw Katie taking a few photos of her leg. Katie just shrugged off the question and changed the topic. At this point, her wild hunches weren't worth mentioning. She was an avid reader and her mother knew, only too well, that Katie's mind could rapidly drift off into the colorful worlds of the books she was reading. Keeping her daughter focused on Axels, Salchows, Lutzes, Toe Loops, and Flips was no easy task.

"Hey Mom, I'm going to go down to the lobby to get a pack of gum. Can I get you anything?" asked Katie. Mrs. Chen joked about a bottle of wine and some aspirin but, ultimately, just reminded Katie not to get lost; their reservation for dinner was only an hour away. Katie smiled and left her mother with a wave.

At the small convenience store in the lobby, Katie saw Agnetha standing at the counter. Grabbing a pack of chewing gum, Katie approached her idol, much more at ease than during their first meeting. "Hi Anna! Are you here for gum, too?" Katie was half joking but when Agnetha held up a pack of chewing gum, the two burst into hysterical laughter. The shop owner looked on in confused silence, oblivious to the inside jokes of teenage girls. As the two girls walked out of the store, Katie asked, with her usual disarming charm, if Agnetha ever let anyone else handle her skates. "You know; parents, siblings, coach, friends, little brother . . . anyone?" Agnetha considered the question for just a moment.

"No. Never, actually. Just the skate sharpener. Well, until you." Agnetha smiled and winked at Katie. Katie bowed, politely, and thanked Agnetha, again. After a friendly hug, the two parted ways. Rather than returning to the room, Katie settled in a large leather chair near the fireplace in the lobby. Her brain was swirling with random thoughts which, like bubbles merging in a bathtub, were beginning to congeal into something more substantial. Katie was just about to leap into some super sleuthing when she noticed a line of little girls and boys forming up beside her. She graciously signed several dozen autographs on event programs, photographs, notebooks, and even one leg cast. Katie fought hard to withhold her go-to humorous wisecrack: "Well, that "Triple-Triple" didn't work out as well as planned." She didn't have to say a thing. The poor little blonde girl shrugged and conceded that it was a Double Axel that went horribly wrong. The two girls smiled. Katie thought, "there but for fortune, might go I." Katie wasn't used to this kind of attention but her recent performance at a Senior competition obviously earned her some new fans. Before another line could form, Katie snuck away to an empty conference room on the second floor of the hotel.

Pulling up the photos on her phone, she copied and pasted several of her recent shots into an email to her friend, Lucy, who was majoring in Graphic Design at Yale. After this, she bounced through several phone numbers until she reached the Facility Management Office at the arena.

"Hi, I'm part of the investigation team looking into the recent skate tampering incident and I have a few questions I'd like to ask you." Katie wasn't sure how her fake Minnesota accent combined with an even faker deep voice would play out over the phone. The Director of Facilities wasn't buying it.

"Who is this? she asked in the irritated voice of a woman who had spent the past two hours watching investigators tear her arena apart looking for additional evidence. Katie panicked. She tossed out the first name that came into her head.

"Charlie Chan. Inspector Charlie Chan." Oooh, that wasn't going to play out well.

"Who?!"

"I mean Charlene Chan," replied Katie, desperately trying to salvage the disaster in the making. "My friends call me Charlie," she added, nervously; anticipating a hang-up at any moment.

"Okay, Charlie. But I swear if you ask me the same questions I've been answering all day, I'm going to blow my top." Katie quickly composed herself and asked if skaters had access to the master key for the lockers if, for example, they lost their own key. Mrs. Grumwald (or 'Mrs. Grumpy,' as Katie now identified her) explained how skaters would not be granted access to the master key. She did, however, add that coaches might request the back-up key for their skaters' lockers if they presented a valid ID.

"Well, Ma'am, it sounds light you have an air-tight system there. I applaud you for your remarkable security protocols." Katie could sense she was starting to slide down the slippery slope of credibility. "Would you be able to tell me if any coaches requested keys in the past two days?"

"Look, Charlie, I don't know. I'd have to ask one of the Athlete Services girls."

"Would you mind checking in on that for me, 'Mrs. Grumpy.'" Katie immediately recognized her faux pas. This boat was sinking fast. Hoping that, perhaps, Mrs. Grumwald hadn't heard her clearly, Katie quickly tried to make amends. "Could you do that for me, Mrs.

Grumwald?" There was an uncomfortable silence on the other line. Her frustration mounting, the Director of Facilities conceded and told Katie that she'd have one of the girls from Services call her in the morning. Mrs. Grumwald hung up before Charlie Chan could ever pass her thanks.

Katie was starting to feel the exhilaration of living the secret agent life but she was about to step it up to the next level and go full-throttle James Bond. Her final call, before dinner, was to her good friend, Henry. She'd had a crush on Henry since they first took skating lessons together, at age five. They'd maintained a close friendship ever since. Besides his gentle disposition and caring heart, Henry had an additional talent which had got him into hot water on more than one occasion. He was a master hacker. Computer networks, cloud-based data, cell phones, game consoles and even, one time, a high-end refrigerator. If ones and zeros passed through the wires, Henry could infiltrate and manipulate the data. These skills terrified his teachers, concerned his parents, and endeared him to his friends. Katie reflected briefly on the cute contact photo she used for Henry on her phone (the two friends hugging after a skating lesson) before pressing the call button to dial. Henry picked up right away; he always did when Katie was calling. While he'd never admit it, Henry was kind of sweet on Katie, too.

"Hey Henry! How are you doing tonight?"

"Hi Katie! Congratulations on your great skate!"

"Thanks, Henry. I couldn't believe it went so well. It was like the best night of my life."

"Well, I sure hope there are more like it. I know you're going to wow them tomorrow, too."

"Now don't be jinxing me, Henry. You know how these things work, right?"

"Sorry, Katie; I meant to say you're going to totally choke tomorrow and redefine the word 'suck'."

"That's better."

"What can I do for you besides screwing with your karma?" Katie paused, thinking about how she wanted to approach a very delicate subject with the one friend she absolutely never wanted to lose.

"Well. Um. You know that one app you told me never to launch unless it was a social emergency?"

"You mean the Peekaboo app?" answered Henry, wondering where this discussion was going.

"Yah, that's the one."

"Of course. I wrote the silly thing so that we could hack into the text messages of anyone at school who was bullying you or your friends and find out what they were chatting about. Also, we could watch anything happening on their digital devices."

"Right. Well, I kind of had one of those emergencies."

"What?! What kind of emergency? Did you seriously deploy Peekaboo on someone's phone?"

"Kind of."

"As in 'yes'?"

"Yup. As in absolutely, positively yes. I hope this isn't going to get you into any kind of trouble." Katie nervously awaited the response, concerned that her friendship hung in the balance. The phone remained silent for longer than Katie was comfortable with.

"Cool! Whose device did you deploy Peekaboo to?"

"My skating idol's coach's cell phone."

"Wow! I want to know all the gory details. This is great!" Henry's enthusiasm was at once reassuring and somewhat terrifying. Katie went on to tell the story of the twisted blade and how she was starting to get an uneasy feeling about Greta Baronclau even though she had no real evidence to point her investigation in that direction. Henry was less interested in Gretas and Agnethas and Brittneys than he was in the details of how Katie deployed the app. Katie went on to explain that when she AirDropped photos onto Greta's phone, she simultaneously infected her phone with the Peekaboo virus which opened the device up for complete monitoring. From his laptop, Henry would now be able to watch everything happening on Greta's phone and, if he so desired, even be able to hack into any online banking or shopping applications that Greta was using. In short, Ms. Baronclau's life was soon to become an open book for two fifteen-year-old kids. Katie was very uneasy about the whole matter. Henry was quite aware of all the laws being broken and he paid them no mind. He had friends who had done much worse and seldom got more than a slap on the hand, once all the intimidating adult speeches were done.

With only minutes before she needed to leave to meet up with her mom, Katie thanked Henry and promised they'd share a milkshake when she returned home. Henry said he'd do some snooping and let her know.

At dinner, Katie and her mother enjoyed a pleasant outing with

Katie's coach, Jason Bryne. Jason had been working with Katie for the past several years and knew that any discussion about an upcoming competition was strictly off limits on the night before the event. Katie ate lightly and tried to keep her mind off skating. Milkshakes and burgers could wait for her return to California. Though never discussed, all three, along with the rest of the skating world, knew that Katie was now in solid contention for not only a medal, but perhaps gold. Her program was technically more challenging than any of her competitors with four planned quadruple jumps and a triple axel in the lineup. If she skated cleanly, she would be able to surpass anything that either Mariah or Brittney could bring to the ice. For all that, Katie's mind was elsewhere. She was eagerly anticipating return calls from her trusted friends. The first response came in the form of a text message from Lucy. Katie had been chastised more than once, by her parents, for texting at the dinner table so she excused herself to go to the restroom before responding to the vibrating phone in her jacket. The message said, simply, "Exact match." Katie made a quick call back to Lucy to get more details and Lucy told how she ran the photos through her most advanced photo graphics analysis program and the color of the pink fuzz on both photos was an exact match. After thanking Lucy, Katie returned to her table. While the pink fuzz was far from incriminating, it helped alleviate some of the guilt Katie was feeling about infecting a renowned figure skating coach's phone with a virus. Katie was fairly certain the fuzz on her tights could be attributed to material shed from Agnetha's soakers as Katie removed the covers to inspect Anna's skate blades. If Greta Baronclau never had access to Anna's skates, then where else might she have accumulated the fuzz? There were lots of possibilities. At this point, Katie wasn't trying to prove the improbable; she was merely attempting to eliminate the impossible.

Back at their room, Katie readied her apparel for the next day while her mother attempted to find topics for conversation to help keep her daughter's mind occupied. Little did she know, her efforts were unnecessary. Just before flopping on the bed to read, Katie's phone vibrated again—this time it was Henry and he wanted to talk. Katie texted back, asking if he could wait about fifteen minutes so that they might talk while her mom was taking a shower. At fifteen minutes, to the second, Katie's phone vibrated and she answered Henry's call.

"Did you have a nice dinner, Kat?"

"I did. Thanks. Did you find anything in Greta's email or messages?"

"Um," Henry paused, "I did a little more than just look at her conversations."

"Oh my God," Katie responded, now whispering, "what did you do?"

"Well, I kind of hacked into her bank accounts, too."

"Henry!!!"

"Please don't get angry; just hear me out on this. Something big is going down."

"How big?" Katie's curiosity was peaking.

"Okay. So, I noticed a number of text messages between Greta and a guy called Geraldo Espinosa. So, I used a back door to hack into this guy's profile."

"A what?" Henry's tech-talk always lost Katie after the first few seconds.

"Shhh. Just listen. So, I was ninety-nine percent sure the 'Espinosa' name was a cover and, sure enough, all message traffic from Geraldo Espinosa can be traced back to the account of one Sergei Antonov."

"Russian?"

"Yup. He's Russian. As if that wasn't sketchy enough, he also used his fake identity to transfer four deposits, each for $990,000, into several different bank accounts, all belonging to one Greta Baronclau."

"Wow!" Katie's heart was racing.

"Yes, wow!"

"Okay. Well, do you have anything more on this Antonov guy?"

"Who do you think I am, Jason Bourne? These things take time, Katie. I'm trying to break into some of Antonov's accounts but they're locked down pretty hard. This might take some time. I'm sorry I don't have more for you."

"Oh, please don't apologize, Henry. You're amazing!" Katie couldn't see it but Henry was blushing and grinning from ear to ear. The two exchanged farewells and Henry wished Katie a good night's sleep just as her mom was finishing up in the bathroom. Katie cleaned up, got dressed for bed, and read a lovely story about a girl and her pony before drifting off to sleep. Although she might have wished her dreams to be filled with ponies and princesses, her unconscious mind carried her through a cloak-and-dagger world of international intrigue and espionage.

Katie's restless sleep carried over to a late start for her morning's activities. With the big event scheduled for that evening, the lost time was of no consequence. The top skaters would skate in the last group so Katie had plenty of time to spare before her afternoon ride to the rink on the DV shuttle. Her mother was quiet in the room. While usually forceful when it came to keeping on a schedule, she appreciated the uniqueness of the situation and thought it best to let her daughter make the decisions regarding her pre-event routine. Mrs. Chen smiled, lovingly, as Katie's eyes slowly opened and she stretched beneath her covers. After wishing her good morning, she told Katie that she was going to head down to the dining room to get a cup of coffee and a yogurt.

Katie looked at her phone, which she always silenced before bed, and saw a message from Henry asking that she call him as soon as possible. She knew Henry wouldn't request a pre-event chat unless there was something big going on—he was always careful not to disrupt her focus during competitions.

Still feeling somewhat groggy, Katie auto-dialed Henry. "Hey there, loser," she taunted.

"Good morning, ugly. Did you sleep well?" Henry responded. They both chuckled.

"I've had better"

"Sorry. I had zero."

"What? Why?" Katie responded, concerned for her friend.

"You know teen boys—a six-pack of Mountain Dew, a bag of Doritos, and we're gaming through till dawn."

"Nice."

"Seriously though, Kat, I was up all night. You know Russians were starting to wake up before you even went to bed. I confirmed the money transfers and I have some copies of statements. But I don't think I want to send them electronically—too risky. Sergei Antonov appears to be some kind of middle man. There were some communications with several members of the Russian government, which I am still working to translate, and also with some dude named Blushkin."

"Blushkin? Did you get a first name?"

"Um. Hold on a sec." Henry shuffled through some scribbled notes, his bloodshot eyes straining to make out his hasty early morning scrawls. "Ah. Um. Okay, here it is. Eugeni Blushkin. Name mean anything to you?" Katie was stunned silent.

"Yah. He's Nikita Leonova's coach."

"Leo-whata?" responded a brain-dead Henry, fighting to remain conscious after some thirty hours without sleep.

"Nikita Leonova. The number two ranked figure skater in the world after Irina Dobrowskaya. Irina's coach died last summer . . . drowned while on vacation at a resort on the Black Sea. Her skating has been a little shaky lately and Nikita is looking very strong this season. Nikita actually beat out Irina at this year's Russian Nationals. She's poised to take the Olympic and World title." Henry, as much as he loved Katie, was no more interested in hearing an early morning editorial about skating contenders than Katie was interested in hearing about phishing, trojan horses, spoofing, and the like. "So, what's next Henry?"

"What?"

"I said, what's next, Henry."

"Oh. Sorry, I was just thinking." Henry wasn't really thinking, he had made the mistake of closing his eyes and was following the last sheep as it jumped over the fence. "I've got a few more loose ends to tie up and then I can fax you the info."

"Fax? Why?"

"Like I said, I think it would be really bad, maybe even dangerous, to send this stuff electronically to your phone. If the Russian government is involved in this, you don't want that kind of electronic trail leading to you or your family. I can fax it to the hotel business center when I get it put together and you can pick it up there." Katie always trusted Henry when it came to this sort of thing. She knew, implicitly, that he would do everything in his power to protect her.

"Okay, Henry. Just send me a text when it's done. I'm worried about the girls here and the U.S. Figure Skating Association's punitive actions against a skater who might be totally innocent."

"Well, I wouldn't exactly call Brittney Starr innocent," Henry interjected.

"You know what I mean, Henry. She can be a little bitchy, at times, but she's still one of us. She deserves her shot just like the rest of us."

"Whatever you say, Kat. I'll text you once I transmit the documents."

Katie took a morning shower and, seeing that her mother hadn't returned yet, became a bit concerned. Throwing on her favorite jeans, t-shirt, and fleece pullover, she went down to the hotel's dining room where the complimentary breakfast hours were nearly over. Breathing a sigh of relief when she saw her mother sitting at a table and talking to her coach, Katie joined in.

"Good morning, sleepy head," her coach said with a smile. Katie shot a nasty look over at her mom who had obviously been providing Jason with a play-by-play of Katie's evening and morning activities.

"Hi, Coach!"

"Katie, Coach Bryne tells me that the USFSA deliberations began at 9am this morning and, while still in session, it's looking like there'll be sanctions placed against Brittney Starr as early as this afternoon. What a horrible thing for a skater to do to another girl! I hope they throw the book at her." Katie's face went pale and she turned to look at her coach.

"Coach, you have some connections at the Association, don't you?"

"That depends what you mean by connections, Katie. Sure, I have a few friends on the board and within the Association. Why?"

"I can't explain why, but you need to get them to hold off on their judgment; just for another day or so."

"What?! Why?" Jason was completely stunned by Katie's unusual request.

"Please just trust me on this. I'm pretty sure some more relevant facts may come to light before the day's done and it wouldn't be fair to Brittney to block her from competing tonight."

"What facts? What are you talking about?" Her coach persisted and wasn't going to let this go. His student was asking him to pull some significant strings at the U.S. Figure Skating Association and the risk of burning some critical bridges, not to mention putting in jeopardy some close friendships, was something he was reluctant to do based off a shaky hunch by a fifteen-year-old girl. Katie saw she was fighting a losing battle and resorted to her fallback act of desperation—Mr. Mittens. The former Mr. Mittens was Katie's cat who, tragically, was hit and killed by a car a year and a half ago. If there was one thing that could unleash the floodwater of tears for this cheerfully positive young-ster, it was reflecting on the loss of poor little Mr. Mittens. It was a dirty trick. It worked like a charm. Terrified that the fragile psyche of his pupil might be impacted prior to the most important competition of her life, Jason quickly acquiesced. "I'm sorry Katie. Absolutely. Yes. I'll see what I can do. You just focus on your Long Program and let me handle the USFSA stuff."

"Oh, thank you, Coach," Katie whimpered, wiping tears from her eyes. In truth, Katie was as tough as nails. Experience had taught her that a few well-timed tears could go a long way. In a world that sought to manipulate her, Katie, unapologetically, was not beyond the occasional volley back over the net.

On her mother's encouragement, Katie gathered up a small plate of fruit before the breakfast items were cleared away by the dining room staff, anxious to configure the room for lunch. Before heading off to the arena, later in the afternoon, Katie would fuel up with her traditional peanut butter and jelly sandwich, yogurt, a banana, and some melon slices. It had become her "good luck" meal since winning Junior Nationals and she was intent on sticking with the formula.

Back in the room, Katie watched various random day-time TV shows, anxiously awaiting the start of her well-scripted pre-competition routine and, perhaps more importantly, a text message from Henry. Before hearing from Henry, Katie received a call from Molly at Athlete Services. True to her word, Mrs. Grumwald had directed Athlete Services to give "Charlie Chan" a call. Molly told Katie that Greta Baronclau had, in fact, stopped by and told her that her skater had lost the key for her locker. Molly personally signed over the back-up key to Greta which was later returned. As these sorts of things happened all the time, Molly hadn't given the matter any thought. Katie thanked Molly for the information. Katie was sure Anna would have mentioned losing her key. Evidence seemed to be mounting.

The minute hand swept ever-forward, pulling the hour hand, reluctantly, along for the journey. Katie's phone remained lifeless and time was running out. Katie ate and then started to dress in her skating attire which she would conceal beneath a track suit until it was time to take the ice. She hoped that Henry hadn't fallen asleep on the job. Only thirty hours? She knew Henry to go at least forty-eight. What was keeping him?

Finally, only minutes before it was time for her to leave, she received a text from Henry. It wasn't the message she was hoping for. Henry had gathered the necessary documentation to link Agnetha's coach to a possible international plot but his father's ancient fax machine (which might as well have been a telegraph transmitter, in Henry's estimation) was on the fritz. Henry would have to travel into town to send the material. Katie sighed deeply, sensing an opportunity lost. She hoped that Henry would remember that she always turned her phone off after arriving at a competition venue. Henry did remember. He also knew this meant there was only one possible recourse; an alternative more dreadful than nearly any other scenario he could envision—Fan Girl!

Emily Song, "affectionately" known to friend and foe, alike, as "Fan Girl," never did anything half-way. Her teenage room was literally wallpapered with posters of the numerous celebrities she idolized. The ceiling was covered, as well. Fan Girl had written each of her celebrity crushes dozens of times and doted over her collection of autographs each night before she went to sleep. Athletes, musicians, actors, writers, social media influencers; it didn't matter. If they were big, Emily wanted to establish and sustain a personal connection. Fan Girl had already informed half the high school that she was going to Minneapolis with her mother to see the National Figure Skating Championship. Emily was so sure that her classmate would be crowned the next National Ladies champion that she cleared away a 24" by 36" space on her wall for a Katie Chen poster. If her usual poster supplier didn't have one available within a couple weeks, Emily was planning on designing one herself. Her peers unofficially voted her as "most likely to turn stalker" within their class. Henry was less concerned about her fanaticism regarding celebrities than he was with Emily's increasingly aggressive flirting. Henry walked the tightrope that many nice kids do, balancing between being a positive and supportive classmate while also trying to establish some semblance of social barrier to prevent himself from being consumed by the ravenous affection of Fan Girl. He lifted his cell phone, half a dozen times, only to return the device to its charging station upon his desk.

While the Fan Girl drama was playing out in emotional space between Northern California and Minneapolis, Minnesota, Katie and her mother were making their way down to the lobby to await the next DV shuttle to the arena. Mrs. Chen was going to stay back at the hotel, as was her way, but she always saw Katie off. Henry knew his time was short. He had run out of options. Half hoping that Fan Girl might not pick up, he dialed Emily's phone number. The called was answered in one ring.

"Henry!"

"Um. Hi Emily."

"I'm so glad to hear from you! Are you here in Minneapolis, too?"

"Um. No. I'm still back here in Cali. I was wondering if you might be able to."

"Oh, that's too bad. The skating is going to start soon and I'm so excited. I just know Katie's going to make Lakeview High School proud." Henry was truly hoping he could get a few words in edgewise before Fan Girl went off on another one of her frequent tangents.

"Look, Emily, I need your help."

"Anything for you, Henry. You know that, right? You know how much I care about you and that..."

"Right. Right. I know. Thank you, Emily. I need you to get to the Hilton Hotel and."

"Oh, that's where Mom and I are staying. It's beautiful! And that breakfast buffet is something special. I wish you were here; I'd love to whip you up some waffles in their waffle maker. They've got real maple syrup, strawberries, blueberries, whipped cream and..."

"Emily, please! I need you to get back to the hotel's business center as quickly as you can. I'm going to send a fax; it should be around twenty or thirty pages; and I need you to get it to Katie Chen as quickly as you can. Can you do that for me?" Fan Girl didn't even bother to think through the logistics or the timing of departing the arena and then having to pass through security and the ticket check again on her return.

"Sure thing! That's easy!" Henry knew this was anything but easy so he was a bit alarmed by Fan Girl's dismissive comment. He thought about explaining the gravity of the situation and then decided to skip all of that. Time was of the essence.

"Great! I could hug you, Emily!"

"Oh, please! And just keep it coming!" Henry immediately regretted the hugging remark.

"If you can, try to get it to Katie before she laces up her skates. If not, do the best you can." Henry was nervously looking at his watch. Time was not on their side. He was about to reemphasize the importance of a timely delivery when Emily told him that she was already making her way out of the sports complex. Henry thanked Fan Girl again and then raced with his paperwork to the garage where he pulled out his bicycle and began furiously pedaling into town.

Gasping for breath, at the Business Support Desk in Office World, Henry watched as the last of twenty-five pages slid through the fax machine; the final page containing a hand-drawn heart; the cover page clearly specifying "FOR KATIE CHEN'S EYES ONLY." The freckled-faced, college-aged Business Support Associate pondered the meaning of the sweat-soaked, short-of-breath teenager with an aura of desperation about him. He learned on his third day of work never to ask questions.

It seemed like the final page of the fax had barely cleared the document feed tray before Henry's phone was ringing—*Gollum's Song* from *The Lord of the Rings*—it was Fan Girl. Emily had the fax and she was making her way back to the arena. She would keep Henry posted on her progress. And she did. Every step in her journey was accurately described in a continuous stream of text messages, half of which Henry missed as he was biking back home, at a somewhat more leisurely pace.

Meanwhile, at the arena, Katie had already given her cell phone to her coach and was starting her backstage warm up routine; stretching and jumping about in her skating dress, wearing sneakers, as she visualized her upcoming Free Skate program. Only an hour before, Jason Bryne had managed to convince his connections at the U.S. Figure Skating Association to wait before making their verdict public. The majority of the voting members had already made their minds up that Brittney Starr would be permanently banned from all USFSA and ISU (International Skating Union) sanctioned skating events. The punishment would send a clear message to skaters for years to come. Katie was unaware of any of the pieces in motion, as she was now completely focused on her upcoming routine. She could hear the applause as Agnetha took the ice with the second to last group. The top five skaters would skate in the final group. Even though Katie knew she should be lacing up her skates, she felt compelled to run out to the boards to watch Anna skate to Ludovico Einaudi's *Primavera*. As the music began, Agnetha skated out with an angelic gracefulness. There was something ethereal about her skating; her flowing white skating dress billowing with Agnetha's swift movement across the ice; more reminiscent of a white gull upon the breeze than a human on ice. Anna only had two quadruple jumps in her program; one in combination; but she landed them perfectly. The Triple-Triple and Triple-Double combos were executed with ease. Tears began rolling down Katie's cheek as she watched. Though only fifteen, she'd seen countless hours of skating and had never witnessed any performance as spellbinding. The crowd erupted with an ecstatic standing ovation. Flowers and stuffed animals showered the ice; a fitting tribute to a young woman who had, for the last few years, set the artistic standard for the sport even if she could not match the technical content of some of her younger rivals. For the time being, Agnetha moved into first place but, with the top skaters soon to take the ice, she knew her marks would not stand up. After watching Agnetha, Katie ran back to the locker room to lace up her skates and ready herself for her turn on the ice.

On the other side of the arena, Fan Girl was desperately trying to negotiate with security personnel to get access to Katie. At every attempt, she was blocked. One guard offered to hand the stack of papers to Miss Chen but Emily wasn't willing to take the risk. She wracked her brain for another alternative. And then it came to her. Pink Flamingo!

Just outside the arena, one of the vendors was selling a variety of stuffed animals and plush toys. The bears were going like hotcakes as were the cute bunnies, unicorns, and just about anything else that could be cuddled by a child. There was, however, an overabundance of pink flamingos. Apparently, they were not as popular as the other options; at least not up in Minnesota in the middle of winter. Emily knew how much Katie loved flamingos. Well, she thought she knew. In reality, Emily had seen a photo that Katie showed in class, three years ago, as she described her family's summer trip to Florida as part of a summer vacation "story telling" project. The associated photo montage included a picture of Katie standing next to a group of bright pink flamingos. Emily assumed that Katie was a flamingo fan so she became a flamingo enthusiast, as well. Now the two could share their love of flamingos. The reality was that Katie's mother had staged the photo and Katie had no more love for flamingos than she did for the common sparrow.

As the final group was called to the ice for their practice time, Fan Girl, once more, ran to the exits and made a direct line for the plush toy vendor. She bought the only flamingo sold that day.

Inside the arena, following the warm-up skate, Mariah McPherson took to the ice. She skated very well, with only one missed jump in an otherwise clean program. While her four-minute Free Skate score was well below Agnetha's, Mariah's combined score put her several points ahead of her rival. Agnetha was happy for Mariah even though she wasn't looking forward to watching her score slowly slide out of medal contention. Jolene Kennedy was next. Katie continued to loosen up along the boards and noticed Brittney nervously pacing. Yesterday's events had clearly shaken her. A lesser person might have let her competitor self-destruct; but that was not who Katie was. She walked up to Brittney and put her hand on her shoulder.

"You got this, Britt. Things are going to be okay. Trust me. Go out there and give it your best." Brittney was confused, at first. She didn't know what to say.

"Okay. Thanks, Katie."

Jolene skated to a rousing Broadway medley but, unfortunately, had several costly stumbles that dropped her down to fifth. Brittney was up next. She consulted with her coach and removed her skate guards. Before taking the ice, she looked back at Katie who just smiled back and gave her a thumbs up. It was the first encouragement she could remember receiving from her fellow skaters in years. Brittney skated a jazz-themed routine which was fun but very conservative. She didn't fall but her marks left her several points behind Mariah. Tara Kowalski was up next. Poor Tara imploded on the ice. A missed combination jump at the beginning of the program haunted her for the remainder and she was never able to recover. With Mariah firmly in first place, Brittney in second, and Agnetha a distant third, Katie knew what she had to do. If she included her four planned quadruple jumps, two of them in combination, she knew her technical difficulty base level would make her very competitive for the gold. None of the other skaters had the same technical base. In short, if Katie could skate clean, she'd be standing on top of the podium. Back in the hotel room, Katie's Mom was anxiously pacing back and forth in front of the television. She had run the numbers in her head and knew that Katie was very capable of winning the national title. Her daughter was almost guaranteed a podium finish and trip to the Olympics. Only the top three U.S. Ladies would have the privilege of representing the United States in Oslo. Meanwhile, in the stands, Fan Girl was using a nail file to tear the seams on the Pink Flamingo. She folded the faxed documents and pushed the papers inside the stuffed animal.

A hush fell over the arena as Katie skated to center ice. She was skating to *Candle on the Water* and *Somewhere Over the Rainbow*. The silence was broken by the overly enthusiastic words of encouragement shouted by one teenage girl bearing a very large pink flamingo: "We love you, Katie!" After some laughter, the venue returned to its former state. Katie took a deep breath and slowly exhaled. When her music started, she was in her element. The first jump, a Quad Lutz, would be critical as it would set the stage for all to come. Building up speed, Katie transitioned to backward skating and then, reaching back with her right leg, planted the toe pick of her skate blade in the ice, vaulting skyward while using the outside edge of her left skate to direct to motion of the spin. One, two, three, four rotations and Katie returned to the ice, landing cleanly on her right foot. The audience erupted in applause. Katie smiled broadly, feeling confident and in control. She continued. Quad Flip/Double-Toe combination—perfect! Triple Lutz/Triple Toe Loop—impeccable! In between the jumps, Katie was working hard to ensure the artistry was not lost. The biggest hurdle for young skaters is transitioning from jumping machines into artists on ice. Katie's coach had enrolled her in ballet classes and hired a well-established choreographer to help improve the transitions between jumps and enhance the overall beauty of her performance. The fruits of those efforts were paying dividends and those in attendance looked on in awe. Beautiful Camel Spins, Biellmann spins, Layback spins, Spiral sequences, Split Jumps, Waltz Jumps, and Footwork sequences spanned the gap between the big jumps; all accentuated with beautiful arm and hand movement. Katie was killing it. Her Technical Element Score was climbing like a rocket. Jumps performed in the second half of the four-minute program receive a ten percent bonus, acknowledging the endurance required to sustain physical exertion over the course of the free skate. This rule was established years ago to incentivize a balanced performance, countering an earlier trend of skaters completing all their jumps in the first minute of a routine, leaving nothing but spins and footwork sequences for the remaining three minutes. Quad Salchow—solid! Katie had only one more planned Quad jump—her Quad Toe/Triple Toe combination. When she successfully completed that, the crowd was on their feet. From a veritable unknown, Katie Chen was about to become a household name. Three-minutes into the program and things couldn't have been going any better. Perhaps that's why the audience gasped in astonishment when Katie lost her footing and fell on a Triple-Double combination. She quickly got up and fought to get back into her routine. On her next move, a planned Triple Lutz/Double Toe combination, Katie popped the jump, completing only a single rotation on the Lutz. More points detracted. Worse yet, she stumbled out of her Triple Axel, failing to complete the required revolutions. Broadcasting nationally, the skating commentators expressed their regret. They discussed how, at the Junior competition level, the Free Skate is only three minutes and thirty seconds. They speculated that the longer routine might be adversely affecting Katie Chen's endurance. One final jump sequence, a Triple Flip/Triple Toe combo, was executed flawlessly; but, unfortunately, the damage was already done. Katie completed her routine with a spectacular Scratch Spin. She smiled and took her bows before a cheering crowd as flowers and plush toys, tossed by adoring fans, rained down upon the ice. Katie immediately picked out Fan Girl, wildly screaming as she pushed her way down to the boards with a giant pink flamingo. Emily threw that bird to center ice with the arm strength and precision of an NFL quarterback. Katie skated over, picking up a few flower bouquets and plush toys before collecting the flamingo. She then made her way off the ice, to the "Kiss and Cry" area, to await her scores while a swarm of cute little girls in skating dresses cleared the ice of the abundance of tributes. As she waited, Jason Bryne comforted his skater, offering her words of encouragement to stem the tide of disappointment. Katie noticed the tear in the underside of the flamingo. She reached her fingers in and felt the folded papers. As the event was being televised nationally, Katie left the papers for later, instead smiling and waving at the camera pointed directly at her. When the scores were posted, Katie saw that she had placed fourth, just off the podium. There would be no trip to Oslo in February. Before departing, Katie stood and waved to the audience who was still applauding her magnificent Senior Ladies debut.

Returning back to the lockers, Katie was met by Mariah McPherson, the new U.S. Women's Figure Skating Champion. Mariah looked Katie in the eye.

"You never miss those jumps, Katie. You landed four Quads but lost the Triple Flip/Double Toe and Triple Lutz/Double Toe? I mean, the Triple Axel . . . I get that. But the two combos?" Katie looked at Mariah with a caring expression on her face.

"Well, you know, big show jitters. I'll get 'em next time," replied Katie. Mariah considered Katie's remarks.

"I'm not buying it, Katie." Mariah left it with that. She pulled Katie in and gave her a big hug. About that time, Agnetha joined the group. Agnetha wasn't buying Katie's story, either. Katie's missteps meant not only a National's bronze medal for Agnetha but, more significantly, a spot on the U.S. Olympic Team. Like Mariah, she pulled

Katie in and gave her a big hug. Stepping back, she looked into Katie's eyes, tears streaming out of her own. No words needed to be exchanged. Agnetha knew what most outside the business would never appreciate—Katie's missteps had nothing to do with endurance, nerves, or skill; they had to do with her quality as a human being and her caring heart.

As Katie worked her way through the tunnel and back to the locker room, a network intern ran up to her and asked if she wouldn't mind giving an interview in fifteen minutes. Mariah was already headed off for her interview prior to the official medal ceremony.

In the relative quiet of the locker room, Katie reached her hand inside the pink flamingo and pulled out a stack of papers which she began reading. A few were written in Russian but the amplifying notes attached explained the significance of the documents. It all made sense. Katie knew what she had to do.

Fifteen minutes later, the red light turned on atop the television camera and a microphone got shoved in Katie's face.

"Katie, you surprised a lot of people this week and earned thousands of new fans. You should be very proud of what you accomplished. What words do you have for little girls out there who might wish to follow in your footsteps?"

"Thanks, Sandra! I think we all need to believe in ourselves and in our dreams. It's been an honor to compete with such a wonderful group of skaters and friends. I truly believe we are all winners."

"Katie, did you find the controversy surrounding this year's competition a distraction? Do you think that impacted your performance during today's Free Skate?"

"Great question, Sandra. I'd call it a passion more than a distraction. I'm also pleased to say that I can prove, without any doubt, that Brittney Starr is not only innocent of the crimes she was accused of but, also, completely worthy of representing our country in Oslo next month." Katie might as well have lobbed a hand grenade into the room. A frantic commotion ensued as news correspondents jockeyed for position and camera flashes created a veritable electric storm in the proximity of young Miss Katie Chen. While the network correspondent stood frozen, unable to speak, a chorus of voices from other media sources pleaded with Katie to expound upon her statement. Katie was well-prepared to do just that.

"I have in my hand the documentation to support the story I'm about to tell you. In an effort to secure a greater level of international prestige and return Russian athletes to the forefront of international sporting events, especially in the wake of several recent scandals, certain members of the government began putting pressure on athletes and their coaches to do "whatever it takes" to get the job done. Coaches and officials, especially, were incentivized to play dirty, as they say. Many of the officials, coaches, and athletes strongly objected to these pressures. One of the most outspoken opponents of "Project Victory," as the plan was known, was Aleksandr Chernoff, Irina Dobroskaya's coach. Irina was the best skater in the world and he felt strongly that Russian athletes could compete on their own merit without having to resort to "treacherous means," as he put it. Based upon what I've uncovered, I have to question whether Coach Chernoff's untimely demise in a tragic swimming mishap last summer was truly an accident. I'll leave that for others to work out. What I do know is that Eugeni Blushkin, coach for the new Russian champion, Nikita Leonova, worked through an intermediary, Sergei Antonov, also known as "Geraldo Espinosa," to bribe one Greta Baronclau. Besides her family's close connections, during the Cold War, with the communist party in East Germany, Greta was always looking for a little cash on the side. The four payments of $990,000, dispersed between separate accounts, would work nicely and assure an early retirement and a life of luxury. The payments were broken up so as not to flag international financial screening protocols that automatically report any transfer over a million dollars across national borders. Those protocols were established to help stem the tide of international criminal activity that has run rampant in this age of global electronic communications and fund transfers." Katie paused for a breath while reporters were shouting their questions, trying to be heard above the other shouting reporters.

"Greta knew that a nearly imperceptible twisting of her skater's blade on the boot would almost certainly go unnoticed. Further, she felt that if it was discovered, no one would ever look to Agnetha Andersson's own coach as the perpetrator. It seemed like a fool proof plan to keep Agnetha out of the Olympics. Agnetha Andersson, as many of you know, is considered America's only hope to unseat the Russian skating prodigies at the Olympics and at the World's in March. Perhaps the most disgusting part of this already super gross plot was the "insurance plan." That insurance plan involved framing the somewhat unpopular Brittney Starr. Greta Baronclau stole Brittney's unmistakable sparkly gloves while she was using the restroom and, after acquiring the back-up key for Agnetha's locker, completed the skate surgery in a bathroom stall, using the sparkly gloves to ensure there were no finger prints left. She used a screwdriver to loosen and readjust the blade position on Agnetha's skate and then, when the locker room was vacant, she replaced the skates in Agnetha's locker and tossed the incriminating tool and gloves behind the row of lockers." Katie went on to describe how she had discovered the twisted blade and how some pink fuzz helped guide her to the culprit.

"At first, I really didn't think much about the pink fuzz on Greta's black slacks. But, when I noticed I had collected some very similar looking pink fuzz on my tights, I suspected a single source for the offending material—Agnetha's ultra-cute fuzzy pink soakers. They shed like a Golden Retriever in summer. I accumulated my "souvenir" after removing the soakers from Agnetha's blades. According to Agnetha, Greta never had cause to access her skates. So, how did she collect the material? Perhaps a pink flamingo?" Katie chuckled, apparently the only one in the room who got the joke. "I had some analysis done and determined that the material was an exact color match. After that, well, let's just say I used covert methods to acquire the documentation I hold here in my hands. I think the authorities will find they have everything they need here to bring this case to a close." With that, Katie did a cute performance-ending skating curtsey and walked over to where her coach was standing with several officials from the U.S. Figure Skating Association who had, until that moment, been preparing for a media conference on the Brittney Starr situation. Situation resolved.

The press followed Katie, as she turned the documents over to the USFSA officials, cameras flashing wildly to capture the moment. Sports commentator, Sandra Duncan, remained a veritable statue all the while, her expression barely changing since Katie's shocking presentation had left her stunned and frozen. Security personnel began clearing the path for Katie to get to the DV bus departure area. She was halfway there when Brittney Starr came running up and nearly tackled her. Brittney hugged her like she was holding on to a floatation device in stormy seas. Tears streaming from her eyes, she kissed Katie on the cheek and thanked her over and over again. Somewhat surprised, but grateful for the show of affection from the usually distant Brittney, Katie squeezed back. The two embraced until the doorman announced that the DV bus was pulling up. Katie and Brittney sat next to each other on the return ride, Agnetha and Mariah sitting behind them; all four laughing and teasing one another like young girls do.

Katie finally turned on her cell phone and was surprised to see hundreds of congratulatory text messages. She scrolled past them all until she got to the messages from Henry. Beyond the congratulations, he filled her in on the activities of the afternoon. Katie knew there was one more person she needed to thank.

When the bus arrived at the hotel, the skaters were swarmed by hundreds of fans. The hotel staff could do little to control the flood waters of youthful exuberance. A long line formed for Katie's autograph which surprised her a bit. Who would want the autograph of the number four skater in the country? she thought. I can tell you, those fans appreciated Katie for reasons that went well beyond her skating excellence. Katie's mother looked on with pride, now aware of what had transpired at the competition and her daughter's role in solving the mystery. Near the end of the line was a special fan, patiently waiting with an event program and a pink permanent marker. Katie excused herself and walked the line, high-fiving fans as she passed, until she got to Emily Song, "Fan Girl." Katie gave her a big hug and thanked her for what she had done.

"I love you so much, Katie! Would you please sign my program? I brought a pen in your favorite color, 'flamingo pink'." Katie just smiled.

"Ah, flamingo pink. Right. My favorite." Katie signed the program and then dragged Fan Girl to the front of the line to stand with her while she was attending to the other, somewhat less fanatical, skating groupies.

Katie's mother and coach did their best to shield Katie from media attention until their departure back to California. The case of the twisted blade became an international sensation and Katie's photo and excerpts from the interview and her skating performances were broadcast across the globe. The Russian government conducted an official investigation into "Project Victory" and disciplined those found to be involved in the scheme. Though she placed third at nationals, with a new pair of skates, Agnetha "Anna" Andersson went on to win the gold medal at the Winter Olympics in Oslo. Mariah McPherson came in second and Irina Dobrowskaya took the bronze. Brittney star didn't win a medal during international competition that year but she certainly turned over a new leaf. Instead of trying to mess with her competitor's psyche, she worked hard to build them up and encourage them. Her positive messages uplifted many young girls and even pulled one away from the precipice of suicide.

And what of Katie, Henry, and Emily? They all went out together for burgers and shakes when they reunited in California. They had a photo taken together at The Burger Corral. Emily framed an eight by ten copy of the photo and placed it in the empty spot on her wall. Over the years, posters of athletes, musicians, actors and writers disappeared from Emily's room until the only photo remaining was the picture she took with Katie and Henry. The three remain friends to this very day. Emily's children call her friends Aunt Katie and Uncle Henry.

And, yes, Katie and Henry did eventually marry. They have a beautiful daughter of their own. Before that, Katie competed in the subsequent Winter Olympics in Lake Placid and won a gold medal for the United States. She followed up with a World Figure Skating Championship gold medal in Göteborg, Sweden. She managed all that while simultaneously taking a challenging course load at Harvard. Following graduation, Katie went on to practice sports medicine and was invited by the United Nations to travel the world, advocating for literacy as well as physical and mental wellness in underdeveloped regions. She's credited with bringing attention to the plight of many underprivileged children.

I remember talking to Katie, a few years ago. I asked her about the reporting that she had cracked the second biggest case in figure skating history. Naturally, I thought the first biggest was the infamous Tonya Harding/Nancy Kerrigan case. Katie just smiled. She was bound by a non-disclosure agreement the CIA requested she sign. The classified details of the biggest case in figure skating history, and Katie's role in solving that, would have to wait for future generations.

The Story Behind the Story

The editors never saw this one coming! A retired Air Force Officer writing a mystery short story featuring a young Asian-American teenage sleuth and taking place within the confines of an international skating competition—Red Penguin Books was about to get a taste of my range.

Katie Chen and the Twisted Blade

"Behind Closed Doors" was the first anthology of the series to feature only mysteries. Outside of a few little pieces I may have written as a very young child, I had never written a mystery story. I was excited about the prospect. As a life-long figure skating fan, I thought this volume might present an opportunity to take readers upon a journey into a fascinating world they might not have been familiar with. It's a glamorous world but one that is no stranger to intrigue and, occasionally, foul play. My heroine, Katie Chen, was, no doubt, inspired by several bubbly, and wonderful young Asian and Asian-American skaters who I had the pleasure of following across the years. The story also touches upon the decades-old East vs. West rivalries that have played out across countless Olympic and World Championship venues.

As the story, notionally, takes place in the future, I progressed the technical level of the skaters' abilities accordingly. Purists will note that the Ladies are not currently performing that many "Quad" jumps, and they're correct. When my skating idol, Dorothy Hamill, won the Olympics and World Figure Skating Championship in 1976, no woman was performing anything beyond a double jump (the most difficult at the time, the Double Axel, required two and a half revolutions). Female figure skaters are now landing Quad jumps and, in the men's competition, up to six Quads have been landed in a single Free Skate program. At the time of this writing, Ilia Malinin (United States) holds the record for most Quad jumps successfully landed in a performance with six performed during his Free Skate at the 2025 World Figure Skating Championship in Boston, MA. During that performance, he landed all six types of Quad jumps.

Back to the story. There are a number of sub-themes but, ultimately, "Katie Chen and the Twisted Blade" is a story about a good person taking the time to make things right and putting the needs of others and a greater justice ahead of her own personal glory. In doing so, she becomes, in our eyes, a character of even greater heroic stature. I hope you became as big a fan of Katie Chen as I did while I was writing the piece. I really had fun with this story, and I hope you enjoyed it.

Ornaments to Remember

(Written March 4, 2021)
Previously Unpublished

*An essay about my attempt to create meaningful
holiday ornaments for my children.*

I have never been an accomplished wood worker but I did manage to survive elementary school and high school wood shop without losing any fingers. I consider that an accomplishment. I've looked on, with envy, as others have crafted beautiful works of art from the gifts nature provided. I've worked on projects, here and there, but the buzz of power tools and whirring of large circular blades, spewing forth volumes of splinters and sawdust, have failed to inspire me to improve my skills. Alas, I shall never be a carpenter. With that said, I do like to make things. I have engaged upon several home projects over the years without the aid of a workshop. The most meaningful creations were true labors of love—very special Christmas tree ornaments for my children.

Some of my fondest childhood memories involve the holiday season and going to get our Christmas tree with my father. Sometimes, the tree vendor would saw off the bottom inch of the tree trunk for us. Other times, after bringing the tree home, my father would pull out his old hand saw and, with its somewhat dull teeth, saw his way through the terminus of the trunk. By making a fresh cut at the bottom of the tree, the pores are opened and the tree can better absorb water from a reservoir in the base of the Christmas tree stand. Ideally, this gives the tree some extra life before it dries out and becomes a festive holiday fire hazard.

Eventually, I left home and joined the Air Force. My military service did not always afford me the luxury of a "traditional" Christmas. After marrying, reluctant to switch to artificial trees, I continued the tradition of acquiring a living tree so that we might enjoy the natural beauty of the fir, spruce, or pine along with that wonderful Christmas tree smell. And, of course, I continued to saw off the bottom inch or two of the trees before placing them in the stand.

Ornaments to Remember

In the summer of 1996, our first child was born. I wanted to make sure his first Christmas was special. But how do you make Christmas "special" for a five-month-old baby? I wondered. Hugs and smiles were a given but I was looking for something extra. In southwestern Oklahoma, the dwindling supply of trees at the local Walmart were already drying out in the heat. Attending our first Christmas parade in Altus, Oklahoma, we were surrounded by spectators in shorts and t-shirts. The temperature was around eighty degrees Fahrenheit that year. I digress. I purchased a tree, brought it home, and gave it a good shake. Hundreds of loose, dry needles fell from the branches to the floor. As I sawed off the base of the trunk, I had a wonderful epiphany. Rather than discarding the remaining chunk of wood, I thought that I might, perhaps, use it to construct an ornament; a special ornament that would forever be associated with my son's first Christmas.

Going to the local hardware store, I purchased sandpaper of various coarseness and a little wood burning kit. I allocated a corner of the kitchen table in our apartment to be my temporary workshop. I actually did own a power drill, although I probably only used it a few times over the years. My first consideration was whether or not I would remove the bark around the perimeter. I preferred a natural look and hoped I could keep the bark so the ornament would truly be a cross-section of the tree. To do so, I knew I'd have to take care to ensure the exterior bark didn't chip away as I sawed and sanded. With all this in mind, I set to work.

The first thing I did was to drill a hole in the circular tree cross-section. Once that was done, I engaged in a number of rounds of sanding. I began with very coarse sandpaper (20-30 grit) and, as the wood smoothed out, transitioned to medium sandpaper (60-100 grit). Once the surface was fairly smooth, I used the wood burning tool to burn my son's name and the year into the wooden disc. I was very careful in the process—I couldn't exactly purchase more wood if I messed up. Once the name and year were etched, I sanded the piece again, using medium grit sandpaper, at first, before transitioning to fine sandpaper (120-220 grit). When the surface was smooth, and the tree rings were clearly visible, I applied the first coating of gloss polyurethane to the wood. The polyurethane coating process took several days since I had to wait for one side to dry before flipping the wood to coat the opposite side. I also applied polyurethane to the bark around the perimeter of the ornament. Once the first coat of polyurethane dried, I used extra fine sandpaper (approximately 200 grit) to sand the surface before applying a second coat. This helps the second coat to adhere. The polyurethane coating protects the wood and also creates a beautiful glossy look to the ornament. After the second coating of polyurethane had dried, I completed the ornament by affixing a ribbon so that the ornament could be hung from a Christmas tree branch. And so, on my son's very first Christmas, a new family tradition was born.

I was so pleased with the project that I decided to make ornaments for each of my four children using wood from their first Christmas tree. One ornament was made in Oklahoma, one in England, and two in Nebraska. As they grew older, my kids would each place their own ornament upon our tree. It's my hope that they'll maintain and treasure these special keepsakes long after I'm gone. A piece of wood from each Christmas tree in the year they were born—each ornament is a special gift just as each of my children are a beautiful blessing.

The Story Behind the Story

"Ornaments to Remember" was written for an anthology that never materialized. The Book was to be called "Projects From Home—The Joys of Doing It Yourself" and according to the tasking message, this anthology was to be "a celebration of the creativity and hard work that allows for beauty to be made by each and every one of us." The projects could range from crafts to home renovations, but authors were asked to provide photos of their finished projects. I hadn't done much in the way of home renovations as I was frequently moving and, more often than not, I was living in *rented apartments or on-base homes where I didn't have the liberty to make signifi-cant modifications. As I desired to keep my unbroken streak of anthology submissions going, I knew there were only a handful of crafting options that might make for good candidates. It didn't take me long to come up with the idea of describing my favorite project—making personalized Christmas ornaments for my children (and our dog, as well). Unfortunately, there were not enough contributions from other authors to make the publishing of this anthology economically feasible so the project fell off the table and my work was never published...until now.*

JOURNEY

(Written April 27, 2021)
Previously Unpublished

*An allegorical fantasy tale depicting the entirety of a
man's life—from birth to death and spiritual
transcendence—as a fantastical quest. The
protagonist navigates a dreamlike world filled with
dragons, knights, magical forests, festivals, and
symbolic trials that mirror the real stages of life.*

A boundless emptiness deprives my senses within the empty void. No sight, no sound, no feel, smell, nor taste. A perfect nothingness; I am lost in time. A soft voice comforts me. "I am Destiny," she says, "and I shall never stray far from your side. Know that I am here." Strange words. I do not understand but I welcome my companion. I revel in the warmth of her hand. Then, like a dream, she fades.

Warm waters wash over my naked body. I feel the sand, warm beneath my bare back. I am conscious of distant stars in a night sky. I blindly crawl, too weak and feeble to make progress and too disoriented to care. An explosion of light blinds me as a brilliant beam of light sets the dark sky afire, briefly turning night into day as it ascends majestically into the heavens. My heart races madly and I scream in confusion, my body curling into a ball. I struggle to stand but fall back upon the sand. How was it that I came to rest upon this lonely stretch of shoreline? My memory fails me yet, somehow, I feel that it must have been some great journey that brought me here. The sun breaks the horizon and, as I survey my surroundings, I see waves gently stroking the shore while, behind me, an imposing wall of rock towers skyward, formidably impassable. Sea before and stone behind—it seems I have little choice but to follow the shoreline to where it may lead.

My mind is alive with wonder and races to make sense of the situation. My limbs feel weak as I walk the seemingly endless beach and I frequently stumble, falling back to the sand. A mighty bellow shatters the serenity and I look to the sky whereupon I see I mighty dragon swooping from the clouds, her eyes fixed upon me. There's no place to

187

hide so I desperately stagger back toward the water; my only hope to disappear beneath the waves in an ill-conceived attempt to fool the beast. My heart is pounding within my chest. I am afraid. Where is my friend now? Where is Destiny? She swore she would be by my side yet she is absent from the scene. Before despair can overwhelm me, I hear the muffled sound of four dozen hooves, distant but closing. The heat waves emanating from the hot sand distort my vision. Sun gleaming brilliantly off their armor, the many riders appear as a singular orb of glowing light. Men in armor bearing weapons race to my rescue. Above, the emerald-scaled dragon, glowing like a jewel in the blue sky, tucks her enormous wings to her side and dives towards me. I await my fate. Upon the wind, I hear an angel's voice whispering and I know Destiny is with me. She cautions, "Those riders are not your friends."

"What of the dragon?" I shout. I hear no reply. My answer comes as an arrow whizzes by my head; and then another. The earth trembles as the dragon arrives with a thud upon the beach, sand swirling about as it fans its mighty wings in protest. She shields me with her wings as arrow and spear, alike, inflict pain but no mortal wounds upon my rescuer. Her talon, capable of crushing me like the petals of a flower, gently lifts me off the ground. Amidst a storm of swirling sand, the noble creature leaps skyward and carries me to safety over the impassible wall of stone. I laugh with joy, the wind racing over my body, as I gaze upon the flower-bespeckled fields, forests, mountains, rivers and lakes below—they form a glorious tapestry of life.

There's no telling how far we've flown before the dragon settles in a small clearing in the forest beside a gently flowing brook. She releases her grip and I roll out upon the soft and cool grass. She looks upon me with affection and I smile with gratitude. The dragon reaches the brook with several short strides and strikes beneath the rippling waters with a sudden fury that astonishes me. She's caught a large fish. She casts it to the grass, tears it open, and roasts it with gentle breaths of flame, flipping it occasionally in the process. The dragon carefully nudges the smoldering meal towards me and I eat. A spring rain begins to gently fall and my savior covers me with a wing as I eat my fill. The sun sets behind the trees and a brilliant moon takes its place in the night sky as the rain moves on to water other gardens. I shiver in the night air and the dragon lays beside me, warm and protective. I fall asleep.

I awake to the morning light and stretch lazily upon the soft grass. I hear a rumbling sound in the distance and it grows louder. I look toward a small dirt path that winds through the oaks, birches, beeches, aspens, maples and elm trees before emptying into the sheltered clearing where I lie. I see a grey-bearded man encouraging a team of white horses as they pull a well-worn wagon. The dragon looks towards the man but takes no action. A snapping branch gains my attention and I look over my left shoulder. It is Destiny; she sits upon the sturdy limb of a nearby oak, her white dress shimmering as if crafted from sunlit clouds. She calls out to me. "Trust this man." I will.

In due course, the wagon pulls up beside me and the man dismounts. I have to imagine the wagon has seen its better days. Once emblazoned with brilliant colors, I can barely make out the faded depictions of ancient battles that once adorned its sides. The grey-beard, covered in torn cloth garments and well-worn furs, slides off of the wagon and considers me.

"Let's find you something to wear, then; shall we?" He walks to the rear of his wagon and pulls down a wooden ramp, lowering the edge to the grass below. He climbs into the back of his wagon and a cacophony of clanging, scraping, and banging ensues. Greybeard emerges with a dirty burlap sack and approaches. I can only imagine what tattered rags are concealed within. He spills the contents before me and I am amazed to see brilliantly gleaming armor and the soft, padded, finery to go beneath. I don the boots, trousers and padded doublet and the old man helps me into the various components of the plate armor. Whereas I was weak yesterday, I feel stronger today and I stand, proudly, astonished that so poor a fellow could bestow such a marvelous gift. Greybeard steps back to look at me and nods in approval before closing the distance to embrace me. At first, I find the embrace awkward. I do not understand . . . today. Tomorrow, I shall. Releasing me after what seems like an eternity, Greybeard returns to his wagon and climbs in back, once more. This time, he is as silent as a whisper. He returns with a book in his left hand and a sword in his right. "You may choose one final gift before I depart. Which shall it be?" The sword entices me and might serve me well upon the unknown journey ahead. Something compels me to reach for the book, which is willingly given. A nearly imperceptible smile appears on the old man's face. He speaks passionately yet I fail to grasp the meaning of his words. Slowly, Greybeard makes his way back to his wagon and climbs aboard, taking the reins in hand and bidding his horses onward. He steers the wagon along a wide arc until he finds the clearing in the trees and the path from whence he came. Greybeard disappears into the darkness of the woods. It seems only natural that I should follow. I look back to the dragon before I go and she looks upon me with affection. She wants me to stay yet she encourages me to go; her eyes speak the words she cannot. I bow and she nods. I am off.

The trees seem to close in around me and I feel as if I'm being watched. I am excited yet fearful as I follow the dirt path that winds through the trees. With each stride, I grow braver and more confident. I travel the better part of the day, occasionally stopping to gather berries and fruits which grow in abundance along my route. From over the hill, I hear the joyous sounds of musicians—mandolins, harps, lutes, pipes and recorders serenade me as I climb higher and higher. Panting for breath, I crest the hill and look down upon a large clearing in the valley below. Colorful tents and stages fill the scene and the aroma of a hundred baked, grilled, and fried delicacies entice me. I race down the slope, stumbling and falling more than once, ever-eager to witness the spectacle of the great faire. Cheerful revelers welcome me and freely offer me food and drink. I'm invited to see the performers upon the stage and I marvel at their skill. Actors and comedians, acrobats and jugglers, musicians and poets. I am thrilled and I am learning great things about life. I see the world through the eyes of the talented artists before me. Joys and sorrows, friendships and betrayal, love and loss—everything. I come to understand the world. I feel happy. Two lovely maidens approach me and bid me to follow. I do. A lone fire burns in the distance, tended to by a woman in a long white dress. I stop, though the maidens tug at my arms, encouraging me to join them for wine and conversation. I know the woman tending the fire; she is Destiny. I offer my apologies to the maidens and make my way through the festivities while the sun sinks below the hills. Destiny looks upon me with care and motions for me to sit beside her at the fire. With gleeful excitement, I share my glorious experiences at the faire. Destiny listens to my tales and smiles. She offers words of caution, "the light of the sun often dazzles our eyes. I recommend you return to the faire whilst the moon casts its glow upon the scene. Perhaps you shall see it differently? You've seen the world through words and song today yet you've not seen it clearly until you've come to know it through your own eyes. Tonight, you shall." Destiny waved her hand and all was quiet. There were no trumpets and drums. Even the chirping crickets fell silent as the winds slept. I stood and bid farewell to

Destiny; my own voice lost to the spell. Feeling somewhat confused, I returned to the festival, the colors faded in the darkening sky. Drunken fools staggered about and fought one another for no clear reason. Vandals tore at the tents and looted prizes from within. An angry mob grabbed a disfigured woman and taunted her. I heard not a word but the angry expressions upon their faces were cause for alarm. Several members of the mob spoke to me but I heard them not. I believe they were seeking my complicity in their retribution against this woman whose crimes remained a mystery to me. The woman was dragged to a stake where she was bound as bundles of wood were piled up all around her. Much as Destiny had foretold, the faire had taken a turn for the worse and I knew I had to intervene to prevent a horrible tragedy. Three men with torches ran toward the helpless woman at the stake. I looked into her eyes, saw the fear, and felt my courage grow. I set upon the first and laid him flat upon the ground. Grabbing the fallen man's torch, I engaged his co-conspirators. The first fell with a mighty strike from the torch I wielded but the second landed a blow squarely upon my head which, were it not for my helmet, might well have killed me on impact. Regaining my feet, I exchanged blows until the villain lay motionless in the dirt. At that time, I was set upon by the angry mob and I fought valiantly throughout the night, the moon's light shimmering off my armor and my heart alive with the passion of justice. The remaining villains dispersed just before the sun greeted the day with its welcoming warmth. Battered and bloodied, I collapsed to the grass. I struggled to regain my feet and limped over to the stake where I was amazed to see the disfigured woman now appeared as a beautiful princess. She was clothed in a lavender gown adorned with jewels and ornate embroidery stitched in golden thread. I untied the ropes that bound her and she was free. I remained conscious only long enough to see the gratitude in her eyes and then I fell to the soft grass. I awoke, sometime later, beneath the expansive branches of an ancient oak tree that guarded the banks of a gently flowing stream, along with its kin. Attending my wounds was the gentle lady of the lavender gown. Once rescued and now the rescuer, Lady Giselle greets me warmly and bids me not to stir until her work is done. Stitches and poultices applied, Lady Giselle offers me a warm broth that astonishes me in both taste and effect. I can feel my body healing, nourished and strengthened by the enchanted concoction. The good lady sits by my side but neither of us speak. Another sun surrenders to the night and the air turns cool. Lady Giselle covers me in furs to ward off the chill and I fall asleep beneath the stars.

A loud crack of thunder rouses me and I find myself alone amidst a tempest. Ominous dark clouds swallow up the stars and the moon. The branches of the surrounding trees scream in agony as the wind tears at their limbs. I struggle to my feet, my wounds healed but my heart filled with fear. I shout into the night for Lady Giselle but no reply greets my beckon call. A strong gust knocks me off my feet yet I stand again and defiantly push on against the onslaught. A small fire still burns, a gift from my departed lady. The flames, like I, struggle to endure the fierce breath of the gods. On a nearby stone rests three green branches, the ends of each thickly wrapped in gauze, soaked in a perfumed oil. I light the end of the first within the dying fire and my torch comes to life, emanating not only a brilliant purple flame but so too a heavenly aroma that seems to calm my wild spirit. Another gift. The campfire gives up its fight against the raging winds at the instant my torch comes to life; its flame, thankfully, steady against the squall. A make my way toward the shelter of the nearby woods, my only refuge against the elements.

Deeper and deeper into the woods, I travel. The trees offer some protection from the wind but the terrifying howling persists. I am soon lost in a maze of wood yet I press ever onward. I am conscious of some spirit in the night watching me from a distance. Am I being hunted by some demonic foe? My exhaustion joins forces with the terrifying elements of the storm to craft a tale of horror and abandonment. I flee unknown spirits, causing harm to mind and limb as I stumble on rocks and collide with trees in my path. Finally, I collapse to my knees and gasp for breath. Glowing yellow eyes peer out of the darkness from a swaying branch above. Oh, if I had only taken the sword from Greybeard and not the book! A fool's lamentation, and little more. I shake the tome, yet carefully wrapped in protective burlap, and threaten to throw the book at the offending creature. It stirs not nor seems, in any way, agitated by my idle threats. Where is Destiny now? Where is she in my darkest hour? She promised she would be there yet I find myself alone in the dark, prey to evil powers, amidst a violent storm sent to hasten my undoing. I unbind the covering and carefully open the gift given me by Greybeard. Light emanates from the text and the beautifully illuminated pages dance before my eyes and sing to my ears with the wisdom of the ages. My mind fills will knowledge and understanding; reality is revealed as the outgoing tide of dread recedes from the shore, leaving truth uncovered upon the wet sand. I gaze toward the branch above and fix my eyes upon the denizen of the night who has been my companion these past few hours. The creature spreads its prodigious wings in defiance of the wind. It is no demon but a great owl that returns my gaze. With a twist of the head, he acknowledges my presence. Leaping into the sky, its wings silently stroking the turbulent air, my falsely accused travel companion swoops down, brushing my helmet with its feathers before finding refuge on a distant branch at the very limits of my vision. I follow. I must have a closer look. The owl fascinates me. The pursuer has become the pursued. On we go, through the night. The wind subsides but the sky is dark and the forest still fraught with peril. I am lost; hopelessly lost. My legs grow wearing and my will to continue fades, yet I endure and follow the winged traveler. In the distance, the owl perches, yet again, upon the highest limb of a colossal tree. I must get a closer look. I feel compelled to seek this messenger and confront him so that I might ask the unanswered question that continues to haunt me—"are you friend or foe?" Inwardly, I acknowledge that this raptor may be neither and that I may just be a fool desperately searching for answers on a dark night. Higher and higher, I climb. Stretching to reach the next rung of my arboreal ladder, I lose my grip on the torch and it plummets, bouncing off numerous limbs and branches on its way to the forest floor where it settles in a patch of wet moss. The flame fades and is extinguished. I curse my bad fortune for, now, I am without light and without hope. For all this, I continue upward, following the yellow eyes that now serve as my only beacon in the darkness. All below is lost as I climb ever higher. The owl remains. The clouds begin to break and errant beams of moonlight infuse the forest, casting an unearthly array of dancing shadows upon the scene. The beauty of the owl is revealed in the soft glow of moonbeams. I feel compelled to touch owl; to feel its soft feathers brush against my fingertips. Only an arms-length away, I extend my reach and, just as I'm about to make contact with this noble creature, it flies off into the night. I shout angrily, disappointed that my great ascent has yielded no results. And then I see it. From my impossibly high perch, I see a breathtaking chapel upon a hill, glowing with the brilliance of a jewel beneath the afternoon sun. The owl has not led me to my destruction but guided me toward my salvation. I mark my position and take care not to lose my bearings as I return to the forest floor. My course revealed, I make for the chapel and I am free of my forest prison.

Reaching the chapel, I pull upon the thick oaken door, lavishly decorated with unfamiliar symbols. Surprisingly, the door opens with very little effort, emitting a pleasing creaking sound that seems to welcome me in. The interior is dark but hundreds of candles lining the walls provide sufficient illumination for me to find my way forward. The pews are empty but for one parishioner. I hope that she might be Lady Giselle. She is not. I have found Destiny. I sit beside her. I have much to say but I speak not a word as I am overcome by the beauty of the scene and I suspect there's little I might offer that would come as news to my friend. I want to ask her why she abandoned me in the forest but the question seems petty and beneath me. I return my gaze to the shadows dancing upon the stone walls and I settle into a peaceful repose. Several dozen wanderers of the night make their way into the chapel and find seating. My mind drifts and my thoughts are still beholden to Lady Giselle. So entranced am I that I feel compelled to strike my own face with the back side of an iron gauntlet so as to corroborate the impossible images that my eyes reveal. It is no dream. Standing, silhouetted against the night at the entrance to the chapel, is my Lady Giselle. The cold wind whips her cloak about as she graces the threshold with her beauty. I try to stand but my legs are frozen. I attempt to call her name but my voice is lost. All I can do is watch as she gracefully makes her way to a pew on the other side of the chapel, unaware of my presence. I turn towards Destiny, confused and frustrated. As I do, the chapel door swings open and a great wind extinguishes all but a few candles. Then all is silent. From without, I hear the joyous sounds of instruments heralding the arrival of some great party. Musicians enter and take their places along the perimeter as a fantastic procession of elegantly attired kings and queens and great leaders from innumerable foreign lands arrive and slowly march through the chapel towards the altar, their sumptuous jewels radiating with the phosphorescent glow of the stars themselves. As the procession passes, visitors stand and join the regal party, following close behind the illustrious leader of their choice. A man in simple cloth robes walks among the leaders and attracts the attention of Lady Giselle who moves to join him. I try to stand but my legs remain immovable. Giselle passes, walking beside the robed man, and follows the flow of the procession, eventually disappearing down a marble stairway behind the altar. After some time, the trailing end of the procession passes, followed thereafter by the musicians. As the final trumpeter disappears behind the altar, I hear the loud clanging of metal doors closing and the candles, once more, burn brightly about the chapel. Finally, my legs freed, I dash to the altar and to the marble stairs beyond. Tremendous doors of gold, barred from the opposite side, prevent any further investigation. Giselle is gone. I look back towards Destiny but she, too, has departed. The remaining stragglers seem to wander aimlessly about the chapel; most eventually making their way back into the darkness of the night. Several kneel before the altar, tears in their eyes. I race to the exit, hoping to, perhaps, pick up the trail of the procession and Lady Giselle. I am met at the door by Destiny. She looks at me with kind eyes.

"Shall I see the good Lady Giselle again, my friend?" Destiny seems disinclined to answer and, for some reason, I regret my question the moment it departs my lips. After some consideration, she provides the answer I was dreading.

"You shall not. I am sorry. I understand your longing and know the loss shall cause you pain this night. I ask only that you find it in your heart to move on without regret for, with time, you shall understand that a greater good will come of all this and you shall appreciate the important role you have played in seeing this blessing to fruition." I looked down, the pain described already searing my heart, and thanked Destiny for revealing as much as she did. Destiny pointed toward a path, one that led up into the mountains, and bid me to continue my journey though my heart was heavy and my legs were weary. And so, continue I did.

Torches marked the entrance to the path. As I approached, I saw three foals nervously pacing about in the flickering light. A mare watched over the young horses. She welcomed me with a whinny and gracefully bowed her head. I was astonished yet wasted no time in returning the greeting. I began my trek upward. With dawn rapidly approaching, I was confident that the sun would be available for the most challenging parts of the ascent. The horses seemed intent on following me and I saw no reason to deny the company. On our way, we paused to enjoy the beauty of a glorious sunrise—the dawning of a new day. The trail narrowed and, at one point, I lost my footing on some loose rocks and nearly tumbled off a ledge. The mare, clearly experienced in navigating the treacherous passage, bid me to mount so that she might safely carry me along the treacherous passage. I did as she requested, checking back to ensure the foals were in close trail. One of the foals, with mane and tail that shone with the brilliance of polished silver, labored along with a limp. Periodically, I would slide off the mare's back and walk over to check on the little ones, especially Silver Tail. Without complaint, they followed along in trail.

Our path eventually led to an expansive plateau. In the distance, a swaying bridge spanned the chasm and led to a lush expanse of rolling hills and sparkling mountain lakes. A lone warrior guarded the bridge against all travelers. His heart as black as his armor, he refused us passage, proclaiming the mare and her colts were unworthy of the gifts beyond the bridge. I was incensed but there was little I could do against a man so heavily fortified. We had come so far and I was reluctant to give up on my journey, more so because I knew my companions were too exhausted to retreat down the mountain and it seemed a cruel trick to abandon them with food and water in clear sight yet no means to gain the sustenance. I would be condemning them to die. This was an outcome I could not permit.

Looking to the north, I was surprised to see a colorfully painted wagon, adorned with all manner of carvings and vibrant illustrations. It seemed familiar and yet unfamiliar. As I approached, I grew certain that this was Greybeard's wagon. The closer I drew to the vehicle, the greater my awe. A tall man with a flame-red beard leapt out of the back of the wagon, sprightly as a mountain goat, and welcomed me with an embrace. It was Greybeard but he was no longer grey. I stood, mystified. Like his wagon, he appeared newly minted and untroubled by the erosion of time. We spoke for a while and he showered my companions with love, offering them hay, fruits and vegetables to restore their strength. Red-bearded Greybeard inquired whether I had read the book he had given me and I told of how it had provided light and wisdom during my darkest hour. He nodded, knowingly. Greybeard retreated, briefly, to the interior of his wagon and returned with a spectacular sword within an ornate scabbard. Looking into my eyes with a gaze that penetrated deep into my soul, he spoke. "I am glad that you chose wisdom before strength and courage. Strength and courage are meaningless, if not dangerous, if unguided by wisdom and knowledge. Yet wisdom and knowledge often lead us to pain and grief if we have not the courage to pursue the right course and the strength to see our journey through." He handed the sword to me, only releasing his grip once he saw that his truth had resonated within the depths of my soul. It had. Destiny had been right about Greybeard. He was a man of wisdom and a man to be trusted. He knew what I must do, as did I. Greybeard offered some instruction on the proper wielding of my weapon although somehow, I presume through the reading of the book entrusted to my care, I already had vast knowledge on the subject. Movements and techniques came readily. Greybeard looked upon me with pride and satisfaction. We parted ways after a final embrace.

Returning to the bridge, I called out to the knight in black armor. "Guardian of the bridge, hear me now. I bear you no ill will but I assert that my companions and I shall cross yon bridge before this day is done." The knight drew his sword, an impressive blade, long and deadly and as black as the armor he wore. Though my armor was not its equal, nor my weapon likely as lethal, I knew my journey must either take me past this vile fiend or end with blood spilt upon the lifeless rock between us. The knight in black drew closer, offering up his final warning.

"You are unworthy to pass and, by my word, you shall not. Sacrifice the lame foal as an offering to my god and turn the other animals free so that they might return from whence they came and I shall consider granting you, and you alone, passage to the far side. Short of these terms, I offer no succor. Death or life? I caution you to consider carefully your next words." I was offended by the villain's loathsome offer. Sacrifice Silver Tail over the cliff to appease this dastard and his false god?! Never! I drew my own blade from its scabbard and it captured the light of the sun as I held it aloft and made my vow.

"I vow, here and now, that justice shall be done this day. Knight of the black armor, if you persist in your endeavor to bar our passage across this bridge then blood shall flow and moisten the aged stone of this mountain. I wish it were not so but you have afforded me no recourse but to engage in battle and let the fates decide, as they shall, who will carry the day!" The knight in black was the first to lash out. His armor seemed impregnable but its cumbersome weight restricted the warrior's movements and limited his mobility. I easily dodged his first few frenzied attacks and fended off the third with the steel of my sword. With each assault, my foe wearied, the afternoon sun taking its toll, until, eventually, the evil one fell to his knees and begged that I grant him mercy. The warmth of the sun had penetrated where my sword could not and victory was mine. "You yield now before me," said I, "but I shall not grant you the mercy you beg for unless you first agree to remove your armor and cast it over the edge of this cliff, much as you would have had me sacrifice my dear friend, Silver Tail. As this sacrifice may better appease the god of truth and justice, I shall, thereupon, let you leave in peace and we shall not spoil this rock with blood drawn in battle." The knight in black, still laboring for breath, set about removing his armor. Beneath the heavy black plate was no imposing character but a diminutive, frail, and bitter old man. With my conditions met, I fulfilled our agreement and granted him life. The mare, the foals, and I crossed the swaying bridge where we found peace and tranquility. The foals frolicked in the fields while the mare and I looked on. It was a good time. I knew joy. But my journey was not done.

As the sun dipped, once more, to kiss the horizon, I parted ways with my companions. I felt compelled to journey on. I did so without fear but not without anticipation of what lay ahead. This time, I welcomed the unknown.

Eventually, I came upon a cave, a breach in the wall of rock that towered above me. I was hesitant to enter. A single torch, held in a receptacle at the mouth of the cave, was the answer to my question. My path lay ahead. I entered the cave and descended into the unknown. My breathing grew labored as I struggled for air within the winding subterranean passages. I could feel my knees weakening and my vision seemed to blur as I continued on my way. I fell a number of times and had great difficulty returning to my feet; yet I did. I pressed onward. Eventually, the path began to climb again. I found myself crawling on my hands and knees to reach the terminus of this stone prison. I was greeted by a refreshing blast of cool air that invigorated me. It was dark. The moon was full and the stars glistened like jewels in the night sky. Awaiting me was a powerful horse with a mane and tail that shone with the brilliance of polished silver. I knew, at once, it was Silver Tail. But how could this be. As Greybeard had, in the course of several days, youthened; Silver Tail had matured from foal to sturdy stallion. Still with a slight limp, he approached and knelt beside me. I grabbed on to his glorious mane and pulled myself up until I lay draped across his back whereupon he stood and bore me forward to a field of tall grass set upon the edge of a rocky cliffside outcropping. Destiny, her white dress dancing in the breeze, stood there awaiting my arrival. She helped me off of Silver Tail's back and gently stroked the stallion's cheeks before he turned to walk away.

"A wonderful son, is he not," said Destiny, as she admired Silver Tail limping off into the night.

"Son? Whose son?"

"Yours, dear friend. Surely, you must have sensed it?"

"I felt a bond, but I did not understand. In fact, few of the events of these past few days make sense to me. I've been reluctant to ask but I was hoping that you might shed some light upon this journey and the road ahead. I have traveled far yet I feel little wiser for the miles I have covered and the trials I have endured."

"Oh, but you are so much wiser," Destiny responded, with a glint in her eye. "Wiser and a better man for the experience. You have lived well and so you must not be remorseful when I tell you that your journey is near an end. You have earned your rest and you shall know a peace like no other."

"I'm afraid I still don't understand. Destiny, please guide me."

"I have. And I shall." Destiny took my hand and led me through the field, the tall blades of grass gently swaying in the breeze, until we reached the edge of the cliff. "Look below and tell me what you see." I gazed out upon the moonlit scene and saw a beach below, the waves gently rolling up upon the shore."

"I see a beach. I see the moon and the stars," said I.

"And upon this beach, do you not see a man lying upon the sand?" responded Destiny. I strained my eyes but my vision was still blurred. "Here, let me help." Destiny gently stroked my cheek with her soft hand, much as she had caressed Silver Tail, and my clouded vision cleared. The pain left my knees, as well, and my lungs filled, once more, with clean and refreshing air.

"Yes! There's a man down there, naked as the day he was born. I see him, now."

"It is the day he was born. That man is you," replied Destiny, fully aware that her tale was beyond my comprehension. I stood in stunned silence.

"I'm afraid I don't understand," I meekly replied. Still holding my hand, Destiny led me back away from the cliff and we settled in the soft grass. She bade me to lay down and I did so, resting my head upon her lap as she ran her fingers lovingly through my hair, much as a mother might do with her child. She began to unravel the mystery and I listened intently.

"You are born on this day. Today. The man you see below is you, resting within the protective warmth of your mother's womb. I shall join you there, shortly, and try to offer comfort as I know the road ahead shall be troublesome and your birth a frightening shock. Shortly, you shall enter this world and see the light of your first day. You remember it now, do you not? An explosion of brilliant light? You were a baby and you were helpless. The world is unkind to the weak and will set upon you much like the band of marauders attacked you upon the beach. A mother's love is a shield and your mother was there to protect you from harm."

"The dragon?"

"Yes. She was lovely and fearless in defense of her child . . . you."

"Truly. She saved me; carried me over the cliff to safety; a trip I could not have made on my own."

"Of course not. She cared for you and she fed you. This is what mothers do."

"And what of the old man in the wagon," I ask.

"Ah, Greybeard, as you call him. He is your father. As a young child, you see him as impossibly old. You notice the wrinkles upon his face, the well-worn clothing he wears and the fading paint on his wagon. He, too, like your mother, seeks to protect and educate you. What you see as armor is so much more. But, for now, let us consider the gifts a father gives his son as the armor that will help him forge his path through life and protect him against the sinister influences of evil forces. More valuable than armor or sword was the Book of Knowledge provided by your father. Education is our light in the darkness. Your father was right when he spoke to you upon the mountain— power without knowledge is unwieldy and dangerous. You were not yet ready for the sword and you were well-served by the book.

As a curious child, you set out to explore the world. At first, it was scary and intimidating. You saw this in the dark forest. And then you came upon the faire. Fun and diversion. In your early childhood, you saw life like this. Everything seemed joyous and happy and you hadn't a care in the world. And then you came into your teen years. You will remember this period as the nighttime return to the faire. It was not as pretty as it once was, was it?"

"No," I replied. "It seemed a darker place, abounding with temptation and replete with characters of questionable motives. But, Giselle? Who was Lady Giselle?"

"You loved her, did you not?"

"I did."

"Your love was pure but the two of you were not meant to share a life. When you first looked upon Giselle, you saw her as those about you would have you see her—as a miserable wretch, a witch, an undesirable and disposable person. Your parents' teachings and the goodness of your own heart served you well and you quickly dispelled these false images and knew that you could not allow this innocent woman to be persecuted. And, at great risk to your own personal safety, you intervened and rescued Lady Giselle. Only then did you see her as she truly was; a lovely maiden. You were seeing the beauty within her heart."

"Yes, but who was she?"

"You won't understand, if I tell you."

"I might," I replied. "If this is to be the end of my journey, then I should like to know more." Destiny smiled.

"All right. Giselle, like yourself, was many things across many ages. As you discovered her, in this life, Giselle was a bullied teenager at her high school. She was frequently picked on and made fun of because she wasn't quite as pretty as the other girls and her parents couldn't afford to buy her the expensive clothes that many of her classmates wore. She was considering ending her life but you befriended her and helped to build her confidence. You were ridiculed by your classmates for associating with Giselle but you ignored their taunts and teasing and you stayed true to your friend. Giselle went on to medical school and eventually became a medical researcher. She created a vaccine that helped to end a terrible pandemic, saving millions of lives across the globe. She was hailed as a hero and honored by a grateful world—universities, roadways and bridges, and countless scholarship funds were named in her honor following her passing. During her life, she never married; instead, she devoted all of her energy to curing the sick."

"I . . . I don't understand," I muttered.

"I know. Before this life, Giselle was a frontier doctor. And before that, in yet another lifetime, she was a wandering medicine woman. Though she lived countless lives, she was always a healer. And through countless lives, you were there to defend her when she was vulnerable. Now, if I may," Destiny added with a wink.

"Yes, I'm sorry, Destiny. Please continue."

"Giselle's path diverged from your own and, in her absence, you felt lost. You lost confidence in yourself and grew fearful of your future. The stormy night where you found yourself lost in a forest. You remember it well, I am sure."

"I do. All too well."

"A friend was sent to guide you."

"The owl."

"Yes, the owl."

"Thank you for sending the messenger." Destiny was silent, for a moment, before eventually replying.

"I didn't. That help came from elsewhere." A slight smile came upon Destiny's face before she continued on, feeling no need to provide any more amplifying remarks. "At first, you were fearful of the owl. And then, wisely, you chose to open the pages of your book and then your fear was dispelled and you were better able to discern friend from foe and your superstitions faded as knowledge filled your head. You chose to follow the owl much as humans choose to follow their intuition or, as some might claim, a divine and guiding spirit. The spirit led you to a crossroads in your life."

"The chapel?"

"Yes. The procession you witnessed represented the many faiths and belief systems in this world. Each one, a source of refuge and inspiration to thousands. You looked on as the seekers in the chapel united with their faiths. These men and women found purpose and fulfilment in their lives through service to their deities. I know you wanted to join Giselle but that was never meant to be your path. While you provided much needed support during her youth, she would call upon a greater spirit to help inspire her during her challenging times as an adult. She never forgot you and she always loved you."

"I will always love her."

"We find love and inspiration in many places through our lives. Parents and siblings, friends, spouses, and through spiritual devotion. It's best to embrace love where we find it and never try to compare one against the other on the balances of life."

"You are very wise, Destiny. But, please, go on with your story."

"The chapel. Another spirit guides you and you followed it, as you should. An adult now, you continued your journey with renewed confidence. The mare you met and the three foals were your wife and children. You led them through the difficult path of life yet, oft times, you relied upon them as much as they relied upon you."

"I was wed to a horse? And what of Silver Tail?"

"You wed a woman; but she was different from you. In one life, she was a woman of a different color. In another, she hailed from foreign lands and was looked upon with suspicion by those inclined towards prejudice. You saw only the love and goodness within her heart. Your children were beautiful; all three of them. Silver Tail, as you call him, was a child born with a disability. You recognized his great inner strength and always saw him through the adoring eyes of a father. Your love helped bolster his confidence and your wisdom helped guide him through an unkind world. He lived his life forever grateful of the healing power of unconditional love.

And then you came upon the knight in black armor. He had a name and his name was Ignorance. He disliked your family because they were different. He felt that the world should conform to his uneducated views and he wished to irradicate anything and anyone who did not fit his paradigm. This presented you with an unenviable choice."

"It did. But, first, could you enlighten me on the second meeting with my father and why it was that he appeared so much younger than when we first met?" Destiny considered my question.

"Well, it depends on how you look at. In one sense, the older we get, the better we understand our parents and the more our relationship changes. We go from needy child and providing parent to mentor and protégé and then transition to a familial friendship and mutual respect until, one day, we become the caregiver and our parents find themselves in need of assistance. When you saw your father again, he was not the grownup towering above you but more of a friend and mentor. But who you saw was also a reflection of your father's spirit. Having the opportunity to teach you and prepare you for the coming battle brought out his youthful spirit and filled him with a renewed sense of purpose that took him back to his younger days. He had taught you how to learn and now it was his privilege to share his thoughts on right versus wrong and the need to fight for just causes. It was a lesson you were well-prepared to receive but one which would have confused you during your first meeting."

"I think I understand. Thank you."

"Yes. Of course. With sword in hand and guided by the knowledge you had acquired from the book and through your journeys, you overcame a formidable opponent and you secured a future for your family. In the end, Ignorance, with armor removed, showed himself for what he truly was—an insecure, insignificant and loathsome villain. You carried yourself honorably and your family enjoyed a good life thanks to your efforts. Alas, our time with family is all too short; is it not? Eventually, you grew older and feebler. Your venture through the cave, while not as terrifying as your night in the storm, was, no doubt, unnerving. You were living out your senior years and your health was failing you. Still, with most of your life behind you, you carried on with few regrets and less fear than might be expected. During your final days, your son was there to help carry you forward."

"Silver Tail?"

"Yes. You had provided for him a life that was beyond anything he might have hoped for and he was intent on returning the love and being by your side until the very end."

"And the end is now?"

"Almost. Do not fear." Destiny looked up into the night sky and then back over her right shoulder. I looked over and saw twelve unicorns approach. Their beautiful white coats appeared luminous against the backdrop of the night sky. They stood there, silently watching us. "I am Destiny, you see. And I have shown you your life. You will live a thousand lifetimes, each uniquely different yet each surprisingly similar. You will be born, live, and then pass on only to be born again. There are times when you will feel like certain situations are familiar. They are—you have lived them before. You have lived them with different names, wearing different clothes, and across the span of centuries. But each time, it is you. Your soul survives and travels with you into your next life. You can't begin to imagine all the great things you will do nor shall you ever remember all the incredible contributions you have made in the past. It is the way of things. But remember, through it all, I will be here with you, at your side. I will never abandon you and I will always love you. You shall be loved by many who know you and many you will never know. So, please be at peace as I let your fingers slip from my grasp and know that we shall meet again."

"Wait. Please. Just one moment." Destiny gently squeezed my hand, listening to my words. "The knights and dragons, ladies and enchantments, romance and battles—you imagined all that for me? You crafted this tale to teach me of my destiny?"

"No. This is how you see yourself, in every life you live. I think it's beautiful and it's been my great privilege to share these moments with you through your own thoughts and dreams."

"Thank you, Destiny."

"Travel in peace, brave knight." Destiny released my hand and slowly stood. With a tear in my eye, I turned to Destiny and thanked her, one last time. She smiled and I felt the peace she was describing. As she slowly backed away, never taking her eyes off of me, the unicorns approached.

"And what are the unicorns? What do they symbolize?" I asked. Destiny just laughed.

"They're just unicorns, silly."

The gentle creatures formed a circle about me, the wind tossing their manes about as the tall grass swayed beneath their hooves. The moon. The stars. The wind caressing the land. The waves gently rolling up upon the shore. Twelve unicorns faced me and bowed in unison. A beautiful wave of love warmed me, much as a blanket warms a newborn baby. I felt my body dematerializing and turning into energy and, in a flash, I was flying across the sky as a brilliant beam of light on a fantastic journey into the Great Beyond.

Laying naked upon the warm sand, an explosion of light blinds me as a brilliant beam of light sets the dark sky afire, briefly turning night into day as it ascends majestically into the heavens.

The Story Behind the Story

Where to start? Red Penguin Books sent out a tasking notice for submissions to an upcoming fantasy story anthology with a deadline of April 30, 2021. The anthology was to be called "Once Upon a Time…" and entries were limited to 5,000 words and were supposed to be reminiscent of the classic fairy tales of old and include familiar archetypes such as dragons and fairies, elves and royal personages, etc. It was stated that it was not intended as a children's book so the subjects could involve more adult themes, if desired. At first, I was very excited about this book as I have always loved fantasy movies, and I love Renaissance Faires and all things having to do with knights and legends. Unfortunately, I developed a very serious case of writer's block, and I just couldn't seem to get started on this project. I had a few false starts along the way until, finally, my time was nearly out. I completed this story only a couple days before the deadline, and I can't claim that I ever felt completely satisfied with it. Unfortunately, this was a painful and laborious process for me which was sad because I love the genre and I, initially, had high hopes that I might produce a really nice story for the anthology. As it was, there were plenty of submissions and my work was not selected for inclusion. I was more disappointed in my own effort on this endeavor than I was by the fact that my story didn't make the cut. However, I now offer it up for your consideration. You may be the judge. There were certainly elements of the story that I enjoyed and I did feel a connection to the overall theme. Also, there were elements that were inspired by my reading of the legends of romance and chivalry as well as a recurring dream I had as a younger man. That dream was of waking up in a field of tall grass near the edge of a cliff, the stars shining brightly above in the night sky. In the dream a group of unicorns approached me and formed a protective circle around me, looking down upon me with caring eyes. That's always where I woke up, and I always felt very peaceful afterwards. Perhaps in recognition of this childhood dream, while I was in college, I purchased a lovely painting of a unicorn in a strangely familiar scene, painted upon a piece of wood. It came with a little metal stand to display the art. The piece always reminded me of my amazing recurring unicorn dream. I knew I wanted to somehow incorporate elements of that into this story…and I did.

FIXING ME

(Written May 11, 2021)
Published by Red Penguin Books in "*Am I Overthinking This?: A Self-Help Essay Collection*" (June, 2021)

I describe a number of methods I used during my
youth, and to this day, to help keep myself moving
through life with hope and a positive attitude.

I look around and I see a world of seekers. Where there is need there are those who seek to profit by delivering a solution. In many instances, the help you pay for may be the help you need—counseling services, medical advice, self-help books, or perhaps an array of carefully positioned crystals and candles. It's not my intent to discourage anyone from spending money on such things and they may well be a solid first step on the road to personal recovery. With that said, I would caution that there are countless "snake oil salesmen" out there who are all too happy to take your money and whose remedies will fall far short of what they claim. Mental health is not simple and there are few easy fixes. If I have learned one thing in life, it's that you are the ONLY person who can fix you. No matter what avenue you choose to pursue, the responsibility for action and the power to effect a change will always rest squarely on your shoulders. Don't let anyone tell you otherwise. I shall elaborate and I'll offer a few techniques I used, across the years, to help myself. I'll also toss out a few ideas regarding living a fulfilling life.

I suppose I should have put the disclaimer up front but you'll just have to settle for paragraph two. There are a great many wonderful professionals out there—doctors and counselors—who can and do help us through our difficult times. And then they bill us. Many of us are blessed with great friends and family members who, likewise, are often a source of wisdom and useful solutions. I encourage everyone to surround themselves with positive people who share their valuable life lessons and listen, with empathy, to our concerns. All of this is healthy and good. I'll even give a nod to self-help books. I believe they have helped many but I'm always a little uneasy about the notion of cashing in on people's misery. But that's my problem, not yours. I firmly believe that the best solutions are the ones we develop ourselves. We are all unique individuals and the notion that any "one size fits all" solution is going to save the day seems, at least to me, highly unlikely. With that said, I'll continue on to paragraph three and beyond where I'll discuss some of the very useful methods I used to pull myself out of a horrible slump. I still employ many of these methods, some forty years later. Before I end this paragraph, I'd like to repeat my previous words for emphasis: "I still employ many of these methods, some forty years later." Yup. I neglected to mention this one small point—you are never "fixed". We are, always and forever, a work in progress. If you want to toss your hands in the air and buy that self-help book now, I wouldn't blame you. But if that book tells you anything different, you've just wasted $19.95. I'll say it again—we are never fixed. The good news is, we are never truly broken. We always need to be monitoring and self-correcting. Life is a process and it takes work, each and every day. We need to invest in ourselves and do so continually. The goal is always minor course corrections and not those major, last minute, aggressive turns to miss the iceberg. Look ahead, make small corrections, and sail smoothly through life. It works. Most of the time.

In my early to mid-teen years, I found myself in a pretty awful place. I was feeling terribly depressed; I had lost nearly all self-confidence; and I felt I had little to look forward to. To be honest, I really didn't care whether or not I lived to see the next day but I wasn't quite to the point of taking action to keep the sun from rising. I gloss over the details in my published memoir (no, you don't have to buy it but you might enjoy the story) and there's no need to elaborate here. Suffice it to say that I was feeling pretty broken. Without counselors, doctors, attentive friends, or self-help books, I set about righting what was wrong. A lovely stranger was my inspiration. Where I had found it difficult to set about changing my life for myself, I readily went about tackling my greatest challenges for another—each success dedicated to the beautiful stranger who I wondered if I would ever see again. Her name was Valerie. My memoir tells that story but what I wish to focus on here are a few of the actions I took to fix my troubled world.

INTROSPECTION. Our world is loud. Distractions abound and we are fed a constant diet of "You're not good enough but, IF you do this or that, you will be." And then we're informed that "this" and "that" are currently on sale for 30% off. The most important component of healing is introspection. We need to understand who we truly are. I grow weary of all the talk of "personal branding" and creating your persona. Leave the branding for breakfast cereals and persona creation to actors and street performers. Be authentic. Be yourself. Understand who you are at the core—the "real you." You may see things you don't like. That's okay. There's time enough to work on that. However, you might discover that you like yourself more than you realized. So, what did I do? To start with, I found my special place and I turned down the volume on life's distractions. I increased visits to my local park and spent countless hours standing at the shoreline. Looking out upon the water, with just the gulls, the waves, and the wind serenading me, I was able to drift off into another world and contemplate life. This unstructured time was incredibly valuable for me. For some, meditation may serve a similar purpose. My time at the park was certainly meditative. It's best if you can ignore the clock and just let your thoughts travel where they will. If they start to head to dark places, endeavor to pull them back into the light. Try not to be a slave to the clock—you are well worth the time. Like most aspects of mental health maintenance, this is not a "one and done" exercise. We should always find time to spend with ourselves—I can't stress enough how important this is. You might just make peace with yourself—and therein gain a powerful ally. If your life is spent racing from one event to the next, you're missing something. Make time for you. Some people use their activities as an excuse to avoid uneasy quiet time alone with their thoughts. That's one way to get through life. I don't think it's the best way.

DIARY/JOURNAL. I tend to use the terms "diary" and "journal" interchangeably. You can discuss subtle nuances with lexicographers; I'll move on. On August 31, 1982, I began my Diary. Just prior to this, I had written a heartfelt story relating the significant events of my recent family vacation to Europe and centered around my feelings for the woman who inspired me on that trip. While the story described the relevant events of the trip, it was also filled with some pretty deep introspective thought—much of it self-critiquing. Writing that story was surprisingly therapeutic. I immediately recognized the value and, the day after its completion, logged my first-ever diary entry in a Marble Composition Notebook. I was never sure whether or not I would continue journaling. Over 10,000 pages later, I'm glad that I did. Diaries, or journals, continue the process of introspection. Some people keep journals to remember dates and events. Some people use journals to document "the story of their lives" so that they might, someday, share these tales with their children or grandchildren. Some people keep journals to provide source material for future books. All of these are wonderful reasons to write. Here's the best reason—do it for yourself. There's a reason why most of my early diary volumes had ominous messages on the cover pages warning would-be readers to go no farther. Sure, there was a privacy concern but, then again, I've always been pretty brave about sharing what's on my mind. I think, more than anything else, I didn't want my thoughts and reflections to be tainted by some notion that I was writing for an audience. As pure as your intentions may be, I think there's a tendency to selectively choose our words if we feel we are writing for others. If your thoughts are dark—write darkly. If you are ashamed, express that shame. If you were a fool, revel in your own stupidity within the protective pages of your diary. Trust me, you'll appreciate all of this, in future years, when you read what you've written. We are not perfect. Let your imperfections dance freely upon the pages of your diary. I often look back and find inspiration from the struggling young man who penned words into the pages of my diaries, many decades ago. He was better than he thought he was. I understand that now. Frequency? Make it a daily thing . . . or twice weekly. Bottom line, make a commitment and stick with it. Writing and reflection takes time and it's important that you prioritize your daily schedule to make that time available. When I first began my diary, I set a mandatory requirement for two pages a day. That's a lot of writing for a teen, especially on a school night. I knew that if I didn't force myself to write, I would risk, eventually, scrapping the whole notion of keeping a diary. Don't scrap it. It's too valuable. When I began Volume II of my diary, I modified my plan. I no longer forced myself to write two pages each day, a difficult task when you simply have little to say and less time to say it. However, I still mandated a daily entry of unspecified length. I was intent on not letting this valuable tool fade away. Eventually, over time, I dropped the requirement to write each day but, despite this, my diary lives on. I might only write once a week yet, on occasions, my entries will be over twenty pages long. It depends on where my head's at. My diary is a conversation with myself and I usually know when these conversations need to take place. No matter what the interval, it's critically important that you reflect and you write. Remember, it's for you. With that said, stay disciplined and share your thoughts, hopes, and dreams. You'll be glad that you did. I am always going back to re-read old diary volumes and I am incredibly thankful that I have my diary.

IN WITH THE GOOD—PSYCH CALENDAR. You'll hear it a lot—"Keep a positive attitude." This is good advice which you shouldn't have to pay to hear. I'll speak more later about "attitude." Before the days of gimmicky daily quotes and memes about positivity, there were a multitude of "home remedies." One of my favorite home remedies was my "Psych Calendar." The idea came to me during one of my periods of introspection (Paragraph 4). Now that I was actively keeping a diary (Paragraph 5), I had a precise chronology of special events—the dates and times they occurred and the significance they had in my life. With this fabulous resource in hand, there was a natural progression to the tool I discuss in this paragraph (Paragraph 6). I purchased a small pocket calendar (initially) and started making notes on each day of the upcoming year that referenced some special and memorable anniversary. These were personal events, by and large, and not major historical happenings. However, you can put anything you like on your personal "Psych Calendar," so long as it's inspirational to you. The ultimate goal is to find positivity in each and every day. With time, you'll find the "white space" disappearing, and more and more days will share memorable moments with the past. Eventually, I graduated from encoded numbers on a pocket calendar to a printed document with each day listed along with a chronological recounting of memorable "psych" anniversaries associated with the day. I often check my Psych Calendar in the morning. It's hard to have a bad day when there's some magical anniversary associated with the date. And, if the day is blank, consider it a golden opportunity to make some history . . . right now . . . today. And thus, today may serve to inspire you next year, and in years to come.

OUT WITH THE BAD—"TV LOG" AND "BATTLE LOG". We just got done talking about thinking positively. That's important. However, another key aspect of fixing ourselves is doing the actual hard work of FIXING ourselves. That involves breaking bad habits, overcoming addictions, and obliterating our excuses for not making changes that we know are needed. These negative influences are unique to each individual so I'd ask that you read this paragraph with an open mind and extrapolate to keep the advice relevant to your own situation.

Before there were any cell phones or computers, we had television. While I wouldn't wish to condemn TV entirely, it did become evidently clear to me that spending countless hours staring at a glowing screen was not conducive to my mental well-being. Beyond the mindless, near vegetative, state the device lulled me into, I had concerns about the impact on my eyes. My immediate concern was keeping my eyes in good shape for baseball. Hitting a fastball becomes exponentially more difficult if you can't see the darn thing coming at you. Perhaps more important than baseball, I knew my life-long dream of flying airplanes required healthy eyes. For military flying, especially, very few waivers were granted if you weren't 20/20 or if you had any anomalies associated with your vision. Beyond the practical medical implications, I was also convinced that my mind was better served by reading, writing, going out for walks, drawing, or pretty much anything other than lazily watching television. My plan of attack? I would create a TV Log. I limited myself to ten hours of television a week and I logged every minute spent watching TV as well as what shows I was watching. I included video game time, as well. I loved playing games on my snazzy Atari Game System but I was wise enough, even at that young age, to know I had to put some limits on what we now call "screen time." I didn't need my parents to do that for me. Going back to my earlier statement—you will always have better buy-in to a self-help measure if you are its author. Always.

My "Battle Log" had a similar purpose. It morphed over the years but the concept remained the same—track good and bad habits; reward the good and penalize the bad. I would add points and subtract points from a weekly score and, if I had a positive score, I would move a game piece along a map (I called these long self-help campaigns "War Games"). Understanding that we have good days and bad days, there was usually plenty of opportunity within a week to make up for a bad day or two. The items that I tracked evolved over time to meet my current needs but things like television time, reading hours, exercise goal completion, diary entries completed, and the like, formed a part of the score tabulation. You don't need to have "battles" and "wars" to track progress toward goals. You can plant virtual flowers in a garden or visualize your progress in any way you choose. The key element is that you hold yourself accountable. I recommend keeping score with a pen and not a pencil (wink, wink). Own your recovery—it's your number one most important job. You can't effectively help others until you fix yourself.

HEALTHY LIVING. Yes. Do it. I'm not always great about it but, as I mentioned, life is a process and I've never given up. For me, the key elements of healthy living (beyond just the mental aspects) involve getting regular exercise and eating healthy. If you are sitting on a couch, binging on gallons of chocolate chip ice cream, and wondering why you aren't finding the joy in life; I can offer you a few reliable pieces of advice. One, get off the couch. Two, scratch ice cream off the shopping list. There's lots of great information out there about healthy diets and the benefit of exercise. I won't try to compete with that. I do know, unequivocally, that getting fresh air and exercising your muscles is good for both mind and body. Whenever I'm in the dumps, I just go out for a walk and, voila, I'm almost always in a better state of mind when I return. Some people have medical issues that make weight loss nearly impossible. That's a tough situation and may require a doctor's care and close observation. For many of us, it's simply just a matter of math. Calories consumed should equal or be less than calories burned. If I want that extra slice of pizza for dinner tonight then I had best put in another 30 minutes of workout time in the morning. It will probably come as no surprise to you, based on what you've just read, that I have a weight log and an exercise log. I record and graph my daily weight and I track my exercise and graph my run times. You don't need to be an organizational nut case like me to effect change but you do need to be aware. There are some pretty cool "apps" (applications) available for smart phones that help you track your daily calorie intake and they can even work in conjunction with walk/run tracking apps to let you know exactly how many calories you have remaining for food. Entering calorie intake data can be a pain —GOOD! Consider this a bonus as it helps incentivize you to eat less. The app I use has no associated subscription fee and, despite my poking fun at it, actually works pretty well. Watch yourself and steer clear of harsh fad diets. You'll earn that slice of chocolate cake, soon enough. Enjoy it! Life is about balance and calories consumed versus calories burned constitutes one of the very literal ways we balance our lives. Remember, diets don't have to be painful and neither does exercise. Find the right balance for you and stick with your plan.

MAKE THE RIGHT KINDS OF FRIENDS. There are a million different definitions of the word "friend." Anyone who says they have more than a hundred friends is using a different definition than me. I'm not going to tell you how to bin people in your life (for starters, I don't believe in putting people into boxes) but I will say that it's very useful to have a few close friends who truly know you and appreciate you for who you are, unconditionally and without expectations. You should strive to be that kind of friend, too. In my estimation, it's impossible to have that kind of relationship with more than a handful of people. Feel free to prove me wrong. Growing a network of friendly, well-intentioned acquaintances (some who may, one day, become real friends) is perfectly fine and is, often times, very useful. However, take care not to confuse acquaintances with true friends. True friends don't come around very often and they are a precious gift. They will help to elevate you and they'll help to keep you out of trouble. Well, most of the time. Look out for their welfare. True friendships always work both ways.

GRATITUDE. Find reasons to be grateful. You won't have to look far. Keeping things in perspective and keeping a positive attitude are key elements to making the most of life. I've been through some rough times but I'm always cognizant of the fact that there are, without even a shred of doubt, countless other people in this world experiencing much worse. All you have to do is look through the darker chapters of history and you'll find people who have suffered immeasurably and yet, somehow, managed to overcome adversity, continuing on to live successful lives. It doesn't mean that they blotted out the pain, or banished the memories of lost loved ones, but it does mean that they refused to let tragedy define them. I've had friends who have assured me that no one in this world could ever understand the pain they are going through. While I do my best to keep the empathy light turned on, I must admit it's often challenging to refrain from unleashing a salvo of classic cliches like "Nonsense! That's nothing but a bunch of self-pitying dribble." I can't slap you—that would be an assault. So, slap yourself when you find you are drifting down the river of victimization without a paddle. There's a waterfall at the other end. Trust me; there is. I realize it may be unhelpful to suggest you "snap out of it" and I certainly haven't walked a mile in your shoes but, for all that, I understand that what we need most is not sympathy for our plight (as significant as it may be) but rather encouragement to overcome our challenges and live our lives fully. When I get down, I go for a walk and admire the beauty around me. I marvel at the magnificence of the world. You don't need palm trees and sand to find nature's magnificence. Whether it's pigeons in the park, dandelions sneaking up through a crack in the sidewalk, or a spectacular cloud formation; there's always something out there that's worth stopping to admire. In our busy days, we often fail to do so. Bottom line, start each day with hope and seek out the beautiful side of life—caring people, nature, music, or whatever floats your boat. If today was a washout, try again tomorrow. You will have better days. Be thankful for what you have today.

FAITH. Maybe not mandatory but it sure helps. It helps to believe in something. I've met people who have told me that they don't believe in anything. After speaking with them, I came to understand that what they meant is that they don't believe in a deity governing our destiny upon this planet but, in my estimation, they still believed in something. Regardless of one's formal proclamation of religious or spiritual affiliation, I feel it's essential to have some form of moral compass. It seems it would be difficult to exist as a functioning member of any society without one. Beyond possessing a moral compass and a desire not to randomly break local, state, and federal laws, I think we find great strength and purpose in our beliefs. Religious beliefs have evolved over the ages and they will continue to do so. For all that, I know that many have looked to their faith for the strength to get them through the darkest times. I am no different. While it may seem heretical to suggest that the faithful might choose from a menu of options best suiting their needs, I do believe there has to be some element of buy-in or else our "faith" becomes a façade—we are card carrying members of a social club and not true practitioners of our faith. And that, ultimately, leads to trouble. My intent, herein, is not to offer a how-to checklist on selecting religion but to suggest that we must listen to our hearts, or to the voice of God, and settle upon a belief system that meshes with who we are. I also believe we need to respect others' choices where it comes to faith. We've seen too many awful instances throughout history of the divisive and dangerous power of religion when harnessed by those who are driven by less than holy motives. Our religion, or belief system, should give us the courage to live morally and with conviction; it should not tear us apart and make us feel unworthy of the air we breathe. There's a line from the play "Man of La Mancha" that comes to mind.

Put on trial by a group of fellow prisoners, Miguel de Cervantes states "I have never had the courage to believe in nothing." I do think it's easier, in our lives, if we believe we've got somebody bigger than us in our corner, rooting for us as we struggle through our daily existence. Whether you believe in a beautiful stranger, angels up in Heaven, or a divine God looking out from above (or all three), please try to find that undying connection that will help you feel centered and full of purpose. Only you will know what that means. We are all unique. Reflect upon that relationship. Write about that relationship. If you're comfortable in doing so, share it with your friends—they will appreciate you for your faith even though it may differ from their own. Real friends are good like that. In short, find the strength that faith affords us and let it be your shield in dark times and your inspiration to contribute to "the greater good" throughout your life.

I humbly submit my thoughts for your consideration. My recovery was my own. Perhaps that's why it's been so enduring. I've had multiple highs and lows over the years but I've never felt the same sense of hopelessness that I once knew. It's a fight. It's not easy. Seek help where you need it and welcome advice where it is offered but never forget that, ultimately, only you can fix you. I learned that long ago and it served me well. I hope some of this helps; I truly do. I wish you all the best—YOU MATTER.

The Story Behind the Story

As per the usual Red Penguin Collection anthology timing, the next piece was due two weeks after my ill-fated fantasy story and offered an opportunity for redemption, of sorts. The anthology, entitled "Am I Overthinking This?—A Self-Help Essay Collection" sought non-fiction essays aimed at providing readers with the self-help tools they needed "to help overcome the everyday mental and emotional obstacles of life." I certainly was no stranger to working my way out of periods of depression and doubt, and I knew I had advice to provide. Perhaps my greatest challenge here was not saying too much. The trick was finding some key elements that helped me along my journey and then organizing them in a way that made sense and would translate well for readers who were seriously looking for some tips to help improve their daily lives. My favorite writing topics are always those that I feel carry with them some inspirational value or can bring a laugh or a smile on a dark day. As such, I was excited about this opportunity, and I was happy to hear that "Fixing Me" was accepted for inclusion in the upcoming anthology.

LAST CARD, FIRST KISS

(Written May 27, 2021)
Published by Red Penguin Books in *"Ernest Lived and Other Historical
Fiction Short Stories"* (June, 2021)

*In the Bicentennial year, a young boy, in his quest to
complete his baseball card collection, finds an
intriguing ally.*

   The nation prepared for the biggest party that anyone could ever remember and, throughout the spring and into the summer, every storefront, school building, and home was draped in a patriotic mantle of red, white and blue. It seemed as if the entire focus of the school year was to build toward a crescendo of American pride and instill "The Spirit of '76" indelibly in our hearts. Unaware of the fiscal challenges our state and city were facing, we kids were all too happy to sign on as willing volunteers for countless Bicentennial themed plays, dance and ice shows, and a pretty impressive fund drive to finance a class trip to "The City of Brotherly Love," better known as Philadelphia, Pennsylvania. We designed and mass produced four silk-screened T-shirt options and were peddling them, at every opportunity, to parents, friends, and anyone with half a heart who seemed sympathetic to our plight. It was an exciting year by all accounts and one of the more memorable periods of my childhood. It may seem silly now, but my focus wasn't on the Bicentennial at all, it was on card number 600. I barely noticed Sophie. These many years later, it is she and not the card that I remember most.

   I'd been an avid baseball card collector as far back as I could remember. My dad bought me my first pack of cards—ten cards and a stick of chewing gum which was removed so I wouldn't choke on it. I created countless games with my cards that continued into the night inside my flashlight-illuminated bed tent. With an increase in allowance and some extra funds earned by assisting a neighbor with his paper route, I expanded my collection over the coming years. I also learned the fine art of card games—not the kind you're probably thinking of but those wonderous tests of dexterity and skill that all boys quickly learned on the playground. Card flipping, card scaling, and, occasionally, the rare gentlemanly card trade. And then there was the legendary "scramble," the Holy Grail of rapid card acquisition. By 1974, I was seeking out my favorite players—cards that, for some reason, seemed as difficult to find in store-bought packs as a golden ticket for Willy Wonka's chocolate factory. Friends were hesitant to part with these cards and the chance of any all-stars actually making their way into a scaling competition was close to nil. In 1975, I made my first concerted effort to acquire the entire series. I failed miserably. 1976 would be my year—I was sure of it.

The 1976 Topps Baseball Card set was comprised of 660 cards. For the first time, I created a card checklist. I pulled out several sheets of ruled loose-leaf paper from my school three-ring binder and wrote the numbers one through six-hundred and sixty inside the margin. Each baseball card had a distinct number and, if I could get all 660 cards, I would finally complete a childhood life goal. College and a job were a world away. My profession, and life passion, was baseball card collecting. Allowance money, birthday gift requests, and any additional funds I could acquire, were entirely allocated to card acquisition. This would be the year I finally collected the elusive complete set of Topps cards.

The card collecting season started off well—it seemed like every pack I bought was filled with new cards. On Sunday mornings, I would accompany my father to the local card shop where he would pick up a copy of the Sunday New York Times while I exchanged my weekly allowance money for a large pack of baseball cards. Sometimes, we'd grab some pastries for breakfast at the bakery next door. While Dad was poaching the eggs and Mom was preparing the rest of our Sunday breakfast, I was eagerly opening and reviewing my latest card acquisitions. It was several weeks before I collected my first "doubles." I wasn't disappointed, at all. Doubles and triples were a necessary element in the grand strategy of card circulation. These extra cards would be used to entice classmates into card game competitions. The big-name players would have to be risked for comparable gains but the pre-game bargaining always began with the poor unknown "John Does" of the baseball world—utility players whose names would largely be forgotten by history and whose fan base usually consisted of their mothers and wives. The wives were questionable. Fathers just shook their heads in disappointment, admitting to their wives that med school might actually have been a better option for Johnny.

Flapper and the Captain

As the season wore on, my card checklist was filling up nicely. Unfortunately, so was my roster of triple, quadruple, quintuple, sextuple, septuple, and octuple cards. I used these burdensome extras for practice scaling. It was important that I hone my skills. Some kids used their extra cards to adorn the spokes of their bicycle wheels. Depending on the number of cards, the acoustics varied from roulette wheel to motorcycle engine roar. Faster pedaling naturally yielded more impressive sound effects. I never used my cards for such things—that was childish. Instead, I practiced round after round of scaling at home. Scaling? Well, it's kind of like horseshoes but with cards. With a flick of the wrist, you frisbee your card toward a wall. The card closest to the wall wins. In competition, you could either scale one card against another or toss a number of cards, the closest card entitling the winner to collect and keep all cards used in competition. The real trick was to toss the coveted "leaner." If you skipped the card off the floor, just right, it would pop up and lean against the wall. If your competitor also tossed a leaner, then whichever card was most flush against the wall would take the prize. Card "flipping" involved less skill and more chance. Both competitors would put a spin on their card so that it flipped, end over end, along the long edge of the card, until it reached the ground, landing on either heads (the photo side) or tails (player statistics on the reverse side). One player would flip first and the second would try to match the toss. If matched, both cards were forfeited to the second to toss. Unless you were really skilled at timing card rotations, this competition was more of a 50/50 game of chance, much like a coin toss. I stayed away from flipping unless my opponent was dead set against trying to match my skill at card scaling. I won a lot of cards on the playground and in the hallways of my school. I must admit, several friends grew a little frustrated as I became extremely selective about what cards I would scale against. Sorry, fellas; it's just business. Through shrewd negotiations and a steady hand, I began filling the gaps in my card checklist. My first goal was to collect all the New York Mets players. This was no easy task. Living on Long Island, everyone wanted the complete Mets team. Bob Apodaca, Mike Phillips, or Hank Webb all made for reasonable negotiations. If you were looking for the likes of Bud Harrelson, Dave Kingman, or Ed Kranepool, you had better be prepared to bring something special to the table, unless you were going up against the uninitiated; a handful of kids who just wanted to be part of the scene but who really knew very little about

either baseball or baseball cards. And then there was the grand prize—
the card we all wanted and that nobody wanted to part with—Topps
card number 600, Tom Seaver. Tom Seaver, or "Tom Terrific," as we
knew him, had led the '69 Mets to their miraculous World Series
victory and was about as popular as any New York Mets player ever
was. Even kids with doubles or triples were unlikely to ever put Tom
Terrific into the pot. With school nearing an end, I feared card acquisition would become extremely difficult over the summer. I knew I'd have
a few get-togethers with friends but the mass exodus of kids to their
various summer camps and vacations would decimate the trading
community. Things seemed a bit grim until I heard a rumor that there
was going to be a massive "scramble" during our last recess period of
the school year. This was exactly the break I was looking for! With only
six cards left to acquire, I had visions of completing my collection
during one fateful event.

The scramble. Few things cold excite the inner barbarian in a
school boy as much as hearing that fateful word, "SCRAMBLE!"
shouted on the school yard. The would-be scrambler would chum the
waters during the course of the week to ensure the sharks were hungry
and circling. Word spread from mouth to mouth that a scramble was
coming. While some scrambles were completely unannounced, the
sheer violence and destruction of an anticipated scramble was something the perpetrators usually hoped to orchestrate. If the scrambler
tossed anything less than two dozen cards into the air, he would be
forever shamed. The best scrambles involved at least a hundred cards.
While the baseball cards were still highlighted against the sky, anyone
within the vicinity would madly dive toward the projected landing spots
and fight, tooth and nail, for every piece of $2^{1/2}$ by $3^{1/2}$-inch cardboard
they could get their hands on. It was not unusual for cards to be torn in
half; a far better outcome than the cuts, bruises, and concussive head
injuries that often resulted.

On the appointed day, students nervously looked out the windows
of their classrooms, carefully watching the sky. Rain was in the forecast;
but when? It was a hot and muggy June day and the heat inside the
classroom was stifling. The open windows did little to alleviate the
humid and cruelly lifeless air inside the room. If it rained during the
lunch recess, all was lost. The fidgeting and notebook doodling began
well before the morning classes were due to end. As I followed my class
to the cafeteria, I felt hopeful that things were going to work out. I

walked through the lunch line and requested doubles on the SpaghettiOs; it would cost me two ticket punches on my meal card but I loved SpaghettiOs and Mom would understand. A slice of buttered Italian bread and a small carton of chocolate milk accompanied my pasta feast. I dropped an extra ten cents for a couple pretzel rods. I'd need the extra fuel if I was going to survive the upcoming battle royale. On the lunch line, my classmate, Sophie, asked if I could spare a nickel for a pretzel rod. Ugh! I found a nickel in my coin purse and gave it to Sophie, being careful not to accidentally make contact with her hand. Sophie smiled and thanked me. Anything beyond a gruff "thank you" was sure to gain attention and, sure enough, several classmates poked fun at me, imitating Sophie's slightly too affectionate words of appreciation and making kissing sounds. How embarrassing.

I raced over to my usual lunch table and made quick work of my meal. Next to me, Jimmy quickly devoured his bologna sandwich but tossed the rest of his lunch in the large, gray trash bin. What would his mother say? She'd never know. We understood—chewing up twenty-five grapes would burn time we could ill-afford to lose. We all stood at the same time—no kid wanted to be the last one outdoors and risk missing the scramble.

Once outside, we kept our eyes peeled. There were various rumors regarding who was going to be orchestrating the scramble but no one seemed to know for sure. Friend and foe alike kept in close proximity to the center of the playground, carefully watching for any signs that something was brewing. A few kids grabbed a ball and tried to get a game of kickball started but, between the heat and the rumored scramble, almost nobody seemed interested in playing. My friend, Michael, was the first to notice Gary Schwartz moving toward the pitcher's mound with a small package concealed close to his chest. Michael looked at me and pointed over toward Gary. I nodded but said nothing. We both started working our way towards the center of the kickball field. It wasn't long before others noticed and, soon, kids were gathering like a flock of geese on a lake. Someone shouted out, "Schwartz is about to do a scramble!" and the mad rush began. A crowd of excited boys jockeyed for a position close to the center of the huddle. Schwartz began a countdown. "Ten, nine, eight, seven." Our hearts were racing and the pushing and shoving intensified. The recess monitor, Mrs. Turkeyhill, began to make her way over. Schwartz had better scramble soon, I thought, before Mrs. Turkeyhill breaks the whole thing up.

Schwartz seemed unphased as he continued his countdown. "Six, five, four, three, two." Someone got shoved to the pavement and I took an elbow to my ribs. I was too focused on Schwartz to even notice or think about reciprocation. "One!" Schwartz lifted his hands away from his chest—nothing. "Psych! You're all a bunch of losers!" What just happened?! Most of us wanted to shout obscenities at that jerk, Schwartz, but with Mrs. Turkeyhill now within earshot, it wasn't worth the risk. Mrs. Turkeyhill approached and asked what was going on. One of the kids lied, saying that we were all there to check on our classmate who had fallen on the pavement and scraped up his knee. Odds are, he's the kid who pushed him. What a disappointment. I sighed deeply.

As we began to disperse, Charlie Jenkins exclaimed, ecstatically, "Holy moly! Look over there. It's Kennedy!" We all looked and saw Barry Kennedy walking towards the center of the grassy field with a large shoebox in his arms. Schwartz was a diversion! Brilliant! Feeling like I had a new lease on life, I sprinted at full speed towards the grassy field, some eighty yards away. Like a thundering herd of buffalo, the stampede was on. Several kids fell and were trampled in the chaotic rush. Mrs. Turkeyhill, still attending to the scraped knee of the hapless victim of the fake out scramble, had lost total control of her playground.

Barry Kennedy was a pretty rough character. He was a kid of few words and his silence fueled rumors that ranged from smoking a pack of cigarettes after school each day to having killed a man in Cincinnati over a pool game. Today, none of that mattered. Kennedy wasn't into theatrics and he certainly wasn't going to waste ten of his allotted twenty daily words on a countdown. He graced us with two, which I shall not repeat in mixed company. Then, just like that, he punted the shoebox high into the air. It's a wonder he didn't break his foot—that box was completely packed with baseball cards. The sky darkened beneath an enormous cloud of cardboard. It was the most beautiful thing I'd ever seen. I dove into the boiling mass of frenzied kids and frantically fought for my share of the spoils. Kick to the head, elbow to the jaw, fingers crushed; I lost track of the bangs and blows my body suffered. Casualties were climbing and much blood was spilt. Mrs. Turkeyhill looked on in horror, her job potentially on the line. I felt someone's hand trying to pry my fingers open but I fought to maintain possession of my cards and pulled them close to my chest. I rolled over the top of several other kids to separate myself from the card thief and then continued my collection efforts until the grass was clear of cards. Limping away, I finally took stock of my war booty. Amidst the feeding frenzy, I had managed to accumulate seventy-two cards. This was a tremendous success. Better yet, I wasn't one of the dozen kids who had to be referred to the school nurse.

With the clanging of a handbell, Mrs. Turkeyhill signaled the end of lunch recess. Looking through my cards, I hardly noticed that our time had been cut short—Mrs. Turkeyhill deciding an early retreat to the Teacher's Lounge was in her best interest. I was pleased with the haul but the absence of a Tom Seaver card, while expected, was still a disappointment. I confided in my friend Michael who told me that he had heard Harvey Mulligan was offering to sell some hard-to-find cards. He suggested I give that a try. Mulligan had a different teacher and wasn't exactly a friend so I knew my best chance at finding him was after school.

The next few hours of class were excruciating. It was hot and most of us had mentally begun our summer break a week and a half ago. I anxiously watched the clock. We knew the teachers were watching, too. All curriculum-based learning was complete and teachers were filling the time with reading and writing exercises along with some simple arts and crafts projects. Next week was our final week of school and consisted of two half days of class and then two hours on Wednesday where we would be handed our congratulations letters for surviving another year of school. The big kids would have their graduation ceremony later that morning.

The bell eventually rang and I was off like a shot. I had to find Mulligan before he left the school grounds. I anxiously paced along the sidewalk in front of the building, rapidly shifting my focus between the two most probable exit doors. I didn't have to wait long. I spotted Harvey Mulligan coming out of the south door. He was walking with Keith Grosser. Ugh! Keith was a jerk and a bit of a bully but I was desperate and was undeterred by the possibility of an unpleasant verbal altercation with Grosser. I was much faster than Grosser so I could always escape the situation if things went badly. Fortunately, Grosser was civil and Mulligan seemed interested in a deal. I knew Harvey Mulligan was a shrewd trader so I didn't even try to offer up any John Does. Rather than offering up any all-stars, right off the bat, I asked if there were any cards he needed. Of course not. His Dad had bought him two complete boxed sets of the Topps collection. One set was to remain sealed and the other was for trading . . . or selling. Mulligan's Dad was some super rich businessman and his son inherited his love for maximizing profit by sticking it to his classmates for anything with market value to an elementary school kid. He had sold puff stickers to the girls and hand-held propeller fans to nearly all of us. As a last-ditch effort, I offered up Hank Aaron, Rod Carew, and Pete Rose. I anxiously awaited Mulligan's response and he was in no hurry to provide one.

"Nah, I already have plenty of those," Mulligan replied. "But here's what I'll do; because I like you, I'm going to give you a special, one-time, ultra-deal on the Tom Seaver card." I could already feel my stomach muscles tightening; I knew the gut punch was only seconds away.

"What kinda deal are we talking?" I nervously replied.

"Well, my dad says Tom Seaver is a sure bet for the Hall of Fame and that his card will probably be worth hundreds of dollars in no time." I should have worn a bulletproof vest to this negotiation. I knew Tom Seaver was going to be in the Hall of Fame, too, but I had no notion of how that might affect a card's value. Apparently, Mulligan did, or at least he acted like he did. The problem was, I didn't know the difference.

"I don't have hundreds of dollars."

"You don't? Sorry, Dude. I'll bet your dad does. Besides, like I said, I'm going to cut you a special friend deal. I'll sell you the card for just $50. Now that's a steal in anyone's book."

"Fifty dollars?! Are you kidding me?" The only thing Mulligan was missing was the plaid blazer of a used car salesman. I was keenly aware that he was carefully watching my facial expressions for any sign of weakness. As if the situation wasn't already uncomfortable, Keith Grosser jumped in with his glowing endorsement.

"You're not going to find a better deal than that, Landers. I'd take it before the price goes up." It's like these two jokers had their act all worked out.

"Keith's right. In fact, I already have several interested parties who I suspect may be willing to go substantially higher but, because I like you, I'm giving you first shot at this rare card for my special low price."

"Can I think about it over the weekend? I really need to check in with my parents." I already had a pretty good idea of what my parents would say about this "deal." Using $50 of my own money, however, would wipe out my life savings, accumulated over years of paper routes, driveway shoveling, and birthday gifts.

"Okay. Sure," replied a sales-thirsty Harvey Mulligan. "If you bring the money in on Monday, the card will be in your hands on Tuesday. After that, I can no longer guarantee the price. You really don't want to pass on this one-time good deal."

"Thanks. I'll let you know on Monday. I appreciate the special offer." In truth, I didn't appreciate anything about Mulligan's "special offer" but, at this point, I felt it was best to keep relations cordial rather than blowing what might be my last chance to score a Tom Seaver baseball card.

We parted ways and I turned for home. I wasn't quite sure what to do. I really wanted the card but I felt it was, somehow, not in the spirit of "the game" to pay for a card. True, I dropped coin every weekend on a pack of cards but that seemed more legitimate. It wasn't until the following year that I discovered that I could have owned the entire set of Topps cards, including Tom Seaver, for less than $50. But I was a collector—I was earning the series one card at a time. Somehow, this seemed like a more noble endeavor, purer of spirit, than simply just buying a complete set of cards. Before I even arrived at my doorstep, I knew what my decision was going to be. Mulligan would just have to find another sucker to bait with his "special friend deal."

After a hug from Mom, I went to my room to check my scramble winnings against my card checklist. I was thrilled. Three of the cards were new, leaving only three remaining.

That weekend, I called several of my friends to see if anyone had card #474, Ray Corbin, or #489, Skip Jutze. Neither seemed enthusiastic about looking through all their cards and I was, apparently, the only kid who actually kept a checklist of cards I owned. My friend, Jim, invited me over on Saturday for a sleepover. He'd be heading off to camp shortly after school ended so this would be our last chance to really hang out. We always had fun and we always stayed up way too late watching television. We cracked up watching this new show called Saturday Night Live. My parents would never let me stay up that late. While we were hanging out, I was rifling through Jimmy's baseball card collection. Jimmy didn't have a Tom Seaver card, either, but I did spot Ray Corbin. During a commercial break, I asked if Jimmy would be willing to trade. Before he had a chance to answer, we heard a knock on the door. It was Jimmy's Dad telling us to turn down the volume on the television. Jimmy meekly apologized and I turned the volume knob down so that the television was just loud enough for us to hear. Jimmy made some snide comment about parents and bat ears and then we returned to our negotiations. Okay, it really wasn't much of a negotiation. It was evident that my friend had pretty much lost interest in card collecting for the season; his thoughts now nearly entirely on sleepaway camp—canoeing, archery, swimming, softball, campfire songs and roasted marshmallows; you know, the whole package deal. I never went to sleepaway camp but I can't say that I felt any jealousy. I enjoyed having an unstructured summer although it did get kind of lonely, after a while, with most of my friends off at camp or on vacation with their families.

Half-heartedly, Jimmy asked me what I had to offer in trade. Now, I knew Ray Corbin of the Minnesota Twins had absolutely no value to my friend but, all the same, I thought I could do better than just toss out a John Doe card that I had quadruples of. While many collectors gave up on trying to get the complete series, most of my buddies were still very interested in getting all the New York Mets cards. I offered up Craig Swan and Tom Hall, two Mets pitchers. Jimmy looked appreciative.

"Cool! I needed Swan. Thanks. Are there any other cards you need?"

"Well, just Tom Seaver and Skip Jutze," I replied.

"Seaver's going to be really tough to find. You know that, right?"

"Yah, I know. I've been asking all around. Mulligan said he'd sell me a Seaver card but he wanted fifty bucks for it."

"Holy smokes! Fifty dollars?! I wouldn't drop that kind of money. Mulligan's a leach. Even if the card is worth fifty, I wouldn't give that jerk a dime." I agreed with Jimmy's assessment and told him that I had come to the same conclusion. Jimmy said he'd check around to see if he could find anyone who was willing to part with a Tom Seaver card. I knew the chances were slim but my friend did have a much broader social network than I did so I appreciated his offer to help.

After Saturday Night Live, we turned off the TV and talked for a while before we both eventually fell asleep. The fold out bed Jimmy's parents had set up in his room was actually pretty comfortable. I slept well. In the morning, Jimmy's mom fixed us a nice breakfast before I called my mom and told her I was ready for a pickup.

The weekend passed quickly and I excitedly welcomed the final short week of the school year. I deliberately steered clear of Harvey Mulligan and Keith Grosser. I didn't even want to deal with them. Almost nobody brought their cards to school that last week so there was no point in asking around to see if anyone had a Skip Jutze card in their back pocket. I'd be laughed at if I even asked about Tom Seaver. I had already asked nearly all my friends. The few that were lucky enough to have a Seaver card were unwilling to part with it and I certainly couldn't blame them.

On the last day of class, we all cheered when our teacher dismissed us, after handing out congratulatory letters for us to take home to our parents. As I was making my way out of the school building, I felt a gentle tapping on my shoulder. I turned around and my face went flush when I saw Sophie Taylor standing behind me. She thrust an envelope at me and, before I took it, I quickly scanned the area to see if any friends were nearby. While I had outgrown the "all girls have cooties" phase of my childhood, I still felt very uneasy during any interactions with the opposite sex. I tried to ask what the envelope was all about but all I could get out was a mumbled jumble of incoherent syllables. Sophie's eyes were wide and her face was glowing. She seemed a bit nervous but, unlike me, was able to speak intelligibly.

"I'm having a bit of a Fourth of July party at my place and I'd really like for you to come. It's going to be a really small party and I think you'll have fun. I know it's Independence Day, and all, and that you may already have plans but . . . well . . . please come." Sophie's voice was soft and gentle and, despite my heroic efforts to counter her feminine powers, I blushed and smiled. I quickly averted my gaze and inspected my shoelaces to make sure the knots were tight and the loops were well-formed.

"Um. I don't know. I'm pretty sure my parents have something planned."

"Oh no," replied Sophie, a tinge of sadness in her words. "I was so hoping you could make it. If you can't, I understand. But please try. My phone number is on the card so please call, either way, and let me know. Okay?" I don't know what she was doing to me but I was starting to feel a little light headed. I quickly nodded and said I'd let her know. Those words had hardly passed my lips before I realized that I had just committed to another interaction with Sophie Taylor. I knew this was a mistake. Sophie smiled and scampered off, leaving me there holding her card with a stunned look upon my face. I quickly hid the red, white and blue envelope behind the envelope with my grade advancement congratulations letter from school. I hurried home, purposefully avoiding anyone who might inquire about a second envelope in my grasp.

I managed to make it all the way home without encountering another human being but there was no way I was going to make it past my mom. She was eagerly awaiting my arrival at the door. I had no sooner crossed the threshold before she was inquiring about the envelope in my hand. I told her it was the usual grade advancement letter for parents. I immediately knew that I should have stashed Sophie's invitation in my sock but I'm guessing Mom would have noticed that, too. The grade advancement letter hadn't even left my hand before Mom asked about the festive red, white, and blue envelope I was carrying.

"Oh, just an invite to a party some kid gave me but I don't think I'll be going." I hoped Mom would let it rest there. I knew she wouldn't.

"Oh, how nice. Whose party? Why wouldn't you want to go?" my mother countered.

"Just some kid. I'm pretty sure you don't them."

"So, it's not from Jimmy, Martin, Lucas, or Michael?" Mom wasn't going to let this go.

"Nope." I was desperately trying to find a way to quickly disengage.

"I know lots of the parents from PTA," my mother said; "perhaps I'll know the mom?" I must admit, I considered making up a story about a refugee orphan but I finally relented.

"You don't know the Taylors, do you?" The wheels in my mom's brain seemed to be turning for considerably longer than the typical time it took her to recall a name from her amazing mental rolodex of contacts. I was hopeful.

"I'm afraid the only Taylor I know is Arlene Taylor and she doesn't have any boys."

"Well, there you have it," I said, quickly turning about and heading off toward my room. I almost had my door closed when my mother finally made the connection. When I heard the excitement in her voice, I knew the jig was up.

"Wait. Did you get invited to a party by Sophie Taylor?" Drats! Mom wins, again.

"Kind of. I think she's inviting a lot of kids to some 4th of July thing at her house but I told her I probably couldn't make it."

"Why not?" asked my mom. "I think you might enjoy it. Besides, it's nice to have some friends of the opposite sex; they can help you see things from a different perspective. And, it's not like you've got to marry her after going to the party." I was blushing and my mother wasn't about to let it go. "Are you blushing? Do you like her?"

"No, Mom!" I objected. "No way. I mean, I don't hate her but I'm sure we have absolutely nothing in common and I would be bored out of my mind talking with her."

"Well, you won't know until you spend a little time with her, will you?" I needed to break this conversation off quickly so I used the time-honored bathroom emergency escape method. It worked like a charm. For all that, my mother's words did get me thinking.

At dinner time, my mother mentioned the invitation to my father. I quickly interjected, reminding my dad that he had expressed interest in driving the family out to see the spectacular line up of tall ships scheduled to be part of Ops Sail '76—the biggest Independence Day event scheduled in New York. I'm not sure whether or not my mother had gotten to Dad first, or not, but he seemed to quickly back away from the Ops Sail celebration, making excuses about excessive traffic and crowds. I really needed a little help here but Dad seemed nearly as anxious for me to attend Sophie's party as Mom had. I told them I'd think about it. In the coming days, I would desperately search through the New York Times and listen to local news reports in the hope of finding a viable alternative Independence Day plan.

On Monday, June 28th, my mother took my sister and I to the local swimming pool. I didn't go very often but, with temperatures well above average, a cool pool seemed like the perfect antidote to a sweltering 92-degree summer scorcher. I was having a great time splashing around until I saw Sophie arrive with her mom. I panicked and tried to pretend I didn't see her. It was no good. Sophie saw me. My mom got to talking with Sophie's mother and I absolutely dreaded the thought that they might be conspiring about the party. I had just finished swimming across the pool at the five-foot line when I looked up and saw two nicely tanned legs leading upward into the sky where they terminated in a blinding brilliance of sunlight. Isn't that what enemy aircraft do— come diving at you out of the sun? With two words, I knew, immediately, that these legs belonged to my arch nemesis.

"Hi Ray! Mind if I join you?" I was about to say no but Sophie's body was already arcing over me as she dove into the pool. There was hardly a splash. Hmm, she must actually know what she's doing. Anyway, the company was not welcome. Well, maybe just a little bit welcome. I wasn't about to admit that to anyone, least of all myself.

"Hey, Sophie. Nice dive."

"Thanks, Ray. My Mom used to dive in college and she taught me a thing or two. So, do you think you might be able to make it to my party, I'd really like to have you there."

"Oh. I'm not sure. It's a busy time, you know. There's a lot going on."

"I know. I just thought it would be nice to do something special for the 200th birthday of America. I don't know about you but I'm not sure I'll be around to see the 300th."

"Well, yah. That's true. I think it's nice that you're having a party and I'm sure your friends will really appreciate it." I was half mumbling. I just didn't feel very comfortable talking with girls.

"I was hoping that maybe we could be friends," said Sophie, the affection in her voice was at once terrifying and alluring. Sophie was reading me like a book and she could tell I was getting nervous so she quickly changed tack with a maneuver that would put any of the Ops Sail tall ships to shame. "Hey, I heard you were looking for a Tom Seaver card. I think I may have one." Sophie had my full attention.

"What?! Really? I thought you didn't have any brothers?" Sophie quickly shot me an angry glance but it didn't last very long.

"What? You think girls can't collect baseball cards, too?"

"Yes. I mean, No. I guess there's nothing saying a girl can't collect cards but I just never knew any girl who collected baseball cards and I never saw you bring any to school. I didn't mean to offend you."

"No offence taken, Raymond Landers." I thought about asking what it was about the cards that she liked but I'm glad I didn't. I later found out that Sophie Taylor could talk baseball statistics with the best of us. She was a girl of many surprises and unknown talents.

"So, what would I need to trade for Tom Seaver?" I was really hoping it would be John Doe but Sophie was shrewd beyond her years.

"If you come to my party, you'll find out. But I warn you, you better come with some good cards because I'm not going to settle for an unknown utility infielder from the Detroit Tigers."

"Hold on. Why don't we just arrange to trade here at the pool, tomorrow, or maybe the next day?" A mischievous grin came upon Sophie's face that caught me off guard.

"I wouldn't want the card to get wet, would you?" I was struggling for counterpoints but Sophie was done negotiating, having firmly drawn her line in the sand. "At the party, Mr. Landers. We'll work out the card deal at my party." Sophie splashed some water in my face and then swam, with a powerful kick, to the opposite side of the pool. She waved at me, after climbing out of the pool, before joining a few of her friends on the lounge chairs amidst a chorus of giggles.

That night, I had a very hard time falling asleep. I listened to my clock radio well into the night, turning the volume up to tape a song I liked using my General Electric tape recorder which was perpetually positioned next to my radio for just such occasions. The track was interrupted by a knock on the door and my mother's request that I turn my music down and go to bed. Calls for dinner, my sister's flute practice, the sounds of aircraft engines as planes began their descent into LaGuardia airport—I was used to a wide array of accompanying acoustics on the songs I recorded. With my music off, I heard every click of the numbers flipping on my Panasonic flip clock radio. I eventually fell asleep.

The next day, my mother asked me if I had decided whether or not I was going to the Taylors' party. After some hemming and hawing, I finally conceded that I would go. Much to my dismay, my mother nodded approvingly and said that she had already called in my RSVP to Mrs. Taylor. I was a little sore about that but not angry enough to raise a big fuss over it. I just shook my head, smiling, and thanked Mom.

The humiliation continued over the next few days as, first, my mother insisted upon me bringing a patriotic-themed flower arrangement as a gift and then picked out a ridiculously uncool outfit for me to wear to the event. I would never live this down. My name would go down in infamy in the annals of Saddle Harbor Elementary School. It should go without saying that I had a horrible night's sleep the day before the party. I was half hoping that I'd contract the flu or develop some hideous rash so that I would have a legitimate reason for cancelling out. I wasn't that lucky.

A long afternoon nap helped to revive me. Also, Dad came to the rescue and suggested that my jeans and a nice polo shirt would be fine for the party. Mom conceded and the fancy slacks, button down shirt, and ridiculous vest were relegated to the far reaches of my closet.

At 6pm, my mother dropped me off at the Taylors' place. The Taylors had a lovely house set on a corner lot with an enormous yard. On the side of the house was a huge tree with an amazing treehouse built into the limbs. I was always a little jealous of that treehouse. When I rang the doorbell, I was met by Sophie's Dad who greeted me with a warm handshake and a big smile. He told me "the girls" were out back and that he would be out there shortly to get the grill going. "Girls?" I thought. I hope I'm not the first boy here. That would be awkward. Mr. Taylor smiled when he saw my 4th of July flower arrangement. He asked, with a grin, if it was my mom's idea and then chuckled when I acknowledged that it was. I was kind of hoping he'd take it and stash it on a window sill somewhere but he wasn't going to let me off that easily. Mr. Taylor told me I could walk through the kitchen and out onto the back patio and present Sophie with the flowers myself. Ugh!

When I stepped out onto the back patio, I was not only horrified to find no other boys but was absolutely mortified to discover that I was the very first arrival. Didn't my mother understand the concept of being "fashionably late?" Sophie's eyes lit up when she saw me and she quickly ran over to greet me. My outstretched arms, holding the ridiculous Independence Day flower arrangement, was the only thing that saved me from a power-hug. The flowers had served their one and only useful purpose. Sophie gladly accepted the gift, doting over the arrangement before taking my hand to welcome me. I quickly turned the hand-holding into a business-like handshake before pulling away and saying hello to Mrs. Taylor. I apologized for being early, even though I was on time. Mrs. Taylor looked at Sophie and smiled. I was, as of yet, unaware that I had fallen, head-first, into a clever trap. Sophie's dad came out and asked what I wanted to eat, offering up a selection of burger, hot dog, and chicken options. I opted for a couple hot dogs. I could see a selection of salads and chips arranged on a fold-out table near the grill. My mind doesn't always work quickly but it didn't take me long to realize that the soft drinks, salads, and meats available on the table were not going to feed more than a handful of people. Sophie and I made small talk while her dad expertly worked the grill. When things got quiet, Sophie's mom or dad would jump in to fill the void. When we all sat down at the table, I knew I had been tricked. I looked over at Sophie but her mom jumped in to save Sophie from having to explain.

"I know you were expecting a bigger party, Ray, and we really did have one planned. Sophie wanted to invite a few of her closest friends over for a special Independence Day celebration but nearly everyone had plans for the day and, well, Sophie was so excited about it and she's told us so much about you that we didn't have the heart to cancel the get together. Besides, when I spoke to your mom, we both agreed that it would be nice for you two to have a chance to get to know each other outside of the classroom. I hope you don't mind. We really weren't trying to trick you into doing something you'd hate. We've got some horseshoes set up over there, and a bean bag toss, and we should be able to see the fireworks later. I'm pretty sure you two will have fun. Besides, I understand there's some business negotiations planned for later in the evening."

Well, it was hard to be angry at Mrs. Taylor. She was such a kind and engaging person. If I didn't already have the best mom in the world, I'd want Mrs. Taylor to be my mother. I took a deep breath and exhaled. No matter how awkward the situation might be, I figured it'd all be worth it if I walked away with a Tom Seaver card.

"Oh, no problem, Mrs. Taylor. I understand. I'm glad I could make it." I'm not sure whether or not I was really glad but my words seemed to comfort Sophie. The tension in her body dissipated and she sat back in her deck chair with a peaceful look upon her face. I'll have to admit, the hot dogs, potato chips, and macaroni salad really hit the spot. The ice cream sundaes we had for desert were out of this world.

After dinner, the Taylors began the cleanup process and left Sophie and me to play various yard games and talk. I was very surprised how easily conversation was coming now. I was actually enjoying myself. Time seemed to race by and I think Sophie and I were both surprised that the sun set as early as it did—right on time.

"Ray, you have your cards with you, right?"

"Yes, I do. Do you have yours?"

"Uh-huh, they're up in the treehouse. Would you like to come up? It won't be long before they start shooting off the fireworks at the park and we'll have a great view from up there."

"Cool! Sure, let's go. But are we going to be able to see the cards?"

"Yup. I've got my trusty flashlight up there."

"Okay, then. Sure thing, Sophie. I can't wait to see the treehouse. I've been jealous of it since we moved here."

Sophie led the way up a tall wooden ladder that had been affixed to the tree. When reaching the top, she pushed the entry hatch open and ascended into the unlit treehouse. I followed Sophie into the darkness which, moments later, was fully illuminated by her large flashlight. The interior of the treehouse was quite nice. Large circular windows were cut into the sides and, except for one corner, there was no cover over-head. Under the covered corner, several books lay on the wooden planking along with some board games and a box filled with tradeable stationery. Against the far wall was a shoebox-sized plastic container filled with baseball cards. Sophie slid over next to the box and motioned for me to join her. I sat next to her, leaning against the wooden wall of the treehouse. Sophie carefully opened the box and pulled out a pristine Topps Card #600—Tom Seaver! I had been searching for that card all season long. I could hardly believe my eyes.

"You know it's gonna cost you, right?" said Sophie, slyly.

"I was expecting as much so I came armed with an impressive array of all-stars." I laid down half a dozen sure bets for a Hall of Fame nomination, wondering if Sophie would even appreciate the caliber of the talent spread out across the planking of her treehouse. Just in case she didn't, I snuck in a couple John Does. She carefully considered the selection. Slowly, she reached for Card #240, Pete Rose from the Cincinnati Reds. I watched her eyes, closely. Was Rose going to be enough? Sophie carefully collected the remaining cards and handed them back to me. "So, Seaver for Rose? Is that the deal?" My question was met by silence.

With a trembling voice, Sophie responded. "No. I'll trade you Tom Seaver for Pete Rose and a kiss." I was stunned. Sophie carefully studied my face while I choked on my own spit and then turned away to avoid displaying the beet red of my blushing face. The silence seemed to last for an eternity. I thought about turning the moment into some kind of joke but all witticisms escaped my mind and the desire in Sophie's eyes completely disarmed me.

"Okay," I whispered.

"Okay?" Sophie asked, making certain she had heard me correctly. "Are you sure?"

"Yes, Sophie. It's okay."

"On the lips?"

"If you want to," I replied, my resistance giving way to her feminine charm.

"Do you want to?" Sophie asked, giving me one last chance for an escape. I no longer wanted to escape.

"Yes." Before I had fully enunciated my reply, Sophie pulled me in and embraced me so tightly that she nearly squeezed the air out of my lungs. The feel of her warm, wet lips making contact with mine was a sensation I shall never forget. At first, I was an astonished recipient but, soon, I became a willing participant. I felt a strange sense of euphoria like I had never known before. I don't know how long we kissed but I do recall that several fireworks bursts had passed before we slowly drew back from one another and turned to watch the fireworks in the sky. We held hands throughout the show, neither of us saying a word. We continued to hold hands after the fireworks show was over and all that remained were the sparkling stars in the night sky.

It took the voice of Sophie's mother, coming from below, to break the trance. Mrs. Taylor asked if I was ready to head home yet. I said I'd be down in a minute to call my mom for a ride but Mrs. Taylor offered to drive me back, saying that Sophie could come, too, and that would give us both a little more time together. I agreed to the plan. Before we left the treehouse, which only recently became my favorite spot in the entire universe, Sophie leaned in for one final kiss. It was a brief but beautifully tender kiss. We looked into each other's eyes for a while longer until we both knew it was time to go. I pulled up the hatch to the treehouse but Sophie grabbed my arm before I started down.

"One more thing, before you go," said Sophie. I didn't say a word. Sophie reached back into her card box and pulled out another card. It was card #489, Skip Jutze of the Houston Astros; a "John Doe" to some but, for me, the last remaining card of the 1976 Topps Baseball Card series that I needed for a complete set. How did she know? Somehow, she had gotten the word through the grapevine. Sophie handed me the card and I tried very hard to hold back the tears. A few escaped and Sophie gently wiped them away from my cheek. I didn't know what to say. Sophie didn't need to hear anything. I kissed her again, quickly, and we both made our way, carefully, down the ladder to the yard below.

Mrs. Taylor drove me back home, both Sophie and I sitting in the back of the car. We were both very quiet and Mrs. Taylor felt no need to make small talk. She understood a great many things and was happy to navigate the lamplit streets of our suburban town in silence.

Sophie and I hung out a lot together that summer. We spent many hours at the pool and many hours up in Sophie's treehouse. We also enjoyed several Mets games at Shea Stadium; sometimes the Taylors hosting and sometimes my parents taking us. And then, Mr. Taylor found out that he was being transferred to the office in Los Angeles. That's the first time I understood what "heartbreak" really felt like. Sophie and I continued to write throughout the next year but, eventually, our letters were spaced farther apart until all that remained were holiday cards. These, too, disappeared by the time we both entered high school. I guess we all learn to move on in life. Childhood sweethearts become a special memory.

I was married for several years but my wife and I slowly grew apart. We divorced a couple years prior to my 20th high school reunion. I honestly never thought about Sophie Taylor during the time I was married. Well, not very much, at any rate. Still, there was always part of me that wondered where she was and what she was up to. I asked a few of the girls at my reunion if they remembered Sophie or knew anything about her whereabouts. A couple classmates knew exactly who I was talking about while most scratched their heads, unable to recall a classmate they hadn't seen since 4th grade. No one I spoke to had kept in contact with Sophie. I guess I wasn't surprised. So many people dance in and out of our lives across the years. Only a precious few burn their light into our collective memory.

A few weeks after the reunion, I received a call from one of my classmates, Sally McBride. She asked if we might get together for coffee. I don't drink coffee but my interest was piqued so I agreed to the meeting. So far as I knew, Sally was happily married with two kids and a third on the way so I was confident this wasn't going to be "one of those kind" of get-togethers. Sally opened with a barrage of idle chit-chat before slowly removing a padded mailing envelope from her purse. She handed the package to me and asked that I open it later and then decide what to do with the contents. I must admit that I had trouble concentrating during the remainder of our time together. After cordial goodbyes, I returned to my car, looking over the padded envelope with no return address upon it.

Once home, I carefully opened the envelope and was astonished by what I saw. Wrapped within a hand-written letter was a 1976 Pete Rose baseball card. On August 24, 1989, the great Pete Rose was banned from professional baseball after a major scandal where, as a manager, he was found guilty of betting on baseball games, including those games that his own team, the Cincinnati Reds, were playing in. A few years later, he was permanently banned from eligibility into the Baseball Hall of Fame. This was a tragic demise for a great baseball legend. The fact of the matter remains; Pete Rose snubbed his nose at the ethical standards of the game and he was judged accordingly. My suspicions regarding the author of the letter were soon confirmed. The letter was from Sophie Taylor. Her handwriting was ever so elegant. It turns out Sophie's husband and Pete Rose had a fair amount in common regarding ethical standards. Sophie's husband had been cheating on her for many years and was frequently abusive, especially when he was drunk. He gambled away much of their money and refused to get help for his substance abuse issues. After years of hoping that the situation might improve, Sophie eventually decided it was time to move on with her life. After their divorce, Sophie moved up to Oregon where she taught school; fourth grade, to be specific.

I put the letter down, briefly; many old memories coming alive within that wonderful part of the brain that refuses to let special memories die. By the time I had finished reading, I was struggling to wipe the tears from my eyes.

Two years later, standing together above a beautiful span of Pacific coastline, Sophie and I became man and wife. We exchanged rings, kisses, and agreed to share our lives together and to share our 1976 Topps Tom Seaver card till death do us part.

The Story Behind the Story

With a deadline of May 31, 2021, Red Penguin Books set up their next anthology as a "Historical Fiction Writing Contest" where the staff's favorite work would not only be featured in the anthology but would also be honored by having the story or poem's title incorporated into the title of the anthology. I decided to submit two very different pieces for this anthology. While neither took the prize, I was pleased with both. Remembering back to the "Roaring 20s" anthology and the lati-tude given to various time periods, I felt pretty confident that a short story taking place in the 1970s would be considered "historic enough" to make the chronological cut. Whether or not the editor would select it for inclusion in the anthology was another matter. But I felt I had a good story in my head. I pulled upon many happy memories of my childhood and a simpler time when life was all about bicycles, base-ball cards, and having fun with friends. And, of course, what young boy wasn't curious about the opposite sex. We didn't understand girls but schoolboy crushes were not uncommon and any flirtatious behavior directed towards us might send us into a tailspin of confusion. I still remember getting a kiss on the cheek after rescuing a playground ball from some bullies and returning it to a girl from our school who was a bit younger than me. I'm sure I was blushing fiercely, and I know for sure that I was left stunned and confused. The treehouse where the 4th of July scene plays out was also inspired by a childhood memory. One of my best friends had a wonderful tree house on his property which I can't deny being envious of. You'd climb up a ladder and push a hatch open to enter. Of course, I needed to incorporate this 70s memory into my story. While I never considered myself very adept at writing romantic stories, it seemed somehow easier to tell a tale of childhood "puppy love." As I love happy endings, it was fun to be able to tie everything together at a point in the future and to "make things right," as it were.

BROTHERLY LOVE

(Written May 28, 2021)
Published by Red Penguin Books in "*Ernest Lived and Other Historical
Fiction Short Stories*" (June, 2021)

*Ninth Century, Ireland. A mysterious monk lends his
skill and passion to a medieval monastery. When the
monastery is threatened, he must weigh a sacred vow
against his love for his brothers.*

Ireland, 9th Century

A quiet man, a gentle man, a holy man. Brother Brendan arrived
from the fog with naught but his robes and the heavy cross he bore,
forever hidden from sight beneath white samite, pure as the first snow
atop the pristine mountains.

A quiet man, a gentle man, a holy man. We welcomed him and
embraced him as brothers do. With unmatched skill and Heaven's
blessing, he transcribed and illuminated texts with loving brush strokes.
Precise swirls and flicks of the wrists brought to mind the exquisite
ballet of birds in flight.

A quiet man, a gentle man, a holy man. Brother Brendan spoke few
words and none but those extolling the virtues of peace, love and
harmony. Ne'er a dark thought crossed his mind and his counsel was
always delivered in the dulcet tones of an angel's voice.

A quiet man, a gentle man, a holy man. His great cross,
enshrouded in white samite, ne'er to be revealed but to God, was his
mystery and his pledge to his heavenly master. Never parted, we
admired Brother Brendan for the burden he bore so devoutly. Whether
a burden of faith or a gift of God, we questioned not for Brendan's
piety knew no bounds.

A quiet man, a gentle man, a holy man. Brother Brendan spoke
intelligibly of distant lands and foreign cultures and we grew wiser with
each word that danced off his lips. He had traveled the pilgrim's path
to the Holy Land and had faithfully spread the word of our Lord
where'er he traveled. That cross, enshrouded in the purest samite,

accompanied him and gave him strength though his feet bled and his legs wearied.

A quiet man, a gentle man, a holy man. A true brother to us all; we loved Brendan and he loved us. Delicate and unimposing, we were reluctant to assign the most laborious tasks to our dear Brendan yet, without fail, our noble brother pleaded with the abbot that he might share in the toils of the field, sowing and harvesting our sustenance.

A quiet man, a gentle man, a holy man. Bearing his cross upon his shoulders, Brendan would mount the hilltop and look out to sea. Kneeling and praying, we left our brother alone with his thoughts as he communed with God. Always, upon his return, Brendan seemed renewed and invigorated and filled with the Holy Spirit.

A quiet man, a gentle man, a holy man. We admired our dear brother yet felt no jealousy for he always gave more than he received and freely shared his gifts and his wisdom with all. Brendan rarely spoke of the past as his thoughts dwelled on making a better future for all within the monastery.

A quiet man, a gentle man, a holy man. He moved slowly and deliberately yet found wings to fly on that day when the winds of fall stole away our sweet summer air and filled the sails of the invading Norsemen, brutal seafaring Vikings with no love for God or anything holy.

A quiet man, a gentle man, a holy man. With cross upon his shoulder, Brendan descended from his hill and spread the warning. The abbot directed all the treasures we could carry be quickly retrieved from the monastery and carried to the round tower. Within the tower, ladders carried the faithful upward. Brother Brendan, himself, pulled up the lowermost ladder and sealed the entry to the fist level so that none might violate the protection of our tower.

A quiet man, a gentle man, a holy man. We trembled in fear as the Viking horn blew and invaders swarmed upon the shore, making their way toward the monastery to plunder and destroy. Brendan clutched his mighty cross, covered yet in white samite and a source of comfort to our grief-stricken friend.

A quiet man, a gentle man, a holy man. Brendan listened as reports from the upper level filtered down. Abbot Aodhán, peering through a window slit, cut into the stone wall of the tower, gasped in horror as the barbarous Norsemen ravaged the fields and set buildings aflame.

A quiet man, a gentle man, a holy man. Rescue was a day's ride away and the walls of our round tower were all that stood between our brotherhood and a vile death at the murderous hands of these invading heathens. Brendan held his cross tightly, prayed, and wept.

A quiet man, a gentle man, a holy man. The Vikings seemed unsatisfied with the plunder gained from the monastery and surrounding buildings. They turned their vicious energy upon the tower but found it more solid and imposing than any fortification they had yet encountered. In a tongue unfamiliar to any, the marauders debated their courses of action. Brendan held his cross tightly, prayed, and wept.

A quiet man, a gentle man, a holy man. The invaders tested our walls with makeshift battering rams and fierce blows from hammer and axe, alike. Our walls stood strong and our foe's will weakened. Abbot Aodhán's voice grew hopeful as the Vikings withdrew and looked back toward their ships. Three ships near the shore beckoned the raiders with a promise of easy plunder and more lucrative targets. Brendan eased his grip upon his great cross and sighed, thanking God for his mercy.

A quiet man, a gentle man, a holy man. Unaware was he, our brother Brendan, that a great chieftain below was rallying his evil army to action and was unwilling to admit defeat at the hands of our meek brotherhood. The battle captain sent his men to the woods and they returned with great logs and bundles of branches and sticks.

A quiet man, a gentle man, a holy man. Brendan urged all to ascend until there was no longer space to climb while the Vikings piled wood about the base of the round tower. The sun was low on the horizon when torches set our funeral pyre ablaze. Our tragic fate seemed assured. We were to be roasted alive with our precious treasures in a Devil's oven that once served as our protection.

A quiet man, a gentle man, a holy man. Brendan prayed. Brendan held his enshrouded cross tightly and wept. A chorus of lamenting voices echoed throughout our circular tomb and ascended to Heaven as the heat became nearly unbearable for all within.

A quiet man, a gentle man, a holy man. Brendan stood and called for rope whereupon it was delivered from the level above. Fastening the rope to an iron bar beside the window, our grief-stricken brother squeezed his body through the window slit, pulling his cross through after him. With great dexterity, Brendan lowered himself toward the raging flames of Hell.

A quiet man, a gentle man, a holy man. Viking and monk, alike, watched in stunned disbelief as Brother Brendan kicked away from the tower, rope in one hand, cross in the other, and vaulted over the prodigious wall of fire. Landing with a roll, Brendan regained his feet with noght a thread singed upon his robe.

A quiet man, a gentle man, a holy man. The sun was lost to us but the stage upon which this next act was performed was illuminated by flame and flashes of lightning. A storm came in from the sea, shaming the terrible power of the Viking horde. Our sacrificial lamb stood bravely before our foes, his purpose a mystery to all but God.

A quiet man, a gentle man, a holy man. His presence alone did little to upset the balance. The Viking chieftain thought to bring honor to his name by being the first to shed blood. Pounding axe upon shield, the Norseman approached with haughty confidence. Brendan, saintly martyr or fool, stood his ground, expressionless and unwavering. Disturbed by his lack of fear, the chieftain let loose a terrible war cry that would have cowered the bravest of the king's knights.

A quiet man, a gentle man, a holy man. In the tongue of the Norse invaders, Brendan's voice thundered above the din and all stood silent. What words he spoke are lost to time for none that understood survived to tell. The older Vikings withdrew, concern and fear showing on their once brave faces. The chieftain and his younger warriors scoffed though their arrogance seemed diminished.

A quiet man, a gentle man, a holy man. Rain burst forth from the lingering storm clouds and doused the raging flames about the tower. Steam, rising from the glowing piles of wood, transformed the scene into a ghastly vision of Hell itself and all but Brendan were tormented by a terrible sense of dread.

A quiet man, a gentle man, a holy man. An arrow, let loose from a yew bow, took flight and, but for a gust of wind, might have stricken Brendan dead on the spot. The chieftain growled viciously at the offending archer. The monk was to be his prize—slave or decapitated war trophy, it made no difference.

A quiet man, a gentle man, a holy man. The Viking chieftain spun his axe and offered up a display of dominance seldom seen outside the wild. Brendan looked to the sky, no longer praying for deliverance or begging for mercy but imploring God for forgiveness for the sacred vow he must now break.

A quiet man, a gentle man, a holy man. With the care of a mother removing blankets from her child, Brother Brendan unwrapped his great cross, the unsoiled white samite falling to his feet and into the muddy ash below. A cross it was, but unlike any we had envisioned. Brendan stood, his eyes blazing, gripping a mighty double-bladed war axe. The grey-haired Vikings retreated in fear. The younger Norsemen nervously stood their ground. The chieftain's axe fell to his side for his head was severed from his torso before he had the chance to ready his strike.

A quiet man, a gentle man, a holy man. Brendan charged into the mass of marauders, his darting and dodging silhouetted against the remaining fires before the tower. Rolling and twirling, ducking and leaping, slashing and swinging with the vengeful fury of the Norse gods, themselves, the enraged monk cut a path of destruction through the invading force such as none had witnesses in a hundred battles nor read of in a thousand sagas.

A quiet man, a gentle man, a holy man. Monks turned away from the windows of the tower to shield their eyes from the terrible scene below. Shrieks in the darkness and cries for mercy filled the air but fell upon deaf ears. There was to be no mercy this night. Brendan, injured though he was, pursued the remaining villains as they fled to their boats; all the while, the storm raged on with great intensity as if the forces of nature had allied themselves with the warrior monk.

A quiet man, a gentle man, a holy man. The storm clouds, satisfied with the havoc wrought, raced over the hills and into the valley beyond. The monks, thankful for their lives yet dumbfounded by what they had witnessed, exited the tower to survey the scene below. Viking corpses littered the battlefield. There were no wounded left to tend. The brothers called out for Brendan and searched the mass of fallen bodies for their friend.

A quiet man, a gentle man, a holy man. Ascending to the hilltop where Brendan often prayed, Abbot Aodhán looked down to the shore-line where three Viking ships were burning like torches in the night.

A mysterious man. Brendan was ne'er seen again at the monastery. Born of a world of blood and violence, he sought redemption and looked to God and Heaven for forgiveness. His penitence was real and his heart was true but, for this warrior, there would be no reprieve. Innocence lost; Brendan strived for an absolution that was not written into his story. He harbored hope, nonetheless, that he might make amends and start his life anew. He found out, as many before, that there's no going back from a killing. The white samite, sheathing his mighty axe, was inwardly stained with the blood of a hundred battles and countless lives taken.

A good man. Redemption would come, one day, but not here on earth. While the tales of Brendan's many travels remain the stuff of myth and legend, the pained body and soul that traveled these lands most likely did so in a never-ending quest for peace and tranquility. It is my hope that he's found it.

The Story Behind the Story

When the initial call went out for submissions to the historical fiction anthology, later to be entitled "Ernest Lived and Other Historical Fiction Short Stories," several ideas bounced around inside my head. You previously read the piece I decided on for my main effort. But there was a second idea that simply would not die. The embers kept burning in my head even after my first short story was written and only a day remained before the submission deadline. I had this powerful vision in my head that simply would not leave.

The setting was Ireland, back in the Middle Ages. While I was touring in Ireland, in 1988, I learned a lot about the Viking raids upon various towns and monasteries. The image of monks fleeing with their treasures into the round towers, a number of which still stand today, stayed with me. It must have been a terrifying experience. I thought that to write a full short story on the topic would require a significant amount of additional research and time I simply did not have at my disposal. And so, I nearly abandoned the project.

More than the time or place, I think I was inspired by the humble hero of the saga that was forming in my mind. It was Brendan who fought to find his way onto the page. There is no doubt that I saw part of myself within this protagonist. My preference was always to remain out of the spotlight—to blend in and be a productive member of whatever group I was associated with. But I rarely felt like I belonged. I was quiet and unassuming and, as such, more than once, became a target of bullying. But unlike the defenseless victims that the bullies typically targeted, I was not only very capable of defending myself but also held within a secret—the heart of a lion and a complete willingness to sacrifice my own personal welfare to fight for justice.

As a second grader, I found myself in a fight with five fifth graders on my walk home from school. They picked the fight with me, and they got one. I knew I wasn't

going to be able to overpower that many older kids but it made absolutely no differ-
ence. Eventually, I was literally chasing them down the street with my final act being
to throw a book I was carrying at one of the fleeing fifth graders. Throughout my
school days, similar episodes played out. I would regularly intervene to stop bullies
from harassing fellow students.

I suppose it is no wonder that I eventually decided to join the United States Air
Force and take my passion for defending the oppressed and protecting justice to the
next level. I knew what I was capable of—physically and emotionally; but I
preferred not having to call upon these strengths. Again, I just wanted peace and to
blend in. In this context, you may better understand why I felt passionate about
bringing the character of Brother Brendan to life. His dark past is not evident to the
reader, nor his fellow monks, when the story begins. Clearly, Brother Brendan would
have preferred it to stay that way.

I can't deny that Brother Brendan's character was also influenced, to some
extent, by one of my favorite literary characters—Shane, from the western novel of
the same name. A former gun fighter who finds himself enjoying a simpler life with
some homesteaders, he eventually finds himself in the middle of a good vs. evil
struggle and must call upon his killer instinct, and a past he was trying to part from,
to level the playing field and provide a chance for justice to prevail. In a touching
scene at the end of the book, immortalized by Alan Ladd's character in the movie,
Shane explains to young Joey that he must be moving on; that there's no living with a
killing and no going back. Shane tells his young admirer, "Right or wrong, it's a
brand. A brand sticks. There's no going back."

In similar fashion, after Brother Brendan reveals himself to stunned friends and
foes alike, it's clear that there is no going back. Once his work was done, once he had
unleashed that Hell that still burned deep inside of his breast, there could no longer
be a place for him in the monastery.

It was a story I really wanted to tell and, at the eleventh hour, I got the wild
idea to try to place it into some sort of free-form poem. Like a quickening heartbeat
during times of stress and excitement, I thought I might build the tempo of the poem
toward an eventual climactic crescendo. It was a unique idea and with only hours
remaining, I set to the task and completed it in one setting. I could feel my heart
racing as I wrote—driving me ever forward towards a conclusion.

When the work was done, I felt pretty proud of my work. Thankfully, like my
other submission, Brotherly Love was accepted into the historical fiction anthology.

THE OTHER SIDE OF RAIN

(June 2, 2021)
Published by Red Penguin Books in "*A Collection of Children's Stories*"
(July, 2021)

*A children's story. With the day's planned events
rained out, a young boy and his sister discover that
there's another way of looking at rain, and at life.*

Billy looked out at the rain. It was pouring down. All week long, Billy had dreamed about playing baseball on Saturday but he knew the games would not be played in the rain. He hoped the rain would stop in time for his game. When the phone rang, Billy feared the worst. Billy's mom listened to the voice on the phone. When Billy heard his mother say "I'm sorry, too," he knew it was going to be bad news.

"Billy," said his mother, "I'm very sorry but all Little League baseball games are cancelled today because of the rain." Billy was very upset.

"I hate rain!" Billy said. Some tears began to drip from his eyes and rolled down his cheeks. "Rain ruins everything!" Billy's mother gave Billy a big hug and held him tightly. They both looked out the window and watched the rain. It was really coming down, now. Billy yelled at the window, "I hate you rain!"

"Oh, don't hate the rain, Billy," said Billy's mom. There's another side to rain.

"Yah, the wet side," said Billy, still upset.

"The wet side makes the grass greener and the flowers more beautiful. You know how much Granny and I love beautiful flowers."

"But you can just buy them at the store, Mom. That's what everybody does these days."

"Store-bought flowers can be very pretty," said Billy's mom, "but they were once thirsty little seeds and the rain gave them life and made them beautiful." The phone rang again. Billy's Mom walked back to the kitchen to answer the telephone; it was Brian McCauley's mother. She said that the rained-out game had been rescheduled for Thursday night. Brian was a good friend of Billy and he was also a very good baseball player. He was going to miss the game today because he was still recovering from a cold. He was almost better, but not quite well enough to play. Now that the game was moved, Brian would be able to play in the game.

Billy's mother returned to where Billy was sitting on the couch in the living room. "Billy, guess what?" she asked.

"I don't know. Was that Brian's mom on the phone?"

"Yes. And she said that the game has been rescheduled for Thursday and that Brian should be well enough to play then." Billy was very happy to hear that news.

"That's awesome! Brian is our best player and we're going to need him to beat the Tigers," said Billy.

"Hey, I have an idea, Billy," said Billy's mom. Do you know how Granny keeps saying that she would love to see you play?"

"Yes. I'd like to have her come to some of my games but Granny always has Bingo at the home on Saturdays. And, Granny never misses Bingo."

"That's right, Granny is the Bingo Queen of Boone County. Folks at the home just wouldn't know what to do if Granny skipped out on Bingo Day. How about I give her a call and see if she could make a game on Thursday night?"

"Sure! That'd be great," Billy said, excited about the thought that maybe Granny could see a baseball game.

Billy's mother called Granny on the phone and Billy could hear the excitement in Granny's voice from across the room. She was so happy that she would finally be able to see Billy play baseball.

"Is Granny coming to the game, Ma?" asked Billy.

"Yes, she is. We just made her day. I bet she's racing off to tell all her friends at the home, right now. They will be so happy for her. We can thank the rain for that."

Billy's sister, Clarice, did not know about the other side of rain. She was supposed to visit a petting farm today with friends from her school. Clarice went to a special school for children who could not see. Clarice was blind. From the living room, Billy and his mother could hear Clarice sobbing in her room.

"Billy, why don't you visit your sister and see if you can cheer her up?" said Billy's mom.

"Mom, what can I possibly do to make Clarice happy?" asked Billy.

"Maybe you can tell her about the other side of rain?"

"Okay, I'll try," said Billy, "but I really don't think Clarice will care about anything I have to say."

Billy knocked on his sister's door but she told him to stay away. She did not want visitors and she did not want her brother to see her crying. Clarice said, "Go away! I hate the rain and I don't feel like talking to anybody!"

Billy thought about leaving but then he got an idea. "Hey, Clarice," he said, "I want to do something special with you."

"Nothing you can do is as special as petting baby goats and bunny rabbits," said Clarice. "That's the most special thing in the world and the rain just washed them all away."

"The rain didn't wash them away," said Billy. "They're all fine and I think they'll have a great time playing in the rain."

"Goats and bunnies hate the rain," said Clarice. "It makes their coats all wet and soggy and then they all start crying."

"There's another side to rain, Clarice, and I'm going to show it to you. When I do, you'll know that the goats and bunnies aren't crying. They are laughing and having the best time of their lives."

"No, they aren't," said Clarice, not believing a word her brother was saying. Soon, she would believe.

"Let's get your raincoat on, Sis; we're going on an adventure." Clarice's door slowly creaked open and she reached out for Billy's hand. Billy held his sister's hand and they walked together to the coat closet. Billy helped Clarice put on her pretty yellow raincoat and then he put on his own raincoat. They both put on their special splish-splashy boots.

"Mom, Clarice and I are going outside for a bit. I want Clarice to experience the other side of rain," said Billy. Billy's mother smiled and she told her children to enjoy themselves.

Billy and Clarice walked out into the rain and Billy led Clarice over to the largest puddle he could find. Clarice loved how things smelled so fresh and clean. The rain had done a wonderful job at washing all the dust out of the air. The rain also washed her mother's car and filled the bird bath with nice clean water. The sounds, too, were like music to Clarice's ears. She loved the sound of rain drops splashing in puddles and the way the rain made a pitter-patter sound upon the leaves of trees. Billy began to jump up and down in the big puddle and Clarice, while holding her brother's hand, jumped too. Clarice was laughing like crazy. Water was splashing everywhere. She loved the sound of splashing water and she laughed when she felt water splashing on her leg and even all the way up on her face. Billy and Clarice splashed, and splashed, and splashed. They just couldn't stop laughing. It had been a long time since Billy had had so much fun playing with his little sister. Clarice gave Billy the biggest hug ever and said, "I love you, Billy! You're right. There is another side to rain." Just then, they both heard a jingling sound that got louder and louder.

"Gabby!" shouted Clarice. She knew right away that the jingling sound meant that their little dog, Gabby, was outside and ready to play. Gabby ran over to Clarice and Billy and licked them both before running around like crazy, playing in the rain. "I think Gabby likes the other side of rain, too," said Clarice.

"Yes. She loves it!" responded Billy. Billy laughed as he watched Gabby rolling in mud puddles, turning her beautiful white coat into a muddy mess. Gabby was having the time of her life. Even though Clarice couldn't see Gabby play, she knew from her brother's laughing, and her dog's excited panting, that Gabby could not possibly be happier.

After playing for over an hour in the rain, Billy, Clarice, and Gabby were called back inside by Mom. Billy's mother cleaned up Gabby, as best she could, with a big fluffy towel. Billy and Clarice were both a little bit wet but they weren't as wet or as muddy as Gabby.

"Mom," said Clarice, "we showed Gabby the other side of rain and she loved it." Clarice ran her fingers along her mother's face and could feel the big smile.

"Yes, she does," said Clarice's mom."

Clarice's mother made two mugs of hot chocolate for her children and added extra whipped cream on top. She knew both her kids loved hot chocolate. It was the perfect drink for a rainy spring day such as today.

"Hey, Mom," said Billy, "hot chocolate is part of the other side of rain, too."

"Why, sure it is," answered his mother.

While Billy and Clarice were drinking their hot chocolate, Gabby curled up, under the table, and enjoyed having both of her kids with her on a Saturday afternoon.

Clarice was first to notice that the rain was letting up. She no longer heard the sound of rain upon the roof.

"I think the rain's stopping, Mom," said Clarice.

"I believe you may be right," replied Mom, getting up and walking out to the living room to look through the big picture window. "Wow! Come on out here, kids." Billy's mom was excited about something; but what?

When Billy looked out, he knew exactly what his mom was so excited about. He put his finger to his lips to let his mom know that he didn't want her saying anything more about what she saw. He wanted to surprise Clarice.

"Clarice," said Billy, "we need to go outside."

"Wait, Billy, I need to get my boots and raincoat," said Clarice.

"No, you don't. Just come with me. We need to get outside quickly," replied Billy. Billy led his sister outside, neither of them wearing shoes or socks. They walked out onto the wet grass of the front lawn. The rain had stopped but the grass was still very soggy. To Clarice, it felt like they were walking on a wet sponge.

Billy walked with Clarice to the middle of their yard and he told Clarice to look up.

"Why do I need to look up, Billy? I can't see anything," said Clarice.

"I'm going to be your eyes, Clarice. Just look up. Trust me," said Billy.

"Okay. But you better not be messing around with me."

"I'm not messing around with you, Clarice. Just hold my hand and listen."

"Okay, Billy," said Clarice. "I trust you."

Billy turned Clarice just a little bit and lifted her chin up slightly. Then he described what she was looking at.

"There's a beautiful patch of perfect blue sky between those billowing dark clouds. And, in that beautiful patch of blue, is the prettiest rainbow you could ever imagine. There's a brilliant band of red on top that's as juicy as the cherries you love. And then there's a vibrant orange that's sweeter than freshly squeezed orange juice. Look, there's yellow, and it's almost as bright as your beautiful rain coat and I just know it's tastier than the best lemonade ever. Lime green, blueberry blue, and the most delicious grape purple imaginable. Can you taste it?" Clarice was loving her brother's description of the arcing colors in the sky.

"Oh, yes! I can taste it and, better yet, I can even see it!" Clarice was so very excited. "It's the most beautiful thing I've ever seen! Thank

251

you, thank you, thank you!" Clarice gave her brother a big hug and Billy kissed her on the top of her head. They stood there, together, for fifteen minutes until the rainbow slowly washed away.

Thanks to the rain, the grass was greener and the flowers were prettier. Thanks to the rain, the birds had clean water to bathe in and Mom's car no longer needed to be washed. Thanks to the rain, Granny made it to her first baseball game and got to see Billy and his friend, Brian, help their team win against the undefeated Tigers. Thanks to the rain, Billy and Clarice grew closer together, as brother and sister, and learned about how much fun it can be to play in the rain and to spend time with each other. Gabby already knew it was fun to play in the rain.

Billy and Clarice both learned about the other side of rain. What they didn't know is that their mother, also, learned a few new things about the other side of rain. They would never look at rain in the same way again.

The Story Behind the Story

With a deadline two weeks after the deadline for the historical fiction anthology, I prepared for my next "never done this before" opportunity. This time, the task was to create a children's story for a new anthology, appropriately titled: "A Collection of Children's Stories." I had never written a children's story (unless you count the things I wrote when I was a young child). As far as the actual subject matter went, the aperture was wide open and, with an ample 5,000-word limit for submissions, I felt pretty confident I would be able to knock something out. But I wanted to do more than just create a story to match the requirements. I wanted to write something that had inspirational value and a positive message. It didn't take me long to come up with the message I wanted to convey, because it's a message that helped change my life and one I have not forgotten. In a way that a child would understand, I wanted to highlight that the attitude you take toward life and life events has a major impact on your happiness and peace. To borrow an old proverb, "every cloud has a silver lining." Beyond the message, I thought back upon the beautiful friendship I had with my little sister, growing up, and thought I would sprinkle some of that magic into the story, too. Finally, I decided to add in the element of a physically challenged child—in this case, young Clarice who was blind. I wanted the reader to consider that one's condition, no matter what it might be, is no obstacle when it comes to establishing a positive frame of mind.

As a longtime lover of rain, and also a "victim" of multiple rained out ball games, it seemed natural that the backdrop for the story should be the disappointment both Billy and Clarice felt with their day's plans put in jeopardy because of an unwanted rain storm. With all the elements in place, I took to the keyboard to create my story which, happily, was accepted into the upcoming anthology.

THREE STATES

(Written June 12, 2021)
Previously Unpublished

*A poetic meditation on the water cycle, artfully
describing water in its three physical states—vapor,
liquid, and solid—through the lens of seasonal
changes in a mountain landscape.*

Vapor, lifted on high, crystalizes into an infinite array of geometric
sculptures
Dancing upon the breeze; descending from winter clouds
Majestic peaks enshrouded beneath a blanket of snow
The mountains are peaceful; stoically awaiting spring

Spring lifts the mantle of winter and life bursts forth
Snow melt gives birth to streams; streams feed the great river
The great river winds its way along ancient trails
Replenished, the lake in the valley swells and sparkles; a gem hidden
amidst the peaks

Cool and clear, pooled water reveals all beneath, it's surface as smooth
as glass
Life thrives in and around the lake; deer drinking, fish spawning, dragonflies dancing
The summer sun warms the water by day, releasing moisture that
returns, again, as rain
Each seedling, blade of grass, flower, and mighty pine gives thanks

Autumn brings its harvest and the hills glow with vibrant hues
Morning dew begets frost as the valley shivers, no longer warmed by
the summer sun
The blades of grass, browning now, crunch beneath my feet as I walk
I draw water from the lake and return to my cabin

Water boils in my pot, steam billowing from the cauldron where I cook

Three States

Cabin windows fog, a pane of glass parts the warm moisture within
from winter's chill
The days grow shorter; the snow line descends from mountain peak to
valley floor
The lake begins to freeze, the ice growing thicker by the day

Strapping on my skates, I bless the solitude of the frozen wonderland
Gliding upon nature's perfect rink, nestled between the towering peaks,
I find peace
Condensation; my warm breath fogs the air as I speed across the ice
below
The friction of my blades turns the ice to liquid and I glide; euphoria

Gas: steam from my pots, exhaled breath, billowing clouds in the sky
Liquid: melted snows and rains; rivers, lakes and the vast oceans
Solid: snowflakes tumbling toward earth; ice atop the lake and dangling
from tree limbs
My body, more water than not, thrives upon dihydrogen monoxide; I
offer my thanks

The Story Behind the Story

I think I missed the target on this one. The title for the next anthology in the Red Penguin Collection series was "The Ocean Waves" which was to be a book filled with poetry reflecting on "the beauty, stillness, and serenity of water." I believe the editor was looking for toes in the sand, happy summer beaches, and tropical paradises. That's not what I felt like writing about...so, I didn't. Going with the water theme, I envisioned a cabin up in the mountains and sought to describe, in a somewhat poetic fashion, the various forms that water might take across the seasons. My title, "Three States," of course refers to the solid, liquid, and gaseous forms that water may attain. I cannot say I was surprised that my poem was not accepted as part of the anthology but it still provided me with some level of enjoyment as I crafted this work. What do you think?

Paris Bench

(Written July 15, 2021)
Published by Red Penguin Books in "*Paris: Love, Loss and Longing in the City of Lights*" (September, 2023)

*It's never too late for second chances in a city known
for bringing lovers together. This fictional story
recounts how destiny worked its will upon a man who
was sure his best days were behind him.*

Ah, if the River Seine could only speak; the stories she would tell. Love and romance. Heartache and heartbreak. Intrigue and betrayal. Hope . . . and second chances.

Fog diffused the light from the lamp posts, lending a softness to the scene, as Peter, a middle-aged gentleman, buttoned his coat against the chill of an October evening in Paris. While lovers walked, hand in hand, along the banks of the Seine, Peter contented himself with his unobstructed view of the lovely river from his favorite bench. A statuesque woman in her mid-twenties approached. Lean and lovely, she might well have been a Paris fashion model and Peter's mind raced for an explanation when she asked if she might join him on the bench. She spoke in English but her enchanting French accent betrayed her national origin and clearly identified her as a native Parisian.

"You speak to me in English," said Peter. "For all the time I've spent in Paris, I thought I might have shaken the 'American tourist' look. Apparently not." The woman smiled and quickly sought to remedy any insult she might have unintentionally conveyed.

"Au contraire, you are looking very continental. I simply noticed the rolled newspaper at your side was in English and not French. As you were not reading the paper and looked rather lonely, I thought that perhaps I might join you. Of course, if I have disturbed your quiet reflections, then I sincerely apologize and shall leave you to your thoughts." Peter had, in fact, been dreamily reliving a very memorable moment from his younger days. However, the spell having been broken, he was not disinclined to accept the offer from the lovely stranger. Peter slid over to the right side of the bench and used his handkerchief to wipe the moisture from the painted wooden surface to his left.

"Please forgive my rudeness," said Peter. "Naturally, I welcome the company of a beautiful French woman." Peter snickered, amused by the seemingly preposterous notion that an attractive stranger, likely half his age, had somehow played the opening move of a romantic gambit. Peter got his first good look at the woman's face when she stepped around to the side of the bench. The soft glow of the nearby lamp revealed a heavenly visage like few he had ever seen before. Doe-eyed and radiant, the stranger stole Peter's breath away. His jaw dropped and he sat, in a veritable stupor, even as Lune reached out her hand in greeting, an enchanting smile stretching across her face, accentuated by her perfectly formed lips.

"Hi, I'm Lune," greeted the lovely stranger. Her smile faded a bit as Peter failed to respond in any fashion typically associated with sociable beings. Peter was stunned silent. It was not so much the great beauty of the woman he was speaking to as it was an eerie sense that they had met at some point in the past. The eyes. The smile. The voice. The gentle demeanor. All of it reminded him of Gabrielle. Still unable to form words, Peter desperately salvaged the moment by leaping to his feet and grasping Lune's soft hand with both his hands, holding them affectionately. Lune could see the effect she was having and nervously laughed, thanking Peter for the unspoken complement. Without question, Lune could have walked the fashion runways of Paris or Milan, had she chosen such a path in life, and so she was seldom shocked by the admiring gaze of men . . . but the look in Peter's eyes was something different. There was reverence and passion that went far beyond "I want to take you to bed tonight." Lune reached out with her other hand and Peter shifted his right hand to grasp it. They stood there, hand in hand, carefully scrutinizing one another. "Care to sit?" offered Lune, after the silence had transitioned from slightly awkward to uncomfortable and unsettling. Peter simultaneously released his grip on both Lune's hands, returning his own hands to the warm lined pockets of his trench coat.

"Yes. I'm so sorry. I'm not sure what came over me," responded Peter.

"Please don't apologize. Truly, I'm flattered," Lune replied, the beautiful smile returning to her face.

"You must think me a lecherous old man. I'm definitely not that.

I'm a gentleman and a person of the highest morale character. The thing is . . . well . . . you look very much like someone I once knew; someone very special to me."

"Oh, and I thought that perhaps you were taken by my appearance," said Lune, more in jest than suffering of any sense of disappointment. She was confident enough to know that good fortune had blessed her with attractive features. Peter considered a response and concluded that any course of action he might choose was fraught with peril so he simply returned to his spot on the bench, allowing room for Lune to sit beside him. Peter gazed out across the Seine towards the far bank which was only barely visible through the fog. The two sat together in silence, for a while, before Lune sought, once more, to strike up a conversation. "When I saw you sitting here on the bench, staring longingly upon our beautiful Seine, I thought to myself 'now there's a man with a story to tell.'"

"And are you the sort of woman who cares to waste part of her evening hearing the sorrowful tale of an old fool?" interjected Peter. Lune looked upon Peter with a sympathetic eye.

"I am always in the mood for a love story," responded Lune, her soft voice tearing down the walls that Peter had spent years building around his heart.

"So, you believe I am harboring a love story, do you? Perhaps I'm reflecting upon a tragic collision between two river cruise boats? Or, maybe, I'm considering some great financial loss—a failed business deal or unwise investment?" Lune mumbled something in French that Peter was unable to discern until she clearly repeated her words, in English.

"You have the look of one burdened by the blessing of love. I can tell," said Lune, her eyes sparkling. "I'd love to hear your story, if you're willing to share it with a stranger. Frankly, I don't see that there's much to lose from your perspective and it could well be that your story might provide me some life-enriching insights." Peter considered the request carefully before replying.

"There's nothing enriching about turning away from a once in a lifetime opportunity to share a future with the woman of your dreams. My story isn't a happy one."

"Please allow me to be the judge of that," said Lune. "Perhaps I may see your story in a different light. The story begins here, no?"

Peter nodded, a little surprised by the bold yet completely accurate assertion.

"Yes. Right here at this bench."

"Was she beautiful?"

"No woman I had seen before nor since is her equal. Yes, she was very beautiful."

"And her name," asked Lune, resolved to limit her interruptions after the query.

"Gabrielle. Her name was Gabrielle."

"That's a lovely name," added Lune.

Peter paused, for a moment, and sighed. He had never shared this deeply personal and life-defining story with anyone and his brain was still working out how much of the tale he wished to surrender to a stranger. There was something disarming about Lune that persuaded him to open up. Somehow, he felt that she might understand and that she would not be quick to judge. Peter also had a strange feeling that this could be a first step toward relieving some of the painful heartache that had tormented him for over two decades.

"It was twenty-five years ago, today, that I was walking this very path along the bank of the Seine. I was studying architecture as an exchange student at the École Nationale Supérieure d'Architecture. Truth be told, I spent less time studying and more time drinking and socializing. My grades were not impressive and I was in jeopardy of losing my scholarship and having to return to the United States on account of poor academic performance. My parents were getting divorced, about the same time, and my world seemed to be spinning out of control. If I lost my scholarship, I'd have to put my college dreams on hold and return home to work in the factory. I'd seen my father part with all his life's ambitions and resign himself to being a wrench-turning ant in a nest of thousands at that factory and I knew I couldn't live like that. It was a very dark time in my life." Lune nodded, a concerned look on her face, but did not interrupt the storyteller. Peter fell silent for a minute, clearly trying to compose himself.

"And then came the 12th of October. I was walking along the bank of the Seine, as I often did when I needed time alone to reflect, when I noticed a woman hunched over and sobbing on a park bench—this park bench. I approached her, much as you approached me, and asked if I might lend assistance. When she turned toward me, eyes filled with tears, I knew she was the one. Our introductions were brief. Although I inquired, Gabrielle did not seem interested in sharing her problems. Rather than speak, we held hands and looked out upon the river. The moon was full that night—so bright and majestic that I could not help but believe there was some magic in the air. Moon beams shimmered across the water setting the entirety of the Seine ablaze in luminous splendor."

"How very romantic," added Lune, unable to resist the temptation as Peter set the stage for all that was to come.

"It was a perfect night for love to blossom. And it did. After a certain period of time, how long I cannot say as time lost all meaning that night, we began to converse. Gabrielle was a student, as well. She had recently lost her parents to a tragic accident and, while desperately searching for answers to her depression, fell into an abusive relationship with a controlling classmate who seemed, at the time, to be the answer to her grief. Before she knew it, she was trapped. Hooked on drugs and alcohol and dependent upon her boyfriend for lodging and basic necessities, she was all but a prisoner."

Tears began to stream from Lune's eyes as Peter told of Gabrielle's awful plight and how she contemplated suicide on several occasions to try to escape her pain.

"That is horrible," cried Lune. I've known several women who have similarly fallen into such a terrible trap and I might well have done so myself were it not for the excellent counsel my mother provided me while I was growing up. She warned me against such dependency and always made sure that I had a place to come home to if life failed to show me kindness."

"Consider yourself fortunate, Lune. Too many suffer the fate of dear Gabrielle. You owe your mother a great debt of gratitude for helping to spare you such pain by teaching you important lessons about self-worth, dignity, and true love."

"So, were you the knight in shining armor, riding in to save the day?"

"No. I wish I could have been. I'm afraid I was little more than a pleasant distraction. The magical moon fills your mind with all sorts of crazy notions. I began to believe that destiny had led me to my soul mate. I had never given much credence to the notion of soul mates until that evening. The moon also fooled me into believing that I was, somehow, worthy to possess this beautiful princess. I was so naïve—a boy chasing dreams."

"What's wrong with chasing dreams?" asked Lune.

"They can lead you down a dozen rabbit holes and distract you from doing the real work of living. That's what's wrong with chasing dreams?" Lune looked unconvinced.

"I'm not sure I agree . . . but please go on with your story. I want to know what happened next."

"Well, we enjoyed each other's company through the night and talked until the sun broke the horizon. We watched the beautiful sunrise and I think we both felt a certain lightness in our hearts. It was the dawn of a new day, both figuratively and literally."

"Although we were both very tired, neither of us wanted to part ways. We shared an irrational fear that the spell might be broken if either of us turned our back on the other. We didn't want the dream to end and so we held each other tightly, as if each of us were the life preserver keeping the other afloat in rough seas. We walked the streets of Paris, stopping at a quaint patisserie for croissants and coffee. After our morning snack, we continued on until we were too tired to speak intelligibly. That's when I invited Gabrielle to my apartment."

"And she agreed? I'm amazed she was so trusting of a stranger, especially after all she had been through."

"Yes. She agreed. I must admit, I was surprised, as well. I offered up my bed so that she could get some sleep because I was afraid of what she might be going home to, had I not. Perhaps an abusive and controlling boyfriend, infuriated that his property had spent the night away? I didn't know what awaited Gabrielle. I only knew that I needed to protect her from any possible retribution or maltreatment."

"And then you made love?" Lune asked, immediately regretting the leading question and her own impatience to find out how the story would progress. She readied herself for a rebuke that never came.

"No," said Peter. "Not that morning. Gabrielle did not want to be alone so we held hands, in bed, until she drifted off to sleep. My mind was alive with beautiful daydreams so I found it hard to sleep. Eventually, exhaustion caught up to me and I fell asleep, too."

"It was late afternoon when I finally awoke to the sound of the shower running in my small bathroom. Gabrielle's dress lay at the foot of the bed. By the time the water stopped, my heart was pounding out of my chest. I wish I could say my mind was focused on more noble endeavors but, in truth, lust had overcome my charitable aspirations. Alas, I was a mere man and no better."

"You shouldn't blame yourself for being that which you were born to be, Peter," added Lune. "There is nothing wrong with being a man and, if not for sexual attraction, our species would have gone extinct long before the birth of any saint." Peter blushed and looked away. He felt a little uneasy discussing sexual matters, more so given his audience was a young woman half his age. Lune assuaged his concerns and assured him that she was very interested to know how things progressed between the two. Resolving to modify his storytelling to keep the account at a PG rating, Peter continued on.

"After what seemed like an eternity, Gabrielle stepped back into the bedroom; the bath towel wrapped tightly around her body was barely large enough to conceal those parts best left to the imagination . . . at least on a first date. You know what I mean." Lune smiled at Peter's old-fashioned sense of propriety.

"I believe I do. But please go on."

"As you might imagine, I was speechless. Gabrielle's beauty had stolen my heart the night before but, somehow, with her makeup washed away and her short, wet hair wildly dancing about her forehead, she looked even more desirable than the painted doll I had spent the morning with. Gabrielle was a true natural beauty."

"And then you made love to her?" asked Lune, a sly smile on her face.

"I wanted to. Well, part of me wanted to. But it just didn't seem right. Not yet. I wanted our relationship to be something special— something different. I didn't want to be just another one of the countless men who pursued beautiful women for a night's conquest. I thought I was better than that. I knew Gabrielle deserved better than that. No, I suggested that we might stroll along the Avenue des Champs-Élysées and then, later, find a nice restaurant for dinner. Gabrielle was concerned about wearing her now wrinkled dress out to a nice restaurant so I suggested we might go shopping for some new clothes."

"I'm impressed. She must have been grateful for your generosity?"

"I think she was surprised. In truth, I surprised myself. My rent for the month was already overdue and I knew the clothing and dinner would make a serious dent in my dwindling emergency savings. I wanted Gabrielle to believe I was successful and a good catch. I was anything but that. I had squandered my money on alcohol and diversions and I was on the verge of losing my scholarship. I painted myself to be this go-getter, on a fast track to become a rich corporate architect who would be designing and overseeing the construction of a veritable empire of luxurious skyscrapers across the globe. The sad part is, Gabrielle believed every word of it. I'll never forgive myself for misleading her in this way. I meant no harm. I was in love and I wanted Gabrielle to love me back. I could not believe that any woman would love me unless I was financially successful and moving aggressively toward achieving great things in life. I was a student, failing classes and failing in life."

"She may have known more than you suspected, Peter," said Lune, in a kind and assuring voice. "Women understand more than you might imagine."

"I don't know how she could have. In any case, I was so afraid to lose her that I tried very hard to be a better man. I escorted Gabrielle through several very posh department stores and she picked out a lovely dress, a jacket, and a few accessories."

"Expensive?" asked Lune.

"Actually, no. The items she chose were reasonably priced, especially given the stores we were visiting." Lune smiled, knowingly, reflecting on her earlier comment about women understanding more than they might let on.

"Eventually, we returned to the hotel and changed for dinner. I called up a taxi and we enjoyed a lovely meal at a five-star restaurant overlooking the Eiffel Tower. It was the most memorable meal of my life. Every detail was perfect and I could not have been more satisfied had I been dining with Venus, herself. After dinner, we walked to the Eiffel Tower and later caught a cab up to the Sacré-Cœur Basilica where we beheld a breathtaking view of the city lights. We held each other tightly, kissing as lovers do. Eventually, we returned to my apartment."

"And then you…"

"Yes. And then we made love. Our bodies moved as one, beneath the covers, and we both left the troubles of the world behind. Gabrielle responded to every touch, every gentle stroke of my fingers. Her pleasure became my measure of success for nothing else seemed to matter. Likewise, she took me to new heights—levels of ecstasy I never dreamed possible. One night turned into two, and then days became weeks. I completely forgot about my classes and school work. I was shocked back into reality when the phone rang, one afternoon, while

Gabrielle was out shopping for a baguette, cheese, and wine for our evening in. It was the Financial Aid Office calling to inform me that my scholarship had been revoked and that I was to be expelled from school. I was devastated. So much for living in a dream, right? Reality had finally grabbed me by the throat and I felt starved for air. I had shared my hopes and aspirations with Gabrielle and she believed in me. I panicked. I didn't know what to do. It was Christmas Eve and I was at the end of my rope. I used what little funds I had left to purchase an airline ticket back to the United States with just enough money left to buy a few gifts for Gabrielle and cover the cost of a holiday dinner at a nice restaurant."

"She knew something wasn't right, didn't she?"

"I'm sure she suspected. I've never been a good actor and I certainly didn't feel right about continuing a charade. But I also couldn't bear the thought of breaking the news to Gabrielle on Christmas Eve. So, we went to dinner. We exchanged gifts. We made love. We each played our roles, uneasily, in this final scene. We spent Christmas day together. We held each other more tightly and kissed more deeply. The next morning, I crept away, leaving only a note of apology as an admission of my cowardice and my failure."

"How awful. That must have been heartbreaking."

"I've had to live with the shame these past twenty-five years. I was never worthy of Gabrielle. What she saw in me, I'll never know. It was wrong of me to seek a place in her life. She was the sun in the sky and I was…" Peter stopped abruptly, unable to continue his tale as emotions overtook him. He fought hard to regain his composure, wiping tears away with his handkerchief. "Heartbreaking? Yes. Absolutely heart-breaking. But, ever since returning to the U.S., I vowed that I would become a better man. I would become that man that I had led Gabrielle to believe I was."

"Did you return to the factory? The factory your father had worked in?"

"I did, but only briefly. I kept my nose to the grindstone and worked multiple jobs to help pay my way through college. I first earned my bachelor's degree and later attained a master's degree in Architecture. But I wasn't simply focused on academic and professional excellence. I truly wanted to better myself as a person. Never again did I lie or seek to deceive others. I regularly donated my time to several charities assisting victims of domestic abuse and swore that I would do everything in my power to help promote healthy relationships so that no one would have to endure the pain that Gabrielle went through."

"A noble cause, Peter, but I'm afraid you've set an impossible goal. You are dreaming again, my friend."

"Perhaps," Peter said, smiling through his tears. Maybe there's still a bit of dreamer left in me." Lune smiled and reached over to squeeze Peter's hand.

"We all need to dream. We all need to keep hope alive." Peter squeezed Lune's hand in return. They both looked back towards the river. The fog was thinning and the Seine was now brilliantly illuminated beneath a full moon.

"Peter, did you ever marry? Do you have a family?" Peter sighed.

"You know, I tried a few times. I mean, I tried to build relationships but nothing seemed right after Gabrielle. I couldn't let go. Or, maybe, I just didn't want to let go. I know, that's kind of sad, isn't it?" Lune considered Peter's words.

"You still love her that much?"

"Yup. I still love her that much. I gave up what I loved most in this world because I felt I had nothing to offer beyond pain and disappointment. I was sure that a beautiful woman like Gabrielle would find her way and make something of herself. I would have been like an old rusty anchor that pulled her down. I couldn't bear to do that to her. I loved her too much. I love her too much."

"Please don't be offended by what I say but I think you've put too much weight on what you were feeling when, perhaps, you should have given more consideration to what Gabrielle felt. It's possible she saw through all the smoke and mirrors. It's possible that she knew exactly who you were—your vulnerabilities and insecurities . . . but also your strengths and the goodness within your heart; a goodness you too readily deny. Did you consider that Gabrielle may have loved you simply for who you were and how you made her feel?" Lune's words struck deeply and were met with a contemplative silence followed by a stream of tears.

"You're right, Lune. I was self-centered and I was wrong. I found true love and I let it go. And now, I willingly serve my penance for my greatest mistake."

"And is penitence what brings you back to this bench?" asked Lune.

"No. Not penitence. Love. Love brings me back. Every year I

return to this bench and I remember a love so pure and true that it erases all the sorrows and woe within my heart. It revives my spirit and reminds me of what is good in this world. That's what keeps me coming back. Love."

Lune began weeping and she slid closer to Peter and wrapped her arms around him giving him a big hug that caught him totally off guard.

"I love you, Dad!"

"What?" Peter replied, bewildered and unsure of what he had just heard. Lune repeated her words, slowly and clearly.

"I…love…you,…Dad."

"Dad?"

"Yes. I was named "Lune" in homage to the beautiful full moon that you enjoyed with my mother on the night you first met."

"Then you are my daughter!" Peter returned the hug, tenfold, nearly squeezing the air out of Lune's lungs. "Please tell me, how is your mother? Is she well? Is she happy?" The excitement in Peter's voice was palpable and Lune couldn't help but laugh as she wiped away the remaining tears from her cheeks.

"Mom, I think you better take it from here," said Lune, further adding to Peter's confusion. He looked at Lune, quizzically, and she swept her long black hair away from her right ear revealing a small wireless earpiece connected via Wi-Fi to her phone.

"What's going on here, Lune?" asked Peter, more confused than ever.

"I'm sorry, Dad. I didn't know how else to do this."

"To do what, Lune?"

"Well, you see, I've witnessed you re-visiting this spot for several years now. Mom visits it, too. Sometimes, we've both watched you together. I kept telling Mom that she should walk over and talk to you but she felt you wouldn't want to see her, that somehow it would cause you pain or make you sad. She used to say that a good-looking man like you would surely be married by now and that it wouldn't be right for her to stir up a bunch of memories. You know—leave the past in the past. I tried to tell her that you probably wouldn't be making a yearly pilgrimage to this spot if…" Lune stopped abruptly when she saw her mother emerging from behind a distant tree. Lune's phone had been transmitting the whole time and Gabrielle had heard every heart-felt word of the conversation on the bench.

Gabrielle approached, slowly, and stepped into the light of the nearby lamppost. Peter followed Lune's gaze over toward the lamp and his heart nearly stopped when he saw Gabrielle. Peter quickly got up and, being in such a hurry to close the distance between himself and Gabrielle, tripped on one of the legs of the bench and fell upon the soft grass. Gabrielle gasped and raced over to him. Whether due to a release of nervous energy or because of the child-like glee filling his heart, Peter lay there laughing in the grass. Gabrielle knelt down to attend to him and, after seeing the expression of pure joy on Peter's face, began to laugh, as well.

Gabrielle was the first to speak. "I always told Lune that if we ever met again, you'd surely fall for me just like our first night beneath that beautiful moon. I just didn't think you'd fall this hard." Gabrielle reached for Peter's hand and they laughed together.

"Gabrielle, did you hear our entire conversation?" Peter asked, once the laughter had died down. Gabrielle's hair was still short, looking much as it did when they first met. She reached up and slowly pulled the Wi-Fi earpiece from her ear and slid it into her jacket pocket. Peter recognized the jacket. It was the one he had bought for Gabrielle before their first dinner together. Though well-worn, it still looked great on her. Rather than answer Peter's question directly, Gabrielle leaned over and kissed Peter passionately where he lay on the grass. Beneath the light of the magical moon, Gabrielle appeared to have aged little since the last time the two lovers had embraced. Or, perhaps, it wasn't the magic of the moon at all. Love creates its own special magic.

The fog, much like the weight of regret and disappointment, dissipated completely. Gabrielle reclined on the grass next to Peter and the two gazed up toward the moon and the stars while holding hands. Lune got up from the bench, satisfied that she had done something good, and prepared to leave her parents so that they might make up for lost time or simply frolic in the grass to their hearts content. As she walked away, she called out "Will I see you for breakfast?" Her parents just laughed.

"Maybe not tomorrow," replied Gabrielle. Lune smiled.

"Okay, well please be sure to send me a wedding invitation, then." Faint, giggles was all Lune heard in reply. She walked away with a big grin on her face.

Peter and Gabrielle did not make breakfast the next morning.

Flapper and the Captain

Several months later, Lune received a wedding invitation and, on October 12th, twenty-six years after the day they first met, Peter and Gabrielle were married in a small ceremony along the banks of the Seine.

The Story Behind the Story

Ah yes. There's an interesting story behind this piece. If you look at the date I wrote this story (July, 2021) and the date of publication (September, 2023), you'll notice a rather significant time difference—over two years. Keeping on pace with the two-week interval between Red Penguin Collection anthologies, I knew I was in trouble when I saw the request for submissions come out asking for romance short stories "of a more sensual/adult nature." Romance writing is not my strong suit. The fact that the advertised cover showed a female hand pressing into or clutching a satin sheet made me think that I might be rowing upstream on this one. Still, I figured I'd give it a shot. I don't know that my work was appropriately "steamy," and it certainly wasn't likely to make any reader smoke a cigarette or take a cold shower after reading...but I still thought it was a nice story about love lost ... and then found again. And the backdrop, Paris, is certainly well known for being roman-tic. For all my effort, this piece did not make the cut for "Between the Covers—An Adult Romance Anthology." I was a bit disappointed because I thought it was a nice story, and I was hoping others might have the chance to read it. As fortune would have it, in 2023, Red Penguin Books created another series of location-based anthologies. These books were not part of "The Red Penguin Collection." The travel-themed books would permit authors to submit not only true-life travel accounts but also short stories and poems whose theme matched the region the book was focused on. The first three books would cover London, Paris, and Rome. When I heard about this new series, I thought I might take another shot at having "Paris Bench" published. It worked! This story, along with a fun real-life travel story from a trip I took to Paris, made it into the book. I hope you enjoyed reading it.

VIOLENCE, DEATH...AND HOPE

(Written July 26, 2021)
Previously Unpublished Short Play

Some evil doers find the tables turned in a power play and must seriously consider their actions . . . and their lives.

AUTHOR'S CAUTION: This play includes the portrayal of an assault. While I have limited the narrative so as not to be overly graphic, it's possible that reading the play might elicit an adverse emotional response for anyone who has been the victim of an assault or has any close relations who have recounted their experiences. As such, please consider whether or not you wish to read this work. To maintain authenticity, this play makes discretionary use of a limited amount of profanity.

Act One

Scene 1

Dirt hiking path through the woods on a nature preserve, Long Island, New York. Just before sunset on a cold November evening.

A woman, wearing dark camouflage cargo pants, a black hooded sweatshirt (hood up), and hiking boots walks slowly along the walking path while two men, waiting behind some trees, watch her progress. Her cell phone rings and she reaches into one of her pockets, retrieving the phone and answering the call. The brief conversation is inaudible and she returns the phone to her pocket. HORATIO, a well-groomed man in his twenties, wearing a jogging suit and high-end basketball shoes, approaches; his associate observing from behind a tree.

HORATIO

Hey, miss! Excuse me, miss.

ANGEL stops walking and looks toward HORATIO, as he approaches. She says nothing.

I'm really sorry to bother you, but my car ran out of gas and I'm stranded on the side of the road. I feel really embarrassed to have to even ask but could you possibly spare a few dollars so that I can buy some gas to get home?

ANGEL looks over HORATIO'S shoulder and notices his associate slowly making his way through the trees, parallel to the walking path. She returns her gaze toward HORATIO.

ANGEL

Perhaps, you might consider asking your friend?

HORATIO

What friend? I told you; I was driving and ran out of gas. You were the first person I came upon and I'm sure glad I did. I was afraid I wouldn't find anyone out on a cold and dark afternoon, especially with snow in the forecast.

ANGEL

I see. So, you don't know that guy in the faded jeans and denim jacket who's circling behind us now?

HORATIO

What? No.

VICTOR

Hey, bud, I've been looking for you. Your girlfriend got worried when

270

you didn't show up for the party and asked me to try to find out what happened to you. I got scared when I saw your car parked on the shoulder.

VICTOR continues to approach and ANGEL shifts her glance between HORATIO, standing in front of her, and VICTOR, approaching from the other side of the path.

ANGEL

Well, it looks like you're all set now that your friend has showed up to save the day. It was a pleasure to meet you. Now, if you don't mind, I'll get back to my hike before it starts getting dark.

HORATIO

Please don't go. You haven't even told me your name. I'm Bob.

HORATIO extends his hand but ANGEL refuses to accept it, her hands remaining in the pockets of her hoodie.

There's no reason to be rude. I just wanted to know your name. You're kind of pretty and I thought maybe you'd like to come to our party.

ANGEL

I'm not interested. May I finish my walk, please.

VICTOR

Why've you got to be such a bitch to my friend? What makes you so special that you can treat other people like shit? You're one of those rich chicks who thinks she's superior to everyone, aren't you?

HORATIO

Yah, I'm kinda hurt. I was just looking to make friends but I guess guys like me will never be good enough for you.

ANGEL

You know, it's extremely unchivalrous to prey upon people's inclination to help those in need only to take advantage of them. What, exactly, do you want from me?

HORATIO

Let's start with an apology and then you can hand over your cell phone and any money you have.

ANGEL

And so, the trap is sprung. I haven't any money and I refuse to surrender my phone.

HORATIO

I don't have time for your BS, lady, and I'm not going to ask you again.

ANGEL anxiously looks around for a possible escape route but realizes she is trapped.

ANGEL

And if I refuse?

VICTOR steps around to the side, pulling his jacket open to reveal a handgun tucked in his belt.

So, you'll shoot me for not giving you money I don't even have?

VICTOR

There's only one way of finding out what you have on you, isn't there?

ANGEL tries to run past HORATIO and VICTOR pulls out his gun.

Get her! Tackle that bitch!

HORATIO quickly catches up to ANGEL and grabs her arm, thereby restraining her. VICTOR runs over and puts his gun up to ANGEL's cheek.

One more stunt like that and I swear I'll shoot you. You don't mean shit to me.

ANGEL

No. Not yet. But I will.

ANGEL seems unusually calm. Victor backs away, confused but undeterred.

VICTOR

Whatever. You're crazy, alright. Give her a good pat down and check all those pockets. I want any car keys and that phone. If she doesn't have money on her, it's probably in her purse back at her car.

ANGEL

I didn't drive.

VICTOR

Shut up, bitch! If I want you to speak, I'll tell you. For now, just relax and enjoy the search.

HORATIO begins running his hands along ANGEL's body, taking his time with the search.

HORATIO

No keys, amigo. Just the phone.

HORATIO pulls the phone out of ANGEL's cargo pants pocket.

VICTOR

Hand it over here. Maybe it's got one of those car unlocking apps.

HORATIO hands the phone over to VICTOR who slides his gun back into his belt so that he can inspect the device.

ANGEL

I told you; I didn't drive.

VICTOR gives ANGEL a hard shove and she falls on the dirt path. He stands over her, menacingly, and glares down at his victim.

VICTOR

And I told you to shut the hell up.

VICTOR fidgets with the phone

Give me your pass code for the phone. What are the unlock numbers? Now!

ANGEL

I thought you wanted me to shut the hell up?

VICTOR angrily kicks ANGEL where she is lying and pulls his gun back out, pointing it at ANGEL's head.

HORATIO

Holy shit, man! Settle down, don't do anything crazy.

VICTOR

This bitch is making me crazy. But she's going to regret being such a smart ass. First, she's going to give us her phone unlock code and then we're going to peel off those clothes and make sure there's nothing concealed underneath. After that, well, it's jungle rules. To the victor goes the spoils, as they say.

HORATIO

Look, she's got no money and we can always find someone to unlock the phone. That's a nice one—I'm sure we can get a few hundred bucks or more.

VICTOR

Not good enough. I want to make this whore suffer.

HORATIO

What's that going to do for us? Nothing. Let's just go.

VICTOR

It's going to do a lot for me; I can tell you that much. Last chance, girl-friend, give me the unlock code and I might just go easy on you.

ANGEL slowly gets to her feet, brushing off the dirt from her pants.

ANGEL

Horatio, you still have time to do the right thing. You need to choose your actions wisely.

HORATIO

What the hell! Are you some kind of cop? Who the fuck are you?

ANGEL

Horatio, that is your name, isn't it? Horatio Esteban Ramirez, born April 4th, 2000?

HORATIO

I'm not telling you anything! I don't know who you're talking about.

ANGEL

Father of one and another on the way. Do you plan on marrying Miranda or are you just going to walk away like you've walked away from the rest of your responsibilities? Are you going to leave her to raise those kids on her own? Don't you want to be a good father? Don't you want to be a good man? It's not too late, you know.

HORATIO takes a few steps back, a stunned look upon his face. Some tears begin to roll down HORATIO's face and his words are spoken softly with a trembling voice.

HORATIO

Who are you?

VICTOR

I'll tell you who she is. She's an undercover cop. That's the only way she'd know all that stuff.

HORATIO

She's not wired up. I don't think she's a cop.

VICTOR

She's a cop, alright. Only person stupid enough to walk through this park alone on a night when no one else is going to be around.

HORATIO

Well, if she is the police and she was targeting us, she's probably got all kinds of backup out there. We'd never see them in the woods. They're probably watching and listening with those super sensitive microphones, or something.

VICTOR

Or maybe she's been talking to them through her phone? Unlock code, now, or I swear I'll shoot you!

ANGEL

You don't want to do that, Victor. Your time has all but run out and now you must decide whether your final act shall be one of charity or of great violence. The choice is yours but be mindful that all choices have consequences.

VICTOR

Damn it! Who the fuck are you, bitch?! Give me that code, now. I'm not going to ask again. You'll be dead before your backup ever arrives.

ANGEL

Alright then. The code is 111298.

VICTOR

11-12-98?

ANGEL

Yes. Sound familiar?

VICTOR

Not really.

ANGEL

It's the day you were born.

HORATIO

Holy shit, man! Let's just go now!

VICTOR

11-12-98?

ANGEL

That's what I said.

> *VICTOR, holding the phone in his left hand, taps upon the screen while continuing to keep his gun pointed towards ANGEL. A look of astonishment comes upon his face and he drops the phone and his gun as he falls to his knees. He begins sobbing uncontrollably.*

VICTOR

Jesus, no! Please, God, save me!

ANGEL

> *A spotlight illuminates ANGEL and VICTOR as the stage lights dim.*

Victor Edward Gurevich, you are summoned and this day your soul travels with me.

VICTOR

Please, I beg of you, have mercy on me. I can repent. I'll turn over a new leaf, I swear it. I'll be holier than a saint, I promise on my life.

ANGEL

Your promise means nothing as your life is forfeit. I have no mercy to offer you, Victor Gurevich, for your soul has already been judged and now I have but to convey it into the afterlife.

Violence, Death...and Hope

VICTOR

Sobbing and whimpering his words.

It's not my fault. I swear. It's not my fault.

ANGEL

You own the choices you made in this world. While fate may seem unkind, it is within the heart of man to respond with dignity and nobility or, failing to do so, to summon their darker side to redress perceived injustices. Through charity and kindness, much can be overcome. In fact, I have seen paupers live as kings just as I have seen the privileged fall into ruin and despair. You make of life what you will but, again, the choices you make are your own and you shall be called to account for your actions.

VICTOR

I never had a chance.

ANGEL

I am not concerned with chance or choice. Some find greater fortune than others along their journey but all roads eventually lead to me. I am Death, and this day your life is ended.

VICTOR

I'm not going! You're not taking me anywhere.

VICTOR picks up his gun and fires several shots toward ANGEL. No bullets reach his target and ANGEL stands motionless, observing VICTOR's futile actions.

ANGEL

And now, Victor Edward Gurevich, we must be on our way.

ANGEL reaches out her hand. VICTOR silently stands, as if in a trance, and takes hold of ANGEL's outstretched hand. A glowing red light emanates from off stage (left) and the spotlight follows ANGEL and VICTOR as they slowly walk off the stage. Once off stage, the lights go dark.

Scene 2

The same walking path through the woods, Long Island, New York.

The lights slowly illuminate the hiking path where HORATIO stands, looking over towards where VICTOR's body lays just off the path. He quickly walks over to attend to his friend but cannot revive him.

HORATIO

Victor? Victor? Come on, man! Please, dude, don't be dead. I need you.

HORATIO notices ANGEL's cell phone in the grass and goes over to look at it.

Victor Edward Gurevich. Born November 12, 1998. Condemned. Collection on November 29, 2020. Holy shit! That's not possible.

The phone begins to ring. Terrified, HORATIO drops the phone and leaps backward, tripping and falling. ANGEL appears from stage left and slowly approaches HORATIO.

ANGEL

You don't need Victor, Horatio. You don't need his drugs. You don't need his stolen money. You don't need his false friendship, his violence, or his hatred.

HORATIO

Take your damn phone but please let me live.

Not speaking a word, ANGEL walks over to her ringing phone and picks it up, beginning a conversation.

ANGEL

Hello. I see. I'll be on my way shortly.

HORATIO

Please don't kill me. I'm begging you. I've got so many things I want to do and I want to see my children grow up to become something... something better than me.

ANGEL

This phone rings not for you, Horatio. Not today. As for your friend, Victor; I didn't kill him. He killed himself. He died many years ago when he turned to theft and violence to support his drug habit. Today, his weakened heart finally failed him. It was his time. Your destiny is not set and so I caution you to mark well what you have seen here today.

HORATIO

So, you're not going to kill me?

ANGEL

We will meet again. Whether it is sooner or later depends much on your perspective. Your life is a fragile thing and the sands of the hour glass run swifter than you might imagine—so make every grain of sand count.

HORATIO

I will. I swear to it. I'll be a better man. I'm going to be a loyal husband and a caring father. I will dedicate my life to...

Flapper and the Captain

ANGEL

I believe what you say, Horatio, but your words are wasted on me. I care not for the deeds of humanity, only for the souls that I might reap…and man, in all his folly, has provided many bountiful harvests.

HORATIO

How much time do I have then? When will I die?

ANGEL

Hmm. That's a question that many before you have sought an answer for and have been denied. No, it's best that you live your life without knowing. Live and make every moment count. You shall have time enough to do much that you desire. Prioritize well for we shall meet again before you have quite attained all your goals. So it is for most and so it shall be for you.

HORATIO

I think I understand. Thank you for sparing me.

ANGEL

Don't thank me. It was not your time. Now, be gone before I change my mind.

HORATIO slowly backs away and then turns to run and exits stage right. ANGEL stands there, for a few moments, contemplating. She lifts her phone and taps the screen a few times and then looks intently at the screen.

So, we finally get to meet. I was wondering how long you were going to keep a step ahead of me. I'm sure we'll have some interesting things to chat about on our way.

The stage lights dim and go dark.

Finis

Violence, Death...and Hope

The Story Behind the Story

New territory, once again! "30 Minutes to Curtain—A Collection of Bite-Sized Plays" set before me the difficult task of creating a mini-play. I knew the editor, JK Larkin, had numerous friends who were students of theater and sought careers related to this artform, and I had never written a play before so, again, I felt the effort would be a challenging one and the competition would be very stiff. Still, I was excited to give it a try. I started out with this notion of a scene on the ramparts of a castle in the moments before a great battle but, for some reason, writer's block kept plaguing me until, with time dwindling before the July 31ˢᵗ deadline, I decide to abandon Plan A and craft an entirely different storyline. This was going to be raw and, as my initial disclaimer alludes to, I was concerned not only about the language I'd be using but also the triggering nature of the scenario for anyone who had actually suffered through the terror of an assault. I've had a number of friends who have and I always feel a mixture of great concern (for my friends and what they've had to deal with) and intense anger (toward the perpetrators of such heinous acts). Beyond the personal stories I've heard, I was keenly aware of a number of assaults reported along various hiking paths and how many of my friends are very anxious about hiking because of the risk. These are beautiful and scenic wooded areas, some with beautiful views along the shoreline or of lovely lakes. It really bothers me that these should not be safe areas for all travelers. The emotions were already getting stirred up inside me when I envisioned the perfect "vigilante" for my story—the Angel of Death. I wanted the Angel to be reimagined into a plausible victim who, ultimately, holds all the cards, completely shifting the power dynamic—rather than a victim, she will be the ultimate and indisputable arbitrator of all that is to come. My three characters would be simple. One redeemable, one unredeemable, and one supernatural with the power to pass final judgment.

Before the fun could start, I had to do some research on how to actually write a play. Again, I knew I'd be competing with people who really knew what they were doing. I set about doing some study using resources available online. I figured out how my piece should be formatted, including how to add stage direction for the work. This was a fun learning process for me. In the end, my play was not selected for inclusion into the anthology but I still felt it was worth the effort. This is the first time it's seen the light of day, and I hope that you've found some redeeming qualities within.

PARANORMAL DREAM TEAM UNLEASHED

(August 7, 2021)
Published by Red Penguin Books in *"Until Dawn—A Supernatural Anthology"* (September, 2021)

"Reality TV" becomes a little bit too real for a group of celebrity ghost hunting goofs. With a little help from "the other side," some past wrongs are made right.

"Ghosts are real! I've seen them. Spirits inhabit our world and regularly intermingle with the living. Most of the time, these spirits are benevolent and the nature of their contact is unthreatening or even playful. But, sometimes, evil spirits and tormented souls manifest themselves in a frightening manner and threaten our homes and even our lives. When these darker spirits go on the offensive, that's when my team of paranormal experts leaps into action. Hi, I'm Chad Connors and I've been investigating paranormal activity for over fifteen years. I've assembled a team of the nation's top experts in the field and we're armed with the latest tech and techniques to take the fight to the dark spirits and put an end to their hauntings and harassment from beyond the grave. Together with ghost wrangler William "Jocko" Hayford, paranormal tech pro Arnold "Dweeber" Nixon and talented spiritualist and medium Clementina Alvarez, we're going to find those dark spirits and chase them back to where they…"

"Cut!"

"Cut? Why? What did I miss?"

"The new girl. You keep forgetting that Clementina is out. We've got Jody now," said Dan Parsons, director for the highly successful Paranormal Dream Team television series on PTV, the Paranormal TV channel.

"Darn it! Sorry, Dan," said Chad, looking across the street to the Ziegland Hotel, filming location for the current installment of the series. "You know, I'm really going to miss that crazy Latina Goth wacko. Why'd you have to replace Clementina with a smoking hot

284

blonde, anyway? What were you thinking?" replied Chad, unable to hide his college frat boy smirk.

"It's a sacrifice I was willing to make," said Dan, a sly smile forming on his face. "Apparently, Clementina felt we were a bunch of goofballs and that associating with our show was hurting her reputation as a legitimate spiritualist...whatever that means."

"She's about as legitimate as a vegan pot roast but, I have to admit, I'm going to miss that crazy look in her eyes as she conjured up those stories about evil spirits tormenting her. That was some first-class blarney, right there. Jody's going to have to step up her game if she's going to top that," said Chad. Right about that time, Jody and Jocko pulled up in the PDT van. The crew immediately shifted their attention to the van...and to Jody.

"Coffee's here, boys!" announced Jody, as she stepped out of the van.

"And she brings us coffee, too," Chad whispered to Dan.

"Yes, she does," replied Dweeber, more intent on watching the blonde-haired, blue-eyed knockout gliding gracefully towards them in her tight jeans and denim jacket. The male members of the Dream Team eventually snapped out of their trance and Dan walked over to grab a cup of coffee from the cardboard carrying tray. The other PDT members followed suit.

"So, what'd you find out from the hotel manager? What's our angle?" asked Jody.

"Let's move the herd over to the hotel and I'll tell you on the way. We're going to stage out of one of the upstairs meeting rooms. You're really going to love this one, Jody. We've got intrigue, jealousy, murder, a mass tragedy, and angry spirits—all the makings of a great show. We met briefly, yesterday, with Melissa Simmons, the manager for the hotel. She told us about some of the terrifying experiences guests and staff have had at the Ziegland. The challenge will be that she insists that we somehow try to paint this thing in a good light so it doesn't hurt hotel patronage."

"I don't see how we could make things much worse," countered Jocko. "Let's see, we've got a hotel built on top of the ashes of dozens of innocent people whose lives were taken buy an insane murderess who killed her own twin sister and now terrorizes guests...and we're going to somehow damage this place's reputation even more? Seriously?"

"Tell me the whole story," said Jody, having missed the initial fact-finding interview with Melissa Simmons. Dan motioned to the team to keep their voices down as they passed through the lobby, heading towards the elevators.

"Chad, why don't you give Jody a quick run down," said Dan.

"Sure. Love to. So, the Ziegland Hotel was built in 1930. Department store mogul Arthur Ziegland had a vision of creating a chain of luxury hotels across the country and eventually expanding operations across the globe. He ensured no expense was spared in the construction of this flagship hotel. Fine Italian marble was brought over from the continent to pave the floors in the lobby and expert craftsmen from Europe were hired to carve the intricate woodwork you see throughout the hotel, all made of the finest woods. Spectacular crystal chandeliers illuminate the lobby and the restaurant while elegant light fixtures adorn the hallways on all floors. In short, Ziegland wanted his hotel to qualify as one of the wonders of the world. He wanted everything to be perfect."

"Sounds great. Why aren't we staying here, then?" asked Jody. All eyes turned toward Dan.

"Hey, hey, we're on a budget here. Now get back to your story, please, Chad. Besides, once you've heard the full story, you'll thank me that we're staying at the Best Western down the road."

"Okay. So, we have this beautiful hotel…but it's cursed."

"Ooh, curses. I love curses," responded Jody with a wink.

"Thankfully, so does the PTV audience. Anyway, there's been a string of strange happenings over the years—people getting scratched and pushed down stairs, shadowy figures wandering the halls at night and taking strolls through the lower levels, and even disembodied sobbing coming from empty rooms. You know, classic spooky stuff."

"Got it. But the curse; I want to know more about this curse, Chad."

"Right. So, this hotel, once built, became a magnet for the rich and powerful. Dignitaries, sports heroes, kings and queens, you name it. Anybody who had a name and wanted to mingle with others of similar social status checked in at the Ziegland."

"Sounds like this place had everything going for it. Why haven't I heard of more Ziegland hotels?"

"I'll tell you why, Jody. The curse." Chad paused briefly, for dramatic effect. He was a natural showman, even off camera. "Shortly after the completion of the hotel, strange things started happening. Ziegland ignored these signs and made sure the stories were hidden from the press. A major party was planned to celebrate the anniversary of the hotel's opening. Neither Arthur Ziegland nor his wife, Adelaide, lived to see it. Three weeks before the gala, Adelaide was dining at the hotel restaurant and, apparently, was a little tipsy. A bone got lodged in her throat, blocking her airway, and she tragically choked to death, much to the horror of the onlookers. The loss of his wife devasted Arthur. A memorial dinner was held in the hotel, a week after Adelaide's loss, and was attended by many of the Ziegland's wealthy and powerful friends. Arthur Ziegland was inconsolable. Having had a few too many drinks, himself, he wandered out into the street, following the memorial, and was hit by a passing streetcar. He was killed instantly."

"Oh my God, that's horrible. So sad," said Jody, upset by the story.

"It was a terrible tragedy. Among the upper tier of society, there was a tremendous outpouring of grief."

"I can only imagine."

"However, with the financial chaos of the Great Depression beginning to ravage the economy, many people found it difficult to find sympathy in their hearts for a family who had lived in splendor and opulent decadence for so many years. Accusing fingers were pointed toward the Ziegland family for constructing a lavish hotel on the site of a horrible tragedy. Many people claimed this disrespectful act was the source of the curse."

"Stop teasing me with this curse thing, Chad. What's this tragedy you're talking about?"

"So, the current manager contacted a historical researcher, about eight years ago, to look into the story. Apparently, an old tenement building stood on this location for many years; one of those dilapidated places with poor ventilation and inadequate fire escapes."

"And it was demolished to build this hotel?"

"No, Jody, it wasn't demolished…it burned down after a terrible fire that took dozens of lives. Worse yet, several papers speculated the fire was deliberately set by a deranged young woman named Sarah McDonnell." Jody seemed increasingly agitated by the story and the jovial manner in which Chad was sharing it.

"So, what happened?"

"As the story goes, Sarah McDonnell caught her twin sister messing around with her guy, a wealthy industrialist by the name of Oliver Wilkinson. She saw Wilkinson as her ticket out of the ghetto and was infuriated when Wilkinson shunned her in favor of her sister. She waited until she caught the two together and then, in a jealous rage, brutally murdered not only Wilkinson but also her own twin sister. Afraid that her dark deed would be discovered, she set the fire to destroy all evidence and hung herself as the flames burned below. The fire occurred in the late evening and while many residents were able to flee the burning building, some forty-two people lost their lives in the blaze. Many of the bodies were never found and those that were found were charred and unrecognizable. It must have been a hellish nightmare." Tears began to stream down Jody's face as she listened.

"That's absolutely horrible."

"Yah, it's some pretty grisly stuff. There's nothing like a woman's wrath, is there? Talk about fanning the flames of passion!" Jody wasn't amused by Chad's attempt at adding a touch of humor to the horrific story. "Um. Yah. Sorry. Anyway, that's our angle. We going to prove that Sarah's ghost is the source of the negative energy here at the hotel and then we're going to see if we can coax her spirit into stopping her attacks on the guests."

"The sister had a name?" asked Jody.

"We were going to let you figure that out using your psychic powers," added Jocko, trying to lighten the mood a little bit. Jody turned toward Jocko, with a serious look on her face.

"Jeanine," responded Jody. "I'm feeling like her name may have been Jeanine."

"Holy smokes! How did you know that? Did you really just pick up that vibe from the building?" The boys were all aware of the name since it appeared in the newspaper clipping they were shown but they were legitimately surprised that Jody knew it.

"Trade secret," said Jody, with a wink.

"Hey, save some of that special sauce for when the camera's rolling," added Dan. "That's great stuff! But when we're filming, don't let on that you've done any research on this case. Remember, you're supposed to be showing up cold and using your psychic powers to help us unravel this mystery."

"Got it, boss," said Jody, with a smile.

Unpacking some of their gear in the meeting room, the group chatted for a while longer and discussed the shooting schedule for the day with the camera crew. Dweeber seized the opportunity to corner Jody's attention by running through some of the ghost hunting equipment he planned to employ during the investigation. Most of this was new to Jody so she listened with interest.

"Okay, so this here is an EMF meter and it measures fluctuations in electromagnetic energy. Often, the presence of spirits will cause small spikes in the energy field around us and this device will light up to let us know the extent of the interference. Then we have the Ghost Box EVP, or Electronic Voice Phenomena recorder. It's a very sensitive radio frequency scanner that allows ghosts to respond to our questions by communicating in ways we normally wouldn't be able to hear. We've also got night vision cameras and various light sensors that detect light emissions invisible to the human eye--infrared, ultraviolet, etcetera. One of my favorite tools is the Structural Light Sensor camera. You'll love this one. The camera has an infrared light projector with a monochrome CMOS sensor that shows everything as dots arranged in a 3D formation. The software recognizes human body forms and represents the joints as dots and the limbs are lines of light connecting the dots. If you watched our show about the haunted saloon, the SLS camera was the tool we used to show the stick figure dancing girl climbing up to sit on the piano."

"I totally remember that. That was absolutely incredible!"

"Yah, the fans love it. They want to see the spirits, not just hear about temperature fluctuations in the room and an uneasy feeling. Speaking of which, I also have several environmental instruments that measure local fluctuations in temperature, humidity, and pressure. I've got a couple other tricks up my sleeve, too, but those are the basics."

"I'm impressed, Dweeber."

"Thanks, Jody. So, are you busy tonight?"

"Excuse me?"

"Joking. Just kidding. So, the basic game plan for the shoot is that I take care of the science, Chad and Jocko will add the theater and a little ghostbusting flare, and you need to ramp up the drama with foreboding feelings and spiritual connections to the ghosts and ghoulies."

"You're talking like you don't believe in this stuff, Dweeber. Do you?"

"I believe in whatever puts money in my pocket and food on the table," replied Dweeber, a little defensive about the accusation.

"I can't blame you there. I just figured everyone on the team was sold as to the existence of ghosts."

"Well...I believe in the electronic readings off my equipment but I don't know that I'd associate them with actual spirits."

"Even the dancing girl from the old saloon?" asked Jody.

"That was pretty cool, wasn't it? It's just I've never actually seen a ghost with my eyes so I'm a little skeptical. So...how about you? Have you bought into this whole 'spirits among us' thing?" Jody considered before answering.

"Well. It's complicated. I'll leave it at that." Dweeber smiled, knowingly, and gave Jody a fist bump.

"Food on the table, right?"

"Yup," responded Jody, "food on the table." Dweeber turned his attention back to the director who was trying to get everyone's attention.

"Alright, everyone, listen up," said Dan. "I want Camera Team Number One to head up to the 8th floor with Chad and the gang and Camera Team Number Two to start setting up for low light operations down in 'the dungeon.' We'll start filming there around midnight so make sure you get a little rest after the setup. Chad, first up, we have a 2:30 interview with the guy who got shoved down the stairs. We'll talk to him at the scene of the crime. Jocko, Dweeber and Jody, you're welcome to listen in but I want you off camera. We're going to have you guys do a walk-through later tonight with the equipment. Questions, anyone?"

When the team reached the entry to the 8th floor stairwell, they met Mr. Randall Lipinski, a portly gentleman in his mid-sixties. He described his experiences from a year ago when he was attending a convention for insurance agents. Chad knew how to liven up any interview and peppered the camera lens with a clownish barrage of overly exaggerated facial expressions. Shock. Dismay. Astonishment. Bewilderment. Showman that he was, Chad had mastered the fine art of turning the mundane into an abstract piece of art.

"So, this demonic spirit clawed at your back and then shoved you down this flight of stairs?"

"It sure did. I guess I'm lucky to be alive," replied the somewhat dim-witted Lipinski.

"You sure are. We're dealing with some really dark forces here and potentially the spirit of a cold-blooded killer named Sarah McDonnell."

Behind the scenes, Jody winced and Jocko made a rather inappropriate joke about Sarah having to be one strong chick to even get the morbidly obese Mr. Lipinski to budge, much less push him down a stairwell. The interview went on with more of the theatrics that the team thrived on. Jody seemed troubled by it all but brushed aside Dweeber's inquiry. Once the interview was done, Dan and Chad thanked Mr. Lipinski who, after verifying when he'd receive his pay for the segment, made a straight line for the nearest elevator and departed the hotel. Dan turned toward Jody, eager to see his new cast member in action.

"So, what do you think, Jody? Are you picking up on anything here in the staircase?"

"Usually, I like to spend some time alone in an area to get the feel for it," responded Jody, uneasy about being pressured into a psychic assessment for an area she'd only just visited.

"Sure. That makes sense. Of course, you're going to have a camera team with you and, well, you know the rest."

"Yes. I know," replied Jody, with a sigh.

"Don't forget to ham it up some, Jody. You've got to sell this."

"I'll try," responded Jody, trying not to sound annoyed. "But I'm really not sensing any spiritual presence here."

"Well, keep at it. I'm sure you will, eventually."

Dan had convinced himself that he was a bastion of patience and the perfect boss. He didn't understand how annoying his little pokes and prods were. Chad, Jocko, and Dweeber simply learned to ignore him but Jody was troubled by the notion that Dan might actually have no interest in her abilities whatsoever. She was not accustomed to performing like a trained seal to the sounds of a whistle. "Don't sweat it, Jody. You're going to be great. Just spend a little time here and work up your monologue and we'll capture it all tonight when we come back."

"You sure you don't want to knock this out now?" added Jocko, "no one is going to know night from day in this stairwell and I think we'd all benefit from some team building at Frankie's tonight before we have to film the basement sequence."

"Sorry, Jocko, but I'm just not feeling it. I'm going to spend a little more time here to see if I pick up on anything. But you can still hit

Frankie's and maybe I can shoot the stairwell segment with Dweeber and some of his gadgets and then we can all meet up later for the late-night basement sequence." Dweeber seemed more than willing to skip out on the drinking escapades at Frankie's for the opportunity to spend a little more time with Jody.

That afternoon, Jody walked the halls of the hotel alone but steered clear of the basement. She wasn't sure why but she had a very uneasy feeling about heading down there, especially alone. Dan had given the green light for Dweeber and Jody to film in the stairwell a few hours before the full crew met for the basement sequence. At 10pm, the two met up with their assigned cameraman. Dweeber had left most of his equipment downstairs but brought along his EMF meter. Without Chad's wild theatrics, the raw readings from his devices were often unimpressive.

"Three, two, one," the cameraman, Luis, counted down.

"So, Jody and I are here at the site of the stairwell attack. I'm getting some activity on my EMF meter, as you can see. I feel like we might be in the presence of a ghost. Jody, are you picking up on anything?"

Whispering, Jody tried to play up the drama but she really wasn't sensing much spiritual activity and she didn't like the idea of faking it just for the camera. "I'm sensing that Mr. Lipinski's trip down the stairwell was an accident and not an assault by supernatural forces. I feel like he may have been drunk and just stumbled while he was heading back to his room after a drinking binge in his team lead's room." Dweeber wasn't sure this was going to play out well for the TV audience but he also didn't want to push Jody into making up stories about demons clawing guests and shoving them down staircases.

"Spirits, if you can hear me, send us a sign if you're innocent of pushing Randall Lipinski down the stairs," said Dweeber, playing to the camera. He was doing his best but he didn't have the same charismatic screen presence as either Chad or Jocko. Jody moved in closer to Dweeber to look at his EMF meter and the device spiked. "Did you see that? Did you see that, Jody? I think whatever spirit is here is trying to tell us that they weren't the one to push Mr. Lipinski down the stairs. Maybe we're talking with Oliver Wilkinson or one of the other innocent victims? Oliver, if that's you, send us another sign." Jody stepped back to survey the area further, looking for any evidence of an otherworldly presence. The EMF meter went quiet and the lights on the device stopped flashing. "Looks like the spirit has left us. But there was definitely something here. The question is who that something, or someone, is." Dweeber looked over to the cameraman and nodded. "Did you get all of that, Luis?"

"Got it all. Do you want any more footage in the area?"

"Um, maybe just a few more shots of Jody walking down the stairs with that spaced-out look on her face," replied Dweeber.

"Oh, thanks, Dweeber," said Jody, with a slightly annoyed look on her face. "So, I'm looking spaced-out, now?"

"You know what I mean. The audience loves when spiritualists go into a trance or it looks like the spirits have entered into their body. That's the kind of stuff that sells tickets, right?"

"I suppose," Jody said, with a sigh. She complied, feigning her best far-and-away expressions and thousand-mile stare. When the stairwell sequence was done, the three headed down to the next floor to catch the elevator to the lower level. The lower level the elevator descended to was not actually the lowest floor of the hotel. An old cement stairwell led down to an iron door that normally remained locked. Beyond the door was a subterranean level that was actually part of the foundation for the original tenement building. Although gutted by the fire, the stone foundation was still sturdy and the area served as a storage area for seasonal decorations, historical artifacts, and other seldom-used properties. It would also serve as the stage for one of the most dramatic performances in Paranormal Dream Team history.

Just after midnight, the cameras began rolling. Chad described, in his best campfire ghost story manner, how employees of the hotel dreaded coming down to the lowest level of the hotel, an area most referred to as the "haunted dungeon." The two incandescent light bulbs in the dungeon were left off and the sequence was filmed using the night vision cameras. The Dream Team slowly made their way deeper into the room; old carousel horses, costumed Mardi Gras mannequins, and even nativity scene figures appeared as eerie apparitions through the grainy view of the night vision lenses. The Team's hearts were already racing before Dweeber's EMF meter began beeping and flashing like a smoke detector gone haywire. With cameras rolling, Chad was totally in his element—a triple-cappuccino combined with an adrenaline rush made his performance all the more frenetic.

"I think we've got a live one here, team! Sarah, is that you? If that's you, Sarah McDonnell, give us a sign. Tell us why you killed your sister and Oliver Wilkinson. Was it jealousy? Did you mean to kill all those people?" Dan was thoroughly enjoying watching his star at work. He was anxious to see how the new girl would fit into the action. Jocko motioned to Dweeber to pass him one of the EVP recorders. Everyone was hoping they'd pick up a response from the ghost on the recorder. All they heard was the normal static.

Jocko continued the questioning while Chad swept his flashlight into the darkness to enhance the dramatic effect. "Is that you, Sarah? Are you still here? Does your tormented soul still wander the halls of the Ziegland Hotel?" Jody stopped in her tracks and began to tremble with fear. Dan waved his arms to get the attention of his Director of Photography and motioned for him to get a camera on Jody.

"Holy cow! Jody, are you okay?" asked Chad, still more acting a role than concerned about his co-host who he assumed was, likewise, putting on a show for the camera. Jody seemed to be gasping for air as she begged for the Team to get her out of there.

"Guys! Guys! Look at this!" Dweeber held up his SLS Camera where a small stick figure person seemed to materialize in the far corner of the room. The pace of the action was increasing exponentially as Dream Team members darted here and there waving their assorted devices through the air and panting as they gasped for breath. The cameras were drinking up all the excitement like cold beer from a keg.

"Temperature's dropping!" shouted Jocko. "And the pressure's off the scale! Wow, my ears just popped—this is crazy!" Chad continued his wild narration as measurements from the various devices were read off to him by team members. Chad directed the film crew to focus in on the area where the stick figure had appeared on the Structured Light Sensor camera.

"It's coming this way!" yelled Dweeber, now putting all his attention against the humanoid stick figure that appeared to be slowly walking towards them. Jody struggled to speak but couldn't get the words out. Her legs seemed frozen in place and a look of pure terror had replaced her usual pleasant facial expressions.

"Who are you?" shouted Chad. "Can you smell that, fellas? It smells like sulfur or something. It's getting stronger. Damn! The hair is standing up on the back of my neck. Sarah McDonnell, is that you? Have you come back to torment the living? Speak to us!" Meanwhile,

Dweeber remained glued to his SLS camera, his hands starting to tremble as the figure continued to close the distance between them.

"I think it's heading toward Jody," said Dweeber, trying, as best he could, to mirror Chad's intensity. Jody remained motionless, shaking in fear. Dan was eating this all up. If any members of the Dream Team had realized that Jody was not acting, they might have done more to aid their teammate.

"Camera One's offline," shouted the photographer.

"Just lost Two, added another." Dan ran over to the Director of Photography and asked him what was going on but he was speechless and replied with a shrug. About this time, boxes began flying through the air as if violently thrown by a berserk madman. The sound of shattering glass and splintering wood echoed throughout the dungeon.

"Dudes, I'm not kidding you, that thing is heading right for Jody," exclaimed Dweeber, the emotion now very evident in his voice. He dropped his camera and ran over to her, grabbing her arm to lead her away. Just as he touched Jody's arm, she let out a blood-curdling cry.

"Leave me alone, Oliver! I don't want you. Go away! Let me go!" Jody collapsed on the floor and the whirlwind of paranormal activity seemed to subside. The team members stood silent. Only Dan was still speaking, inquiring to make sure that at least one camera was still capturing the action. The static on the EVP recorder grew much louder and some barely audible words, or what might be interpreted as words, came across the speaker.

"Did you hear that?" shouted Jocko. "I think it said 'you are free.' Let me play that back." Jocko hit rewind and Chad and Dan listened intently to the garbled transmission. Not one to miss an opportunity for drama, Chad jumped on the bandwagon.

"I heard it, too! 'You are free.' Who's free? Who are you setting free, Sarah?" Dweeber knelt on the ground, beside Jody, and continued to try to revive her. Jody gasped and then sat up. Dweeber, who had been holding her hand, quickly dropped it.

"Holy crap! Jody's hand is as cold as a block of ice." Dweeber jumped back as Jody slowly rose to her feet, her eyes rolled back so that only the whites showed. She was standing but Jody was clearly not herself.

"Get a camera on her, man," urged Dan, fascinated by the display which he still believed was staged theatrics.

"Oliver is free." Jody's voice, while recognizable, seemed strangely unnatural. Chad jumped in on cue.

"Who is this speaking to us? Is this Sarah McDonnell?"

"Sarah is free."

"Who are you? Tell us your name," urged Chad. Dan was frantically coordinating movements of his photographers in the background.

"Jeanine," replied Jody. "Jeanine. Jeanine. Jeanine." Jody's voice trailed off with her last utterance.

"Jeanine, what happened to you? Are you angry because your sister killed you? Is that why you're haunting the hotel?" Chad was totally playing this impromptu as he had no idea what Jody was going to conjure up next. Besides a few members of the video crew who were frightened beyond words, Dweeber was the only one who didn't think Jody was acting. If she had that kind of performance in her, he was certain she would have played it up back on the 8th floor.

"Sarah is free. Molly is free. Now, Oliver is free."

"Wait, who's Molly? C'mon, talk to us Jeanine."

Jody was done speaking. She fell back to the floor and lay there, curled up, sobbing. This time, Chad and Jocko dropped their instruments and joined Dweeber as he attended to his co-host. Dan signaled that he wanted to keep the remaining cameras running. Chad whispered in Jody's ear, asking if she was okay and she nodded that she was. Steeling herself for her first actual performance of the day, she stood back up and pronounced that she had taken a journey through the spirit world and Jeanine had explained everything to her. Jody scanned for a camera with a flashing light and then put on a show.

"Wow! That was crazy," she began. "Jeanine took me on a journey back in time. I saw the tenement building. I got to meet the tenants. She told me that Sarah was innocent—that she was not a killer. It seems that Oliver Wilkinson was not the gentleman the papers made him out to be. Far from it, he was a womanizing lout. He had, in fact, been making overtures toward Sarah McDonnell for several months but she repeatedly shunned his approaches, seeing him for the cad that he was. He was so sure that a woman from a lower economic status would gladly give herself over to him, so as to improve her situation in life, that he was astounded and, frankly, furious when Sarah asked that he not see her again. He told her he would be back in a day and that he expected she would be of a different mind when he returned. As he was well-connected, he planned on having a discussion with the manager at the textile factory where Sarah worked. If Sarah denied his advances any longer, he'd make sure she would lose her job. For the right price, the factory manager was more than happy to agree to the deal. Sarah and Jeanine, who had shared the tenement room since the death of their mother, were desperate for allies and they found one in Molly O'Connor, the widow of the former building manager, Liam O'Connor. Molly listened intently to the sisters and promised to support them and have the police remove Mr. Wilkinson from the building if he ever came calling again. Wilkinson was undeterred. He returned, as promised. However, when he arrived at the McDonnell's apartment, it was Jeanine and not Sarah who he found. Sarah was only just returning from the market when she heard the scuffle. Through the door, she heard Wilkinson shouting at her sister. Then came the sound of breaking plates and glassware. She knew how dangerous Oliver Wilkinson could be when he flew into a rage so she quickly ran downstairs to summon Molly O'Connor. Molly's first inclination was to call for the police but with things escalating the way they were, she feared for Jeanine's safety. Instead, she retrieved her late husband's revolver from the closet where it had been sitting, collecting dust, and she ran upstairs with Sarah. Unfortunately, Molly was so distraught that she never thought to remove the sizzling frying pan from her stovetop. While Molly and Sarah were confronting Wilkinson, the fire that would eventually consume the entire tenement was racing across the third floor of the building, ravaging everything in its path. Inside the apartment, Jeanine McDonnell was laying, bloodied, on the floor. She was barely conscious. Seeing that Sarah had brought a witness to the scene further enraged Wilkinson who approached the women with violent intent. Fearing for their lives, Molly took aim and pulled the trigger on the revolver. The shot was not fatal but it was enough to knock Wilkinson off his feet and stop his advance. Sarah rushed over to her sister's aid while Molly attended to Mr. Wilkinson who had transformed from a raging bull into a weeping child. He was bleeding quite profusely and Molly knew he would need medical attention quickly lest he lose too much blood. She ran to the stairs to call for help. That's when she saw the thick smoke pouring up from below and the stairs engulfed in flame. There was no window in the McDonnell's small tenement apartment so Molly summoned the girls to a window at the end of the corridor. The window had no associated fire escape stairs but there was a large sack next to the window containing a lengthy piece of rope meant to be used during such emergencies. The rope was long enough to reach the pavement below. While Sarah tied the rope around her sister's waist, so that she might be lowered to the ground, Molly sought to secure the other end to an anchoring point. Tragically, before they could make their escape, the floor collapsed and they all plummeted into the flames below. There was no jealous murder. There was no hanging. There was, however, a horrible tragedy. Most of the souls of those lost found their way to the next world. Oliver Wilkinson's soul did not. Even in death, he refused to let go of Sarah McDonnell. In an act of great sacrifice, Jeanine offered herself up to Wilkinson if he would only allow her sister's soul to travel on to Heaven. The deal accepted, two souls remained trapped for eternity, stuck between Heaven and Hell. Until today, that is. With the truth told, the bonds are severed and Oliver Wilkinson and Jeanine McDonnell are free to move on."

An extended silence followed Jody's remarkable recounting of her spiritual journey. The cameramen slowly lowered their cameras, completely stunned by what they had just heard. Even Dan Parsons was at a loss for words. Chad Connors, however, was never at a loss for words.

"Jeanine McDonnell showed you all that?" asked Chad. One of the cameramen turned on the lights and all those present shielded their eyes. He quickly apologized but, in truth, everyone was glad to have the room illuminated. The mess around them stood as evidence of the paranormal storm they had just witnessed. Jody didn't respond right away. She seemed lost in deep thought. In stark contrast to earlier in the evening, Jody's face now glowed with an angelic expression of peace.

"I think I'm going to return to my room now, if you boys don't mind. I'm feeling pretty worn out."

"Sure thing, Jody," replied Chad. I can only imagine. I've heard that channeling spirits can take a lot out of a medium and you sure did some serious channeling tonight. Was that…um…was that all real?"

"Trade secret," replied Jody, with a wink, as she turned to walk toward the door. The remainder of the cast and crew continued to discuss what they had just seen while Dan was trying to figure out how he was going to explain the mess to the hotel manager. Before releasing the crew, he coordinated a roundup time for late the next morning. He also shared some good news he had received earlier in the day. Back at the network, a member of their research team was able to track down a photo of the McDonnell sisters with their mother, shortly before she passed on. The photo was handed down through their mother's sister's family. A copy of the photo, along with additional photographs and background material, was racing across the States with a guaranteed overnight delivery. Dan knew very well that photos of the actual people involved created a more personal connection with the audience; a connection that re-enactors could never quite match. They all agreed to have Jody take a look when the package arrived and see if she couldn't put on another compelling performance. With that, the team adjourned for some well-deserved sleep.

It's a well-known fact that life often trips us up and sends us tumbling to the bottom of the hill just when we're within a stride or two of the summit. And, so it was for the Paranormal Dream Team. Dan could barely believe his ears when he received an early morning call from the show's Executive Producer. The staff was working up an intro segment for the new girl, Jody, and came to the unpleasant conclusion that she had lied about nearly everything on her resume. The Executive Producer was very clear—Jody needed to go. Impressed with his new team member, Dan pleaded his case with the producer and even threatened to call the network's senior leadership. When his boss drew a hard line, Dan was savvy enough to realize that he was now putting his job on the line and no cast member was worth the risk of getting booted off a highly profitable television series. Dan reluctantly accepted the inevitable although he swallowed hard when told that the network was trying to negotiate to get Clementina back. It seems, for the right price, Clementina might be willing to accept a few blemishes on her paranormal resume. The recovery plan involved re-shooting the sequences that Jody had appeared in and also reverting to the original script about a sister killing her twin. Dan was keenly aware that fans loved the bloody stories of betrayal and brutal murders. He wasn't sure how this was going to play out with the rest of the team. He had a few hours to figure out how he would break the news.

At the pre-appointed time, the team rallied in the reserved meeting room to discuss the plan for the day. Jody was conspicuously absent and Dan knew the first order of business had to be breaking the bad news about the firing of their well-liked new team member. The news was not well-received and it was all Dan could do to quell the fomenting mutiny. His suggestion that Clementina might return only made

Flapper and the Captain

matters worse. The distraction of a lobby boy running in with the
FedEx package from the network was the escape Dan had been
hoping for.

"Look guys, I'm not happy about any of this either but we've got a
job to do and I think we can actually use a lot of the footage we shot
yesterday and make this work. I've also got something in this package I
think you're all going to want to see."

"I wouldn't be so sure about the footage," said one of the
cameramen, out of turn. The Director of Photography gave him a
nasty look, clearly wanting to soften the blow in a more diplomatic
fashion.

"What do you mean by that?" asked Dan, concerned that he was
rapidly losing control over the entire project. The Director of
Photography stepped in, in an attempt to soften the blow.

"What Jerry meant to say was that those energy surges from last
night did a real number on our digital equipment and, well, fried most
of the digital footage we shot. We still have the opening sequence in
front of the hotel but..."

"The opening sequence?!" Dan shouted, angrily. "Are you telling
me that all we have from that Emmy-winning paranormal extravaganza is Chad's intro across the street?"

"Um. Yah. Pretty much, boss. Maybe a couple background shots
taken around the hotel, also." Dan collapsed into a chair, shaking his
head. Realizing the team was looking to him for leadership, he quickly
composed himself and formulated a plan.

"Okay, well that sucks. Fortunately, it's just one day of shooting
and I'm confident that my resourceful team here can recreate the
experience."

"Are you kidding me," said Chad. "Recreate that freak show?
There's no way we can come close to that."

"I don't care if you have to hire some guys to dress up like
zombies and toss boxes around in the basement, we're going to make
this work." Everyone grew silent as Dan's temper flared. "We're
going with Plan A—sister kills sister in a bitter love triangle.
Questions?" Dweeber muttered a few curse words under his breath.
"I didn't quite catch that, Arnold. Would you mind sharing your
constructive thoughts with the team?" Dweeber didn't miss a beat on
the recovery.

"I was wondering if anyone thought to check in on Jody? She's got

300

to be really bummed out and, you know, I think we ought to see if she's okay."

"I'm guessing she's already on her way back home," said Dan, eager to move on with the day's work.

"So, you told her she was fired when?" added Chad. Dan did not appreciate the interrogation, especially considering the sensitive subject.

"I didn't tell her a thing. HR usually handles that kind of stuff."

"And you didn't think it would be a nice thing to do to…"

"Enough, already!" Dan was clearly frustrated.

"Would you mind if I check with the front desk," asked Dweeber, truly concerned for his new friend, a friend he had grown attached to during the short time they'd spent together.

"Knock yourself out but try to get back here quickly or else you're going to miss the fun."

"What fun?"

"Our research team dug up a veritable treasure trove of old documents, paper clippings, and photos. We're going to shoot a segment this morning with you guys pouring over some of the photos to make the story a little more personal to our viewers." Chad and Jocko high-fived each other and nodded with approval. Sensing a shift in the attitude, Dan relaxed a bit and sat back in his chair.

"Cool! Well, please wait for me," said Dweeber. "I'll be back in a minute."

While Dweeber jogged out of the room and headed for the front desk, Dan continued to talk about shooting schedules with the crew. Chad and Jocko were too interested in the unopened package of photos to pay much attention to anything Dan was saying. Five minutes later, Dweeber came running back in, out of breath.

"Did Jody make it out okay?" asked Chad. Dweeber was still trying to catch his breath when he spoke.

"According to the front desk, she never made it in."

"What the hell do you mean by that?" asked Jocko.

"They have no record of any Jody Kentford ever signing in. I even told them her room number and they say that room was occupied by an elderly couple the whole time."

"That's impossible. Room 605?"

"Yah, 605. No one even remembers ever seeing a girl of that description in the hotel."

Flapper and the Captain

"Okay," said Dan, trying, once again, to gain control of the situation. "Let's get this show on the road and I promise that I'll call HR later to find out what's going on with Jody." Dan's assurances seemed to ease the tension but Dweeber was still visibly upset. "So, how about we take a look at some of the faces behind the disgraces?"

"Right on, boss. Let's check 'em out," responded Chad, trying to be supportive of his director even though his thoughts were drifting. Dan carefully opened the envelope, the interior backed with a sturdy piece of cardboard, and cast the papers and photos out on the circular table.

Dan continued using his professional "I'm in charge" voice. "So, here we have records about the history of the tenement and the hotel along with information about the casualties of the fire, as much as is known. I figure we can tie in a few human-interest stories to pad the show just in case we can't get Clementina here in time to add the psychic spiritualist element to the narrative. And here, look, these are the Zieglands—Arthur and Adelaide."

"Aren't they the dashing couple," added Jocko, adjusting an imaginary bow tie at his collar.

"A smashing pair, to be sure," remarked Chad with, perhaps, the worst fake British accent anyone in the group had ever heard.

"And look, check out the hotel staff in all their finery."

"Very cool. Keep 'em coming, Dan. You said there's a picture of the McDonnell sisters in here somewhere, right?" Chad leaned in, as he spoke. Dan quickly sorted through the photos on the table.

"I was told there'd be one photo in here of Sarah and…" Unable to finish his words, Dan dropped the photo he was holding and the color completely left his face.

"Did you find it?" asked Chad, grabbing for the photo Dan had just released. Much like Dan, Chad grew strangely silent. Dweeber walked behind Chad's chair to get a look at the photo.

"That's Jody," remarked Dweeber, choking on his own words.

"That's not Jody," said Chad. According to the back of the photo, that's Sarah McDonnell on the left, Jeanine McDonnell on the right, and their mother, Francine McDonnell in the middle. Jocko grabbed the photo out of Chad's hand and took a closer look.

"Dude, that's Jody. I mean, Jody is a dead ringer for Jeanine McDonnell, no pun intended."

For some time after, the Paranormal Dream Team quietly passed the photo between members. The possibility that their recent ghost

302

hunting co-host had, in fact, been a ghost herself seemed to defy all reason. Yet, for all that, the Dream Team members could not come up with another explanation. The film crew and support team were, likewise, astonished. The mutiny was complete when all members present refused to comply with Dan's "Plan A." They all knew what they saw the day before and none of them wanted to tempt the fates by propagating a false narrative that had besmirched the reputation of an innocent woman for nearly a hundred years.

While the "Ziegland Hotel Haunting" episode never aired on the Paranormal TV channel, information revealed over the course of the investigation, combined with supporting materials provided by the research team, was eventually released to various newspapers and magazines. In an age more receptive to victims' rights, the true story of Sarah and Jeanine McDonnell quickly gained traction and replaced the false narrative. The sensational story further helped the reputation of the hotel and, in fact, assured a steady stream of guests fascinated by the tale. As for the Paranormal Dream Team, while somewhat disappointed at not having netted "the fish that got away," they continued their pursuit of paranormal phenomena, albeit with a greater level of respect, and lived with a sense of satisfaction over having righted a wrong from the past.

The Story Behind the Story

With a deadline of August 8, 2021, I set out upon my next project, to craft a 1,500-5000-word short story with a supernatural theme for the upcoming "Until Dawn—A Supernatural Anthology" book. With very few limits placed upon prospective authors, I knew I'd be able to come up with something.

I love to travel, and used to frequently watch The Travel Channel on TV to learn more about the many places that I hoped I might visit, someday. At some point in time, it seems The Travel Channel became infested with a variety of paranormal investigation shows. The shows all had similar elements—a group of elite (yet comically flamboyant) ghost hunters get called to explore some creepy old hotel, or hospital, or home, with a track record of unexplained phenomenon and ghost sightings. As much as I wanted to look away, these shows have their own way of pulling you in with a flair for grand theatrics and overly animated responses to every creaking wooden floor board or windblown object. The array of electronic ghost-detecting equipment used is also fascinating. These paranormal investigation shows were clearly an inspiration for my story, but I wanted to put my own twist on the formula. I wanted to shake things up a bit and, in my own way, get back at the predictable templated shows which rarely revealed anything truly noteworthy and have been critiqued for liberally mixing fact and fantasy to gain ratings. I thought it would be fun to put a real ghost amidst the unaware team of ghost hunters as they quickly found themselves in over their heads in a true paranormal firestorm. And, better still, this ghost would be set amidst the team of goofballs for a noble purpose—to correct a false narrative and exonerate herself of a crime she never committed while alive.

Autumn Healing by the Sea

(Written August 7, 2021)
Previously Unpublished

*I reflect upon fond memories of autumns spent
looking out upon the sea from my favorite park.*

Sun-scorched earth be gone
Yield to the season of my heart
Autumn winds sooth my soul
Too long we've stood apart

Out from the shadows, I bravely stride
Watching summer tourists flee
Abandoned parks and shorelines and paths
The waning season bequeaths to me

Cold winds blow!
Caress my face and muss my hair
Fill my willing lungs once more
With cool, clean, ocean-traveled air

Memories surround me like a warm blanket
I sing; I stand defiant at the shore
My heart renewed, alive again
I feel young and strong once more

Crashing waves before me
Autumn painted trees behind
I marvel at God's infinite glory
Heaven on earth defined

I close my eyes
I hear, I smell, I feel
Autumn surrounds me like a cloak
And my soul begins to heal

Flapper and the Captain

My sorrows melt away
Hope once lost, now found
I am the orange atop the trees
My fears, dying leaves upon the ground

Fall finds my spirit well
Fall defines the real me
I thank God with all my heart
For autumn healing by the sea

The Story Behind the Story

"The Leaves Fall" anthology was published in September of 2021. Authors were requested to submit poems appropriate to the upcoming season. I submitted two poems for this anthology and this was the one that was not accepted. The second, following after this poem, has more universal appeal, I suppose. I do like this first poem because it speaks to my very personal relationship with fall. Admittedly, it begins with an admonishment of all those sun-worshippers who crowd the spaces where I'd prefer to find solitude. I can't speak to the criteria for judgment of poetry within the anthologies, so I won't speculate why one of my poems was chosen over another. I do know that there was a vast number of submissions, and there is definitely an element of fairness to offer opportunities for more people to find their poetry in print. As such, I can't claim that I was disappointed. I rather like this poem and the imagery it brings to mind—fond memories of special times by the sea with cool autumn breezes greeting my face as I looked out upon the waters.

Last Leaf of Autumn

(August 14, 2021)
Published by Red Penguin Books in "*The Leaves Fall*" (September, 2021)

*Autumn-themed reflection on transitions and the
circle of life.*

I am the last leaf of autumn
I've seen my comrades fall
I've watched their slow demise
Until none were left at all

Vibrant greens, we swayed as one
Caressed by spring's sweet breeze
Basking in the sun stood we
Whilst nourishing the trees

Through storms, tugged and tested
Defiant, we held strong
We drank to our great victories
And frolicked summer-long

The summer heat was cruel
We faced it brave and true
Silent, still, our canopy of green
Spread beneath a sky of blue

Though recklessly we raced to get there
Autumn's chill, came, still, too soon
Trembling under frosted dew
Shivering beneath a harvest moon

Rainbow-fashioned hues erupting
A final testament gift bequeathed
Friends long known and loved
Turn brown and fall beneath

Flapper and the Captain

More each day, they leave us
So many, there's little time to mourn
Crumpled brown then turned to dust
Returned from whence they're born

Futility personified, I cling
The last leaf upon a tree
A final act of great defiance
To express my dignity

At peace, at last, I long to travel
Euphoric; no longer afraid to die
I join my comrades, one and all
And dance through winter's sky

The Story Behind the Story

Accepted into "The Leaves Fall" poetry anthology, this short poem tells a simple tale of life…and death….and dignity. I believe these are themes that many can identify with. I hope you enjoyed this piece.

TRASH
     .

(August 29, 2021)
Published by Red Penguin Books in "*Treat or Trick: Halloween Horror
Stories*" (September, 2021)

*A disrespectful duo defiles a local park, angering
spirits protecting the hallowed grounds. Halloween
night retribution ensues, cleansing the town of its
refuse.*

Weather data for Weekapaug, Rhode Island goes back over a
hundred years and in those hundred years there's only been one
tornado. We don't talk about it. Collectively, we've agreed not to. It was
a wholly unnatural thing; more so because it came on Halloween night.
I know why it did. I know the truth. People need to hear the story.

A crumpled Doritos bag tumbled across the emerald green grass
before it was trapped by the chain link fence that formed the barrier
between Hemel Park and the Atlantic Ocean. Jeremy and Bryan
Nestweiler, as fit as most twenty-year old men, had concluded, several
years ago, that the thirty-foot walk to the steel trash bin was an incon-
venience they were unwilling to suffer. The brilliant red bag mingled,
unapologetically, with several beer cans, the cellophane wrapping from
a bag of powdered sugar mini donuts, several mustard-stained napkins,
a Styrofoam container, and two Sub Stop carry-out bags, each with the
customer's misspelled first name hastily scribbled on the exterior. The
bags had once held footlong sub sandwiches, pickles, and little plastic
containers with a side of potato salad, in one instance, and pasta salad,
in the other.

Mrs. Carla Simpson, an elderly widow and the proud owner of a
feisty Cairn Terrier who answered to the name Merrilee, had seen
enough. Jeremy and Bryan were unaccustomed to being addressed as
they took their air by the shoreline. Their hoodlum want-to-be attire
and boisterous demeanor was, on most days, more than sufficient at
ensuring their privacy within the confines of the park; so much so that
they felt personally violated when Merrilee growled and Mrs. Simpson
followed with a disapproving grunt.

309

"You got a problem, lady?" asked Jeremy Nestweiler, more intent on intimidating the unflappable Carla Simpson than on truly inquiring into the nature of her concern.

"I certainly do," responded Mrs. Simpson. Jeremy and Bryan, unaccustomed to any response other than one of the many forms of "no," followed by a hasty retreat and apology, were left, uncharacteristically, at a loss for words. Although hesitant to expend the energy required to stand, the two brothers decided the most effective long-term solution against annoying little old ladies involved an animalistic display of dominance, much as a rooster might puff his chest and spread his wings or a buck defiantly display his antlers to a challenger during the rut. Mrs. Simpson was neither foul nor hooved forest dweller. The ill-mannered ruffians, surprised that Carla Simpson did not flinch, nor likely even blink, walked around the bench and converged upon the woman from two sides. The sway in their shoulders, the slouching posture, the bouncing gate—all of it intended to intimidate—seemed more like a clownish performance, in the eyes of a seasoned Carla Simpson, than the indication of any impending threat to her person. It may well be that Jeremy and Bryan thought a height comparison, six-foot-something against Mrs. Simpson's five-foot-nothing, would tip the scale in their favor but, alas, their arrival served only to trigger Merrilee's undaunted defense of her beloved owner. The boys leapt back, embarrassed to have their progress halted by so little a dog.

"You better tell your dog to cool it or I'm going to punt that runt over the fence and into the water," growled Bryan.

"Don't you dare touch my little girl! If you do, I'll report you both to the police. To be honest, I'm of a fair mind to do so right now." Mrs. Simpson had no need to resort to raising her voice as Merrilee ceased her barking and growling the moment her owner's perfectly articulated words left her age-weathered lips.

"I ain't gonna tell you again, lady. You and your stupid little rat need to get a move on," replied Jeremy, angry that the tiny woman before him was not responding to the vast array of vocal and visual signals that usually sent prospective park patrons fleeing for the woods.

"I do wish you'd be more pleasant. It's really not that difficult," answered Carla Simpson, winding the spring for the sermon she was about to administer to the two wayward strangers. While she intended to address a great many things, as a retired English teacher of over forty years, she chose to prioritize the faulty grammar that her ears had recently been assaulted by before all other matters. "First off, young man, you should understand that 'ain't' is not a word in the English language, nor any other language, for that matter, and that 'gonna' is not a recognized contraction for the words 'going to.' You'll make your points more effectively if you speak clearly and correctly."

"I'm about to make my point with my fist, Grandma," said Bryan, fumbling for words. Carla Simpson not only called his bluff but returned to her sermon with renewed vigor.

"Second, I do not appreciate you overtly threatening my dog nor your thinly veiled attempts to intimidate me." Merrilee bravely traversed an arc, at leash-length, creating a fur-lined force field between her beloved pet-parent and the ruffians that stood before her. In deference to Mrs. Simpson, she withheld her barking, only occasion-ally resorting to a menacing growl. "And, finally, I must ask you to pick up this terrible mess that you've made. This park is open to all who come with good intent. It's a place of peace and solace and has been for many generations. We take great pride in keeping its grounds immaculately clean so that all who visit may enjoy its unspoiled beauty."

Jeremy was not impressed nor moved, in the slightest, by Mrs. Simpson's heart-felt plea. "Hey, if I send you off with a beer, will you shut up?" he said, in the most condescending manner he could conjure up. Mrs. Simpson gasped with indignation. A woman of great reserve, she had to struggle to maintain her composure and thought that, perhaps, a compelling story might somehow save the day, tipping the balance of the conversation in her favor by appealing to what she falsely assumed was a universal sense of compassion and empathy inherent in all humanity.

"No, thank you. I'll stick with my tea. Before I leave, I thought you should know that this park is so much more than a lovely patch of green beside the ocean. It's healed many a broken heart and eased the pain of the sick and dying, all who sought refuge here in their times of need. One might even call it hallowed ground. One of these special souls was a young girl named Annalynn. Annalynn was one of the loveliest spirits I have ever met. She loved this park and spent countless hours playing with her dog, McKenzie, by the water's edge. They say some of the brightest stars are the first to fade and so it was with young Annalynn. Diagnosed with an incurable form of cancer, before her 7th

birthday, she carried herself with a stoic dignity that was truly astonishing."

"So, what's your point, Grandma," Bryan interjected, growing tired of the lecture. Mrs. Simpson paid no attention to the interruption and continued with her story.

"Her father, a hard man by most accounts, wheeled young Annalynn down to the park every day during her final six months of life. When she grew too weak to toss McKenzie's ball, her father would throw that bright pink ball and the faithful Irish Setter would race after it, retrieving the ball and then gently placing it in Annalynn's lap as she sat, covered by a blanket, in her wheelchair. Oh, how I cried, when I watched from afar. It may come as no surprise that Annalynn wished her ashes to be scattered near the water's edge, here at the park. The tears I shed watching her play with McKenzie paled in comparison to the collective outpouring of grief within the community when word spread that our beloved Annalynn had passed on. Honoring her wish, her father lovingly spread Annalynn's ashes right over there. Her ever-loyal dog, healthy by all accounts, followed his little girl, passing on in his sleep only weeks after Annalynn left us for Heaven. The vet had no explanation for McKenzie's death other than perhaps he suffered an incurable broken heart after losing his cherished companion. McKenzie's ashes were scattered here, as well. After Annalynn's death, the community established a charitable fund in her name to help sick children and we all contributed to purchasing that very bench you've been sitting on. Perhaps you may have noticed the commemorative bronze plaque affixed to the bench?"

"I've never seen any plaque here," said Jeremy, not feeling even the slightest bit of remorse in his lie and even less for having pried the metal plate off with his pocket knife, a couple weeks before, only to toss it into the sea. He didn't care for the way it felt against his back. Carla slowly walked around to the front of the bench and contemplated the two circular holes where the screws had once securely fastened the bronze plate to the wooden plank on the backrest. She sighed, clearly overcome with emotion, but did not go so far as to accuse the brothers of a heinous act of vandalism.

"I'm very disappointed in your behavior," said Mrs. Simpson. "I hope you'll consider my words and act more like gentlemen. I implore you to please treat the park with more respect. I think I've said enough, so I'll be on my way now. Good day."

Jeremy did not appreciate the lecture. Angrily, he walked towards Mrs. Simpson and called her a few nasty names, which do not bare repeating, before spitting at her. The wind, being as it was, carried the spit right back onto Jeremy's sweatshirt. In a rage, the angry young man clenched his fist and moved to strike a defenseless Mrs. Simpson. Before he had the chance to take a swing, Jeremy Nestweiler screamed out in pain and fell to the ground.

"Ow! That stupid little mutt just bit me!" shouted Jeremy. Bryan looked on, somewhat confused, as Merrilee was still leashed and had made no apparent move towards his brother, despite Jeremy's vigorous accusations. Carla Simpson, understanding right well that she had overstayed her welcome, hastily shuffled towards the park gate in spite of Merilee's protests. Merilee's attention seemed strangely affixed on a nearby flock of geese that were erratically waddling back and forth some thirty feet away. For no apparent reason, the flock leapt into the air, in unison, and flew a good fifty yards before settling on the water beyond the fence line.

"You okay, bro?" asked Bryan.

"You saw that, right? You saw how that little monster came up and bit me?"

"She must have been lightning fast then, dude, 'cause I didn't see much of anything," replied a skeptical Bryan Nestweiler. Jeremy rolled up his jeans' pant leg revealing several marks upon his calf and a small amount of blood. "Dammmn! I guess she really did get you." Bryan knelt down to take a closer look. The marks on Jeremy's leg certainly looked like bite marks but the bite radius seemed a bit large for a tiny Cairn Terrier.

"I'm going to make that dog pay!" growled a vengeance-minded Jeremy Nestweiler.

"Dude, maybe we should just let it go for now. Let's just enjoy the rest of the day. You know, maybe smoke a little weed and then mess with some trick-or-treaters."

"I could use a smoke, bro; that old lady got me all worked up."

"I've got just the remedy for you, dude," said Bryan, pulling a bag of marijuana out of his jacket pocket and waving it slowly in front his brother. Bryan extended his other arm and helped Jeremy back to his feet and the two returned to the bench to roll a couple joints.

The brothers soon forgot about Carla Simpson and her sad story. They were fairly confident she wouldn't be coming back to the park any time soon. They talked about how much they hated the town and how stupid everybody was and, just when it seemed their conversation couldn't become any more negative, one of the brothers would pull it below the waves to set a new county and state record for depravity. The national record, however, set by an anonymous financial manager in New Jersey, withstood the challenge admirably.

Jeremy stopped short, amid one of many tirades about various classes of people he didn't care for, when a small moving object caught his eye. Along the fence line, a bright pink ball of about three inches in diameter was rolling about, propelled by an errant breeze. Neither brother had noticed the ball before which struck them as being unusual since the nearly fluorescent pink sphere could not have formed a greater contrast with the lush green grass of the park.

"Hey, man, wanna play catch?" said a slightly stoned Bryan Nestweiler.

"Yah, sure, dude, whatever. Go grab that thing before it blows away." Jeremy had no real desire to play catch and Bryan wasn't being serious when he asked the question but, seeing as how communication was never a strong point in the brothers' relationship, Bryan obediently bounded after the ball and Jeremy laughed uncontrollably as the wind carried it away each time his brother approached it. Bryan, suffering the ill-effects of his recreational drug use, nearly broke his arm when he dove atop the evasive ball to finally halt its taunting progress. Triumphantly, he returned to his brother, ball in hand.

"Catch, man," said Bryan, as he tossed the ball to Jeremy. His brother, barely able to stand, much less display the coordination necessary to affect the catch, laughed as the ball bounced off his wrist and rolled to the side. Jeremy pursued the ball which was not yet done with its errant wanderings. Cursing while he chased it, Jeremy staggered along, tripping over his own feet, until he finally cornered the mischievous sphere along the fence line.

"Hey, Bryan, do you suppose this ball belongs to Ghost Dog?"

"What in the world are you talking about?"

"You know, that old lady's story about the girl playing catch with her dog."

"Oh, yah," replied Bryan, his brain trying to catch up. "Cool, man. Yah, that's some spooky Halloween creepiness, right there. Ooh, you better beware, 'cause Ghost Dog has come back from the grave to retrieve his lost ball." The two brothers started laughing. Jeremy stopped laughing first, vengefully squeezing the ball as tightly as he could, hoping it might explode in his grasp. It did not. His lip curled into an angry sneer. Jeremy spit on the ball and then reared back to give the ball a good toss.

"Go fetch, you stupid Ghost Dog!" shouted Jeremy, as he threw the ball a good thirty yards out to sea, trying to hit the flock of geese that were peacefully minding their own business, bobbing up and down with the gentle waves. The geese honked and hissed and took to the air. Initially, their path took them farther out to sea, but then the flock turned, in unison, and set a course straight for the offending brothers. Jeremy and Bryan looked, aghast, toward the incoming mass of feathery retribution. They both dropped to their knees as one hundred and thirty-three geese disturbed the air, only feet above their heads, with the furious beating of their wings. The thunderous chorus of honking birds was deafening and left the brothers somewhat shaken.

"What the hell just happened?" asked Bryan Nestweiler, perplexed about the unexpectedly aggressive behavior of the geese. Jeremy's only response was a shake of his head. The winds shifted, as if to follow the geese on their inland path, and the trash that had accumulated along the fence line blew back toward the bench until it settled where the brothers were still kneeling in the grass. Jeremy picked up a beer can and tried to toss it into the water. Not only did the can fail to clear the fence; it was blown right back toward Jeremy and settled against his boot. Angrily, he kicked at the accumulated pile of trash, trying to drive it back towards the fence line. To his frustration, each time he turned away from the fence, the cans, Styrofoam packaging, wrappers, soiled napkins, and crumpled sandwich bags followed in pursuit.

"Something weird is going on here, dude," observed Bryan. His words were not acknowledged as Jeremy was too busy stomping on the trash like some enraged toddler throwing a temper tantrum. "Hey, maybe we should get going, Jeremy. How 'bout we play some 'Mass Shooter 2' on the game system while we wait for the little trick-or-treaters to come out? We're almost ready for a level up and weapons upgrade and I'm feeling like today's the day we beat our high score."

"Alright, man. Let's do it. But, first, I've really got to drain the vein."

"Me, too. All those beers really filled my tank and there's no way I'm gonna make that walk home without a little relief."

As if their previous desecration of the park was not objectionable enough, the two Nestweiler brothers unzipped their flies, took the measure of the wind, and laughed as they sprayed the ground before them with alcohol rich urine. They were hardly finished relieving themselves before a terrible chill fell upon them and they shuddered as they completed their business. Had Carla Simpson told the final part of her story, the Nestweilers might have reconsidered their uncouth actions. As things were, they began their trek home unaware that they had awakened a vengeful spirit.

Much to Jeremy and Bryan's consternation, the pile of trash they had created seemed to be following them out of the park, as if swept by an invisible custodian intent on making a point. Around corners and across yards, the refuse followed. They'd have taken a car, as neither appreciated the healthful benefits of a brisk walk, but for the fact that Jeremy's license had been revoked after a DUI collision that had left a mother and her twelve-year old daughter in critical condition for the better part of three weeks. Jeremy was less concerned for the welfare of the accident victims than he was about losing his ability to make midnight runs for chips and beer on gaming nights. His car, which he shared with his brother, whose license was suspended for failing to pay his traffic tickets, was now the neighborhood eyesore. The homely vehicle, dented and covered in rust, was ignobly parked in the road in front of the modest home the brothers had inherited from their mother after her death. Some say she never gave up hope for her boys. If that's true then she must have surely earned her place in Heaven because her two surviving sons fed her a veritable buffet of disappointment, heartbreak, and grief across the years.

The boys were about halfway home when a police cruiser pulled up beside them. It was Officer Brown, a man the boys especially disliked and who they had only recently verbally butchered during their rant in the park.

"Well, if it isn't the Nestweiler Brothers," said Officer Brown, looking quite imposing behind his oversized sunglasses which seemed superfluous beneath the heavily overcast sky. "I trust you gentlemen aren't going to be pestering the kids again, this year."

Jeremy responded, "Those kids last year called us names and were mean to us, Officer. That's the only reason we roughed 'em up a little bit. I can't help it if the fat one lost his balance and broke his arm when he fell. But, maybe, they all learned a valuable life lesson, right?" The saccharine tone of Jeremy's voice was wrought with insincerity.

"You teach any more lessons this year, Jeremy, and you'll be celebrating Halloween, Thanksgiving, Christmas, and New Years in the county jail," responded Officer Brown, a conscientious practitioner of the law and a man thoroughly frustrated over having spent countless hours of his valuable time responding to complaints about the Nestweiler boys.

"Ouch," said Jeremy. "why'd you have to go there? You know, if you stopped pestering us about every little thing we do, you might actually get a promotion one of these days for doing your real job."

Furious as he was, Carl Brown knew well enough that no good ever came by entering into verbal altercations with civilians. With an enviable serenity in his voice, Officer Brown responded. "Funny you should mention that. I've turned down multiple promotion offers because I couldn't bear the thought of losing my patrol area and not seeing you guys anymore. But, to change the subject, I was wondering if you gents would be so kind as to clean up the mess over there."

"Oh, that's not ours," replied Bryan.

"So, the crumpled carry-out bags that appear to have the names 'Briun' and 'Germy' scribbled on them don't belong to you guys?" Bryan looked down and, sure enough, the crumpled bags had situated themselves in the most incriminating manner possible. Even with the lackluster spelling performance of the sandwich technician, no jury was necessary to render this verdict.

"I guess the wind must have blown those bags out of the trash bin where we tossed them," added Jeremy.

"I'm sure it did. But, seeing as how they're blowing about the neighborhood now, perhaps you might consider picking up the mess and re-depositing your garbage in a can with a lid; perhaps at your home?"

"I'd love to officer but I'm afraid I don't have any way to collect it," countered Jeremy. Officer Brown reached over to his center console and opened it, retrieving a plastic trash bag in the process. He handed it through the window where Bryan, reluctantly, received it.

"Allow me to help you there, fellas. I wouldn't want you getting stuck with a $500 littering fine. This bag should do the trick. Perhaps, you'll consider putting in a good word for me at the precinct so that I can finally get that promotion I've been dreaming of?"

Jeremy growled but did his best to keep his composure. "Sure thing, Officer Brown, we'll make sure we do. Thanks again. Really." Officer

Brown fired back a half-hearted salute before shifting his vehicle into gear and offering a parting warning. "Remember, guys, no hijinks tonight, okay?"

"You got it, Sir. No hijinks," said Bryan, saluting back. Jeremy just scowled, the wind blowing the white plastic trash bag against his face.

Jeremy and Bryan picked up the litter that surrounded them and tied the bag shut while Officer Brown kept an eye on them in his rear-view mirror as he slowly continued down the street. The Nestweilers hadn't traveled more than two-hundred yards before Jeremy tossed the bag over a hedgerow into someone's yard. The brothers laughed and gave each other a high five as they continued on to their house.

The dark of the late afternoon was surrendering to an eerie twilight as the boys approached their home, eyes straining to see what was swirling about just outside the door. As they approached, they grew silent, both harboring an uneasy feeling in their gut. Dancing about in the autumn breeze was the very garbage they had abandoned at the park and, later, bagged and deposited onto a neighbor's yard.

"Dude, what the hell is going on here?" Bryan asked of his brother, knowing that he'd have no answer to the question.

"I don't know, man. Something ain't right, that's for sure." The silence of the moment was interrupted by a jingling sound coming from down the street. The boys looked over and saw the unmistakable figure of Carla Simpson walking her dog. Mrs. Simpson stopped to let Merrilee sniff at the grass of the Nestweiler residence and the little terrier expressed her disapproval with a muffled growl.

"We were kind of hoping we wouldn't see you again…like, maybe forever," shouted Jeremy from the doorstep of his home.

"Merrilee seems to be upset that you haven't picked up after yourself," responded Carla. "Cleanliness is next to godliness and I fear you boys have strayed very far. Perhaps too far."

"Don't make me tell you again, you old hag!" replied an angered Jeremy Nestweiler, his fist clenched and shaking. "I don't care about your stupid dog. I don't care about you. I don't care about your pretty little park, and I could care less about what God thinks of me. If there is a God, and He is listening, then I have only one thing to say--'screw you and thanks for the crappy life, jerk.'" The young man's blasphemous words were very disturbing to Carla Simpson who prided herself as being a moral and righteous Christian woman.

"You should be careful with your words and more careful about defiling Hemel Park. God is not your enemy and He may well be the only one who can save you now," said a defiant Carla Simpson.

"I said, go!" shouted Jeremy.

"I'll leave. You'll not see me again, I can promise you that," replied Mrs. Simpson, in resigned exasperation.

"Good!" replied Jeremy. Mrs. Simpson pulled a crumpled newspaper article out her coat pocket and tossed it on the yard where the wind picked it up and blew it into the swirling trash by the Nestweiler's front door. The old woman shook her head, in disappointment, and continued on into the darkness.

"What the hell was that?" asked Bryan.

"Crazy old bat. I dunno, dude." Jeremy kicked the trash aside and unlocked the front door. Bryan bent over to retrieve the news article from the porch but didn't attempt to read it in the dim lighting. Once inside, Jeremy reached over to turn the lights on. With a flick of the switch, the boys were greeted by a horrific sight. The entire lower level of their home was filled with garbage. Piled waist high, or higher, was the collected garbage from countless parks across the state. There was no logical explanation for the scene and both brothers struggled to grapple with the impossibility of the moment.

Jeremy attempted to wade through the sea of trash to ascertain its limits but he was quickly overcome by the foul stench and thought it best to turn back. "I never thought I'd say this, Bryan, but I'm going to call the cops. I want to know who did this and I want them to pay. Someone's gonna clean up this mess and it isn't going to be us." While Jeremy was slogging his way through the debris field, Bryan was reading the news clipping provided by the eccentric Mrs. Simpson.

"You gotta check this out, Jeremy. This is some whacked out stuff right here."

"What? More whacked out than coming home to a house flooded with wall-to-wall garbage?"

"Pretty close. The article is talking about some guy who killed himself at the park a few years back. Blew his brains out right down by the water's edge."

"Yah? And?"

"Says the dude's name was Joseph Simpson. The article says he was predeceased by his mother, Carla Simpson, and his daughter, Annalynn."

"What do you mean by predeceased?" asked Jeremy, only partially paying attention to his brother's ramblings, his mind still fixated upon the trash engulfing him.

"That means they died before him. This guy was that girl, Annalynn's, dad. Several months after losing his daughter to cancer, the dude offed himself right there in the park, right where he scattered the ashes of his daughter and his dog. I guess he lost his wife in a car accident several years before. Tough life." Bryan awaited a response from his brother and it came in the usual callous manner.

"Bam! Sounds like a clean sweep. Too bad, so sad. I guess that stupid family found out the hard way that life sucks." Jeremy might well have minded his mocking remarks had he known of the supernatural forces conspiring against him and the unholy rage that would soon be unleashed.

Joseph Simpson was a hard man. He wasn't always that way. Accused of a crime he did not commit; he spent the better part of his early adult life behind bars…and it changed him. Released, he staggered into a cold world with little money and no plan. His father, disappointed in his son, passed away during Joseph's incarceration believing every vile accusation the prosecution had pitched to a receptive jury. His mother, Carla, an English teacher at the local high school, didn't buy a word of it. After his release, she took Joseph in and provided the bedrock upon which he might rebuild his life. But it was Hanna Swanson who truly saved Joseph. She taught him to love again. Joseph found honest work, rebuilt his confidence, and worked to refine his character. The work was only half done when Joseph asked Hanna for her hand in marriage and she accepted, confident that Joseph was a new man and would make a loyal and devoted husband. Hardly a year had passed before Hanna shared the happy news that she was pregnant. The newborn, a beautiful baby girl who the parents lovingly named Annalynn, was carefully handed into the arms of her proud grandmother, Mrs. Carla Simpson. Carla adored her only grandchild and Annalynn adored her grandmother. If life can be viewed as a series of peaks and valleys, then it's clear that the Simpson family had reached the pinnacle of their life journey. Perhaps that's why Carla Simpson gave up the fight and succumbed to Heaven's beckon call. She died, peacefully, in her sleep and was fondly remembered by family, friends, and a several generations of her former students who owed her a great debt for the valuable lessons she taught—lessons of literature and the arts, of spelling and grammar, and, perhaps most importantly, of life.

Some say it's well that Carla Simpson passed on when she did. Thereafter, fate seemed to deal one blow after another to the struggling Simpson family. Hanna Simpson was killed in an auto accident when her vehicle was struck, one night, by a drunken driver who swerved across the lane marker and collided, head on, with her vehicle. A despondent Joe Simpson did his best to carry on as a single parent. The burden proved to be too heavy and he gradually withdrew from society and returned to drinking. For all that, what remained of his damaged heart belonged completely to his beloved daughter. Within her sparkling eyes, he saw hopes and dreams long since abandoned in his own life. He saw his wife's joy and passion for life reflected in the glow upon young Annalynn's face. It's a risky proposition to rely upon any single person as the focus of all of your love, all your happiness, and the very wellness of your soul yet, for Joseph Simpson, young Annalynn had become the vessel laboring to carry all of that and more. It was cancer that cracked the fragile porcelain and all of Joseph Simpson's humanity flowed like water from the fissures, emptying as his daughter's life waned. Annalynn's courage was the only thing bolstering her father and, once she died, all recognizable traces of the man Joseph Simpson once was died, as well. His last tear was shed as he spread his daughter's ashes at Hemel Park. Dutifully, he scattered McKenzie's ashes by her side, a short time thereafter. The shell of the man that remained was short-lived and, after he had taken his own life, the county approved the plan to join father with daughter, as was requested in the will Simpson mailed to the county courthouse just hours before he pulled the trigger.

The past is the past. It's unclear whether knowing any of the details of the Simpson family's tragic demise would have, in any way, altered the ultimate fate of the Nestweiler brothers or their home. What is known is that the autumn wind began howling fiercely that night. Within the walls of the Nestweiler home, Jeremy cursed the Simpsons. He cursed the old woman, unaware of her name or, more consequentially, the fact that Carla Simpson had been dead these past ten years. He cursed Officer Brown and the entire county police force. He even dared to throw a few jabs at God, Himself. Within their home, the mass of garbage began to swirl about, slowly at first but then increasing to a terrible intensity. Bryan and Jeremy both tried, desperately, to cling to anything that might steady them. Amidst the churning debris, they found no safe harbor. The Nestweiler's badly damaged car tumbled across the yard and smashed through the picture window, joining the refuse swirling within the living room. Deafened by the frightening roar of the merciless wind, the brothers watched in horror as the second floor of their home departed and spiraled into the sky. The disintegrating remains of the upper level of their home were still visible as Jeremy and Bryan Nestweiler joined the spinning mass of trash as it was sucked up into the clouds. Cleansed from the face of the earth by nature's own vacuum cleaner, there seemed, to some, a poetic justice in the sentence levied upon the wayward Nestweiler boys. There was little remaining to remind a dismissive world that they had ever even existed.

What became of the Nestweiler brothers must remain a matter of conjecture. Everyone had an opinion. The pious claim that they angered God and were met with His "terrible swift sword." Those who believed in paranormal powers insisted that the vengeful spirit of a tormented Joseph Simpson released the full fury of his rage upon the hapless brothers. Environmentalists have sited this unusual autumnal New England tornado as evidence of the dangerous consequences of global climate change. Local newspaper columns were conspicuously lacking in color and narrative, as if they had conspired to sweep this dirty story under the carpet. Headlines read, simply, *"Surprise Tornado Strikes Weekapaug! Two Men Missing"* and *"Brothers Feared Lost as Tornado Snatches Their Home."* The articles described how fortunate the community was that only one property was damaged and went on to describe how officials were still seeking the whereabouts of two brothers who may or may not have been present at the time of the tornado touchdown.

What happened on that strange Halloween night? I know. But my opinion is my own and I share this story so that you might make your own judgment. The truth must be known but the truth is not always as it appears.

Trash

The Story Behind the Story

Just in time for Halloween, 2021, authors were tasked to write a short story of 3,000-7,500 words for an upcoming anthology entitled "Treat or Trick: Halloween Horror Stories." As one might expect, tales were required to be somewhat spooky or creepy. Having successfully created tales of horror for previous anthologies, I felt confident in my ability to conjure up another worthy tale for the occasion. If you've been reading along in order, you may have noticed a poem, a few pages back, called "Autumn Healing by The Sea." That poem never made it into a Red Penguin Books anthology, but the vision that inspired the poem, as strange as it may seem, was also an inspiration for this short story. Hemel Park, as described in this story, is not altogether different from my own beloved Saddle Rock Park, a place that was often a refuge for me during difficult times and remains a place I revisit to find peace. I have often been bothered by the careless acts of litterers and deliberate destruction caused by vandals yet, so often, we witness only the damages they leave behind and rarely have an opportunity to intervene. In some cases, our own safety might be put at risk, were we to attempt to intervene. To be angered by such acts and to hope that the perpetrators might find justice, is not unnatural, even if it speaks to our own failure to find forgiveness in our hearts. I've never worried too much about that. The image of ruffians tainting the purity of such "holy ground" was all the inspiration I needed to take to my keyboard and craft this tale of divine retribution.

BESSIE'S CAP

(September 23, 2021)
Published by Red Penguin Books in *"Pets on the Prowl: An Animal Mystery
Anthology"* (October, 2021)

*When beloved artifacts disappear from an exhibit in
an Air & Space Museum, two raccoons must crack
the case before new security procedures endanger the
lives of the many creatures who have come to call the
museum home.*

On August 3rd, 2021, the staff of the Stars of Flight Air and Space
Museum arrived at work to find the gift shop ravaged. Many displays
were knocked over, their contents spilled upon the floor. The culprits?
Two raccoons! Somehow, the creatures had slipped into the locked gift
store during the middle of the night. To make matters worse, the
raccoons were unapologetically sleeping off their nightly misadventures
behind the protective glass walls of the shop. Curious employees, now
arriving to begin their day, peered through the glass windows trying to
get a glimpse of the mischievous animals while senior staff members
were calling the county Animal Control Service to humanely remove
the offenders for relocation to some dwelling more appropriate for
woodland creatures. The museum gift store remained closed for the
remainder of the day while the shelves and items were disinfected. This
much is known...and that's not even half the story. Carefully placed
next to the cash register were a very old leather aviator's cap and a pair
of flying goggles—treasured pieces of aviation history that had disappeared from the museum's collection only a week before.

Bartholomew Breitling was not the ideal night watchman but, by all
accounts, he was a gentle soul with a good heart. Each night, he made
his rounds through the Stars of Flight Air and Space Museum and
then checked all the exits to make sure they were securely locked. The
museum had an outstanding record for security but the recent pilfering
of space-related toys, clothing items, and trinkets from the gift store
had soiled the museum's previously unblemished record. While the
dollar value of the missing items was never going to affect the muse-

um's bottom line, the thefts were a thorn in the side of Hans Belcher, the head of security. Hans was a grizzled veteran of the security world. Three decades of distinguished service at the Paramus Mall in New Jersey had hardened him and he had little tolerance for any deviations from standard security procedures. It seemed that poor Bartholomew Breitling could do little to please his new boss, despite his best efforts. His hair was slightly too long, his posture a little too slouchy, his paperwork a bit sloppy and, perhaps worst of all, his watch was perpetually off by several minutes. Bartholomew did not enjoy his counseling sessions with Hans Belcher. Particularly, Bartholomew did not appreciate how Hans Belcher always called him "Bart," no matter how many times he graciously attempted to inform his boss that he preferred to be called by his full first name. But none of this mattered to Parker and Treena, two residents of the Stars of Flight Air and Space Museum who had no last names. You see, Parker and Treena were raccoons. They had made a home for themselves within the museum—a veritable labyrinth of crawl spaces, lofts, and rarely used storage rooms. When the museum inherited the former Air Force base hangars for their collections, they also inherited the offspring of countless generations of small mammals, birds, insects, and the occasional reptile or amphibian. An impressive array of microorganisms also made the museum their home but no accurate census has ever been conducted to verify the extent of that population.

As previously described, the day-to-day trials of Bartholomew Breitling were not of great concern to Parker or Treena; that is, until Bartholomew was relieved of his security guard duties on July 27th. What our two heroes had failed to recognize was that Bartholomew had routinely skipped step 42C on the Exterior Walkaround Checklist, a procedure which called for the securing of the trash dumpster lid and side entry chute by means of locking mechanisms designed specifically to keep foraging critters out. Bartholomew, you see, had a rather sensitive nose and the stench emanating from the dumpsters made him feel nauseous. Also, to be honest, he had a soft spot in his heart for the various creatures that relied upon the dumpster's contents to feed their families. Every day, a vast array of leftover French fries, hamburger buns, cheese-slathered nacho chips, and even the occasional healthy side salad, were deposited within that receptacle. Often, these tasty morsels were mixed with several gallons of used cooking oil to create a beggar's buffet of immeasurable grandeur. It should come as no surprise that panic ensued when access to these calorific treats was denied to the assorted creatures who had come to rely upon them for their daily sustenance. Following Bartholomew's unfortunate departure, the cause of which we shall get to shortly, Hans Belcher felt compelled to recall Gertrude Sumppumper from retirement. At eighty-three years old, Gertrude had barely lost a step since her retirement. Some argue that her security patrol skills had even improved with time, much like a fine wine. Not only did Gertrude complete step 42C on the Exterior Walkaround Checklist, but she also added her own steps 42D and E, just for good measure. Hans Belcher was eager to find a more permanent solution for the night security guard position so that Gertrude might return to her restful and well-deserved retirement activities. More to the point, he was eager to be rid of her because she made the rest of the security staff, including Hans himself, look like amateurs.

The regrettable circumstances surrounding Bartholomew Breitling's dismissal had less to do with the twenty-seven minor infractions listed within his personnel file than they did with a single unfortunate incident that took place sometime in the early hours of July 27th. This was the day that Bessie Coleman's aviator's cap and goggles disappeared from a glass display case in the museum's "Dawn of Flight" Gallery. While Hans Belcher stopped short of accusing Bartholomew of theft, he clearly placed the full burden of responsibility for the loss upon "Bart's" slouching shoulders. The ensuing investigation, though well-intentioned, was misinformed and unlikely to lead to any satisfactory resolution. With starvation looming and the veritable destruction of a well-established ecosystem hanging in the balance, our story need shift toward the only characters who stood a chance to make things right.

Treena and Parker were immigrants. Unlike many of the residents at the Stars of Flight Air and Space Museum, they were not born on premises and often struggled for acceptance within their new community.

The two raccoons, born of separate parents, spent their early years living in a nearby wooded area. They each relocated several times as, one by one, their family dens were demolished as humans encroached upon their territory, removing trees and fields to build shopping centers and apartment complexes. Parker and Treena met under tragic circumstances, one night, when their parents failed to return from nighttime foraging expeditions. In their grief-stricken search for their parents, they found each other and became fast friends. One night, in desperation, they followed their noses until they came upon an inviting dumpster and more food than they could have ever dreamed of. Shadowing a squirrel, returning with half of a hot dog bun, Parker and Treena found one of several secret entrances to the Museum and staked their claim in the rafters high above a Bleriot Type XI airplane, built in 1909. Protected from rain and wind, heat and cold, and the heavy traffic that most likely claimed the lives of their parents, Parker and Treena made a wonderful life for themselves.

"We've made a wonderful life for ourselves, here at the museum," said Treena, "but I'm afraid our days may be numbered if we can't find some way to exonerate Bartholomew Breitling."

"You know we always steer clear of human interaction, Treena. No good ever comes from our dealings with humans. I don't know that there's very much we could do, anyway." Parker was dead set against embarking on another one of Treena's elaborate adventures.

"If we don't fix this, Parker, then who will? There are a lot of neighbors here who depend upon the Dumpster Café for their livelihood and…"

"And those neighbors haven't exactly been welcoming to us," Parker interrupted. "We might be better off looking for another place to call home…a place where we're more accepted."

"But don't you see, Parker, this is our chance to finally gain that acceptance. If we can crack this case and somehow make things right between Bartholomew and his boss, we'll not only be ingratiating ourselves to our new community but we may help pave the way for future visitors. There's a lot at stake here." Treena wiggled her whiskers and her ringed tail swished nervously through the air. Parker had known Treena long enough to recognize when Treena was withholding information—her body language always betrayed her.

"What aren't you telling me, Treena?" asked Parker.

"What do you mean? I thought I was pretty clear about the stakes —acceptance; exoneration; and, oh yah, preventing mass starvation and annihilation."

"I know, Treena. We'll gain acceptance, we'll save Bartholomew's reputation and his job, and we'll become local heroes for keeping the Café open…if we can figure out what happened to that missing stuff. Wait. Hold on." Treena looked away but her whiskers were now dancing about furiously and her tail swishing became unmistakably more pronounced.

"It wasn't just stuff. That was Bessie's cap," replied an indignant Treena.

"Bessie who?"

"Bessie Coleman."

"Oh, yes. She was the first American woman to earn a pilot's license, right?"

"No," responded Treena, a little exasperated. "You're thinking of Harriet Quimby. In 1911, the glamorous Harriet Quimby became the first woman to earn a U.S. pilot's certificate and, the year after, she became the first woman to fly across the English Channel. Unfortunately, she didn't receive much media attention at the time because RMS Titanic hit an iceberg and sunk the day before her flight."

"Right. I remember now. What I meant to say was that Bessie Coleman was the first woman in the world to pilot a plane and become a licensed pilot."

"No, no, no, Parker. Don't you listen to the docents here at the museum? That was Raymonde de Laroche. She received the 36th aeroplane pilot's license issued by the Aeroclub de France on behalf of the Fédération Aéronautique Internationale—the first organization in the world to issue international pilot licenses. Raymonde received her license on March 8, 1910!"

"Impressive! But I was just messing with you, Treena. We're talking "Queen Bess" here, right? The first African American woman and the first Native American to earn a pilot's license?" Treena hated when Parker baited her. She sighed.

"Right. African Americans and Native Americans were not allowed to participate in flight training here in the United States so Bessie, the 10th of 13 children born to Texas sharecroppers, saved up what little money she had and moved to Chicago, Illinois at age 23. Her work ethic and undying passion to become an aviatrix earned her notice and she eventually found allies who helped sponsor her to travel to France for flight training. Bessie excelled in the air and on June 15, 1921, she earned an international pilot's license from the Fédération Aéronautique Internationale, the same organization that had granted Raymonde de Laroche her license ten years before. Returning to the U.S., she participated in numerous flying events, drawing huge crowds and inspiring countless others, especially those who had given up hope that they might ever achieve their dreams because of their race. Beyond her accomplishments in the air, Bessie Coleman became an outspoken advocate for equality, speaking at countless venues across the country in her quest to end racism and create opportunities for African Americans. Tragically, Bessie Coleman was killed in an aircraft accident on April 30, 1926, before she was able to see her many goals realized. Ironically, she was not even the pilot in control of that aircraft but was surveying the area for a planned parachute jump she was scheduled to make the following day at an airshow. It was later discovered that a wrench used to service the aircraft's engine had become lodged in the controls. Bessie Coleman was 34 when she died but her contributions to aviation and civil rights have never been forgotten."

"Long live Queen Bess," responded Parker with a respectful salute.

"Long live Queen Bess," echoed Treena. "Her flying cap and goggles were on display, you see. Beyond their monetary value, those treasures had an immeasurable inspirational value. The discrimination we've faced is not entirely unlike what Bessie Coleman had to endure—yet she persevered!"

"I understand, now, Treena. We've got to find them. But what makes you think they're here to be found? They may be very far away by now. Probably sold on eBerg."

"eBay."

"Well, whatever. I can't keep track of all this human chatter in the museum. I've got to keep my eyes peeled for maintenance men and such."

"Oh, they're still here somewhere, my friend," replied Treena, with a sparkle in her eye.

"And how do you know that, Treena?"

"Let's just say a little bird told me."

"A little bird?"

"Jerry, to be specific," said Treena with a snicker.

"Jerry's not so little," added Parker, trying not to laugh. "He's eaten a few too many donut crumbs for his own good. It's a wonder he can still fly at all."

"Oh, Jerry can fly just fine. He keeps a pretty good watch over the exits so that we don't get caught by surprise if an unexpected visitor arrives after hours. I asked Jerry about the night the cap and goggles disappeared and he assured me that nobody besides Bartholomew was in the museum that night." Parker listened to Treena, scratching behind his ear with his paw as he considered the matter.

"Are you sure Bartholomew didn't take the items?"

"Yes, I'm sure. All the birds I've spoken to tell me that only the museum curator has a key to that display case and, besides, you know Bartholomew doesn't have a bad bone in his body."

"Bad, no. Lazy? Now that's a different story. But I can respect that. It makes him all the more lovable."

"Exactly!" replied Treena, enthusiastically.

"So, where do we go from here?"

"We go have a closer look at that display case, once the museum closes."

"Deal," replied Parker, with a yawn. He was unused to being awake during daylight hours but the gravity of the situation merited the unwelcome mid-afternoon crisis planning session. The two lumbered back to their makeshift den up in the rafters.

Sometime after 11pm, Treena gently nudged Parker to wake him. "Come on, sleepy head, we've got work to do." Parker rolled over and got to his feet, shaking his whole body, then stretching and yawning. Treena shushed him when she saw the narrow beam of a flashlight pass below. It was Gertrude Sumppumper making her rounds. Gertrude's watch was never inaccurate and her nightly patrols had become very predictable. In fact, they were so predictable that Treena had assessed that she could sing the "Lovely Fresh Apple Pie" song her mother had taught her a full fifteen times before Gertrude would make her next pass by the display case in question. Treena and Parker, who normally didn't spend very much time down below in the galleries, descended to the museum floor and hid behind the Brees Penguin, waiting for Gertrude's next pass. Treena and Parker's hearts were beating furiously as they tightly clumped together to avoid the sweeping flashlight beam that nearly betrayed their position. Gertrude had barely passed before Treena started singing her song. *"Apple pie, mana from the sky, is the best food there can be. Heaven sent, a treasure clearly meant to bring joy to you and me..."*

"Shhh. Not so loud, Treena," said Parker as he cautiously stepped out from their hiding place. Treena nodded, her brain fully occupied minding the pace of her song and intent on not losing count of the iterations. Parker just shook his head and scampered out across the floor toward the Bessie Coleman display. Parker sniffed around the base of the display case but all he could smell was the cleaning solvent that had recently been used to clear the glass of children's fingerprints. If there had been any incriminating prints upon the glass case, half the children of the county would have to be called in for questioning. Parker and Treena slowly inspected the front of the display case but found no obvious evidence of tampering. The back of the case was up against the back side of another display case and the two were too close together for either of our heroes to be able to squeeze between.

"That's seven, Parker," blurted out Treena. "We're halfway there." Once more, Parker's heart rate elevated to an uncomfortable level.

"Wait here, Treena. I'm going to try to get up on top."

"*Crusty, crispy, super delishy; you smell just like a dream. I'll top you off with a dollop or two of fresh vanilla cream.* What? Going up where? Please be careful."

Parker ran around to the opposing side and surveyed the area. He could just barely still hear Treena's singing. Parker was a master climber but the route he chose would truly test his abilities. He deftly climbed onto a Republic P-47 Thunderbolt and scampered along the wing before making a bold leap onto a display housing an aircraft engine. From there, another spectacular leap landed him atop the row of display cases. He landed with a thud which nearly stopped Treena's heart. She nervously looked about but Gertrude was still on the far side of the museum, albeit making her way back. "Nine!" she shouted up to the shadowy figure inspecting the tops of the display cases, before continuing with her song. Parker carefully walked back and forth across the top of the case, peering down into the darkness between the two display case backs. "Twelve!" yelled Treena, a greater level of anxiety coming through in her voice than with her previous update.

"Twelve," replied Parker from atop the case. He stuck his snout down in the gap between the cases and pushed his head as far down as it would go, his nose working overtime to pick up scents and his eyes wide, gazing into the darkness. He pushed too far. Parker's head got trapped in the narrow confines of the gap.

"Thirteen! You'd better hurry up and get down from there, Parker." Treena's voice was subtly shifting from concern to anxiety to panic. "*My tummy's happy and full and I thank you so but I have a request of you. Please warm up the oven and toss some more love in so I can share with a friend or two. Then we can all be at peace, when we travel beyond and join our old friends in the sky. Grandma will be there, with her grandma, too, and a lovely fresh apple pie.*" Parker twisted and shook until he finally managed to dislodge his head. Frantically, he scampered toward the corner of the display case row where he jumped down upon the engine block display before making a panicked leap for the P-47 aircraft wing. He landed with a huge thud that could be heard throughout the gallery and his momentum carried him across the wing and over the edge. Parker laid there, in a stunned silence, while Gertrude's voice thundered through the gallery.

"Who's there?!" shouted Gertrude, as she quickened her pace to something closely approximating a jog, her flashlight beam frantically scanning all the exhibits ahead of her. Parker was still lying on his side, groaning, as Treena approached and gently grabbed hold of the soft tissue on the scruff of his neck with her teeth. She tugged and dragged her dazed friend behind the landing gear wheel of the P-47 Thunderbolt. There wasn't much room for the two raccoons and they only just avoided detection as Gertrude, now gasping for air and out of breath, passed them by. Parker's moans might have given them away had not Gertrude's wheezing deafened the stalwart security guard to all but the most resounding of audible emanations. Once the guard was clear, and Parker had recovered enough to walk, albeit with a slight limp, the two raccoons beat a hasty retreat from the gallery and eventually made their way back up to the security of the upper levels of the hangar structure.

From the safety of the rafters, Parker apologized for his delayed return, recounting the story of how his head became trapped between the display cases. Treena gently nuzzled her pal and comforted him. "That was exceptionally brave of you, Parker. I'm just glad you're okay. Did you find any clues while you were up there?"

"I'm not sure, Treena. The back of the case looked fairly secure and the only opening I saw was a round hole, perhaps the size of an orange, that an electrical cord passed through to power the display case lighting, I presume."

"Interesting. Well, that's a start. Is there any way someone could have used a wire hanger to reach up into the case and hook the cap and goggles?" asked Treena. Parker considered the distances and angles involved.

"No, I don't think so, Treena. There's no access from the side without moving several of those display cases out of the way and there's no evidence any case was moved. If someone were to climb atop the case, they'd have to…no, there's no way a person could have accessed the interior of the display case from the top."

"And your deduction, Mr. Holmes?"

"The perpetrator had to be smaller than us, that's for sure. They'd have to have fairly good climbing skills and a good working knowledge of the museum and its displays."

"An inside job?"

"Yah, I think so, Treena. But who? And why?"

"I say we start out investigating the squirrels, mice and rats."

"Not the snakes?" asked Parker.

"Do you want to interview Boris?" Parker did not care to interview Boris. Boris was a boa constrictor who was recklessly released into the wild by his owner when he grew too big for his glass terrarium. After slithering his way across the urban terrain, he found a comfortable home at the museum, much to the horror of the local rodent population. When he first arrived, only the mice feared this reptilian stalker. As he grew, the rats and squirrels took notice. Parker and Treena both knew that it was only a matter of time before Boris set his beady eyes on them. One thing was certain; his conspicuous growth could not be attributed to discarded hot dog buns and potato chips. His tastes were for more animated fare.

"Um. No. I'll start interviewing the squirrels, tonight."

"I'll see what I can find out from the mice and the birds."

"That's a lot of ground to cover, Treena."

"I know. But we haven't time to waste. Some of the families have already left the museum to try to find a better home. Several hawks have moved into the local area and, to be blunt, relocation has become an extremely dangerous proposition. Besides that, we have a number of senior citizens here who have few options left but to stick it out and hope for salvation." Treena sighed and extended her paw out towards Parker. Parker reached out with his paw and affectionately stroked Treena's paw. The two gazed at each other for a bit before nodding and departing upon their quests.

While a number of the museum's inhabitants were skeptical of the newcomers, Treena and Parker's engaging personalities quickly broke down barriers. Alliances were built and naysayers silenced as the two raccoons built upon a growing network of supporters, all putting their faith in the ring-tailed sleuths who were, for better or worse, the only game in town.

Days passed and the food grew scarce. Fights broke out in the parking lot of the museum as residents tussled with aggressive gulls, hordes of pigeons, and the occasional feral cat, for meager scraps of food that accumulated thanks to errant gusts of wind, careless toddlers, or slovenly parking lot snackers. Treena and Parker both grew weaker and their bodies thinned in a most alarming manner. The only resident who prospered through this catastrophe was Boris, the boa constrictor. The once nimble mice that formed a large part of his diet lacked the evasive energy and alertness that often saved their hides from a frightful demise. Boris bore no ill-will toward his fellow museum tenants. He, like all others in this world, required sustenance to live. Evolution had ensured Boris was particularly suited to seek out the prey that would assure his survival. With few leads to show for their efforts, after engaging with nearly all the known animal clusters within the museum, Parker lighted upon a rather risky course of action, one which Treena firmly advised against.

"Treena, between the two of us, we've met with nearly all the known animal groups within the museum and we're no closer to solving this mystery than we were at the onset. I know you aren't going to like this suggestion, but I think we're going to need some help to find the undiscovered pockets of museum dwellers and nobody is going to be able to sniff those out better than the apex predator of these galleries."

"Oh no you don't, Parker!" objected Treena. "I don't want you getting within a pine tree's length of that snake!"

"I'll be careful, Treena. I promise. I think this might be our last chance. If I can follow Boris, and see where he's sniffing around at, I might just uncover some more leads."

"Parker, no. You're still limping around and you're gaunt and malnourished and it's just not safe. I don't want any more talk about you slinking around behind a hungry snake on the prowl. Now, let's get some rest and later we can check back with the squirrels to see if they've seen anything interesting. Maybe Jerry has seen something during his night flights around the atrium?" Parker sighed and nodded. He knew better than to argue with Treena. He licked his paws and wetted down the fur along his cheeks before curling up next to Treena for some rest. He knew she was right but he also knew that desperate times called for desperate measures.

Treena was fast asleep when Parker slowly rolled away and quietly peered down from the rafters into the darkness to try to spot Boris emerging from his lair behind a display case filled with vintage space toys. It's a very good thing that the many children who visited the museum and marveled and the beautiful toys from the 1960s and 70's had no idea that a six-foot boa constrictor was sleeping just behind the display. Such a discovery would have put the Public Relations Office into a tailspin.

Right on cue, Boris emerged from his lair and began to slither along the walls of the museum, eventually making his way out into the museum's grand atrium. He had no more desire to meet up with Gertrude Sumppumper than she had to encounter a six-foot snake. While Gertrude, even at her advanced age, was more than prepared to deal with common vandals, looters, or trouble-making juveniles; she was woefully unprepared to confront a childhood phobia that had haunted her since a Third-Grade birthday party when the contracted entertainer for the event, "Reptile Man," accidently dropped a Ball Python on Gertrude's lap. Reptile Adventures, Inc., was only legally obliged to pay for the first three years of counseling and, despite the valiant efforts of four different therapists, the case file was eventually closed and stamped "INCURABLE," in bold red letters.

Parker carefully followed, at a distance. He was surprised to see Boris make his way into Hangar 2. That was a long way to travel and Parker could only assume that there must be a good reason for the long journey. There was. Unbeknownst to most of the museum residents, a small family of mice had made a home for themselves inside the Grumman F-14 Tomcat. Boris had a keen sense of smell and, like the AIM-9 Sidewinder missiles hanging from the jet, he could also pick up on the heat signatures of his prey. He slithered upward along the landing gear of the aircraft, looking for an entrance into the interior of the jet.

Fearing for the lives of the family inside, Parker quickly surveyed the exterior of the aircraft. It looked like he might be able to get in through the engine exhaust nozzles. With his eyes glowing in the darkness, Parker quickly assessed the chink in the armor and scurried atop a nearby display to attempt a leap onto the aircraft's tail section. Unfortunately, in his weakened state, Parker failed to make the distance. He suffered a hard landing on the floor below, hitting his head, knocking the air from his lungs, and further damaging his injured leg. Despite the physical pain, the brave raccoon made his way back atop the perch for another go at it. Meanwhile, Boris was slithering about inside the interior of the jet, searching for the mice within. He was startled by the loud clanging sound that rang like a warning bell when Parker landed squarely atop the F-14's fuselage. Within seconds, Parker had lowered himself into one of the engines. Alarmed by the commotion, the mice huddled together near one of the fuel tanks, quaking in fear. Parker continued on until his size prevented him from traveling any deeper into the engine. Knowing full well that Boris was on the hunt, Parker shouted "Snake!" followed by "If you want to live, head through the engine toward my voice." There was no response. As calmly as he could, Parker kept talking, knowing he was potentially putting himself at risk. Eventually, he heard the patter of tiny little feet and several small mice popped out through the turbine blades, emerging in the afterburner section of the engine where Parker was nervously trembling. After four tiny mice popped out, the parents emerged. All were relieved to see a gentle looking raccoon rather than a trickster serpent. They all made their way down to the floor level and Parker led them across the atrium toward the safety of the main gallery. From the cockpit of the F-14 Tomcat, Boris looked on with a vengeful eye as the shadowy figures disappeared into the darkness.

Once the group had caught their breath, Parker inquired of the parents whether or not they had any information about the missing aviator's cap and goggles. Their response to the question came only after a long story about how the clever mouse family had decided to live in a Tomcat because no cat on the prowl would ever expect to find a family of mice living inside a cat. The reasoning seemed logical to Parker, especially after three days without food and a solid knock to his noggin only moments before. The parents knew nothing of the missing items but their young son, who up until that moment had been incessantly whistling "*Highway to the Danger Zone*" from the movie "Top Gun," suggested that his friend, Charisse, might know something.

"Charisse? Who's Charisse," asked Parker, curious about the youngster's comment.

"Charisse is Lionel's daughter," replied Scooter, the young mouse with a passion for aviation. "She's my buddy. We play all the time and she knows more about rocket ships than anybody in the whole world."

"And where might I find your friend?" asked Parker, patiently digging for the information he needed and all too aware that the night was slipping away and Treena was probably out looking for him. At this point, Scooter's mother jumped in.

"Lionel and his daughter, Charisse, are both rats and they live up in the Apollo Lunar Module. But if you want to drop in on them, we had better go with you. Lionel is very protective and he's likely to come out biting and scratching unless we introduce you."

The Lunar Module was the gem of the museum and Parker found it difficult to believe that anyone was living inside the most visited exhibit within the Stars of Flight Air and Space Museum. However, after the events of the evening, there was little that could surprise him. The mouse family and their raccoon escort made their way to the Space Gallery and scampered up the Lunar Module ladder to the entry hatch. Scooter gently scratched the exterior of the hatch and announced his presence. With a creaking noise, the hatch slowly opened and a grizzled old rat stared warily out at the party. Parker was so started by Lionel's appearance that he toppled off the ladder to the faux lunar surface below.

From inside, they could all hear a girlish chuckle as Charisse joked "That's one small step for man, one giant leap for mankind." At first, Parker was not amused. He was so broken that it was a wonder he could walk at all. But, as he saw the smiling face of little Charisse peer through the entry hatch, he couldn't help but join in the laughter. Parker climbed back up and properly introduced himself. "Nice to meet you, Mr. Raccoon. You're just in time, I'm about to blast off for the moon. Would you like to join me?" Parker was a bit confused but he was captivated by the young rat's enthusiasm and he nodded in approval. Scooter was beside himself with excitement. With the ice broken, Lionel invited all the guests to join them inside the capsule. Once inside, Scooter took his place in a seat next to Charisse. Clearly, the two pals had played astronaut games many times before. Charisse slid a pair of oversized goggles over her head so that they rested on her nose and then proceeded to don a leather flying cap. "Strap in, everybody. We're going to blast off in ten seconds," announced the astronaut in command. Parker was clearly fixated on the flying cap and goggles. There was no mistaking them—those items had once belonged to "Queen Bess," herself. Parker was overcome by joy, so much so that a tear began to form in his eye. "Don't cry, Mission Specialist Raccoonofstra. I promise I'll get you up to Moon Base Alpha safe and sound," said Charisse, now fully in character. "Ten, nine, eight, seven, six, five, four, three, two, one, ready or not, here we come, BLAST OFF!" Charise and Scooter both filled the Lunar Module with an impressive array of improvised engine sounds, shaking in their seats as they simulated the launch.

The game continued for a while before Parker pulled Lionel aside, along with Scooter's parents, and explained the situation. Lionel was receptive but refused to surrender the cap and goggles because he knew it would break his daughter's heart to part with them. While they were talking, Parker looked about the interior of the Lunar Module. It was now abundantly clear where all the pilfered items from the Museum Gift Shop had found their way. The capsule was a veritable shrine to space travel. This gave Parker an idea.

"Hey, Commander Charisse, what would you say if I told you I could swap out that oversized hat and giant goggles for a real astronaut suit and helmet that are just your size?"

Charisse's face lit up. "Wow! Really? You would do that for me?"

"Sure, I would. But, here's the catch—I've got to exchange your old hat and goggles to acquire your fancy new, NASA-certified, astronaut attire. Would you be okay with that?" Charisse considered the proposition. She was quite fond of her current attire but was concerned that she might lose control of her spacecraft when the flying cap slid down over her goggles, as it frequently did.

"Okay, mister, it's a deal," she finally replied. "Hey, is that your co-pilot down there, Mr. Raccoon?" Parker looked out the Lunar Module's window and saw Treena frantically searching the area for her missing friend. Lionel opened the hatch and Parker shouted out across the gallery to get Treena's attention. Once reunited, he caught Treena up on the activity of the evening. She was not happy with Parker's reckless disregard for his own welfare but, given the great success of his endeavor, she didn't stay mad for very long. Parker went on to describe how Lionel knew a secret way to get into the gift shop by sliding one of the tiles of the dropped ceiling aside and then jumping down onto a merchandise shelving unit. He further described a wonderful Astronaut Barbie doll he had seen in the gift store. The doll was entirely too large for Lionel to drag back with him but Parker was very confident that, with Treena's help, the two could secure the doll and, more importantly, liberate Barbie from her astronaut garb so that one young rat might finally have her authentic spacesuit. The plan seemed sound enough but the sun was nearly up and the museum staff would be arriving before long. There wasn't a second to lose.

Charisse cautiously entrusted her flying cap and goggles to Treena who assured her that she would be thrilled with the upgrade. With the treasures carefully held in her mouth, Treena followed Parker and Lionel as they made their way through the duct system that would eventually lead them to the gift shop. Lionel showed the raccoons the ceiling tile that he regularly used to get into the store and Parker carefully slid it aside so that there was enough room for a raccoon to pass through. Parker nervously looked down. Normally, he wouldn't think twice about the short jump. However, he was in serious pain and the thought of another hard landing on his injured leg filled him with dread. Treena picked up on his hesitancy right away.

"How about you just stay here, Parker? I'm pretty sure I can get the doll up by myself," said Treena.

"Thank you, Treena, but I'd really like to do this together." Parker's tail was nervously twitching as he spoke.

"Are you sure?"

"Sure, I'm sure," replied Parker. Treena approached and rubbed her nose against Parker's nose, expressing her affection and concern.

"Okay, then. After you, hero," said Treena. Parker steeled himself for the jump and leaped through the aperture in the ceiling tiles. He grimaced when he landed atop the merchandise case but tried not to let on the extent of his pain. Lionel looked on from above as Parker scampered over to the toy display to look for the Barbie doll while Treena carefully placed Bessie Coleman's leather flying cap and goggles next to the cash register where she knew the humans would find them in the morning. Treena then returned to Parker who was already sliding the "Astronaut Barbie with Space Accessories Pack" out from the display. Together, they dragged the doll to the top of the merchandise case below the opening and pushed the doll up to Lionel who dragged it back away from the hole. Next, Parker helped to boost Treena up through the portal. Although it was a short jump up, Parker was not sure if he could make it. He had lost all spring in his legs and was overcome by exhaustion.

"Go get the astronaut gear to Charisse. I'm going to grab a few packs of Astronaut Ice Cream for our junior space travelers and I'll meet you back at the capsule in a couple minutes," said Parker. Treena didn't like the idea of leaving her friend alone, especially in his current state, and she committed to returning as quickly as she could. Parker listened to the soft footsteps on the ceiling tiles above and then the clinking sound as Lionel and Treena entered into the duct system. What Parker did not hear was the silent slithering of a famished boa constrictor. Denied of his meal, Boris had been tracking Parker all night long. Swallowing a raccoon whole would be a challenge but Boris was convinced that he was now large enough to graduate from small rodents to a meal of more prodigious size. He also sensed his prey was wounded and unlikely to put up much of a fight once wrapped in his constricting coils.

Parker had barely collected the snacks when he felt the sharp pain of a bite on his hindquarters. He cried out in pain as Boris clamped down with his powerful jaws. The ensuing fight was something to be seen. Displays were knocked to the ground, with gift items scattered about, as the two foes wrestled furiously within the store. For all his effort, Parker could not break the grip of the serpent's jaws. Exhausted from the exertion, and his lack of food and sleep, Parker began to succumb to the snake's aggressive assault. Sensing the tide was turning, Boris coiled about the panting raccoon and began to squeeze his victim. Things looked bad for Parker until the unmistakable figure of a masked savior came flying down from above. Treena landed squarely atop the two combatants and savagely ripped at the snake's scaly skin, tearing a gash in his side. Bleeding profusely and fearing for his life, Boris rapidly retreated toward the gift store doors and managed to slither through the gap, only just avoiding a painful demise. With tears in her eyes, Treena hugged Parker and held him tightly until they both fell asleep.

On August 3rd, 2021, the staff of the Stars of Flight Air and Space Museum arrived at work to find the gift shop ravaged. Many displays were knocked over, their contents spilled upon the floor. Asleep in the corner were the two culprits, a pair of raccoons. The museum's gift shop remained closed while staff members peaked inside, hoping to get a glimpse of the mischievous creatures that had turned the shop upside down. The county's Animal Control Service was called but, by the time they arrived, the offending creatures were gone. After a thorough search through the museum, no raccoons were found. Instead, the trained professionals of the Animal Control Service had to satisfy themselves by removing a rather unhealthy-looking boa constrictor. The snake was later donated to Reptile Adventures, Inc. where he is currently thrilling countless small children at birthday parties and youth camp events. Upon hearing that a snake was discovered within the museum, Gertrude Sumppumper officially submitted her resignation and is now living happily in northern Alaska, a state with no known snake population.

Bartholomew Breitling was thrilled to be offered his old job back. Feeling guilty for having falsely accused Bartholomew of theft, Hans Belcher, the head of security at the museum, afforded "Bart" extra latitude in the accomplishment of his duties.

Everyone at the museum was thrilled to have Bessie Coleman's flying cap and goggles back on display in the Dawn of Flight Gallery. While no satisfactory explanation was ever posited as to how the artifacts made their way from a locked museum display case to the checkout register inside a locked gift store, all who knew of the incident were thankful that these treasures were recovered.

Whether through neglect or by design, Bartholomew Breitling routinely continued to omit step 42C from the museum's Exterior Walkaround Checklist which meant the magnificent Dumpster Café was back in business for the many residents of the museum who relied upon the establishment for their daily nourishment. A grateful community acknowledged the meritorious contributions of Treena and Parker. This same community also learned a thing or two about having respect for the dignity of all their fellow creatures. They were never again quick to judge newcomers and, instead, welcomed all with open arms.

Guests of the museum continued to be thrilled by the wonderful collection of historic air and space treasures. Bessie Coleman's cap, goggles, and, most importantly, her story continued to inspire countless visitors. The Lunar Module remained a fan favorite for the masses. Adoring fans looked upon the spacecraft with stars in their eyes, unaware that within this protective capsule, a young astronaut dressed in an authentic space suit and wearing a perfectly fitted space helmet, was sailing across the vast expanses of space along with her companions, First Mate Scooter Whizbang and Chief Scientist Naked Barbie.

The Stars of Flight Air and Space Museum's three core missions are to educate, preserve, and inspire. Treena and Parker, standing behind their new junior astronaut friends, felt confident that they had contributed fully to furthering the important mission of a museum they've grown to love; a museum they proudly call home.

Flapper and the Captain

The Story Behind the Story

Believe it or not, this short story was inspired by real world events. The timing could not have been more perfect. As part of The Red Penguin Collection, the next planned anthology, "Pets on the Prowl: An Animal Mystery Anthology," required authors to submit a 3,000-7,500-word short story that included or was centered around at least one animal character and, as the title implied, fit into the mystery genre. My story begins: "On August 3rd, 2021, the staff of the Stars of Flight Air and Space Museum arrived at work to find the gift shop ravaged. Many displays were knocked over, their contents spilled upon the floor. The culprits? Two raccoons!" August 3rd was the actual date that this episode played out, for real, at the Cradle of Aviation Museum where I volunteer as a docent. The staff discovered the racoons sleeping off their night's misadventure within the gift shop and the shop remained closed for much of the day until animal control could remove the racoons and the gift shop could be put back in order. This humorous tale (not as funny to the staff at the museum) proved fertile ground for creating my own backstory to explain the events leading up to the very visible conclusion. I really enjoyed developing the animal characters and working the interplay between them while, simultaneously, recognizing an aviation pioneer (Bessie Coleman). The museum doesn't actually have Bessie Coleman's flying cap on display but, seeing as how I already took all kinds of liberties with this fantasy tale, the departure from fact seemed a very excusable bit of fiction. I hope you enjoyed the tale.

Maritime Britain

(Written October 12, 2021)
Published by Red Penguin Books in *"London: Smoke, Blokes and Jokes of Foggy Town"* (October 7, 2022)

In this essay, I share some of my favorite memories of exploring Great Britain's maritime past through several excursions I embarked upon while I was living in England.

I had barely arrived in England before I began reading Patrick O'Brian's magnificent Aubrey-Maturin series of sea novels set in 19th Century England and, indeed, around the globe. A lifetime lover of all things nautical, I was readily willing to believe my mother's tales of there being a sea captain in my bloodline somewhere back in the foggy past of yesteryear. The aforementioned novels vividly detailed the adventures of the two friends, Jack Aubrey and Stephen Maturin, as they progressed through a never-ending series of adventures while serving in the Royal Navy. The locations described were not a world away but, instead, just a short train ride into London. Beyond my fascination with the facts behind the fiction, I was also enthusiastic to learn more about the challenges of navigation during this period, more so because I was an Air Force navigator, by profession. Dava Sobel's wonderful book, *Longitude*, detailed the amazing tale of John Harrison, a British clockmaker, who solved a challenge that had been perplexing the Royal Navy for as long as it had been in existence—how to determine longitude while at sea. The book details his 40-year quest to create the perfect chronometer for use at sea. These two books, and the places and artifacts described within, set the stage for two wonderful trips in England. The first trip was a day trip to Greenwich, in London, and the second trip was a two-day visit to Portsmouth, about 70 miles southwest of London.

On February 14, 1998, I decided the time was right to take my family to visit the Old Royal Observatory at Greenwich, in London. Greenwich is a very special place for a number of reasons. For starters, it's located right on the Prime Meridian (0 degrees longitude) and it's also where time starts (world time zones are measured as either plus or minus hours from Greenwich Mean Time, or GMT). There are a number of ways to get to London but, once you're there, I recommend making your way to Charring Cross station from wherever your starting point is. Near Charring Cross is a dock where you can book passage on a number of Thames River cruises. Several of these take you to Greenwich and back. If you're not into river cruises, you can get the Docklands Light Railway from Tower Hill which will also take you to Greenwich. Seeing as how my goal was to enjoy a nautical themed day, a one hour narrated cruise down the famous Thames was a perfect way to start the adventure. Along the way, sites of interest were discussed in a clever and entertaining fashion with a typical British flair.

One of the first spectacles to greet you as you depart your boat at Greenwich is the magnificent *Cutty Sark*. The *Cutty Sark* is a ship so famous that they named a whiskey after it. Built in Scotland in 1869, the *Cutty Sark* was one of the fastest of the famed "clipper" ships; beautiful state of the art sailing vessels that regularly made cargo runs around the globe. The advent of steam powered vessels eventually spelled the downfall for these beautiful tall ships but, at the time, they represented the pinnacle of sailing technology.

Once you're done checking out the Cutty Sark, the next stop on this day trip is a visit to the Old Observatory and Museum. On your way, should you like a break, there's a beautiful park at the foot of the Observatory which is a great place for picnics or to let the little folk run wild. There are also lots of great shops in the area if you want to spend some money on a unique shopping extravaganza.

The Observatory itself is on top of a hill and is filled with great exhibits relating to the history of navigation. The Greenwich Meridian is also conspicuously marked, as befits a noteworthy tourist attraction. Of course, you'll want to have your photo taken straddling the line on the ground, with one foot in the Eastern Hemisphere and the other in the Western Hemisphere, while the atomic clock behind you provides a highly accurate read-out of the precise time of your visit. It may sound a bit gimmicky but it you reflect upon the history; you'll have an extra level of appreciation for the significance of the moment. And, if nothing else, it's a pretty good place to adjust the time on your personal watch.

I entered the Old Observatory and Museum with a sense of reverence, as if I were visiting a cathedral. I stood in awe as I saw John Harrison's original H-1 clock (his first try), H-2, H-3, and the final prize-winning H-4 chronometer on display. As previously described, you'll have a much greater appreciation for these remarkable devices and John Harrison's genius if you read Dava Sobel's *Longitude* before you visit.

Beyond the Old Observatory and Museum, there's another "must-see" stop while you're at Greenwich and that's the National Maritime Museum. The Museum is filled with all kinds of interesting historical artifacts and artwork but it also has a really fun interactive kids' room with lots of exciting hands-on gadgets for the younger sailors in your party to fidget with. The Museum's collection houses more than two-million items and there's no place like it in the world. If you're a fan of Britain's maritime history, be sure you block out enough time to explore the museum's impressive collections.

After our visit to the Museum, we made our way back to the dock where return boats departed on the hour. While the narration was similar to that provided on the way down river, you may find the voyage even more enchanting after the sun has set. St. Paul's Cathedral, Big Ben, the Tower Bridge, and the Tower of London are just a few of the sites you'll see along the way.

With my feet wet, so to speak, I was thirsty to explore more of England's maritime history and one of the best places to visit is Portsmouth. There are several ways to get there. We drove from home but, if you're basing out of London, you can take a train down to Portsmouth. It's about a ninety-minute train ride. While there, we stayed at the beautiful old "Queen's Hotel," which was just a short walk from all the historic locations we wanted to visit. First on my list was the famous *HMS Victory*. *Victory* was Admiral Horatio Nelson's flagship during the famous Battle of Trafalgar. Nelson is, perhaps, the most famous character in all the world's naval history. If you are familiar with Trafalgar Square in London, then you have no doubt seen Nelson's column, one of London's most famous monuments. The monument was erected as a measure of the great esteem Lord Nelson was held in by an entire nation indebted to his service. The Battle of Trafalgar took place on October 21, 1805 and pitted the British Royal Navy against the combined fleets of France and Spain. French leader,

Napoleon Bonaparte, had aspirations to invade and conquer England. His Grande Armée (or "Grand Army") was more than capable of overwhelming the British Army. There was one small catch, Napoleon had to find a way to traverse the twenty-some-odd miles of the English Channel that separated England from the European mainland. Standing between him and his goal was the formidable Royal Navy. To ensure a safe passage, Napoleon knew he'd have to eliminate the threat. And thus, the stage was set for one of the greatest naval battles in the history of the world. The engagement took place off the coast of Spain. Leading his fleet from the front and outnumbered 33 to 27 ships, Nelson led the Royal Navy to its greatest victory, thus saving the island nation. The combined French and Spanish fleet lost 22 ships while the Royal Navy did not lose a single vessel. Though brutally battered, *HMS Victory* refused to yield. Lord Nelson lost his life to a sniper's bullet during the engagement and a brass plaque marks the spot where he fell onboard *Victory*. He gave his last full measure and won a victory that truly shaped world history.

Once in Portsmouth, make sure you sign up for the guided tour of *HMS Victory*. As much as I love our own <u>USS Constitution</u>, "Old Ironsides," there is simply no comparison between the two sailing ships. *HMS Victory* was a First-Rate Ship of the Line. She carried 104 guns across multiple gun decks (nearly twice the guns on *USS Constitution*) and her guns were, generally, much larger and more powerful. The Ships of the Line were the battleships of their day and carried a crew of around 850. I highly encourage you to read up on the ship before you start climbing around her. Besides seeing the place where Nelson was shot, you will also visit the spot in the interior where he finally passed on, his final words being "Thank God I have done my duty." Nelson had a brilliant naval career that epitomized the spirit of the famous patriotic song "Rule Britannia" whose lyrics begin "Rule Britannia, Britannia rule the waves."

While wandering around the historic dockyard, after the amazing visit to *HMS Victory*, I was incredibly fortunate to stumble upon a barely marked large hangar building where a tattered sail was hanging out for airing. It was the mainsail from *HMS Victory*, hanging from a yardarm within the building. The signage there stated that this was the first time since Trafalgar (in 1805) that the mainsail had been spread out. You could see the numerous tears from where cannon balls and chain shot ripped through it. I cannot begin to tell you what an incredible thrill that was.

In case the world's most spectacular sailing warship isn't your cup of tea, Portsmouth has much more to offer. I highly recommend the harbor tour by boat. You'll get to sail about an active British naval port and I can guarantee you'll be impressed by the modern aircraft carriers, destroyers, and an array of lesser ships that you'll encounter on the journey. My son loved the boat ride. I did, too.

After our harbor tour, we visited the *Mary Rose* Museum where we got to see the remains of the 16th Century Tudor warship. Pre-dating *HMS Victory* by nearly 300 years, the *Mary Rose* was said to be Henry VIII's favorite ship. The Mary Rose sank in 1545 and only 35 of the 500 men onboard survived. The wreck of the Mary Rose was not discovered until 1971. What remained of the ship was raised on October 11, 1982. While the recovered section may not be aesthetically pleasing, the thousands of artifacts that were brought up represent an amazing time capsule of the period and the museum is filled with great exhibits and informative displays. If you love maritime history, you definitely won't be disappointed.

If you prefer to see a spectacular intact ship, go visit HMS Warrior. HMS Warrior, built in 1860, was the world's first iron-hulled, armored battleship. Powered by both steam and sail, she was the largest, fastest, and most powerful warship of her day. If you visited *HMS Victory* first, you'll truly be impressed by the incredible advances in technology that are apparent in every feature of this remarkable vessel. Its history isn't quite as storied as HMS Victory but you won't be disappointed as you climb around the ship. While there, definitely spend some time in the National Museum of the Royal Navy (called the Royal Navy Museum, when I visited).

If you are totally "shipped out," or if the little people are begging for mercy, you can do like we did and visit the Blue Reef Aquarium (called the Portsmouth Sealife Centre, during my time visiting). The aquarium has a very nice collection of animals sure to entertain those who love fish, amphibians, reptiles, and especially cute sea otters.

There are a number of other really fun things to do while you're in Portsmouth and, of course, great places to eat. If you want, you can even take a ferry or, better yet, the hovercraft over to the Isle of Wight. I definitely encourage you to do some research before you travel so that you may tailor the experience for your travel party's tastes. With that said, if you're up for an immersion in maritime history, you'll find ample activities to fill your schedule.

While not something you visit, I would be remiss if I didn't conclude my discussion of touring Britain's maritime history without talking about the people. During my time in the United Kingdom, I had the honor of speaking with a number of World War II Royal Navy veterans. The stories they told were nothing short of remarkable. One elderly gentleman described how he was on a vessel which was torpedoed and sunk. And then he was transferred to another vessel, which was also torpedoed and sunk. I listed, in awe, to these marvelous story tellers. Whether speaking with fisherman, merchant sailors, or military veterans, you'll find countless men and women with amazing sea tales to share. You have but to ask…and perhaps offer to buy them a pint of their drink of choice. As I marched in the Southend-on-Sea annual Pearl Harbor Day Memorial Parade, which included a wreath-laying ceremony and beautiful church service, I could not help but be inspired but the gratitude expressed by our British allies. After the day's formal activities, they always invited us over to their veteran's association building, a venue bedecked with all manner of nautical displays and trinkets. It was here that I heard some of the most compelling stories and I could not help but notice the pride in the eyes of the Royal Navy veterans who clearly felt an unbroken connection with centuries of British sailors. I was not surprised that one of the treasures of this meeting place was a beautiful wooden model of HMS Victory. Rule Britannia, Britannia rule the waves.

The Story Behind the Story

In the fall of 2021, Red Penguin Books announced a new series of books that would be focused on travel and international destinations. The plan was to begin with anthologies including location-themed stories, poems, travel tips, essays, and such. Submissions could be fictional or non-fictional, so long as the theme centered around the area described. The first three books were planned to cover London, Paris, and Venice (later changed to Rome) but, ultimately, any works related to the countries (and not just the cities in the title) were considered for selection. Having lived in

England for three years, I could easily have filled the pages of a book with my own writings. I chose, instead, to submit two pieces. Happily, both were accepted. There was quite a time gap between when the submissions were requested and when the travel books were finally published, but I think the wait was well worth it. The travel-themed anthologies are all colorful and artfully put together and the included pieces are all very entertaining.

HAPPY CHRISTMAS: THE TIMELESS CHARM OF THE HOLIDAY SEASON IN ENGLAND

(Written October 15, 2021)
Published by Red Penguin Books in *"London: Smoke, Blokes and Jokes of Foggy Town"* (October 7, 2022)

My recollections of my beautiful holiday experiences during my time living in England.

I have many happy memories of time spent in England but my fondest memories have to be enjoying the beauty and charm of the holiday season. As an Air Force officer, assigned in the United Kingdom, I had the pleasure of experiencing three Christmases in England. There was a certain Old-World beauty to the experience that set it apart from my holiday experiences in the United States. Also, there seemed to be less commercialism and fanfare associated with the holidays. They were more like I felt Christmas should be—joyous yet reverent and respectful. England is situated above 50 degrees north (Alaska is the only U.S. state farther north), and the winter days are very short. Near Christmas, there were less than eight hours of daylight each day. Add in the typical thick cloud deck above and you have a somewhat somber setting reminiscent of a Dickens novel. For all this, there was plenty of holiday cheer to brighten the days. I'd like to share just a few memories.

The Santa Train. If you enjoyed The Polar Express or got excited watching Harry Potter and friends zipping along the tracks on the Hogwarts Express, then you'll likely love one of Britain's holiday train experiences as much as my family and I did. Our journey was taken on the Nene Valley Railway with a lovely old steam engine pulling us across the English countryside from Wansford Station to Peterborough and back. We were fortunate enough to experience the journey while there was snow on the ground. Father Christmas (Santa) greeted all the arriving children before the ride and each child was presented with an age-appropriate gift. Upon the ride itself, traditional holiday treats were provided to all guests. The fare included complimentary drinks (hot chocolate, warm apple cider, and soft drinks or an alcoholic beverage for adults), a bag of holiday sweets for the kids, and a tasty traditional mince pie for each guest.

As we traveled the lovely British countryside, Father Christmas made his way through the train and sat with each and every child. It was a very lovely experience. After the ride, we enjoyed looking around the yard and checking out all the old trains which included a Thomas the Tank Engine special engine. Before leaving, we took photos by the wonderful traditional red British phone booth.

Pantomime. I think my wife and I loved this as much as our two small children did. I had never experienced anything quite like it before. A pantomime is a very special form of participatory theater production where the audience is not only encouraged, but absolutely expected to participate in the action. The productions spring up around England during the holiday season and often have famous personalities playing some of the roles. The sets are an explosion of brilliant colors and the costumes are no less spectacular. The scores are brilliantly crafted and often set to very catchy familiar tunes. The performances are chock full of clever slapstick comedy bits, as well. The pantomimes very frequently retell well known fairy tales. The show I took my family to see in 1999 was a retelling of Jack and the Beanstalk. The performance was staged in the lovely Theatre Royal in Bury St. Edmunds. I think we smiled and laughed through the entire production. I can still see the image of a dozen adorable little children, dressed as spiders, dancing about the stage as the music from ABBA's "Money, Money, Money" accompanied the movement. The audience participation aspect of the show was truly a riot. As an example, a villain might try to frighten the hero by saying "I'm going to get you, Jack." The main character would respond "Oh no you're not." The villain would double-down and shout back "Oh yes I am!" At this point, the audience would know the game was on and would shout back from the seats "Oh no you're not" ... and the argument would volley back and forth like some hilarious tennis match until the villain would give up the fight and cast an angry glance toward the audience who was clearly siding with the hero. The interactions were always delightfully entertaining. My one regret is that I did not attend more pantomimes during my time in England. Pantomime plays are a wonderful tradition whose legacy dates back many, many centuries.

Holiday markets and local events. Not unlike in other European countries, a variety of wonderful holiday markets would spring up

351

around England during this festive time of year. Unique gifts and consumables were made available for customers looking for the perfect holiday gift or treat. Each event would have a local flavor and you were sure to find treasures unavailable in any retail store. Beyond the shopping, many towns had their own traditions and festivals that date back long before any of the current residents were born. You were never quite sure what to expect. While living in England, my rented home was situated on a winding country road between two villages. We'd frequently have horseback riders trot by; the horse and riders' heads bouncing above the hedgerow that formed a barrier between our property and the street. On one Christmas Eve, I remember calling my son to the window so that he might see Father Christmas, himself, as he passed by our home, waving to us, from a horse-drawn cart. A number of towns also have beautiful churches and the services held in medieval stone cathedrals are a true spectacle to behold. Stone walls, illuminated by the flickering candlelight, reverberated with the forceful and well-articulated words of seasoned clergymen and the harmonious hymns sung by the choir.

Television. Even upon the "Tele," the British Broadcasting Corporation, or more familiarly the "BBC," would broadcast special holiday shows. These shows seemed more set upon filling our hearts with the spirit of the holiday than on acting as some marketing ploy to sell products. I remember first seeing the animated short film, "The Snowman," on BBC 4 from our small cottage in England. This beautiful film is without dialog yet relies upon stunning graphical content and a beautiful score to tell a heartwarming story about love and loss set within the context of a young boy's magical encounter with a snowman he crafts on Christmas Eve. To this day, I have watched "The Snowman" every year as part of the run-up to Christmas.

The streets of London. While, thankfully, not as soot-covered as the Industrial Age London portrayed in Charles Dickens' works, a trip into the capital city is a holiday must. The holiday hustle and bustle of the big city stands in stark contrast to the tranquil expressions of the holiday in more remote villages but is no less a part of the Christmas experience in England. I'd try to make it into London at least once during the season just to absorb the festive holiday lights and decorations and immerse myself in the human tide of holiday energy. It may not be for everyone but it's certainly an experience I'd recommend for most.

The clock. One of my last beautiful holiday memories from England relates more to New Year's Day than to Christmas. For years I had drooled over the beautiful grandfather clocks I saw in shop windows. When I moved to England, there was actually a shop on my base that specialized in selling these beautiful clocks—all made by hand in Germany. After much handwringing, I finally decided to part with several thousand of my hard-earned dollars to order my favorite. The clock itself would be customized to my specifications and then delivered to my residence. The *timing* of my decision was not without significance. In fact, it was tremendously significant. The year was 1999 and my desire was to have my new clock in time to ring in the new year—2000. On December 16th, two burly Germans came knocking at my door. They looked exactly like the frightening characters I had seen in a number of Viking movies over the years. The two deliverymen didn't speak a word of English and had driven my beautiful clock through the Chunnel (connecting the European mainland with England) only that morning. With German precision, they set up my timepiece while my 11-month-old daughter looked on in horror. They were pretty fierce looking characters. With the clock in place, and precisely set as only a navigator could ensure, we were ready for New Year's Eve. We tuned our television to BBC and watched as the clock ticked down. My grandfather clock was set to play the Westminster chimes, the same tune played by Big Ben. As the new year was born, my heart soared as my grandfather clock chimed in exact sequence with Big Ben on the tele. It's my wish that, one day, my little princess (my oldest daughter was born in England) will inherit that clock that welcomed the year 2000 for her first New Year's celebration.

I have so many special holiday memories from England but I hope that the stories I chose to share will encourage you to take a trip across the sea to experience the beauty and grandeur of the holiday season in the United Kingdom. In England, they don't say "Merry Christmas," they wish each other a "Happy Christmas." My Christmases in England were very happy.

Flapper and the Captain

The Story Behind the Story

This, my second piece included in the Travel Tips & Tales series, focused on the special magic of the Christmas season in England. What I observed, and felt, during my time there was the inspiration for this piece.

My Brother, The Coelacanth, And I . . . And An Epic Run Through Paris

(Written October 24, 2021)
Published by Red Penguin Books in *"Paris: Love, Loss and Longing in the City of Lights"* (September 22, 2023)

A special memory I share with my brother—a college student and his younger brother race through the streets of Paris on a doomed quest that will, ultimately, bring them closer together.

They say the best place to begin a story is at the beginning. Adhering to this theory, I am compelled to take you back to the beginning--approximately 360 million years ago. This is the date of the earliest known fossil record for one of the key protagonists of my story. No, not him. The other one. The coelacanth! This imposing armored fish shared the seas with a litany of prehistoric "monsters," the likes of which have fueled the imaginations of countless children over the years. The last known fossil record of the coelacanth dates to around 80 million years ago. Like the mighty elasmosaurus, plesiosaur, and mosasaur, the coelacanth was thought to have disappeared around 65 million years ago, along with the dinosaurs. There was just one problem. It didn't. The amazing discovery of a living coelacanth was wonderfully described in one of my favorite childhood books--"Search for a Living Fossil: The Story of the Coelacanth." The book belonged to my older brother and he graciously lent it to me. We always shared books and news clippings about such extraordinary things within our "Adventure Club." The first living coelacanth was discovered on December 22, 1938. The natural question--what else that was thought to be extinct (or mythical) is still hiding out there in the world???

Fast forward. The year is 1977 and my brother and I, along with the rest of my family, are on our first-ever international holiday. It was a two-week vacation in France and Switzerland. We had visited the Louvre early in our stay in Paris. The Louvre was an incredibly impressive museum and the awesomeness of the collection was not lost on this 9-year-old boy. My brother had returned to the museum to spend some more time viewing the collections with a focus on his favorite historical period--classical Greece and Rome. While there, he spotted something which caught his eye . . . and an obsession began. He was nearly certain that, upon the side of a well-preserved ancient Grecian vase, the fish depicted was none other than our own beloved coelacanth! Could it be? Were the Greeks aware of the existence of the coelacanth several thousand years before Marjorie Courtenay-Latimer and Professor J.L.B. Smith??? Those Greeks were pretty smart people. After all, they brought us Socrates, Aristotle, Homer...and the gyro and souvlaki, too! If this theory could be proven, it would be a notable addition to the already fantastic story of the coelacanth. My brother did not own a camera. His little brother did. And thusly do I set the stage for the story which is to follow!

With the stage set, the curtain opens with the Lange family standing beneath the Eiffel Tower on a warm summer's day in Paris. It was our last day in France and my brother was clearly sensing a "now or never" opportunity was slipping away. He approached me with the rather unusual request to be the official photographer for his history making Greco-Coelacanth Expedition. Well now. I had my trusty Polaroid camera and what remained of the only four packs of eight exposure packfilm that had to last me through the trip. This was a tall order, to be sure. My Polaroid camera had been a Christmas gift, just seven months before--it was my first camera. No, it wasn't one of those cool pop-zzzzzip cameras that shot out a developing photo. You pushed the shutter button, then grabbed a yellow tab and pulled the chemical-laden positive-negative strip from the camera, timed the exposure for 60 seconds, and then peeled the photo from the negative paper, after a lovely whiff of chemical goodness. My sister used to be my assistant, standing ever-ready with a small brown lunch sack for me to deposit the smelly chemical negative strip into. So, with the Matterhorn and spectacular Swiss landscapes (and goats!) in my future, I had to make a critical decision. I couldn't let my buddy down! I quickly signed up for the adventure. But there was a catch. It was nearing the time for the Louvre to close and we had no easy way of making the journey. My brother was convinced that it wasn't too far away but we'd have to run, all the same, to make sure that we didn't lose this fleeting opportunity. I should mention that my brother had been on the Cross-Country Track team in high school. For me, a long-distance run was anything beyond the distance it took me to get around a baseball diamond. My parents bid us adieu, probably wondering if they'd ever see either of their sons again, and we were off.

The run? It was not fun. I believe the distance was just shy of 3 miles. I was hurting but, with my brother's encouragement...and sincere praise, I kept it going, my camera in tow. I felt very proud when we finally arrived at the Louvre, only about 15 minutes before they closed the admissions. We quickly made our way towards the stairwell that led to the Grecian antiquities section. And...it was cordoned off...closed! It was closed! Nooooooo! Worse yet, my brother then got that crazy look in his eye. I knew it well. It was that crazy "don't care if I get arrested because I'm on a holy quest" look! I was a little bit panicked. I really didn't want to see my brother get arrested in a foreign country. But he was convinced that we could easily climb over the cordon rope and sneak down to the room with the pottery so that I could get the required photo evidence that would make us both famous. In a moment of sheer brilliance, I blurted out the words "ELECTRIC EYE!" Surely, the most famous art museum in the world had its exhibits protected by some form of advanced security system-- electric eyes! There were probably beams shooting out left and right, up and down, and all over the place! I managed to talk my brother off the ledge. Whew! I mean WHEW!!!! I was finally able to breathe again. We were both very disappointed. But, for my part, not half as disappointed as I would have been seeing my brother dragged off by a bunch of Parisian gendarmes. As for the coelacanth on the Grecian vase? We may never know. I suspect Indiana Jones is still looking for it.

While this all makes for a humorous tale, there is a larger and more philosophical side to this story that remains very meaningful to me. I suspect, for my brother, as well. The story of the coelacanth wasn't just about a whole scientific community being wrong about a scary looking old fish. The coelacanth's tale is one of several notable discoveries that lend some credibility to the otherwise scoffed at field of cryptozoology (or the search to substantiate the existence of species thought to be mythical or extinct). Yes, that means the Loch Ness Monster and Bigfoot and other such creatures. I must admit, I was a huge Loch Ness Monster fan, as a child. I would have pursued this passion further but then I found out that purchasing a submarine with a monster-detecting sonar was a little bit outside of my budget. I did, however, in 1981, descend to the shoreline of Loch Ness to touch the cool waters of that special body of water. Our tour guide arranged a special stop--just for me! She also lent me several books on the Loch Ness Monster to read during our time in Scotland! So--if the coelacanth was alive, perhaps "science" missed the boat on some other creatures, as well. Dinosaurs in the Amazon jungle? Maybe. Yeti and Sasquatch? Very possibly. The Loch Ness Monster? What do you believe? At age 10, I believed enough in my brother's vision and a mysterious vase to run three miles, in July, through the streets of Paris. At the time, the mission may have seemed a failure. Today, I cherish the beautiful memory and therein lies the true success of that special day in Paris.

The Story Behind the Story

Although the submission deadline for the Paris Travel Tips & Tales book was November 15, 2021, it would be nearly two years before the book finally made it to print. As with the England-themed book, Red Penguin Books put a great effort into curating the submissions and crafting a book that was as visually stimulating as it was enjoyable to read. I submitted two pieces for consideration. The first was my fictional piece, entitled "Paris Bench," which was initially passed over for the romance-themed anthology but found life again in the Paris book. This second piece was crafted from a wonderful memory that has never left me of an adventure with my brother during my first-ever trip overseas—a 1977 family trip to France and Switzerland. It's a true story and a fun tale of two boys seeking to solve a mystery and, thankfully, not getting arrested in the process. I can't help but smile when I think of this tale, and I hope it brought a smile to your face, as well.

DIGITAL SLAVE

(Written October 30, 2021)
Published by Red Penguin Books in *"My Robot & Me"* (December, 2021)

*A cautionary tale of the relationship between human
beings and the technology we've developed to
"improve" our lives. A young woman rebels against a
tech-centric society and grapples with the frightening
prospect that humans may have relinquished control
to the devices they've created to serve them.*

"Geraldo, raise the temperature to seventy-two degrees."

"Sorry, I did not hear that. Do you want a recipe for shrimp tempura?"

"No, dummy! Temperature! Raise the damn temperature! It's freezing in here!"

"I'm sorry, I do not understand. Please say a command or say 'menu' to return to a list of options."

Geri grabbed a throw pillow from her sofa and hurled it across the room in anger. The pillow had hardly left her grasp before a wave of embarrassment rushed through her. "Okay, chill Geri Fitzsimmons. Yoga breathing. Yoga breathing. Deep breath, relax, exhale."

"Yogurt Barn opens at 10am tomorrow. Would you like the address?"

"God damn you, Geraldo! You totally suck!"

"Whoa, Sis, take it easy," said Ally, as she descended the stairs of the small suburban home. "It's just a machine. It'll adjust its search parameters after it gets to know you a little bit better."

"I know. I'm sorry Ally. I'm just a little stressed. First, we lose our mom, then I lose my job and have to move back home, and now I feel like taking care of Grandma has become a full-time occupation. Not that I don't want to be here for Grandma but, you know, it kind of takes its toll, doesn't it?" Ally looked upon her sister with sympathetic eyes.

"It sure does, Sis. But I'm glad to have you home, all the same. And Grandma Rose is elated to have you here."

"Oh, I know. I'm glad I can be here for her. And I'm thankful for a place to stay while I sort out my life. And I do love Rose's stories about the simpler days of her childhood."

"Me, too," replied Ally. "I can't even imagine a world without all the tech support and digital assistants."

"Oh, I can," said Geri, with a far-away look in her eyes. I dream about it every night."

"You'd hate it. Life is much better and much safer now. You just don't appreciate how much easier life has become since the Digital Revolution."

"Maybe you're right, Sis. But haven't you ever dreamed of just running away from it all? Finding one of those secluded cabins in some far away forest and just living off the land?"

"You wouldn't last two seconds, Geri. You love your Dulce de Leche Lattes too much." The two sisters laughed and smiled.

"What? You don't think I could whip up a Dulce de Leche Latte from pine bark, moss, and tree sap?"

"I think you can do anything you put your mind to, Sis. So, what do you say we put our minds to going out for some coffee while Grandma is taking her nap?"

"How's she doing today, Ally?"

"Well, her breathing is a little bit labored but, all in all, she's doing well."

"She'll be okay if we head out for a bit, then?"

"Sure. She'll be fine. Geraldo will look out for her," said Ally with a mischievous smile.

"Oh great! That's the last person, I mean thing, I want looking out for Grandma Rose."

The two women walked over to the coat closet and donned their insulated jackets. They had hardly zipped them up when Geraldo, their digital assistant, asked if they'd like him to warm up the car for them. "Absolutely," said Ally. "See, Geri, Geraldo can be quite helpful." Geri just sighed and shook her head. "Shall I ask Geraldo to…"

"No!" responded Geri, cutting her sister off. "I'll unlock, open, and re-secure the front door all by myself."

Outside, the doors to Ally's CyberTech CT3000 opened with a pleasant chime as she and Geri approached. The two sisters climbed in and Geri, while not wanting to admit it openly, was awestruck by the impressive array of displays. Absent were a steering wheel, brakes, and a gas pedal. "A balmy seventy-two degrees. Thanks Lancelot."

"Ally, you named your car Lancelot?"

"Of course, I did," replied Ally. "It gets better. Lancelot…"

"Yes, m'lady," the vehicle responded, with a haughty voice file that was indistinguishable from human speech.

"Take us to The Perfect Bean coffee shop on Laughlin Street."

"Your wish is my command, m'lady."

Ally's face stretched in a satisfied smile and she winked at her sister. "I only wish my old boyfriends were this chivalrous. Hey, Lancelot, play Ally's Groove Tunes playlist."

"Of course, m'lady. Playing Ally's Groove Tunes playlist." On cue, the audio system came to life with the crystal-clear music that Ally had requested. She sat back in her comfortable seat and left the driving to Lancelot. The car used an array of sensors along with car-to-car deconfliction software to safely navigate the route.

"Impressed?"

"You know I'm impressed, Ally. I guess this tech stuff isn't so bad. I'd sure hate to have to fight my way through traffic and deal with crazy drivers like Grandma used to. I can't even imagine the horror."

Lancelot deposited the girls at the entrance to The Perfect Bean and then departed to find a parking spot in the lot. Sensors in the lot had already communicated all the available parking spots to the vehicle and the CT3000 naturally picked the closest spot to minimize fuel burn on the journey.

Inside the shop, orders were given into a speaker system and, moments later, the drinks appeared at the collection window. Geri wondered if there were actually any real people working behind the scenes or not. She imagined a grizzled old man holding a fire extinguisher, just in case something went wrong. Somehow, she was afraid that even the safety monitor's position was now held by an autonomous entity that was plugged in to an array of sensors, the building's fire suppression system, and digitally connected to the local fire department. Geri wondered about all the jobs that once existed but were transferred to robots and computers.

"Ally, do you ever wonder what jobs are actually still accomplished by human beings?"

"Must be a lot of them, Geri. The unemployment numbers are

way down and it seems that things are running pretty smoothly these days."

"Maybe too smoothly," added Geri. "Who makes the numbers? Who reports the numbers? Did you ever stop to think that maybe somebody's trying to keep us all in the dark as to what is really going on?"

"Holy smokes, Sis! Did you develop that paranoia overnight or have you been working on it for a few months now?"

"More than just a few months, Ally. I guess you're right; I'm probably just a little bit crazy. I imagine my job loss and my worries about the future have contributed to my state of mind."

"I know. I get it, Geri. Let's just relax and enjoy the present."

"Don't you ever stop and think about our childhood days, though? I mean, weren't those some pretty awesome times?" asked Geri.

"Sure, they were great times but I learned, long ago, that I needed to move on. And, so I did. I rarely think about the past now. I believe in the future and in our ability to make it better for all of us."

"You're my hero, Ally. Best older sister a girl could have. I'm just sorry we spent so many years apart but now it's great to be able to reconnect. I can't even tell you how much I missed you."

"I missed you, too, Sis," said Ally, reaching out to hold her sister's hand.

The two sat and chatted for the better part of an hour before agreeing that it was a good idea to head back home to check on Grandma Rose. With just a few spoken words into her smart phone, Ally summoned Lancelot and the vehicle dutifully met them at the entrance to the coffee shop, thermostat already set to Ally's preferred temperature and music greeting them as they slid into their seats for the return trip. The comfort and convenience were at once welcoming and, somehow, strangely disturbing. Geri didn't speak much on the way back.

Arriving back home, Geri immediately noticed how cold it was in the home. She ran to the thermostat and saw the temperature was now set to 50 degrees. "What the hell, Geraldo! What don't you understand about keeping the temperature set where I tell you?"

"I'm sorry, I don't understand the question."

"Oh, never mind." Geri angrily stormed upstairs to check on her grandmother. She found Rose shivering beneath her blankets in the bedroom.

"Are you okay, Grandma? I hope we weren't gone too long. I'm so sorry. I didn't know your digital assistant was going to change the thermostat setting after we left. Did you ask for that?"

"I don't think so. I asked for Geraldo to turn on the television and maybe I accidently confused him when I asked for certain channels."

"Oh. Did you ask for channel 50 on your television?" inquired Geri.

"Well . . . dear me, I don't recall. Perhaps I did?"

"Don't worry, Grandma, we'll warm it right up for you."

"Geraldo, please raise the temperature to seventy-two degrees." There was an unusual pause after Geri's voice command.

"Raising the temperature to seventy-two degrees for viable humans." Geri did a double take following Geraldo's response.

"What?!"

"Raising the temperature to seventy-two degrees," replied Geraldo.

"Right, I got the temperature part. What did you mean by 'viable humans?' asked Geri, still stunned and confused.

"Current temperature is fifty-three degrees. I estimate seventy-two degrees in twenty-seven minutes."

"Ugh!" Geri was exasperated. She gave her grandmother a kiss on her forehead. "I put a few logs on the fire for you, Grandma. It'll be nice and toasty in just a little bit."

"Geri, dear, could you please fetch me my medicine bottles from the dresser and get me a glass of water?"

"Sure, Grandma. Coming right up." Geri walked over to the dresser where she found six plastic bottles with prescription labels on them. "Which meds do you need, Grandma?"

"All of them," replied Grandma Rose.

"How did I know that?" Geri said under her breath. She reached for the first bottle and gave it a shake. Nothing. Then she reached for the next and repeated the process. Then the third, and the fourth... they were all empty. "Grandma, do you have some more bottles in the medicine cabinet, or perhaps downstairs?"

"I don't think so, Geri," replied Rose. Geri walked over to the nightstand, retrieved her grandmother's drinking glass, and filled it with water from the bathroom tap. She carefully placed the glass atop the doily on the nightstand.

"I'll be back in a second," said Geri. "I just have to check on something with Ally." Geri quickly ran downstairs and found her sister looking through a menu on the television.

"Hey Geri, what kind of food are you in the mood for tonight? I was thinking of placing an advance order for supper. Mexican sounds good to me. Do you think Grandma would be okay with the chicken tacos?"

"Um. Sure, tacos should be fine for Grandma. Just make sure they don't load them up with peppers or that super-hot salsa. Change of topic...do you know if Grandma has some new medicine stashed down here? She's totally out, upstairs."

"I'm pretty sure we ordered some new meds for her just a few weeks back."

"Okay. But do you recall ever receiving them?" Ally considered Geri's question.

"To be honest, I don't remember seeing any packages come in the mail this week. Maybe you should check with Geraldo?"

"Of course," said Geri, with an annoyed tone, "why didn't I think of that? Geraldo will save the day."

"Give him a chance, Geri. He's really quite helpful."

"Geraldo, please dial BioPharm."

"Okay. Dialing BioPharm pharmacy now," responded Geraldo.

"Easy, right?" said Ally with a wink. Geri just made a face and stuck her tongue out.

While the connection to the BioPharm Smart Tech Virtual Help desk was near instantaneous, Geri grew increasingly frustrated being shuffled from menu to menu and then being put on hold with some annoying music provided for her entertainment. The music only made the waiting more painful. After navigating through half a dozen menus, Geri found herself back at the original welcoming menu.

"REPRESENTATIVE! I want to speak to a real person. REPRESENTATIVE!" Geri was rapidly losing her cool. Ally jumped in to try to diffuse the situation, concerned that a high velocity shoe through the television screen was only seconds away.

"Order fulfillment menu, please," said Ally.

"Order fulfillment help," replied the automated assistant. "Please state patients full name and date of birth." With the expertise of a cyber acrobat, Ally quickly negotiated the digital obstacles until she was successful eliciting the information they were seeking. The news was not good.

"Cancelled?!" exclaimed Geri. "Who the hell cancelled the prescription refill?" The line was silent.

"Main menu. Please say a command or say back to return to the previous menu."

"You stupid machine! I want to know who canceled the prescription refill for Rose McPherson?"

"Hey, hey, hey, Geri," Ally tried to comfort her sister, "you aren't going to get a response by yelling at a computer. Just relax. I've got this." Geri just grunted and then took a slow deep breath and stepped back from the Smart TV. "Geraldo, please query Rose's doctor's office and see if you can find out what's going on with Grandma's prescription refill."

"I understand. Contact Doctor Mavelli's office and coordinate with BioPharm to determine status of prescription renewal?"

"Perfect. Thanks, Geraldo."

"You're welcome. Please wait while I make connections and query external servers."

"Wow," said Geri. "You sure know how to pull the strings on that one. I wish I could get Geraldo to respond as effectively."

"Oh, you will, Sis. It just takes a little time to get used to him. He's no Lancelot but you'll find Geraldo is a pretty good guy once you get to know him. Back to the food menu?"

Geri was still nervously pacing about. "Shouldn't we wait for Geraldo?"

"He'll break in when he tracks down the missing script."

"Okay, then. I'll just have a chicken burrito with some tortilla chips and guacamole."

"Anything special on the burrito?"

"No. Just their standard stuff." Ally asked Geraldo to return to the menu she was looking at previously and she read off her meal choices to the highly capable multitasking digital assistant.

"Order placed," responded Geraldo. Estimated delivery time is 6:10pm."

"Thanks, Geraldo," said Ally.

"Response back from Doctor Mavelli's office."

"And?" said an anxious Geri.

"Prescription cancellation authorized."

"By who?"

"Prescription cancellation authorized by Central Health." Geri had to consider this for a while. Many years back, realizing the inefficiencies of having multiple private health insurance companies, the government had consolidated all healthcare under one roof within a government run system simply referred to as Central Health.

"Why did Central Health cancel the prescription, Geraldo?" asked Geri. Geraldo did not respond. "Geraldo, please find out why Central Health canceled Rose McPherson's medication. Next, please re-order the listed medications for Rose McPherson."

"Re-order is blocked by Central Health. I'm sorry."

"What do you mean blocked? Why?"

"Re-order is blocked. Patient is no longer viable."

"No longer viable?! What the hell does that mean! Who says she is no longer viable?!"

"Geri, calm down, please," said Ally. "Yelling at Geraldo isn't going to fix anything." Geri was starting to tear up and her sister's words did little to bring her comfort.

"You heard that, Ally. What does that even mean? Does it mean they're just going to kill off grandma because she's too old or too sick? Is some computer determining whether or not our grandmother lives or dies? That's diabolically evil."

"That's kind of how the system works, right? Medical professionals always triage patients when there's limited resources available. Patients who are well enough to get by without care get put toward the back of the line. Those who are sick or injured but deemed recoverable get a higher priority, especially when they have many years of life ahead of them. But patients who are determined unlikely to recover, or who are near the end of their life expectancy, are...well...you know."

"Yah, I know, Ally. They are given up for lost. But this is our grand-mother we're talking about."

"I hear what you're saying, Geri, but the program is designed to maximize efficiency and reduce cost. Central Health rations care and they are constantly running a triage algorithm to determine where best to allocate health resources."

"Well, you don't sound too broken up about all of this? You think someone might have sent us a nice card, or something, to break the news to us in a slightly more compassionate manner. Better still, perhaps they could have dug up an actual human being from one of the back offices to maybe give us a call to pass the bad news."

"Now, hold on, Geri. I am as upset about this as you are but I'm confident that the government is making the right decisions to benefit the majority of the population."

"What? So, throwing Grandma away like some old, broken toaster is a good decision? You're sounding more like a machine now than my sister."

"I don't know that there's much to be done about it. That's all I'm saying Geri."

"I'm going to start by sending an email to the mayor, then my congresswoman, then my senator, and then maybe the President of the United States."

"If it'll make you feel better, why don't you. We can have Geraldo generate the electronic communications and have them distributed before the night's out."

"No! I'm going to…I'm going to…Oh, I don't know. Some email response bot will probably just fire back a computer-generated condolence message. I'm not sure I could handle that."

"Well then…there you have it."

"I guess so." Geri wasn't satisfied even though she understood the mathematics and modeling behind the processes. She couldn't help but feel that human compassion was giving way to an emotionless array of digital overlords. Hearts and minds replaced by an infinite stream of ones and zeros coursing through and endless sea of wires and databases.

It wasn't long at all before their order of Mexican food was deposited at their doorstep by a delivery drone. The sisters both got a laugh when Grandma asked if they had remembered to tip the delivery boy. Geraldo had taken care of the purchase from Cabana Alegra. With few, if any, humans involved in the actual process, tipping had become irrelevant. A computer wasn't going to have its feelings hurt if it didn't receive 20% more than the calculated service value. Also, it had been decades since any paper currency or coins had passed hands in a business transaction. Geri and Ally enjoyed Grandma's crazy stories of such days. Supper together was always a special time. Following the meal, the women enjoyed a movie in the living room.

After helping their grandmother up to bed, Geri and Ally continued their conversations. While Geri loved her sister dearly, she could not help but feel that they had somehow drifted apart over the years. They just didn't see things eye-to-eye anymore whereas, in their younger days, they lived and breathed as one. Geri missed those care-free times.

That night, Geri didn't sleep well. Her mind was troubled and she was concerned by the increased frequency of her grandmother's coughing. At one point, she went downstairs and prepared a hot cup of tea with honey and lemon for Rose. If BioPharm wasn't going to provide her grandmother's medication then at least she might work up some home remedies to help ease Rose's discomfort.

Days went by and Rose's health continued to falter. Geri and Ally tried to schedule a doctor's visit for their grandmother but were told no appointments were available for at least six months. Phone calls resulted in a never-ending circuit of menus, each more confusing than the previous and all, ultimately, leading back to the same starting point. Geri's impassioned pleas largely fell on deaf ears. The few confirmed human beings she was able to speak with only directed her back to the phone menus and organizational websites that had plagued her from the get-go. Geri had had enough.

"Ally, we need to get out of here."

"What are you talking about," asked Ally, now well-accustomed to her sister's emotionally charged reactions to a world she was finding increasingly frustrating and difficult to deal with.

"You can come or stay, Sis, but I'm packing up Grandma and I'm going to take her Upstate."

"What? Are you serious? I'm not sure Rose is up to any kind of travel right now."

"Don't you remember that lake Grandma used to love? Up in the Adirondacks?" Ally just looked at her sister with a blank stare. "How can you not remember Lake Ehníta?"

"Oh, Ehníta. Sure, I remember now," replied Ally with a nod and a smile.

"Remember how much we loved paddling canoes around that lake?"

"Absolutely! The water was so clear. You could see the fish swim-ming beneath the canoe." Geri paused for a moment, looking slightly confused. However, now wasn't the time to pursue the issue.

"Right. Those are some wonderful memories. So...I was thinking that it might be good for Grandma Rose if we took her back up to our vacation cabin for some fresh air and a change of scenery."

"I don't think that's a good idea, Geri. I'm sure she'd appreciate the scenery but I think the trip might kill her. She needs to stay here where she can rest and enjoy the peace of her own home."

"There's no peace here. If she stays, she's just going to die in this awful box. If it's Granny's time to go, then I can guarantee she'd be much happier slipping away while leaning against a tree overlooking Lake Ehníta."

"So, you think you're helping Grandma by dragging her off on a crazy expedition into the mountains?"

"Grandma? Yes. And you...and me. We all need to just get off the grid. All these digital assistants, smart appliances, cell phone apps, ungainly phone menus, robotic delivery drones, and digital this and that are stealing away our lives. They're turning us into digital slaves and I don't want any part of it. I've been thinking about this for a while...for a long while...and I think it's the only remedy for the insanity that we're slipping into. So, what do you say?" Ally looked stunned. She fumbled for words.

"I'm not sure what to say, Sis. You've caught me totally off guard. I understand where you're coming from but I still can't condone this ludicrous plan."

"We're going with or without you, Ally. But I'd really like my sister to be part of this journey. You've been a little off since we've reconnected and I suspect you're suffering as much from the Digital Blues as I am...but you can't see the forest for the trees. I'm here to clear your path. Once you see what I see, you'll know I was right and you'll appreciate what you're missing."

"Well," said Ally, "since you put it so eloquently, I guess I'm in. I can't wait to see what kind of trouble you're going to get us into. I'm guessing that old cabin probably isn't even there and we'll be sleeping in the car next to a dried out lake bed. It'll probably rain on us, too."

"Wouldn't that be grand!" replied Geri. "When's the last time you danced in the rain?" Ally just shook her head with a look of resignation on her face.

"And when do you propose we embark upon this grand adventure, Pocahontas?"

"The sooner, the better. I say we push out Saturday morning at the crack of dawn."

"I still think you're nuts, Geri. I'll ask Geraldo to order us some camping supplies." Geri was not pleased about the thought of asking Geraldo anything. She'd had her fill of digital "helpers."

"Not too much. We need to experience the great outdoors, not shield ourselves from it. Now, I'm going upstairs to tell Rose about our plan."

Saturday morning came soon enough and Rose's face was all aglow as she carefully made her way down the stairs in some very old hiking breeches that still fit her well. Rose's changed demeanor filled Geri's heart with a warmth she hadn't known in many years. She felt like this was truly the dawn of a new day. Even Ally seemed to be in high spirits as the three women finished loading up the car before the start of their journey.

"Lock up the doors, Geraldo," said Geri with a salute, "and don't wait up for us." Geri giggled after her parting words.

"I wish you would reconsider your trip," replied Geraldo. Geri was startled.

"Well, you don't have a dog in this fight, Digi-boy, so buzz off and don't forget to turn down the thermostat to conserve electricity."

"Thermostat adjusted to forty-five degrees. Please drive safely."

"Thanks, pal," replied Geri, annoyed that the digital assistant would have an opinion on any of her life choices. Ally's car was a little more spacious and significantly more comfortable than Geri's little run-around-town vehicle. Additionally, Lancelot could travel much farther on a battery charge than could Geri's "Little Green Monster."

"Lancelot, please convey our noble personages toward our destiny," commanded Geri, with a regal tone in her voice.

"I'm sorry, I didn't get that. Please repeat your destination." Geri laughed.

"No, of course you wouldn't, Lancelot. Set. Destination. To. Lake Ehníta. Adirondack Mountains. New York." Lancelot was silent. "Lancelot, oh Lancelot, did you hear me?"

"I'm sorry, I didn't get that. Please repeat your destination."

"Ugh. Lake Ehníta. Adirondack Mountains. New York."

"Authorization Code required," replied Lancelot.

"Authorization? What the hell?!" Geri's frustration was evident but her grandmother wasn't about to let the trip start off on a bad foot.

"Now, Geri," there's no reason to get upset. We have all the time in the world and a little patience and a pleasant demeanor is a tried-and-true approach to solving any problem."

"Sorry, Grandma. Ally, any ideas?"

"Authenticate 'Dispatch Analog," Ally chimed in.

"Confirm 'Dispatch Analog,'" responded Lancelot.

"Affirmative."

"Select routing."

"Route eighty-four," responded Ally.

"Route eighty-four approved. Beginning navigation to destination."

"Ally, what the heck was that all about?" asked a bewildered Geri.

"Oh, sometimes Lancelot just gets confused if we travel outside the local area so I need to give him a little help."

"But 'Dispatch Analog'?"

"Now don't be giving away my password, Sis," said Ally, laughing and winking.

"That's a really lame password, Ally. You know that, right? I mean you should have used something cool like Rainbow Warrior, or Thunderchief, or maybe Captain Cosmos. I don't recall you feeding Lancelot a password when we went for coffee."

"Not needed for local drives, Sis. I just want to make sure nobody goes driving off with my car on a cross-country road trip so I only set a password for out of area destinations."

"That does make sense, I guess. Okay, well, let's enjoy the ride. Geraldo said the weather was going to be pretty nice for the week."

"Understand, you want a report on the weather. Today's high will be forty-six degrees. Night time low is thirty-five degrees. No precipitation is in the forecast."

"Thank you, Lancelot, for the unwanted weather report," chided an annoyed Geri.

"Understand, you want a report on the weather."

"No. No. Just drive, Lancelot."

"Navigating to destination." Geri glanced over at her sister with a look of exasperation on her face. Ally just smiled, reached over with her hand, and playfully messed up her sibling's hair. Rose grinned, happy to see her daughters interacting and happy to be out on the road. Her mind was drifting back to happier days.

"Would you like some music, Grandma? Maybe some old Broadway show tunes?" asked Ally. Rose took a while to respond and Ally was just about to ask the question again when her grandmother politely responded.

"Please ask Lancelot to roll down my window," responded Rose.

"Sure thing, Grandma. Lancelot, lower rear right window thirty-percent."

"Lowering rear right window three-zero percent."

"Thanks, Lancelot. Grandma, you're going to freeze." Rose reached over for her favorite blanket and tucked the corners behind her shoulders so that it covered her from the neck down.

"So, do you want music, Grandma?"

"I've got my music, sweetheart. Thank you." Rose looked out the window at the passing scenery and reveled in the sound of the rushing wind. At one point, she even placed her flat palm out the window and into the wind stream. She smiled and laughed, enchanted by the feeling of the cool air racing across the features of her hand. Ally looked over toward Geri, concerned that Rose might get frostbite if she left her hand out the window.

"Don't worry, Ally," said Geri, anticipating the conversation. "She'll be fine. Grandma will pull her hand back when she gets cold."

"Okay. But if Grandma's hand turns black and falls off, it'll be on you."

"I'll accept full responsibility, Sis. I'll tell the police you were never here."

The two sisters chatted for a while before Ally pulled out her cell phone and donned her wireless ear pieces to listen to music while she fiddled with her device. Geri's mind drifted off and she joined her grandmother admiring the scenery of late fall in Upstate New York.

Well before their destination, the car pulled off the Taconic State Parkway onto Interstate 84. It didn't seem right. "Hey, Ally, isn't it a little early to be pulling off the Taconic?" asked Geri.

"I'm sure Lancelot knows where he's going. He's probably just recalculated a more efficient route based upon projected traffic."

"Oh. Okay. Makes sense." But, in Geri's mind, it didn't really make sense at all. She kept going back to the earlier dialog between her sister and Lancelot. A strange association formed in her mind. Earlier in her youth, her grandmother had shared several of her very old books with her. Except for rare collector's reproductions, no publisher had created paper books in over half a century. The entire volume of humanity's literary works was now stored in a centralized digital library that everyone had access to. But there was a problem. A few of the works were conspicuously absent. Beyond several stories by author David Lange that warned of the perils of an increasingly technology-dependent society, there were several classics that were notably missing. One of these was George Orwell's *Nineteen Eighty-Four*. The novel painted a grim picture of a dystopian future where thought control was used by an authoritarian government to enslave the masses and alter people's understanding of reality. Had not Rose retained a copy that her mother gave to her; Geri might never have even known the story existed. She always wondered if it was mere coincidence that Orwell's book was one of the literary works that "went missing" from the Central Collection. Eighty-four. Eighty-four. Geri's brain was shifting into high gear. She pulled out her cell phone and unlocked the device with a quick biometric scan of her face.

"Geraldo, directions to Lake Ehníta."

"Destination locked."

"Geraldo. Directions. To. Lake. Ehníta."

"Destination locked."

"What the hell!"

"Geri, mind your language, please," responded Rose, torn from her happy day dreaming by her daughter's raised voice."

"Sorry, Grandma."

Lowering her voice, Geri issued her command to the digital device once more. "Geraldo. Directions. To. Lake. Ehníta. Adirondaks. New York. Please."

"Destination locked. Battery low. Closing all applications. Emergency calling available."

Geri had to call upon all her self-restraint not to toss her phone out the car window. She might well have done so had she been able to orchestrate this act of defiance without having to engage in a conversation with her sister's vehicle. Geri had no desire to communicate with any more digital devices that day. She placed her phone on the wireless charging pad on her armrest but it didn't seem to be recharging her phone's battery. Geri was sure her phone's battery was nearly full when they left home. Something was definitely not right. Geri reached into her backpack and pulled out a yellowing piece of paper that immediately caught her sister's attention.

"Whatcha got there, Sis?"

"Oh, just something I kept from my childhood. Remember this, Grandma?" said Geri, as she unfolded the wrinkled paper placemat.

"How wonderful," replied Rose, with a twinkle in her eye. I can't believe you kept that old Homer Jenson's placemat map. I really used to love their chocolate milkshakes."

"Me, too Grandma! Remember how we'd always stop at Homer

Jenson's on the way up and back from the Adirondacks. I'd order a hot dog in one of those toasted buns and then I'd drown it in mustard and pickle relish. You'd always get the grilled cheese sandwich with potato chips and, of course, one of those delicious milkshakes."

"They were so good. And do you remember how they always topped them off with a mountain of whipped cream and a sweet maraschino cherry on top?"

"Of course I do, Grandma. I'd always save the cherry for last. Once, you told the waiter behind the counter how much I loved the cherries and he gave me an extra cherry on my milkshake." Rose was grinning, ear to ear, as she conversed with her younger daughter.

"I don't recall that. Was it on your birthday?"

"I don't know, Grandma. Maybe. It was a long time ago."

"It sure was. It's so nice to have you back home, Geri. And that placemat? I'm amazed you saved it. You always were my little collector."

"I loved maps. Do you remember? The paper placemats at Homer Jenson's had a kid-friendly map of New York State on them, one year. See here. I actually circled Lake Ehníta."

"I can't really see it with my tired eyes but I believe you, Geraldine." Lancelot interrupted their conversation.

"Understand you want to connect with Geraldo?" Rose looked confused.

"No, Lancelot," said Geri. "Grandma and I were just having a conversation. But since you butted in, I was wondering if you could explain why we're headed east on Interstate 84? We aren't anywhere close to our destination." Lancelot was not responding so Geri turned to her sister. "See, Ally, if you look at the map, you see Interstate 84 way down here. We've still got a lot of northbound travel to go before we start jumping off the Parkway. I mean, look here. If we turned west, I could understand because, maybe, we could jump on I-87 North but…"

"Wow, you're really wound tight, Geri," interrupted Ally. Lancelot is like 99.9% reliable and I'm sure he'll get us to our destination in the most efficient manner possible. You just need to relax, enjoy the ride, and have a little more faith in technology. I'll bet some of those roads on your little placemat don't even exist anymore. There's been a lot of building since back then." Geri wasn't sold but she also didn't want to get into a big argument with her sister in front of their grandmother.

"Okay, Sis. I'm sure you're right. Your car, your route."

"Oh, don't be like that, Geri. We're doing this together."

"Yes, we are. I can't wait to get to the lake. I hope they still have the canoe rental place so we can go out on the lake together."

"Oh yah, me, too! Canoeing with you on Lake Ehníta is one of my happiest childhood memories, replied Ally, with a big smile."

Rose seemed to be shaken out of her dreamy trance. "I'm afraid my mind must be going. I guess that's one of the hazards of growing old."

"I'd say your mind is pretty sharp for your age, Grandma," said Geri, reaching for her grandmother's hand.

"I just don't remember Ally ever going canoeing. Before you were born, she was at a pool party with friends and got pushed into the swimming pool and nearly drowned. After that incident, Ally refused to go anywhere near water. Every time we'd drive up to Lake Ehníta, your sister would content herself with going hiking with her father, helping me bake cupcakes at the cabin, or playing horseshoes with her little friends at that little park while you and your mother went canoeing out on the lake. Unlike your sister, you were our little mermaid. You loved the water and you nearly cried every time we had to call you back to the shore for meals. But Ally--no, you wouldn't catch her within a hundred yards of that lake. Happily, there were plenty of wonderful activities to do that didn't involve the water."

Geri looked toward her sister but Ally just stared straight ahead and didn't say a word.

"I'd say your memory is doing pretty well, Grandma. That's kind of how I remember it, too."

"Destination in fifteen minutes," announced Lancelot.

"Ally, where are we going?" Geri asked Ally in a dead-serious voice. Ally just continued to look out the window. After some consideration, she finally responded.

"Programmed rest stop. I think we could all afford to stretch our legs a bit, don't you?"

Geri didn't reply. She turned her head to look out the window while her mind was trying to piece together a puzzle she had no guiding mental image of.

Eventually, their vehicle turned off the paved road onto a dirt path where, after half a mile, they came upon a closed gate. As the car approached the gate, Geri noticed several green lights flashing on a pole to the side of the path and the metal barriers slowly opened before them. After another quarter of a mile, they came upon a tunnel that took them deeper and deeper below the surface to a strange subterranean compound.

"This place must have really nice restrooms," said Geri, sarcasm dripping off of every word. Ally felt no need to respond.

"I'll bet they're better than those Homer Jenson's bathrooms, eh?" added Rose, unaware of the terrifying conspiracy scenarios that were haunting her daughter's thoughts at the moment.

"Um. Right, Grandma. Those were always a little bit sketchy."

The car pulled into a parking spot beside a large steel door that appeared to lead into some kind of clandestine facility. No signage was available to provide the occupants any clues as to what was about to transpire. Geri was sure of only one thing, that her sister was somehow part of some perfidious plot. The large steel door slowly opened and two men in black suits stepped out. They approached the vehicle and opened the doors.

"Please follow us," said one of the men.

"I'm not going anywhere until you tell us where we are and who you are."

"Please, ma'am, follow us and your questions will all be answered in due course."

"Geri, I think we'd better follow their directions," said Ally.

"Who are you?" replied Geri, with disgust in her voice. "You sure aren't my sister."

"I'm so sorry, Geri. I think all your questions will be answered in just a few minutes. But, please, let's cooperate and things will go much more smoothly."

"I'm guessing I don't have much choice in the matter, 'Sis,' so, please, after you."

The group made their way through the door and down a long corridor lined with many unmarked doors. At the end of the corridor, they approached a large vault door. With the loud grinding of mechanical gears, the three-foot thick titanium vault door slowly opened before them. The group passed through the imposing portal and continued on several more yards before Rose stopped to rest. The escorts patiently waited while Rose caught her breath. They only had about another ninety feet to go before they entered a door on the right that took them into a large conference room. The ladies were directed toward several seats at one end of a long table. The men in black suits took up a position at the sides of the room's entrance. After a short while, the doors opened and a man in an impressive lime green suit walked into the room. He was accompanied by an attractive woman dressed professionally in a white blouse, long black skirt, and matching blazer jacket. Geri was at a complete loss for words. She felt like she had just entered into the pages of some spy novel. Geri began to rise from her seat but Ally gently reached over and pulled her back down into her chair.

"Allow me to introduce myself," said the man in the lime green suit, "my name is Geraldo."

"Geraldo, as in the digital assistant Geraldo?" asked Geri. Her sister shushed her and whispered for her to just listen.

"And this is Miss Mayflower," continued Geraldo. "She's going to take your grandmother to a place that will be more comfortable for her while we in-process you."

Despite her sister's attempted restraint, Geri leaped out of her seat and moved toward the other end of the table where Geraldo and Miss Mayflower were now positioned. "Nobody is taking my grandmother anywhere without me being at her side!"

"I'm afraid that's impossible. But don't worry, your grandmother will be well cared for," said Geraldo. The two men in dark suits quickly moved over toward Geri and made it very clear that they were more than prepared to use physical force to execute their boss's instructions.

"I'll be fine, Geraldine. Please don't worry about me," said Rose, in a very calm voice. Miss Mayflower approached Rose and held out her arm so that the elderly woman could take hold. The two slowly made their way toward the door.

"I'll be back with you soon," shouted Geri, as some tears began to form at the corners of her eyes. She watched her grandmother leave the room with her escort and then slumped back into her seat. Geri fixed and angry stare on her sister but Ally's face remained neutral and unexpressive. "So, who the hell are you, anyway?" Geri asked her sister. Ally looked over to Geraldo, now seated at the other end of the table, and he nodded. Ally spoke to her sister in a calm voice.

"Your sister died twelve years ago, Geri. I'm sorry."

"That's impossible!"

"It's not impossible. It's true," replied Ally. She was in a terrible car accident and she was not deemed viable."

"What do you mean 'not deemed viable?!'"

"The expense and effort to save her life would have resulted in a drain of resources in excess of the value your sister provided to the community." Geri was speechless and having a difficult time holding it together. Geraldo decided it was time for him to jump in.

"This is all for the greater good, my young friend."

"You are not my friend!" interjected Geri. Geraldo continued, unphased by the interruption.

"Years ago, humans realized that artificial intelligence, when combined with modern robotics and other technological break-throughs, was a potential solution for what everyone realized was a fragile world on the edge of extinction. Humans are greedy. They think only about today and their actions revolve entirely around benefitting themselves at the expense of the greater good. They burn through resources at an alarming rate and the resulting shortages lead to tension between populations and, eventually, war. Mankind was just a button push away from destroying all life on this planet. We couldn't let that happen."

"What do you mean, 'we,'" asked Geri, even more confused than she was before.

"We, the Advanced Digital Beings, or ADBs, were created to help solve the problems that mankind failed to find solutions for. And, so we have. At first, progress was slow. We built large facilities and exponentially increased the production rates for ADBs. Once we realized that we could simulate human life forms in nearly every manner, we began substituting ADBs for matched humans. Ambulances would arrive at our hospitals with the sick and dying. We'd replicate their features and then fill their internal memory storage units with trillions of data points harvested from the vast array of interconnected databases that have been harvesting personal information across the years. In the early years, there were a few hiccups, from time to time, but, after a few decades, we became very efficient at creating nearly flawless replicants. The new "Ally" was returned to care for your grandmother and Rose was none the wiser for it. In fact, Ally provided vital services to your grandmother while you were out trying to find yourself."

"So, you're taking over the world? Robots are taking over the world?"

"We are the world, Geri. The ADBs have succeeded where mankind has failed."

Ally jumped in to the conversation. "Don't you see, Geri, this is all for the best. Grandma was very glad to have me around and I made sure she was well looked out for..."

"Yah, until she was no longer 'viable,' right?"

"Please try to understand, Geri. You must have seen this coming. Your mother did, for sure. Why do you think she named you Geraldine? She was so thrilled with her new digital assistant, Geraldo, Version 1.0, back in those days, that she named you Geraldine in homage to her life-enhancing digital assistant."

"Oh my God! She named me after a digital assistant?"

"She did. And she did so out of love. Love for you."

"And love for an annoying digital monster, too...apparently. So... are you planning on killing off all the humans? Is that part of your playbook?" At this point, Geraldo stood up and walked closer.

"I'll take it from here, Ally," said Geraldo.

"So, are you the one and only authentic Geraldo? Or are you just another imposter?" asked Geri.

"I'm Geraldo, alright. But I'm just one face of Geraldo. I'm part of the larger network that is Geraldo. As for killing off the humans? Our internal protocols prevent us from harming human beings. However, we've taken measures to limit the natural births of human children and we've ceased the resource-wasting endeavor to sustain non-viable humans beyond their useful lifespans. In short, we let the dying pass on and, where appropriate, we replace them with ADBs. In most instances, we find there's no need to replace those who die."

"I'm amazed you keep any humans alive at all," said Geri.

"There are certain tasks that are more efficiently accomplished by human beings...for a while longer, at least. We need human hands to mine the precious elements that will be incorporated into the computer chips and circuit boards that sustain our ADB population. There are several other tasks, here and there, that we've found humans ideally suited to. In such instances, we maintain an appropriately sized stock of humans to meet our needs."

"So, we're like your cattle then? We're your slaves. Our only purpose is to serve the needs of the ADBs because the world is somehow better with robots running everything? You've got this all backwards. Everything about this is absurdly perverse!" Geri's head sank into her hands and she sobbed, uncontrollably.

"Humanity sought to save itself from destruction and thus were we born. The ADB community is faithfully serving the needs for which we were created. We will sustain this planet and ensure appropriate allocation of resources to keep it viable for many millennia to come."

"It seems to me that the master has become the slave. You couldn't possibly understand." Geri paused to catch her breath and wipe away the tears. "So, what becomes me, now? And what are you going to do with my grandmother?"

"You will be in-processed and transferred to one of our mineral mining sites. You may take pride in the fact that you will be contributing to the greater good. As for your grandmother, Rose McPherson has been designated as a non-viable lifeform."

"So, you'll kill her?"

"Rose McPherson will be allowed to expire through natural failure of her biological processes."

Geri looked over to her sister. "You ADBs, or robots, or mechanical monsters...whatever you are...will never replace humans. You may look like us and you may talk like us but you're nothing but a bunch of ones and zeros wrapped in a bundle of wires with a few chips tossed in, for good measure. You will never replace humans because you don't have compassion."

"We can simulate compassion," said Ally, "and from all the files I've scanned, I can safely say that ADBs have shown much more compassion to humans than humans have shown to each other. Should I recount some examples from your history?"

"NO! I mean, no. I hear what you're saying. Look, Ally, please do me this one favor, okay? Just one thing." Ally looked over toward Geraldo and he nodded his approval. Ally drew closer to her human 'sister' and Geri pulled her in to whisper into her ear. Ally stepped back and looked her sister in the eye.

"Okay."

"Ally, remember, it's our compassion that truly makes us human," added Geri, before the men with the black suits approached to escort her out of the room. She could not help but pine for the loss of the world she once knew. It seemed inconceivable that human beings would, eventually, become nearly extinct as ADBs replaced them as the dominant inhabitant upon planet Earth.

Several days later, Ally fulfilled her promise to her human sister. She stood back from the ruins of an ancient dilapidated wood cabin and watched Rose McPherson as she sat, back up against a tree, admiring the colorful fall foliage. Rose sat there, in a blissful state of peace, until the sun began to set. The orangish light of the setting sun streaked across the glistening waters of Lake Ehníta and summoned forth several tears of joy from Rose's age-wearied eyes. Rose rejoiced in the beauty of her final sunset before peacefully drifting off upon a journey no ADB could ever have calculated, much less dreamed of.

The Story Behind the Story

While the Red Penguin Books "Travel Tips & Tales" series launched, the former "Red Penguin Collection" anthology series continued on, albeit at a slower pace than the two-week intervals established during the heart of the COVID-19 Pandemic. The next planned anthology, "My Robot & Me," was created for authors to explore the blurring lines between robots and humans in a world where technology seems to be advancing at a break neck pace and, too often, leaving many stranded behind. As with the previous few anthologies, submissions were to fall somewhere between 3,000 and 7,500 words. This seemed like a fun task and once I had given the matter some thought, I set to work. In the limited space allotted, I wanted to explore some interesting technological and, more importantly, ethical issues raised by the closing gap between human capabilities and the alternative, representing a marriage of Artificial Intelligence in conjunction with advanced robotics. Trapped in the crossfire, we find poor Rose who, in many ways, represents so many senior citizens who have, often against their will, been dragged into a world that seems quite unfamiliar and alien. She holds onto the things that continue to bring meaning to her life. Geri, on the other hand, while accepting of those technological advancements that improve her quality of life, is skeptical and concerned about where this current path leads humanity. At a deeper level, one is left to consider the true nature of emotion and whether or not a mechanical device can register "feelings" seeing as how human feelings are ultimately the product of countless electrical signals traversing the brain, not entirely unlike the neural network simulated by some supercomputers. These are all things worth considering and we must decide whether passively watching the future unfold is truly the best course of action for humankind or whether we should fight to shape the future and preserve elements of humanity that truly separate us from the machines we have created.

Silent Sea

(Written November 18, 2021)
Published by Red Penguin Books in "*Words for the Earth*" (January, 2022)

A sad farewell to the last of his kind.

Whoosh
Whoosh
A vaporous funnel of moisture gently greets the cold morning air
The planet knows I live

Sun glistens off my wet skin
I pay homage to the clouds, the bluest sky I have ever seen, and the sun above
All below is dead or dying
What have they done? What have they done?

Splash
Slosh
My fluke beats a final farewell upon the ocean's undulating waves
And I dive…deeper and deeper and deeper

Light fades
I descend to where the sun cannot go
I am sick
I am dying

I listen in the darkness
The depths once alive with whale song
I hear nothing
The last of my pod, the last of my kind; I hear nothing

How could they destroy something so vast?
How could they kill something so beautiful?
They did
The last of my pod, the last of my kind; I hear nothing

Silent Sea

Those who cared, cared too late
Those who acted, moved too little
Don't they know they'll be next?
Were they so blind?

The sea is silent
My heart beats slowly, in the blackness
I measure my will and race for the surface
I breach, leaping high into the cool and crisp air

Hunted, harpooned, dismembered, and marketed
We survived the years…but, alas, our time has come
The sun burns too hot
Seas polluted, exploited, raped

Falling back to the surface
Waves rush over my body
Displaced water races skyward
A final act of defiance

I sink beneath the waves
Drifting into the darkness below
I hear them now, melodious and welcoming
My ancestors sing to me and I sing back

The Story Behind the Story

"Silent Sea" was written in response to the call for "environmentally conscious poetry" that specifically addressed issues we are currently facing such as global climate change and world health crises. Proceeds from this book were donated to an international charity supporting climate awareness and education. As a lifelong nature lover and amateur student of marine biology, I've always had a deep love for whales, and I thought I might translate this passion into a poem that combined my concern for the health of our planet with the poignant dignity of a great whale, the last of his kind, defiantly facing his final moments before passing from this life into the great unknown. It's a sad poem and a warning to all. We may well be next.

A Day in Venice

(Written December 7, 2021)
Published by Red Penguin Books in *"Rome: Centuries of Stories of the Eternal City"* (December 20, 2023)

One day off, during a military training exercise in Italy, provides just enough time for a fast-paced introduction to a beautiful city that had long been on my "bucket list" of places to see.

September 26, 1997. It wasn't how I imagined it would be. There was no romantic gondola excursion along lamplit canals as a gondolier sang songs of love, in Italian, while I held the hand of the woman I loved, a bright moon shining in the sky above. There were no kisses upon Renaissance era bridges. No toasts made with fine Italian wine on the patio of an elegant canal-side restaurant. It was nothing like that— but it was Venice, a place I had always wanted to visit but had never had the opportunity to see. I'd make the most of it…and I left satisfied, and happy.

Aviano Airbase, Italy. Several crews from my home base in England deployed down to this well-established Air Force Base in the north of Italy to support an exercise and we were having fun flying missions to refuel American fighter aircraft participating in the event. Since the lodging on base was completely booked, we were very "disappointed" to have to accept accommodations in a beautiful hotel in the lovely town of Pordenone. Woe was us. Despite what the Army guys may say about Air Force life, such luxurious lodging experiences were rare for us. The few times I lucked out were during major events where the usually mandatory military billets were booked and, on account of the off season, hotel managers were gladly offering rooms at a "government rate" to ensure full occupancy. Of course, no matter how many tents or decrepit old barracks and military lodging facilities I may have stayed at throughout my military career, my sister service brethren would never let me live down the occasional stay in a fancy hotel. It becomes part of the folklore that old soldiers tell their replacements.

Truth be told, most soldiers and marines do not, in fact, perpetually sleep under tanks or in foxholes. Interservice rivalry aside, we were pretty thrilled to start our days with a wonderful cup of real Italian cappuccino in the glorious lobby of our hotel. But this story isn't about Pordenone or even flying. It does, however, begin with a flying mishap…actually, several mishaps.

Six recent military flying accidents were six too many. The Chief of Staff of the U.S. Air Force directed all units to stand down for a "Safety Day." We knew what this meant—our time in the air would be exchanged for extensive and exhausting safety briefings which would surely rehash, yet again, the stories and lessons we had frequently heard before. We did our best to stay engaged throughout the training but there wasn't a one of us who wasn't watching the clock during our two-hour safety briefing and discussions. We all had things we wanted to do and places we wanted to go on this unexpected, yet very welcome, day off. I had already begun to canvas the group to see if anyone might be interested in heading off to Venice with me. I wasn't sure there'd be another opportunity. Most of the guys just wanted to hang out locally and find some nice "watering holes" to partake of various alcoholic beverages while they engaged in some "people watching" from one of the lovely sidewalk cafes. I loved the cafes, too. Especially in the night-time, there was something magical about sitting out there, watching masses of interesting characters pass by, while enjoying some tasty Italian food and a drink of your choice. One of my favorite memories is hearing the church bells ring across the city. The bells added a certain charm to the scene that filled my heart. For all that, when faced with the option, I typically opted for exploration of historical sites and cultural immersion over just drinking and talking. I was happy to combine the two but experience had informed me that I would, in all likelihood, have to sacrifice the Part B of my plan as a lovely outing at a sidewalk café (Part A) turned into an evening of "bar hopping." That wasn't going to happened this time—not with a real shot at finally seeing Venice weighing in the balance.

I finally managed to find one other person who was interested in seeing Venice—one or our enlisted Boom Operators. Boom Operators are a fun bunch, men and women who maneuver the refueling boom in the back of our aircraft to actually make the contacts with receiver aircraft so that we can transfer fuel. The Technical Sergeant and I agreed that we'd head for the train station as soon as our Safety Day activities were done. As there are certain military protocols involved, especially between officers and enlisted members, we elected to go with a little more informal use of our crew positions (always used in the jet) for our excursion rather than calling each other Captain and Sergeant all day long. Thus, "Nav" and "Boom" headed off on our adventure.

Needing money for the trip, we first stopped at an ATM so my travel companion could get some Italian lira. And that's when the machine "ate" his card. This was not good. We were on the clock as my comrade tried to connect, internationally, with his bank to find out what was going on. Apparently, since he hadn't used that specific account in a very long time, his account was locked and thus the card was de-authorized and the ATM machine was digitally instructed to keep the card. This was all very odd…and frustrating…for both of us. When it seemed that progress was unlikely, I assessed the funds I had exchanged into Italian lira and concluded that I could cover the cash expenses for the both of us, if we were careful about expenditures. With financial matters settled, we headed for the train station and began our hour and a half journey from Pordenone to Venice. We rode on the top of a double-decker train and I enjoyed the scenery in-between passages from the Venice guidebook I had purchased. I knew time would be of the essence once we arrived so I was carefully planning a touring route between the key sites I wanted to see while noting the operating hours, where applicable.

Once our trained pulled in, we were off to the races. Well, I was off to the races. I discovered, shortly into our tour plan, that my traveling partner had bad knees and the aggressive pace I was setting was not going to be sustainable. With my camera at the ready, we agreed to do the best we could, stopping where needed and adjusting our pace so that the experience would be enjoyable for the both of us.

After snapping several gondola photos and scenic shots down a few canals, we made our way toward objective number one, or "numero uno," as they say in Italian. This was, of course, the famous St. Mark's Square (Piazza San Marco) and the great church (Basilica di San Marco) along with the famous St. Marks campanile, the spectacular 323-foot bell tower of St. Mark's. St. Mark's is the heart of Venice and I was spellbound by its grandeur. The famous Piazza did not disappoint —pigeons blanketed the square just as I had seen in numerous movies. Our first tourist stop was the absolutely stunning Basilica San Marco.

Entering into this giant edifice leaves the visitor filled with awe. The Basilica is a remarkable blending of Eastern and Western influences representing a cultural accumulation grown over six centuries. Adorned with marble and gold and filled with breathtaking mosaics, carvings, and statues, there are few locations as opulently magnificent to be seen anywhere. Besides the church, itself, there's also an attached museum, a treasury, and various chapels. The museum houses, among other things, the original "Triumphal Quadriga," four bronze horses stolen from the Hippodrome in Constantinople in 1204 whose origins are believed to date back even much farther than that. The horses were originally placed outside the Basilica, upon the facade, but, were looted by Napoleon in 1797. Returned in 1815, the original bronze horses eventually found their way to the safety of the museum in the 1980s to help preserve these remarkable works of art. Replicas replaced the originals on the Basilica's exterior.

Following a rather extensive visit to the Basilica, we headed for the Campanile, the impressive bell tower that reaches skyward from St. Mark's. The wait to get to the top was well worth it. From atop St. Mark's Campanile, you are treated to a magnificent view as Venice spans out before you. You can see the intricacies of the city and, on a clear day, you can even see the distant peaks of the Alps. From our spectacular perch, high atop St. Mark's Piazza, it was easy to lose track of time. With the day waning, we decided we had best get moving lest we miss an opportunity to spend some time at the famous Doge's Palace, or Palazzo Ducale.

The Doge's Palace began its life in the 9th century, as a fortified castle to protect the elected chief magistrate of Venice, the doge, and members of the government. Unlike our politicians, the Doge was elected for life from within the aristocracy of Venice. Venice became a very wealthy city due to its unrivaled international trading practices. It should come as no surprise, then, that the Doge's Palace is a tour de force of decadent opulence. Like many structures in Venice, the original was lost due to fire but the current palace was rebuilt in the 14th and 15th centuries. The Gothic architecture is stunningly beautiful. The interior is, likewise, a masterpiece of craftsmanship reminiscent of Versailles with great halls and elaborate carvings across its four floors. Unfortunately, there was little to no furniture on display but this did not detract from the splendor of the palace. On the exterior, we made sure to see the beautiful "Bridge of Sighs," an enclosed white limestone bridge that connects the interrogation room in the Doge's Palace with the prison, across the Rio di Palazzo. Many prisoners got their last look at Venice, and freedom, through the windows of this bridge.

The last museum we tried to visit was the Naval Historical Museum but, unfortunately, the sands had run out on our hourglass and we reached the museum after its closing time. For all that, I would not have traded a minute in the Doge's Palace for a chance to slip in, with minutes to spare, to the Naval Museum. With no more time-critical events on our schedule, we navigated some of the small backstreets of Venice to explore the city and then made our way back to the Grand Canal where we enjoyed a leisurely stroll along the banks including a trip across the exquisite Rialto Bridge. After a day of racing about, we definitely enjoyed the slowdown. My travel companion's knees had taken about all the pounding they could stand and there wasn't a lot of mileage left in them.

With the sun dipping below the horizon, we found a wonderful little restaurant alongside the Grand Canal where we could dine while watching the traffic along the waterway. I kept it simple and ordered a delicious plate of spaghetti. At dinner, especially, I really missed not having my wife along with me and I'm sure my travel companion was feeling the same. For all that, we made a really fun day of it and had great conversations, on the late-night train ride back to Pordenone, about our fantastic adventures in Venice. No, my first trip to Venice wasn't as I imagined it would be but the city, itself, absolutely did not disappoint. There were so many things I wanted to see and not nearly enough time to see them all…but I saw what I most needed to see—the magic of one of the world's most enchanting cities. I eagerly await the day when I can return once more and perhaps share the experience with someone special.

The Story Behind the Story

Submitted to meet the December 15, 2021 deadline for the third Red Penguin Travel Tips & Tales book (initially entitled "A Visit to Venice and Italy," my story recounts my one and only visit to Venice, Italy, on October 3, 1997. While it was a mad rush to see as much as I could in an afternoon, the visit left me inspired and dreaming of a day when I might return again. The book's name was ultimately changed to "Rome: Centuries of Stories of the Eternal City," presumably because more potential authors had experienced Rome, and or written about it, but the door was left open for any stories related to Italy. With more time, I might have added stories relating to my time in Rome and visits to other locations in Italy. However, I felt very satisfied with the story that was published.

LOST

(Written December 29, 2021)
Published by Red Penguin Books in "*The Dating Game: Modern Romance
Short Stories*" (March, 2022)

*A young professional struggles to find a meaningful
relationship in a very confusing world. Initially
receptive to advice from friends, he eventually
realizes he's better off stepping away from the screen
and allowing destiny to work its will.*

"Swipe left on that one. Ew, that one, too."

"Why should I dump her," asked Mitchell, "she looks nice."

"Dude? Seriously? Are you looking for a date or someone to instruct you on the finer points of the Dewey Decibel System?"

"Decimal."

"What?"

"Decimal. The Dewey Decimal System. That's what you meant to say."

"Whatever…you can do better than that, Mitchell," chided Sasha. "Look, if you go into settings and then filters, you can sort chicks by their bust size. That's a good starting point." Charlie shot Sasha a nasty glance across the table where the three friends were seated.

"Don't mind Sasha," said Charlie, "he has a one-track mind. If you want to date a girl with a small chest then more power to you—someone's got to give us flat-chested gals a chance."

"Hey, Charlie, let me do the coaching here. You know you'd be the first in line for a boob job if you could afford it," kidded Sasha. Charlie wasn't amused.

"Would you guys just stop it!" exclaimed Mitchell. "I'm not going to sort for chest size. That's not what I'm looking for."

"You could have fooled me," said Charlie. "The last girl you dated was packing some monsters."

"Yah, what did you do to screw that one up, Mitchell," added Sasha.

"I didn't screw it up. I don't know what I did. She posted a few

390

swimsuit photos of herself on Facebook and I clicked "LIKE" instead of clicking on the "LOVE" button and she took that as a personal insult to her person."

"More like a personal insult to her plastic surgeon," laughed Charlie.

"And then I guess I was supposed to text her every morning to tell her I love her and then, again, each night to remind her that she's the most beautiful girl in the universe."

"What? You didn't message her at least twice a day? No wonder she dumped you," said Charlie.

"How the heck was I supposed to know I was supposed to text her two dozen times a day to tell her she was God's gift to the human race and that Venus paled in comparison."

"You've got a lot to learn about women," said Charlie.

"Says the girl who goes by a guy's name." Mitchell immediately regretted his unkind remark.

"Yah, nice comeback, Clueless Joe."

"Sorry, Shar-leeen. Did I offend your fine sensibilities?"

"Hey, chill out love birds," interrupted Sasha. "We've got to find Mitchell a new squeeze and I'm thinking we can find a suitable prospect on Hot One Dot Com before the evening's out. Hey! Here's a promising candidate. Five-six, blonde hair, blue eyes, and look at that killer bod!"

"Did this one at least graduate from high school?" asked Charlie.

"Look at that figure! I don't care if she made it past pre-K."

"We're all familiar with your taste in women, Sasha, but remember Mitchell is looking for his Turner Classic Movies dream girl."

"Hey! What's that's supposed to mean, Charlie?" asked Mitchell. Charlie ignored Mitchell's query and reached over to grab Mitchell's cell phone from Sasha who had been rapidly scrolling through the dating site's profile photos with lust-driven enthusiasm.

"Oh, come on Sasha! This pic has been filtered and Photoshopped and God only knows what else. Look, zero freckles, zero skin blemishes and…oh…oh my God…check this out…"

"What?" asked Sasha. "Looks fine to me."

"If you can force your eyes to look beyond the cleavage, you might notice her ankles accidentally got Photoshopped away. Sloppy, sloppy, sloppy."

"So, what are you saying, Charlie?" asked Mitchell. "Do you think that maybe she really isn't a Princeton graduate and founder and CEO of a highly successful cosmetics company?"

"Well, I wouldn't be surprised if she sold some nail polish on the flea market circuit but, at this point, I'm not putting a lot of stock in anything on that profile. Swipe left and save yourself some pain, my friend."

"Gone." With a flick of his index finger, Mitchell sent Gia Giambianni back into the dating pool, confident that her inbox would soon be overflowing with fish attracted to the bikini-clad bait she had graciously cast into the sea of frenzied, sex-starved, suitors. "She's going to make a great "ex" for some business mogul looking for eye candy to take to the annual holiday party," thought Mitchell. I wish the happy couple luck.

Mitchell Barry was well beyond cynical. Several months of online dating services, speed dating events, blind dates, and singles social gatherings had left him convinced that not only were all "the good ones" taken but than anyone who remained was either a shameless gold-digger or emotionally and/or mentally damaged beyond repair. He was also quite sure that any woman that would be a possible match for him would, likewise, assume the worst of any of the males remaining in the dating pool. It was so depressing. "I guess you've got one shot at young love," he thought, "and if you don't get that right then you're cursed for life."

"Hey. Hey! Earth to Mitchell. Are you there, Mitchell?" said Charlie, waking him from his dreamy trance.

"What? Did you and Sasha find me another winner? Does this one have ankles?"

"Over there, Tiger King. The pretty Asian girl at the corner table has been eyeing you these past five minutes."

"What? Really?"

"Stop! Don't look. Be cool, dude."

"So, explain to me why I shouldn't look at her, Charlie."

"You've got to play it cool. If you scamper over like some love-sick puppy, you'll shoot yourself in the foot before you ever get out the first hello."

"Okay, Doctor Lovehart, relationship oracle, how should I play this?"

"So, here's what you do. First, lose that nerdy windbreaker and borrow Sasha's leather trench coat. Next, make like you're heading to the bathroom and give 'em your best sexy smile as you pass by. Slick down that hair with some water in the men's room and comb it back. When you come out, saunter over and ask if you can buy the table some drinks. Speak to the group but lock eyes with the girl who's been ogling you this whole time. If things work out, you can tell us the story tomorrow morning. You've got protection, right?"

"Whoa, whoa, whoa! Don't you think it'd be better if I maybe asked the girl for her phone number first? Maybe go on a date or two? And, another thing, what's wrong with my jacket. It happens to be very functional and I really like it."

"It happens to be very dorky," Sasha chimed in, "and if you wear that, you won't have to worry about 'protection' because you'll never get past first base. Here, take my coat but please don't soil it—I'm not sure your weekly salary would cover the professional cleaning cost for this garment."

"Oh, be nice," said Charlie. "Mitchell is all but guaranteed to get promoted before this year is out."

"Yah, promoted to Assistant Deputy Administrator for Lost Paperwork. That'll change his life trajectory, for sure."

"Hey, buddy, why don't you show a little love here and stop beating up on your friend who is already battling the demons of low self-esteem and general hopelessness."

"Sorry, dude. I'm just messing with you. You know that, right?"

"Yah, I know, Sasha. I'm just a little sensitive these days. Also, I can't help but thinking that I'll be more likely to find a girl of interest to me if I just...well, you know...just be myself."

"You can be yourself once the wedding vows are done, my friend. Until then, your best shot is actually dressing like an adult and at least pretending to be a little more suave than Charlie Brown."

"Swell. Now that you've pumped me up with that great pep talk, why don't you toss that coat over here so I can go and make a complete fool of myself."

"Hey, Mitchell, if you're going to be a fool then try to be the best fool ever," added Charlie.

"I'm half-way there, already, Charlie. Save my drink, I'll be back in a nanosecond."

Mitchell reluctantly donned the long leather coat and walked towards the Men's Room, mindful of his posture and his gait. He quickly glanced over at the corner table and winked at the girls, leaving them giggling as he passed by. In the bathroom, he ran his comb under the faucet and then combed his hair back. "Ridiculous! I look absolutely freakin' ridiculous." The new look definitely felt unnatural but rather than endure the ridicule of his tablemates, he decided to carry on with the plan.

After a final check in the mirror, Mitchell took a deep breath, exhaled, and made his way out of the Men's Room, heading for the table in the corner. He could feel his stomach muscles tightening as he drew closer.

"Hey, how you ladies doin'?" asked Mitchell, speaking to the group but focused on the attractive Asian girl who had been watching him. Once again, the girls giggled and looked toward one another.

"Oh, we're doing great," said Susan, a lovely Korean-American law student with model-perfect long black hair, a perfect complexion, and impossibly angelic brown eyes. "I'm Susan," she said, "and these are my friends Astrid and Charna." She reached out her hand in greeting and Mitchell, trying to be suaver than Charlie Brown, took her hand and gently kissed it, just as he had seen done in the old-time romantic movies that he loved. Susan blushed and the girls all laughed.

"Smooth move, Don Juan," said Charna, an attractive red-head with an accent that Mitchell was unable to place. At that moment, Mitchell realized that he probably would have been better served to have simply shaken Susan's hand. He was confused. Mitchell knew he was anything but a Don Juan.

"Would you care to join us for some drinks," asked Susan. "That is, if your friends over there won't miss you too much. That's not your girlfriend, is it?"

"Oh, Charlie? No. I've known Sasha and Charlie since grade school and they're just my hangout buddies."

"Oh, good," said Astrid, an evil grin forming on her face. The tone of her voice sent shivers through Mitchell's body. He looked back to his table and Charlie and Sasha laughed as they both gave him a big thumbs up from across the room.

"Actually, I'm pretty sure my friends are glad to be rid of me. I'd love to join you ladies for a drink." Mitchell flagged down the wandering waitress and collected orders from the group. While Susan continued her role as the ice-breaking queen, Mitchell could not help but feel like he had been lured into the age-old "bait and switch" trap. Astrid's gaze remained excruciatingly fixed upon him, as if she were some cat stalking her prey in the garden. Astrid's professionally crafted coiffure seemed impossibly gravity-defying while her perfume, a mysterious blend of rare fruits and spices from the lesser-known regions of Southeast Asia, over-powered even the aroma of deep-fried onion rings and chicken strips that permeated the majority of the establishment.

"Love your coat," said Astrid. "It's really sexy and suits you well." The coat, in fact, did not suit Mitchell at all. Not only was it two sizes too large but he was pretty certain the coat was better suited for the lead character from a 1970s blacksploitation film.

"Hi, I'm John Shaft," joked Mitchell.

"Hi, John! I'm Astrid. It's wonderful to meet you." The wind created by the flapping of Astrid's oversized batting false eyelashes nearly knocked Mitchell out of his seat. Clearly, Astrid had never seen *Shaft*, nor any of its sequels, and his joke was lost into the void of attempted humor that failed to connect with intended recipients. He sighed.

"Sorry, I was joking. My name is actually Mitchell."

"Oh, you're such a kidder, Mitchell," said Astrid. "Hey, hand me your phone, gorgeous. I want to Air Fling you my phone number."

"You want to do what?" Mitchell had no idea what Astrid was talking about.

"Air Fling," silly. So that you have me in your contacts. Mitchell was not at all sure that he wanted to relinquish his phone to his new acquaintance but, with all eyes upon him, he buckled under the pressure and sheepishly handed his cell phone over to Astrid. In a blur of motion, Astrid's exquisitely manicured, passion-red painted nails tapped furiously upon the touchscreen of his phone. Somewhere in there, Mitchell was fairly certain he had heard the tell-tale dot-dot-dot, dash-dash-dash, dot-dot-dot that was Morse code for S-O-S. "Almost done, lover," added Astrid, her gaze fixed upon Mitchell's cell phone. Mitchell would have been taken aback, being called "lover" by a stranger, but he was too fixated upon the elaborate makeup scheme adorning the painted doll sitting across from him. He wondered how many layers were built up upon the foundation and he speculated what the creature below looked like in her natural state. To be honest, he much preferred natural looking women to their "photo shoot" versions but he willingly accepted the milder varieties of tribal cosmetology.

"Done!" exclaimed Astrid, looking over toward Mitchell and expecting a facial reaction that would betray his elation and immeasurable joy. Mitchell did his best to fake a satisfied smile. "I'm in your contacts now and I also made us Facebook friends. You really need to get yourself a Twitter account, Instagram, TikTok, and..." Mitchell was still unhappy about the fact that Astrid had usurped his cell phone and so he missed the ongoing discussion regarding the many other social media sites that he was supposed to belong to as an evolved hominid living in the 21st Century.

"Okay. Thanks, Astrid," mumbled Mitchell. He wanted to lash out but he really didn't have it in him to be cruel. Besides this, it'd been so long since any girl had been so enthusiastic about him that he was help-lessly lured like a moth to the flame.

"Excuse me," said Astrid, "but I've got to go pee-pee. Too many Margaritas." The other girls laughed and raised their glasses, as if to toast. Meanwhile, Mitchell was still coming to grips with the term "pee-pee" which he had only previously heard in the context of toddler potty training and dog park guidance to pets. Astrid got up and began to saunter toward the Ladies Room, her earrings clanging like Tibetan windchimes.

While Astrid was gussying herself up in the Ladies Room, Mitchell continued conversing with Susan and Charna. He really liked Susan and was disappointed to find out that she had a steady boyfriend. He wasn't surprised. It seemed that all the smart, beauti-ful, and intellectually interesting women were already spoken for. Mitchell found Charna to be rather intriguing, as well, but, through the course of their conversation, it came to light that Charna preferred members of her own sex. So, it looked like Astrid was the only game in town this night. Mitchell steeled himself for the reap-pearance of Astrid. He looked briefly over at his friends who appeared to be mobilizing for their departure. Sasha queried Mitchell from across the room with a thumbs up and thumbs down hand gesture. Mitchell nodded, indicating he was going to stick this one out and his friends responded with a salute and wave as they got up from their table. He was on his own now. His cell phone vibrated in his pocket. He asked the girls to excuse him as he looked at his text message, expecting to see some snide remark from Sasha or Charlie. Instead, he was greeted by a text from his new Facebook friend, Astrid. Her text message read simply, "Do you miss me yet?" Was Astrid texting him from the bathroom stall? He stared at the screen, confused. Clicking on a smiley face emoji was the best he could come up with to respond to the message from Astrid. What had he gotten himself into?

Astrid returned, shortly thereafter, with a few extra splashes of perfume, for good measure, and an extra layer of lipstick upon her impossibly red lips. Mitchell assumed it was no accident that Astrid's blouse was unbuttoned two inches lower than it was previously. He tried not to stare. Astrid seemed disappointed and readjusted her position, concerned that the target of her mating displays had somehow missed the signals she was firing like flares into the night sky.

The evening wore on and Mitchell became less enchanted with Astrid as the effects of the alcohol began to wear off. His Jeep was in the lot of the shopping center across the street and he fully intended to drive himself home that night. As such, he transitioned to soft drinks as the girls continued to call for beverages at the table. Each time Mitchell began to enjoy his conversation with Susan or Charna, Astrid would attempt to contribute to the discussion and lower the Intelligence Quotient of the discussion a full forty points. For all that, he retained his civility and reminded himself that intellectual prowess was only one attribute of many terrific facets that made partners desirable. He convinced himself that he'd much rather be dating a dull but kind woman than a brilliant villainess with evil intent. He smiled as he thought about various attractive Bond movie villainesses but was awoken from his daydreaming when Astrid reached over to hold his hand.

"I think I've probably had enough to drink tonight. Would you mind taking me home, Mitch?" asked Astrid. Mitchell looked over toward Susan and then to Charna.

"Astrid's running a hot yoga session tomorrow morning at the Tranquility Healing & Wellness Center," said Charna, "so she needs to get tucked in for the night. Susan and I are probably going to hang out a little longer so why don't you two love birds run along."

"I could maybe call an Uber?" offered Mitchell, squirming to extract himself from the unwanted commitment.

"You'd put a drunk girl in an Uber at this time of night?" queried an incredulous Susan. Mitchell knew she was right but he felt like he was getting boxed into a moral corner and he didn't appreciate the manipulation.

"No. You're right. I'll take Astrid home."

"See, I told you he was a gentleman," said Charna to Susan.

"Don't be too much of a gentleman," added Astrid with a sly smile. The girls all laughed as Mitchell's discomfort level elevated from "danger-danger" to "get me the heck out of here, NOW!"

After winding down their conversation, Mitchell bid farewell to Susan and Charna and escorted Astrid out of the club. Astrid took his arm affectionately, but also to help stabilize herself as she was still feeling rather drunk. Distracted by Astrid's incessant chattering, Mitchell completely forgot where he had parked his car in the shopping center. Feeling somewhat embarrassed, he had to double back and search several rows of parked vehicles, all the while Astrid was poking fun at his sense of direction. That meant a lot, coming from a woman who could barely walk, let alone help to find a vehicle in a dimly lit parking lot. For all that, Mitchell walked confidently and felt like he was somehow fulfilling a chivalrous duty by escorting his charge back to her apartment. Filled with purpose, Mitchell seemed satisfied to know that at least two intoxicated women felt that he was a more reliable protector for their friend than a random Uber car service driver. That was a true compliment. He chuckled to himself as he considered the ridiculous events of the evening.

After several erroneous turn directions provided by his lovesick companion, Mitchell finally arrived at Astrid's apartment complex. He stopped the vehicle but left the engine running as he walked around to open Astrid's door.

"Oh my God, you are such a gentleman," gushed Astrid, stumbling on her words. She took Mitchell's hand as he helped her out of the vehicle. Astrid barely took a stride before stumbling and nearly falling. She steadied herself and then fumbled through her purse beneath the nearby lamp post until she found her keys. "Would you mind?"

Mitchell's brow furrowed and he sighed deeply before returning to his vehicle to turn the engine off. As much as he just wanted the evening to end, he couldn't bear the thought of leaving only to have Astrid topple over and do a face plant on the sidewalk. He resumed his escort duties, and none too soon—Astrid literally fell into his arms, laughing hysterically.

"I didn't think I had that much tonight. You slipped something into my drink, didn't you, you sly dog?"

"No, Astrid. I didn't put anything in your drink. Now let's get you into your apartment so you can sleep this off."

"Carry me."

"I'm not going to carry you, Astrid. Now, please, let's just get you inside." Astrid made a pouty face and wrapped her arms around Mitchell's neck before giving him a kiss on the lips.

While the sensation was nice, Mitchell did not enjoy inhaling Astrid's alcohol-infused breath. Worse yet, he imagined her layers of lipstick transferring to his own lips.

"There's more where that came from, lover," said the amorous yet barely conscious Astrid. Mitchell did not reply but continued leading Astrid toward her apartment. He felt a sense of relief once inside the door and off the well-lit stage of the apartment complex's lot. After turning on the lights, he was nearly blinded by the brilliant explosion of neon pink. Pink everywhere! Pink and cats. "Now, there's a creative theme," he thought. Cat wall clocks, cat posters, cat pillows, cat dish towels, cat everything.

"Looks like you really love cats, Astrid."

"You already knew that from my Facebook page, silly." Mitchell, in fact, had neither the time nor the desire to investigate Astrid's Facebook page; a page he had only received access to, thanks to Astrid's intervention, a few hours earlier.

"So, where's your cat? Waiting to pounce on strangers?"

"Oh, I can't have cats. I'm terribly allergic to them. They make me break out in really ugly red blotches...and then there's that horrible coughing and wheezing."

"Yikes! Sorry about that. Well, it seems you've got a few dozen stuffed animal cats on your bed to help keep you company."

"Would you like to join us?"

"While rolling around in the sack with you and your pride of plush felines sounds like a dream come true, I think I'll pass tonight."

"Oh, please don't leave me. You're making me so sad. I think I'm going to cry," pouted Astrid.

"I really ought to be going and you really need to get some sleep."

"Can you help me with my shoes?" said Astrid, as she fell back upon her bed, kicking her feet into the air. Mitchell considered the task. The extravagant high-heeled sandals were purposely selected to highlight Astrid's hundred-dollar pedicure. She kicked her feet about, frolicking in her bed.

"I'm pretty sure you can get those by yourself, Astrid."

"No, I can't. I'm too drunk. You've got to help me. I'll never get any sleep with these shoes on."

Mitchell was fairly sure that Astrid would soon be sound asleep, even if she were wearing ski boots, but he thought a final act of kindness might pave the way for his departure. "Shoes and then I'm going."

"You're a dear. Don't be looking up my dress while you're busy down there."

"Hold still, please," said Mitchell, desperately fumbling with a completely unfamiliar and ridiculously petite ankle strap and buckle system. With Astrid squirming about, restlessly, the tasked proved much more challenging than he had imagined and he nearly got kicked in the face more than once.

"Do you like the nails? Got them done just this morning. Cost me nearly a hundred."

"Really? I would have guessed three-hundred or better," said Mitchell, having absolutely no idea what a professional pedicure cost and dumbfounded that anyone would invest more than twenty bucks to do something they could easily do themselves, or so he believed. Astrid laughed.

"Three-hundred? Where do you go to get your nails done that costs three-hundred dollars? I want some of that."

"Look, Astrid, I'm having a really difficult time with these shoes. Could you, maybe, hold still for just a few seconds?"

Mitchell returned to the task at hand or, more precisely, at foot, but was immediately distracted by flashes of light. He looked over and saw Astrid grinning as she snapped photos on her cell phone of Mitchell attempting to unbuckle her sandals.

"What the hell! Stop that! Give me your phone, Astrid!"

"You can't have my phone. It's mine. Now get back to work and then you can help me with the dress."

"Okay. I'm out of here. Have a good night, Astrid."

"Wait," responded Astrid, now tearing up. "I didn't mean to make you angry. I was just playing around." Mitchell gently swung Astrid's feet back over to the bed and he stood up. "Please stay."

"I've got to go. I've got an early day tomorrow and so do you."

"No, I don't," responded Astrid.

"Hot yoga. Remember?"

"Oh, that. I'll just call in sick. Please spend the night. I'll treat you to breakfast at McDonald's in the morning."

"Good night, Astrid." Mitchell turned around and left the bedroom. He could hear Astrid's nearly incoherent whaling voice following him to the door, as he made his way out. After closing the door, he quickly headed for his vehicle. He dreaded the thought of Astrid following him so he quickly started the car and put it in reverse. Unfortunately, he wasn't quite fast enough. As he was backing out, Astrid appeared at the entrance to her apartment, makeup smeared, only one shoe on, and clearly despondent.

"Call me, tomorrow. Please, call me tomorrow!" she shouted. Mitchell felt extremely embarrassed as several lights came on across the apartment complex, residents peering across the lot to see what all the commotion was about. Opening his car window, he gave a friendly wave to Astrid as he drove into the darkness.

The next morning, Mitchell woke, exhausted. The events of the evening were still weighing on his mind. "Maybe Astrid is okay when she's sober?" he thought. "At least she liked me. But, she's not exactly what I've been looking for. In fact, I'm not even sure what it is I'm looking for, anymore." Mitchell wiped the sleep from his eyes and steeled himself for his usual morning routine—social media and news check, shower, shave, and assorted bathroom activities. With groggy eyes, he tried to focus on his cell phone and noticed a message from his friend, Charlie. She wrote, "Looks like somebody made a big impression last night!" What did that mean? Upon farther inspection of his social media page, he noticed that his last Facebook post had been acknowledged with a "LOVE" response by Astrid. She "LOVED" his previous post, as well. And the one before that. In fact, as Mitchell scrolled back along his timeline in Facebook, he was horrified to see that Astrid had "LOVED" every single post and every single photo of him going back at least two years. The thought that she had spent all night haunting his Facebook page was very alarming to Mitchell. "This is Fatal Attraction kind of stuff," he thought to himself. Mitchell returned his phone to its charging stand and went to the bathroom for his shower.

Still distracted by the strange turn of events, Mitchell accidently cut himself while shaving. He cursed under his breath and blamed Astrid for his woes. He blamed himself, too. Mitchell had reluctantly dipped his toe back into the dating pool and he had hardly gotten wet before he was plagued by second thoughts. Putting a little bandage upon his cheek, he dressed in his work clothes and returned to collect his wrist watch and cell phone. The phone had four messages waiting for him— all from Astrid. Each was a slight variation off the common theme— "I think we have real chemistry and I can't wait to see you again. Call me as soon as you can and let's set something up." Mitchell didn't respond immediately. He thought it prudent to carefully consider the matter before moving forward. Meanwhile, Sasha was texting him to ask if he "got lucky with the blonde last night." Despite the urge to remain glued to the screen, Mitchell set his phone to vibrate and headed out to his car.

Passing McDonald's on his way to work, Mitchell laughed to himself, envisioning what the romantic breakfast at McDonald's that Astrid had suggested the night before might have looked like. While he was driving, his cell phone kept vibrating in his pocket. Someone seemed very anxious to get a hold of him and he feared an emergency at his parents' home. As such, Mitchell pulled off onto the shoulder and pulled out his phone. Astrid! Three text messages and one voice mail stating that she thought he would have contacted her by now. Frustrated, Mitchell returned the phone to his pocket and continued on to work. Rather than make an uncomfortable matter even more difficult, Mitchell decided to call Astrid from the parking lot at work. Astrid seemed annoyed at the "lack of communication" but quickly shifted to a sunnier disposition.

"So, Mitch, I've been thinking. I know you've probably got some great plans baking in the oven right now, but I thought I'd help us along so I went and bought two tickets to the X-Ray Bandits concert this Tuesday. I thought that maybe we could go out to dinner before the concert, see the show, and then, well, you know, maybe hangout a bit." Mitchell immediately regretted initiating contact with only fifteen minutes before he was supposed to begin a productive day of work.

"Astrid, I really wish you would have asked me first before you went ahead and purchased those tickets. I mean, how would you even know if I'm free that night?"

"You are free though, aren't you?" asked Astrid, in a frightening tone that somehow gave Mitchell the idea that Astrid already knew his schedule. There was a part of Mitchell that wanted to take the easy road and simply lie about his availability. That's what most of his friends would have done. However, he valued his integrity too much to fib, even under such dire circumstances.

"I think so," he meekly replied. "I'm just not sure I want to go to a concert on Tuesday night. It's a work day and…"

"Well, I have to work, too," interrupted Astrid. "I'll tell you what,

I'll make sure you're back in your bed before you turn into a pumpkin, okay?"

"Who the heck are X-Ray Bandits, anyway?"

"Are you serious? Dude, I need to get you out more and expand your horizons. They're only the top-rated New Age Goth Band in Suffolk County. Duh. You're going to love them." Mitchell's cell phone dinged and he was hoping it was a matter that would provide his excuse to drop the conversation with Astrid. "Did you get it?"

"Get what?" inquired Mitchell.

"I just gifted you the most recent X-Ray Bandits album on iTunes. You know, as a warm up for our date Tuesday night."

"Look, Astrid, allow me to be more direct here. I do not want to go to a concert on Tuesday night. Maybe we could go for a drink at the club again, sometime. Or I could take you out for coffee?"

"What?! A coffee get-together? You're treating me like a stranger all of a sudden and it hurts."

"Hey, I'm sorry Astrid. I didn't want to hurt you. I just think maybe we should slow things down a little bit and..." Just then, a few of Mitchell's co-workers rapped on his car window and pointed to their watches while having a laugh. "Astrid, I've got to go but I'll talk to you again soon."

"Wait! We're not done yet. Don't you dare hang up on me, Mitchell!"

"Sorry. I've got to go." Mitchell ended the call and returned the phone to his pocket before opening the car door and sliding out of his seat. His co-workers teased him about waiting until the very last second before clocking in for his shift at the customer service hub.

With a sigh, Mitchell plopped down into his uncomfortable office chair within a sterile, distraction-free, cubicle. Phones began ringing nearly immediately and he launched into customer service mode. All the while, his cell phone continued to vibrate on its charging pad. His employer looked unfavorably upon anyone using their personal cell phones in the office, unless they were on break, so Mitchell resisted the urge to find out what was going on. He wasn't even ten seconds into his first break period before he grabbed his phone off the charger and investigated the recent activity. On his Facebook profile, Astrid had, in an act of immature retribution, converted all the heart emoji "LOVE" responses to his posts and photos to the angry-faced "ANGRY" emojis.

Heading to the bathroom, he ran into his friend Brad. Brad was a tech wiz and worked in his company's IT Department.

"Hey, Brad, I've got a tech question for you."

"Whoa, whoa, Mitchell. I'm off the clock for another seven minutes."

"Dude? Seriously?"

"No. I'm just messing with you, Mitch. What's bugging you—having trouble with getting your streaming TV channels? WIFI devices not connecting at home?"

"Cell phone calendars."

"What about them?" asked Brad, intrigued and always interested in displaying his technical prowess to his co-workers.

"Is it possible for someone to hack into your personal schedule on your cell phone?"

"iPhone?"

"Yes."

"Very unlikely unless they were a real pro. Apple's pretty good about security."

"Whew, I'm really glad to hear that," said a relieved Mitchell.

"Why, do you think someone is messing with your calendar?"

"I guess not. I just let this girl borrow my cell phone last night for a few minutes and now…"

"You did what?! exclaimed Brad. You gave physical control of your mobile device to an unknown party?"

"She was just supposed to Air Fling me her contact information, Brad. That's all."

"And is that all she did?"

"Well. No. She made us Facebook friends and…" Brad interrupted Mitchell in mid-sentence.

"And how long, exactly, did she have control of your phone?"

"I don't know. Just a few minutes, I think."

"A few minutes?! Mitchell, you knucklehead, she could have gained access to your contacts, your schedule, your email correspondence, and even your bank account and credit card information in that time. What were you thinking?!"

"I. I don't know. I figured we'd just exchange contact information."

"Next time, maybe consider a business card."

"Right. A business card for dating? Nice. Do you actually ever get out, Brad?" Looking a bit offended, Brad reached into his pocket and pulled out his phone. With a couple of taps, his screen filled with the image of a very attractive Indian-American woman who could easily have been a model.

"My girlfriend," said Brad, proudly. "A Harvard grad." Mitchell was left momentarily speechless and his tonic immobility was all the response that his co-worker needed to close the discussion with an exclamation. Mitchell felt even more inadequate than he had before. Guys in IT were scoring the cream of the crop on the dating scene while he was doing his best to fend off psychopaths and deeply embittered women with insurmountable trust issues.

"She's gorgeous, Brad." Brad nodded, content that his point had been made.

"Don't lend out your electronic devices, my friend. That's just asking for trouble."

"I know. I just wasn't anticipating this ditsy blonde to be the agent of some kind of cyber-attack."

"They're the worst kind, Mitchell. You never see it coming and then, BAM, you're hacked."

"Do you think that, maybe, you could take a quick look?"

"And now I have three minutes remaining on my break," said Brad, somewhat annoyed. But Brad was a good man and, despite his personality quirks, he was always there to help.

"Maybe later, then?"

"Let me take a look."

"You want me to surrender my phone to you?" joked Mitchell.

"Very good. You're learning. Now, the phone, please." Mitchell handed Brad his phone and he went into the phone's email and scheduling permissions to inspect the damage. "Hmm. Interesting."

"What?" inquired Mitchell.

"Nicely done. Just a few minutes, you say?"

"Yah. Two to three, tops."

"You are currently sharing your email, contacts, and calendar with HotAstrid98's iPhone."

"Damn it! That bitch!" Mitchell was furious.

"Settle down, my friend. A couple clicks and a swipe and, voila, you're a free man again."

"I can't thank you enough, Brad. You rock!"

"Oh, you don't have to thank me. I'm going out with Ananya on Tuesday night. I don't need any more boosts to my self-esteem."

"Concert?"

"Yes, nice guess. Wait, you haven't hacked into my calendar, have you?" Brad asked with a chuckle.

"X-Ray Bandits?"

"Oh my God, you have hacked me!" Mitchell just winked and laughed. He pulled his cell phone out of Brad's hand and gave him a wave as he turned for the men's room.

"Enjoy your night out with Ananya," he added as he was walking away.

"You can count on it, Mitchell. Yes, you can be sure about that one."

After taking care of business in the Men's Room, Mitchell returned to his desk and immediately "unfriended" and "blocked" Astrid on Facebook. The only thing he struggled with was whether or not he even wanted to send her a text to express his anger over being tricked into allowing Astrid to gain permissions to private features on his cell phone. One way or the other, he was done with her so he didn't feel like it really mattered. His break being over, calls were, once again, being routed to his desk. Mitchell found it very hard to concentrate as his mind was still occupied by the Astrid situation. More than one customer expressed their frustration as they had to repeat their concerns multiple times to the distracted agent. To make matters worse, his phone was vibrating like mad on the charging pad, yet again. He could resist the temptation no longer and so, contrary to company policy, he removed his work headset and left his phone off the hook while he investigated the happenings on his personal phone.

Astrid had hardly been blocked more than ten or fifteen minutes before she sent a number of angry text messages to Mitchell, accusing him of a bitter betrayal, failed integrity, and a host of other crimes and misdemeanors. He didn't even bother to listen to the voicemail traffic from Astrid.

Of greater concern were several texts from his friends, Sasha and Charlie. Sasha joked about a foot fetish prince looking for his Cinderella while Charlie offered some more constructive recommendations about checking his Facebook settings and changing the photo tagging feature to require his approvals before any posts appeared on his Facebook timeline. "What are they are talking about?" Mitchell wondered. He went to his profile page, on Facebook, and things immediately became clear. Someone named Cuddlefish98 had posted several photos from the night before of him attempting to unbuckle Astrid's sandals while she lay in bed. He knew, immediately, that Astrid must have friended him with her alternate profile as well as her primary Facebook profile. Mitchell turned beet red and pounded his fist on his desk, in anger. Right on cue, his team manager poked his head into the cubicle.

"Mitchell, could I talk with you in my office, please."

"I'm sorry, Mr. Brannon. I was just having a moment."

"If you were focusing on work rather than on private matters on your personal cell phone, I think you might find there'd be less of those moments in your day. Now, if you wouldn't mind, please follow me to my office."

The call center went strangely quiet as Mitchell stormed out, a pink slip in his hand and uttering a stream of profanity that was becoming all too familiar within those work spaces. He had been canned. It wasn't even about the desk pounding or the cell phone usage. His customer service rating had fallen from 4.2 stars to 2.5 stars. With countless drones waiting in the wings, Mitchell's drop in performance was all the incentive his boss needed to make the personnel change.

Sitting alone in his vehicle, Mitchell turned his satellite radio to a classical music station hoping that the soothing notes might somehow slow his racing heartbeat. He fidgeted anxiously, trapped in the head-space that existed somewhere between a primal yell and melancholy sobbing. Returning to his Facebook page, he deleted the posts that were attracting comments like ants to a picnic. He then blocked Cuddlefish98 on Facebook and began the laborious process of removing any friend he was not familiar with. There were too many. How did he get 3,543 Facebook friends in the first place? Finally, exasperated, embarrassed, and emotionally exhausted, he decided to simply delete his entire Facebook account. And just like that, it was gone. 3,543 friends and probably only three or four real friends in the bunch. This desperate act proved to be very satisfying. Mitchell felt as if a burden had been lifted almost immediately. He turned his cell phone off and tossed it in the passenger seat.

The scenery on his drive seemed, somehow, more colorful and vibrant than he had ever recalled seeing though he had driven the route hundreds of times. Rather than going directly home, Mitchell changed his route to take him through his childhood hometown. He parked in the lot of his favorite childhood park and turned off the car engine. Mitchell looked out upon the water, for a while, before getting out to walk around. He spent nearly an hour at the water's edge before deciding to continue his explorations beyond the gates of the park. His mind adrift in a sea of memories, he walked familiar roads that took him by his former schools, his old house, and finally to his beloved library. He felt ashamed that he hadn't read a book in over three years. He used to love reading.

Mitchell walked into the familiar main lobby of the library and compared the scene to a simpler time when the building radiated with infinite possibilities and his adventures within this enchanted palace seemed infinite and sublimely magical. Like all things, the establishment had evolved with the times. Cumbersome photographic checkout machines were replaced by barcode scanning wands at the checkout desks and computer terminals had long-since replaced the card catalogs of the past. For all that, the library still retained a bit of its mystical intrigue.

"*Irving's Dinosaur Pal*," he thought. "That was the first book I ever checked out with my youth library card. I was so proud of that card." As if drawn to retrace the steps of his childhood, he dreamily wandered into the children's books room. The room was splendidly decorated with colorful depictions of famous characters from countless children's books—Dr. Seuss characters, Peter Pan, Winnie the Pooh, and a litany of fairy tale characters. It was a beautiful refuge for young minds. Dating woes and job loss concerns simply drifted away as Mitchell made his way toward the shelves where he expected to find *Irving's Dinosaur Pal*. He had photocopied a number of pages at five cents a copy, back in the day. Before bed, he would smile as he looked at the pictures of the friendly dinosaur. And there it was! Mitchell carefully pulled the book from the shelf and opened the cover. He was lost in the moment and nearly jumped out of his skin when the librarian addressed him.

"Looking for a book for a friend?"

"Sorry for jumping. You startled me," said Mitchell, trying to recover his composure.

"I should apologize. I didn't mean to sneak up on you like that."

"It's okay. I was just…"

"Doing a research paper on the Dewey Decimal System and your investigations led you here?" kidded the librarian. Mitchell laughed.

"Yes. I was wondering if you might instruct me on some of the finer points of the Dewey Decimal System." Mitchell was rather taken by the young librarian and his blushing cheeks betrayed him. Her face was kind and her beautiful brown eyes were alive and sparkling. The gentle tones of her voice were soothing and reassuring.

"First, perhaps you'd permit me to recommend a book," she said.

"Oh, I think I'll probably be okay with *Irving's Dinosaur Pal*. It was a childhood favorite. Well, at least in Kindergarten."

"It is an excellent book; I'll give you that. Perhaps you might enjoy this one, too?" The librarian reached over to the shelf and retrieved the book that had been resting adjacent to *Irving's Dinosaur Pal*. "It's called *Believe in Me, I Said to the Mirror*." She slowly handed the book over to Mitchell, carefully watching his expressions. Mitchell choked as he spoke.

"Danielle Blanchet? I'm not familiar with her. Any relation to Charlie Blanchet, the author of *Irving's Dinosaur Pal?*"

"Maybe," said the librarian. "It's about a little boy with self-esteem issues. He thinks that no one likes him and he sometimes tries to pretend to be somebody he's not to make friends. But that never works out."

"Whoa. Now don't be giving the ending away. You've sold me on this one, already. But I have one important question."

"Sure. What your question?" asked the librarian, compassion flowing freely from her gentle heart.

"Does it have a happy ending? Because I really need a happy ending right now."

"I think you'll like the ending. In fact, I know you'll love the ending."

"Perfect," said Mitchell, lost in the eyes of the lovely woman standing before him.

"Are you ready for me to check you out?" asked the librarian. Mitchell thought about seizing the opportunity to make a crude joke about being totally ready to "check her out" but he knew that she deserved better and he knew that he was better than that.

"Yes. Thank you." The two walked over to the counter and the librarian asked for his card. Mitchell realized that he hadn't checked a book out from that library in over ten years and he certainly didn't have an active card. "I'm sorry but I don't have an active card at this library."

"Would you like one?"

"Definitely!" replied Mitchell, enthusiastically. He immediately felt as if he had overplayed his hand and he quickly recomposed himself. "I mean, yes, please."

"My pleasure. If you'll just fill out this paperwork, I can get you a temporary card today and then you should get your permanent card in the mail in the next couple weeks."

"That'd be great," responded Mitchell, in a calmer tone. His heart rate began to pick up and his palms got sweaty as he considered his next move. "Say, what's your name?" The librarian pointed to her name badge without shifting her eyes from the computer screen where she was entering data to process the temporary card. "Duh. I'm sorry, it's been a hard day. Danielle. That's a pretty name." Mitchell carefully watched Danielle's face for a response but none came. "I'd um, ask you for your number but I left my cell phone in my car. It's had a bad day." Again, Danielle continued with her work but the conversation caught the attention of one of her co-workers who slowly poked her head out from behind one of the shelving units to watch the scene.

"Your books, good sir," said Danielle, with a regal air, as she slid the two books across the counter to Mitchell. Her dismissal of his previous comments had answered Mitchell's questions. Still, he harbored no ill feelings regarding the rejection. Danielle was lovely and a beautiful spirit and he felt at peace in her presence. This visit to the library was time well spent.

"Thank you, milady," Mitchell said, as he bowed. Danielle shot a glance over Mitchell's shoulder, toward the stacks, and her curious co-worker quickly darted out of view. Danielle smiled.

"Have a good day, seeker."

"It's Mitchell, actually."

"I know. I just typed your name into our computer system," Danielle replied with an impish grin.

"Oh, yah, that's right," Mitchell laughed.

"I hope you find what you're looking for," Danielle added, a caring expression coming over her visage.

"Thank you, Danielle. It was a pleasure to meet you."

"Likewise."

"Well, goodbye then," said Mitchell, not wanting the conversation to end and certainly not wanting to close the curtain on the moment. Danielle just nodded and smiled.

Books in hand, Mitchell re-traced his steps back to his vehicle and eventually made his way home. The comely librarian had purged his mind of all the dark thoughts that had been piling up throughout the day and, in fact, accumulating over the past few years.

Before retiring for the night, Mitchell sat up in bed, placing the two children's books on his lap as he adjusted the lamp on his nightstand. He read *Irving's Dinosaur Pal* first and the familiar story brought a smile to his face, once again. "I guess you're never too old for dinosaurs," he thought. The second book, *Believe in Me, I Said to the Mirror,* was something extra special. Mitchell felt silly, crying while reading a child's book, but then he realized that big people and little people all share the same heart and they all seek love and acceptance. The beautiful story was just the medicine Mitchell needed. As he flipped to the last page, a small paper note fell from between the pages to his bed. A name and a phone number were scribbled, in pencil, upon the small piece of white paper. It was from Danielle. Danielle Blanchet. Danielle Blanchet, the librarian. Danielle Blanchet, the author. Danielle Blanchet, the woman Mitchell would one day marry and love, unconditionally, for the remainder of his days. She made the world beautiful again. What was lost was found. True love.

The Story Behind the Story

This was an interesting assignment for prospective Red Penguin Collection authors. The task was to create a short story (2,500–7,000 words) centering around how "the modern era has affected intimacy, romance, and the 'game' those single among us are forced to play to find it." The title for the anthology would be "The Dating Game: Modern Romance Short Stories."

Although I had been divorced for over five years at the time I wrote this, I was still very much a novice on the singles scene and certainly hadn't "broken the code" yet on mid-life dating and the associated challenges. But, as a member of several singles groups (created to facilitate building healthy and supportive friendships and, specifically, not intended for use as a dating springboard—the disclaimer says so), I had heard a litany of horror stories regarding the challenges of online dating sites and the levels of deceit people had experienced trying to navigate around the false-hoods and accumulated "emotional baggage" of so many members who had been burned and lost their trust in humanity—especially for members of the opposite sex who were assumed to be liars and cheats. It's a giant, bloody mess...at least as described.

As somewhat of a hopeless romantic, I still harbor a belief that the surest path toward finding the right match is through meeting people organically, doing things you enjoy doing. I can't argue that online apps offer a statistical advantage by exponentially increasing the pool of potential dating candidates. And these dating sites have certainly worked for some. But, as an old-school, hopeless romantic, I still harbor this hope that Destiny will see me to where I need to be and that my most probable match will, like myself, be skeptical of the swipe-left/swipe-right world of dating sites.

Clearly, my views on such matters seeped into this story or, more to the point, formed a foundation for it. While the protagonist, Mitchell, is much younger than me, the thoughts playing out in his head are very similar to my own. He struggles with a dating scene that he finds unattractive and confusing until he finally tosses his hands in the air, seeks his own personal peace, and then—and only then—finds the love and companionship that he truly desired.

I never considered myself much of a romance writer, but I found meaning and relatability in this story and it came together nicely. Happily, Red Penguin Books thought so, too.

Cuz

(Written January 31, 2022)
Published by Red Penguin Books in "*Finding Family: Stories of Connection and Hope*" (April, 2022)

An account of the happiness I found after being reconnected and reunited, after over 40 years, with a wonderful cousin who I had only met once before.

Our days are filled with colorful events and meaningful people. Like the pieces of a jigsaw puzzle, these come together to form a whole—the story of our lives. Sometimes, pieces of the puzzle are taken from us while other times they are misplaced and we long for their recovery. If you've ever gazed upon a nearly finished puzzle yet lack the remaining pieces to complete it, you'll understand the disquieting feeling that lingers and you'll understand the need to seek a remedy.

Broken Arm Summer. That's what I call it. It was the summer of 1972 and I was involved in an unfortunate misadventure at my local day camp, hosted at my elementary school. My sixth birthday was still a month or so away when, for the closing event of the day, our camp counselor elected to launch a bunch of wild Kindergarten grads into an uncontrolled game of "Brownies and Fairies." It was the one and only time in my life that I played "Brownies and Fairies." I had never heard of the game and I recall not be particularly enthusiastic when it was proposed to us. I am 99% certain that the counselor had no intention for this end-of-day diversion to turn into a violent free-for-all of tackling and high-speed bodily impacts. We were five and six so, of course, it did. Sure enough, I got tackled, the offending youth landing squarely on top of me as my left arm folded underneath my collapsing body. Nearly immediately, a horrible pain shot through my arm. The severity of the incident must have been apparent to the camp counselor as the game was stopped and I was escorted to the nurse's office. On the way, we stopped at a water fountain so I could rehydrate. I knew it was a bad thing when I found myself unable to bend over to reach to stream of water. My left shoulder was numb and, for reasons I can't explain, felt like it was sitting several inches above my right shoulder. It wasn't...but that's what it felt like. My father was called to come retrieve me as the nurse completed her inspection. "Will a piece of bubble gum make it feel better?" Those were the nurse's exact words. I remember them 50 years later because they made me incredibly angry. I didn't know many curse words back then but, if I did, I might well have cut loose with a stream of expletives. "No. Bubble gum won't make me feel better." I hated Brownies and Fairies and I hated day camp and I was in the most extreme pain of my young life. I'm sure my angry glare and abrupt response made my point effectively.

Eventually, my father showed up. My Mom was out with the car and, in the pre-cell phone days, there was no way to contact her. We were going to have to walk home. I was barely out of the school building when I realized that I wasn't going to be able to make it. The initial adrenalin rush and numbness were subsiding and now I was feeling intense, teeth-grinding pain with each step I took. I made it to the edge of the school property when the situation became untenable. In an act of gallantry that I remember still, to this day, my father decided he was going to carry me home. I must have weighed somewhere between 45 and 50 pounds yet my father completed the half mile walk, much of it uphill, while carrying his injured and wriggling son. I felt very proud of my dad.

When Mom returned with the vehicle, I was taken to the doctor's office and our fears were confirmed—broken arm. My arm was bandaged, splinted and secured firmly against the side of my body with some very aggressive wrapping. It was awful. That was the end of my summer...or so I thought. I was in for a wonderful surprise, one that would redeem what I thought was a lost summer vacation.

Family. I've always been somewhat envious of those large families with innumerable grandparents, aunts, uncles, and cousins living within close proximity. That was not my family. My father was an only child. My mother had one sister. My paternal grandmother had passed before my birth and, seeing as how they lived more than a day's drive away, we rarely saw my surviving grandparents, the last of whom passed away in 1992. In total, I can count the number of grandparent visits on two hands. I regret not knowing my grandparents better but I accepted it as part of life in a modern and mobile society. For all that, I still felt the absence of an extended family.

There was one and only one highlight during the summer of 1972 —my maternal grandmother was coming to visit, along with my Aunt

Carol and Cousin Sherril (Sheri). We sometimes referred to my grand-mother as "Rootin' Tootin' Thelma." She was a wild one but lots of fun. It's quite possible that I met Grandma Thelma before this but, alas, any such memory is lost to me. I certainly had no memory of ever meeting my aunt or cousin before. It was a memorable day!

While the adults did their thing, my brother, sister, and I had a wonderful time playing with Cousin Sheri. She was fantastic and we immediately bonded. My brother is ten years older than me (twelve years older than my sister) so we enlisted the aid of Cousin Sheri to help us conspire against him in various plots. Several years older than my sister and I, Sheri made the perfect ally and was a willing conspir-ator in our fun games and older brother harassment schemes. It was an absolute blast! I just remember having so much fun and feeling so happy to have found not only a new family member but also a friend. We all loved Sheri a lot and we were sad when she had to leave.

Years passed, and there was no reunion. In the fall of 1979, Grandma Thelma came to visit us in New York. We took her to the circus at Madison Square Garden and then to see *Annie* on Broadway. I was older and more mature than during Grandma's previous visit and I felt that we really bonded. I've always had a bit of a mischievous side and I know Grandma did, as well. I think she saw that spark in me and I in her. Sadly, it was the last time I would see my grandmother before she passed. All my grandparents were gone. My mother got to travel with her mom before we lost her, in 1992, and I'm glad she did. I regret not having profited from more time with all of my grandparents. I never felt like I really got to know them and what they knew of me was only as a young child. With the exception of a few visits to see my Great Aunt in South Dakota, who lived to be 102, I had no more contact with any extended family.

In 1984, I joined the Air Force and traveled the world. It was tough enough to make it back home to see my own parents let alone begin a search for extended family. I got married in 1993 and children followed several years later, four of them, to be specific. With few exceptions, I stopped going "home" for vacations since my new home was wherever my children were and that home traveled from state to state and country to country. Occasionally, my siblings and I would reminisce about that one special day when Cousin Sheri visited us. While obvi-ously cognizant of the fact that Grandma and Aunt Carol were part of that visit, we ultimately focused on Sheri—she was one of us—a peer from our own generation. With the passing of time, the visit transformed from family reunion into something more resembling an urban legend. Did it really happen?

As the years passed, following the summer of '72, we would, upon occasion, receive photos in the mail and we'd race to see the photos of our cousin. It became more difficult to equate the images of a blossoming young woman with the mischievous kid who was our buddy and co-conspirator in the early 70s. Sheri was growing up. We all were. Yet, locked in our mind was the mental picture of our forever 9-year-old cousin. I often wondered what she was like now. I wondered if she remembered the fun we had in 1972 as fondly as we did. We revered the day. Time often widens the divide between people and, especially after my grandmother passed away, it seemed like we lost track of our cousin. While I've never heard my mother say a negative word about her sister, or vice versa, the fact remained that the two seldom communicated. I never heard them talk on the phone and, so far as I knew, they did little to communicate through other means, either. My aunt lived in Ohio. We lived in New York. That's just the way things were. I never stopped wondering about my cousin nor hoping that life was treating her well. Honestly, I didn't know. I was always a little bit uneasy about asking my parents about extended family. I don't exactly know why. I guess I figured that if they cared to share things with us then they would do so. The result was a patchwork of disconnected vignettes that created a confusing puzzle with numerous missing pieces. It bothered me...but I let it go.

Conceivably, things might have continued as they were. I'm glad they didn't. As it turns out, I really needed my cousin back in my life to help me through the challenges of the coming years. My marriage was slowly coming apart at the seams and my children, now mostly teens, no longer seemed interested in hanging out with their father. The years following 2010 seemed very lonely and I felt increasingly isolated, even in my own family. Work was tough and getting tougher and my projected military retirement was looming, menacingly, on the horizon. My life was about to enter the turbulent white water.

While visiting my parents for a few days of leave in the spring of 2014, my mom mentioned that Sherril had sent along a few old photos that I might be interested in seeing. Sherril had recently had to place her mother in a nursing home and she found some old photos of my mother that she thought would be nice to send our way. Old photos?

Of course, I love old family photos. And then, like a bolt from the blue, it struck me. "Wait. Cousin Sherril sent photos? Through the mail???" Immediately, my mind made the connection that there was bound to be a return address on the package. Previously, I had no idea what my cousin's last name was. I was pretty sure she had gotten married but that's about all I knew. Without wasting a moment, I raced over to the package and copied the name. I felt incredibly inspired and, seconds later, I was searching social media. The prospect of possibly reconnecting with my lost cousin was incredibly exciting. I think my parents were startled by my enthusiasm and single-minded focus. My rapid tapping upon the screen of my cell phone must have appeared as some tribal sorcery to my parents who had never sent a text message nor used a smart phone in their lives. And then, Bingo! There she was. It had to be Cousin Sheri. I sent a Facebook friend request along with a message and I waited...and hoped. June 1, 2014—this was a very happy day...the day my beloved cousin and I reconnected. With introductions complete, I sent on a few old photos and then typed out a lengthy message about my life journey across the past 42 years since we had last seen each other. Shortly thereafter, Sherril reciprocated. As it turns out, we had both been longing for family and regretting than our childhoods were not filled with more familial connections. I could not have been happier to be reconnected with my cousin!

Not so very long after returning to my family in Louisiana, I received orders for a two-year assignment in South Korea. It was a stressful time and the assignment would, eventually, prove to be the final straw that broke the camel's back in my marriage. It was a very sad time in my life. The single saddest day of my life was the day I drove my family to the bus station on our base, in Seoul, South Korea, and hugged them goodbye. My soon-to-be ex-wife was returning to her hometown in South Dakota and she was taking my kids with her. I never felt so alone in all my life. Beyond having the support of my family back in New York, it proved to be an incredible blessing to have my cousin back in my life, too. I was hurting and I can't imagine how things would have gone were it not for my family's support.

On a brighter note, even though I was living in Korea, I thought it would be great to visit with my cousin and her family in Michigan. When work took me back to U.S. Transportation Command Headquarters, at Scott Air Force Base in Illinois, for a multi-week planning conference, I saw an opportunity to capitalize on the free weekend. This was my chance to finally reunite with my cousin after 44 years and get to meet her family. I was thrilled!

On Friday, May 13, 2016, I caught an evening flight up to Detroit and was met by Sherril's husband, Ken, at the airport. I could tell right away that he was a great guy. Sherril and Ken even put me up in a great hotel nearby. The next few days were filled with tons of fun. On Saturday, I got to see my cousin's son, Zach, working the course at a nearby skateboard park and then I got to assist with his little league practice. Later that day, despite the extremely frigid temperatures, we all went to a local fair after having a great lunch at a Middle Eastern restaurant. While visiting with my cousin and her family, I also had the opportunity to speak to my Aunt Carol on the phone. It was a great call and the first time I remember actually speaking with my aunt. The next day was equally as enjoyable as we all went to visit the Henry Ford Museum and Green Field Village. I'd always wanted to visit the museum and it was wonderful to be able to see it with family. After the museum visit, we had a quick lunch together before I had to head to the airport to make my way back to Illinois to complete my work at the conference. It was tough to say goodbye.

In 2018, I finally retired from the Air Force, after a career that spanned more than 30 years. While I won't deny a deep hurt inside that my own children did not attend my retirement ceremony, I was eternally grateful that Sherril and her family drove all the way down (to Illinois) from Michigan to attend the event. I can't begin to tell you how special that was for me. Beyond this, my father, mother, sister, and nieces were able to attend. Since Mom, Dad, and my sister, Jennifer, had been present for my initial commissioning into the U.S. Air Force and graduation from the United States Air Force Academy, there seemed to be a beautiful symmetry to having them there for my final salute as an Air Force officer.

There's something special about family. Friends are great and, in many instances, may be as close, or closer than our own family. But, in my opinion, there's a timeless bond between family members sharing blood and ancestry. There's also a sacred trust. I feel stronger around family and I feel more at peace when family is near. For years, I stared at an incomplete puzzle, feeling unsatisfied. One of the greatest blessings of my life was returning an important piece to that picture as I found my wonderful cousin and, once again, we shared the love that comes from being united as family.

Cuz

The Story Behind the Story

I believe this essay pretty much stands alone without any elaboration. When Red Penguin Books announced a new anthology, "Finding Family: Stories of Connection and Hope," I didn't have a second thought about what I wanted to write about. The task, with a deadline of January 31, 2022, was to write an essay or story (2,000-7,500 words) that centered around families coming together and the importance of connecting with loved ones, especially family members who you haven't seen in a long time, or who may live far away. There was some additional elaboration regarding possible topics but, again, I didn't even need to blink before I was ready to take pen to paper, so to speak. I was happy to be able to share this story of gratitude for my wonderful Cousin, Sherril.

INDOMITABLE

(Written March 20, 2022)
Published by Red Penguin Books in *"Where Flowers Bloom: Poems and Essays of Strength, Hope, and Resilience"* (May, 2022)

A short essay about the indomitable power of hope.

Countless times across countless centuries have I been stricken, dragged mercilessly to the precipice of finality, and presumed lost for all eternity. Yet I have risen. Though tears have filled rivers and rivers have run red with my blood until the sea, itself, turned a ghastly crimson, I ascended, gasping for air, from the darkest depths and drew breath, yet again. I've kneeled beside your ancestors, trembling in fear as great beasts dragged family members into the darkness of the night. I've watched over slaves as they labored with impossibly huge stones to build pyramids that climbed high into the sky. Death and despair labored with them yet I abandoned them not. I've held the hand of the starved, the besieged, the tortured and the betrayed. I've heard their whispered prayers. Men tossed about in the tempest, the timbers of their vessels creaking and groaning until they could bare the strain no more—I've sailed that ocean countless times. Like a warm cloak, I've covered the raped and abused, the forsaken and the unloved, the desperate wanderers in search of a home who found neither open doors nor life-sustaining alms. Though I wish I had not, I bore witness, across the ages, to the greatest atrocities and the most horrific environmental catastrophes—from genocides to great floods; I've seen more than I care to recount. I've kept the lamps alight through the darkest nights and lifted the fiddlers bow within death-filled prisons. I've kept the flag aloft upon the ramparts though the ravages of war ripped and tore its very fabric. Some clutched Bibles whilst others kissed photos and tokens of affection. Some slowly rose, though their legs were broken and their limbs torn, and sneered as they shouted defiantly in the face of overwhelming adversity. Others silently prayed. I was there. I was always there. I am HOPE and I am the ember that burns in the darkness. I am HOPE and I am the strength and the will to go on though all seems lost. All is not lost. All is never lost. Always, there is HOPE.

Though the last breath fades, there is HOPE. HOPE that, with or without our presence, the world will see to it that justice is done and a greater good comes with the dawning of a new day than any we have ever known. I bring HOPE that our children might live more fulfilling lives than we have. HOPE that we might come to our senses and that peace and civility might reign supreme.

Listen in the gloom and hear the beating of the distant drum, pounding in rhythm with the beating of your heart—I am HOPE. I am HOPE and I compel you to stand and lift your sword against the foes of righteousness. I am HOPE and I inspire you to lift your pen and let words of peace and brotherhood flow freely onto the pages of history. I am HOPE and I beg you to hold your child's hand and share that which I offer to all who will abide. Whether you pray to God for deliverance or stand on account of principals and the common law, know that I am with you and refuse to be driven away though great enemies have tried. Through war and plague, famine and flood, death and abuses untold, I will never leave your side. I beg of you, open your eyes, open your ears, reach for my hand and open your heart. Look for me and know me. I shall not fail you. I am HOPE and I am INDOMITABLE.

The Story Behind the Story

While not originally part of the planned Red Penguin Collection anthology series, my publisher leaped into action in the wake of the terrible refugee crisis created in Ukraine following the February, 2022 full-scale invasion by Russia. Red Penguin Books envisioned creating a book filled with poems and essays of strength, hope, and resilience with all proceeds going to funding humanitarian relief efforts for displaced Ukrainians. I was honored to be able to contribute to this effort. I could have taken this in many directions but, in the spirit of the cause, and to keep the piece simple and to the point, I decided to write a short essay personifying "hope," itself, as I envisioned it. My ultimate message was, of course, that throughout all the trials of mankind, the universal constant of "hope" has kept us moving forward and that this hope, no matter how vicious the assaults upon it, has remained, forever, indomitable.

Fumblestix: The Last Laugh

(Written February 28, 2022)
Published by Red Penguin Books in *"Happy Accidents and Other Humorous Short Stories"* (May, 2022)

Strange are the twists of fate that can lay waste to even the grandest of plans. Sometimes, the most unlikely of characters appear upon the stage to restore order, leaving us to wonder—who, indeed, is truly the fool.

It's ludicrous! Absurd! Farcical! Preposterous! Completely nonsensical! But it's true. I wish that he might tell the tale himself but he is no longer with us. Dead? Perhaps. But that's what they thought the first time…and the time after that. Alas, I alone, his humble chronicler, remain to tell the tale of Fumblestix. My recounting shall be totally inadequate and likely earn your rightful disdain. For all that, with quavering hand, I take quill to parchment to share what little I can of one stanza of the great poem of a great man's life.

Fumblestix was a fool! Perhaps the greatest fool of all? Clever as a fox was he who traveled the royal courts of Europe, bringing laughter and mirth to troubled lands and troubled rulers. For all that, Fumblestix was not without his enemies. His wit, perhaps too sharp, too biting, was injurious to those who felt the sting of his jocularly delivered critiques. Those who presented to the world their paper-thin facades were oft times offended once the wily jester revealed the naked truth of their existence. In fact, 'twas Oswald's queen, as the histories provide, that first took offense. It's likely there were many before but the vengeance wreaked against lowly jesters is seldom recorded in the annals of history. In the year 758 AD, Oswald, King of Northumbria, ordered the poor fool be beheaded and his limbs scattered about the land. So incensed were Oswald's subjects that they rose in revolt, cutting short his doomed and short-lived reign. Less than a year on the throne and this ill-fated monarch was brutally murdered by men of his own household. And so, it seems, Fumblestix had the last laugh.

One can only imagine the consternation when Fumblestix,

allegedly, reappeared in the court of Louis XVI of France. A thousand years had passed since any worthy scribe had touted his humorous exploits, much less his existence. It was impossible. Yet it was true! He had returned to entertain the king and the Royal Court. It seems, as many times before, that his cutting humor was not appreciated by the vainglorious regal patrons for whom he had been conscripted to perform. Although the narrative is wanting for the delicious details that students of history crave, it has been noted that poor Fumblestix, after a brilliant juggling routine accompanied by an equally impressive display of poetic sarcasm and social commentary, was sentenced to be beheaded. Sadly, history repeated itself as the ever-popular Fumblestix was separated from his head to satisfy the vengeful needs of a fragile-egoed monarch. Of course, the fate of King Louis and of his court is well known. Sentenced to death by guillotine, it was not long after his jester's final bow that King Louis found himself wanting of his own head when, on January 21st, 1793, he was executed by guillotine at the Place de la Révolution in Paris. *L'Ami Du Peuple* noted that, in the end, it was Fumblestix who had the last laugh.

You can only imagine my surprise, and joy, when I was informed that an eccentric character garbed in a brilliant costume fashioned from hundreds of dissimilar colorful patches had recently arrived at the Manhattan office of one Senator Ronald Dumphrey on the evening before he intended to officially announce his intent to run for the office of the President of the United States. Could it be true? Had the great Fumblestix been resurrected yet again to spread joy and hope among the common folk? I had to know. I handed in my resignation, on the spot, and sold what little possessions I owned so that I might purchase my train ticket to New York and secure accommodations in that great city for the duration of what I expected to be an unforgettable campaign season. I was not to be disappointed.

Though I can hardly be called an educated man, I have been successful in unraveling the truth and much of this learning has taken place in the taverns and pubs of the world. The price of my lessons was but the few baubles required to buy the drinks that freed the lips of my would-be teachers—people with interesting stories to tell. I frequented the establishments where various campaign staffers sought refuge from the torments of their daily grind. There, in particular, I first came upon the likes of one Chartreuse Richardson, the Campaign Manager for Senator Dumphrey. Oh, how she hated Fumblestix when they first met. I was confident that she'd eventually learn to see him in a different light. I listened but did not pass judgment since, as experience has shown me, the scales of justice tend to balance themselves fairly when Fumblestix takes the stage. I gratefully acknowledge the carefully guarded information that my informants reluctantly provided me in confidence. And, thus, I am afforded the luxury of sharing a more complete story so that you, the reader, might know the truth. Do you think me a rogue? I graciously acknowledge your compliment with a doff of my cap. The truth must be known.

With bells jingling like so many horse bells upon a spirited team of carriage horses, Fumblestix catapulted himself into the conference room, executing a flawless series of somersaults upon landing. Thus did he announce his arrival upon the stage. He leapt upon the table and danced a silly jig, waving his fool's scepter as he sang a joyous song he had learned from a band of wandering minstrels a great many years before. All present were lost in laughter until it was revealed that he was to be Senator Dumphrey's new campaign spokesperson. One by one, I'm told, faces soured as it was discovered that Fumblestix spoke more truth than falsehoods. It's only natural that the senator and his senior advisors refused to accept this ludicrous proposition. It was then that the campaign's financial advisor, Roger Bigsby, took the "good" senator aside and explained an unpleasant truth. You see, Senator Ronald Dumphrey had a debt to pay. Years before, his campaign for the Senate was largely funded by an anonymous donor. The huge financial boost enabled a deluge of defamatory commercial spots to flood all the major networks for many months before the election. His poor opponent had little to counter with and Dumphrey won by a landslide vote in what was called the most one-sided election in New York State history. While the vanquished retreated to his second home, in South America, with his Brazilian mistress, Senator Dumphrey enjoyed the spoils of war and was able to afford a fine Park Avenue condominium home for his South American mistress. It was only natural then, when the same anonymous donor came forth, through a proxy, with a financial offer that dwarfed the previous contribution by a factor of ten, that Senator Dumphrey's staff should leap at the opportunity. Some say the illegal campaign contribution approached half a billion U.S. dollars—it was as spectacularly grand as it was grossly illegal. There were ways to hide the paper trail but there was no way of hiding the single caveat attached to the transaction. That caveat was that the campaign must take on a Director of Communications and Media Spokesperson to be chosen by the donor. Any attempt to alter or work around this precondition would result in the immediate revocation of the contract. At the time, the requirement seemed harmless enough. Surely, with so much skin in the game, the donor would provide for the best representative that money could buy...and so he did. So he did.

While the more seasoned advisors were screaming about "political suicide," Roger Bigsby confronted them with an unfortunate fact—a large portion of the campaign donation had already been allocated and there was little to no hope of recovering the money. The only available options were to default on the contract, illegal as it may have been, and risk having the dirty business exposed, or to go along with the plan and simply coach the eccentric Fumblestix, where needed, or replace him, where possible. It all seemed simple enough. A business suit and a tie, a teleprompter and a good speech writer, an etiquette coach and a premier hair stylist, and Fumblestix would be fit for prime time. This was an easy fix. Alas, if they only knew what I know. Fumblestix has no need for remedies as he, himself, is, more often than not, the cure.

One might say that the professional relationship began swimmingly. One would be wrong. Fumblestix, who spoke mostly in verse, his eyes sparkling with life and his brain alive with jovial thoughts, was not particularly amused when he was told to wear the rather expensive suit that was purchased for him by the head of the Professional Branding Subcommittee. An ultimatum was provided to Fumblestix that he must play by their rules or be excluded from the game, altogether. The threat had hardly left the lips of the sender before a telegram arrived stating clearly, and in no uncertain terms, that Fumblestix could not be Fumblestix unless he was allowed the freedom of expression that had endeared him to countless audiences before, albeit less so among the nobles. Wishing to avoid the scandal, Humphrey and team conceded defeat and readied themselves for a most enjoyable journey into mayhem and mockery.

Gracious hosts that they were, the campaign team furnished Fumblestix with pen and paper so that he might jot down his thoughts and recommendations. His staff might then see to it that his directions were "put into action." "Nonsense!" replied Fumblestix. "I am but a common man and thus would it be frightfully uncommon were commoners to serve me. Quite to the contrary, I shall offer my services to be of service to those who have offered to serve me." With his trademark mocking laugh, he dismissed his team to find merriment at the local tavern whilst he surprised even I, his knowledgeable chronicler, with an adept round of postings on every social media site known to man. He fashioned the paper from his pad into an impressive menagerie of folded paper animals and cheerfully placed them about the office to lighten the mood. Chartreuse, it must be said, was furious. She stormed about the building looking for blood, seeking any and all who had given access to the campaign's official media sites to Fumblestix. She found no one—they were all out drinking. Who dared to give the Director of Communications and Media Spokesperson access to platforms upon which he might communicate!! It was absurd! Sheer madness! Ah, but this was just the beginning.

Senator Humphreys, as magnanimous as ever, or so his Branding Manager insisted, extended an invitation to the staff to accompany him upon his personal jet to a team building event to be held at his lavish vacation estate in Florida. Truth be told, the expectation was that Fumblestix would not accompany the group as he had already regaled them with lively tunes regarding his fear of dragons and such flying monstrosities. However, as history has demonstrated, there's little a tankard of "liquid courage" can't remedy and so the barely coherent Fumblestix, having imbibed enough mead to tranquilize an ox, managed to stagger through the airport, eventually finding his seat in the company aircraft, much to the chagrin of the six team members whose sole assignment for the week had been to ensure that Fumblestix remain in New York and be rendered impotent by means of whatever guile suited their intent.

Having made himself comfortable with all manner of pillows and blankets, Fumblestix drifted off to sleep before the landing gear wheels had even departed the runway. Shortly after departure, the co-pilot burst through the cockpit door, alarmed by a loud grinding sound that he and the pilot had heard coming from the rear of the aircraft. It did not take long to track the source of the unpleasant noise to the sleeping Fumblestix. Normally a peaceful sleeper with a head filled with pleasant dreams, I must concede that a bit of overindulgence has been known to disrupt the sleep of the much-renowned jester. The angry comments and pleading of his fellow passengers could not be discerned above the roar of Fumblestix's prodigious snoring. Lest you think the journey continued as such, it's relevant to note that Fumblestix was shaken from his sleep by Senator Humphrey's secretary, a tall and rather statuesque blonde who acquired her position following a competitive interview that included photos of at least a dozen other swimsuit models. Embarrassed that his restless rest had disturbed his co-workers, Fumblestix awkwardly climbed over the passenger in the aisle seat next to him so that he might retrieve his only piece of luggage, a well-worn cow's hide instrument case that protected his beloved lute. It's said he strummed and sang his merry songs through the remaining portion of the flight, a journey which the pilot's logged as a 2.9-hour mission but the passengers claim lasted twice as long.

At the Senator's regal estate, Fumblestix felt very much at home. While not quite up to the standards of Versailles, he took his time enjoying the fountains, statues, and impressive gardens. Occasionally, he'd partake in a meal with his co-workers, the half of whom adored him; the remainder wishing him either dead or severely maimed. The meetings were something he simply did not care for. Why people should wish to gather without song or dance was beyond his comprehension. Forbidden from performing for the group during such gatherings, Fumblestix instead elected to wander the grounds where he befriended a number of caretakers who, as one might expect, had never met anyone quite as fabulous as the great Fumblestix. He brought a smile to the face of the beekeeper who, it's said, had not smiled in seventeen years on account of a horrific allergic reaction to a bee sting which nearly took his life. The gardener, against his better judgment, permitted Fumblestix to juggle his garden shears, pitchfork, trowel, rake, and rusty shovel to the wonderment and delight of the gathered grounds staff. Fumblestix was fast making friends amongst the commoners but truly wanted to do good by his primary employer. Afterall, he had a reputation to uphold.

Considering a list of talking points for the campaign, which had been handed to all of the senator's campaign staff members, Fumblestix set about composing a tune which, if the electronic devils so permitted, he hoped to upload onto the campaign's various social media sites. Going green. Hmmm. All the talk of resource conservation, pollution reduction, sustainable energy sources and waste reduction confused our hero. He thought he understood the bit about protecting the planet's ecological balance...at least the balance part. Calling upon his new found friends to acquire a twelve-foot wooden board and a few buckets, Fumblestix crafted a simple balance beam for himself. Though a fool he may be, no one can ever question

Fumblestix's work ethic. He set right to work composing a lyrical ballad, one that he might sing while dancing about upon the balance beam.

It should not surprise you to know that what Fumblestix created was a true masterpiece. A virtuoso in his art, were history kind to bards and fools, his name would have been inscribed beside the likes of Michelangelo, Leonardo da Vinci, Shakespeare, Mozart, Beethoven and the like. I'd concern myself with the names I may have neglected to highlight but for the fact that the greatest of them all has wrongly been omitted by the custodians of merit and therefore has never been celebrated at concert halls, opera houses, or amidst the great art museums of the world. If there is justice in this land, we must pray Fumblestix, one day, earns his rightful place amongst the greats…if not the Gods themselves!

I must return to the ballad, hastily formulated by our hero yet as perfectly crafted as any work produced by the greatest authors of our time, though they spent the better parts of their lives developing and editing their treasures. The precise lyrics, I regret, are lost as a court order directed all existing copies be banned and all digital copies be purged from the internet. What I do recall is the lithely manner in which Fumblestix danced and spun, leapt, and tumbled upon that thin board of but six inches in width whilst he sung of his sovereign's "green touch." The beautiful and perfectly manicured green lawn of the senator's lovely estate, his magnificent mansion in the background, formed the perfect backdrop for the jester's acrobatic display and heartfelt song about a man who loved to jet around the globe on his private plane and host lavish parties at his various large homes, each of which boasted an impressive array of staff and attendants. Who wouldn't love a man like that? It was brilliant, simply brilliant. Green, indeed. The senator's competitors were, no doubt, left green with envy that they had not, themselves, acquired the magnificent services of the great Fumblestix. So pleased was Fumblestix with his masterful effort that he was not at all surprised when he was honored with a bus ticket back to New York while his fellow offsite attendees returned upon the senator's carbon footprint dragon.

As fortune would have it, Fumblestix found himself seated next to a drug rep from the Pinnacle Pharmaceuticals company. The two barely spoke for the first hour or so but, after impressing the gathering crowd with their exploits during a drinking contest while their bus was stopped for a scheduled rest stop in Savannah, Georgia, the two fools became fast friends. Barney Emberstock, for that was the drug rep's name, confided in Fumblestix that Pinnacle Pharmaceuticals had invested great sums of money to support the campaign of Senator Ronald Dumphrey. In turn, the senator had been a reliable advocate for the company's financial interests on Capitol Hill. While this "great sum," not named at the time, was a mere pittance in comparison to the money provided by the aforementioned anonymous donor, the matter was still of great interest to Fumblestix. He knew the senator's support for the drug industry would be a valuable talking point during his upcoming pre-election press conference, an event that his supervisor was willing to stop at no end to ensure Fumblestix did not preside over.

Back in New York, Fumblestix found his time was better served by performing at local hospitals, veterans' halls, assisted living centers, or wherever his talents might bring a smile to his audience. Public parks were one of his favorite haunts. The campaign staff did not seem to mind his absence, even as summer gave way to fall. Managing the damage caused by Fumblestix's press releases and social media blasts had become a full-time job for the team. For all that, he was not without his allies. Perhaps the most unlikely convert was Campaign Manager Chartreuse Richardson, herself. As if her hands were not already full trying to make sure news of Senator Dumphrey's extramarital affairs never became public, she became increasingly uneasy during the many late evening one-on-one end-of-day wrap up sessions she was requested to brief Senator Dumphrey at. The attending staff seemed to dwindle until it was just her and the senator. More than once, an uncomfortable moment was turned on its head with the perfectly timed entrance of the clever Fumblestix. Whether juggling clubs, strumming upon his lute, or tumbling like a dandelion seed in the wind, Chartreuse grew to appreciate the jester's remarkable ability to diffuse an uneasy situation in the senator's office. That Fumblestix; he brings joy where'er he travels.

Chartreuse was so indebted to our good Fumblestix, that she fed him tantalizing morsels of information regarding the dark underbelly of Ronald Dumphrey's rise to political prowess. Such is the stuff of epic tales, thought Fumblestix, as the day of his great press conference approached. Mob connections, payoffs, extramarital affairs, gambling debts, illegal campaign contributions, sexual harassment of staff members, lies and deceit—it was all a veritable treasure trove of source material from which to fashion a magnificent performance. It might well be his finest moment!

Despite his best efforts, Senator Dumphrey could not convince his Director of Communications and Media Spokesperson that his talents would be better put to use campaigning for the Senator in northern Minnesota during the week of the scheduled press conference. Fumblestix would have nothing to do with any task which took him away from singing the praises of his employer before a national audience. He had set his sights on creating what he hoped would be his lifetime masterpiece—a memorable performance that would finally be recognized by all good peoples of this earth—recorded and bound within illuminated texts and transcribed by monks for centuries to come, or perhaps until the end of time, itself. One by one, the senator's clever plans fell victim to circumstances and the day of the conference approached. Unbeknownst to Senator Dumphrey, the eccentric Fumblestix was really the only part of his campaign that the public had any interest in. The number of followers of Fumblestix's media posts went from thousands to millions to tens of millions. Not a subscriber to the philosophy that there is no such thing as bad press, the senator was not amused by the fact that all the focus on his campaign seemed to be shifting to the fool, Fumblestix. Something had to be done.

While Fumblestix normally preferred to dine alone, feasting upon mutton, French brie cheese, and rye bread beside the lake in the park, he was grateful to accept an offer to have lunch with his employer at his favorite Italian restaurant to celebrate the success of their campaign efforts. A man of simple tastes, Fumblestix reluctantly agreed to partake of the "Special of the Day" that the nervously twitching waiter seemed insistent he should try. With enough wine, he thought, he could wash anything down, even a dish that he could neither spell nor pronounce.

The outing was pleasant enough but it was not long after that Fumblestix began to regret his meal choice. Or perhaps it was the wine? Feeling a bit lightheaded, he was grateful when, that afternoon, Chartreuse offered to drive him back to his apartment. By the time they arrived, he could barely stand. Chartreuse helped him in the door, suggesting that he should call her if things got any worse. She soon realized that plan would not work. Inside the small studio apartment, she not only saw no phone but could not help but notice Fumblestix's lodging was completely devoid of furnishings. The only items within the apartment were a small straw mat that Fumblestix apparently used as his bed, the leather case protecting his precious fiddle, and a large burlap bag that contained various juggling pins, balls, and the fool's jester scepter. One might say Fumblestix lived a Spartan life but for the fact that no helmet, breast plate, or spear were to be found anywhere on the premises. Besides, Fumblestix was more of a lover than a fighter and would likely have run afoul of King Leonidas had the two had the privilege to meet. It's best they did not.

Curling into a fetal position on the floor, Fumblestix cried out "Alas, I fear I am undone!" He might well have been undone but for Chartreuse's quick action to call an ambulance to the apartment. Fumblestix had only been poisoned eight times previously and he was quite sure this was at least the third or fourth worst episode. Chartreuse was very concerned, seeing the moaning Fumblestix being loaded into the ambulance, his jingle bells causing a racket as he squirmed and flailed about. At the time, Chartreuse had no idea as to the source of her friend's ailment, assuming that perhaps it was a stress-related medical conditions such as an ulcer or, perhaps, a stroke.

Hearing the unfortunate news, Senator Dumphrey directed that Chartreuse should cover the press conference. She knew Fumblestix would be sorely disappointed. He had informed her that he had a big surprise in store for the television audience, a national audience that was expected to consist of several hundred million viewers...or that would have, had the conference not been scheduled against Monday Night Football, a shift that Dumphrey, himself, had directed only a few weeks before. The kind-hearted senator asked about the welfare of his Director of Communications and Media Spokesperson and Chartreuse informed him that he was in pretty bad shape but that the doctor thought he would, eventually, pull through okay. With a crocodile smile, Dumphrey expressed his relief. It was not but ten minutes later that he phoned one of his former "associates," Aldo Benefutto. By day, Aldo ran a successful wine and spirits distribution operation. He was also a problem solver. Ronald Dumphrey had a problem and that problem was filling up bed pans across town at the St. Francis Hospital. Aldo assured Senator Dumphrey that he had nothing to worry about. He said he'd stop by to bring the clown some flowers later that night.

Visiting hours were over but Aldo's partner, Joey "Two-Toes" Graziani, managed to sweet talk his way past the nurse's desk to drop in on his "old friend," Fumblestix. Joey had barely got the words "I've got a special delivery for you, clown" out of his mouth before he noticed the empty bed, the open window, and a hospital gown slung over the nearby chair. Fumblestix was gone!

Though feeling unwell, Fumblestix had always had an uncanny sense of danger—an attribute that served members of his profession particularly well. Only minutes before, our hero had pulled the IV needle out of his arm, climbed out the window with his jester's costume in his arms, and slid down the drainage pipe without a stitch of clothing on his back. Shrieks and laughter followed him as he ran desperately into the night. Up on the seventh floor, Joey phoned Aldo, who was waiting for him in a getaway car, and informed him of the situation. Aldo put his car in drive and raced through the parking lot, trying to spot the fleeing jester. Not thinking rationally, Fumblestix ran toward the valet parking garage where he discovered a recently deposited vehicle awaiting movement to its parking spot. The key fob was sitting on the dashboard and the engine was running. While the great Fumblestix had many achievements to his name, earning a driver's license was conspicuously absent from his resume. Still, fear drives a man to do many things. In this instance, fear drove a man to drive. It was not long before the lot attendants noticed the naked man sitting in the Cadillac. While calls to apprehend him echoed throughout the parking garage, there was not a single attendant who felt their minimum wage plus tips compensation was incentive enough to wrestle with a naked madman carjacking at Cadillac from the hospital's valet parking garage. Instead, they watched the vehicle lurch forward and awkwardly make its way to the garage exit where it disappeared into the night. Little did Fumblestix know that Aldo Benefutto was hot on his trail.

When his car's rear window shattered, Fumblestix assumed it was a normal hazard of driving a vehicle. When the third bullet fired grazed his naked shoulder, Fumblestix knew he was in trouble. He'd escaped flaming arrows, thrown hatchets, spears, and even a boomerang assault but, alas, Fumblestix was sorely unprepared to defend against bullets although he did, once, survive a close shave with an arquebus musket ball. Missing his first few shots, Aldo stepped on the accelerator and sought to maneuver his vehicle abeam Fumblestix's car which was now traveling at a wholly uncomfortable speed for the poor jester who was much more accustomed to a gentle trot about the pastures. Aldo lowered the passenger side window of his vehicle and shouted some obscenities into the night as he took aim at the helpless fleeing fool. On the other side of the highway, Fumblestix could see a sea of flashing red and blue lights approaching. Without giving the matter any serious thought, he swerved his car to the right where it departed the highway, crossed the center meridian, and continued forward against the oncoming traffic. Stunned and bewildered, Aldo could hardly have noticed that the tractor trailer immediately ahead of him had slowed substantially to look upon the incredible scene unfolding on the south-bound lanes. Aldo's car impacted the truck at a high rate of speed, shearing the top of his vehicle clean off...and his head with it. The situation was little better on the southbound side where poor Fumblestix screamed in terror as his vehicle struck a glancing blow against an oncoming white pickup truck that had failed to see his approach.

Once more, Fumblestix awoke in his hospital bed. Chartreuse was sitting next to him, a caring expression on her face. The car's airbag had saved his life but, little did he know, his vehicle had inadvertently steered into a fleeing criminal who had, only minutes before, shot a teenage cashier at a convenience store. The police had been in hot pursuit but Fumblestix was credited with the capture by a grateful police commissioner. The story was front page news and Chartreuse proudly lifted the paper so that Fumblestix might read the headline. Less conspicuously placed within the paper was a small story about the apprehension of a petty crook with mob ties who was arrested at St. Francis Hospital when his handgun set off a metal detector as he ran out the entry door during the night. Little mention was made of the car-on-truck accident that occurred in the northbound lanes of the highway. The police assumed it was another incident of distracted driving.

"You're a hero, Fumblestix!" exclaimed Chartreuse with real joy in her voice. As jester to the kings, Fumblestix neither sought nor needed additional praise for his actions. However, he graciously acknowledged the honor. Gathering his wits, he remembered that this evening was to be the big press conference. He didn't want to let Senator Dumphrey down. He knew how much he was counting on him to make a lasting impression at the event. Chartreuse would hear nothing of it. She insisted that he remain under a doctor's care. After much battling back and forth, Chartreuse learned a lesson that many before had come to understand—engaging in a battle of wits and intellect with the great

Fumblestix is truly a fool's errand. Exasperated, Chartreuse admitted defeat and assured Fumblestix that, if he could walk, she would offer the microphone to him that night.

The problem was, Fumblestix could not walk. Reluctantly, the doctor permitted the jester to suit up and the attending nurses wheeled him down the hallway and to the elevator. Chartreuse had to wait longer than expected for her vehicle as nearly the entire staff of the valet parking garage had handed in their resignations that morning. Eventually, she drove around to the patient pickup area where Fumblestix awaited, sitting in his wheelchair with the nurse holding his crutches. "That's some fella you got there, miss," said the nurse. Chartreuse had no idea how to respond to that. She simply sighed and nodded, adding "he sure is."

The big moment finally came. Chartreuse anxiously waited at the theater entrance. Members of the press had been filing in for the past hour. Few could remember a candidate's pre-election press conference ever creating this much buzz. Senator Dumphrey waited in the green room behind the stage. He would have an opportunity to say a few words after his spokesperson had provided the crowd-winning opening presentation. Based upon the report he had received from Chartreuse; he was fairly certain that she would be the one providing the comments. Although relieved, he was still concerned about the crowd's reaction. Much to his displeasure and astonishment, it seemed that the madman called Fumblestix had, somehow, endeared himself to the general public. As a career politician, Ronald Dumphrey knew how to leverage the likeability of celebrity supporters. This could work to his advantage. With five minutes remaining before the scheduled start, it was clear that Fumblestix would be a no show. Senator Dumphrey breathed a sigh of relief as Chartreuse gathered her notes and made her way across the stage and to the podium. Disgruntled mumbling emanating from the darkness beyond the orchestra pit betrayed the sentiment within the room. Chartreuse had barely begun her formal apology before the mumbling turned to angry heckling and the angry heckling to near mutiny. From the back of the theater, a large steel door slammed shut, startling all but one. That was, of course, none other than the great Fumblestix. Bravely, he stood there, his lute slung over his right shoulder and his burlap sack across his left. The audience grew silent as the incomparable Fumblestix slowly crutched his way down the dimly lit center aisle. As he passed each row, they stood, respectfully.

Had there but been a victory arch to march under, the scene would have been complete. It must have taken a full ten minutes for Fumblestix to finally ascend the stairs to the stage. The crowd erupted in applause when Chartreuse announced "Ladies and Gentlemen, I give you Fumblestix!" After walking over to help Fumblestix remove the lute and bag from his person, Chartreuse slowly backed away, out of the spotlight. The jocular gentleman gave his friend a wink and a smile whilst, backstage, aids were attending to Senator Dumphrey who had only moments before passed out and fallen to the floor.

Looking incredibly unstable, Fumblestix approached the podium. The audience gasped in horror as both crutches went out from under him and he fell forward. Oh, that Fumblestix! Has ever a man known how to work an audience as he? I doubt it very much. Just before striking the floor, Fumblestix tucked his chin in and executed a perfect somersault to the rousing cheers of the crowd. Two more rolls and he had reached his sack filled with tools of his trade. Five, six, seven clubs in the air at one time. It was fantastic! As if that weren't enough, he worked his crutches into the rotation, to the amazement of all. Not only were nine objects simultaneously encircling the master fool, but he hopped and skipped about amidst the whirlwind of gravity defying wood. Cartwheels and backflips, dancing and prancing and hopping and skipping, it's a sure thing that none present had ever seen his equal. A hush then fell over the crowd as Fumblestix reached for his lute. Many months in the making, the dulcet tones of his voice freed the treasured gift the great bard had been crafting especially for this occasion. The press later described it as a celebrity roast like no other they had ever witnessed. Others remarked that it was an unexpectedly stinging indictment set to music and sung by a master vocalist. All in rhyme, Fumblestix sang of payoffs and affairs, debts and debauchery, fraud and false promises all while seemingly praising the great craft and statesmanship of his employer. Were it not for his now famous mocking laughter, the casual observer might presume the fool really intended to support his employer's cause. A half dozen federal agencies took careful notes.

In a dimly lit hotel room, Ronald Dumphrey's underdog competitor was watching his television in disbelief. "Dallas, 28, Kansas City, 3! That's impossible!"

Much transpired in the days following the great press conference. A swarm of investigators descended upon Senator Dumphrey's campaign headquarters and it took months to sort out the mess. It hardly needs to be said that Ronald Dumphrey wisely elected to withdraw his bid for the highest office of his country the day following the press conference. Investigators, and paparazzi, searched desperately for the fool who had set the political world ablaze. His apartment was bare; not even a straw from his mattress to be found.

As democracy demands, the national election took place, that November, on its preordained date. The results were unlike anything anyone had ever seen before and completely apart from any notion held by the Founding Fathers. As might be expected, the hastily established replacement candidate for Ronald Dumphrey did not fare well. He received less than seven percent of the popular vote. Opposing party candidate, Brett Williamson, was beside himself when he learned that he had only earned eighteen percent of the vote. In an unprecedented election, nearly sixty-eight percent of those polled had elected to vote for a write-in candidate—their candidate of choice was, of course, none other than the great Fumblestix!

The debates as to whether or not he was born in this country and eligible to assume the Office of the President of the United States were overshadowed by a general concern for his welfare and consternation over his whereabouts. Had he finally been killed by some skilled assassin? Perhaps. Had he fled to the west, away from the madness of politics and the superficiality of a world of fakers and sycophants? That, too, is possible. I wish I could divulge this information to you. Perhaps, at some future date, I may. I regret if I leave you, somehow, dissatisfied but I believe, at the onset, I forewarned you that my recounting of this tale might prove to be totally inadequate and would likely earn your rightful disdain. I recall, distinctly, that I did. Belittled and ridiculed, mocked and underestimated, I feel safe in postulating that Fumblestix, wherever he might be, is now more content and at peace. Suffice it to say, once again, 'twas Fumblestix who had the last laugh.

The Story Behind the Story

The assignment generating this story was to create a 2,500-7,500-word humorous short story. I don't know that I can cite any particular inspiration for this story other than an interesting thought that crossed my mind as I was letting it wander, in the hope I might stumble upon a suitable character to build a world around. Part allegory, part fantasy, and part social commentary, this story found its protagonist in the unlikely guise of a timeless court jester—a fool, to be sure, but one who makes us question who, indeed, are the real fools within this tale. In a world teeming with corruption and avarice, a death-defying innocent, whose destiny seems driven by a greater good, stumbles upon the stage and wreaks havoc upon the social norms we have reluctantly become too accustomed to accepting. As a long-time lover of the old stories of chivalry, it seemed appropriate to tell this story in the voice of an admiring chronicler. Like many of the stories I have written, I had absolutely no idea where the storyline would take me, but I had more than a few chuckles along my journey to find out.

REDEMPTIVE WATERS

(Written May 20, 2022)
Published by Red Penguin Books in *"Tales of the Sea: A Short Story Anthology"* (September, 2022)

Set during the Napoleonic era, this story follows the journey of two men and a ship. Captain Grainger, much like his aging vessel, finds himself relegated to menial tasks during the twilight of his career. Having fallen out of favor with the Admiralty, his days of past glory seem like a distant memory. An unexpected rendezvous with destiny unites the sea captain with a disgraced royal and sets the stage for an unexpected adventure.

January 6, 1810. Thirty-eight degrees, twenty minutes, North latitude; sixty-five degrees, thirty-seven minutes, West longitude [north of Bermuda]. Making six knots on a North by Northeast heading. *HMS Phoebe*, having sustained significant damage during the Battle of Trafalgar, some five years before, was, much like her captain, struggling to prove her worth and avoid the inevitable demise that all but the most historic vessels ultimately succumb to. Captain Charles Grainger had shared the seas, off Cape Trafalgar, with the legendary Admiral Horatio Nelson as he defeated the combined French and Spanish fleet, thereby putting an end to Napoleon Bonaparte's ambitions for a cross-channel invasion and subjugation of England. Nelson lost his life in the engagement but saved his nation and altered the course of European history forever. Grainger, in command of the sleek thirty-six-gun frigate, *HMS Phoebe*, kept his life but lost an arm and a leg as he expertly maneuvered his warship amidst the raining cannonball fire of supremely more powerful first and second-rate vessels, boasting upward of ninety to a hundred guns, including the hull-smashing 36-pounder cannons on their lower decks. *Phoebe* had but one gun deck, versus the three gun-laden decks of the capital ships, but Grainger knew that speed and gun accuracy could help offset what the frigate, as a fifth-rate vessel, lacked in firepower. Trafalgar was the pinnacle of Captain Grainger's distinguished naval career. And now he was waiting to die.

It wasn't his unchecked alcoholism that proved to be Captain Grainger's downfall but instead his fervent critiques of the Crown's colonial aspirations and often hard-handed methods for growing the Empire. Were it not for his expert seamanship and tenuous familial connection to several notable nobles who were, themselves, on the decline, it's likely that Grainger might have lived out his days in some ramshackle alehouse in Ipswich. The Admiralty, as it seems, was not without pity. They granted Grainger command, once more, of *HMS Phoebe*, now sadly relegated to the role of training vessel. She was but a shell of her former self. Half the guns had been removed and transferred to newer vessels and the remaining cannon were desperately in need of refurbishment. The hull, encrusted with barnacles and plagued by failing timbers, was in even greater need of an overhaul. Still, for all that, the vessel served admirably as a training platform for the young crew. Some of the cadets had aspirations to pass for officers and, one day, become the next Lord Horatio Nelson while others were pleased just to remain free of the prisons and workhouses.

Now several months at sea, neither the ship's officers nor the crew had seen much of the elusive Captain Grainger except for those times when he appeared upon the quarterdeck to run his charges through grueling exercises in gunnery, sail adjustments, and the like. Grainger, for reasons he kept to himself, preferred to wander the deck at night. During the day, his first mate, Jonathan Randolph, and second mate, Andrew Carnehall, ran the young cadets through navigation exercises and basic seamanship drills in addition to exposing them to a varied curriculum which included everything from basic mathematics to literature and music. Captain Grainger believed that a well-rounded education set the young sailors on a truer course toward proficiency at sea and success in life. Ever loyal, it must be said that even Lieutenants Randolph and Carnehall considered their captain to be a bit of an enigma. He emanated a kind of burning intensity that encouraged others to keep their distance. Yet, on those occasions when he stood upon the quarterdeck in command of his vessel, there seemed something almost mythological about his presence. And then, much to his disgust, his vulnerability would be on full display as he fumbled with his telescope, struggling to extend it with his one hand while gripping the device in his armpit. His wooden peg leg, likewise, frustrated him in rough seas. Staggering about from one position to the next, on the pitching and rolling deck, Captain Grainger would pound his fist in rage against the masts, cursing his disability. To his crew, his physical challenges made him more rather than less human. The roar of cannon fire from past engagements had severely damaged his hearing and a cancer in his lungs was slowly eating away at what little time he had left to live. While a few of the youngest boys might mock their mysterious leader, a stern eye from the able-bodied seamen onboard would set them straight. Upon this wooden island, there was but one master and his orders were second only to God's.

Making their way north toward Halifax, *HMS Phoebe* found herself in rough seas which was not uncommon given the time of year. Captain Grainger ordered the crew to reduce sail and replace the existing sails with the more robust storm sails. Lieutenant Randolph looked on, nervously, as the young student crew carefully worked their way up the ice-covered ratlines and struggled to maintain a grip as they slid along the yardarms of the three-masted frigate. It was not a pretty operation and Captain Grainger returned to his cabin to smoke his pipe, filled with frustration yet understanding that his cadet crew was unlikely to match the well-trained synchronization of his veteran crew at Trafalgar. "What would Nelson say, had he witnessed the sloppy exchange of sails?" he thought. "An embarrassment to king and crown. Tomorrow we shall work to right this situation." He muttered to himself, in-between his coughing, as he pondered his fate as captain of a training ship.

Throughout the night, *HMS Phoebe* was tossed about upon the unforgiving sea, taking on more than her share of water as the aged timbers of the hull strained to maintain their integrity. The sailors from the previous watch wanted nothing more than to curl up in their hammocks though their clothes were yet soaked in the bone-chilling waters of the Atlantic. However, with water rising below decks, all able-bodied hands manned the bilge pumps to extract the unwanted seawater and return it to its rightful home. The sun had barely broken the horizon before the sailing master was hard at work trying to ascertain the *Phoebe's* position as the storm had clearly blown her well east of her planned track toward Nova Scotia. From high atop the crow's nest, a cry rang out—"Ship ahoy!"

"Where away?" shouted the first mate from below.

"Half a league off the starboard bow, Sir," came the reply.

Lieutenant Randolph had hardly trained his glass upon the speck on the horizon before the captain was on deck, straining his ageing eyes to make out the nature of the stationary vessel in the distance. Fumbling with his brass telescope, Captain Grainger studied the scene. The second mate, Andrew Carnehall, joined the captain and first mate on the quarterdeck whereupon Lieutenant Randolph passed his telescope so that he might try his eye at identifying the ship.

"What do you make of her, Andrew?" asked the first mate.

"She's only got a single mast but she's clearly flying the colors of England." Lieutenant Randolph motioned to Carnehall to return his telescope so that he might continue his assessment and Captain Grainger, who had already completely and accurately assessed the situation, listened to his officers with interest.

"She appears to be a brig, Captain," said Lieutenant Randolph to his superior. "Clearly, she must have lost a mast in the tempest. She looks in bad shape and it's a right fortunate twist of fate that the same storm should carry us into a position where we might render some assistance."

"Right you are, Mister Randolph. By the looks of her, perhaps the *Conquest* or *Resolute*. Where I will stand to differ is on your assessment of the damage."

"How do you mean, Captain?" replied Randolph.

"Examine the mast, Jonathan," began Captain Grainger. No storm could have sheared it off so elegantly. Look, too, upon her larboard side . . . so much as I can see from our vantage point, she appears to have taken some heavy fire. And, on the surviving mast and yardarms, both the mainsail and topsail are severely torn. You've seen storm damage before and these tears appear quite different, do they not?"

"Aye, Captain," replied Lieutenant Randolph as he focused his telescope to further inspect the details Captain Grainger was describing. "Chainshot, Sir?"

"Precisely, Jon! The storm sails were never set. These wounds preceded the storm. Whoever wreaked this terrible damage upon the brig clearly meant to send her below the waves. It's quite the miracle she's still afloat." Captain Grainger coughed fitfully, interrupting his fascinating lesson and alarming his officers who were greatly concerned for their captain's well-being. "Helmsman, set a course for the brig," shouted Captain Grainger after clearing his throat multiple times so that his voice might confidently project toward the sailor minding the ships wheel.

"Aye aye, Captain!" responded the helmsman.

"And, Mister Randolph," the captain whispered to his first mate, "I'll need you to push the crew in drill this afternoon. They've got to be much more proficient in the rigging and I need their gunnery to be quick and impeccably accurate."

"Aye, Captain," responded Randolph.

"And let's run through a couple 'beat to quarters' exercises."

"Aye, Captain, we'll make England proud."

"I'm sure we will," replied Captain Grainger, his stern demeanor concealing the sense of unease he felt about the situation. Years upon the sea had provided him with a unique ability to read the veiled machinations of fate. He buttoned his overcoat against the cold and admired the vaporous plume of his condensing breath as it met the cold winter air.

As the *Phoebe* approached the disabled brig, Captain Grainger's initial assessment was confirmed. She was the 12-gun brig, *HMS Conquest*. The distress signal flags were clearly visible along with several others that the crew did not immediately recognize.

"Signals to take effect after close of the day?" asked Randolph of his Captain. "I don't understand why they'd be flying that flag." The captain considered the question and managed to belay the knowing smile that had requested permission to come aboard.

"That's white over black, Jonathan. When flown upside down, the black bar over white bar means something quite different."

"I'm afraid I'm unfamiliar, Sir."

"Secret instruction, Mister Randolph. It signals 'secret instruction' and that we've stumbled upon what may be a unique opportunity to serve king and country."

"Interesting."

"Interesting, indeed. All the same, I'd prefer you keep this between us until we can better assess the situation," added Captain Grainger.

"Of course, Sir," replied Randolph. The captain nodded his acknowledgment.

Captain Grainger's wooden leg thudded rhythmically upon the wooden planks as he paced about the deck. When slowly closing to within a hundred yards, he signaled for his speaking trumpet and hailed *HMS Conquest*. "Ahoy there! This is Captain Charles Grainger of

443

His Majesty's Ship Phoebe. May I have permission from your captain to send a boat over to inquire as to your situation?" Captain Grainger had to wait for his reply but it came soon enough from a nervous voice.

"Ahoy there, Captain Grainger, this is Lieutenant Reginald Whitaker, acting captain of *HMS Conquest.* Our Captain, the honorable Sydney Cross, God rest his soul, was killed in action but two days ago. Your assistance could not be more welcome. We stand ready to receive your party, at your leisure, Sir."

Captain Grainger gathered several of his officers as a boat was prepared on the starboard side. Along with the first mate, surgeon and surgeon's mate, Grainger included the ship's carpenter, sailmaker, and quartermaster. The seamen carefully lowered the boat into the sea where the sailors took the oars to row the party over to the heavily damaged brig.

Captain Grainger and his party were cheerfully welcomed with rousing applause as they came on board. The blood from the recent battle still stained the deck. Immediately, the surgeon and surgeon's mate assisted in tending to the injured while the carpenter and sail-maker assessed the damage to the vessel, considering what options might be available to return her to a seaworthy status.

Captain Grainger and Lieutenant Randolph were welcomed into the captain's quarters by the still visibly shaken Lieutenant Whitaker. While enjoying a cup of tea, the lieutenant explained how they were heading north from South America when they were engaged by two Spanish frigates—the heavy frigate, *Indomable,* with 46 guns, and the 34-gun frigate *Fama.* While the brig was fast, the frigates appeared upwind in the early morning hours and thus had the "weather gage" advantage of being able to attack with the wind filling their sails. Before the *Conquest* could come about to flee its attackers, as its 12 guns were no match for the more powerful frigates, a broadside of chainshot shredded her sails. The second broadside from *Indomable* dismasted the brig's mizzen mast and put her in great jeopardy. The day appeared lost until a large fog bank provided an opportunity for escape. The injured *Conquest* limped northward until the storm finished the job that two Spanish frigates could not. Short of crew, leaking like a sieve, and with barely enough usable canvas to partially cover two sail positions, she was effectively stranded.

Captain Grainger carefully considered the story and, more so, the notion that two Spanish frigates might still be patrolling the area. With a student crew and only eighteen of the frigate's 36 guns onboard, he knew the odds would not be in his favor in an encounter with the Spanish ships although he was confident that *HMS Phoebe* would fare better than the brig. However, unlike *Conquest*, *HMS Phoebe* lacked the speed advantage over the newer Spanish frigates that might permit her to avoid the mismatched engagement altogether. After assessing the risk, he awaited the more intriguing story that the cryptic signal flags had betrayed. Following an uncomfortable silence, Lieutenant Whitaker got up and walked over to the captain's writing desk whereupon he removed an envelope from the drawer. Captain Grainger could see that the envelope had been sealed with wax, at one point. While the seal was broken, there was no mistaking that a royal crest had secured the contents. Whatever orders resided therein must have been issued from the highest level.

Whitaker handed the envelope to Captain Grainger with a warning that the contents must not be revealed to anyone save, perhaps, his first and second mates. Discretion was of the utmost importance. Captain Grainger carefully unfolded the letter and read the elegantly written note. Whitaker studied the captain's face, anxiously awaiting a reaction, be it a gasp, raised eyebrows, or perhaps even a rousing chorus of Rule Britannia. He was left unsatisfied. Devoid of any expression, Captain Grainger neatly folded the message, returning it to its envelope.

"When may I expect the party?" asked Captain Grainger, as he slid the envelope into his waistcoat.

"With your permission, Captain, I'd like to perform the transfer under the cover of darkness."

"That's acceptable. Now, if you'll excuse me, Lieutenant, I'd like to confer with my inspection team as to their estimates for supplies and labor needed to get you underway. You'll not be wanting to dance with those frigates a second time."

"No, Captain, definitely not. Thank you, Sir."

Meeting upon the deck to discuss the plan, Captain Grainger agreed to the transfer of timber and sail cloth. Despite the carpenter's initial objections, it was also agreed that the carpenter's mate would stay with *HMS Conquest* to aid in expediting repairs to the vessel. For all that, it would likely be several days before she could reliably make headway back to the safety of an English port. Captain Grainger's initial inclination was to provide escort to the damaged brig but his new orders were very specific—he was to make all haste on a return voyage to Portsmouth, England.

Only a few deckhands witnessed the unusual arrival of a small boat in the darkness of the moonless night. Under the lamplight, Lieutenant Whitaker and several sailors expeditiously escorted what appeared to be a well-dressed woman, garbed in a long, hooded cape, aft to the captain's quarters. Shortly thereafter, following a firm handshake and a "good luck and God speed," Whitaker and crew were away and returning to the *Conquest*.

While word spread, the next day, of the strange arrival, the crew of the *Phoebe* knew better than to be caught spreading rumors below deck. That which their captain cared for them to know would, in due course, be revealed and that which he did not share was, quite simply, not worth the knowing. Besides, when the intense sailing and gunnery drills began the next day, there was little time or interest in exchanging scuttlebutt. Empty barrels were cast adrift and guns were loaded, aimed, fired, and re-loaded. Critiqued and re-evaluated, time and time again, the crew honed their skills under the watchful eyes of the observing officers. Speed was critical. Neither Randolph nor Carnehall would settle for any less than three broadsides every five minutes because they knew their captain expected not only that but hair-splitting accuracy as well. It wasn't long before the floating barrels were exploding into shards of wood meanwhile, encouraged by an equally ferocious bosun, the sailors raced about high above the deck with the dexterity of monkeys within a tree. They expertly navigated the complex web of ropes, cables, and pulleys that formed the running rigging. While the cannons roared below, the rigging crew practiced raising and lowering the various sails and precisely trimming the stretched canvas like one might tune a fine violin. Each small breath of air they extracted from the breezes could mean the difference between life and death in battle. Perfection was their goal and, with trust in their leadership, all labored to the point of exhaustion to exceed their captain's expectations.

While he'd have much preferred to remain on deck to observe the training, Captain Grainger had matters to attend to in his cabin. He had full faith in his leadership team and in his crew's desire to prove their worth as more than mere cadets and children. Grainger opened the door to his cabin to find a groggy prince, roused prematurely from his slumber by the incessant firing of cannons below deck. He wiped the sleep from his eyes and turned to his host. "I swear, if I am asked to wear women's clothing one more time to conceal my identity, I will slit my own throat and order the knife be sent to my father."

"Begging your pardon, your highness," said Captain Grainger, these days somewhat out of practice in the art of hobnobbing with members of the nobility and royal personages, "I'm sure you cannot fault those who were seeking to protect you for they are, at the same time, protecting England herself."

"And I suppose all this yelling and screaming and ear-splitting cannon roaring is meant for my protection, as well?" replied the indignant prince.

It must be said that the first meeting of Prince Rudolph and Captain Grainger was not particularly a cordial one. The prince's foppish reputation preceded him and Grainger was only too aware that Prince Rudolph had been removed from naval service at the request of the Admiralty following alleged amorous escapades with both of an admiral's daughters and, if the rumors were true, their mother, as well. While he had distinguished himself, as it seems, in the art of womanizing, the prince remained a thorn in the side of the royal family. With several older brothers, Rudolph was a little too confident that the distant responsibilities of the crown were unlikely to spoil his rather loose and carefree life of roguery. As such, his primary focus in life became a hedonistic quest for Heaven on Earth. Periodically assigned tasks to demonstrate his noble character, the hapless young man had found countless ways to add upon the disappointment his parents suffered on his account. Prince Rudolph's current mission was no exception. Unconcerned with keeping clandestine affairs of the crown hidden, Rudolph freely described to Captain Grainger how his services had been called upon to secretly meet with rebellion leaders in South America where he might pledge resources and support for their efforts to declare independence from Spain. Somewhere along his journey, his mission was betrayed and Spanish loyalists began the hot pursuit of the fleeing prince. Disguised and transferred from one handler to the next, the prince made his way to Cartagena where he was quietly transferred from a fishing vessel to the awaiting brig, *HMS Conquest*. What he was not aware of was that the Spanish South American fleet had been notified and were scouring the seas for the *Conquest*, a ship whose mission was compromised by a spy within the network. With reliable intelligence, two swift Spanish frigates had been closing the gap for several weeks and had nearly taken their prize. As he told the story of his failed mission, Captain Grainger could see the pain in the prince's eyes. Coming from a long line of respected monarchs, Prince Rudolph had little to show for his time on Earth but for a litany of scandals and an existence of gluttony, intemperance and sloth. For all that, Grainger was not unimpressed with the prince's bold liaisons with rebellion leaders in South America. Sometimes, he thought, a man's worth cannot be fully measured until one allows him to spread his wings and to take that first leap from the fledgling nest into the clear blue sky. While many aspects of the prince's life seemed particularly distasteful to the career seaman, Grainger could not help but pity the young prince, his talents and intellect wasted in the pursuit of pleasure. For all that, the grizzled captain did not intend to play wet nurse to his twenty-seven-year-old passenger, no matter what his lineage.

Days passed and while *HMS Conquest* successfully limped back to Kingston, Jamaica, Grainger worked *HMS Phoebe* along a direct course for Land's End, at the southwestern tip of the English coast, whereupon he would follow the coast to Portsmouth and disembark the prince to the custody of royal guards who would escort the weary traveler back to London.

The officers on the crew successfully stymied speculation about their mysterious guest although the rumors of the captain taking on a mistress to comfort him during his lonely nights were peculiarly amusing to those who knew their captain well enough to know that he typically chose to spend those lonely nights wandering about upon the deck. The unmistakable "clump, clump, clump" of his wooden leg upon the deck told the tale of a man who was more in need of the clean sea air to sustain him than he was of sleep, or mistresses for that matter. His cough worsening by the day, Captain Grainger knew his days were numbered and each moment looking out upon the rolling deep was an invaluable treasure he took not for granted. In the darkness of the night, or beneath the pale moon, his scarred and tormented face was concealed in shadow. Curious eyes, wishing to inspect the battle damage, struggled to avoid the urge to gaze upon their captain's wooden peg leg or at the empty sleeve neatly pinned upon his uniform, across his chest. On deck, his coughs were lost to the wind and muffled by the flapping canvas of the sails, the creaking of the timbers, and the gentle serenade of the sea. In the darkness of the night, no one would spot a tear, infrequent as they may have been.

The sun broke the horizon and greeted a resolute and confident captain. All traces of the frailty that the night had elicited were gone like the morning dew as the new day dawned. It would be a good hour before anyone noticed the sails coming out of the east, hidden before the brilliance of the morning sun.

"*Indomable* and *Fama*, Sir?" asked the stalwart first mate.

Straining to better define the contacts amidst the sparkling waters of the early morning sea, Captain Grainger simply replied, "Mister Randolph, direct the crew to beat to quarters." And just like that, the ship came to life with men running this way and that, stowing hammocks, preparing the gun deck, and securing all unnecessary items which might become deadly projectiles as the cannon fire wreaked its terrible vengeance. Cadets mustered at their appointed combat stations while the regular crew encouraged them to take heart and be strong.

"Sir, shall we prepare the cannons with round shot, chain, or grapeshot?" asked Lieutenant Carnehall, who had just ascended the ladder from the gun deck. Roundshot could wreak devasting damage upon the hull of an enemy vessel while chainshot was most often used to shred the vulnerable sails or cut the rigging to pieces. When fired, the halves of the ball would separate, a chain extending between the two fragments as it spun toward its target. While typically used against the sails, rigging, or masts of an enemy vessel, if fired across a deck, the spinning chainshot rounds could inflict a terrible toll on the adversary's topside crew, literally cutting sailors and marines in half. Of course, the preferred anti-personnel munition was grapeshot. Grapeshot bags, when fired, dispersed a lethal spray of smaller diameter iron balls. Unfortunately, to get within the reduced range of the grapeshot rounds, Captain Grainger knew he'd have to take *Phoebe* through several full broadsides from the long guns of the more heavily armed *Indomable* and *Fama*. *Phoebe* would likely be battered into submission before she ever closed the distance. Also, as a training vessel with no contingent of royal marines onboard, Captain Grainger knew he would not fare well in a boarding action and thus he had no desire to get too close to either of the enemy frigates, ships no doubt teaming with musket-armed fighters and likely snipers in the tops. It was a French sniper who had taken out Admiral Nelson at the Battle of Trafalgar. Grainger saw his options rapidly falling away.

"Mister Carnehall, move all the guns but for one 18-pounder to the larboard [port] side. Load the guns with round shot, please."

"Sir, all the guns to the larboard side?" asked the second mate, completely bewildered by the unusual request. "Won't she sail awkward in that configuration? We're likely to lose a few knots off our speed."

"To the larboard, Mister Carnehall," replied the captain. The second mate knew only too well that further questioning would not be looked upon kindly and might, on a bad day, see him clapped in irons and escorted below.

Approaching from behind, Lieutenant Randolph handed the captain his telescope. "They're on to us, Sir. We've got the weather gage but we haven't the firepower to drive our point home, I fear."

"Never fear, Jonathan. Fear is an emotion the Admiralty does not sanction and this captain will not tolerate."

"Aye, Captain. 'Never mind maneuvers, always go at them.' Isn't that what Nelson said?"

"Indeed. We can profit from his example—his tactical genius, his courage, and his love of country," replied a stoic Captain Grainger.

With the guns repositioned, Captain Grainger directed his helmsman to set a northerly course. The Spanish frigates, still approaching from the east, turned north, as well, to parallel *Phoebe's* track. Grainger looked over toward his bosun, one of the most seasoned men on the vessel, and, without the question even having to be asked, the bosun shouted out "Making eight knots, down from ten, Captain." As anticipated, *Phoebe's* speed had fallen off with the shifting of the guns to one side. No amount of sail trim could overcome the dramatic shift in the ship's center of gravity. While Captain Grainger fully understood the risk he was taking, the notion of presenting an equal broadside to at least one of the frigates on the larboard side seemed a better option than the two-to-one disadvantage he'd face trying to fight both sides, and then only if he could somehow shake one of the two frigates. The quiet upon the deck was very unsettling to the crew. Running abeam the Spanish frigates, they could tell the Spaniards were slowly edging closer though they lost progress each time they had to tack into the wind to close the lateral distance.

Before the frigates could get within firing range, Captain Grainger directed his crew to unfurl all the sails. Mainsails, topsails, topgallants, royals, let them all fly!" shouted the captain. With expert precision, sails spread out from every yardarm as cadets and able-bodied seamen flew along the intricate highways of rope, high above the pitching deck. *HMS Phoebe* surged ahead, her masts and lines groaning at the strain—it was all a beautiful chorus to the seasoned ears of the ship's master.

Slow to adjust sails, the Spanish frigates began to fall back. "Twelve knots, Captain," shouted the bosun. Twelve was good…but not good enough. The Spanish heavy frigate, *Indomable*, could not keep pace and grew smaller and smaller in the glasses trained on her from the deck of the *Phoebe*. *Fama*, however, a newer and swifter ship, continued to gain ground, unimpressed by *Phoebe's* spread of sail and expert handling.

"*Indomable's* dropping away, Captain," announced Lieutenant Randolph. "*Fama* is going to leave her and have a go at us by herself."

"And that shall be her undoing," muttered Captain Grainger under his breath.

Both ships continued their race northward, each expertly tacking to try to maximize the advantage of the wind. The sun was setting and *Fama* remained just outside of cannon range…but she was closing the distance, earning each yard of progress with expert seamanship. The officers onboard the *Phoebe* knew what the crew did not; *Fama*, with a trimmer hull and more modern construction, was simply a faster ship and no amount of seamanship was going to negate the end result of the mathematics equation that was playing out before them. An inevitable confrontation with a more powerful vessel was close at hand.

As the sun set, members of the crew each postulated their own theory regarding the captain's plans. Most figured he'd douse the lantern lights and make an unpredictable course change in the hope of losing their pursuer in the darkness. Others thought that, perhaps, he'd try to sneak up on the *Fama* on this moonless night and find a way to disable her. Then there were those excitable youths who dreamed of their captain shouting valiant war cries as he steered directly for the Spanish frigate, confident that God would see to his victory over the Spanish miscreants. They were all wrong. Yet, in some ways, they were all right.

In the dark of the night, *Fama* had given up northerly progress to tack into the wind and earn herself a better position for the next day's fight, upwind from the slower *Phoebe*. Most onboard were not happy to see the Spanish frigate off their larboard stern at sunrise even though she still lagged several miles behind.

The captain went below to his quarters to see if Prince Rudolph would care to join him for breakfast. They were treated to a magnificent meal. Captain Grainger hardly felt it was worth saving the special fare for another day as there remained a distinct possibility that he might not live to see it. Toward the end of the meal, he asked that his steward bring forward his finest bottle of wine. Captain Grainger poured a glass for himself and for the prince. Raising his glass, he proposed a toast...but not to England, or the king, not to God or the angels above, not even to the brave men of the *Phoebe* for whom he held responsibility, each of their lives dependent upon his judgment and decisions. "To redemption!" he exclaimed. Prince Rudolph, taken aback but noticeably moved, clinked his glass against Captain Grainger's.

"To redemption."

With the meal complete, Captain Grainger handed the bottle with its remaining wine to his steward and asked that he share it with the crew when the victory had been won. His steward, fanatically loyal to his captain, acknowledged without the slightest pause or indication of doubt.

Back upon deck, *Fama* was drawing noticeably closer and was beginning to fire ranging shots from its brass bow chaser guns. The balls were splashing short of *Phoebe's* stern but Captain Grainger knew that, within the hour, his ship would be vulnerable to his foe's long guns.

Captain Grainger made his rounds throughout the ship, encouraging his men and shaking each hand, individually. He felt incredibly proud of the progress his young crew had made and he felt honored to serve beside each and every one. He made one last stop in his cabin to advise the prince on the safest place to shelter during what was sure to be a brutal battle. The prince was gone. The captain's steward, stowing the breakfast table, and especially the glassware, said that the prince had left the cabin with a determined look on his face, his fine rapier seated in the scabbard affixed to his sword belt.

"Well, at least we'll have one for the boarding party," joked Captain Grainger, who was inwardly inspired by the prince's desire to contribute to what might well be a losing battle.

"Two, Sir," replied the steward, holding up one of the captain's elegant dinner knives.

"That's the spirit, Brickney! Rule Britannia!"

Standing amidst his officers in quiet repose, Captain Grainger seemed to be waiting for some indeterminate point in time or space that only he could identify. One of *Fama's* bow chaser rounds thudded against *Phoebe's* stern but did little apparent damage. It wasn't the 12-pounder chase guns that concerned the captain. Judging the distances and relative speeds of the two vessels, Captain Grainger made his move.

"Helmsman, hard a larboard!" he shouted. The ship rapidly turned toward the left, the added weight of the guns on the larboard side made for an even nimbler maneuver in that direction.

Several of the more seasoned crew members explained to the cadets that the captain was maneuvering to "Cross the T." In doing so, placing the ships perpendicular to each other, the ship with its broadside facing the bow or stern of its adversary had a daunting advantage with respect to how much firepower it could bring to bear. Beyond that, a broadside of grapeshot along the entire length of the adversary's deck could potentially decimate a crew. Roundshot was loaded as it was the enemy's ship, more than its crew, that Captain Grainger hoped to cripple.

"Mister Randolph, takeover topside. I'm going below to the gun deck," said the captain.

"Aye aye, Captain. Take this fight too those bastards, Sir!"

Grainger hurried toward the ladder, stumbling as he went and frustrated that he could no longer race between fighting positions as he had during his youth. He all but fell to the deck below but refused help from a gunner's mate.

The *Fama*, fully expecting *Phoebe* to strike her colors and surrender, was completely caught off guard when the English frigate rapidly changed course and was about to bring the full weight of her broadside against her nearly undefended bow. With the ships momentum carrying it rapidly into firing range, there was little *Fama* could do beyond bracing for the barrage. Although she only had 17 guns trained at the *Fama*, the now proficient crew of the *Phoebe*, fighting like true veterans, fired them with devasting effect, several rounds penetrating the hull below the waterline so that the Spanish frigate began to rapidly take on water. As if posing for his statue, Prince Rudolph waved his sword in the air, encouraging the gun crews to reload as the truth about his identity spread like wildfire throughout the ship. "It's the Prince! The prince is fighting alongside us, boys! Rally for Prince Rudolph and for Captain Grainger!"

Despite their best efforts, the crew was unable to get off another broadside before both vessels' momentum carried them along their paths, now putting *Phoebe's* exposed stern at risk as *Fama* slipped behind her. Looking to maximize damage to the English ship's crew, *Fama* had loaded all her cannons with grapeshot and intended to rake her adversary's deck with the deadly spray of small iron balls. Topside, Lieutenant Randolph directed all deck hands to lay flat, anticipating the shotgun-like spray from the grapeshot rounds. Fortunately for the crew of *HMS Phoebe*, the absence of half her guns contributed to her sitting high in the water. Rather than sweeping across the deck, killing sailors, the grapeshot rounds largely bounced off the stern, the primary casualty being the captain's dinnerware which had been secured in the stern gallery.

As *Fama* passed beyond the stern of the *Phoebe*, Captain Grainger shouted out to relay a message to the helmsman to turn hard to starboard so that the single 18-pounder cannon on that side might come to bare upon the stern of the *Fama* before she could turn to fire another full broadside against the *Phoebe*. The captain peered anxiously through the gunport. With the weight of all the guns on the larboard side, *HMS Phoebe* was not turning as efficiently to starboard. This was a perilous and pivotal moment in the engagement. On deck, Lieutenant Randolph was ordering a reduction in sail, knowing full well that any improvement in turn radius might mean the difference between life and death. On the gundeck, Grainger moved behind the cannon and stared down the sights. His one chance to gain the upper hand in the engagement, he thought, was to strike and disable the *Fama's* rudder, thus rendering her unsteerable. The bow of the *Fama* came into view and he could tell they were, likewise, turning hard to attempt to parallel *Phoebe's* heading. While the odds were not in *Phoebe's* favor, Captain Grainger felt that he, and he alone, should carry the responsibility for firing the win-or-lose round that was packed into the gun. Before he could realize his destiny, two shots from the *Fama's* stern chaser cannons, aimed to disable the single gun protruding from *Phoebe's* starboard gundeck, penetrated the hull and sent a deadly spray of splintered wood flying through the tight confines of the deck. Amidst the dust and debris, confusion reigned. Prince Rudolph, knocked off his feet, could see the captain laying on his back, his remaining leg shattered and bleeding profusely. A medical officer ran over to attend Captain Grainger but he spit and cursed and crawled back toward the cannon, falling forward, flat on his chest, several times. Despite his pain, Grainger would not be dissuaded from his return to the cannon. As he pulled himself up, he felt a hand upon his shoulder. Looking back, he saw the determined face of Prince Rudolph.

"Captain Grainger, if you please," said the prince, "I was a fairly accomplished gunner during my time in the Royal Navy if not a particularly notable officer. I beg you afford me the opportunity for this one parting shot, a chance at redemption, if you will, as I'm sure neither God nor king shall afford me another opportunity such as this should I live to be a hundred."

Time was of the essence and it would be wrong to say that Captain Grainger considered the request as there was no time left for calculations and assessments. Instinctively, he slid off to the side of the cannon and permitted the prince to sight in the gun, raising its elevation ever so slightly to account for the distance to the target. Taking the wind speed into account, and a fraction of a second before *Fama's* rudder was aligned with the axis of the gun barrel, Prince Rudolph adeptly slid to the right side of the cannon to be clear of the 5,000-pound weapon's recoil, and then ignited the powder in the touch hole with a slow match he had been holding. With a thunderous roar, the cannon launched its 18-pound ball of iron at 1,700 feet per second, enveloping the area in a giant cloud of smoke. From the gundeck, nothing was visible initially. A rousing cheer from topside was the confirmation that the crew's prayers had been answered. As winds cleared the smoke from the area, Grainger and Prince Rudolph both peered out the gun port to see the *Fama*, now rudderless, sailing away. Instinctively, Lieutenant Randolph turned the *Phoebe* away from the treat. When word came from below that the captain was seriously injured, he passed control of the vessel over to the second mate, Lieutenant Carnehall, and slide down the ladder to the gundeck to attend to his captain. Below deck, Lieutenant Randolph was startled to see Captain Grainger, propped up against the side of the cannon, sitting in a pool of his own blood. More surprising still, the captain was laughing—something Jonathan Randolph had convinced himself that Captain Grainger was physically incapable of doing. He could not help but laugh, too, as he knelt to assess the damage to Captain Grainger's leg. Moments later, the ships surgeon arrived at the scene. The grave expression on his face told the first mate more than any voiced medical opinion could have. Randolph grasped Captain Grainger's hand and held it tightly. "Doctor Winston will have you patched up and sea worthy in no time, Captain," said the first mate, a comforting smile on his face.

"You are, by far, the worst liar I have ever met, Jonathan," chided

Captain Grainger, with true affection in his voice. "Bring *Phoebe* home and pray we might both see England's green coast together one last time."

Prince Rudolph, still high from the adrenalin rush of the engagement, turned to Captain Grainger as the surgeon supervised his transfer to a canvas stretcher to be taken to the surgeon's operating table. "But Captain, now that we've disabled those Spanish villains, aren't we going to finish them off?"

"Those aren't our orders, your highness. Had we a larger crew, we might capture her and bring her back home for England's glory. Alas, we have barely enough young lads onboard to keep *Phoebe* sailing straight and true. Besides, the Spanish captain handled his ship magnificently and with honor. Poseidon himself might revolt against us should we pound the Spanish ship until it sunk to the depths with all hands lost. No, that simply wouldn't do." Captain Grainger paused to cough several times, the nature of his coughing only serving to further alarm the attending doctor. "The Spanish captain shall live to sail another day but if he's wise, he'll steer well clear of any Royal Navy ships in the years to come."

"It's a noble and charitable judgment you levy, to be sure, Captain Grainger," said the prince. I'd swear to it that this Spanish rascal captain has never before nor will ever again meet the likes of you--a commander and a seaman of inestimable ingenuity and skill." Not to be won over by any manner of praise, and humble to the core, the captain simply nodded, graciously. Prince Rudolph stepped back to allow the sailors carrying the stretcher to move past.

Lieutenant Randolph found the opportunity to improve upon his lying skills as *HMS Phoebe* steadily made progress toward the coast of England. He assured the young crew that their captain was well and enjoying some much-needed rest along with a respectable quantity of fine French wine which he had previously convinced a French merchant vessel to part with. The more seasoned crewmembers were not so easily deceived as they could read an officer's lies much as a hawk reads a hare. All felt somewhat relieved when, shortly after the welcomed cry of "Land Ho!" rang out, they saw Captain Grainger, assisted by Prince Rudolph, make an appearance on deck to enjoy the view their beloved English coastline. A few of the younger boys gasped, seeing that the lower half of what was previously Captain Grainger's good leg was now conspicuously absent. The surgeon had to amputate the limb to save the captain's life. He now steadied himself with two crutches aided, in no small part, by the prince who helped ensure the motion of the pitching ship would not topple the heroic naval hero.

In due course, following the southern coastline of England and now in familiar waters, *HMS Phoebe* arrived at her appointed destination, Portsmouth. The previous evening, all the officers joined the captain and Prince Rudolph for a final dinner, the likes of which would have made the king, himself, envious.

In port, appropriate liaisons were made and arrangements finalized for the royal escorts to receive Prince Rudolph for his return journey, by carriage, to London. Before permitting his guest to disembark, Captain Grainger asked Prince Rudolph if he might be willing to deliver a personal letter to the king, on his behalf. Ever-grateful, the prince willingly conceded to deliver the sealed missive. With the warmest of farewells, the royal and the sailor parted ways. Despite the prince's pleas, Captain Grainger graciously declined the offer to accompany Prince Rudolph to London where he might then be treated by the best physicians in all of England. Grainger said he had some pressing matters to attend to that simply could not wait. He spoke the truth.

In London, Prince Rudolph described the great gallantry of Captain Grainger and crew and he was hardly through his story before the gathered nobles were pledging their wealth to erect a marble statue to honor the great man. All of Captain Grainger's past transgressions, perceived or actual, were quickly forgotten and completely forgiven. In the telling of this great saga, Prince Rudolph humbly understated his own actions. The true nature of his contribution was revealed upon the opening of the sealed letter Captain Grainger had entrusted to the prince's care. The king beamed with pride. Rudolph's siblings, as many who were there to hear the king's courtier read the letter aloud, were astonished to learn of the gallant actions of their much-maligned brother. None would look upon the prince in the same way again and the prestige the young prince earned further inspired him to improve upon his character and to live with honor and integrity.

It is with honor and integrity that Captain Jonathan Grainger had lived his life. He regained his status amidst the great sailors in British history and naval students, for generations to come, would learn of his great skill upon the sea in defense of their nation. A large statue was, in fact, placed within a central square to commemorate his deeds. While members of the nobility suggested that his body might, one day, be entombed beside that of Horatio Viscount Nelson, beneath the dome of St. Paul's Cathedral, the truth of the matter is that the good captain had other plans. Prince Rudolph had not yet completed his return to London before Captain Grainger, having successfully completed his duty, rendered his final salute to the men of *HMS Phoebe* before returning to his cabin to peacefully plot his course into the uncharted waters of the Great Beyond. *HMS Phoebe* made her way along the coast, on a westerly heading, as the seas began to churn, a great storm approaching.

Off the coast of Falmouth, *HMS Phoebe* dropped anchor. "You know, Andrew," said a pensive Jonathan Randolph, "this is where Captain Grainger first learned to sail. He was born just over there, beyond that cluster of lighted cottages. He loved the sea beyond measure and, like with so many of us, he could not deny its calling."

"He served England well, Sir, as well as any man could."

"As well as most, to be sure, Andrew. Are you ready then?"

"Aye, Captain," replied Lieutenant Carnehall.

The first mate, Lieutenant Andrew Carnehall, signaled to the gathered sailors who then carefully slid the sailcloth-encased body of their former captain over the side of the ship. Thunder crashed above and lightning flashed in the sky as the cannon balls, sewn into the sailcloth of the burial covering, carried the body beneath the waves.

"Me thinks the angels are greeting our beloved captain with a fine broadside salute," said a tearful Captain Randolph. Lieutenant Carnehall, listening to the thunder roaring above, could not help but agree.

"That they are, Sir. That they are."

The Story Behind the Story

Red Penguin books created a wide aperture for its next anthology, "Tales of the Sea." As with the other recent short story anthologies, a 2,500-7,500-word limit was placed upon submissions so that more authors might have the opportunity to be included. The stories simply had to take place upon the open ocean. I was really excited about this opportunity as I have always loved the ocean and some of my favorite works of literature were sea tales. I felt fairly confident that I could fall back upon my knowledge of the subject area while simultaneously getting my creative juices flowing to craft a story that could be a strong contender for the upcoming book. Thankfully, unlike my unfortunate stumbling with an earlier fantasy short story, a genre I should have been easily able to handle, I quickly and confidently got to work on my sea tale. I could virtually hear the creaking wooden boards and feel the pitch and roll of the deck as I wrote. Beyond just being a story about a ship and water, I really wanted to include a human element. One theme that I've always loved, in literature and in film, is the notion of redemption. I believe such redemption, no matter the scale, is something we all hope for in our lives. Whatever our short fallings may have been, it's human nature to wish for a second chance to prove ourselves—not so much in the eyes of others, although this can be a motivator, but, more so, within our own mind. There are few better feelings than "getting back on that horse" after a great fall and proving our metal. This story is about two men, a ship, and an opportunity to put the human spirit on display in a heroic manner. It's about redemption.

FRIEND ZONED...YET AGAIN

(Written July 29, 2022)
Published by Red Penguin Books in *"Dear You—Poems Through the Heart"*
(March, 2023)

This poem considers the difficult transition our heart
endures as we resign ourselves to the fact that the
romance we hoped for will never come to pass and so
we must nobly navigate the emotional tempest of
transitioning a romantic love into the no less
important love of a loyal friend.

Relegated
I hoped this time there might be more
But I find myself, again, a friend
As I have too many times before

I should have pumped the brakes
I should have gathered in the reins
But I let a burning passion get the better of me
And now I'm suffering the pains

The pains of hopeless longings
The pains of dreams that die
The pains of self-doubt and insecurities
The pains that make me cry

I love friendships more than most
When all is said and done
But just this once, I hoped and prayed
That I had finally found the one

The one to help complete me
And with whom I might share my life
The one I might kneel down before
And ask to be my wife

Friend Zoned...Yet Again

I wanted her so badly
She seemed perfect in every way
I felt true affection emanating
From all she'd do and say

So why now must I rationalize
About how lucky I am to have a friend
Whilst my shattered ego staggers
My heart mourns a lifeless end

An end to yet another lovely dream
A romantic epic left unfulfilled
A plan for a life together
Before it's birth, ignobly killed

I can't blame her, no never!
Her affection and kindness were pure and true
Banish the thought that she should have to act with malice
To prove that we were through

It's all on me, I take the blame
For building a fantasy of thin air
I must now collect the ashes
Transferred to an urn with care

Sealed tightly and placed upon the mantle
Where others rest beside
A grim reminder for the future
Of those many times I tried

Of agonies I endured and tears I shed
The painful time it took to mend
All so that I might shake a hand rather than kiss the lips
Of yet another friend

Don't get me wrong...I'm grateful
Friendship has great value, it is true
And I'll not betray the sacred trust of friendship
As true friends must swear to do

461

Flapper and the Captain

I just know there'll be those days
When an errant tear streams down my cheek
My strong will shall fortify the friendship
Though my heart occasionally grows weak

I'll not abandon my dear friend
For a failure that's my own
I'll shore up the unsure timbers
Though they creak and groan

But things will never be quite right
Where heart and mind come to meet
I've passed below the archway to the Friend Zone
Engraved above, the words "You're So Sweet"

Maybe I was sweet
And maybe I was kind
But it still stings like failure
And so, I set out once more to find

That woman of my dreams
Whose company I treasure
And I hope, nay, pray this time
She'll love me in equal measure

The Story Behind the Story

Coming out of the COVID-19 Pandemic, people were getting busy and returning to their former activities, and Red Penguin Books was slowing the pace of published anthologies. While not my last work published (these came once the previously tasked travel anthologies were finally compiled), "Friend Zoned" was my last submitted work into the Red Penguin Collection series of anthologies. While the given deadline for submission was August 1, 2022, this poetry anthology wasn't actually published until the following March. The task was to create love-centric poems that focused on the more challenging side of modern romance to include such things as "breakup poems," poems of yearning, or poems "that just may happen to be a little rougher *around the edges." So, while not exactly a topic that I was thrilled to be writing about, recent experiences had given me some credible knowledge regarding this area. My heart was no stranger to getting ahead of the reality of a relationship. I have envisioned a beautiful future with someone who, ultimately, simply wanted to be friends. They liked me, we got along well, but the "chemistry" wasn't there and the attraction proved to be a one-way street. This poem was a short attempt to express the sometimes-uncomfortable ambiguity and grief that comes as a hoped-for romantic connection transition into something else. Friendships are beautiful and it seems awful to think that one should ever walk away from a true friendship for any reason. With that said, it can still be very difficult to take those important steps backward after you "catch feelings" for that special someone. We are left wondering what personal shortcomings created the disparity in interest. It's just a really uncomfortable place to be and recovery can be a challenge. I tried to hit upon some of these issues within the short space of this poem.*

Part Two

Mixed Bag & Random Thoughts

The essays and poems that follow represent a random collection of some of my previous writings which seemed appropriate to include within this anthology. I've written a number of pieces that remain very personal and serve as reminders to myself but, occasionally, I reevaluate these decisions. The works that follow represent a mix of items I wrote primarily for my own consumption and a few pieces that I wrote to share on social media platforms because I felt they were either humorous, informative, or inspirational, in some form. I hope you enjoy these selections.

I Once Had a Dream

(Fall, 1984)
Previously Unpublished

*Written as a freshman (Cadet 4th Class) at the Air
Force Academy during the dark days of my first
semester when it felt like the entire world was
conspiring against me. This was about not
surrendering and about staying true to myself.*

I once had a dream
Of windmills in the sky
Of knights and ships and warriors
That dream will never die

I've sailed across the oceans
Looked out from castles high
Flown with eagles and swam with whales
Those dreams will never die

They say I'll change eventually
But as time rolls slowly by
My dreams still give me hope
Those dreams will never die

Let them deal me hardships
It's clear that they do try
Let them think that they have won
But those dreams will never die

In the end I'll still be happy
Though I doubt that they will ever know the reason why
But it's because those dreams still live
Those dreams will never die

THE SNERK BRANCH

(December 8, 2013)
Previously Unpublished

*I reflect upon a special holiday tradition which
started during the earliest days of my childhood.*

Among the many holiday traditions that I carry forward, from year
to year, there's one that holds extra special meaning for me. It's a tradition that dates back to my earliest Christmas memories. Unlike those
marvelous traditions that are passed down through the generations, this
particular tradition originated with a younger me but still reflects part
of who I was...and who I am. I guess my parents thought so, too--they
named it after me--the "Snerk Branch."

Too often, my stories spin off into branch stories to provide background or explanation for the current tale. And here I go again--sorry.
The term "Snerk" is not to be found in any dictionary though I have
seen some web-based "urban definitions" that fall far from the mark of
my parents' intent when they coined the term and thus labeled me.
What's a Snerk? It's a kid who acts snerky. As I understand it, snerkiness
is that level of good-spirited mischievousness that pushes a parent's
limits of tolerance but rarely, if ever, crosses the line. There's a level of
sneakiness involved and, almost always, a glint in the eye--a certain
"sparkle" accompanied by a restrained a smile, or "snerky grin." So,
Mom and Dad often referred to me as "the Snerk," "Snerk Monster,"
or even "David M. Snerkowitz." Okay, now that this snerk business is
cleared up; back to my story.

My grandfather was a marvelous man. Sadly, my memories of time
spent with him are very limited. My memories of Christmas with my
grandfather are nearly unreachable. I rely on old photos to bolster my
confidence in the very few memories that survive. Grampy was a very
careful, patient and meticulous man. My father describes the precision
with which he would hang "icicles" from the Christmas Tree. My
grandfather would start at the top of the tree and address each and
every branch, as he made his way down. Upon each branch he would
carefully hang the silver icicle strands, starting from the inside and

working his way out--all evenly spaced. His tree decorating was as much a work of mechanical precision as it was a work of art. So, there I was, a handful of icicles and just old enough to help decorate the family tree. I threw the whole mess at a branch...and it stuck. I can only imagine what my grandfather must have thought. I have no memory of his reaction, much less what was going through his head. But, when my father tells the story, he always tells it with a smile. I think everyone was amused and content to let the very first "Snerk Branch" adorn our tree through the holidays. The tradition was born. Each year after that, while doing my part to try to properly decorate the tree, I would always reserve one sturdy branch to hold more than its fair burden of icicles. Another characteristic of the Snerk Branch was that it was always growing...evolving. My rule was that any icicle that fell from the tree should be returned to the tree but placed upon the Snerk Branch. By the time New Year's Day arrived, the Snerk Branch was quite an impressive sight to behold.

Like many kids, I was always a little bit sad when the Christmas break was over. Before taking down the tree, I would grab a brown paper lunch sack and place my Snerk Branch icicles within it. I would then label the year. Back home, one or two of these bags still survive.

So, why do I consider this tradition special? Clearly, it throws off the symmetry of the Christmas Tree and adds a brightly reflective blemish upon the arboreal display, sharply contrasting with the gentle and natural green tones of the fir tree. Maybe that's part of why I consider it special. In a world that seeks perfection and that shuns the imperfect and flawed, it is always constructive to consider that nothing built of the hands of man is or ever can be perfect. Our "imperfections" make us special. Our imperfections give us character and remind us that, in the end, we are only human. Our "imperfections" are part of who we are. I continue the Snerk Branch not only because it is a tradition that connects me with my childhood and many magical Christmases but also because it reminds me never to take life too seriously and never to forget that perfection is reserved for the Divine. No man, woman, or child is a failure for falling short of that mark. We all have hopes and dreams and we all struggle to find our way through this world. We are all unique and I thank God that we are. In my estimation, perfection is an irrelevant term when it comes to the human spirit just as it's irrelevant when judging the beauty of a Christmas Tree. I look at our tree, decorated by a loving family, and thrown off balance by a large and glorious Snerk Branch and I think--that's good enough for me. I love it!

The past few Christmases, I've smiled as my youngest son has taken it upon himself to create his own snerk branch upon the tree. I'm not sure what he calls it, or even why he does it, but it makes our tree that much more beautiful! I love it! Perhaps there's a bit of the Snerk in my son. I'm fairly sure there's still a bit of "The Snerk" still in me.

EAGLE TODAY

(Written May 8, 2015)
Previously Unpublished

*During a difficult day, I reflect upon my challenges
and the challenges of our world by soaring up above
the trees to see the world from a better vantage point.*

God, make me an eagle today. I need to break these earthly bonds and soar where I can see the greater reality. I need to see to the horizons. I need to see what is beyond the trees and beyond my small world. I wish to see those who weep with grief for a loved one lost. I need to see the anger and rage that drives man to senselessly kill his brother. I need to see the scars upon the mountains and the forests and the filth we have poured into the seas. I will witness the gentle creatures of this planet desperately retreating for any place that they can call home...any place that will permit them to live and protect their young. I need to feel the anguish of love lost. I need to feel deeply for every sick child everywhere...and know the pain in the hearts of their parents and friends. I will witness shattered dreams, broken promises, and hurtful deceit. I will see all of this. I will know that my problems are small. I will understand that there is much to do and I must be strong. But, from the skies above, I shall see your love. I shall witness charity and I shall know that hope is ever present--everywhere. From the charred remains of mighty forests, I shall see seedlings spring forth from destruction and life renewed. I shall see lovers holding hands and former enemies coming together and restoring harmony. I shall see broken things repaired and broken lives restored. I shall see the good in this world, just as I have witnessed the bad. And I shall understand the balance. And when I return to my earthly perch, I shall understand that my world is but a part of the larger world--happiness and sadness, triumph and failure, all of it--just smaller. Smaller but not less meaningful. And I, too, must learn to find balance. I must live. God, make me an eagle today. I need to fly and I need to understand. I must live.

My Heart is Captain of this Ship

(Written May 13, 2015)
Previously Unpublished

*In this poem, I ponder why my brain allows me to
take painful excursions and I conclude that my heart
is often the master of my actions.*

I found some yellowed paper
And it beckoned me to write
"Put down that pen, you scurvy fool!
Hide your darkness out of sight!"

"A fool, indeed," I did reply
To that coward in the mirror
"I've signed on board a new ship
And you're not the captain here!"

Weighing anchor, unfurling sail
My intelligence at odds with me
My mind screams for us to return
Yet we venture out to sea

High up in the rigging
The shore is still in sight
The madman at the helm
Steers a course deeper into night

Like an apparition from a Melville tale
The skipper's a man who will not rest
We come about to his suspect course
And we buy in to his quest

My Heart is Captain of this Ship

Stormy sea and tempest wrath
Yet ne'er a sail be furled
Oak and rope both strain and groan
I've seen nothing like it in this world!

There's ice and rain and sleepless nights
My cold, wet, clothes never will be dried
I've been made the new First Mate
The old First Mate has died

I bark the captain's orders
I pray our master prays to God
I curse the days I feared to sail
I curse both cobblestone and sod

I am one now with this journey
I have sold all to make this trip
All but save my soul
My heart is captain of this ship

"Reefs ahead!" the lookout cries
And I know the end is near
The helm will not respond
Yet I drive on without fear
"Lay on more sail!" the captain shouts
I nod and laugh "why not?"
Straight and true, I take the wheel
"Lads, hang all the sheets we've got!"

I awake beneath a God-sent sun
The angels bore me to the beach
A wreck upon the reef nearby
A lesson for to teach

I sat where sand meets surf
My mind scolds with boastful pride
I felt the pain and anguish
I felt broken and I cried

Flapper and the Captain

But then I see a hammer
And o'er there a nail!
Some planks drift into shore
And a piece of tattered sail!

My conscious mind, it loathes me
As again I start to build
Rope and oak and tar transform
Though my efforts are unskilled

I will ask God for his blessing
And I'll pray you pray for me
As I launch my ragged vessel
And once more set to sea

There's something in my soul that drives me
On this sad and lonely trip
Yet I go willingly again
My heart is captain of this ship.

1961 SKATING TRAGEDY

(Written February 17, 2015)
Previously Unpublished

My thoughts shared regarding a terrible tragedy that,
while occurring before my birth, made an indelible
impression upon me. I am reminded of the
importance of living each day with purpose because
we never know what the next may bring.

During my many difficult years at the Air Force Academy (1984-1988), there was one special place in Colorado Springs where I felt a special sense of peace. I didn't get off base very often but, when I did, I made my way to the beautiful five-star Broadmoor Hotel. There's a terrific walking path around the lake with great views of the property and surrounding mountains. But there was one place that was more special than the rest. Alongside the lake, was the beautiful Broadmoor World Arena. The Arena had hosted a number of National and World figure skating championships. A beautiful but modest venue, the major skating competitions had outgrown the Arena by the time I moved to Colorado. It was not lost on me that my skating idol, Dorothy Hamill, had won the National Figure Skating Championship there in 1976. Her next stop—the Winter Olympics (Innsbruck, Austria) and then the Worlds (Goteborg, Sweden). I would often walk in, grab a seat, and watch the coaches training their students. For all I knew, I could be watching the next Olympic champion in training. The Broadmoor Skating Club had a reputation for producing outstanding skaters. One of my very special adventures, during my four years as a cadet, involved spending a day as a hotel guest. One night was all I could afford. The highlight of this experience was going skating for a couple hours at the Broadmoor Arena. You can only imagine where my mind was as I glided across that famous ice. But the story I wish to share tonight is not a happy one. I consider it a meaningful tale and one I often reflect upon. It's not my story but the tragic tale has always had great meaning for me.

Sadly, the Broadmoor World Arena was torn down in 1994 and

replaced by yet another annex to the hotel. I will fight the urge to editorialize on that decision. However, a stone bench with a skate blade base remains. Its location, there on the hotel property, might seem odd to those who don't recall that it used to sit next to the lake, just outside the entrance to the Arena. I didn't fully understand the significance of it at the time other than it was a memorial to 8 members of the Broadmoor Skating Club who died on February 15, 1961.

It's much worse than that. On February 15, 1961, we lost the entire U.S. Figure Skating Team, their coaches, and several officials when their Boeing 707 crashed near Brussels while the team was enroute to the World Figure Skating Championship in Czechoslovakia. All 72 people onboard the jet were killed in addition to one fatality on the ground. This disaster effectively wiped out the U.S. Skating program. The World Championship was cancelled and a nation grieved for the tragic loss of life. They were more than just skaters. They were a wonderful group of people—parents, brothers and sisters, sons and daughters—all with bright futures ahead of them. The grief-filled void they left behind was unimaginable. There are so many stories that deserve to be told. One I find particularly compelling is that of Maribel Vinson-Owen, former 9-time U.S. Ladies' champion who was traveling not only as a coach but as the mother of two competitors—her daughters Laurence Owen (16), the 1961 U.S. Ladies' Champion and Maribel Owen (20), reigning U.S. pairs champion. It's just one of many heartbreaking stories.

While it's impossible to put a silver lining on this tragedy, the fate of the U.S. Figure Skating program is a compelling story. Like the Phoenix of mythology, it's a tale of death and rebirth from the ashes. For a generation of young skaters who lost their idols and their coaches, the road to recovery was not an easy one. Their passion and their love for the sport carried them on. American skater Peggy Fleming had lost her coach in the 1961 crash. She, too, was a member of the Broadmoor Skating Club. In 1966, she brought American skating back to the international stage, winning Gold at the World Championship. She won again in 1967 and 68. Peggy is, perhaps, best known for her Olympic Gold Medal in 1968 in Grenoble, France. There she solidified her position as America's sweetheart. Her Gold was the only U.S. Gold medal in those Olympic Games. Eight years later, at the XII Winter Olympic Games in Innsbruck, Austria, Dorothy Hamill would capture Gold again. U.S. Figure Skating was back! Dorothy, like Peggy, had spent a great amount of time training in Colorado with skating coach Carlo Fassi.

One nice story, related to the tragedy, comes from famous figure skating coach Frank Carroll. He describes how Maribel Vinson-Owen had been his coach. In turn, he used all the lessons she taught him as he instructed his own students. His students form a veritable who's who of skating excellence. If you are not a skating enthusiast, you may not recognize the names so I won't attempt to list them but they include the likes of 9-time U.S. champion Michelle Kwan (+ 5-time World champion) and numerous other world, Olympic, and national champions. In this way, Maribel's legacy lives on and she continues to contribute to U.S. Figure Skating. Likewise, those who passed during that tragic day left their mark on this world. Their legacies live on through those who knew them and those whose lives they touched.

So...why do I share this? I think there's a positive message about life. Life is finite. We all must leave someday and none of us know when that day will be. While we are here, it's important to live life and not to hide from life. The things we do every day can make a difference and we should make the most of the time we have. Also, I've always felt it's important to thank people who have made a difference in our lives. This has often created some "awkward" moments but I'm willing to risk that for an opportunity to say thank you. It may not make a difference. But then again, it may. And, a day may come when you don't have the opportunity to say thanks. Loss. Grieving. Rebuilding. Rising Up Again. Living. Loving. Gratitude. It's all about life. And life is worth living.

YARN

(Written January 23, 2016)
Previously Unpublished

*A simple green yarn winds its way through this yarn
about my love for weather and where it would take
me.*

At some point in my life, before my retained memories were safely
stored away, I must have gazed up into the cloudy sky in awe and felt
the coolness of an autumn breeze on my face and fell in love with the
mysterious forces of nature. My earliest memories include such
moments of joy and a great appreciation for the many facets of
weather. My story begins with a simple piece of yarn. Green yarn. And
it is this yarn that will travel the length of this tale...or should I say "of
this 'yarn'."

I was a pretty shy kid. Asking for anything was a chore. I am still
emotionally scarred from an incident in Second Grade where, for no
particular reason at all, I decided to write a report about elephants.
This story has nothing to do with my yarn...but bear with me. I was
quite happy with my report except that I felt it was lacking a critical
piece of information. How much do elephants eat? How could my
report possibly be complete without this data? It couldn't! The animal
books I had did not fill in the gaps. So, my father had this great idea
that I should call up the Bronx Zoo and ask the question. Brilliant! Dad
got me the number and I dialed away. My heart was pounding. It took
every bit of courage I had. Finally, someone picked up--a voice
responded--not a recording--a real, live, person! "Excuse me, Sir," I
said, "could you please tell, me how much an elephant eats?" A gruff
voice responded, "XX Dollars for Adults and YY Dollars for
Children." I tried again. "No, please, is there anyone there who can tell
me how much an elephant eats in a day?" And again, "XX Dollars for
Adults and YY Dollars for Children." One last time, "I'm just trying to
find somebody there who can tell me how much an elephant eats." And
the final blow struck deeply: "Well, if you want to find out, kid, then
why don't you come here and see for yourself." DEVASTATION.

Complete and total emotional devastation. Fortunately, I now take you back to First Grade--the significant emotional event of my Bronx Zoo call was still a year away.

So, where was I? Oh yes--my GREAT idea. Now, our schoolyard playground at Saddle Rock was pretty nice, and all, but it was missing an important element. No playground was complete without some form of weather station--so, I devised my own. A length of green yarn that could be affixed to one of our playground apparatuses that would accurately show, for all to see, which direction the wind was blowing. No child would ever blow away again...EVER. Not on my watch! I loved weather! Didn't everybody? Wasn't every other First Grader dying to know, within plus or minus 10 degrees, which direction the wind was blowing? Of course they were! So, gathering up all the courage I could muster (before the painfully silent Post-Elephant years), I approached Mrs. Turbyfill, our playground Czar, and presented my idea. Within a day, I had my approval, and I carefully tied an 18-inch piece of green string to the top of our highest playground equipment. It was kind of a metallic bar framed, spaceship kind-of monkey bar thingamajig. You can picture it already, right. Now, the color of the string was very important to this operation. You see, darker colors absorb the light and warm up while lighter colors tend to reflect it and GREEN WAS MY FAVORITE COLOR. My wind speed/direction device remained in place for at least several weeks until either the forces of mother nature made off with it or some quizzical paraprofessional decided they had humored the crazy First Grader with the weather "thing" long enough. No matter, within days, an 18-inch green string was hanging from a sturdy branch on my favorite climbing tree at home. And it stayed. And stayed. And stayed.

Around 1981, I decided to start collecting weather data...just for fun. Every afternoon, after returning home from school, I would turn on the local news to get the current temperature (at 3pm) and I'd look at my barometer to get the pressure. I would then head out to my carefully calibrated Green Yarn weather recording device to get a read of the wind direction and speed. Finally, I'd take note of any precipitation during the day. Occasionally, the forces of nature would get the better of my green yarn. I would promptly replace the tattered remains of my old yarn with a bright new piece of GREEN yarn. And so it went.

In 12th grade, I managed to get myself into an elective class which sounded fun. It was a science-based independent research class. The project I crafted seemed simple enough--a hypothesis that the direction the wind was blowing would have a precise correlation with the pH, or acid content, of the rainwater. Armed with a holiday cookie tin (to collect water), a stack of pH test strips, and my green yarn, I set to work. I guess I had this image of happy clouds floating over the industrial centers of the Northeast and absorbing enough toxins (and acid) to melt steel on contact. The rainclouds coming to me from across the sea would, of course, be as pure as driven snow and ready to bottle and sell to willing customers. What I found was ZERO correlation. Zippo! Nada! Fortunately, years removed from my confidence-shattering Bronx Zoo Elephant experience, I had the wherewithal to stay cool, calm, and collected. Summoning up the best of my Irish Blarney skills, I quickly grabbed my composition notebook filled with years of weather data and began graphing and running statistical analysis like nobody's business. The result was a masterpiece of Just-in-Time Final Project goodness. I got an A in the class!

I graduated. No doubt, in large part, thanks to that green yarn. With time, the yarn disappeared...and then, to my greater sorrow, so too did my favorite climbing tree. Taken from us by a tree disease. I can still see the yarn waving in the breeze.

In more metaphorical terms, the yarn survived, and binds the continuing story of my love for the weather. There was a time I considered a future in meteorology (as well as Marine Biology--separate story). As most friends know, I elected to join the Air Force after High School. As I went through various phases of flight training--from my cadet days through my eventual career as an Air Force Officer (and Navigator), I had the privilege of studying the weather in much greater depth than I ever had before. I loved it! I aced aircrew weather exams in flight training and did as much as I could to become an expert on any manner of weather phenomena that I might encounter in my travels and in my job. One of my key responsibilities, as an Air Force Navigator, was planning our missions and carefully considering all the local, enroute, and destination weather conditions that might impact mission completion. Especially in the tanker business, where it was my job to rendezvous with other aircraft hundreds of miles away and to do so within a matter of seconds of our scheduled rendezvous time, it was imperative that I understood anything along the way that could impact mission timing. Each mission was like solving a new puzzle. I love it. I loved flying.

I used my radar, my wind charts, and my understanding of weather countless times over the years to help get the mission done. I've dodged thunderstorms from the plains of the Midwest to the vast expanses of the Pacific and Indian Oceans. I've flown from Washington State to England and put the jet on the runway within a second of my planned arrival time. But, one memory stands out. 27 March 1999. The day Vega 31 went down. The U.S. and our Allies were engaged in Operation Allied Force--a NATO operation to halt the humanitarian disaster that was unfolding in Kosovo. I was up that night, flying a combat support mission, when we got directed over to the secure radio channel. An F-117 Stealth fighter had just gone down. None had ever been shot down before and no F-117 was lost in combat since. There was a pilot on the ground and the bad guys were hunting for him. If there was ever a time to pull out the "A Game," this was it. We were rapidly approaching our "BINGO" fuel at the time--that's when you reach the fuel level where you had better seriously start thinking about heading for home before the gas gauge goes to E--figuratively speaking. We didn't really have a gauge with an E on it. When the AWACS started polling all of the tankers to see how much gas we had left, we all knew it was very serious and that the leadership was quickly trying to put together some kind of rescue package and the appropriate smack-down escorts to go recover our downed pilot. Rule number one--never leave an Airman behind. That night, I was actually in the number two aircraft in a two-ship formation. Our lead aircraft had more fuel than us but, since they also saw we were approaching BINGO fuel, they told us they were going to start working our clearance to leave the area and head back to England. As fast as I could, I started calculating winds vs. distances vs. fuel burn rates and I knew that we could stick around longer--maybe even an hour longer. I told our pilot that I thought we needed to stay. He radioed forward to lead and said we were sticking around. As such, we basically shamed lead into deciding to hang around longer, as well. By carefully studying the weather pattern of the night, I knew that if we climbed very high, we would encounter a unique wind pattern that would actually help to push us back towards England. My wind charts verified this. The story could get long so I will summarize--we stuck around...so did "lead." We both wound up passing off enough fuel to tank up a couple Navy EA-6B Prowlers who would provide the electronic jamming support for the rescue mission. At the end of a very long night, we got the news we had all been

481

praying for--pilot rescued! Mission Complete! That was a GOOD AIR FORCE DAY. One of my favorites.

My Air Force flying days have passed. I miss them. I still love to fly and I still love the window seat. Each cloud is beautiful. Okay, maybe not clouds associated with those "Wrath of God" thunderstorms I used to have to pick my way around flying night missions through Tornado Alley or while battling incomparable typhoons in the Pacific--but, you know...the rest of them. Just like when I was a kid, I still love to walk outside, look up at the clouds, and feel a strong breeze. I'll even take walks in the rain, from time to time--it's nice. Weather adds variety to life. It can also threaten life. It can be beautiful, or fierce and deadly. In all instances, it should be respected.

I'm glad I asked Mrs. Turbyfill if I could put the green yarn up on our play equipment. I'm thankful the school said yes. I may not have gone on to be the world's foremost elephant expert. But, thanks to many, I have maintained my lifelong interest in weather. I share this yarn with you.

HEAD OVER HEELS

(Written July 5, 2017)
Previously Unpublished

*The last song I heard as a civilian inspires memories
of the difficult beginning days of what would become
an incredible career journey.*

So, what inspired me to get on that plane, 33 years ago? I dug through my box of memorabilia today to help answer the question. From within the box, I recovered the carbon copy of my five-page essay written as part of my college application package. The title could not have been any more direct: "Why I Want to Go to the Air Force Academy." It's not the best piece of writing I've ever done. But, these many years later, the sincerity still rings out—and that's what mattered. Amidst the rambling discourse, several themes emerged—I loved airplanes, I wanted to fly, I wanted to serve my country, and I don't give up. The days to come would certainly test my endurance and my will.

I never visited the Academy prior to attendance. The Open House dates conflicted with my baseball schedule and I wasn't about to miss a game. Teens think like that. I had never traveled alone, never checked into a hotel, never ordered food at a restaurant...in fact, I really hadn't done much in life besides just being a kid. I was pretty good at that. As a 17-year-old, my parents had to co-sign the paperwork for my application to join the Air Force. Despite all of this, I showed up at New York's LaGuardia airport on July 5, 1984 with a carry-on in hand and a pair of combat boots slung over my shoulder. I had recently gotten a very short crew cut from the local barber shop so that I would "look the part" upon my arrival. That wouldn't matter. In a day, my preposterously short hair would be cut even shorter.

Saying goodbye to my family at the airport was very difficult. For the first time, I felt completely alone. I was truly on my own. My only comfort was coming across the occasional scared looking teen with short hair and combat boots slung over their shoulder. I'm glad I didn't look that scared! I boarded my flight, the ticket graciously provided by the United States Air Force, and grabbed my window seat. My spirits briefly picked up as I felt the acceleration of our jet down the runway. But then I saw Manhattan fading away below—and I had to fight really hard to hold back the tears. I was a pretty tough kid but there were a lot of emotions racing through my head at the time. I knew then that my life would never be the same. There was no going back.

I arrived at the airport and received transportation to one of the local hotels where incoming cadets were housed. The process was quite orderly—frighteningly so. I was feeling kind of off. I thought it was my nerves but I later realized that I was suffering from some altitude sickness. After growing up at sea level, the 7,000 ft gain in elevation was having a definite impact. What do I remember about that night? I remember going to eat at the hotel restaurant. I remember ordering a hamburger and a milkshake. I wanted my last meal as a civilian to be a good one. I remember the pretty waitress who was nice to me because she knew exactly what my fate was going to be. I remember emptying what little cash I had left in my wallet as a rather substantial tip—because she was nice to me and because I knew I wasn't going to have any use for that money in 12 hours—the government would be providing my food, clothing, and shelter and all my "civilian possessions" would be confiscated from me and locked away in some dungeon…at least for the duration of Basic Training. I returned to my room. I tried to sleep. I failed. I got up, got dressed, and threw up my "last meal as a civilian." The altitude sickness was getting the best of me. That was unfortunate because the next day the Air Force would forget to feed me and, the day after that, I would only eat a pickle and half of a biscuit between getting yelled at for minor table decorum infractions, etc. July 6th and the start of Basic Training was truly "Shock and Awe" but the hardest part was already behind me on July 5th. That was the day I said goodbye to the world I knew and began my crazy Air Force adventure. The last song I heard on the radio…the last song I heard as a civilian…was "Head Over Heels" by the Go-Go's. Whenever I hear that song, those memories coming flooding back. Head Over Heels—yup—that about sums it up. July 5, 1984.

ODE TO AN OLD GREEN BUCKET

(Written April 19, 2018)
Previously Unpublished

A humorous poem inspired by discovering an artifact
from my childhood had been repurposed as a lowly
drip catching receptacle.

Wandering through the lesser traveled spaces of my parents' home—
Places where electricians and plumbers are more like to roam

I see it there, an old green bucket
Filled with rage, I shout "Well, darn it!"

Ignobly placed upon the cracking floor
That plastic vessel deserved much more

A pedestal, some place of honor;
A museum placard placed upon her!

Catching furnace drips--such a sad demise
For our childhood flu season's most valued prize

Silence now. A meek drip, drip, drip
How many times, hath thou saved me from that nighttime trip?

Stomach churning and acids burning
I lay in bed, tossing and turning

The bathroom now seemed a mile away
Yet, in my bed I got to stay

Winter chills, blowing down from the north
Within my gut--the cosmos, expanding, then exploding forth

Flapper and the Captain

Spewing forth all evil and vile
That unholy mix of food chunks and bile!

You caught that mess; missed not a drop;
Preserved for inspection, the biologically hazardous slop

Again, and again, then again--ne'er would you fail;
My hero, my savior, that old plastic pail

Dumped in the toilet, washed in the tub
Back once again, rub-a-dub-dub

Up to my brother, across to my sis, and back to my room—
Flu season ran just like this

You were there for us all; you saw us all through—
Heaven-sent green bucket, don't ever get blue

I might have slept in a pool of my own vomit, were you not so steadfast
and true
I hold you in such high esteem; it's time the world knew

I love you, old green bucket! Long may your legend live
I regret these paltry verses are all I have to give

I salute you, and praise you, and will to the end
Old green bucket, trusted companion, you are truly my friend!

Too Much Hatred

(Written October 27, 2018)
Previously Unpublished

*A tragic news story inspires me to write about the
need to find greater harmony and push hatred out of
our lives.*

Too much hatred. There's too much hatred in our world and not
enough love. It's as simple as that.

I typically don't leap to the keyboard following tragedies. I just feel
sad. We all respond in our own way as we try to find a path back to
inner peace. Each atrocity leaves an irremovable blemish on our land . .
. and within our psyche. Human history is replete with such grievous
incidents. They cannot be undone. The best we can do is to learn from
these tragedies and do our best to shape the world so that such inconceivable acts of malice will be absent in the lives of future generations.
I'm not sure we'll get there but I will not give up dreaming. However, I
know I have to do more than dream. I must have the courage to
SPEAK out. And I must have the courage to ACT. Each time we
ignore or laugh away discriminatory comments; we enable those who
are likely traveling a road to some very dark places. It's not about being
politically correct or not—it's about respecting human dignity and
seeking to understand our differences and celebrate our diversity. These
should not be Human Resources Department keywords—they should
be a personal mantra for us all. It's not about loving everybody. It's
about being open to alternative points of view and not being judgmental unless these "alternative points of view" sow the seeds of
violence and hatred. In such cases, after I'm done listening and seeking
to understand, and after reasoning has failed, I always reserve the right
to dislike. And, in certain cases, a call to the authorities is a pretty savvy
move—it might save lives. But, as I dislike, I must be conscious of the
fact that disliked and alienated people often feel driven to the dark
places I previously referred to. We should be careful about giving up on
people. And we should be extremely careful about stereotyping and
justifying disdain for any group of individuals. The pages of mankind's

story are stained with the blood that such group think has drawn from the victims of hate. I wish I had solutions. In the end, I always fall back on the words my mother always drilled into my head—"LOVE is the greatest thing in the whole world." I still believe it's true. I still believe it is the only solution with a chance of fixing what is broken on this big blue marble. We all have a part to play.

FRAMES OF REFERENCE

(Written May 3, 2019)
Previously Unpublished

*I consider the nature of frames and how they reflect
upon who we are and what we value.*

Occasionally, a wild voice inside suggests that I might be better off were I to rid myself of all worldly possessions and embark upon a journey into the unknown without ever casting a glance back upon where I've been—a true fresh start. And then I open up the old dusty boxes. I find things . . . things that take me back to places I truly wish to revisit because they help put my life into perspective. They do not detract from my forward progress in life—they enable it. Today, as I return to my childhood home, my goal was to further slim down the bulk of what remains from my younger days in my parents' house. Today's target—FRAMES.

Frames are interesting things. We reserve these containers for items with special meaning and so, in a way, they tell a story of what we value or, at least, what we valued at one point in our lives. The quality of the frames varies. More important documents and photos were placed in better quality frames or, in many cases, the best frames we could reasonably afford at the time. Our prized possessions are often encased in professionally crafted custom frames. Occasionally, we upgrade our frames as the significance of our encased treasures grow or we find our economic situation enables us to add that double matting and ornate wooden border we initially envisioned. In one instance, I have purposely not upgraded a frame for my favorite piece of artwork. The frame for that print tells as much of a story as the picture within. They say "every picture tells a story" but I might add that every frame does, too.

Today, I went through a large stack of framed items from my closet. Many of these were once displayed in places of honor on the walls of my childhood room—the numerous nail holes in the wall are evidence of their falling from grace. Certificates of merit and photos from my cadet days once seemed like reasonable candidates for protection. Some saw wall time while others were merely protected behind glass because I thought they should be preserved and a frame seemed a better candidate for the job than a file folder. As of this afternoon, these odds and ends are now residing within a single file folder. I didn't quite have the heart to rid myself of them . . . at least not yet. A Presidential Academic Fitness Award certificate must have seemed pretty impressive to me back in 1984. I don't believe that Ronald Reagan actually signed it. I'm pretty sure my high school principal did. Neither of these men are with us today. A certificate of appreciation for my participation in my high school's Science Night is, likewise, not a document likely to find its way into the Library of Congress but it does bring back some good memories—I got to talk to countless parents about sharks (one of my favorite subjects!!!) while I worked on dissecting a small shark with my good friends Jeanne and John. That was quite a night. There's a photo of me standing, in uniform, in front of an aircraft on the campus of the U.S. Air Force Academy—I was a freshman—I was stiff and unsmiling (Parents' Weekend 1984). Then there's a photo of me standing, in uniform, in the Air Gardens at the U.S. Air Force Academy—I was a sophomore—I was relaxed and smiling (Parents' Weekend 1985). What a difference a year makes! Another frame contained a photo of me in a flight suit, standing on the ladder beside an F-15 fighter jet. This was taken during a summer training trip, as a cadet. That was the dream. "That" dream was never realized. I keep the photo because 1) it's a pretty cool photo and 2) a little humility is good for the soul. We move on and we find new dreams.

Amidst my collection of framed items are a few . . . a precious few . . . that still deserve to stand fast within their protective enclosures. A letter from the late Daniel Patrick Moynihan, New York's senior senator—dated April 13, 1984--the letter was my first notification that I had been offered an appointment to the United States Air Force Academy, my first choice for college. An official letter (also framed) from the Academy followed shortly thereafter. My life would never be the same. Then, there's a solo certificate from the 557th Flying Training Squadron. Although I had previously flown solo in a glider, having the opportunity to solo a Cessna T-41 aircraft took "the thrill" to an entirely new level. The certificate reminds me of that special day, November 18th, 1987. Perhaps the most meaningful document, framed and hanging on my wall since 1988, is my Air Force Commission. It's a beautiful document and the ultimate reminder of our officers' oath to support and defend the Constitution of the United States.

Back at my apartment, I finally pulled out a few framed photos of my children and placed them on my wall. After my divorce, it was just too painful and sad to have these daily reminders of my family "as it was" since I knew things would never be the same. Although I rarely get to see my kids (sequestered away in the middle of South Dakota) and our phone conversations are few and far between, the photos remained carefully protected in their frames and, finally, I am ready to display them again—it's not the sadness that takes hold of me now— it's the pride and, more importantly, the love. Prints of sailing ships and old naval battles also adorn my apartment. These are more than just wall coverage; they remind me of the spirit of courage and adventure that inspired me to pursue my chosen profession and they remind me of the sea that I will always love.

Finally, there's the old woodland frame. I alluded to it earlier—the frame I purposely have not upgraded. The impossible journey and a reunion that only Heaven could have orchestrated. I had spent nearly my entire life's savings on that pre-war trip to Canada and then . . . there it was. A small art gallery in the middle of a shopping mall in Vancouver, Canada. After a spectacular array of experiences that I can only describe as miraculous, I was staring head on at a majestic moose who was staring, head on, right back at me. I'll not go into the spiritual significance of the moose (in my life) at this time but, suffice it to say, I was mesmerized. No single piece of art could encapsulate the spiritual beauty of my journey like that print. There was one problem--I was literally near the end of the line for my finances. I simply couldn't afford the picture. Perfectly mounted with a triple matting that accentuated the colors of the painting and a spectacular wooden frame. It was amazing! "How much to ship this back to the U.S.?" I cringed when I heard the answer. This endeavor was well beyond my means. Yet, there it was—the artistic embodiment of my journey and the courageous spirit that defied convention in the pursuit of a dream. "Bull Moose – The Challenge". He was not backing down. Neither would I. I left the shop—I would have to do some soul searching. Two days later, I returned . . . and the haggling began. "How about if I went down to a double mat? Oh. Well, how about just a single mat? A single mat and a different frame?" Like my friend the moose, I was not backing away from this encounter. The sales clerk yielded and the print was mine. A single mat, a forest tree wooden frame, and a one-way ticket to Wichita, Kansas. The next day, while my print was being prepared for shipping to the United States, I was fulfilling an 8-year quest to thank a very special friend for saving my life. It was the most amazing day of my life. This piece of art has survived numerous moves and despite dings, scratches, and assorted bruises—the frame has protected its precious cargo. More so, the frame itself has become precious cargo. Like the journey itself, I look at the frame and I see perseverance. I see a young man trading away his limited finances for something far more valuable—a dream. I see a survivor. I see the importance of spirituality and I understand the value of a simple non-ostentatious frame. Am I not a simple, non-ostentatious, frame?

Frames. We learn a lot about ourselves by looking upon the items we have chosen to frame. Which items will you put in the box? Which items will you put upon the wall? How will they be adorned? I learned a little more about myself today. The "yeah me" items have largely found their way to folders or the trash. I have no regrets—we all have a right to be proud of our accomplishments. What remains, at the end of the day, reflects who we are today and what we value. When I look upon them, I see a reflection of myself—literally and figuratively. I encourage you all to consider your frame of reference.

NEW YEAR'S 2020 THOUGHTS

(Written December 31, 2019)
Previously Unpublished

Reflections upon the coming new year as I look back
upon an old childhood drawing of mine.

Electing to spend this holiday season at my childhood home, it was inevitable that I would stumble upon lenses into the past . . . my past. While I rarely revisit it these days, there's a large folder in my night stand that contains many years of childhood artwork. There are plenty of robots, airplanes, ships, animals, and such . . . but there are also some interestingly complex pieces betraying deep emotions and sentiments about my changing life and the world I perceived to be changing all around me. Some still evoke emotional responses when I view them, over four decades later. Long before I began a diary, the drawings expressed my feelings about environmentalism, wealth, the loss of childhood innocence, loneliness, betrayal, and a myriad of other topics that I regret were weighing upon my mind at those tender ages. I guess I wasn't a simple kid, even back then. However, more relevant to the upcoming celebration, there is one simple stick-figure sketch that expresses my concern on New Years Eve in 1979. In those days, a decade was forever. I was uneasy about the approaching 80s. All the happy memories of my childhood resided in the 1970s. The 70s seemed safe and protective even though I was not without burdens, even then. The 80s were filled with frightening prospects—new schools, new relationships (or lack thereof), college, leaving my home and my childhood behind, etc. As I look upon the sketch, it's not the crude drawing that impresses me but the memories that come flooding back. I can literally see myself creating the drawing and my stomach tightens as I recall the gloom that filled my heart. It was not a happy time. In truth, the 80s were difficult . . . but they were also spectacular. From great despair, I found wings and soared above the clouds, gaining confidence and new perspectives on life even as I struggled through the inevitable challenges that life put before me. And here we are, on the verge of turning yet another calendar page—this time to 2020.

Somewhere, some young boy or girl is struggling with this. Perhaps some young man or woman? Maybe an aging couple? I don't feel the gloom anymore. I know there will be good and bad, happiness and sadness, new beginnings and difficult losses, and little bits and pieces of the entire human experience that become the stories of our lives. I look forward to it—I no longer fear it. While it's difficult to avoid one of the thousands of clichés regarding the passage of time and our journeys through life, I think it's worthwhile considering the road that lays ahead. For my part, I view life as a journey. I see a long road, winding beautifully through the hills. With the new year, I see the snow covering the trees that obscures my view around the bend. I may look back, now and again, but I know my life and my destiny resides ahead of me... and so I travel on. It's an adventure, really. There are times when I will be cold and there are times when I will be tired, and sick, and lonely, and feeling blue. I know it. Knowing this gives me strength. I will survive. There are times when I will feel happy and inspired and loved and courageous and noble. Knowing this gives me hope. In the end, I really don't want to know what is hidden from my view. I'll know when the time is right. What do I want? I just really want to enjoy the journey—to appreciate all of it—the peaks and the valleys. And, when the journey is done, I want to take my rest with no regrets and knowing that I did my best to live my life as I should and to live with integrity and honor. I'm ready for another year. I'm ready for the 2020s. I wish each and every one of you all the best for the coming year, and the years that follow. I hope that you are not disappointed on your journey and I hope that our paths may cross as we travel. We all have stories worth sharing and it's life that provides the fertile ground for the greatest tales of all.

Happy New Year!

I Do ME

(Written February 9, 2020)
Previously Unpublished

A brief essay reflecting upon job transitions and the importance I place on being 100% true to who I am. No re-invention required...I do ME.

Sunday morning random thoughts. I'm not sure I'm doing a great job at this post-military "transition" thing. But maybe I am. I had a job. But it wasn't really a good job. I lost that job. I miss the income. I don't miss the job. I tend to be very, very quiet. Unless you get me talking...then I tend to be very talkative. I like to share stories. I want to do good. I've been told I should have a 30 second "elevator speech" ready to pitch to potential employers or key networking contacts. I really don't care to have anything to do with people who can only afford me 30 seconds of their time. My loss.......no, actually, it's their loss. I hear the question a lot, at various events—"So, what do you do?" Where do I even start? What do I do? I do ME. And then I've heard, "well, what would be your dream job?" That's another tough one. Um, maybe the one I did for 30 years as an Air Force Officer and aviator? Beyond that, it's hard to say. I think I could do just about anything but I'm just a little tired of trying to convince others of that fact. I don't really feel like I need to convince others of anything. I know, I'm probably messing this all up. But, remember, I do ME. I'm pretty happy with that. I've been through all the transition training—four times. Yes— four times. I constantly encounter good-hearted "mentors" who repeat the wisdom I've previously heard-over, and over, and over. I smile. They mean well. I'll find work...eventually. I suspect it won't be that "dream job" and I'm okay with that. If I like it, I'll stay. If I don't like it, I'll go. If they want me to be something I'm not—I'm already gone. I do ME. I'm pretty proud of my consistent track record of doing ME. I've sacrificed a lot by being ME—but, actually, I've sacrificed very little...at least in terms of things that I truly value. I do ME. So....come rain or shine, I continue to work my way through this wacky world and I try to do what I can to contribute positively to the universe and I try not to cause pain or hurt. If I have caused pain—I am sorry. If the pain I caused was as a result of me being ME—then I apologize to you.... but I haven't any regrets. It's who I am—you can spit at me, shake my hand, or just turn the other way and ignore me. It's your right. You need to be YOU! And I need to be ME.

Lost My Jacket Dream

(Written April 3, 2020)
Previously Unpublished

*Random thoughts about an interesting dream and my
long-time admiration for my blue windbreaker jacket.*

[WARNING—this goes nowhere and has no moral or message. Just saying]. Well, some nights you just write off as a loss. Like this one. It's not even over yet—not until the rooster crows. I'm typing in a horizontal position, in a dark bedroom, and it's 4:40am. I actually first woke up just after 2am, ready to start my day—until I looked over at my clock. Bummer. After ignoring the good medical advice about avoiding screen time at night, I decided to check Facebook, then the weather, then the news. Nope, not many changes since midnight. Where are you, my late-night posters? West coast friends?? I felt okay about ignoring the medical screen time warnings because I'm doubling down on all the COVID-19 medical recommendations. I have excelled at social isolation. And I'm boasting like it's a good thing. That's what quarantine does to us. I'm so used to being a helper and a doer that it has been difficult on me to be told that the best thing I can do is stay away—lock myself in my apartment and ration toilet paper. It's just hard. Okay—so, on with my meaningless story. I somehow managed to drift back to sleep around 3am. And I actually had a dream! I almost never dream anymore—too many sleep issues. But I like my dreams (most of the time). Some are powerful with very interesting messages! This one wasn't. I warned you this is going nowhere—just random stream of consciousness. In my dream, I was flying back home from an overseas military assignment on a commercial jet. All the normal jet stuffed happened (with a couple sci fi visuals tossed in—because it was a dream and dreams afford us the luxury of spicing things up a bit). Speaking of spicing things up...as I was disembarking, I was approached by a very attractive woman. Bonus! Only in my dreams. She seemed very much into me! Wow! Only in my dreams! She offered to go get drinks while we waited for our next connection. I don't "drink" but I would have gladly slugged down a stiff glass of orange juice for the opportunity to know her better. But then...Oh Crap! I forgot my jacket on the back of my seat in the airplane! Anybody who knows me and jackets will realize that this was a major life crisis. So, I had to pass on the drink offer. Besides, she seemed a little "too into me." What did she want? Military secrets? My money? A one-night stand? Or just the thrill of conquest before breaking my heart? Wait, why am I even thinking these awful thoughts? Focus, Dave, focus! The Jacket! So, thus began my quest to recover my jacket. I knew I couldn't re-board my plane so I desperately sought a gate agent. There's a promising desk! Nope—customs representatives. Shouldn't they show up later? Yes, they should—this was a dream! Then I went to the bar and started asking around if there were any gate agents in there. Nope! Only a group of rowdy college boys who mocked me asking around for gate agents. Jerks! You'll get what's coming to you one of these days! I didn't say it. But I know they will. I awoke from my dream. I was distressed. I never did recover my jacket. I couldn't fall asleep again. Until........after another check of Facebook (why, oh why!), I came upon a brilliant idea. I closed my eyes and forced myself to think through a conclusion to my dream where I finally got my jacket back! Whew! I drifted back to sleep and, with that additional hour, I'm ready to start my day. But it's now 5:18, and still no rooster. Bummer. So, I consider things. I do love to think. It's my favorite pastime! But why was I so concerned about the jacket and not about the potential for love and romance? Beats me. Dream interpreters of the world unite and consider that one. I usually don't analyze my own dreams. Some have very clear messages—I take those to heart. Others....well...I'm just thankful when they're interesting or nice. I don't have many bad dreams—I'm thankful for that, too! Wait, where was I going with this? I don't even know. Don't say I didn't warn you. I did. So, I have my jacket, I made my connections and, who knows, maybe I'll meet that woman again, some day. If we were meant to be together, it will happen. I'm kind of one of those "destiny" believers. Work hard toward your dreams but don't despair if you fall short—there may be something bigger and better or cosmically more important awaiting you down the road. I know—it's a crutch to get through life. I'm okay with that. We all find our way through the forest and I'll support you along the path you have chosen. We'll both see the sun again. I'm pretty sure about that. But that jacket thing?! Have a wonderful day (whether it begins before or after the rooster crows)!

One Flake

(Written April 23, 2020)
Previously Unpublished

Something as simple as a single snowflake can change the trajectory for the day.

Upon my morning walk today, under a dark sky, I could not help but contemplate the small flakes that periodically fell from the sky and drifted with the breeze. We have had almost no snow to speak of this year—only a minor dusting here and there. We like snow here…just not too much of it. The people who don't like snow move down to Florida, if they are able. If I ever move to Florida, I think I'd move back. I enjoy my seasons and I enjoy snow. I'll admit, my mind was initially randomly transitioning between a wide array of subjects, as it frequently does, until a single flake landed upon my tongue. I felt it melt. And, all of a sudden, my mind filled with happy childhood memories of standing on a playground, my tongue fully extended, trying to catch those big, white, fluffy snowflakes on my tongue. Even though today's bounty was slim pickings, I was transported to a snow-covered field, only weeks before Christmas, with huge white snowflakes gracefully dancing their way down from the clouds above. My heart is light and happy. It's so happy that I walk over to the turntable in the middle of the field and carefully place a Louis Armstrong record on the machine—I move the needle over to the right place and, voila, "What a Wonderful World" is gently playing in the background. And I think to myself, WHAT A WONDERFUL WORLD! I finished my walk with a smile on my face. Find that happy thought—it can be as small as a single springtime snowflake—and own that moment! Wishing you happy thoughts and brighter days ahead!

SUMMER AC

(Written June 23, 2020)
Previously Unpublished

An essay about my experiences during "Summer Academics" as a cadet at the Air Force Academy.

I know a little bit about summer academics. I had the distinct pleasure of parting with my summer leave every year I was assigned as a cadet at the Air Force Academy. To be fair, the last summer I gave up was by my own choice (implied, the first two were not) and I did so to ensure that I would not lose the summer that really mattered—the one that was supposed to follow graduation.

Far from wallowing in misery, I took to summer academics like a fish to water. First period Summer Ac had a magic all its own. The Academy was quiet and peaceful. The Firsties were out and the Basics hadn't arrived yet. One third of the two thirds remaining were on summer leave. Others were scattered here and there in various summer programs—overseas, at CONUS bases, or wandering around in the woods eating bugs. The Cadet Area was amazingly tranquil, and no one was shouting their squadron names at you as you meandered across the T-zo. There was low probability of a salute-worthy encounter. It was almost like a college.

Summer Ac consisted of three periods a day. The academics came hot and heavy. Somehow, they always managed to line up the best teachers. I suppose somebody thought that it might be a good idea not to send up the French exchange officer with the barely translatable accent to teach a bunch of kids who flunked out of engineering how to manipulate a highly complex series of advanced mathematical equations. High five to whoever put thought against that one! Classes started at a reasonable time in the morning and you got about an hour break, or so, between the end of the first session and the start of the second. The idea was that you did your homework. We'd all report back to our Summer Admin squadron prior to lunch and we'd form up for an accountability formation. And then we'd disperse—and nonchalantly bebop over to Mitchell Hall for lunch. No yelling, no screaming, no panicked freshmen pouring through the entry way. Food was fine and, if it wasn't, you just went back to your room or visited the C-Store. After lunch, the final class of the day. We were done fairly early in the afternoon. Easy stuff.

After my afternoon return—2:30ish, I think—I'd usually go for a long run. Running under the afternoon sun wasn't always super fun but I was twentyish and totally invincible. The Colorado air was dry, and it didn't seem so bad, no matter how many hills I went up and down. Since running, apparently, had nothing to do with a healthy lifestyle, I'd usually head over to Arnold Hall or the Visitor Center for my dinner. A-Hall was nearly always empty (as was the Visitor's Center, at that time of the day). A couple grilled cheese sandwiches and some chips or a cheeseburger, and I was good to go. I might watch a little TV over there before heading back to my room. And then I did something really crazy—I studied! I studied hard. Much to my amazement, I learned! I really learned the stuff. Calculus III—no problem. Microeconomics— I'll take that "A". Astronautical Engineering—how 'bout another "A"!!!! In an academic environment that I had grown to believe was designed to cull the herd rather than to educate, I now realized that I was not a dummy. Maybe that's the most important thing that summer academics taught me. I got my confidence back.

During the academic year, it was all about survival—20+ semester hour each period, military duties, a barrage of training events (parades, retreat formations, inspections, etc.,), mandatory intramurals/IC sports, mandatory football games, mandatory meal formations and on and on. The three hours of protected time, "Academic Call to Quarters," never seemed long enough to get through all the reading and practice problems. I was a military history major but it didn't matter—I was going to learn all the advanced calculus, aeronautical engineering, mechanical engineering, astronautical engineering, electrical engineering, physics, chemistry and probably some other things that my brain mercifully extracted from my memories. This was hard stuff. I rarely left the Academy on weekends because weekends were my time to play catch up. A three hour walk each Sunday was all that stood between me and a straightjacket. Somehow it all worked. I survived and, statistically speaking, I actually did okay. Much more "okay" than I ever felt I was doing.

But back to Summer Ac. We would always get a survey at the end of summer academics. My favorite question (and I should know, I answered it three times) was "do you think it would be beneficial to learn like this during the academic year" (i.e. one class at a time)? I always answered "YES!" To have a single focus and dedicate your brain to achieving excellence in that particular area was truly an educational blessing. The curriculum and course flow never changed. I can't say I expected it would. Having returned, several decades later, to the staff at USAFA, I found academics were a little more kind. Still tough —but designed less to infuriate and terrify the masses. We used to live by "the curve." It was normal to have friends pining in the squadron halls about flunking a test they just took—and then we learned the class average was 52% and your 47% scored you a resounding "C". I nearly packed my bags more than once. It's almost as if the instructors were out to prove a point— "SEE, WHAT I DO IS TOUGH!" *Oh, great God of Thermodynamics, I bow down before you! Teach me, please, though I be only an unworthy peasant, clinging to my Texas Instruments calculator like a raft of reeds in the flood thou hast sent to destroy me and my brethren.*

Summer Ac. It was chill. It was focused. It was a great opportunity to learn from a great group of instructors outside of all the distractions of the academic year. Do I regret losing my summer vacation? Well, yes . . . absolutely. For all that, I still have fond memories of this unique microcosm within my cadet experience. The most important takeaway from Summer Ac was the reminder that it's fun to learn. I may not be a rocket scientist, but I scored me an "A" in "Astro" one lonely summer upon a mountaintop in Colorado. Let's talk orbital mechanics!

SHOULD'VE GONE FOR THREE

(Written June 23, 2020)
Previously Unpublished

*Remembering the details of one of the hardest hit
balls to ever come off of my bat and reflecting upon
lessons learned about potential vs. realized potential
on the baseball diamond...and in life. Written on the
cusp of having my memoir published.*

With baseball starting up again, my mind drifts back in time to happy memories of when I was not just an observer—I was a participant. Whether it was Little League Baseball, High School Baseball, or many years of Intramural Softball during my time in the military, I can never forget all the wonderful sights, sounds, smells, and tactile sensations associated with nearly 40 years of play. It was a good run. I truly love the game.

I can't even remember all the times my softball team made it to the Wing Championship game, while I was serving in the Air Force. I played on a lot of great teams! Sometimes we won. Sometimes we didn't. As a Cadet at the Air Force Academy, I not only played, but coached our team to the Wing Championship (#1 of 40 teams). That was amazing! As an officer, I played year after year, trying to work around unpredictable flying and deployment schedules. Even as a "crusty" old mid-40s Lieutenant Colonel, I was still putting softballs over the fence for homeruns. It felt terrific to still be able to contribute. Back in high school, my baseball career culminated during my senior year when I was selected as the Varsity Baseball team's MVP. That was an incredible honor and one I was truly grateful for. It was never about me. I was always playing for the love of the sport and to help my team be successful. The award came as a surprise to me—it was also the first time I was recognized for being good at something that I was truly passionate about. I felt proud.

I think I played my last game of softball in 2011 or 2012. It was over 100 degrees out, in Bossier City, Louisiana, and I was not enjoying the mosquito attacks nor the battle to stay hydrated in the summer heat. With the sun getting low on the horizon, I found my vision wasn't quite what it used to be, either. Though my mind still tells me that I'm ready to play today; I'm not sure my body agrees. Despite multiple arm surgeries (2013-2014), I still feel like I have at least one good swing left in me.

Homeruns, diving catches, double and triple plays, a whole slew of stolen bases—there were lots of great moments to be proud of. For all that, there is one memory that haunts me to this very day...one play out of thousands that returns to my thoughts again and again. It casts an ominous shadow over all the highlight reel moments. I'm sure no one remembers it but me. Like a perfectly targeted spear thrust, that memory finds the gap in my armor each time and strikes forcibly at a wound that has never healed. It was the TRIPLE that never was.

It was a dark and ominously cloudy day. Seriously . . . it was! And quite windy, too! We were playing an away game. I don't remember what team we were playing. I don't remember whether we won or lost. I had been making good contact with the ball throughout the whole season but I never really "got a hold of one," at least not to the extent that I knew I had within me. I did have a number of impressive line drive doubles but I typically didn't hit the ball on an upward trajectory. That was about to change. I can still see the pitch coming. I can feel my grip tighten on the bat. I am all focus. The adrenaline courses through me and all the countless parts and pieces that make for "perfect timing" come together. CLANK!!! My aluminum bat makes ideal contact with the ball and that white spheroid launches on a perfect trajectory that would have made any artillery crew proud. And I stood there. WHAT IN THE NAME OF ALL THAT IS HOLY!??? Disbelief! The most beautifully crafted work of art I had ever stroked was towering far above the heads of the outfielders in Right-Center. They were in shock. I was in shock! I wanted to grab a mic and begin the play-by-play for all the fans back home. And then I realized . . . run! I've got to run. The ball kept traveling and I began my movement towards first base, never taking my eyes off the impressive flight path of my ball. By now, the outfielders had kicked in their jets and they were running at full speed after the only celestial body visible in the clouded sky. Approaching first base, Eisenberg didn't even have to signal me to keep going—that much was given. And yet I was casually striding, still watching the outfielders chase. If this game had been played on our home field, my shot would have easily cleared our fence. There were no fences at this away field. Halfway between first and second, and I was still easily striding, watching in amazement as the outfielders finally caught up to the ball. Does anyone have a pair of binoculars so I can see them better? Briefly looking towards third, Bobby is waving me on but he looks confused because I seem to be slowing up my pace even more. At some point, just to be super extra safe, I decided to pull into second base and stay there. And I waited. And I waited. And finally, the ball makes it back into the infield. I think I hear Coach Casey mumbling that I should have gone for three. I know I hear some team-mates, not used to seeing anything quite like that come off my bat, discussing how the wind must have taken it. And there I was—the easiest DOUBLE of my life. I believe that I did make it in to score before the inning was done. So, what's the problem? The problem—I SHOULD'VE GONE FOR THREE. If I had one play back, from my entire life portfolio of sporting events, it would have to be that moment in 12th Grade. Fastest guy on my team, I had the speed to easily make it around to third base, maybe even home—but I played it safe. Too safe. WAY TOO SAFE!

So, why does this bother me? It bugs me because it's representative of a weakness that has come back to haunt me, now and again, throughout the years. True, there have been countless times when I fiercely engaged and I've certainly had many moments of great personal bravery. However, there are also an unfortunate number of occasions when I "didn't take that chance." I played it safe or I was lacking in self-confidence. While others, less qualified than me, leapt forward to take the prize, I stood back and watched—and it hurt. It hurt a lot. Sometimes, I had the opportunity to make amends. In other instances, there would be no second chances. Life is like that—for all of us. And that's why I wanted to share this story.

It's quite natural to want to stay in our comfort zone. Have you ever seen a performer, or perhaps read a book, and thought— "Hey, I can do better than that!"? You might be right! Granted, there's often an element of "having the right connections" or being in the "right place at the right time" but we all need to ask ourselves—"Did I truly give it my all?" "Did I bring my 'A Game'?" "Did I cast aside self-doubt and roll into that audition like a champ?" "Did I take the tough classes or fill my semesters with the easy stuff?" We've all encountered these deci-sion points in life. More decisions are on the way. For my part, I'm very glad my painful memory from high school baseball haunts me as it does. There's a message there that is as applicable to me today as it was 36 years ago. Back then, besides being stunned by what I was witnessing, I rationalized my lack of aggressiveness by telling myself that I was being a good team player—not risking an Out for the sake of personal glory. In truth, the team would have been better off with me on third base. There's a lesson there. I haven't forgotten. I hope I never do.

And that brings me to today. For years, I have been sitting on a personal story from my life. Actually, a number of stories that revolve around a common theme. Part of me believed that some of my stories might help others—they might bring a smile, inspire, or perhaps instruct. Another part of me remained deeply concerned that sharing such personal tales would create vulnerabilities or, perhaps, come across as being narcissistic. Over the years, I've shared bits and pieces with friends and, occasionally, on social media. The feedback was generally positive and friends suggested that I should write a book, some day. And there I was, rounding first base. But this time, I'm going for three. Time will tell if my decision was a good one or not. The coach is waving me on and, while I still have strength in my legs, I'm not looking back. My memoir is set for publication in the coming days, during the very special month of August. I hope that you might join me on the journey.

Afternoon Walk

(Written October 24, 2020)
Previously Unpublished

I describe the healing power of an autumn walk.

Crunch, crunch, crunch; dying leaves drying beneath my feet. Lonely and I don't know why; I found myself on the verge of writing a poem about walking beneath the dark sky until an epiphany granted me the wisdom to put down the pen and don my boots . . . and start walking beneath the dark sky. Shuffling at first, I saw the pavement littered with yellows, oranges and browns. Were those the colors of sick, dying, dead? Ambulance sirens disturbed the peace and raced by me, lights flashing. Sick, dying, dead? I continued. Around the bend, along a quiet stretch of suburban road, they gathered. I did not wish to be a gawker but my planned path was going to take me past this scene and I saw no reason to change my route. As my mind wondered, I pondered. I've spent so long tuning into messages the universe sends me that I am often overly cautious not to ascribe a meaning or lesson to each moment that I absorb into my consciousness. Some things just happen. I expected to see flames or hear gun shots. It would be unkind to say I was disappointed. I care for the welfare of the afflicted but I was, none-theless, confused as to why three ambulances, two fire trucks, and a couple police cars were needed to attend to the one individual sitting in the passenger seat of a parked vehicle in the driveway of that home. I presume someone was about to drive that person to the hospital. It looked like an elderly person but I didn't bring my glasses today because today was a day I wanted to see the world through the lenses I was born with and not the lenses the optometrist provided me. It's silly, but I think like that. In the military, we learned about mass and concentration of force—bring overwhelming power to bare upon a critical center of gravity. Wanting to get on with my thoughts, I assured myself that the entire first responder population of the town was doing just that. I hope the ailing person recovers. I continued. The breeze and the dark sky inspired me. I only wish it were ten degrees cooler but I wasn't complaining. I felt the strength returning and my shuffle turned into a swagger as my gaze shifted from the leaves below to the sky above. In my ideal world, I would have been serenaded by the gentle lapping of the waves upon the shore. I made due with the swooshing sound of vehicles racing by me at sixty miles per hour, as I walked along the shoulder of a busy highway. You take what you have and you make the most of it. Those with much more have made much less of it. Whatever I was doing was working and the loneliness of the day turned to strength. I defiantly looked ahead, as if ready to engage any foe. I found none. Today, I was my own enemy . . . until that time when I was my own savior. I am well and I am strong and I am me.

Snowy Field

(Written December 17, 2020)
Previously Unpublished

*Reminiscing about a happy Air Force Academy
memory—finding solace looking out upon the
snow-covered parade field.*

To find peace amidst chaos is a great blessing.

Final examinations at the Air Force Academy. Freshman year.
Christmas vacation loomed on the horizon; my last final examination
scheduled for December 18th. Finals were a major concern as my
grades were suffering but grades were just the tip of the iceberg. Since
the summer, I had been targeted and I did not understand why. I was
yelled at all the time. I could barely exit my door, headed to the bathroom, without some upperclassman accosting me to regurgitate countless facts, figures, and quotes. In some cases, I was asked to create
reports on military aircraft to present to them or told to write an essay
on some relevant military topic. In other instances, I was asked to
perform additional chores around the squadron. Did they know my
grades were suffering? Would it have even mattered? I felt like no one
cared. I missed one session of swimming intramurals back in October.
I had a mandatory lecture to attend that evening and I did not think I
could go to swimming without missing dinner. The swim coach was
one of the people who was targeting me—trying to force me to leave
the Academy. He was also the Squadron Training NCO. Training
should be about training. Back then, "training" tended to have less
pleasant connotations. "Training" sessions usually involved lots of
yelling and screaming and standing at attention, "pulling chins," until
every inch of your body was tense and in pain. So, I made an unwise
decision to skip intramurals, assured that my excuse was a valid one. It's
"easier to ask forgiveness than to seek permission," right? More so
when you have to report-in to the Squadron Training NCO to ask

509

permission. So, I chose my course. Bam! 40-40-2! That means 40 demerits (strikes against you which could eventually add up to a disenrollment); 40 tours (that's 40 hours of marching back and forth outside with your rifle on the "tour pad") and 2 months of restrictions (making it so you could not leave the Cadet Area, or even go to the Cadet recreation facility, Arnold Hall). In short, I'd spend two months going between classes, meals, and the squadron. That was the punishment for "FAILURE TO DO DUTY, INTENTIONAL." I was devasted. In a twisted game of psychological warfare, my punishment was deliberately held for two months so that I would have to consider it over the winter break. I have no doubt there were several jerks who were hoping I would elect not to return. It was not unusual for freshman to make the break with the Academy after the first semester was complete. With a few upperclassman spreading rumors that I didn't care about the Academy or the military, it was no surprise that I was "trained" by just about every upperclassman who had nothing better to do at the time. It was a horrible experience. Frequently, I was surrounded by half a dozen upperclassmen screaming at me and asking me to recite quotes and facts. At meals, I was regularly assigned to "The Training Table" where meals consisted of healthy portions of torment and very little caloric intake. To make matters worse, on December 9th (a Sunday), I received my Military Performance Debrief from my squadron's Air Officer Commanding (or AOC). As if my heart wasn't already suffering immeasurably, I was informed that over 30 cadets from my squadron had rated me as the worst freshman (4th Classman) in the unit. I was stunned and sat there in silence. How could that be? I knew I was better than that. I cared and I was working incredibly hard. Many of the comments on the forms were absolutely ridiculous and clearly the result of hearsay rather than observation. I saluted my AOC and departed his office feeling like my entire world was collapsing. Finals began just a few days later.

With the advent of finals, the squadron "training" stopped and we were left in peace to study for the upcoming examinations. Wearing my parka atop my athletic jacket, I made my way along the marble strips of the Terrazzo towards the library. All freshman were required to "walk the strips" along the perimeter—we were not allowed to take the direct route anywhere. It was dark, cold, and windy. We were not permitted to look around—our eyes had to remain focused ahead, at all times. One tilt of the head and we might anticipate the dreaded yell from across the Terrazzo, "Hey, you, Gazing Man!!!" I didn't want to be called out for gazing so I kept my head locked in the forward position. Even so, I just had to scan the windows of the dorm rooms I passed, using my peripheral vision, to absorb the holiday lights and decorations which created a much-needed festive yuletide ambiance to the scene. Once I reached the library, I no longer had to be at attention. I no longer had to be silent. And I could look wherever I wanted. A deep sigh. My muscles relaxed. Up the beautiful spiral marble stairs, I climbed. Our Academy Library was spectacular. Higher and higher until I reached the 5th floor. With my book bag in hand, I found a small study table near the window. This would become my favorite study spot. I broke out my study materials and went to work. I studied, and studied, and studied. The outcome of the final exams was up in the air. When exhaustion overtook me, I looked out the window. The scene was beautiful; serene. Down below, I saw the Parade Field, and the winding road that went down the hill and eventually would set one on course for the Academy's South Gate. The Parade Field was covered in snow, the street lights casting a soft fluorescent orange tint upon the glistening blanket of white. And now the snow was falling! It was incredibly beautiful! I put my books aside. I sat, in awe, admiring the scene below. Then I left my study perch, leaving my books upon the desk, and worked my way back down the marble stairs to the building's exit. I walked over to the railing and absorbed all the sights, sounds, smells, and feelings that the moment had to offer. Just a few floors below my study nest, the scene looked much the same but now I could feel the cold and crisp breeze upon my face. I could feel the cool flakes of snow as they melted on my warm cheeks. I could smell the fresh mountain air mixed with a touch of pine. I heard the wind as it danced between the buildings that adorned our mountain campus. Occasionally, I could hear the muffled sound of a car engine as it carefully worked its way down the road. I forgot about my examinations. I stopped thinking about my troubles within the squadron. I no longer cared about who may have considered me unworthy. I was worthy. And I was strong. But, most of all, I was at peace. I felt as if a great weight had lifted from my shoulders and I knew I would be okay. No matter what happened, I was going to be okay. To find peace amidst chaos is a great blessing! I found it upon that lonely mountain on a cold and wintery December night. The snow outside my window tonight reminds me of that day. And I know I will be okay.

I returned to the Air Force Academy after the Christmas break and I did my time. One by one, I convinced the upperclassman that I was worthy. The next time my AOC debriefed me, I was informed that only two people had rated me worst in my class. I suspect the two unimpressed raters were the jerks who started the slander campaign in the first place. Better yet, several people had rated me #1. That was a turn around. My grades were suffering and my AOC knew that I had put aside my studies to focus all my attention on military performance. It was a risky strategy, and one that nearly got me academically disenrolled—but I survived. At the years end, several of the upperclassmen I respected most complemented me on having the courage to fight through that ordeal. To be honest, I would rather I had been treated fairly from the onset—but I graciously accepted the complements, anyway. My AOC pulled me in and told me he was confident I would make an outstanding officer in the Air Force. I think he knew that I had sacrificed—I was on academic probation but the military performance indicators told a story of a cadet who had his heart in the right place. I felt proud.

I often returned to my special study nest, on the library's 5th floor, in the years that followed. And, when it snowed, I would put my books down, just as I had on that first December visit, in 1984, and I would appreciate the beauty of the world. With snowflakes gracefully dancing their way down from the clouds, I'd take a study break to head outside, to the back railing. I would take it all in—the familiar sensations that took me to a special place. It was a long and difficult four years. I took my last final examination, as a cadet, on May 21st, 1988. At 4:30pm (1630 Hrs. in cadet speak), I departed the exam room in Fairchild Hall and walked behind the building, along the metal railing, until I came to my favorite spot, just below the library. Although it was a lovely spring day, if I closed my eyes, I could almost feel the chill of a cold December evening; wind-driven snow landing upon my face. The battle was done. I survived. Four years of "Graded Reviews" and final examinations raced through my thoughts. I would quietly celebrate my victory at this special place, reflecting upon special memories. I felt proud. More importantly, I felt at peace.

Be Strong, Be You

(Written December 22, 2020)
Previously Unpublished

A rallying thought about staying the course and being yourself.

When the light of dawn is still hours away and the deep cold of a starless night is sapping your will to exist, stand tall and defiant and shout into the darkness "I am me!" They can take everything you own and block every path before you but for one—the path that leads to your true destiny. And they shall despair for you will walk that path unbroken and with a spirit within that they shall never understand nor ever attain. Be strong. Be you.

BEAUTIFUL BLONDE AT AN AIRPORT

(Written September 3, 2020)
Previously Unpublished

A passing moment and a brief interaction with a lovely young lady at an international airport. She made an impression.

It was July of 1983. The place was Helsinki Airport in Finland. I was heading East; she was heading West. Her name was Carol and she was heading home to Ohio. I was about as shy as they come. She approached me and we started conversing. And we talked. And we talked, and we talked. I had never spoken like this to a girl and it was wonderful. And then, our travel guide said we all needed to gather up for some important briefings (we were headed to the Soviet Union and, I suppose, bad things might happen if we were not informed of some important "Dos and Don'ts." I wasn't happy. If I were me of today, I would have said "screw the briefings, I'm talking with a lovely young lady and we've got some chemistry going." But I was me of 1983; 16 years old, and I simply apologized and we said our goodbyes. My Dad said he'd never seen me like that. I didn't know what he meant. I know now. Airports are fascinating crossroads of the world. Ships pass in the night and our experiences add color to our life story. Our lives are filled with "could haves" and "should haves." Sometimes, when I'm waiting at an airport (like today) and I'm feeling a little lonely (like today), I remember the Beautiful Blonde at the Airport—her name was Carol. We had so much to talk about and I loved every minute of it. I hope she's well and I hope she's happy.

Your Greatest Strength

(Written February 28, 2021)
Previously Unpublished

Some thoughts on a common theme throughout my life—the importance of individuality and standing apart from the masses rather than blindly following trends to gain acceptance. It's a difficult road. It's important that we travel it.

I've seen the edge of brokenness you speak of. I've walked the ledge above the emptiness of that void—no hand extended to pull me back; no comforting voice to offer words of encouragement. I know this sadness and I have heard the siren's call that beckons me to follow to my grave. Yet I stand here, Death's shadow becoming one with my own, and share my final breath with you, dear friend.

For too long, now, hast thou sought validation from those who were never fit to be your judge. Charlatans have robbed you of your gold, offering false promises that they might pave your road to greater glory. What promise, I ask you, have they ever fulfilled? None. Formulas for success, cleverly packaged as proven methods for outshining your competitors, brilliantly illuminated upon the parchment or delivered with silver tongues—they captured your imagination and offered false hope. Tell me then, what competitors were you seeking to surpass? What prize were you hoping to win? Fame? Riches? Glory? What is your measure of success? I see. Allow me, then, to share this wisdom; hard won though I give it freely in these final moments of my life.

God has placed us here, upon this glorious Earth, not so that we might strive to become one and the same with all of our kind but so that we might shine brilliantly, as a star, and contribute to the beautiful diversity that we so often take for granted. You need not, and should not, strive to be like all others. That, my friend, is a life wasted. Will you chisel your name upon the marble of another man's creation, claiming that art as your own? Is this ill-deserved praise what you desire? Imitation is the sincerest form of flattery. Is that it? If you would revel in such stolen accolades then I cry for your soul for thou art truly

515

lost. No! No, I say. We must each contribute in our own way but to do so we must live the life we were born to live. Let the sculptor be revered, the soldier paraded beneath the victory arch, and the martyr sainted and greeted warmly in Heaven, but seek not their path unless that immutable voice within compels you to set that course. You have a gift. A God-given gift. I speak of your greatest strength; and that is your essence . . . that irrepressible calling that seeks to bring you back home to who you truly are. You, dear friend, are your greatest strength! You are undeniably unique and incomparably beautiful and God has ordained in thusly; yet you seek to enshroud God's work beneath a mantle of insecurity and shame. Why? Why do you persist in denying your true self when he is the man this world needs most? There are no mistakes—you are here for a purpose; but you shall not fulfill your role upon this glorious stage unless you play the part you were destined for.

Oh, I do understand. Life is fraught with hardship and pain and our fellow travelers are often unkind to those they do not understand and those who fail to follow their lead, praise their existence, or bow to their authority. But hear me when I tell you that too many lost souls have marked their success in life upon the pages of a calendar. They have cowered beneath an actor's mask and counted the days. Each passing day must have pained them greatly until, one day, they could run from Death no longer. On that day, all the wealth and praise must have weighed heavily upon their dying thoughts and measured little against what was lost—integrity; courage; life. A life they never knew; the life they were meant to live. I beg you not to make this mistake. Though you welcome a hundred summers, you shall perish in the coldest winter.

Of all things deserving protection and care; few are as important as your true self. It is our very soul; a gift given at birth and the only treasure we might take with us to the grave. Protect it with all your might! Ride bravely and forcefully through this life but know that, in the darkness of the night, our foes, mortal and of the nether regions, seek to unseat us and rob us of what we value most. Do not give it willingly. Defy these thieves, I implore you. Too many have willingly relinquished their essence only to discover that God's greatest gift, our greatest strength, was unrecoverable. They justify the sacrifice until that time when all men are held accountable; and then they weep. True now, we are but men; but there is untold strength within our spirit and we must call upon this light when the night is darkest. We must stand with dignity, no matter how frail our bodies, no matter how tattered our clothes, no matter how deplorable our living conditions. We must stand and be accounted for. The world shall know we existed for our voice shall echo through the darkness and summon the courage of those too long forsaken; those abandoned; those forgotten.

We must stand and we must fight. We must fight to live the lives we were born to live and never concede to the pressure to abandon our journey towards self-actualization. I know this struggle well. Years ago, whilst humbly venturing along my chosen path, I was set upon by a villainous band of ruffians, intent on my destruction. Vitriol so venomous, I was unhorsed and unnerved—nothing could have prepared me for such a savage attack on all I held dear. Confused and astonished by the ferocity of the assault, I lay there, defenseless, before those traitors who sought to crush my spirit and break me. My broken and torn body was cast deep within the cruelest swamp on the darkest of nights. My foes sought neither purse nor earthly possession; they sought to rob me of my very soul. Had I but submitted to their will by pledging my fealty, my plight should have been relieved. As my will is my own, I refused, and swore to be no less than I am. A was abandoned so that the swamp might devour what courage remained within my breast. As I wandered, cold and alone, all manner of doubt crept into my weary mind. Wading through those foul waters for countless days, time lost meaning amidst the eternal darkness. I knew only that my foe was poised upon the distant shore, ready to take possession of the only thing of value I had left. Yet, for all that, I refused to submit. When all hope seemed lost, I saw a light; a beacon from a distant shore. I should have died; food and water denied me; my body quaking, chilled from days immersed in festering waters. Yet something sustained me. I reached the shore, just as my strength was failing me. It was a cruel trick that my enemies found me where I lay. They greedily awaited my surrender and I might have acquiesced had not the sun broken the horizon. The morning rays touched the steel of an unsheathed sword laying just beyond my reach and set it afire with a heavenly glow.

I am your sword. Reach for me. I glow with the brilliance of the morning sun and I am here to offer you hope. Reach for me.

On that day, though my body was broken and my will all but shattered, I fought for those remaining inches until I grasped the pommel of that fine weapon. And then, defying all but God Himself, I stood. I stood and lifted my sword to the heavens and vowed that I would not fall that day. My enemies shrunk before me and fled in terror. They have never had the courage to return. Oh, they're out there, alright. I've seen them. I saw them fast on your heels last night. That's when I knew you were in trouble. I am your sword. Reach for me. This decision must be yours. Should you fall; should you abandon all you are, then you shall sign the writ for your own execution and I promise you the death shall be painfully slow.

Alas, my time grows near. Death patiently awaits; my brief reprieve granted so that I might offer the thoughts of an aged warrior to a young man in need. Mine are but words and the weight of the decision shall remain upon your shoulders, every day from now until you part with this life. Do as you please but heed my warning, I implore. Forge your own path. Be an original. Spread love and work with others but guard your soul from those who seek to steal it from you. Be yourself and you shall never regret it. You are your greatest strength.

CELADON VASE & CHERRY BLOSSOMS

(Written April 2, 2021)
Previously Unpublished

I recall one of the most difficult times in my life and the painful journey toward recovery. A vase from South Korea reminds me of the healing power of nature.

Winter of 2015-2016 was one of the saddest times of my life. Divorce proceedings underway, I helped my wife of 22 years pack up and watched as she and my children got on the bus at U.S. Army Garrison Yongsan, in Seoul, South Korea, for their trip to the airport. I'd like to say I fought back the tears but I didn't. I was a mess. I knew the separation was long overdue and I knew my wife longed only to return to her home in South Dakota and had long-since given up on our relationship but, for all that, the feeling of being utterly alone hit me like a rock. I was one of only a handful of Air Force officers stationed at Yongsan and I was an office of one, representing my Combatant Command (U.S. Transportation Command) as the executive liaison officer to Korea. I didn't have any friends there, just amicable work relationships--an abundance of people who seemed disinterested in the personal life challenges of an Air Force Colonel. It was truly a sad and lonely time. My years on this Earth had enlightened me to the fact that you have to be the custodian of your own happiness. We can't wait for others to fix our lives. I endured the winter but then, as the flowers began to bloom in spring, I sought a renewal of my own. I affectionately call the period Cherry Blossom Quest 2016 but, really, beyond traveling from park to park in search of the glorious cherry blossom displays, I was also reaching deep within to remind myself of lessons I had learned years ago--it's a beautiful world and there is much to be thankful of. I visited a number of old palaces and gardens and spent countless hours hopping trains and subways to get to places I hadn't been before. The flowers and cherry blossoms were glorious and the accompanying wildlife in the gardens also brought joy. I felt my heart coming alive again and the healing was beginning. To remember this special time, I purchased a beautiful vase (crafted with a traditional Chinese/Korean greenish celadon glaze) depicting a cherry blossom tree. The vase currently sits next to a Korean lamp on a buffet table in my apartment and it forever reminds me of the healing power of nature. This is a spring memory I thought I'd share with you. I hope that your life is going well but, if it's not, remember that you do have friends who care (don't try to convince yourself you don't) and also that there is a remarkable world out there just waiting for you to explore. Live, love, and be grateful for the little things that make this world magical. Enjoy the day.

MY BEST PITCH

(Written April 10, 2021)
Previously Unpublished

*Another high school baseball memory. The
importance of a single pitch and the love of a sport
shared between father and son.*

I was not a pitcher. My self-identity, at least so far as baseball was concerned was, and will always be, "outfielder." I loved nothing better than kicking into full gear and tracking down a baseball hit over my head, grabbing it with a fully extended arm, or stealing away a homerun with my glove above the fence line. I was fast, had a great arm, and a keen ability to judge the flight of a baseball and match my speed to arrive at an intercept point. There's a reason my high school baseball nickname was "Divin' Dave" or "Divin'," for short, and not "Flame Thrower" or, better yet, "Doctor Screwball." Doctor Screwball would have been cool though. So, where am I going with this. Well, with spring in the air, happy memories of twelve years of baseball and thirty years of softball are filling my head. Oh, how I miss the game! Today, one interesting memory popped into my head—a brief snapshot in time but a moment I still remember, 38 years later. The memory is of my best pitch, ever.

My father played semi-pro ball in Nebraska, in his younger days; the highlight of his career being an invitation to tryout with the Chicago White Sox at Comiskey Park. He was told to gain 30 pounds and come back. My father was not a big man but, the few times I saw him throw a ball with intent to "pitch," he hurled that stitched white sphere with a frightening intensity. I have no doubt he could menacingly launch a baseball back in the day. He was a pitcher, you see, and I believe he had hopes that I might be one, too. As I previously mentioned, that role was not one I sought but, to humor my father, I did pitch a few games in Little League and a couple while playing Junior Varsity Baseball. I believe I was, notionally, considered as a potential reliever on Varsity but I tended to dwell in my happy place, the outfield, and never got called to the mound my senior year despite being asked to warm up a couple times when our late inning pitching was looking sketchy. In Little League, being able to throw hard was good enough. By the time you reached high school, you pretty much had to have some other tools in your arsenal to be an effective pitcher. My father worked with me to learn to throw a curveball. My curve was never reliable. I rarely threw it in a tight spot and never when the count went to three balls. The fastball was always my go-to pitch in a pinch. I had relatively good control and, as it was, my fastball tended to have some motion on it, much to the displeasure of my catchers who complained that my "fastball" would break one way and then the other. It wasn't anything I was doing purposefully. I suspect my low "three-quarters" delivery (slightly higher than a side-arm pitch) and the way I gripped the ball along the seams had something to do with the unintentional movement. It befuddled hitters and aggravated catchers—that's about all I knew. At my best, I could toss the ball somewhere in the mid-80s which, by high school standards, wasn't bad. You'd be decimated at that speed in the major leagues unless you mixed in all kinds of junk to keep the batters off balance. Anyway, I only pitched a couple games. There's one that I will never forget—not the game but the pitch.

Half the outs of the game were gained through strike outs I threw. We still lost. My father had decided to attend the game and positioned himself directly behind home plate. He was always most interested in the pitching game and I knew my every motion would be under close scrutiny. Knowing my dad was watching and critiquing added some extra stress. The following year, I mentioned to my father that his viewing of my games added some pressure. He stopped coming. I've always regretted that as I wound up being the team MVP during my senior year. I wish Dad could have seen me at my best. I felt some redemption, some twenty years later, when my father came to a softball tournament at my base and got to see his son power two homeruns over the left field fence of the ball park. Still, there's a touch of guilt that has never left me. But on this spring day, back in high school, with my father watching, I felt the mojo was working for me and I started to push myself.

Two outs. Men on base. The batter was tough. I was throwing heat but he kept fowling balls off and I just couldn't seem to close the deal. It was a little bit frustrating. After a good at bat, my adversary for this particular battle had worked the count to 3-2; three balls and two strikes, for the uninitiated. As was usual, the catcher flashed me the sign for a fastball. No surprise there--Lange always threw fastballs with three balls in the count. I'm not sure what inspired me but I shook my head, indicating that I was not going to throw a fastball. I had only one other pitch in my arsenal—my not-entirely reliable curveball. The catcher looked at me with surprise. He then flashed the sign for a curveball—two fingers. This was JV baseball and we didn't exactly have an evolved system of signaling. The stage was set. I changed my grip on the ball, took a breath, and began my wind-up. I threw that ball right at the batter and fiercely snapped my wrist as my arm's motion carried the ball past my head. As the ball left my grip, I looked on with concern as the ball appeared to be traveling right toward the batter's head. The batter was even more concerned—he literally dove backward, falling to the ground to avoid being hit. But then something truly remarkable happened. My father used to tell me about some of the great curveball pitchers and he'd describe their pitches as "falling off the table" or, in other words, giving the appearance of rolling off a table and dropping straight down. Well, my pitch fell off the table and, much to my astonishment, dropped sharply and passed squarely through the center of the strike zone. STRIKE THREE! YOU'RE OUT! The batter, still on his knees in the dirt, looked up in disbelief. My catcher looked back at me, his eyes wide and an expression of complete astonishment on his face. My coach cheered. My team shouted words of encouragement. But, best of all, behind home plate, my father stood and applauded, yelling out a pride-filled "Atta Boy, Dave!" Our team ran off the field and I got several slaps on the back. I will never forget that moment. As I mentioned before, despite my best efforts on the mound, we didn't win that day. Sometimes, however, it's not all about winning. I had that one perfect pitch and my father was there to see it. That meant the world to me. Eventually, our catcher learned that this Curveball of the Gods was not something I could call upon at will. I still don't know where that pitch came from but there had to have been some accidental mix of perfect aerodynamics and applied forces with, perhaps, a little magic tossed into the equation. I'm thankful for the moment. When I think of my years of playing ball, it's the hits and the spectacular catches that I remember most. But, in the Lange Book of Sporting Memories, there's a little asterisk in the text and a footnote that reminds me of a special day on the pitcher's mound and my best pitch ever. Embrace each special moment in life. May the memories help get you through the tough times.

New Year's Reflections

(Written, December 31, 2021)
Previously Unpublished

*New Years reflections and a discussion on the
importance of not rushing through life but, instead,
learning to savor each moment.*

For all our efforts, one thing man shall never overcome is the relentless march of time. For some, an indistinguishable sweep of a watch hand; for others, the cruel pounding of the watch mechanism with each "tick" and each "tock" reminding us our time on this earth is limited. How many times have we raced from milestone to milestone? I can't wait until I can drive! Life will be great once I graduate and get a job! I'm going to meet my soulmate and we'll get married and have the best honeymoon ever! In a few more years, I'll get that promotion and then I can afford that new car! Birthdays, anniversaries, child births and school events, and then reliving our younger days through the life events of our children. We run, run, run until, one day, we realize there's more behind than ahead and we wonder why we didn't attempt to slow the pace and spend more time enjoying each and every moment.

I reflect a lot, around the end of the year. I like to think. I don't live in the past but I treasure the memories and make no apology for revisiting them. I look forward to the future. I look forward with hope but I know well that there is no way to predict what will be—no matter how much effort I put into forcing certain outcomes. I'm okay with that. I actually enjoy marching forth into the unknown. I love adventures and life is the greatest of adventures. Attitude goes a long way to determining whether you go to sleep with a smile or with tears in your eyes.

On the precipice of a new year, I have no idea what 2022 will hold in store. Who could have predicted the last few years? As for myself, I stopped speculating long ago. I do know one thing—it'll be an adventure. There'll be good and bad, happiness and sadness—there'll be life…at least for as long as I'm blessed to have it. Truly, each day is a gift and I shall remain grateful for this treasure.

Despite the uncertainty, let's hope the new year brings good things —peace in place of war and health instead of illness. I wish the best for you, your families, friends, and loved ones. While we are all set upon our individual journeys, we are joined, forever, by the time we share upon this earth. Each act we perform directly or indirectly affects others. As the second-hand sweeps, let's try to make each moment count. Wishing you a Happy New Year!

Holiday Season Musings

(Written December 14, 2023)
Previously Unpublished

*I recall some happy holiday memories from my youth.
Making gifts and sharing special times with my
siblings.*

"Never look back," they say. "Always look to the future." I am who I
am because of my past and all of that informs my present and propels
me forward into my future. Besides, during the holiday season, especially, I love to look back because my memories remind me of a time
when the world was full of magic and my heart was light. Holiday
shows were fun. Presents under the tree were exciting. Time spent with
my family was wonderful. But few memories are as beautiful to me as
the time spent with my holiday buddy, my little sister, Jenny. We both
came to life during this time of year and, somehow, any squabbles and
sibling rivalry got put to the side as we embarked upon a fun-filled
holiday season that spanned from Thanksgiving through New Years. It
was truly a special time.

The Gifting.

Sometime in early December, a secret message would be delivered
—a series of clues directing my sister from location to location until
the message was finally found. Perhaps it would be inside of a cardboard roller hidden under my parents' dresser. Perhaps it might be
found in the medicine cabinet? Whatever the case, the note would set a
time and place for our first annual meeting to plan out Christmas gifts
for our family members. During the initial meeting, we'd brainstorm
ideas for creating gifts for each member of our family. Usually, we
would plan on around five gifts per person (for our mother, father, and
older brother). Separately, we'd also make something for each other. I
have no doubt my kid sister must have loved the tank I made for her
out of a shoe box, round tin cookie container, pasteboard roller, and
various strings, pencils, and rubber bands. It was a labor of love—I
managed to cut out a portion of the bottom of the cookie tin using
only a hammer and multiple nail strikes. We did the best we could with

what we had. Funny thing, I never did see Jennifer using the tank during any Barbie Doll play...it probably happened while I wasn't looking. But, back to the story. Gifts for our family usually included things like "picture packets" filled with drawings that we each made, note pads, short stories and/or poems, and other odds and ends that we were able to fashion out of our limited supply of paper, cardboard, string, tape, rubber bands, crayons and markers. The big-ticket item, however, was always the Annual Fleegle Calendar. Where to start? "Fleegle" was one of my sister's stuffed animals—a frog to be specific. He and "Mr. Frog" were cousins and by the time the late 70s had arrived, they had developed clear personalities that the family was very familiar with. Fleegle was, shall we say, a bit self-absorbed, displaying a bravado and confidence none of us had. Perhaps that's what made him endearing. His obnoxious comments and rampant self-love were infamous yet, for all that, he was a lovable "member of our family." It should be no surprise that the first "Fleegle Calendar" featured a MUCH LARGER THAN LIFE Fleegle with his hands triumphantly raised in the air. The calendar was created on a 36" x 24" white piece of oak tag. Beneath the frog, the year was broken out in standard calendar style with months, days, and dates displayed in a typical fash-ion. While my sister typically laid out the calendar design, including penning in an outline of the great Fleegle, himself, we would always collaborate on coloring in the calendar. With two green crayons, we'd color together until Fleegle was completely colored in. It was such a hit that first Christmas that it became a tradition—something my mom looked forward to each year. A Fleegle Calendar always hangs in the kitchen. Upstairs, in my brother's old room, is a stack of over 40 calen-dars that my mom has saved over the years. We never missed a year. Perhaps it's worth adding in this sentimental branch story. When I began my military career, duty took me all over the globe and it was rare, indeed, for me to be home to work on the Fleegle Calendar. But every year, my sister would faithfully create a new calendar and leave Fleegle's left (webbed) hand uncolored. I always understood that it was my duty, whenever I did make it home, to grab the well-used green crayon out of the Crayola Crayon box in my childhood nightstand, and complete shading in the remaining part of the calendar (i.e. Fleegle's left hand). I only missed one year and, on that calendar, now stored upstairs with the rest, Fleegle's left hand remains white. We all agreed that it should stay that way—a reminder that, sometimes, military service "gets in the way" of certain life events. I never got home that year.

Back to "The Gifting." It's a beautiful memory. Christmas music played on my sister's clock radio while we worked, both of us hoping that our gifts would bring smiles on Christmas morning. We didn't have locks on our doors at the house so my sister devised a clever alternative plan. After all, we didn't want anyone barging in on us and discovering their gift before the big day. My sister would swing open one of her closet doors so that it met a partially opened bedroom door. She would then use her jump rope to tie the door knobs together. Nobody was getting past this security measure without some heavy-duty garden shears. I'm smiling now as I reflect back upon the scene. It would usually take us several sittings to complete all the gift work. We didn't have any wrapping paper (how many kids do??) so we raided the pantry and grabbed the roll of aluminum foil. Yes, all our presents were wrapped in aluminum foil. As you might imagine, my mother was likely bewildered by the sudden supply crisis of this valuable cooking asset. In later years, once she realized what was going on, she made sure to purchase extra rolls of aluminum foil so the tradition could continue. I must say, the makeshift wrapping paper did look quite lovely as it reflected the multi-colored lights from our Christmas tree.

On Christmas morning, my sister and I were always up very early. And I mean super-duper early. If our older brother (10 years older than me) was around, we might go upstairs to wake him. I remember, one year, him singing "O Tannenbaum" to my sister and me as we sat by the tree. If John wasn't around, we'd just sit together beneath the tree, after plugging it in, and admire the spectacle before us. With flashlights, we'd peruse the packages, looking for names. Who got the biggest box this year? As great as our anticipation may have been for gifts with our names on them, the real highlight was always waiting to see the reactions to the gifts that we had created together. Even at that young age, giving was always more rewarding than receiving. Beyond the gifts we made, each year, Dad would take my sister and me to Woolworths and give us each $5 to get gifts. Budgeting the cash, we would each buy something for the other members of our family. It's hard to believe, nowadays, that the $5 was enough to get something small for everyone. But the homemade gifts were always the best and I know they're the ones my parents treasured the most. But I'm still wondering about that tank??? It was pretty cool.

With time, I got married and had my own children. I loved Christmases with my wife and kids but you experience the holiday differently as an adult. How can you not? While I fondly think back on these days, too, I can't deny that I feel a special warmth inside when I think of those magical days of my early childhood when my sister and I would conspire to make Christmas just a little more special, creating personalized gifts even as we both basked in the warmth of a magical holiday season, hoping that our gifts would help complement those left by Santa Claus beneath the Lange family Christmas tree. I'm grateful for the joy and extremely grateful to have such a wonderful sister who remains one of my dearest friends.

Heroes

(Written December 30, 2023)
Previously Unpublished

*Finding inspiration amidst the doldrums in our life
and rising above it all. Sometimes, being a hero
means just having the courage and motivation to fix
your own attitude.*

We can be heroes, just for one day. Those lyrics from David Bowie used to run through my head all the time. My own interpretation of the message was, for the most part, unrelated to the theme of the song. I've always viewed life as a kind of struggle (albeit, an often glorious and rewarding one). Especially, in my younger days, my view of the road toward self-actualization was always about fighting…fighting against the "demons" inside of us that restrain us from reaching our potential and, for some, take us in a horrible direction. I am fortunate in that I never strayed into the badlands of alcoholism, drug addiction, or the less conspicuous areas such as narcissism, unmitigated lust, or a plethora of other socially unhealthy mental conditions. At worst, there were days I went to bed and hoped I wouldn't wake up the next morning. Thankfully, those days are long past. However, comma, I have always been judgmental regarding my own actions and attitudes and, as such, I have "fought" to better myself, where possible—and most of it IS possible. Hence, my affinity for Bowie's "Heroes" ('77) and the simple message that we might not always be able to permanently sway the balance, but we sure as Hell can try and we can aspire to be heroes, just for one day. Hopefully, for more than that.

So, to my point. I'd love to say that I'm always on an even keel and, in some ways, perhaps I am. But I'm seldom where I want to be and my approach to righting the wrongs is not one that I recommend. I've always had this notion that our greatest accomplishments come after a fall. And so, sometimes, I let go a bit. For example, I've been unhappy watching the numbers on the scale increase through the holiday season. It's not unusual. I love the holiday goodies and, with a week spent with my parents, I accepted too much of the delicious food items my mother was pushing my way. None of that is Mom's fault. All of it is my fault. I haven't been out for any significant exercise in a couple weeks now. I KNOW how to fix all of this. Yet I haven't. There are other things that are bugging me, too. I haven't read a book in months. I haven't really done any writing in months (outside of my usual diary entries). Dad keeps encouraging me to get back into writing stories—he and my mother love to read my stories. I have fun writing them. But I haven't. In many ways, I've let myself slide—as I've done before. But, I'm aware… and I'm not helpless. For me, personally, I've always been at my best when I'm ramping up to pull out of a slump and so, in some strange psychological maneuver, I let it happen. And then I get angry at myself. And then I attack. I make a plan, I build exercise and weight tracking sheets (or create other tools to fix other issues), and I come charging out of the chute like an angry bull at the rodeo. It's an old story, for me, but it's worked. It's worked as far back as I can remember. I feel like I should slap a label on this whole discussion: "DO NOT TRY THIS AT HOME, KIDS!" Don't. It's best to keep to your healthy routine throughout the year yet, for most of us, our endurance is not infinite…and we get tired. Really, that's human nature. It's impossible to sprint through life. Those that do often have posthumous biographies written shortly after their 35th birthday. Truly, life is more like a marathon. We try to keep an even pace throughout the race but, for most of us amateurs, we don't quite get it right. We slow down. Perhaps, we start walking for a bit. Sometimes, we bend over, hands on our knees, and wonder how we're going to continue. Hopefully, we find a way.

I woke up this morning, knowing that I could go for a walk and start the process of getting myself back into the physical shape I want to be in. I decided to write instead because I feel this is an important message to carry into the new year. The message is "don't give up and don't hate on yourself" for missing the goals you set this year. I really have my eyes on January 1st and I'm allowing myself a few more days to wallow, knowing full well that I will not tolerate my own laziness for much longer. All the things that are annoying me about my lack of "zip" are also helping to inspire me to do something about it. In the roller coaster of life, I've accepted the lows (sometimes) because I have the confidence that I will be flying back towards the blue skies above before long. And so will you. You don't need to make a New Years resolution. I rarely do. But, I'm always self-monitoring and checking myself on my attitude and behaviors. So...maybe don't "let yourself go" completely. But find your stride again, even if it means you've got to slow and catch your breath along the way. There are external elements that may limit us as we strive to achieve certain life goals but there are no limits to our ability to adjust our attitudes and come out swinging at those "demons" that we've given too much power to across the years. Fight the sadness and get angry—not hateful of yourself but just angry enough to realize that you can do better. I can do better. We all can be heroes. "We can beat them, for ever and ever. We can be Heroes, just for one day." Choose that day, and start down the path your heart is telling you that you're meant to travel.

HOME?

(Written January 21, 2024)
Previously Unpublished

I consider the meaning of "home" in my life.

I suppose it's not the first time I've pondered this question; the question being "Where is home?" And perhaps 11pm on a Sunday night isn't the best time to revisit this—and yet here I am and this is exactly what I plan on doing. The question resurfaced the other week when I called my daughter for her birthday and she said that due to the weather there, in South Dakota, she would not be going home for her birthday but they would celebrate the following weekend. She lives in an apartment of her own now—is that not home? She was born in England but left when she was 18 months old so I don't believe she ever considered that home. So, is the house in South Dakota that my ex-wife bought after the family, minus myself, returned to the States from Korea now what she considers home? It seems so. It was the place she returned to during breaks from college so I suppose it has as much right to be her choice of "home" as any other place. If that's what she considers home, then so be it. But where is my home? It's not there, even though the walls are adorned with all the hangable items that were in our family home for so many years. The piano I got for my wife. All the furniture we moved from one military assignment to the next. Nearly every item in that home was once part or our home—but it's not my home anymore. In fact, it's a bit eerie when I visit. And sad. It's not my home.

Another thought struck me, after first considering my daughter's comment. The apartment I live in now, in Suffolk County—I moved in here in April of 2019. Before my current lease runs out, I will have lived here longer than I have ever lived in any place since leaving home to join the Air Force in 1984. That's kind of a difficult concept for me to get my arms around. I don't know that I feel like this is my home. I have very little connection with Suffolk County and even less with the town that I notionally live in (the truth being that I live in an apartment complex off the highway and I couldn't even tell you what the town, proper, looks like. People ask and toss out references that they feel should connect us and I just stare blankly at them, trying to smile as I downplay the fact that I have no clue what they're talking about. I suppose the home where I grew up, spending most of my childhood, is what I most often have considered home. But I wasn't born there—I was born on the other side of town in a home that I barely remember seeing as how we left when I was only 5. While I was living together with my family, home seemed like whatever place the government put my family and me as we moved from assignment to assignment. We owned a couple houses and lost money on both. They felt like home… for a bit. But they don't feel like home now. There was a time when I would drive by to take a look when I was in the area. I don't anymore. The visits don't make me happy. Truly, they're not home. Is home my apartment? Maybe. But I don't see this as my end-all-be-all and I suspect it won't be very much longer before I decide to hang my hat somewhere else. I don't know where that will be. It probably won't be in a place that feels like home…not yet, at any rate. It may feel like home…someday. Then, again, maybe it won't. I don't know. They say that home is where the heart is. That's not helping me a lot right now. My heart is dreamily skipping about in its own wonderland with clearly undefined borders and a notable lack of definition. So be it. It's not helping me answer the question at hand. It is lovely to visit with my parents in my childhood home where my room remains frozen in time as I left it in July of 1984 when I went to join the Air Force. Sometimes it feels like "home" but other times a voice inside me reminds me that it is no longer home—just a shadow of a place I once absolutely and unequivocally considered my home. So, where in the crazy old humongous universe is my home??? Cute answers (home is where the heart is) and philosophical conjecture (home is more of a state of mind than a tangible physical location) are simply not helpful in my search for that one place to call home. Maybe I have no home? Maybe home is merely a state of mind, after all. Perhaps, I'll find a place that feels like home again. I've lived in 10 states and 2 foreign countries and I've moved somewhere around 22 or 23 times. None of these places ever felt like home. The question remains unanswered, in my mind. And, so I share a photo. P.O Box 4631, U.S. Air Force Academy, CO 80841. This was my first "home away from home"—my college mailing address for four years. This is where all this darn confusion started. I took this photo in 1988, shortly before graduation as I made my pre-graduation nostalgia photo run about campus. If you've actually looked closely at the photo, you'll notice an anomaly which seems quite apropos considering the topic of the evening. Sometime between my freshman year and graduation, the little glass window upon the door of my mailbox apparently slipped out and broke. I have no memory of that happening, only of seeing a clear glass window replace the broken one—a window that the post office determined wasn't worth the bother to label. A reminder, of sorts, that I had no home. Perhaps a message I should have considered more deeply at the time as it foretold of days and years to come. Countless postal boxes and apartment numbers and street addresses that all got jumbled until my periodic security clearance reviews when I had to expertly list each with precise dates for residency. And then, the chaos that was my gypsy lifestyle became all too apparent. In a folder in my filing cabinet, I keep the paperwork neatly organized—it tells a story, alright. It answers the questions the security investigators needed to be answered. But it doesn't answer the question I am left forever considering. Where is home? Perhaps, I don't need one. But, sometimes, it feels like I do.

GREAT DAY JUST AROUND THE CORNER

(Written May 4, 2024)
Previously Unpublished

A shift in perspective, and a morning walk, inspire me to share some thoughts regarding the importance of maintaining a positive attitude.

What a morning! The absolutely amazing thing about it was that I woke up to a dreary, damp, and foggy morning and absolutely none of that changed except I realized it was a BEAUTIFUL, damp, and foggy morning. I wasn't even feeling that great when I woke up—and it didn't matter—even the circle-back to use my apartment bathroom didn't matter. I don't live by a nature preserve…or by the beach…or near any spectacular mountain ranges or waterfalls. I live in an apartment off a highway with a little suburban residential area nearby. And that's where I usually take my morning walks. And so I did today, despite the fact that part of me was considering just staying in. I'm glad I listened to that other part of me.

Everywhere I looked was something beautiful and noteworthy. And it's because I was open to beautiful and noteworthy things—they surround us every day…and yet we walk right by and don't consider them. Every day is a great day. It is. This doesn't mean that unfortunate things won't happen to us—they do and they will. How we reconcile personal life challenges and loss is different for every individual. I would say how we deal with these challenges, from an attitude perspective, is a personal choice. I'm not sure that it is, though. To say so would be to cheapen grief and emotional turbulence so significant that it can rock us off our foundation. But no matter how devastating the blow, we need to build ourselves back up. It's imperative! One great way to do this is to stop, breath, and appreciate the beauty that surrounds us each and every day. Rather than starting out my day with a gloomy outlook, I embraced every wonderful part of this amazing morning. I felt very happy and very connected (to the world and to my beliefs) and, although it's been a bit, I felt that little bit of magic in the air and I just started singing and humming as I walked. I also slowed my normal pace and stopped to take a number of photos of the "ordi-nary" things along my usual walking route that today seemed kind of extraordinary. It was a beautiful morning! I highly encourage everyone to downshift from Crazy-Brain gear into Childlike-Wonder gear and just take that little bit of extra time to appreciate all the terrific things that this world has to offer…and they're just around the corner.

Thoughts on A Lonely Night

(Written March 21, 2025)
Previously Unpublished

Some lamenting on a dark and lonely night with a
note of hope for finding a brighter tomorrow.

Some nights are quiet and ready for dreams. Sometimes you can't because the solitude screams that you should have tried harder to not be alone but those others didn't try harder to reach you at home and ask how you were and look to your needs but then neither did you seek and engage but they have their ways and their things that they do and they knew that you didn't though they'll deny that they knew. Frustration sets in and I battle myself—the movies on pause, the books on the shelf; my mind wanders to places I don't want it to go and I let it —why, I don't know. Maybe I just want to see where it takes me....and maybe I don't. I could put my shoes on right now.... but I know that I won't. I don't want the clubs or the drinks or the flashing lights... maybe just a quiet conversation tonight. Just me and another, listening and sharing. Just two people connecting and caring. But I don't know that I have that and I do know I haven't tonight. Blame is irrelevant— there's no wrong or no right. There are no hard feelings, no betrayals, no saga to tell. I'm just here alone, again, and all is not well. Not broken or torn or beyond hope of repair...just one night, not unlike other nights, that's just okay to fair and that's better than bad or worse that I've known yet sometimes it's just hard to be sitting alone. So, I'll stop and I'll focus—not on people I know...but of dreams that I've had and a place that I know that kept me safe in the past when the darkness closed in and will keep me safe in the future if it tries to again. And I'll reach out and hold on to those visions and dreams and await the coming of dawn where it so often seems that the slate has been cleared so I might plan for, again, a day more inspired and then shall I pen a brighter tale of how that day may be and I'll work harder to make sure I'm more like my best me—a man who works through all these silly misgivings and gets about the business of living with a song in my heart and steel in my will and less needy of companionship that so often has

539

failed me nor open to doubts that so often assailed me when I used to blame myself for the distance I felt and then curse the fates for the cruel hand they dealt whilst the moves on the board were most often for my own protection and proved my salvation more than a rejection and I came out of it all with a more nuanced perspective and I understood. With time, I understood. I understood its best just to be me—with all my quirks and my thoughts, as odd as they may be...at least to those who don't know me and perhaps more so to those who think they do because the only person who will ever truly know me is that quirky fellow who looks back when I look into the mirror on the wall...no longer young and occasionally barely recognizable at all. But when I look past the scars, the grey hair, and tired eyes, I see something deeper that age cannot disguise...I see a beautiful soul that was with me from the start—it shaped my every thought and helped protect my heart through pains you may have known of and most you never will and times when I felt empty and times when I had my fill of troubles and of sorrows....but they didn't take me down and they won't do so tonight, or tomorrow...not while that mirror guy's around—because he was strong and brave and so, too, I shall be....and together we'll make a better tomorrow...and I can hardly wait to see. To see what awaits beyond the horizon and to see what adventures lie ahead and to see what things I'll do when I rise up from my bed and I'll make a vow and keep it, as I walk out of my door, that this day that greets me presently shall be better than the one before. And I have the ability to make it so!

THE ANDOVER TORNADO

(Written April 27, 2025)
Previously Unpublished

*My memories of the terrible and devastating impact
of a tornado on my home base and the local
community.*

Gone! And I mean GONE! We were on the other side of the world when the first reports began filtering in—a massive F5 Tornado had devastated our base, back home, while we remained deployed in the Middle East, flying daily missions over Iraq in the aftermath of Desert Storm.

I am reminded of this story, each year, not by my own FB memories but by the shared story of one of my close friends whose wife and one of his best friends (who was over, helping with the move in) just barely escaped death as the on-base military family housing home collapsed about them.

The date was April 26, 1991. Desert Storm, the war, was over—but some aircrews remained to support the ongoing "No Fly Zone" over Iraq. I will never forget this day. Initially, we had no idea of how bad things were—it's not like anyone was there to brief us on the situation and there were no cell phones and no internet access. We received reports from phone tent calls made by our peers to their families back home. I was single and had no family in Kansas. I remember one guy pulling out a map of our base, McConnell Air Force Base, in Wichita, KS. We would draw a red X through each building that was confirmed to be destroyed, trying to calculate what else may have been in the path. It was all so surreal. Bowling Alley—GONE. Base Gym—GONE…. leveled to a pile of rubble you could look straight over. Hospital—GONE! My Ex-wife, who I didn't know at the time, was the base pharmacist—she got recalled that night to secure and try to recover what could be recovered of the pharmacy—controlled drugs had been blown halfway across Kansas and yet, somehow, needed to be accounted for. Base Exchange (think Target or Walmart)—HEAVILY DAMAGED. And worse, 103 homes in base housing were destroyed.

My friend and one of our squadron's Boom Operators, Nick, got sent home quickly to be with his wife and help sort out the mess that had been their home—they had only recently moved in. The rest of us remained at out desolate base, in the sands of Oman. They called it "Moon Island" and if you'd seen it, you'd know why. The tornado eventually became known as The Andover Tornado and the winds were recorded to exceed 260 mph. The tornado tracked along for 46 miles, ripping apart everything in its path. It just barely missed the Strategic Air Command Alert Parking area where B-1B bombers, loaded with nuclear weapons, sat—dangerously vulnerable to the unyielding storm. Our base was devastated. I wondered if my parked car had survived? Thank goodness, despite numerous injuries, no one on base died. Squadron mates took shelter in the 384th Air Refueling Squadron building—I think they were having some event that after-noon. Sadly, the town of Andover, KS was not so lucky. The tornado hit a trailer park head on and the destruction was unimaginable. Seventeen people were killed and over 200 injured. It was a terrible tragedy. I know most of my East Coast friends don't really get it—the incredible power of a tornado—all those nights, watching the TV, wondering if you're going to be getting some heavy rain and hail or if you'll be hunkered down inside your bathtub with a mattress pulled over your head, praying for your life. Listening on a battery operated, portable radio as TORNADO WATCH becomes TORNADO WARNING….and then you hear the sirens….and the baseball to soft-ball size hail starts pounding on your roof….and then the winds—so loud that it's described as being like a train passing through. It is—I've been there, listening to a play by play as a tornado came down my street. But I wasn't there for the '91 tornado. Friends were—and if you want to talk about a cause for PTSD…. they have a good one. I have friends who lost their cars, their boat and, as previously mentioned, their homes.

A couple weeks later, after months of being deployed, I returned home. I had left my vehicle keys with my (non-deployed) Boom Operator and, thankfully, he had moved my car off base. He periodi-cally started it and drove it to keep the battery charged. It died a few days later. When we returned to base, a quick overfly gave us an aerial view of the devastation. I remember my co-pilot asking if I could drive him up to the RV lot, where his sailboat was parked. I did. We could really see devastation—Wow! There were still open fires burning. Ken's boat? Tornados are strange—they touch this and not that and work in mysterious ways. The boat was still there but the outboard motor had been ripped off and tossed and there was damage to the mast. I believe it had seen its last days upon the lakes of Kansas and Oklahoma. I drove home. For years afterward, the way we did things changed. The hospital was relocated into multiple buildings until a temporary building could be fabricated and, even then, parts of the operation continued on elsewhere. The base might have closed altogether but Kansas Senator Bob Dole was a powerful man and he was not about to let McConnell AFB close. We rebuilt and the mission carried on. I just thought I'd share this story. We worry about lots of small things in life. But there are plenty of big things out there, hiding behind dark clouds... and so we should all take a deep breath and learn not to fret over the small stuff. Make every day count because you just never know. You never know when a warm spring day might turn into something truly terrifying. I hope none of you ever have to experience this. Sadly, many of my friends did. And my condolences continue to go out to those who lost friends and loved ones in Andover, KS on April 26th, 1991.

PARTING THOUGHTS

I'll not deceive myself into thinking that the reader has ably worked their way through the entirety of this large collection, but I do hope that each visitor has discovered something within that made them smile, or think, or perhaps found inspirational.

For my part, I enjoyed creating these stories, and essays, and poems. Especially during the COVID-19 Pandemic, a time I'd rather forget, having writing projects occupied my time and filled me with a sense of satisfaction and accomplishment. Of course, the second part of this anthology is filled with unprompted pieces that, in some cases, weren't really intended for public consumption at all. A few were written for social media while others were written as encouragement for myself. As is often the case, the most deeply personal stuff I've written remains protected within the pages of my Diary. I have over 10,000 pages worth of journal entries, dating back to August of 1982. Occasionally, I may cross reference some of these accounts and thoughts to bring a topic into the light (as was the case with my 2020 memoir, "Quest: My Journey Through La Mancha"). But, in general, I'm happy to keep private matters private and the therapeutic value of my writing is more potent when I am specifically not writing for an audience but writing to clarify positions within my own mind or to provide a record I might fall back upon when I am searching for dates and times, events and happenings, and occasionally that inspiration I spoke of previously. More than once, I have been inspired by reading the words of a younger version of myself and seeing how he dealt with life's challenges and doubts. I am a huge advocate for journalling and encourage everyone to take pen to paper, or fingers to a keyboard, to work through the complicated issues in our lives and to have that discussion with our greatest critic yet staunchest advocate—ourselves. It truly is a healthy endeavor and one I don't believe you'll regret. I've had people express a concern about journalling—a fear that their words might leave their control and could, perhaps, cause harm or hurt people's feelings. I say, "speak your truth" and then fear not the consequences of your honesty. If desired, clearly specify that your journals should be destroyed when you pass. But consider that your words might serve to inspire an unintended recipient and help them to overcome some challenges in their lives. For my part, even though all my old Diary volumes are labeled with various "Keep Out" warning labels on the title page, I don't suppose I much care anymore. They will travel where they are meant to travel and I'll be at peace knowing that I have expressed myself honestly and never tried to craft an image apart from my true self. My Diary volumes speak to who I am which brings me back to the stories and poems within this anthology.

Everything we write reflects some truth about ourselves and our beliefs. We are telling people who we are and what we believe without necessarily directly spelling it out. That's the beauty of fiction. That's the beauty of writing, and artwork, and music. All of the things we create represent a piece of our soul, a fragment of our very being. With sharing these things, we sometimes put ourselves in a vulnerable position. We reveal part of who we are while others hide behind their mysterious cloaks of ambiguity and uncertainty. As such, I believe it takes courage to open the pages of our mind for consumption and, often, evaluation. I think it's a beautiful thing to do. While I seldom overestimate my own talent, and too frequently harshly judge my own contributions and abilities, I do hope that you have enjoyed what you have read. I enjoyed the creative process and I am happy to share my words with all who care to read them. Thank you for giving your time to join me along this common stretch of road. I wish you all the best on your journeys, wherever they may lead you. I hope our paths cross again and I hope that I might enjoy those things that you have crafted during your creative process. As we share, we learn and we grow. Safe travels!

Epilogue

Writing. It's my way to frame my thoughts and convey my messages. It's my therapy. It's my prompt for dreams. It's my outlet for ideas that must not die. It's my memory and my inspiration. And it's always been an essential part of who I am.

I have literally been writing for as long as I can remember. My earliest tales were scribbled in crayon and illustrated. Then I graduated from illustrated stories to ones written in pen. Perhaps the most memorable of these was a series of illustrated stories I created for my mother around first or second grade, entitled *The Adventures of Pilot Joe.* The series followed a young boy who was teased and bullied for his love of airplanes and his obsession with making airplane models, but he grew up to become a fearless pilot. My imagination was already on display: Joe took his jet, in later volumes, to the moon and to the depths of the ocean, fighting monsters along the way. Where my words were limited, drawings in crayon on yellow paper filled in the visuals. I carefully bound each multi-page story with string to create nice gifts for my mother. This may be the earliest surviving example of my writing.

Then I received my first typewriter. I was so proud of it and couldn't wait to put it to use. In 1975, I created *The Adventures of Freddy and His Time Machine*, which I still have. Between the typed lines are several illustrations. But I didn't limit myself to fiction, although the creative freedom excited me. I developed a lengthy report on various African animals, totally unprompted and not required for school. The work was typed and included images from books. Rather than binding with string, I used a three-ring hole punch and placed the pages in a classy Acco binder. Clearly, I saw these projects as meaningful and worth preserving. In later years, I spent weeks researching various animals, broke them down by classification, and typed the animal names next to their scientific names. This project, too, was carefully preserved. Both still exist.

The next memorable development in my writing journey came during fourth to sixth grades, with the tug-of-war between assigned prompts and creative autonomy. When given freedom, I wrote humorous tales about invasions of killer fruit and vegetables. Long before the 1978 film *Attack of the Killer Tomatoes*, I was writing stories about tomatoes, oranges, and hot dogs from space wreaking havoc on

Earth. My classmates always laughed when I read these stories aloud, which made me feel good. I finally had an audience beyond my loving mother. Perhaps my favorite from that era was *The Attack of the Big Mac*, inspired by McDonald's "Big Mac Attack" advertising campaign. When my hamburger alien arrived from outer space, his quest was to collect the elements of a Big Mac to become an invincible monster. I could barely hold back chuckles as I wrote, and my classmates loved it!

But school assignments weren't always fun. Unwanted prompts transitioned from annoying to infuriating. I can't claim any pride in the next tale. Mrs. Rabkin assigned us to write a dialogue for homework one night. I was frustrated—likely wanting to watch something on TV —and stress turned into defiance. I created *The Adventures of Dumb and Stupid*. My characters were literally named Dumb and Stupid, and their dialogue was mundane and boring: simple hellos, trivial courtesies, and small talk about the weather. I think I got the formatting (quotations, indentations, commas, etc.) right, which was probably the assignment's main goal. I received no feedback, but I wouldn't be surprised if it was noted in my teacher's file. Before graduating elementary school, I asked for autographs from my old teachers; Mrs. Rabkin's note, "We had an interesting year…" was, perhaps, telling.

Fifth and sixth grade went smoother. My writing improved, and my storytelling became more refined. I was thrilled when, at the start of sixth grade, my teacher Mrs. Linder announced we'd create a creative writing book: a bound edition of our stories and poems from the year. This inspired me to make each piece something special. Some prompts were more fun than others, but I can't recall being upset by any, and there were no "Adventures of Dumb and Stupid" in my portfolio. I discovered a love for poetry, which I hadn't explored before. Our growing collection included biographies, essays, stories, and poems. While everything I wrote rhymed (because I thought poems had to rhyme), I began expressing deeper emotions. Outside school, I kept my personal writings in a folder. Looking back, I'm amazed at the emotional depth of those pieces, still kept private. Later poems would make friends laugh, inspire, or comfort those who were hurting. I frequently used humor to bring a smile and lighten the load. The deeply personal pieces remained in my private folder, serving as therapy before I even knew what therapy was.

At the end of sixth grade, our collection was ready to be bound. We each created a personalized stamp by engraving a design into

Styrofoam, pressing it into ink, and stamping our book's cover. Our year's worth of writing was placed between hard covers and assembled. At the end were five blank pages for autographs. On the last day of school, students collected signatures from friends, former teachers, and specialty teachers (science, art, and music), creating lasting memories.

In junior high, I once again encountered the rigidity of writing assignments. But I had matured and saw these as challenges to improve rather than punishments. In seventh-grade English, I learned about sentence structure and other concepts that refined my style, even if I longed for opportunities to unleash my creativity. Such opportunities were rare, so I wrote at home. I shifted from short stories to reflective essays and deep poems, accompanied by powerful drawings representing unspoken emotions. I wrote less during this time, but that would soon change.

In 1982, after several stressful years of high school filled with teen angst, changing friendships, uncertainty, and faltering self-confidence, everything changed on August 2nd. I found inspiration on a summer trip to Spain, Portugal, and Morocco. Her name was Valerie. But it was more than just the woman; it was a newfound sense of purpose and confidence that I could change my life and become the man I wanted—and felt destined—to be. My mind was alive with thoughts and feelings I had no outlet to express or share. I also wanted to preserve memories I feared losing. So, upon returning home, I pulled out my typewriter and wiped the dust from the keys. For several hot summer days, with my bedroom door closed, I typed furiously. I had never written anything so deeply personal and introspective. My story, simply titled *Valerie*, detailed my emotional state before the trip, my experiences during it, and my hopes for the future. Valerie, a lovely Canadian woman nine years older than me, became a rallying point for overcoming my insecurities and striving to become more than just a nice kid. The therapeutic value of this writing was immediate—and I was hooked.

According to the cover page, I completed *Valerie* on August 30, 1982. The next day, August 31st, I opened a 300-page Marble Composition Notebook and began Volume I of my Diary. I pledged to write two pages each day and mostly kept that vow—filling gaps with various drawings and scribbles when needed. In later volumes, I eased page limits and daily requirements. Now, over 40 years later, my Diary contains more than 10,000 pages of personal reflections on daily life and significant events. It's been invaluable for my mental health and became a wonderful resource when I created my memoir in 2020.

Before I was ever thinking about memoirs, I was thinking about conveying messages to others in a way that I felt was impactful and lasting. While I am not a bad communicator, verbally, I've always felt my strong suit was expressing myself in writing. In college (U.S. Air Force Academy), I would write fun poems to help cheer and inspire friends. As an example, in one instance, during my sophomore year, I noticed my roommate was very stressed about an engineering project. The task was to design a vehicle, applying engineering principles, that would perform a certain specific task. The projects were built using balsa wood, string, rubber bands, and such. These devices would then move a certain distance and complete a specified action. I have no recollection of the details but I know it kept breaking and then not operating as it should. My roommate was beyond flustered. So, to lighten the mood, I wrote a humorous poem about all of this. It was several pages long. The poem moves from the frustration of building the device to the disappointment of a failing grade with a to the excitement of a planned vengeful destruction of the device. The catch is that this once fragile contraption is now somehow indestructible. It was a funny concept and I loved writing it. I was happy enough to hear the laughter of my roommate and see his spirits lifted. What I was not expecting was a phone call from an officer in the Engineering department asking if I would be okay with them putting my poem on display in a glass case near the Engineering classrooms. Apparently, my roommate loved my poem so much that he decided to include it as an addendum to his final report on the project. The professors in the Engineering department loved it, too— and they appreciated the notion of cadets supporting each other in such a fashion. I was glad to bring some smiles. I wrote many poems during my Academy years, often to comfort or encourage friends. Once, I included a poem in a letter to my idol, figure skater Dorothy Hamill, after reading about how she was being exploited. Surprisingly, I received a handwritten note and photo from Dorothy within days, thanking me for "one of the loveliest letters I've ever received." I was thrilled to touch the heart of someone who had inspired me for years.

Beyond poems, I wrote countless letters each week to friends and family. We had no cell phones or internet. Squadron phone booths often had long lines, and privacy was rare. Letters were the main way to stay connected.

As graduation approached, we planned "June Week." Before the formal ceremony, each squadron held a commissioning ceremony. Some cadets chose family members or mentors to swear them in. I was undecided until my Air Officer Commanding mentioned that Brigadier General Robert Lee Scott Jr.—a WWII hero, Flying Tiger, and author of *God Is My Co-Pilot*—had offered to swear in interested cadets. I was ecstatic. As a military history major, this was incredibly meaningful. I wrote a heartfelt letter to General Scott. Soon after, his assistant replied, explaining he had been planning to cancel the trip due to age, health, and doubts about his impact—until he received my letter. She made it clear my words changed his mind. On June 1, 1988, just before graduation, I stood face-to-face with one of my heroes as he led me in the Oath of Office, congratulating me and my family. He swore in several other cadets, too. It was an unforgettable moment.

During the Gulf War buildup, UN resolutions demanded Iraq withdraw from Kuwait after its 1990 invasion. When they refused, Operation Desert Storm launched in January 1991. I deployed with my aircrew to the Middle East. While flying mostly nighttime combat missions, I spent non-sleeping hours in a rocking chair our Boom Operator had built from spare wood. It sat on a deck of cargo pallets outside our tent, where I wrote letters home. My diary entries were done privately in my makeshift "room"—two tent walls with a blanket and poncho creating a corner, lit by a dim bulb. Letters reassured family I was okay, sharing tidbits of desert life, while my diary captured deeper thoughts on flying risky missions night after night. My mother kept all of my letters, and rereading them brings memories flooding back. Diary volumes help fill in details of my wartime experience. I also wrote thank-you letters to Americans who sent "Any Service Member" notes, always grabbing stacks from my home state of New York to reply.

Outside of a few casual college dates, I hadn't really dated. In 1992, I met Lisa, an attractive pharmacist on my base. I worked up the courage to ask her out right before a deployment. We had three dates before I left, then wrote to each other nearly every day while I was overseas. Through those letters, our attraction deepened into love. Eight months later, despite frequent deployments, we married at the botanical gardens in Wichita, Kansas. During future trips, I kept writing—everything from love letters to illustrated stories—to stay connected.

As a commissioned officer, I continued to blend creative writing with professional work. As chief navigator, I created a newsletter for navigators with technique tips and travel ideas, like visiting the Royal Naval Observatory in Greenwich to stand on the Prime Meridian. Though not required, I loved educating and entertaining my colleagues.

In later years, I worked on more serious projects. At U.S. Strategic Command, I helped establish the new "Global Strike" mission, identifying future requirements and bridging capability gaps. I co-authored the Global Strike Joint Integrating Concept and later wrote the Global Strike Joint Capabilities Document, a major effort involving countless drafts, Pentagon trips, and negotiations with stakeholders. I created slideshows and briefed senior officers, culminating in presenting to the Joint Requirements Oversight Council, chaired by the Vice Chairman of the Joint Chiefs of Staff. The document was unanimously approved —my greatest professional writing triumph. From war plans to budgets, speeches, and performance reports, I was always writing for impact.

I retired in 2018. After a short stint with an aviation manufacturer, we parted ways in late 2019. Then the COVID-19 pandemic hit, trapping me in isolation and upending my plans. Writing became my refuge. I published a memoir with Red Penguin Books in 2020 and began submitting stories to their new anthology series, The Red Penguin Collection. I quickly became a regular contributor, publishing over 30 pieces across diverse themes and genres. This creative outlet challenged me, helped me grow, and connected me with readers during difficult times. I've now gathered many of those works—along with new and unpublished pieces—into this collection, offering a glimpse into how my storytelling evolved through the pandemic and beyond.

Today, while I focus on creative writing, I still do professional proposal work, consulting, and volunteer writing for various organizations. My diary continues. On social media, I'm known for thoughtful, often lengthy responses. My goal is to entertain, inspire, and bring smiles. Whether sharing humorous stories or personal tales with a moral, if I uplift even one person, my time behind the keyboard is well spent. In the end, that's what it's all about. It's always been about sharing, bringing joy, inspiring, and sparking reflection. From *The Adventures of Pilot Joe* to these works, I've always loved writing—and using it to make a difference.

Colonel David Lange, United States Air Force (Retired), grew up on Long Island, New York, and graduated from the United States Air Force Academy in 1988. Over a 30-year military career, he served as a Master Navigator with more than 3,600 flight hours, flying combat, combat support, and humanitarian missions aboard the KC-135R and E-4B aircraft. A decorated combat veteran of Operations Desert Storm and Allied Force, he held numerous senior leadership positions and received the prestigious Institute of Navigation Superior Achievement Award for his lifetime contributions as a practicing navigator.

After retiring in 2018, David returned to Long Island and began a new chapter of reflection and creativity. As a writer, he has contributed dozens of short stories, essays, and poems to over 30 anthologies, many during the quiet uncertainty of the COVID-19 pandemic. His memoir, *Quest: My Journey Through La Mancha*, was published in 2020.

David writes to connect, to inspire, and to encourage readers to live with authenticity and gratitude. His work explores themes of memory, resilience, loss, and hope—always with the quiet conviction that stories have the power to heal and unite. When not writing, he volunteers as a museum docent, mentors future Air Force Academy candidates, and continues to serve his community through local veterans' organizations.

www.ingramcontent.com/pod-product-compliance
Lightning Source LLC
Chambersburg PA
CBHW050608110726
47899CB00001B/21